"As complicated as a Chinese puzzle . . .
there isn't a slow-moving page!"

Worcester Sunday Telegram

Cruz Despues—An undercover investigator too eager to bust the drug ring wide open, his first big lead was his last.

Sgt. Ray Ycaza—Veteran of Vietnam and the Barrio, he hates the filth that reaps profits from the blood and suffering of addicts and victims of drug-induced crimes. But even more, he hates the scum who'd lured Despues to a seamy bar and casually snuffed out his life.

Rachel—She knew what it was to love a cop. That's why she'd never marry one.

"The Desperate Adversaries, by an author who has established an audience that runs into millions in the United States and Europe, is the first novel of stature to be written about the Los Angeles County Sheriff's Department."

Los Angeles Times

The Desperate Adversaries

Jack Hoffenberg

AVON
PUBLISHERS OF BARD, CAMELOT, DISCUS, EQUINOX AND FLARE BOOKS

AVON BOOKS
A division of
The Hearst Corporation
959 Eighth Avenue
New York, New York 10019

ISBN: 0-380-00702-9

First Avon Printing, October, 1976

Printed in the U.S.A.

"Desperate remedies are necessary
to cure desperate diseases."

AN APPRECIATION AND DEDICATION

This is a work of fiction, the characters and events drawn by the author's imagination.

However, none of it would have been possible without the generous permission of Los Angeles County Sheriff Peter J. Pitchess and Undersheriff James F. Downey, who allowed me my first glimpse into law enforcement at work.

Over a period of several months, the most rewarding hours were those spent riding days, nights, and weekends with uniformed and plainclothes deputies who, happily, showed me no special or favored treatment; and eventually came to accept me as one of their own.

I rode, listened, and observed. I saw crimes committed and perpetrators apprehended and booked; but even more important and impressive were the many instances when deputies were called upon to render aid to the sick, injured, lost, helpless, and bewildered; victims of no crime, but of the complexities of life.

I saw a curious blend of professionalism and compassion in an atmosphere of pure hostility and marveled at the patience of men driven close to the walls of desperation. And came away with a new understanding of those few who stand on that thin line between the world of criminality and the vast public they serve, and serve well.

It is difficult to express my full admiration and deep respect for those men and women of the Los Angeles Sheriff's Department whom I was privileged to meet, talk with, and observe at work; or for the division chiefs, bureau and station commanders who made it possible. Unable to name them all, I would like to show my appreciation by dedicating this book to them, with gratitude.

And to Jerry Epstein, who opened the first door.

JACK HOFFENBERG

Studio City, California

Prologue

His name was Cruz Despues, Mexican-American, young, olive-complexioned, extremely good-looking and with a body that marks the well-trained athlete. During his football career at Garfield High in East Los Angeles, he had picked up the nickname Casey, and it was carried along until well after he was graduated at the age of seventeen. He continued to play football for East Los Angeles State College, but gave it up at the end of his junior year because the sport was becoming more important than his education, which meant far more to him.

At twenty-one, with a bachelor's degree, Casey suddenly decided on a course of action that surprised not only himself but also his family, who had assumed he would enter law school. Instead, he applied for and was accepted as a trainee in the Los Angeles County Sheriff's Department. Within eighteen months he was on active patrol, popular with his colleagues as well as the people on the streets, with whom he had an excellent rapport.

A little more than a year later, after an interview with his station commander, Casey transferred from Patrol to the Narcotics Bureau where there was a great need for bright, intelligent deputies with investigative talents that Casey had already shown he possessed. More relevant was his deep feeling that the annual increase in drug abuse was becoming an almost incurable cancer among his people.

By the time he was twenty-six, Casey Despues had been married for three years to Louisa Orduna, whom he had known since their high-school days, and was the father of a two-year-old son, Paul. Louisa was then four months into her second pregnancy and worried considerably about her husband's assignment as an undercover narcotics detective, for which he had opted and at which he was extraordinarily well suited. His record for arrests and convictions was very high, as attested to by the numerous commendations in his personnel file, praising his dedication, spirit of cooperation, and willingness to devote long, irregular hours to the tedium of investigation and surveillance, consorting with known, dangerous peddlers, trying to stem the flow and use of hard narcotics, particularly among the young.

On a summer night in 1973, shortly after dinner, Casey received a phone call, not unlike many he had received in the past. It was then seven thirty. Paul was in bed, and Casey was drying the dinner dishes as Louisa rinsed them. He put down the towel and answered the phone on the fourth ring.

"Casey? Casey Despues?" the strange female voice greeted him. A Chicano by her inflection.

"Yes. Who is it?"

"You know Carlotta Jiminez?"

Warily, "I know her." He did, indeed. He had busted Carlotta Jiminez as an addict-pusher selling to high-school students, then helped her get on a rehabilitation program and eventual probation.

"I know. She tol' me you know her pretty good. She say you're a pretty good cop. You treat her okay."

"Well—who is this?"

"Name don' mean nothin'. Call me Lilly."

"Okay, Lilly. What's this all about?"

"I wanna do you a favor, man."

"A favor? Why me, if you don't know me?"

"Well, hey, man, because I know what you do, an' Carlotta tell me you the guy I should tell it to."

"Tell me what?"

"About this dude, you know, a heavy dealer—"

He turned wary again. "Somebody you want to get even with, Lilly?"

"Well, maybe, but he ought to be put away, you see. He's no damn good, that dude."

2

"You say he's a heavy dealer? How heavy?"

"Oh, big, man. Big. Three days ago, like he think I'm sleepin', an' I hear him in the next room, he's talkin' on the phone to some guy about a deal for a whole pound of smack. That's big, no?"

A whole pound of heroin was big indeed. Bigger than anything Casey had run into in over six months. "To buy or sell?" he asked.

"To buy, man. He's talkin' big numbers."

"You know who he was talking to?"

"Chure. I seen 'em together three-four time. Old friends, you know?"

"They have names, Lilly?"

"Chure, man—hey, lissen. I got to hang up now. He come back an' catch me, he beat my ass good."

"Hey, wait—"

"I can't talk no more now. You know Moreno's Café?"

"I know it."

"Okay. You meet me there tonight, eleven o'clock, I give you the whole thing. He'll go out 'roun' ten, like he always do. I'll meet you outside on Moreno's parking lot in the back. Okay?"

"How will I know you?"

"You come in by the back, the alley, see, exac'ly eleven o'clock. I'll come out an' meet you. I be wearin' blue-jean pants an' a white top. Okay?"

"Eleven o'clo—" Casey heard the click! as she rang off and stood staring at the dead phone in his hand.

Real thing? Setup? Some anonymous joker getting her kicks this way?

In the kitchen, Louisa had finished drying the last of the dishes and was putting the pots and pans away. He went into his bedroom and checked through a drawer, trying to find a telephone number for Carlotta Jiminez, found the slip, went back to the phone, and dialed the number. The operator came on after several rings and informed him that the number had been disconnected. Information could give him no new number for Carlotta, which did not surprise him in the least.

The thought of a whole pound of heroin floating around excited him, too great an opportunity to allow slip away from him. At current prices it represented between twelve and fifteen thousand dollars at street value. Sixteen ounces; 454 grams to be shot into how many veins, how many overdoses that would kill?

3

He thought about it, then dialed another number and waited. Six rings later, he heard a voice he recognized at once. "Hello."

"Russ? Casey Despues."

"Hi, Casey. What's doing?"

He took great pains to repeat the conversation he had engaged in with the unknown Lilly. "Who is this Carlotta Jiminez, Casey?" Russ McNeely asked.

"Oh, a crazy kid who once freaked out. I busted her for possession and sale, then talked the judge into getting her on a rehab program and give her probation. Comes from a nice family. As far as I know, she's been straight ever since."

"Can you get in touch with her?"

"I just tried. Number's been disconnected."

"So if she's that straight, what's her connection with this Lilly?"

"I don't know, Russ. These kids are hard as hell to keep up with and know more about each other than we'll ever find out. The way I figure it, this Lilly probably took a good beating from her dude and wants the score evened up. We're talking about a whole pound of smack, Russ."

"I don't know, Casey. You've been pretty damned active lately. It could be a setup. I'd feel a lot better about it if you had some back-up going in."

"Jesus, Russ, it would be kind of tough to work somebody inside this late, and outside back-up in a little joint like Moreno's would be too easy to spot. If I had somebody with me in the car, chances are she'd be afraid to even come out and talk to me. I'd hate like hell to blow anything as big as this. I can handle it. Hell, it's only information I'm after, no buy yet, and it could give me another good informant in the area."

"Well—" There was a long pause on the other end, then McNeely said, "If that's your gut feeling, Casey, okay. Call me as soon as it goes down. I'll want to know you're all right."

Casey went back to the bedroom where Louisa was lying down to rest. He lay beside her, talking to her in his "selling" voice, trying to erase the anxiety he knew she would be feeling, aware that she had heard the two one-sided conversations. And just as aware that he wasn't succeeding too well.

At ten o'clock he arose from the bed, dressed in his working "uniform"; slouch felt hat with floppy brim, loose shirt hanging outside his blue-denim slacks, suede ankle-high boots, long hair flowing below his collar line. He clipped his 9-mm.

automatic to his pants belt in the center of his back, covered it with the tails of his shirt. He kissed Louisa, then went into Paul's small room, drew the covers up to his neck, and kissed him. He walked through the room where Louisa was lying on the bed and said, "I'll be back soon. This won't take long."

As always, she said, "Take care," and he left.

Moreno's Café was no more than twenty minutes from where Casey lived, at the bottom of a hillside group of homes known locally as "the Alps." He drove slowly, visualizing the neighborhood beer joint where, during his patrol days in East Los Angeles, he had had frequent occasions to respond to the place to quell disturbances and, just as frequently, to make an arrest. The café was in an area that for years had been deteriorating through the neglect of its indifferent, uncaring residents, the majority on welfare, a few on full- or part-time jobs, all renters. It was also an area of many illegal aliens, with whom he was not now concerned.

Inside, he could recall easily, the bar, accommodating about a dozen stools, ran along the entire left wall. Perhaps another dozen or more oilcloth-covered tables, a jukebox, two pinball machines, a cigarette machine, and a sadly worn pool table made up the rest of the interior furnishings. A kitchen, storeroom, and rest rooms lined the back hallway that led to the rear parking lot and alley entrance.

Casey took a full thirty minutes to reach Moreno's, then circled the block cautiously, casing the aging one-story building. In front, cars of varying makes and ages lined the curbs on both sides of the street. A single wooden door, its entrance, was closed. Windows on both sides of the door were painted in a deep orange to give the patrons inside a certain privacy.

At exactly eleven o'clock, Casey pulled his two-year-old Mustang into the rear parking lot from the alley. There were nine cars parked at different angles, all ignoring the crudely painted white marker lines. He pulled into a space between a '67 Ford pickup truck and a '66 Chevy sedan that showed signs of long, hard wear. In front, just under the sign that hung lopsidedly over the rear door and beneath a dim, single, unshaded bulb, was another sign that read:

PARKING—MORENO ONLY

He cut the motor and sat staring at the door for a moment, then saw it open; the girl, short, a bit overweight, dressed in blue-jean pants and a skimpy white topper,

5

emerged, stared at the Mustang, and then walked directly to its right side. Casey leaned over and unlocked the door. She opened it and slipped in quickly, filling it with a musky odor. Her complexion was dark, either by heritage or the sun, her bare midriff bulging a little too much for the slacks belt to contain, her crotch provocatively exposed by the tightness of her pants.

She smiled, showing two even rows of white teeth, but her face and bare arms, he took quick note, were free of bruise or puncture marks. "Hey," she greeted, "you Casey, hey?"

"I'm Casey—"

"You okay, man. You don' look like no cop. Too young. Too good-lookin'."

"I'm a cop, Lilly. What have you got for me?"

She seemed enamored of him and leaned closer, pressing one thigh against him. "I got plenny for you, man. I give it all to you. Me, too," she added, laughing.

"Come on, Lilly. I can't be wasting time. We've got things to talk about, okay?"

"Okay, man. Hey, you know Roberto Perez, the dude they call Bobby the Snake?"

"No. Never heard of him. Who is he?"

"He's my dude, the one I tol' you about."

"I thought I knew most of the big operators around here."

"Maybe you don' know Bobby so good because he not here long. Came up from Juarez two-three month ago. He say he kill a cop down there, come to L.A. while it cool off."

Casey's interest heightened. "What about this deal of his? When does it go down? Who's his connection?"

"Hey, don' rush me—"

"Come on, Lilly, I can't sit around out here rapping with you. Somebody will come out and spot us, and you'll be in a lot of trouble."

"Not Lilly, man. These my people. Bobby don' never come here."

"Okay, give it to me. Name, place, time."

"Okay. Luis Ortega, he gonna sell to Bobby. A whole pound. Friday night, ten o'clock, my place."

"Where?"

"Laveque Street, 11242, street apartment."

"Up in the Alps?"

"Yeah, right near Rambroz. You know?"

"I know. Lilly, are you giving this to me straight?"

"You bet. That Snake dude, he's no good, a damn freak."

"What did he do to make you want to turn him in?"

"I tol' you, he's a freak. He make me drop acid, other pills, then he do all kind bad things to me, make me do it to him."

"Don't tell me he raped you, huh?"

"No rape. Other things. Dirty stuff."

"All right. I get the picture. Where is Carlotta Jiminez hanging out these days?"

"Carlotta? She take off with a dude; they shacked up down in Carson some place."

"No phone?"

"No. I see her aroun' here last week. I tell her what dirty stuff Bobby been doin' to me. She tell me to tell you, you take care of him."

"Okay, Lilly, we'll take care of him. Listen, about Friday night, what kind of a car does Luis Ortega drive?"

"Las' one I know, a blue Caddy. He got a lot of cars, steal 'em to run his stuff with. He got picked up, the cops confi— con—"

"Confiscate the car," Casey supplied.

"Yeah. That's it. Take it away, keep it. He make sure they don' get his big Linc'n 'rental."

"Okay, Friday night is the night after tomorrow night. I'll set it up. Don't change your mind and blow this, Lilly. If you do, I'll come looking for you. Understand?"

"I understan', man. I don' bullshit you." She grinned, then broke into a childish giggle. "Hey, you bust him good, then come back. I ball the hell out of you, okay?"

He grinned back at her, felt her hand ride high up on his right thigh, caressing his genitals. "One thing at a time, Lilly," he said. "Will you be a witness for me?"

She drew back, sobering quickly. "No, man. No way. You wanna get me killed?"

He had expected that response and wasn't disappointed. Bobby the Snake and Luis Ortega taken out, there would be others who would happily blow up a witness for the prosecution if only for the principle of it.

"Okay, Lilly," he said. "At nine thirty on Friday night, you find some excuse to leave the house. Come here to Moreno's, maybe, and be seen while we nail your friend Bobby and Luis Ortega. Okay?"

She smiled broadly. "Chure, man. I do it like you say."

She got out of the Mustang and started toward the rear

entrance. For a moment, Casey sat watching her jiggling buttocks until she disappeared inside, then reached for the ignition key.

At that moment, a dark figure in the rear of the '66 Chevy rose up from the floor into a crouch and rested his right hand on the door ledge. He fired the gun he held in that hand twice. The first bullet hit Casey Despues in his left temple, and as his head jerked violently to the right, the second shot ripped across the short space between the two cars and lodged in the base of his neck, about an inch below the jawline. The deputy's upper body fell forward and to the right, and he died there. The time: 11:24 P.M.

Miguel Moreno, sixteen, was alone in the kitchen where he was washing the dishes and glasses that had accumulated during the evening when he heard the two shots. For a few seconds he stood rooted at the sink, a plate in one hand, dishrag in the other, having recognized the sounds as gunfire. In the bar in the front, separated from the kitchen by a twenty-two-foot hallway with a storeroom and rest rooms between, he heard the blaring jukebox and little else, not even the water pouring out of the spigot over the sink in front of him.

His first thought was not so much for the two sharp reports, but for his motorbike that was chained to a steel post on the parking lot outside the curtained window over the sink. When perhaps fifteen seconds had passed, he reached up, parted the burlap curtain in the center about three inches, and peered out. With relief, he saw his motorbike at its normal place. Then his eyes caught the movement of a figure leaning into the opened door of a Mustang.

Captured by the drama of the scene, he watched as the figure drew back, examined briefly something he had taken from inside the car, then moved swiftly to an old Chevy sedan, got into it, and started the motor without turning on its lights. The man seemed to be in no hurry as he backed the car out into the alley, headed it west and sped off. Miguel Moreno then ran into the bar and told his father, Carlos Moreno, what he had heard and seen.

At that same moment, in the house across the alley whose rear bedroom windows faced the Moreno parking lot, Enrique and Silvia Morales were preparing for bed. Over the music of their small radio, they heard the two shots. Quickly, Enrique turned off the overhead light, plunging the room into darkness, then went to the window and looked out. Silvia ran into the next room to make certain their three children were safe. At first, Enrique saw nothing as his eyes swept the alley from side to side, then the Moreno parking lot. Now his eyes captured the bare movement of the dark figure leaning inside the Mustang, searching for something. Moments later, as he continued to watch, Silvia padded across the linoleum in her bare feet and stood nervously beside him.

"What is it, Enri?" she asked in a trembling voice. "The children gangs?"

"No. One man. A thief, I think. He shot someone and is robbing him."

"Madre de Dios! *He is still there?*"

"Yes. See for yourself."

And while Silvia watched, Enrique went to the telephone and asked the operator to connect him with the policía. When the East Los Angeles Sheriff's Station answered, Enrique reported what he had seen, calmly gave the address, but refused to give his own name, address, or phone number and hung up. When he returned to the rear bedroom window, the Chevy was pulling away down the alley, its lights still not turned on.

At the East Los Angeles Sheriff's Station, the night-watch deputy who had taken the message from the unidentified caller now took the second call relating to the same incident and address, Moreno's Café.

Deputies Bob Gordon and Sol Gomez, in Car 21-Edward, were no more than twelve blocks from the location when they took the call on their radio. "Twenty-one-Edward, a nine twenty-three has just occurred at twenty-one sixty-three Brooklyn. Rear parking lot, Moreno's Café. You have a Code Three."

Gordon flicked on his red lights and siren while Gomez hastily rogered the call and began recording it on his patrol report. Within a matter of seconds they were at the scene where some two dozen or more men, women, and now youths stood within sight of the Mustang and dead body, some perched on the hoods and roofs of the nearby parked cars for a better look.

While Gomez examined the body to ensure there was no longer any life in it, taking care not to touch any surface that might obliterate a fingerprint, Gordon was on the radio relaying word to his station that they had a 187, homicide, on their hands. He gave the victim's position and what physical *description he could observe, the license number of the Mustang, observing that the deceased's pockets had been turned out, no identification on his person.*

Now a second patrol car, 20-Adam, came on the scene, followed by 21-Sam, Patrol Sergeant Bill Cisneros at the wheel. While the 20-Adam deputies and Sol Gomez roped off the pertinent area and began questioning the bar patrons and curious neighbors attracted to the parking lot by the sirens and red lights, Cisneros talked with Bob Gordon and got the rest of the story as he knew it, which was little enough at that point. Then Cisneros reached in behind the body and found the empty clip-on holster under the victim's shirttail. It bore no identifying name or initials.

Holding the holster by its closure strap while he examined it, Cisneros saw Gomez approaching with Miguel Moreno, Carlos Moreno at his son's right, protesting in Spanish. While Gomez held Carlos off to one side, Cisneros began questioning Miguel at length.

Meanwhile, Paul Harris and Dale Cramer, out of Car 20-Adam, had been knocking on doors, and Cramer came up with Enrique Morales, who finally admitted he had seen a part of the action and had phoned to the East Los Angeles desk.

Cisneros continued to question Miguel Moreno until several East Los Angeles detectives arrived, almost together with newspaper reporters and photographers from the Los Angeles Times *and* Herald-Examiner, *only moments ahead of the Homicide detectives, a lieutenant and deputies from their headquarters downtown. The reporters fanned out among the crowd while the photographers began shooting pictures of the overall scene, not permitted to get close to the car or body until after the medical examiner's people had arrived. The Homicide men were now in charge, taking all available information from Gomez and Gordon, the original handling crew, and Sergeant Cisneros.*

A call came through from the Station with a name and address to match the Mustang's license, obtained from the Department of Motor Vehicles in Sacramento, but no one present recognized the name of Cruz Despues since Casey, an undercover narcotics detective, operated out of Narcotics Bureau headquarters in the Hall of Justice Building downtown; and although he was known to the East Los Angeles narcotics crew, they were not on the scene.

The meager description of the Chevy furnished by Miguel Moreno had been broadcast: probably a '65 or '66 four-

door sedan, light body, dark top, crumpled rear right fender and taillight, license number unknown, involved in robbery-homicide, driver thought to be a black man, possibly dark-complexioned Chicano, wearing dark clothes, no further identification. The medical examiner's man had gone through his medical routine, and the body was removed to the morgue in an ambulance. The investigation continued.

At 0124, Car 23-Boy came upon the '66 Chevy, abandoned in an alley less than a mile from the scene of the shooting. A tow car was called in to haul the vehicle to the East Los Angeles Station for examination. It had been reported stolen from a supermarket lot ten minutes after the closing hour of ten P.M. by its owner, an employee of the food store. The car had been expertly hot-wired.

At 0130 the East Los Angeles night-watch lieutenant received a call from Sergeant Russ McNeely, supervisor of the Zone II Major Crime Violator crew of the Sheriff's Narcotics Bureau. McNeely informed Lieutenant Carl Mead of his earlier conversation with one of his undercover men, who had not called him within a reasonable time, Cruz Despues, working the East Los Angeles area.

"Despues? Cruz Despues? One of your guys?" Mead asked in a voice raised by a full octave.

Now McNeely sensed that something had gone wrong. "Yes. What's happened, Lieutenant? Have you got something on him?"

"Yeah, and it's all bad. Your man was blown up at approximately twenty-three thirty on the parking lot at Moreno's Café."

"Oh, Christ, no!"

"I hate to have to give it to you this way, McNeely. Have you got anything more you can give the Homicide dicks?"

"They're there now?"

"All over the place."

"I'll be there as soon as I can. It'll take me a while. I've got to come in from Manhattan Beach."

"Okay, I'll tell them. I'm sure they'll still be there."

McNeely reported in and drove to Moreno's Café with Homicide detectives Duane Rader and Pete Flannery. They again questioned Carlos and Miguel and nine of the patrons who had been present at the time of the shooting, searching for information about a woman or girl known by the name of Lilly. The only description they could offer was that which Casey Despues had given Russ McNeely during their phone

11

conversation: that she wore a pair of blue pants and a white topper.

This drew nothing. Either out of fear or an ethnic reluctance to talk to Anglo cops, the resistance to their questioning was patently refusal to impart anything that might cause the arrest of one who might possibly be from their own community. Rader went out to raise Sergeant Cisneros on his radio and asked him to come to Moreno's and bring Deputy Gomez with him. When they arrived within minutes, Cisneros and Gomez took over the interrogation in Spanish while McNeely, Rader, and Flannery looked on.

To a man, those questioned denied seeing a woman or girl so dressed, that they knew anyone by the name of Lilly.

At 0400, the deputies gave up and returned to the station.

The medical examiner removed two .38 slugs from the victim's skull and neck. These were turned over to Ballistics for examination and possible matching identification. The results were negative.

Every deputy working Narcotics, every Homicide detective, every uniformed patrolman in the East Los Angeles area, began contacting informants, seeking any possible lead to the killer, the woman who had phoned Casey, his missing 9-mm. automatic, wallet containing his deputy's star and I.D. And for Carlotta Jiminez. All their combined efforts came to naught except for Carlotta, who had been picked up by a patrol team working out of the Firestone station. Carlotta tearfully denied any knowledge of the woman who called herself Lilly, admitted that many of her high-school friends had known of her one brush with the law, and that Casey had helped her get on a rehab program and probation, for which she had been duly grateful. She agreed without hesitation to take a polygraph test and was found to have been telling the truth.

And so, on a bright, sunny day in July 1973, the body of Cruz Despues, released to his family, lay in a casket in an East Los Angeles mortuary awaiting burial, his killer still unknown. What was known was that Casey had been close to something important or someone big in narcotics, someone who had penetrated his true identity and ordered his removal.

There was, of course, a large funeral at St. Vincent's, well covered by the print and electronic media, attended by his grieving widow, the parents of both, their brothers and sisters. *The top-ranking department officials and every deputy who could be spared from his duties were present, along with representatives of the Los Angeles Police Department, California Highway Patrol, and other police departments from nearby and distant cities. Members of the Los Angeles City Council, the mayor, the entire Police Commission, and members of the Board of Supervisors mingled with leaders of the Mexican-American community. There were, quite expectedly, many friends of the two families, school friends, relatives, and the curious. The motorcade to the cemetery attracted several thousand persons as it made its way slowly through the streets, members of the numerous East Los Angeles gangs among them, grinning in silent satisfaction at the demise of a hated "pig."*

In certain Eastern cities, it would be called an "inspector's funeral," honoring a law-enforcement officer who had been shot down in the line of duty; but to the uniformed and plainclothes officers in attendance, to the homicide detectives mingling with the crowds in fruitless search of the killer, it was a "dead cop's funeral," in which any of those present might be the principal victim at any given moment on any given day or night. And each understood very clearly that when and if the killer was apprehended at some later date, a large segment of the public would become more intently concerned and preoccupied with his civil rights than those of the widow, son, and unborn child Cruz Despues had left behind.

Lawyers, paid or appointed by the state, would move into the arena, begin seeking delays and continuances, protesting that prepublicity denied their client the right of a fair trial, and demand a change of venue. If found guilty, there would come the lengthy appeals process that would last several years; and all that while the grass would be growing greener and thicker over Casey Despues's grave. And even then, should all appeals of the killer fail, he would be eligible for parole in seven years. In no event would he pay the supreme penalty for the young life he had taken.

In time, the name of Cruz Despues would grow dim in the public mind, then fade away. His widow, son, and second child, parents, brother, and two sisters would remember. Former school and football team friends would remember occasionally. His priest and schoolteachers, too, until time would finally erode those memories.

But longer than most, his brother deputies would remember; particularly the Homicide men, to whom any homicide, more so of one of their own, remains an open, festering

13

wound that will never heal until the perpetrator has been found. And the Narcotics men with whom he had worked, who would never cease in the search of the killer who had snuffed out Cruz Despues's life.

They would remember.

Chapter One

1●

Promptly at eight-thirty P.M. the girl walked into the lobby of the Yardarm in Redondo Beach, smartly trim in a tailored suit of medium blue slacks and matching jacket that buttoned snugly over her shapely hips, light blue shirt-blouse with a white scarf knotted carelessly at her throat. She was about five-four, with a figure designed to go with the form-hugging costume, a blue-trimmed white purse slung over her left shoulder, blue alligator shoes peeping out from beneath the slightly flared cuffs of her slacks.

She looked to be about twenty-two, but was, in fact, twenty-six, possessing all the assurance of a clean-featured face, the somewhat arrogant tilt of her chin, dark hair falling straight to shoulder length and flared slightly upward at the bottom. There was about her an air of innocent candor mixed with a touch of little-girl mischief, sexuality with grace, and the hint of a certain cool control of herself.

In the foyer, men and women, dressed casually in the manner of an affluent beach community, stood in groups of two and four waiting to claim their table reservations. To one side, five men in business suits also waited, obviously not local residents, probably in Southern California for a conference or convention; talking animatedly, a partially consumed drink in each hand; now following a waitress summoned by the hostess to show them to their table. When the hostess turned to approach the single girl, leather-covered menus cradled in the crook of her left arm and a question in her arched eyebrows, the girl smiled lightly and said, "I'm meeting a friend in the bar."

The bar, in the room to her right, was well patronized, but she saw the man at the far end of the room when he raised an arm to attract her attention. As she made her way down the aisle that separated the tables and booths from the long bar on the left, eyes followed her with appreciation. The man who waited for her rose from his seat in the booth, at the same time signaling a waitress who was passing by.

"Hello, Whitey," the girl said in greeting. "Been waiting long?"

He seemed not to be much taller than she, shoulders hunched forward as he leaned across the table, slender, with blondish hair and pinched, almost simian features. He wore a brown-and-tan plaid sport jacket with dark brown slacks that were expensive, if not well fitting, and a beige sports shirt with a dark green tie.

"Hey, Terry," he replied. "Just got here a few minutes ago, in time to have one beer. How about you?"

To the waiting girl, she said, "I'll have a daiquiri, please."

The waitress took the order as Terry sat down and fished in her shoulder bag for a pack of cigarettes, but found no matches. Whitey lit her cigarette for her with a pad he took from the table, then sat back against the comfortable leather of the small booth, his eyes examining her with deep interest. "That's a cool set of threads you've got there, mama. They never came from Ohrbach's."

She accepted the compliment with a smile. "Thank you, Whitey. I'd guess you don't shop there, either."

He grinned appreciatively. "No way, baby."

"How're you doing?"

"Okay. You?"

The waitress returned with the beer and a daiquiri. Whitey paid with a twenty he ostentatiously peeled from a respectable sheaf of bills. "Never better," he said, then took a cigarette from his own pack and lit it. The waitress returned with his change, and he left a dollar on the tray for her. "Time was," he said as she left, "when she'd have to do a hell of a lot more for a buck than carry a couple of drinks thirty feet."

Terry laughed. "Come on, Whitey, you're not going to tell

me you're old enough to remember the big depression my old man used to tell us kids about."

"No, but I can remember some pretty rough times." He raised his glass and said, "Here's to it."

She sipped at her drink and studied him for a moment. He was what she would have called on the lean, hungry side, guessing he was somewhere between twenty-eight and thirty, sallow complexion with hollowed cheeks. On his left hand he wore an onyx ring with a diamond in the upper right corner, a thin, expensive gold watch on his wrist. The time was 8:50.

"Are we going to do the two tonight?" she asked in a soft voice when he put his glass down.

"Yeah. Sure. Like I said. Nine hundred apiece."

Her face reflected mild disappointment. "I thought you were going to give me a break on two."

He shook his head from side to side. "Look, Terry, in these quantities I can't make out on less than nine. You know what forty to forty-five per cent coke is going for in New York today? Anywhere from a goddamn thousand to eleven hundred an ounce."

"I know what the going prices are as well as you do, but this is L.A., not Fun City. I've been paying seven-fifty, eight hundred tops."

"Yeah, but how about the quality? The stuff you been buying, that's no more than fifteen to twenty per cent, twenty-five if you're lucky. What you're getting from me, you can step another two-three times, and it'll still be better'n anything you can pick up on the street."

"The point is, Whitey, I don't deal on the street, and neither does my guy. I want relevant stuff, and my guy is willing to pay for it, but nine hundred is kind of steep."

"Well, that's how it is." He sipped more beer, then said, "Unless he wants to deal heavier."

"How much heavier?"

"Say eight pieces or a pound; sixty-four hundred dollars for eight, twelve thousand for the pound. Figures down to eight hundred dollars apiece in half-pound lots, seven fifty in pounds. Can he handle that much?"

"No problem. The thing is, can your guy deal that much on a regular basis?"

"Hell, yeah, mama. He's got the best goddamn connections in and outside the country. Top quality. Comes in pure, direct from South America."

"Pure is before he mills it down."

"Hell, he only puts a two-cut on the coke, a four on the

17

smack. Leaves plenty of room for another two or even three on the coke and a hell of a lot more on the smack. That's how he built up to where he is, on top, by giving top quality."

She considered that for a few moments, then said, "Okay, Whitey. I'll go for the two pieces for eighteen hundred. I'll talk to my guy about the other. If you give us a break, I can almost guarantee he'll go for it."

Whitey smiled and said, "Sure, baby. I'll talk to my guy. I know I can work it out." He paused, then added, "If I do, how about giving me a break, huh?" His hand moved over and slid along her elegant thigh, massaging it lightly.

"Well," she said, returning his smile, "if we can do the other thing right, maybe we can work that out, too."

"Hey, sure. Look, why don't we get out of here, go over to my pad—"

"I'd like to, but I came down here tonight to pick up the two pieces and take them back to my guy. I promised to meet him at his place at ten thirty."

"Ah, kiss the mother off till tomorrow, can't you?"

"No way. He's got to deal some of it off to a dude who's hurting."

Whitey showed his annoyance. "You ballin' this guy or something?"

She laughed prettily. "That's funny. Really funny. And what's it to you who I ball?" When he started to speak, she said, "Look, he's like sixty-five years old, married, two grown daughters. All I do is score the stuff for him. He handles the rest of it. Big with the movie, TV, and record people, like I told you."

"He's that big, how come you're doing his scoring for him?"

"I told you the first time I scored the balloon off you for a taste. He tested it out and went for the ounce, now two ounces. He's big enough that he can't risk exposing himself to make the buys himself. I'm his bird dog, and I've got a right to make a living, too, haven't I? When the narcs took out Phil Sutton two months ago, they took our best connection. That's how I got to you. You knew Phil pretty well, didn't you?"

"Phil? Sure. I used to score off him a long time ago, the dumb bastard. They're goin'a throw the book at him with a couple of felonies on his rap sheet."

"Well, it's a high-risk business. I'll bet the dude's got plenty salted away, though."

"Not if I remember Phil. He's a gambler and spender. If

he's got any of it left, he'll need it after this trip to the joint."

"I guess so, but that's the breaks. Hey, let's do it, okay? I've got to drive all the way out to Malibu. Where do we do it?"

"My car. You got the bread?"

"Sure. Take a look." She opened her purse and took out a manila envelope, opened the flap below the edge of the table, and let him see the eighteen one-hundred-dollar bills. "Eighteen hundred. What about our next deal?"

"You name it. Half pound or pound?"

"I'll let you know. Where can I reach you? Each time, you've given me a different number."

He grinned slyly. "Security. Those are public phones I use, and I never use the same booth twice. Tell you what: You give me your number and tell me when, I'll lay a bell into you, okay?"

She removed a small memorandum book and pen from her purse, ripped out a sheet and scrawled 678-7742 on it, then pushed it over to him. "Don't lose that," she said. "The number's unlisted."

He took it, studied the number, folded the slip of paper over once, and put it in his jacket pocket. "Your pad?" he asked.

"No. It's where I do business. If I don't answer on the third ring, my answering service picks it up and takes a message."

"I don't like leaving messages. Give me a day and the time, and you be there."

"Okay. Say, tomorrow morning, eleven o'clock?"

"Okay. Let's go."

As they walked out into the fresh air, she stopped, reached into her purse, and took out a cigarette, searched for a match book and came up empty-handed. "Give me a light, will you, Whitey?"

He took the book of matches from his jacket pocket and held one to the tip of her cigarette. "Where are you parked?"

She waved toward the left side of the parking lot. "Over there in the front row. The red Datsun. See it?"

"Yeah. I'm on the other side. I'll come around and pull up in front of you, pass it to you, and take the bread."

They parted, walking in opposite directions.

In the green Plymouth sedan six spaces east of the red Datsun, Russ McNeely and Harry Deliso had been waiting patiently since eight thirty, after following Terry Dunn to the

Yardarm. In the row directly behind them, Steve Barrett and Perry Roberts also waited in Steve's Buick Skylark. Barrett and Roberts had each gone inside the Yardarm once during the past hour, returned, and reported to McNeely and Deliso that everything appeared to be going well.

In their respective vehicles, both in position to observe the entrance to the restaurant, they continued to wait, a monotonous chore that was part of the job for which training and experience had equipped them. It was September in Los Angeles, and the inner city as well as the coastline had come through a three-day Santa Ana heat wave, not an unusual occurrence at that time of year, with the weatherman's promise that relief was in sight, possibly by the next day.

At 9:40, Deliso said, "There they are," but McNeely had seen them come through the doorway, saw Terry stop and fumble in her shoulder bag, saw Whitey Lloyd lighting her cigarette; the signal that told them there would be no arrest tonight, that she had set him up for a bigger buy.

Using his walkie-talkie, McNeely spoke to Barrett and Roberts in the Skylark. "Okay, they're going to do it now, but we won't bust him. Do you copy?"

Barrett came back with, "We see them. Copy you loud and clear."

The four men watched as Terry came toward the red Datsun, unlocked and opened the left door, and stood beside it, waiting. Moments later, the black-over-silver Stingray came throatily down the aisle and braked in front of the Datsun. Terry walked to the driver's side, handed over the envelope with the eighteen one-hundred-dollar bills to Whitey Lloyd. He lifted the flap, riffled through the currency without counting it, then handed over a brown, tightly taped bag and with a wave roared out of the parking lot.

On her first two buys, Lloyd had used a '72 Chevy sedan and McNeely now recorded the license of the Stingray. Terry got into the Datsun, started the engine, and pulled out. Warily, in case Whitey had left a watcher behind, the men in the Plymouth and Skylark made no move to contact her there. On the walkie-talkie, McNeely said, "Go, Steve. Don't take him. All we want is to find out where his pad is." Barrett and Roberts took off in the direction taken by the Stingray. Moments later, McNeely and Deliso pulled out.

At the sheriff's station in Lennox, Terry Dunn, who was in fact Sharon Freeman, a sworn undercover narcotic agent and a deputy, was waiting when McNeely said, "Okay, Sherry?"

Beaming a smile, "Like a cat lapping milk." She held up

the brown bag, then tore away the tape and removed two Pliofilm bags of cocaine. Deliso took them from her and got out two plastic Narcoban envelopes for a quick field test of the crystalline powder. From each Pliofilm bag, he dropped a few grains into each of the transparent envelopes, then broke the tips of the vials that contained fluid. As the mixture of fluids touched the white crystals, the liquid turned a deep, rich blue.

"Bingo!" Deliso exclaimed. "Like before. Heavy stuff, man."

McNeely and Sherry looked and nodded agreement. McNeely said, "What's the deal, Sherry?"

"He's going to call me here tomorrow morning at eleven on the seven-seven-four-two number. I can set him up for a half pound at sixty-four hundred dollars or a pound for twelve thousand, either way you want it. I'd guess it will take him a day or two to get it together from his connection."

"It's that solid?"

"You'd better believe it." She smiled and added, "He thinks I'm going to be a part of the deal."

McNeely thought for a moment, then said, "I'll call downtown first thing in the morning and see how much we can put together. He's into us for well over a thousand now. This crook is a hell of a lot bigger than any of us thought. His connection must be something else again."

"He's got to be a monster," Sharon said with heightened enthusiasm. "When he sprang that half pound and pound bit on me, I thought I'd flip."

"High-grade and dealing heavy. Okay. I'll talk like a Dutch uncle to Barker and see if they'll go for the pound. Whatever happens on this next deal, we'll bust Lloyd and squeeze him. With a felony rap behind him, he'll be looking at a ten-to-twenty. That ought to send a few vibes up his spine."

"I tried him out on Phil Sutton. He knew him a long time ago, he claims, but that was the extent of his reaction. I don't think there was any connection there."

McNeely shrugged. "It doesn't matter. Sutton's in on a federal rap. If Lloyd goes up, he'll do his time in a state joint. And if he gives us his chief honcho, maybe we can deal him a simple possession instead of possession for sale."

"I hope so," Sharon said. "If some softheaded judge gives Whitey probation, and he runs into me somewhere on the street or in a drugstore or supermarket, bang! bang! I'm dead. Like Casey Despues."

The mention of Casey sobered them for a moment; then

McNeely said with a vague smile, "Would you rather go back to nursing fat, baldheaded business tycoons on a 727 or 747?"

"Bite your tongue, McNeely. And besides, they weren't all fat or baldheaded. Just normal everyday chauvinistic pigs on the loose from their wives for a few days."

"Take off, you sexy broad. At least you've given Whitey some pleasant dreams for a future shack job."

"Ugh. Mr. Repulsive."

"Don't knock it, kid. He's the kind who keeps you in great-looking pants suits and miniskirts."

"Hey, Russ," she teased, "could be I'm finally getting through to you?"

Deliso said, "If you feel you're missing the target, Sherry, I'm moonlighting for Russ these days."

"Boo to you, lover boy. Go back to wrestling your beach bunnies and stewardesses."

"Yeah, yeah. You'd better beat it before I start trying to break one of the department's sacred commandments."

"Okay, Harry. Good night, Russ. See you tomorrow."

Deliso had finished filling in the information on the face of the evidence envelopes, placed the cocaine in one to send along to the Criminalistics Lab for more thorough testing. In the other, he placed the photocopies of the eighteen County-advanced bills, then locked both away in the evidence vault. The package on Whitey Lloyd was growing.

"Come on, Harry," McNeely said. "I'll buy you one drink at Charlie's, then home and let the ocean lull me to sleep."

"What about Steve and Perry?"

"If they've tailed the crook to his pad, we'll know about it in the morning."

For several miles, Steve Barrett and Perry Roberts had some difficulty tailing Lloyd's Stingray along streets that had very little traffic, dropping back as far as they could and still keeping its taillights in view. Once on the Harbor Freeway, with a heavy increase in passenger-car and truck traffic, the problem lessened. Lloyd chose the extreme left lane and stepped up to just below the maximum limit. Barrett took the middle right lane and allowed several cars between the Buick and Stingray. Lloyd seemed to be in no special hurry to get to wherever he was going.

A few miles to the north, however, the situation changed dramatically when a bright yellow Porsche shot past them on the left, then cut back in front, traveling close to eighty miles an hour. Seconds later they heard the wail of a siren behind them, then caught the twirling red lights in their rear- and side-view mirrors as a California Highway Patrol car flashed by in pursuit of the yellow Porsche.

Up ahead, the Stingray accelerated and swung across the middle lanes into the extreme right lane. Roberts said, "The chippie scared him. He's running."

Barrett tried to swing right to get behind Lloyd, but oncoming truck traffic in that slow lane blocked him. Cars ahead of the Buick in the left lanes prevented him from speeding forward. By the time their view of the right lane was clear, they had passed the downtown Los Angeles off-ramp, and the Stingray was nowhere in sight. Forced to continue on, they took the next off-ramp south, but by now there was little chance of locating the Stingray and Lloyd. They circled around, found another on-ramp, and continued on to Lennox station where they found McNeely and Deliso walking out to the parking lot. "What's doing?" McNeely greeted.

"Lost him," Barrett said disconsolately. "Probably orbiting the goddamned moon by now."

"Great," McNeely chided. "Maybe I ought to send both of you back for a refresher course in tailing."

"Bullshit, Sergeant, sir," Barrett retorted. "You try keeping on top of a souped-up Stingray in a Buick with sixty-nine thousand miles on it. My own personal, privately owned car, at that."

"Okay, Barney Oldfield, cool it. I ran his tags. The car is registered in the name of Mark Trowbridge, probably phony, at a Woodland Hills address that doesn't exist."

Roberts said, "You put a want out on the car?"

"Hell, no. We want him for dealing, not a vehicle code violation."

"So what else is doing?"

"Nothing until tomorrow morning when he calls in to Sherry. Let's have a drink at Charlie's and call it a night. Tomorrow is another day."

2●

At 11:45 that night, Whitey Lloyd had been sitting in his car waiting at the corner of Warren Canyon Road just off Benedict Canyon Drive for over an hour, crouched as low as possible behind the wheel. Across the drive, the second house from the corner was dark, and his only hope was that a patrol car wouldn't come cruising along and ask him why he was parked in a remote residential area, a suspicious act in itself. And with an envelope containing eighteen hundred dollars plus seven hundred more in his wallet.

Occasionally, a car would flash by heading northward toward Mulholland Drive or south toward Sunset Boulevard, breaking the monotony of his lonely vigil. He lighted another cigarette, guarding the glowing tip with the palm of one hand. And waited.

At 12:40, he saw the '71 Cadillac he was waiting for. It pulled into Warren Canyon Road across the drive and into the driveway of the darkened house. He started the Stingray's motor, shot across Benedict Canyon Drive, and entered the private driveway just as the two men were getting out of the parked Caddy. He pulled up behind it and cut his lights. As he got out, the taller, heavier of the two men moved his hand upward and under the left armpit of his jacket.

"Eddie, Moose," Lloyd called out, "hold it. It's me. Whitey. Whitey Lloyd."

They allowed him to approach, both coldly silent, eyeing him with a mixture of angry dismay and surprise. Eddie Butler said, "How did you know about this place?"

"I've known about it for five-six months."

"How, you bastard?"

Lloyd grinned weakly. "Hey, come on now, it's no big deal. Call it an accident. One night I was driving past Anderson's on Hollywood Boulevard and saw both of you coming out with a couple of dudes. When you split from them, I followed you here, just for the hell of it."

The big man, Moose Peterson, had relaxed somewhat, standing loosely, his feet slightly apart. "You ever tell anybody about our pad?"

"No," Lloyd said, "never. I swear to Christ. I kept it to myself in case of an emergency. Like now."

"Why here?" Butler asked. "Why didn't you call Connie like you're supposed to? You know you could get yourself blown up, pulling a goddamned cops-and-robbers act on us."

"Come on, Eddie. I wouldn't have done it if it wasn't important. If I'd called Connie, it'd be two days before I'd even hear from you. I need something in a hurry."

Peterson said, "I ought to break both your fuckin' legs, you dumb bastard."

Whitey blanched, knowing Moose could do just that, and without exerting himself unduly. "Look," he said, "can't we go inside. I've got to talk to you."

"Okay," Butler said, "let's go. And it by God better be important." He led the way across the graveled path to the house, unlocked the front door, using two keys. Inside, he hit the light switch, and Whitey followed him past the large living room into the den, Moose Peterson directly behind him. Butler motioned Lloyd to a green leather chair and sat in the matching one facing him. Peterson went to the bar and sat on a tall stool.

"Okay, Whitey, what the hell is so important?" Butler asked. There was no warmth in his eyes or voice.

"I'm on a deal. The biggest I've ever run into. Clean and easy, and I need some help from—"

"Never mind the window dressing. What's your problem?" Butler cut him off impatiently.

"Okay. There's this chick I've been dealing for a month now. Strictly a class deal. She scores for a dude who's big with the movie, TV, and rock groups. She's been scoring off Phil Sutton, who got busted by the narcs six weeks ago, okay? I ran across her through a dude I've been dealing to who was scoring off Phil, too.

"I sold her a taste, and her guy liked it. She came on for a piece, and tonight for the two pieces I got from you the other day. Okay. Now she's ready to do more, and that's the problem."

"So *what's* the problem?" Butler asked. "You could have called Connie and ordered it, couldn't you, without coming here—"

"The problem," Whitey said with a show of exaggerated patience, "is that I can't front the bread for up to a pound, and if I don't show with it, I lose her. She needs product, good stuff. In her league, price is practically no object. She'll go for the pound, even more, on a regular basis if I can keep supplying her."

Butler's eyes widened with incredulity. "Let me get you straight. You're asking us to front a *pound* of coke to you on credit?"

Lloyd nodded. "This one time, Eddie. If I can do this pound, I'll be able to come up with the bread I need from now on. This once is all I'm asking, Eddie."

Peterson, sipping the drink he had poured for himself, snorted with contempt. Butler shook his head from side to side. "No way, Whitey," he said. "You're just blowing soap bubbles. This is strictly a cash business, and you know it. We've never fronted anything for anybody, not even our biggest customers, and you're way down on our list. You want to deal for any amount, the bread's got to be out in front."

"Will you just listen, Eddie," Whitey pleaded hoarsely.

"This is the biggest break I've ever tied into. It could be for you guys, too, the kind of real action you want. I know it can go up to kilo lots, give me a little time. Or do you want me to look somewhere else?"

Butler grinned, malevolence showing. "Where the fuck you think you can find that kind of action without the bread up front, man? That's asshole talk, and you know it."

"Look, Eddie, you been dealing me how long, four-five years, right? Did I ever stiff you once? Cash on the line every time, right?"

"Sure, and we appreciate the patronage, Whitey, but the cash was always up front. Spoons, balloons, a half ounce, two whole ounces the last time. All for cash. Now you're talking big, a whole pound, and you expect us to front it for you?"

"Eddie, why don't you look at what's behind this deal. This is the cleanest, easiest thing you ever saw, and I've been around long enough to know clean from dirty. I stand to make a nice bundle and take it from there. It's big, and it can go a hell of a lot bigger in that crowd. For all of us. It's just that right now I'm short and can't front the deal. If you're worried about it I'll rent or borrow another car and let you hold my Stingray for collateral, along with the pink slip. It's only five months old, less than six thousand miles on it, cost me over seven grand."

"We're not in the used-car business, Whitey, and we don't do business on credit. Forget it. You're way the hell out of line."

"Okay." Lloyd started up out of the chair. "If that's what I get after all the bread I've laid on you guys—"

Moose Peterson said, "Wait a minute, Whitey. Sit down." And to Butler, "Eddie, can I talk to you a minute?"

Butler looked annoyed, then nodded his assent. Both men went out into the hallway toward the living room.

"What is it, Moose?"

"Look, we'd better see if we can't square this thing some way. That little bastard's found out where we live. He knows Connie's number. He may even know more than that, and I don't like the idea of turning him loose with a bug up his ass. Don would blow his stack if he knew this creep was running loose and mad enough to shoot his mouth off in the wrong places."

"Well—I don't know, Moose. What the hell do you think Don would say if we fronted a pound of coke to a guy who never bought more than two ounces in his whole life? If Don was in town, I'd let him pass on it, but he won't be back for another week."

"It's too risky, Eddie. That asshole could get some freaky notion in his head, sore as he is right now. In a pinch, he could even turn us."

"You're saying we ought to go with this?"

"Well, it could work out, and we could keep an eye on him until his deal goes down. We front the pound, let him know we'll be on his tail all the time. We see it go down, he comes over to our car, pays off, we split. If it works, he'll make himself a fast profit, and we don't have to front him anymore."

"Could be." Butler thought for a moment, then, "Okay, but we don't turn it over to him until he's ready to go down with his deal. It'll be over and done before Don ever hears about it."

In the den, Lloyd waited with the feeling that he was making progress. If he failed in this effort, he would be forced to use his ace in the hole; the four thousand dollars hidden in his stash to be used only in the event of desperate emergency. That, plus the eighteen hundred paid him by Terry Dunn earlier and the seven hundred in his wallet. Plus what he could get for the Stingray. Getaway money, if necessary; to pay a bail bondsman's fee if, God forbid, he got busted; or in a case like this, a last resort, to put up every dime he could scrape together.

He hoped they wouldn't go for his offer to turn the Stingray over to them, and he hated the thought of putting up every cent he owned. Even at that, he would be short, and his only remaining hope would then be to try to tap Lee Michele for the balance; but— He knew she had it. Every cent she could put aside went into her savings account at the bank where she worked. But he had serious doubts that Lee would help him in any financial venture. Share her bed and body, yes, and welcome, but when it came to money, no way. It would probably all be over in a minute if she suspected he was involved in dope. Even borrowing her Chevy had been a hassle.

He went to the bar and poured a bourbon and water for himself, trying to think of alternatives, failing. A dope dealer making a touch? Not a chance. Not even a loan shark would make him a loan, no matter how much interest he was willing to pay. Everything now depended on the outcome of the conversation in the other room. Let it be. Let it be. He refused to give any thought to the stash of dope he had in his apartment; that, along with his cash, was his insurance, and the thought of risking any of it was foreign to him.

He tossed off the drink and fixed another, thinking of the brighter side. If this deal went down, there would be others to follow, with a sweet profit in each pound deal. He'd work it up to kilo lots and have it made in no time. He would make a cool play for Terry Dunn, dump Lee Michele, move into a better pad. Maybe at the marina. Buy a nice, comfortable sailboat. That luscious broad and a tie-in with the movie-TV-record freaks. The top of the list. Jesus, let it come through, just this one time, and he'd be sitting up there with the best of them. He might even make a connection of his own down South, travel to Mexico and South America, head up his own organization. Like Butler and Peterson and their chief honcho, whoever the hell he was.

Then Eddie and Moose were back, Eddie, as always, the spokesman, Moose the cold-eyed silent one. "Okay, Whitey," Butler said, "we'll go along with you this one time. And you'd better watch yourself because Moose'll be keeping an eye on you. You turn the stuff over, cop the bread, let the broad split. You go to Moose's car and pay off. Got it?"

Immense relief was reflected in Lloyd's happy smile. "Got it, and thanks, Eddie. Where can I pick it up?"

"You don't. Moose drops it off at your pad, then follows you to make the meet. He'll be behind you somewhere, keeping you in sight."

"When?"

"Wednesday night. There'll be a fifteen per cent hike in the price and don't complain. You buy on credit, you pay a service charge. You'll still come out with a nice profit."

Lloyd was in no position to argue or dicker. "Okay. Wednesday night. Make it around seven, seven-fifteen. I'll set up the meet for eight-thirty. The Crenshaw Shopping Center. Stores are open until nine o'clock."

"Okay, Whitey. Just remember, you screw up this deal, you won't have any place to hide. It'll be your ass."

"Don't worry, Eddie. This one is like money in the bank."

At a little past noon on the following day, Moose Peterson and Eddie Butler drove to San Pedro, checking carefully to make certain they were not being followed. They turned off Harbor Boulevard into Sixth Street and entered the open gates to the Hernandez Auto Works, a large block-long, half-block-wide yard of auto carcasses, small repair shops, and a body-painting shed. They parked the '71 Cadillac beside the office, then went to the large warehouse building behind it. Inside, they walked along a narrow aisle of bins to a door and knocked.

When Simon Hernandez called out, "Yes?" Butler opened the door, and both men entered. "Hello, Simon," Butler greeted. Peterson remained silent.

Of the two, neither of whom he liked, Hernandez despised the taller, heavier one, Peterson, a man whose cold, pale eyes spoke of unknown, untold cruelty. His very presence caused Hernandez to shudder slightly as he used to, as a child in his native Mexico, at the sight of a snake. Butler, the smaller one, Simon regarded with caution, the more clever of the two, since the large man always deferred to him, yet no less dangerous.

"Yes?" Hernandez replied to the greeting without warmth.

Butler said, "I need a pound of coke for a special customer. How is our inventory?"

"It is low, the coke, perhaps less than two kilos. The heroin, we have perhaps three or four."

"Jesus," Butler said, "that's pretty damn low. We'll have to do something about it. Right now, I need a pound."

Hernandez said, "Now? At once?"

"By Wednesday afternoon, early."

"Let me see what we have here." Hernandez stood up and took a ring of keys from his pocket, then locked the outside door. Butler and Peterson followed as he went to the wall panel behind his desk, slid it to one side, then fitted a key into the door that stood exposed. Behind the door was a long, narrow room that ran the full width of the office, about ten feet deep, windowless. To the right was a wall sectioned off into bins that were filled with miscellaneous cartons of auto parts. Hernandez unlatched and swung an end bottom section aside, lifted a steel floor plate, reached inside, and removed a carton. He placed it on a long table and waved a hand toward the two men.

Butler examined the contents, several sacks of white powder, picked one up, and noted the tag tied to it, reading aloud, "Sixteen ounces. This ought to do it."

"You wish to take it with you now?"

"No, Simon, not now. Pack this in a small carton, and Moose will return for it Wednesday around three o'clock."

"You will be with him?"

"No. I'll be busy."

"Then will you sign for it now?"

"Okay." Hernandez took a small black ledger from the same floor opening, recorded the date, time, and amount, then gave it to Butler, who scrawled his name beside the entry. The book was then replaced, steel plate held open while Moose brought the carton from the table and put it back into the opening. Hernandez lowered the plate and relocked it, then positioned the bin and locked that into place.

The transaction completed, they returned to the office. Butler said, "We'll have to play it close for a while, Simon, until we can bring some more stuff in. You get a chance, have your people repackage what you've got there into half and quarter pounds, okay?"

Hernandez shrugged. "As you wish."

"Good. See you later, Simon."

They went out, and Simon Hernandez once again felt relief. He lit a thin cigar, then went over the list of spare-parts deliveries that had been made the day before, comparing them with the typed invoices that were ready to be mailed out to his garage customers.

Outside in the Cadillac, Eddie Butler said, "I still don't feel too good about this deal. I'd hate like hell for Don to find out about it."

"Hell, Eddie," Peterson replied, "I don't see that anything can go wrong. Whitey's small time, but he's a careful dealer. He knows his people. This could work into a good deal all around, like he says."

"Yeah, but there's always a first time. I just hope to hell it goes down fast. Don never did like working with little dealers."

"Don't worry. I'll be sittin' on top of him from the time I turn it over to him until the payoff."

3●

Next morning, McNeely phoned Lieutenant Bob Barker, who headed Zone II of the Narcotics bureau, in charge of sheriff's Lennox, Firestone, and West Hollywood narcotics crews. Barker told McNeely to stand by while he talked with Captain John Esau, the bureau commander. Half an hour later Barker called back with the captain's decision to go for the pound of cocaine at twelve thousand dollars which, since they intended to arrest Lloyd on this turnover, would make a much stronger case than a half-pound buy.

At ten-thirty, attractively miniskirted, legs beautifully sheathed in sheer flesh-tone nylons, Sharon Freeman appeared at the station, drawing sighs and whistles from McNeely's Major Violator crew of four and three of the regular station crew of six, who paused in their labors to admire her.

In the far corner of the large room, beyond the personal and equipment lockers and filing cabinets and behind the desk of Laurie Kelly, secretary to both crews, stood a telephone booth. Inside on the ledge were four telephones that were patched into a Sony cassette recorder. Each phone was hooked into its own outside line that bypassed the central station switchboard. The numbers were 678-7742, 678-4310, 678-5696, and 678-8847 and were unlisted, used only by the crews in contacting, or being contacted by, special informants, dealers, and others with whom it was necessary to discuss confidential matters of business.

On the wall above each telephone was a separate pressure-sensitized label with precise instructions. The first read:

678-7742

TO BE ANSWERED BY A FEMALE,
"678-7742"

The others:

678-4310

TO BE ANSWERED BY A FEMALE,
"WESTVIEW DEVELOPMENT. MAY
I HELP YOU?"

678-5696

TO BE ANSWERED BY A MALE,
"SOUTH BAY HEALTH CLUB"

678-8847

TO BE ANSWERED BY A MALE,
"JOHNNIE'S BAR"

From time to time the instructions, as one fell into disuse, were changed according to need of the crew members. The one used most often was the 678-7742 number, given to Whitey Lloyd by Sharon.

This was the "catch up" time of day when most dope dealers were generally off the streets, either making contacts or asleep. Their working hours would not begin until later in the day and go well into the night, which made it a very long day for the narcotics crew members, working broken hours and much overtime. Now, while they were engaged in bringing their daily logs up to date, typing supplementary reports, making telephone calls, recording mileage and overtime, Sharon waited at Laurie Kelly's desk sipping at a cup of coffee drawn from the pot kept active throughout the day.

"What's doing, Sherry?" Laurie asked in the familiar catchall greeting used by the men.

"I'm waiting for an eleven o'clock on seven-seven-four-two."

"That Lloyd character?"

"Yes."

"Getting any closer?"

"Any closer and he'll be breathing inside my bra."

"Ah, you kids get all the breaks."

"I'll give you Lloyd for a birthday present. A card-carrying creep with breath to match. I'd hate to be alone with him in a room unless I had my gun on me."

"With that outfit, he could spot a needle."

"This isn't for him. I'm working with the West Hollywood guys on a dude who's taking me to lunch. A real smoothie type. Strictly Sunset Strip clients."

Laurie, older and considerably plainer than Sharon, sighed. "Like I said, you kids get all the breaks. Look at these characters around here. Most of them look like the creeps they deal with."

At that moment, the 678-7742 phone rang, and on the second ring Sharon stepped into the booth, closed the door, and activated the tape recorder. She lifted the receiver and spoke the number.

"Terry?"

"Yes. Whitey?"

"Yeah. How you doing?"

"Fine. Hey, listen, I talked with my guy last night, and it's okay."

"How heavy?"

"The pound this time. Twelve thousand, right? Can you do it?"

"Sure. It's all set."

"Hey, that's great. When can we do it?"

"I'll need two days to get it together. Say, Wednesday night?"

"Okay. I'll have the bread lined up by then. Where?"

"I'll call you on Wednesday around six o'clock and lay it out for you. This same number?"

"Sure. Same quality, Whitey?"

"Guaranteed. Jesus, don't you trust me yet?"

She laughed provocatively. "As much as you trust me."

"Well, hell, that's good. Hey, how about you and me?"

"What about?"

"You know. Like you deliver to your guy, then meet me later."

"Sounds good to me. Your pad?"

"Sure, baby, where else. You'll like it."

"Where?"

"I'll take you there when we meet after you deliver to your guy and I unload the bread."

"Yes, okay. Whitey—?"

"What?"

"I'm a little nervous carrying all that bread with me. Would you mind if I brought somebody along with me to ride shotgun? I'd hate to get ripped off for the bread or the stuff."

"Oh, baby, you got nothing to worry about. I don't like shotguns. Hell, I don't use one myself—"

"Sure, but you carry a piece on you, don't you?"

"Well, yeah, but if you want, I'll ride along behind you while you deliver."

"Uh—no, I can't do that, Whitey. My guy would blow his gourd."

"Well, hell, baby, two's okay, but three's a crowd, and I don't like witnesses, you know?"

"Okay, then, we'll do it your way."

"Only way to go. I'll call you Wednesday at six."

"Right on." She hung up and deactivated the Sony, rewound the tape, removed the cassette, and replaced it with a fresh one.

The major crew, McNeely, Deliso, Roberts, and Barrett, were waiting. Joe Paul, the fifth member, was in court testifying. Sharon placed the cassette into the desk recorder and started the playback. They listened intently until it had run its course, then rewound and played it again. At its conclusion McNeely said, "At least he didn't mention anything about being tailed last night. It must have been the chippie who scared him."

Barrett said, "He's a cagey bastard, wouldn't come across with the address of his pad."

"Well, so far, so good," McNeely said. "We'll get it set up for Wednesday night and make the bust."

On Wednesday night at six-ten, Lloyd's call came through, and Sharon was there to take it. "Terry?"

"Yes, Whitey."

"You all set?"

"Yes. Where and what time?"

"You know the Crenshaw Shopping Center?"

"I know it."

"Okay. Eight-thirty, behind the Safeway supermarket."

"Eight-thirty, Safeway. Okay."

"It'll probably be crowded. Park somewhere as close as you can get. The red Datsun?"

"Yes."

"I'll be in the Stingray. I'll find you. If you spot me first, flash your headlights once."

"Right. See you soon."

"And after?"

"Sure, as soon as I make the delivery. See you."

At 7:45, she parked the red Datsun two rows behind the huge Safeway supermarket. The entire conglomeration of shops would remain open until nine o'clock, and parking space was virtually at a premium, a vital factor in Lloyd's operation. In a mobile, single-minded crowd of people driving and walking to and from stores to shop and load bags and packages into car trunks, almost any other activity would go unnoticed; this despite the well-known fact that patrol cars occasionally cruised by, alert for robbers and purse snatchers.

In the Plymouth parked in the row directly behind the Datsun were Russ McNeely and Harry Deliso; Steve Barrett and Perry Roberts were in the Skylark in the front row; to the right of the Datsun, in the same row, were Joe Paul and Vic Lopez, the latter borrowed from Bill Hamlin's crew, in Joe's Olds 88. Only the Plymouth was radio-equipped, the three cars in contact by walkie-talkie. On the front seat of the Plymouth, an additional receiver was tied to the same frequency as the Fargo transmitter in Sharon's left boot, a tape recorder hooked into the receiver. McNeely and Deliso were thus able to listen in and record the conversation between Sharon and Whitey Lloyd, but there was no way by which they could contact her by voice.

"I'm in position," Sharon said into her bra mike as she parked. "Do you copy me, Russ?"

In reply, McNeely flashed his headlights on and off. By

walkie-talkie, he contacted the men in the Skylark and Oldsmobile, who reported their positions.

"Okay," McNeely said. "When I get the signal from Sherry, I'll flash it to you and we move in according to plan. Keep your eyes on the Plymouth. And watch it. He'll probably be wearing a gun."

The other cars acknowledged with a "Ten-four."

It was 2010. Ten past eight. They waited without talking or smoking, watching out of either side of their cars for a possible watcher sent on ahead to scout the location, but none appeared to be other than normal traffic.

At eight twenty-seven, Sharon's voice came through on the Plymouth's receiver. "I see him on my right, the silver Stingray. This row is packed like sardines in a can, Russ. He'll probably come around and up the aisle behind me, in front of you. When he does, why don't you pull out and let him have your space behind me while you cruise around."

McNeely flashed his headlights on and off, signaling that he understood and would comply. As the Stingray drove slowly by the Datsun, Sharon flashed the agreed signal. Lloyd saw it, waved a hand in her direction, and continued on. Sharon said, "Okay, he's made me and is going around."

McNeely watched and saw the Stingray on the up leg in the aisle behind Sharon. As it approached, McNeely started his motor and turned on his headlights. Lloyd braked the Stingray and waited. When McNeely pulled out to his right, Lloyd pulled up, then backed into the vacated space, cut his engine, and flicked his lights off and on, then off again.

Sharon said, "Here I go," into her bra mike, got out of the Datsun, walked back across the aisle to the sports car, and got in as the Plymouth began to circle the area slowly. On its receiver, McNeely and Deliso began to pick up Lloyd's greeting and the ensuing conversation as Deliso activated the tape recorder.

LLOYD (exuberantly): Hey, Terry, baby, you look great. What's doing?

SHARON: Okay, Whitey. You?

LLOYD: Super. Never better. How was the last stuff?

SHARON: It checked out fine. Very relevant.

LLOYD: You bet. Best goddamn stuff you'll find on the street anywhere in the country.

SHARON: *Sure, Whitey, but like I told you, we don't deal on the street, remember? Our people can pay, and they want the best.*

LLOYD: *Well, that's what you're getting from me. (A pause, then) Man, I'd like to have a list like yours.*

SHARON: *You're doing all right, aren't you?*

LLOYD: *Yeah, sure, but I don't like having to depend on somebody else. I'd like to break out on my own.*

SHARON: *You mean dealing in pounds isn't big enough to keep you in Stingrays?*

LLOYD: *Hell, I don't deal pounds to everybody. If I did, I'd have my own organization, hit the real big time.*

SHARON: *Well, who knows? If we put a few more deals like this one together, maybe you can, with the right connection.*

LLOYD: *Yeah, that's one of the problems, to get a connection like my guy's got.*

SHARON: *Can't you get to him?*

LLOYD: *No way. My guy wouldn't let me get anywhere near to him. He's as big a secret as where they mill the stuff.*

SHARON: *Okay, let's do it, shall we? My guy's a little anxious, me handling this kind of a deal all by myself.*

LLOYD: *Hey, nothing to be afraid of, for Christ's sake. You're goin'a meet me later, right?*

SHARON: *Sure, Whitey. I said I would.*

LLOYD (eagerly now): *Where?*

SHARON: *Uh—how about the Yardarm bar, like last time? Say about eleven thirty or twelve.*

LLOYD: *Hey, great. We can have a drink before we go to my pad.*

SHARON: *Fine. The sooner we do it, the sooner I'll be through.*

LLOYD: *Yeah. You got the twelve?*

SHARON: *Right here. (A pause of seven seconds, then) It's all there. Count it if you like.*

LLOYD: *Jesus Christ. Now ain't that pretty. (A pause of thirteen seconds, then) Hell, I give up. It's too damned dark in here. I trust you. Here's the stuff.*

SHARON *(after a few moments)*: *That's a pretty small package for a whole pound, isn't it? Is it all there?*

LLOYD: *It's all there, packed tight. I checked the weight myself, every gram of it.*

SHARON *(laughing)*: *Okay, now I'll trust you. Hey, now, it's the same-quality product, right?*

LLOYD: *Guaranteed, like I told you. Came in on the same shipment as the last load.*

The word "product" was the agreed upon signal that the exchange had been made. McNeely, on the walkie-talkie, flashed the word to the Skylark and Oldsmobile. "Let's go!"

At that moment, he was on the upleg swing of the rear aisle and slowly braked the Plymouth behind the Stingray as though looking for a parking space. Sharon stalled as the Skylark came up the aisle in front. Joe Paul and Vic Lopez were out of the Olds and approaching on foot as though they were on their way into the supermarket. In the Stingray, Lloyd had turned his attention to the possibility of another deal. "How about next time? When do you think your guy will be ready?"

"Let's see how this one goes, Whitey. I'd guess another pound in about two weeks. If he puts a two-cut on this, that'll give him three pounds to get rid of, but with his people I don't think that's going to be much of a problem."

"You know, if we could step this up to a key a month, or every six weeks—"

Deliso and McNeely were out of the Plymouth, crouched low between the Stingray and a Mercury on its left side. Joe Paul and Vic Lopez were just then making their way between the right side of the Stingray and a Ford station wagon. Then Lloyd became aware of the Skylark blocking the Stingray from the front, two men getting out, coming toward him.

"Hey!" he called out, starting to open the door on his side, "What the hell you guys—"

McNeely pounced then, pulled the door wide open, and

grabbed Lloyd's left arm. Lloyd pulled back, reaching up under his left arm with his right. Sharon screamed, "Watch it, Russ! Gun!"

McNeely's head and shoulders were inside the car now, his right hand curled around Lloyd's neck, a tight grip on his right wrist. Then Joe Paul had the door open on the passenger side, gripped Sharon's right arm, and tugged her out of the car, and shoved her back out of Lloyd's sight. Vic Lopez leaped into the seat vacated by Sharon, the two-inch barrel of his detective special at Lloyd's right temple. "Freeze, Lloyd. Sheriff's Narcotics. Hands over your head, and don't make a move that'll get you blown up."

Resistance was foolhardy, and he knew it. McNeely's hand found Lloyd's gun in the holster under his left arm and removed it, gave it to Harry Deliso. Dejected, Lloyd slumped down in his seat, snarling, "Oh, Jesus! Jesus Christ! That lousy bitch! I trusted her—"

"Outside, Lloyd. Keep your hands over your head and your mouth shut."

He came out on McNeely's side, shoulders trembling, knees buckling. "Turn around. Hands on top of the car, feet spread out and back," Deliso ordered.

Cursing, wild-eyed with anger and frustration, surrounded by six deputies, he obeyed. Deliso patted him down expertly, removed the manila envelope with the 120 hundred-dollar bills in it, and handed it to McNeely. Satisfied that he had no other weapons, he cuffed Lloyd's hands behind him, led him to the rear seat of the Plymouth, and got in beside him as McNeely slid behind the wheel. Deliso then began reading Lloyd his rights.

It had been swift, efficient, and was over in a matter of seconds, so quickly that the entire drama went almost unnoticed except for two elderly couples who were removing large sacks of groceries from their shopping carts, placing them into the trunks of their cars and on the rear seats. For a moment or two they stared at the proceedings, then turned back to their preoccupation with their purchases.

And, except for the man who sat behind the wheel of the '71 Cadillac two rows behind the action, stunned by the scene he had witnessed, pounding the steering wheel and mouthing silent curses under his breath.

In the Plymouth, Whitey Lloyd continued to curse "Terry Dunn," using every foul expletive in his street vocabulary, in which he was expert. When they had driven a few blocks, Deliso turned to him and said, "Okay, Lloyd, I'm going to tell you this just one time and no more. You keep your god-damned dirty mouth shut until we get to where we're going, or I'll knock your teeth down your throat." When Lloyd stared balefully at him without replying, Deliso said, "You want a cigarette?"

"How the fuck can I smoke with my hands behind my back?"

"I'll hold it for you. It's good for jangled nerves, and yours are pretty jangled right now."

"Ah, you mother—"

"Ah-ah. You want the cigarette or your teeth to swallow?"

Lloyd surrendered. "Okay."

"Nice thinking. Relax." Harry puffed a cigarette to life and placed it between Lloyd's lips.

McNeely, behind the wheel, listened and remained silent. His turn would come when they had Lloyd inside the station. Sharon, her part of the game over now, had slipped away from the shopping center in the Datsun and was headed for her apartment in Hollywood.

In the second row behind where the Stingray had been parked, Moose Peterson sat in sullen, impotent anger as he witnessed the entire proceedings, unable to warn Lloyd of impending doom as he saw the men coming from three sides to surround the silver and black car. Any signal by voice or horn would focus attention on himself, and that, of course, was unthinkable. He got out of his Cadillac and walked to the trunk, opened it, able to see better from a standing position, fading into the background of normal activity until it was all over.

When the last car pulled out of the parking lot, he got back into the car and at a safe distance followed the parade of officers back to Lennox, saw them remove the handcuffed Whitey Lloyd and take him inside the station. Driving away, he wondered how he would break the news to Eddie; how they would break the news to Don Reed; how much of a lac-ing he and Eddie would have to take for fronting a pound of cocaine to Lloyd on their own, a loss they could never hope to recoup.

Ah, Jesus, Moose reflected wearily. *It's getting so you don't know who the hell you can trust these days.*

At Lennox station, Barrett and Roberts gave the Stingray a top-to-bottom, front-to-rear search and found no further incriminating evidence other than that the registration card in the glove compartment did not match up with the name Whitey Lloyd. They marked the car to be held for impounding, locked it, and returned to the Narcotics office. Vic Lopez took off for home, leaving the cleanup details to the major crew.

The handcuffs were removed by Deliso. Roberts ordered Lloyd to empty his pockets onto a bare table: wallet with $723 in it; some loose bills and change in his side trouser pocket; credit-card folder with a driver's license in the name of Whitey Lloyd and another in the name of Mark Trowbridge, each showing a different address; cigarettes, match book, keys, gold pen and pencil set, a few inconsequential papers. Off came the ring and watch. To the pile was added the .32 automatic, its clip removed, bullets ejected, the holster. Beside these items, Steve Barrett added the small carton that contained a bag of heavy Pliofilm with the pound of cocaine sealed inside. Steve opened the bag and removed a pinch of the crystals for the Narcoban test, which showed approximately the same strength as the previous buys made by Sharon.

"Okay, Lloyd," Roberts ordered, "stand up and strip down to your shorts."

Each item of his clothing, including shoes and socks, were carefully examined. "Turn around, drop your shorts, spread your legs and bend over. Rest your elbows on the desk." When Lloyd, grim-faced and tight-lipped, complied, Roberts checked his body for any foreign matter that might be taped to his flesh, the bottoms of his feet, or inserted in his anal orifice. Satisfied, Lloyd was told to dress again.

There had been little or no conversation during the body search, Lloyd accepting it with sullen hostility as a necessary procedure according to law, one with which he was familiar. The preliminary paperwork concluded, McNeely took over.

"Sit there, Whitey," he said, indicating the chair beside his desk.

"What about bail?" Lloyd said.

"That will be set sometime after we get the complaint from the D.A.'s office."

"How about my phone call?"

"Let's not rush things. After you've been booked, printed, and photographed, ask the jailer. He'll let you make it then." McNeely glanced at the penciled preliminary arrest report for a few moments, then said, "All right, Whitey. We've placed you under arrest for possession of a dangerous narcotic, sale of a dangerous narcotic, three counts, and possession of a concealed dangerous weapon by an ex-felon. You were read your rights in the presence of a witnessing officer at the time of your arrest and said you understood those rights. Am I correct?"

"Okay, okay."

"Do you want to talk to me about this case?"

"What's to talk about, for Christ's sake. You brought in a broad and rigged me for a bust. You rip me off for my bread, then ask me do I want a lawyer. What the fuck am I supposed to pay him with?"

"You're entitled to a court-appointed lawyer, free of charge, remember?"

Lloyd snorted contemptuously. "Sure. Some punk kid fresh out of law school who couldn't find a case for himself inside a goddamn prison. Or an old flake with a case load of a thousand freebies."

McNeely smiled and said softly, "Look, Whitey, nobody held a gun to your head and forced you into dealing dope, and this isn't your first bust. It was your own choice, but you keep forgetting there are rules on both sides of the game. You play by yours, we play by ours."

"Oh, come on, man, spare me the pig-shit lecture, will you? Can I have one of my cigarettes, or do I need a goddam writ of habeas corpus?"

McNeely slid the pack of Marlboros and match book across the desk within Lloyd's reach. As he lit up, sucking deeply, exhaling slowly, McNeely said, "I'm not here to lecture you, Whitey. You're a junk dealer with a felony prior, caught with a heavy load, enough to win you a possible ten-to-twenty. That's what you've got staring you in the face. The ballgame is over. You're thirty-one. If you cop the minimum, you'll be forty-one when you get out, fifty-one if you go the full route, less whatever time you can earn on good behavior."

"Bullshit, man. I can make a good case of entrapment out of this."

"Don't give us that jailhouse-lawyer crap, Whitey. We've got you cold on three separate buys, all witnessed. With judges getting tougher on you dealers for profit, you could very well go the full twenty. Think about it."

Lloyd was thinking of little else, puffing harder on his cigarette, considering the odds that were working against him. And even if he could somehow get a free ride, how could he square himself with Butler and Peterson? Inner tension produced beads of sweat on his forehead, and his jawline tightened, showing hard ridges. Now his eyes were narrowed to mere slits as he assessed his situation. "He did it, didn't he?" he said suddenly.

"Who did what?" McNeely asked.

"Phil. Phil Sutton, the bastard. He got busted and turned me to make a deal. That's how that bitch Terry Dunn framed me, wasn't it?"

Deliso, leaning against the desk, grabbed Lloyd by his shirt front and pulled him up to his feet. "Listen, Trashmouth, one more crack like that and you're going to be picking yourself off the floor. Now you sit there and answer questions or not, but knock off the slime."

He let go, and Lloyd fell back into his chair. "All right," McNeely said, "let's all cool it." He gathered up the bills and loose change found on Lloyd's person and began counting the money slowly and carefully as Lloyd watched and accepted the count as accurate and initialed the report. The money was placed into an evidence envelope except for the loose bills and change, which were returned to Lloyd along with his watch, ring, wallet, and loose papers. "All right, let's get you properly booked and settled down for the night. The van will be here tomorrow morning around eight-thirty to give you a ride down to county jail."

"Hey, wait a minute—"

"What's on your mind, Whitey?"

Indecisively, Lloyd looked from McNeely to Barrett, to Roberts, to Paul, to Deliso, then back to McNeely, running the tip of his tongue over his lower lip. "Look, man, is there some way we can make a deal?"

McNeely studied him quietly for a moment, then said, "I don't know, Whitey. There's such a thing as cooperation, but we can't make any definite promises to you."

"Come on, man, don't hand me that bullshit. I know the scam. It wouldn't be the first time, and it won't be the last. You can talk to the D.A., and he can talk to the judge."

Behind his back, Paul, Roberts, and Deliso exchanged knowing winks. Everything was beginning to fall into line.

McNeely said, "Sure we can, but it all depends on what you're offering us. We're not talking about a two-bit pusher or a street hype, Whitey. You're a heavy dealer and—"

"Look, I know I can't buy a free ride. I'm willing to do some time—"

"Well, that's very nice of you. What are you offering to trade?"

"I want to know first how far you'll front for me."

McNeely shook his head negatively. "No guarantees, Whitey. You're con wise enough to know that. You come up with something big enough, and we'll consider talking to the D.A. If you score say, eighty or ninety on the exam, we might drop the gun charge and ask him to let you cop a plea on possession instead of sale. I'd guess, and it's only a guess, of course, you might draw a year in county."

Lloyd was leaning forward now, sweating heavily, his shirt streaked with it, thinking hard, trying to come to a decision. "Well?" McNeely prompted.

He shook the question off. "I'll pass for now," he said. "I want to think it over."

"Okay, do that. When you're ready to talk to us, have the jailer downtown phone me. Come along now, and let's get you tucked in for the night."

4 •

It was nearing eleven when Russ McNeely reached Manhattan Beach, turned off Highland Avenue into Eighteenth Place, then into Ocean Drive, and activated the electronically controlled garage door beneath his house. Parked, he climbed the flight of stairs to the upper level and, once inside, felt the weariness of the long day bear its full weight upon him. He stripped off his jacket and shirt, went to the small bar in the living room, and poured some Scotch into a tall glass, added two cubes of ice and some water, then threw open the two large sliding-glass doors that led to the sundeck overlooking the beach and black ocean beyond.

Past his middle thirties, McNeely had the athletic body of a man who had taken exceptionally good care of himself. He stood half an inch over the six-foot mark, his trim 190 pounds evenly distributed over a slender frame that showed no evidence of fat. His hair was still very dark, showing no sign of recession or graying. His face was long and angular with well-spaced brown eyes, straight nose, and even teeth. As frequently as he could, he rose early and ran along the beach for a mile or two, took a swim in the cold ocean, then ran back to his house to shower, shave, and dress for the day. Breakfast was held down to the minimum orange juice, toast, and coffee, a concession to the heavier lunch and dinner that would follow. Only when he was due for his regular departmental physical did he give any thought to cutting down on his smoking.

Drink in hand, he went to the far end of the deck and looked toward the house on his right, noting the absence of lights, an indication that Rachel Nugent hadn't returned from her buying trip to New York. Then he sat in one of the two terrycloth-covered lounge chairs and stared out into the mist that had rolled in from the west some hours earlier.

The Whitey Lloyd thing, he thought with satisfaction, was done for the moment, and now he was inwardly stirred by the possibilities to which it could lead; mainly, the bigger dealer on top, Lloyd's connection. Someone high enough in the system to supply cocaine and heroin in pound, possibly kilo, lots.

Although it was standard procedure to learn from a user who his pusher was, get the pusher to turn his connection, and keep moving up the ladder in this tedious, time- and energy-consuming manner, it was a truly rare event when the people on top, the bankrollers, principal distributors, or top-echelon dealers were caught in the net. The higher up one moved, the farther removed and insulated were the top operators, the chief honchos. Now with the possibility of a major dealer on hand, there was that bare, outside chance.

And, of course, at the higher levels, the dangers increased, requiring careful investigation and undercover work in which McNeely would be hesitant to use Sharon Freeman, Patti Hendrix, or any of the other female undercover deputies. He weighed the thought of trying to work one of the department's top operators into the scheme of things, Johnny Segura. But the department would hesitate to pull Johnny out of his present undercover work, where he was having great success locating stolen guns, in order to break a narcotics case. In any event, depending on what Lloyd turned up if he decided to talk, he could make his definite plans later.

Sutton, a dealer who was a step higher than Lloyd, had led them in this direction, along with the names of several other dealers, for which he had received a lighter sentence than the fifteen years he could have gotten. From here, with luck, they might reach the top. What pleased McNeely most of all was that they were dealing in cocaine, the highest-priced narcotic on the market, which had proliferated considerably in the county in recent years. It took big money to bring it in from South America and Mexico in quantity, big money to pay for it at the user level. Any opening above Whitey Lloyd would be very rewarding.

He finished his drink and went into the master bedroom that faced the ocean, stripped, then went to the bathroom and showered. He fell into bed and was asleep at once.

As it had happened many times in the past, and for no specific reason he could attribute it to, Russ McNeely came out of his deep sleep as suddenly alert as though he had slept the night through. And, lying there in the darkness, he knew instinctively that no more than an hour or two had passed since he had fallen asleep.

He turned on his right side and touched the button in the base of the lamp; the lights came on. The clock showed 0210. Before switching it off, he saw the triple-sectioned frame that held separate pictures of his mother, Nora, who had died in 1956 when he was twenty-one, and of his father, Peter, still alive at the age of seventy-three, retired now. The third section, now blank, had contained the photograph of himself and Carol, taken on their wedding day, but he had removed it after she left California to return to Chicago in 1965; a meaningless gesture since the blank space only served to bring her back to his mind more vividly than before. One could destroy a picture, but never a memory. He turned the lamp off.

September. Two dates most prominent in his mind. He and Carol Simon were married during the month of September, and she had left him in September, six years later, their divorce final a little over a year later.

He lay quietly for a few moments, then reached for a cigarette. Hardly moving, he watched the red tip glowing in the darkness, taking no pleasure in the smoke that seared his throat; wishing Rachel were back. She had given him an indefinite "week or ten days" return date. Eight days had elapsed since, and he missed her.

From beyond the open door facing the ocean he could hear the surf rolling softly up onto the beach, saw the curtains billowing inward as the breeze stirred them, the night air cool despite the Santa Ana heat wave that had brought discomfort to the entire southland for the past three days. Then he thought of his father, Peter, to whom he had not written in several months, feeling a measure of deep guilt.

Chapter Two

1 •

Russell Dennis McNeely was born to Nora Foley McNeely at 11:59 on the night of March 17, 1935, at St. Anthony's Hospital, marking the fourth celebration of that momentous day for his proud and happy father, Sergeant Peter Liam McNeely of the Ninth Precinct in the Bridgeport section of Chicago's South Side.

The first celebration had come in a bar nearest St. Anthony's to which he repaired after being assured by the doctor and several staff members that Nora was in capable hands, despite his protests that she had miscarried twice before and had had a "turrible, turrible pregnancy." The second celebration took place shortly before he was to take his place in the great St. Patrick's Day march when Peter was unofficially notified by Captain Matthew Fitzpatrick that he had been promoted to the rank of lieutenant.

Following the annual parade, and after a call to the hospital to be informed that Nora had not yet delivered and was being well taken care of, he was invited to the office of his political patron, Alderman James (little Jim) Herlihy, five-two, 140 pounds, but tall and heavy on the political scene, for a private celebration with his oldest and dearest friend,

Ralph Simon, to prematurely welcome Peter's son into the world.

Shortly after midnight, accompanied by Ralph, Peter was informed of the arrival of a healthy seven-pound five-ounce son, the last infant born in Chicago on St. Patrick's Day. Which called for a very special celebration that took place at the swank house of Kitty Borden, reputed to run the most orderly house in the disorderly Eleventh Ward. At four A.M., Peter fell into the bed of Sandy Nichols, one of Kitty's recent imports from Waukegan.

As he rolled away from Sandy in alcoholic euphoria later, it was his only regret that his father, the late Sergeant Dennis Liam McNeely, was not alive to witness this happy day.

He awoke the following morning with a monumental hangover that two stiff drinks and three cups of coffee helped calm, get him on his feet, dressed, and to the station. After reporting in, he drove to St. Anthony's to see his son. Nora was still having a bad time of it and, after talking to her doctor, learned she would never bear another child. This came as a blow to Peter, softened by the doctor's assurance that his son was as near perfect an infant as the doctor had ever seen. Nora would recover, but her condition would remain "delicate."

More astute and ambitious than his old country father or his older brother Timothy, also a cop, who had been shot down in a gunfight with a holdup man in '29, or his younger brother Sean, who had died of alcoholism, Peter McNeely had learned early in his police career that loyalty to his ward committeeman and alderman was not enough to move onward and upward through the ranks.

On his daily rounds afoot as a beat patrolman, he made it a point to personally meet and know the important as well as lesser citizens he encountered; owners of taverns, restaurants, butchers, bakers, priests, nuns, doctors, lawyers, the men in the fire station, schoolteachers, the clerks on the city payroll, the factory workers.

He met the landlords and their tenants, remembered their names and occupations, their wives, husbands, sons, and daughters. He also knew the bookmakers, gamblers, hustlers, brothel owners, and madams; the wastrels, pimps, their women, the con men. He moved about settling disputes, arrested the belligerent drunk and disorderly, listened with sympathy to complaints and problems, suffered their losses, celebrated their joyful occasions, rustled up fuel for the cold, food for the hungry, scrounged jobs for the unemployed, advised them where to go, whom to see.

In special cases, he brought them to see his precinct captain, Matt Fitzpatrick, who was brother-in-law to Arch Halloran, considered to be, next to the Man himself, the political muscle down at the Hall.

Peter McNeely knew his people. More important, the people knew Peter McNeely, a fact not lost on Fitzpatrick, fifth-term Alderman Jim Herlihy, and in time, the great Arch Halloran. There was a need for men like Peter in the Party, for there were contributions to be gathered in, tickets sold to organization-sponsored corned-beef parties and picnics, food and beer to be solicited, arrangements made for testimonial dinners, rallies of all manner, ads to be sold in the ward book, and the people turned out to support the annual policeman's ball. And if some of the cash collected managed to become mixed in with Peter's own personal funds, it was so carefully managed that no one seemed to notice.

Peter took on these chores voluntarily and cheerfully, as enthusiastically as he herded every eligible voter in his precinct to the polls every election day to vote not only in strength, but properly.

And, many suspected, often.

Perhaps his most notable achievement, early in his plan to improve his lot, was to bring Ralph Simon to the attention of Jim Herlihy. Ralph was then a struggling insurance agent who, on Peter's advice, mortgaged his home to make an astonishing cash contribution of five thousand dollars to support one of Arch Halloran's candidates for the state senate. In turn, Ralph became a favored son and soon began working directly with the men downtown who handed out the city's not inconsiderable insurance business. Shortly afterward, although the Simons continued to live in their modest Bridgeport home, Ralph was doing business from a handsome suite of offices in the Loop.

Russ McNeely grew up in Bridgeport, a workingman's community of cheaply constructed bungalows and flats designed for middle- and lower-income families, business establishments, schools, parks, social and political clubs, churches, bars and poolrooms, all close to the dilapidated Ninth Precinct station in the 3500 block of South Lowe Avenue. It was home for thousands who held political jobs, worked in factories, breweries, the stockyards, in construction, drove trucks, repaired cars, cleaned clothes, sold food, and provided other services for Bridgeport. It lay four or five miles southwest of the famous Loop, populated by Irish, Germans, Lithuanians, Poles, and Italians. Blacks were seen only seldom, passing through on their way to and from their ghetto to the east, a few Latins among them.

Russ grew up on South Lowe Avenue in a house that was not unlike those that surrounded it. The inside, however, was furnished better than most and had two additional rooms built on, one a private den for Peter, whose political activities required more privacy than he could otherwise get, another a sewing room and catchall for Nora. The McNeelys also had the Widow Connelley as their twice-weekly cleaning woman to help the delicate Nora with the heavier household work.

Russ came to know his neighbors very well, and as in the case of Peter, the people came to know Russ. At ten, working a newspaper route in the early-morning hours, he met many on their way to work, their children by association at Armour Elementary on West Thirty-third Place. He was the son of Lieutenant Peter McNeely, who was everybody's friend.

By virtue of Peter's political prominence and police authority, the McNeelys were looked up to with respect, even admiration. People came calling for advice, seeking a champion for a cause, small favors, or merely to enjoy coffee and cake and exchange gossip with Nora, who seldom left the house.

Politicians of all ranks came at night for varying reasons, aspiring officeholders vying for Peter's not inconsiderable support. Questionable characters came in search of counsel, for clout or muscle at the Hall, to buy or offer a deal; lawyers to have a few degrees of heat taken off clients who had run afoul of the law. Ward workers came to plan political strategies over beer, and church representatives came for donations.

The McNeely door was open to all.

From earliest memory, Russell's closest playmates were Ralph and Charlotte Simon's two children, Bobby and Carol, who was a year younger than her brother. Both were extremely studious and reserved, primarily because Charlotte, now that Ralph had attained considerable wealth and stature, despised Bridgeport, and kept an extraordinarily close watch on her children and those with whom they associated.

Bobby Simon was a complex boy with a remarkable talent

for fixing things; toasters, electric fans, mechanical toys, radios, sewing machines, and later, motorbikes. He was interested in science fiction and scientific developments of any kind. In the section of the garage where Ralph had built a workbench for Bobby, strange mechanical creations proliferated, some that worked but did nothing, some that failed. He talked often of becoming an aeronautical engineer, spoke of someday flying in outer space, this long before space flight became reality, and was deeply involved in technological flights of fancy that sometimes frightened his family, schoolteachers, and contemporaries.

Ralph Simon indulged Bobby in his mechanical pursuits, but only as a child's hobby. He had definite plans for Bobby in his own growing and lucrative insurance business.

By contrast, Russell, spurred by Peter, leaned toward athletics, and his favorite sports were track and field, tennis, and basketball. In tennis, he found Carol, tall, slender, and alert, an adept partner. When studies and school athletics permitted, Russell spent much of his free time with the Ninth Precinct men where he became a favorite. On the streets, patrol cars stopped to offer him a lift to or from school, or to the precinct. They taught him the mysteries of the police radio codes and answered his never-ending flow of questions. Bobby Simon built him a radio that was tuned in on the police band, which gave him a constant contact with the police activity on the streets.

With Peter's police and political activities keeping him busy by day and most nights, Russell's earlier years came under the direct influence of his gentle mother, Nora, who had never fully recovered from the strain of his birth and adored him as he did her. Between visitors, most of her thoughts were centered on her son and his future. She did her utmost, without forcing it, to guide his reading toward history, philosophy, and the Bible, secretly hoping he might one day turn away from Peter's single-minded ambition and elect medicine as a career; or, an even dearer wish, the priesthood.

But Peter had seen through Nora's subtle efforts and began an even more concentrated effort to move Russell in the direction of the department. By the time he was ready to move on to Holden High, Russell was very well versed in matters of police regulations, routines, arrest, and investigative procedures, and it was Peter's boast that Russell could go on the force at that time.

Vacation time was divided between nearby park athletics and visiting the station to watch the human slag brought in and booked for every manner of offense and crime. He saw physical brutality on both sides of the coin: prisoners brought in cuffed and bloodied, their cries of pain echoing from the back room where some were taken for "further questioning"; and officers who had been assaulted on the street, in a bar, or a gambling joint while making an arrest. He had seen death by violence and heard the often spoken words, "If it's me or him, it'll goddamn well be him first."

At Holden High, Russ had already begun making a name for himself in track and field. Tall, with uncanny ability in that arena, he was encouraged to go out for basketball, at which he excelled. In his junior year he became the team's leading scorer and a year later was named all-city forward by the prestigious *Tribune*.

He saw less of Carol now and more of Bobby who, lacking in athletic ability, nevertheless remained close to Russell, joining him and his teammates after practice, bringing Carol to the games, always quiet, but always there.

Bobby, determined to attend the Illinois Institute of Technology, was having his problems with Ralph, equally determined he would enter the University of Illinois as a business economics major. That summer, when Charlotte, Carol, and Ralph went off for their annual month-long vacation to visit Charlotte's family at their Mille Laks home in Wisconsin, Bobby insisted on remaining at home. He was working on a unique monorail system he hoped would someday become the means of rapid transit and needed the rest of the summer to complete it. Ralph gave in on Bobby's promise to enter the University of Illinois in the fall.

It was a traumatic summer for Bobby and Russell could do little to cheer his friend up. Then, on the day the Simons were due back from Wisconsin, Russell dropped by the Simon garage where Bobby was working on his uncompleted monorail system, an elaborate, complicated model that stretched the entire length of one side wall. He was in a very depressed mood, and the Simons' maid, Clara, asked Russ to "for heaven's sake do something to cheer that boy up. He ain't et a decent meal all week long, and his folks are due back tonight."

He found Bobby staring listlessly at his project. "How's it going, Bobby?"

"No good, Russ. If I had another couple of months, I know I could make the damn thing work. If I could only talk to him—"

"Come on, Bobby. Let's go to the park. The guys want to get a game up."

"No. Hell, I don't feel like it."

"Come on," Russ urged. "You know how much better I do when you're there watching me."

He allowed himself to be persuaded, and they walked to the park where the two sides waited for Russ. They played for two hours, Russ scoring thirty-two points, cheered on by Bobby, whose mood had improved. Later, they had hamburgers and Cokes at a nearby stand, but as the afternoon sped on, Bobby became edgy again. It was five o'clock when they reached the Simon home and Clara was ready to leave for the day. A roast was in the oven awaiting the arrival of the returning vacationers, and she cautioned Bobby to be sure to turn the oven off at six o'clock. Russell went home to bathe and change for dinner.

Peter, as it frequently happened, was late for his meal. At 7:45, while they were still at the table, the phone rang. Russ got up and took it in Peter's den.

"Hello—"

"Russ—your father—is Peter there?" It was Ralph Simon, his choked voice almost unrecognizable.

"Yes—Mr. Simon?"

"Please, Russ. Your father—"

Peter was there then and took the receiver. "Ralph—?" He listened, then said, "Right away, Ralph," and hung up. "Go back to the table," he said to Russ. "Hurry up. I'll want you and mother to go with me."

"What is it, Dad? He sounded terrible."

"Go on. I'll tell you later." When Russ went out, Peter began dialing.

He returned to the table two minutes later. "Something's happened at the Simons'. I want both of you to come with me."

"What is it, Peter?" Nora asked, alarmed by his tone of voice.

"It's bad—"

"It's Bobby," Russ said intuitively.

"It's Bobby. Let's not waste time talking. Charlotte will need you, Nora. Russ, you see what you can do to comfort Carol."

The Simon house was only four blocks away, and Peter drove them there. By the time they reached the house, police cars were blocking the street, an ambulance stood in the driveway, and curious neighbors stood on the opposite side looking on, whispering, staring in awe. The officers made a path for the McNeelys. Inside, Charlotte sat on the sofa weeping softly, wringing her hands. Nora went to her at once, but Charlotte seemed oblivious to her and the quiet confusion around her. Ralph, his face blank with shock, was talking to Doctor Page, while two precinct detectives stood close by and listened. Only then did Russ learn what had really happened.

The Simons had returned at seven-twenty. Ralph honked the horn to summon Bobby to raise the garage door, but Bobby had not responded. Carol then got out of the car and opened the door. And saw her brother's body dangling from the end of the rope that had been tied to an overhead beam.

At that point, Peter said, "Carol's in her room, son. Go to her."

In the hallway that led to the bedrooms, Russ saw the two ambulance attendants wheeling out Bobby's blanket-covered body. He felt faint for the few moments it took to pass him, then recovered somewhat and went to Carol's door. He knocked, but there was no reply. He knocked again and called out, "Carol?"

Then he heard footsteps as she came to the door. "Russ?"

"Yes. It's me."

"Are you alone?"

"Yes. Can I come in?"

The key turned, and the door opened. She stood there, red-eyed and forlorn, wearing a black dress she had changed into, one he had never seen before. It hung loosely on her and gave her the appearance of a sad scarecrow. He held out a hand to her, but she stepped in close, her head on his chest and began crying again.

"Carol—I'm sorry, Carol—we were together in the park this after-afternoon—" and he was conscious of the tears that began to fill his eyes.

She said, "He did it. My father. He killed Bobby—"

"Carol, don't say—"

"He did. If he had only let him do what he wanted, the only important thing he ever asked for. Damn him! God-damn him! I'll never forgive him, never talk to him as long as I live!"

At the funeral, small and private, Carol insisted that Russ sit beside her. She held his hand tightly during the service and later, at the cemetery, as Bobby's casket was lowered into the ground, burrowed her face into the sleeve of his jacket, weeping almost uncontrollably, unwilling to witness the finality to her brother's life. When they returned to the Simon home, she went to her room, locked the door, and remained there until all but her parents had left.

There was less than a month left before his final year at Holden High, and Russ spent most of that time with Carol, feeling a sense of responsibility toward her, a hint of guilt for having left Bobby alone in his depressed mood on that tragic day. Carol had made a truce of sorts with Charlotte, whom she blamed for never interceding with Ralph on Bobby's behalf. As for Ralph, she refused to even mention his name.

Then in September, the Simons moved out of Bridgeport to a large house on Sheridan Road just off Lake Shore Drive, swiftly and suddenly, as though they could rid themselves of the memory of Bobby's suicide. Carol was enrolled in a private school where she would be boarding.

His senior year was Russell's finest in basketball. When the season ended, he was again named all-city forward and received a warm note of congratulations from Carol, adding, "I miss you so much."

In 1953 he was eighteen, a full summer ahead before entering the University of Illinois. Carol, he learned from Peter, had gone off to Europe for the summer on a tour with a precollege group, but he had little time to think about her. Almost at once, he was besieged by scholarship offers from numerous basketball-minded universities, but firmly resolved that basketball was secondary to his education and police career, electing the University of Illinois as his firm choice. He loafed through the rest of the summer, enjoying his first near-adult status and social activity that athletic prominence brought him. He was invited into homes distant from Bridgeport, saw the inside of country and yacht clubs whose grandeur he had never suspected. There were dinner parties, dances, and beach outings. There were girls, exciting and enticing, who were ready and willing. And it was the finest summer he had ever known. When he found the time, he and his former Holden teammates got together in the park, schoolyard, and gymnasium to work out on the basketball courts.

That summer, Peter was in a particularly good frame of mind. His neighbor and good friend, a powerful political figure, had in July become chairman of the Cook County Democratic Central Committee, a man for whom he had worked assiduously. By that time, Captain Matt Fitzpatrick had been dead three years, and his replacement, Lieutenant

Kevin Delahanty, was being retired for physical disability following a stroke in April. It came as no surprise to anyone when Acting Captain Peter McNeely was named to the permanent rank and became precinct commander in August.

In September, driving the new Ford convertible Peter and Nora presented him with, Russ entered U of I. He made the freshman basketball team against some of the stiffest competition he had run into thus far and still managed to keep his grades at a highly respectable level. In his sophomore year, he emerged as a sports celebrity, acquiring a personal cheering section, with a great number of his father's precinct men present to root for "the captain's kid." It was a very gratifying season, with Peter complaining jokingly that Russ was better known, in and outside the state, than he himself in Bridgeport.

As skill developed self-assurance, and with much sports-page publicity, Russ found the pressures tightening. Strange men began seeking him out, hinting of a career in professional basketball. Even stranger men sought him out on behalf of shadowy syndicate gamblers, hinting at the fortune he could make by controlling the point spread. He rejected all such offers and began avoiding even the social invitations that came his way, restricting his free time to more frequent hours with Nora, who had been ailing, and with his teammates.

July of 1955 brought a special joy for Peter and Ralph Simon. Their good and close friend, the chairman of the Cook County Democratic Central Committee and a resident of South Lowe Avenue, ran a successful race and was elected mayor of Chicago. As could be easily predicted, Peter delivered Bridgeport solidly in the Democratic column.

In the summer before his senior year was to begin, Russ made the unpleasant discovery that Peter had a very special outside life apart from his usual political activities.

It came on a Saturday night when he and Jerry Phillips, Ben Chambers, Mark Parletta, and Scotty Ryner, the "first team," were returning from a day at the Columbia Yacht Club where Scotty's father, a wealthy land developer and sports buff, had entertained them on his luxury yacht and later at dinner.

On their way home in the Ryner limousine, Scotty suggested they top the night off with a visit to Kitty Borden's place on Halstead Street. All were agreeable. Russ was intrigued, having heard much of the Borden establishment and its talented ladies, but in his financial state, had never patronized it. Scotty, however, was well known and on their arrival was welcomed with a hearty embrace from the redoubtable Kitty herself. Scotty introduced his companions by first name only, and the foursome was shown to Kitty's private parlor for a social drink. Kitty excused herself then and returned moments later with four of her "hostesses." Russ chose the saucy redhead named Roxanne.

In her second-floor room, far more elegant than Russ had seen in the few sexual adventures he had experienced among the professional ranks, Roxanne slipped out of her single garment and began helping him undress. "You're kinda cute, you know?" she chattered. "Haven't I seen you somewhere before?"

"I don't think so. I've never been here before."

"This isn't the only place I've worked," she smiled. "I'm sure I've seen you. Or your picture, maybe. Are you somebody I ought to know."

"Could be. I play basketball for the university."

Naked, she turned toward him, eyes wide open in surprise, or revelation. "Basketball! Sure, that's it! You're McNeely, the hot forward. Peter's kid."

He stood stock still, staring at her, and she became suddenly flustered and tried to cover her own embarrassment. "I—uh—didn't mean anything—"

"You know my father?" he said quietly.

"Ah—look now—I didn't mean—it's—well, everybody knows your father is Captain McNeely, don't they?"

"How well do you know him?" Russ persisted.

"Well—listen, let's don't make a big thing of it, huh? I'm sorry. I didn't mean anything by it. It was a slip. I'll make it up to you—"

"No, thanks." He began dressing again.

"Look, are you going to tell Kitty about this? You do, and I'll be out on the street again."

"I won't tell anybody anything. Just keep it to yourself, please."

She watched in anguished silence while he finished dressing. To play the game out, he insisted on paying her and went downstairs to wait for his friends, pacing the parlor in discomfort. Then Kitty came in, saw him, and said with a smile, "So soon? You must have been in a hurry."

When he didn't answer, turning his back on her, she went out without another word.

That was on a Saturday night, and the following afternoon Peter said, "Let's take a walk, son. Something I want to talk to you about."

"Why not here?" Russ asked.

"I think you know why not here." They went out and walked down the block where Russ learned that Peter's sources of information were not entirely restricted to police work. "That thing at Kitty's place last night," Peter began, "I don't want you to get any wrong ideas about things."

"I don't think I have any wrong ideas at all."

"I can tell by your tone."

"Look, Dad, I'd rather not discuss it."

"But I do. I'm a cop. I go into places like Kitty Borden's on business—"

"If it's business, why is the place still wide open? Why isn't it raided like the others who don't pay off?"

"Ah, boy, you've learned a lot in your short life, haven't you, maybe too much."

"I hear things. I overhear others. I'm willing to turn deaf to some of the things I hear, even see, but I can't overlook my father patronizing a whorehouse, your name tossed around by whores—"

"That's enough, Russ. You're old enough to have certain rights, but I'll not stand for you criticizing me for taking something that every man needs that he can't get at home. Someday when you're older, as old as I am, and you still have a certain drive, a need in you that only an able woman can satisfy, you'll—"

"Look, Dad, I don't need that kind of patronizing advice about something in the distant future. I'm thinking of my mother, cheated out of—"

"Now, goddamn it, if you want to talk about being cheated, boy, think about this. Your birth made your mother the invalid she is today. If you want to point the finger of blame, try pointing it in the right direction."

Russ turned white. It was the first time he had ever had the inclination to strike his father, even destroy him. For a moment he stared at Peter, everybody's friend, and saw him as a vague shadow of the man he thought he knew so well and now realized he didn't really know him at all. Without replying to Peter's accusation, whether directed at himself or his mother, he turned and walked back to the house alone, his mind in a state of turmoil.

For days he remained at home and close to Nora while Peter was on duty. At night, he found sufficient reasons to

58

remain away, and if Peter took special notice of Russell's absences, he pretended to show no sign of it.

Then one day, Russ phoned the Simon house to learn if Carol was in town. Charlotte answered and told him Carol was indeed in Chicago, but had taken a summer job with the Anderson, Campbell & Deland advertising agency as a researcher in their merchandising and marketing division. Also, that she would be taking her final year in economics at the university. He phoned Carol at her office and arranged to meet her for dinner that very night.

It had been almost four years since he had seen her and was stunned by the picture she presented. The girl had vanished, and the woman had taken her place. Tall, leggy, with dark, luminous eyes that were her most attractive facial feature, she had matured into a remarkable beauty. She was dressed in a black silk dress with matching jacket that set off her summer tan to its noblest effect. The childlike softness he had known was replaced by fresh, sleek lines and adult charm. For a while, she made him doubt his own self-assurance, feeling a certain inarticulate oafishness. And it was nakedly obvious she was enjoying his momentary awkwardness and did what she must to put him at ease; she ignored his outstretched hand, moved in, raised up on her toes, and kissed him resoundingly on his mouth. It worked magnificently.

They dined at a beach club to which Russ held a guest card given him by an attorney who handled the legal affairs of a number of prominent professional sports figures. Carol was properly impressed by their surroundings and the deference shown them. She ordered a bloody mary, and Russ took a Scotch on the rocks. By the time he downed it, he was returned to normal calm, the slight tremors he had felt at their meeting vanished.

"What are you grinning about?" he asked as she ordered a second bloody mary.

"Us," she said. "Look at us. From Bridgeport to the Essex Club. We're so—so adult."

"All it takes is time."

"More than time. You're getting famous."

"That won't last long. As soon as college is over, the publicity will die down, and the guest cards will stop. One more year and it will all be over."

"What about all those offers you've been getting from the pros?"

"You know about those rumors?"

"According to the papers, they're more than rumors."

"That's all they are at this point. I listen, but that's about all. I'm still headed for the department."

"Oh, Russ," she said chidingly, "haven't you gotten over that yet?"

The disappointment in her voice was apparent. "No, I'm still serious as I've always been about it."

"I thought you'd be past that stage by now, wasting what you've got playing cops and robbers."

"Carol, try to understand. Basketball is a great sport, but even with the possible financial rewards it promises, I can't see it as a worthwhile contribution to a full life. I want to do something more meaningful—"

"But the police! My God, Russ, don't you read the papers, the corruption that goes on, investigations, suspensions—"

"All the more reason, isn't it, for a new generation to move in and correct the situation this crime-ridden city has lived with for so long?"

"Oh, you sound like a textbook lecture out of a police-science course. I simply can't see you as a crusader, the great knight in shining armor. I really can't."

"Then let's say it's what I want to do, need to do to feel useful to society. If I, and others like me, won't do it, who will make the changes necessary to clean it all up?"

She shook her head from side to side, smiling. "People will never change Chicago as much as Chicago will go on changing people. That's how it's been, and that's how it will keep on being."

The subject changed with the arrival of the menus, but Russ had the feeling it was only a temporary recess. Over their meal they spoke of other mutual friends of the past, of events that had transpired since the Simons had moved from Bridgeport to Sheridan Road. And Russ got his second surprise. Carol was not living at home, but had taken an apartment by herself on Lincoln Road.

After dinner, Carol insisted that Russ must see her new place, and they drove there. It was a one-bedroom affair, tastefully furnished, with Charlotte's help, she admitted, and, obviously, with Ralph's money. In the kitchen, she poured brandy and put a pot of coffee on, and they settled down in the living room for more talk; her final year of schooling with the promise of a fulltime job at A C & D after graduation. They touched on many subjects except for the one both kept in the background: Bobby's suicide and Carol's relationship to Ralph. Then they were back to the more intimate questions of self, and suddenly it was two in the morning.

"Lord," Russ said, "I've been so interested, I didn't realize how late it's gotten."

"I'm glad. I've missed you so much. You're my single contact with my—our—other lives. I wanted so many times to write you or call—"

"Why didn't you?"

"I didn't know if the celebrated McNeely was still the same Russ McNeely I played tennis with so long ago. I was afraid, timid about being rejected."

"Carol, for God's sake! How could you even think I could change that much. Look, I plan to see you a lot now, and at the university."

"You'll be too busy for me, won't you?"

"Never. I want you at every home game, and I'll see that you get tickets. Promise?"

"I promise. Thank you, Russ."

"Hey, it'll be a great year. Like old times, but better."

"Yes, much better."

"I'd better go now, or you'll never get to work in the morning. This morning."

"Wrong. It is now Saturday. We're closed except for the small crew in the mail room and production department, on half day."

"Well, then—"

She said it boldly, evenly, easily. "Stay, Russ. Please?" There's plenty of room."

"But only one bed."

"It's big enough for two. Stay, please?"

So the affair began, exhilarating, beautiful. It continued through the summer until Russ had to report for basketball practice, putting a severe crimp in his free time. But they managed an evening now and then and occasionally full nights over weekends together on Lincoln Road.

That winter, the best season Russ had known, Carol, as promised, attended every game. In December, after defeating Michigan State in a hair-raising thriller by one point, Russ drove Carol to her apartment, intending to be home by midnight. They fell asleep side by side on the living-room sofa, shoes off, weary from the long, exciting evening. The phone rang, awaking both. Russ's watch told him the hour, four-forty A.M. Carol went to the phone, then came back to the sofa perturbed. "It's your father, Russ," she said. "How would he know you were here?"

As Peter had learned of his visit to Kitty Borden's place, Russ assumed as he went to the phone. "What is it, Dad?"

"You'd better get dressed and come home," Peter told him. "Your mother died in her sleep an hour ago."

When he arrived on South Lowe Avenue, Ralph Simon was already there along with several other of Peter's intimate friends and Father Mulcahy; and Russ wondered guiltily if Ralph knew, or suspected, that he was involved intimately with Carol. There was no sign that he possessed such knowledge as he shook Russ's hand and murmured his condolences, apologizing for Charlotte's absence at this early-morning hour. But he was so stunned by Nora's death that he had little room for conjecture in that direction. He went into his mother's bedroom and stared down at her wan, chalky face and silently prayed for her. Later, as more people began arriving, he walked about in a daze, unable to remember the names of those who had once been so familiar to him; precinct men, politicians, ward workers, neighbors, his own school friends from Armour, Holden High, and the university.

The funeral was a massive affair that filled St. Anthony's to overflowing with civic officials, the politically prominent, police and fraternal associates, and a host of friends. The mayor, a neighbor, was absent, but sent his aides to represent him along with an impressive wreath. Later, he joined the steady procession that filled the house, calling to privately express his deep sorrow.

Then it was over. Peter and Russ were alone in the emptiness left behind by Nora's absence, neither able to express to the other the full depth of his feelings. Peter seemed to bear the loss far better than Russ and tried several times to open a conversation, as though this would restore the closeness they had felt before the Kitty Borden episode; but Russ was too deep into his personal grief to listen to platitudes and religious clichés on life and death.

The Widow Connelley was installed in Nora's sewing room as full-time housekeeper and cook. Peter returned to his precinct, Russ to complete the school year. Understandably, his strength on the team diminished considerably, his interest and dedication on the wane. In the final half-dozen games he spent much of the playing time on the bench. In the last game, he didn't suit up. Any thought that he might pursue a career in the pro ranks vanished.

Upon graduating in June, he entered the Police Training Academy. Not surprisingly, he found few challenges in the academic portions of his schedule. He took a more serious interest in the physical program, excelled in field problems and on the firing range. In what spare time he could find, he concentrated on boxing, wrestling, and judo, played hard at handball and tennis. He saw Carol as often as time would permit since she, too, was now working full time at A C & D and found it necessary to put in a certain amount of overtime.

Russ's first assignment as a rookie cop that cold winter was on the West Side in a high-crime area. His midnight-to-eight shift made it virtually impossible to meet Carol with any measure of regularity, nor did he see Peter very much. Then, one Sunday, he was surprised to learn from Peter that Mrs. Connelley had left, complaining of arthritis, and intended to move to Florida to live with her younger sister and brother-in-law. A week passed before the suspicion arose in Russ's mind that perhaps Peter had had a hand in Mrs. Connelley's decision.

That suspicion was fortified by the arrival of Mrs. Connelley's replacement, Mrs. Elizabeth Frazier, also a widow, a much younger woman, perhaps thirty or thirty-two, with red-tinted hair, an attractive figure, and showing some concern over the way Russ examined her. She moved into Nora's old sewing room and became established at once; but the meals she prepared were as far from Mrs. Connelley's art as her ability at housekeeping. Within a month, Russ suggested that he would find it more convenient if he found an apartment closer to his precinct. Peter made no objections. "You're your own man now," Peter said. "It's your decision to make." Russ made the move on the following weekend.

His first partner in that drafty patrol car was John Czernak, a fourteen-year veteran of the old school—phlegmatic, tough, and contemptuous of all rookies. A man of strong prejudices, bad breath, and offensive body odors, he was even proud of his inborn bigotry.

Together, they plodded through each eight-hour tour of duty, making a normal number of arrests for drunkenness, peace disturbances, and traffic violations. Czernak showed little patience and handled his arrestees with muscle, insult, and physical abuse, particularly among blacks, whom he openly despised; all in his "look kid, this is the way we do it in this precinct" manner.

Russ hated the hours he spent together with Czernak; hated him for his anger at the world and humanity in general, his overuse of the baton and lack of compassion toward victim and culprit alike, a brutal, sadistic man in every sense of the word. When Lieutenant Andersley, after a month, asked, "How's it going, McNeely?" he answered, "Fairly well sir, although I'd like, if possible, to see how some of the other officers work."

Andersley smiled and said, "Okay, McNeely, I'll see what I can work out."

A few days later he was assigned to Mickey McCormick, younger, more temperate and friendly, with six years behind him. When, after a while, Czernak's name came up between them McCormick said with a grin, "You were the Polack's penance, Russ."

"What the hell does that mean, Mickey?"

"Just between us, old John was raking it in a little too fast and not sharing, so they threw you at him, figuring it'd slow him down some, cut in on his weekly sideline take."

"Jesus, Mickey, is it that bad?"

"In spots. Captain Braden's a pretty good man. So is Chip Andersley, but it's hard as hell to break down a system that's two years older than God."

"But why me? What was my penance for?"

"Maybe it's because you're Cap McNeely's boy. You know, that's something you've got to live down, too. For all old John knew, you could've been a shoofly for Internal Affairs." And with a side glance, "Are you, Russ?"

"If you think that, Mickey, you can always ask Chip for a partner with more guts and intelligence."

"No. I'll go along with you. I'm not on the take or on anybody's pad, so we ought to cut it together."

Out of the area of the theoretical and into that of reality, they worked well together, sharing each experience as Russ had been unable to do with Czernak. In those cold, early-morning hours, they cruised streets and alleys seeking burglars, checked bars for juveniles, picked up addicts, settled family disputes, were involved in one high-speed hit-run chase, came on an armed robbery and subdued the lone gunman without firing a shot, rescued a family of four from a burning tenement before the firemen arrived, and spent countless hours writing reports and testifying in court.

There were the long, monotonous hours of driving without incident, perhaps preventing crime merely by making themselves visible, always waiting for the call that might come a few seconds later to stimulate the flow of adrenalin in their veins. Russ found nothing extraordinary about his work, little he had not anticipated. It pleased him when he could be of help to a victim, to assist the injured; even more so when he could take a lawbreaker off the streets, particularly a dope pusher caught in the act of selling. More and more the numbers of addicts and addict-pushers grew.

Then his schedule was changed to the eight A.M. to four P.M. shift, and he was assigned a new partner, Walter Canady, a twelve-year man who took his work seriously. Married, with three children, Canady showed a certain amount of morbidity, constantly reflecting on the murder of unsuspecting officers shot down by those who saw every policeman as a racist enemy. But Canady knew his job and took pride in his professional skill. He "went by the book" and seldom deviated from its text. His uniform was always pressed, shoes shined, hair combed, a man who always stood out at roll call as an example of what a cop should look like in public.

Canady approved of his younger partner's sense of professionalism and showed it by giving him every opportunity to exercise his judgment in the arrests they made; even to whether to make the arrest or not.

Russ learned much about the reality of police work, but there was that side of it that was not only too realistic but unpleasant. Apart from the authority behind his badge and the power to arrest or not arrest, there were the bribes offered in exchange for freedom, the powerful political influences and outside pressures under which the police operated, the judges who could be pushed this way or that, reports manipulated, evidence mysteriously lost, witnesses unable to be found when needed, transfers made on whim.

Lawyers, nominally officers of the court, clogged those same courts with postponements, motions for change of venue, claims of pressing engagements in other courts, illness, appeals, and every possible legal or illegal delay. That many of his fellow officers were on the take in the streets, or on the precinct pad, soon became glaringly obvious. Too many had too much money to spend, wore expensive civilian clothes, drove expensive cars, and furnished protection and advance information of planned raids. Their rewards came in cash, tax-free, merchandise, liquor, food and travel gifts. But there were many honest cops who were not on the take, although they looked aside at the payoff system and would not report those offenders. Russ was grateful that Canady was among the latter.

And then came his first head-on meeting with violent death. It was shortly after they had stopped for a quick sandwich and coffee, a Saturday on which they had been busy from the very start of their shift; a gang fight in a playground with two youths stabbed and four others injured; then a tenement fire caused by a defective oil heater in which they assisted another team and firemen in rescuing fourteen adults and nine children, most of them overcome by smoke inhalation; then a barroom brawl that required assistance from three other patrol cars before the two perpetrators could be subdued and arrested.

At 2:10, sandwiches and coffee disposed of, they began cruising with a "what next?" attitude. Ten minutes later, a young black boy came running out of a single dwelling and almost ran in front of the car. Canady slammed on the brakes so hard, they almost skidded into the terrified child. Russ leaped out and grabbed him, unable to understand his excited, garbled words, but his thin arm, pointing toward the house, gave some sense of direction, if not meaning, to his terror.

With a glance back at Canady, he ran toward the house, plowing through a gathering crowd of neighbors and passersby. He went through the open door, gun drawn, swiftly examined the rooms on the first floor. Canady was behind him now as he mounted the stairs to the second level cautiously. On the landing he saw four doors, one open. He went to that door first and looked inside. What he saw, he knew at once, was what had sent the screaming boy flying.

The girl was young, no more than seventeen. She lay partly on her left side, head back on the rumpled bed clothes that showed signs of the struggle that had taken place. Her clothes had been torn from her and lay scattered on the floor, dress, bra, one stocking, shoes, her cinnamon-brown body totally nude. The other stocking was tied around her throat and was red with blood, much of it smeared over her face and young breasts. The look on her face was very much like that on the face of the youngster, pure terror, but in frozen silence.

The figure was one of exciting youth ripening into early maturity of womanhood, given her in one of nature's more bountiful moods, now despoiled by a man who had not been satisfied with rape alone. For two things, even at a quick

66

glance, became immediately obvious: she had been raped, her throat cut. And she was dead. There was a flow of semen, not yet fully dried, in a line from her vagina to the inside of her upper thighs. And no human with even a breath of life in him could look as dead as this young girl.

Then Russ realized that he was alone in the room with the corpse and for a moment was frightened. He turned toward the door and heard Canady's footsteps returning. "On their way," he panted. He had merely peered inside the room and run into the patrol car to pass the word along.

It was the first case of its type Russ had seen, and he stood shaking his head from side to side, staring wordlessly at his partner, eyes glazed. Canady said, "Look, Russ, you go down and keep those people from coming inside the house. And get yourself some fresh air."

He obeyed mechanically, went down the steps slowly, heavily, struggling to retain the food that kept creeping up into his throat. He was outside for perhaps a minute when a second patrol car arrived and began dispersing the people gathering in front of the house. Russ knew neither of the officers, nor did they know him. Then an unmarked car braked in at the curb, and two detectives got out. One said to Russ, "What've you got here?" and he merely pointed a thumb and said, "Upstairs. Bedroom."

More uniformed cops arrived, and when they mounted the outside steps, Russ went inside and upstairs. The detectives were examining the scene, staring at the girl, touching nothing except with their eyes, which they used as cameras. The physical examination of any evidence would be made by the homicide experts. Moving to the bed, Russ could see the marks he had been too dazed to see before: nail marks scratched on her breasts, thighs, and arms; a small bloody rip along her left cheek; bruises on her face, forehead, and rib cage; imprint of teeth bitten deeply into her lower lip; and the horrid, ugly slash on her throat that was partially covered by the bloodied stocking used to strangle her.

He heard one of the detectives say, "Strangled and raped her, or raped her and strangled her, but why did the sonofabitch have to use the knife?" And then he began to visualize the struggle, the desperation of this girl as she battled her assailant, and wondered about the man. Young, middle-aged, old? Sober, drunk, or under the influence of drugs? Was it only for sex, or money as well? Had he broken in or known the victim? And where were the other occupants of the house?

Then the homicide men arrived. While they questioned Canady and Russ, the police photographer and print man came in, then two more men from Homicide, one a lieutenant. The body was photographed where it lay, then from every possible angle, the lieutenant directing. "Get a close-up on that semen. In close on the throat. See if you can bring those scratch marks up. Get some more light in here." The photographer placed a narrow six-inch ruler next to each visible mark to give recognizable dimension to the close-up shots.

Detectives began examining the torn, strewn clothing, making certain they touched nothing that had a surface on which a telltale print might have been left behind. The print man was busy lifting visible prints and dusting for latents, emitting small sighs of delight with each that showed up.

Downstairs, reporters had appeared demanding news, but the cops at the door guarded the premises zealously. It was still their show, and they refused to yield an inch or a useful word or hint. All they said was, "Back off. Wait for the lieutenant."

A young, stern-looking assistant medical examiner arrived and told the officers present what they already knew. "She's dead. Strangulation and throat cut. Beyond a doubt, raped. Maybe some concussion, but not sufficient to cause death."

Two white-coated attendants brought in a stretcher, placed the stiffening young body on it, straightened out her perfectly formed legs, encased her in blankets, strapped her down, and took her away. The final rites of autopsy would be performed at the morgue.

Inside, the detectives began the search for physical evidence, searching through the clothes in her closet, opening bureau drawers to peer through the pitiful few undergarments, cosmetics, a few pieces of cheap jewelry. They checked the other rooms in the house, while outside, others were talking with neighbors.

Her name, they learned, was Nancy Jackson, and she was eighteen. She worked in a variety store about a mile away. Her mother was a day worker for a white family across town, her father unemployed and probably in a bar somewhere. She had three brothers and a sister. One brother was in the army, one in jail, the other a long-haul truck driver. The sister was a waitress in a restaurant.

Russ began to write his report, day, date, time, address, name of victim, age, the names of the uniformed and plainclothes detectives on the scene, guessing at their time and order of arrival. By now it was in the hands of the detectives, their case. Before long they would know everything everyone knew about her. Except for the rapist-killer, about whom they knew nothing.

And then it struck him. Where was the boy who had run from the house, a thin, very dark youngster about ten or eleven who in no way seemed to be related to the cinnamon-colored victim?

He mentioned this to a detective sergeant who, busy at the moment, said, "Go down and see if you can find him. Bring him back with you."

But downstairs, the boy was nowhere in sight. Nor could he find anyone who had seen him, knew him from the description Russ gave. Canady, his part over for the moment, joined him in the search, talking with people who had already been interviewed by the detectives. No one knew of the existence of the boy, and all were certain that there was no one of that age or description who lived in the house. It didn't seem possible that not one person had seen or heard that screaming boy, and their every effort to locate him was negative.

It was the lieutenant's opinion that the boy was a stranger to the area, that he had probably come from a neighborhood nearby looking for a house to enter to take money or something else of value. He had come upon this one, entered, found it empty, and searched it—then came upon the body and fled, screaming his fright just at the moment when Canady and Russ came by.

A detail of officers were sent to prowl for the boy, Canady and Russ with them. They returned empty-handed. And, by four o'clock, they were back at the precinct, reports turned in and gone off duty.

But the memory of that young, nude, despoiled body was fixed indelibly in Russ's mind when he returned to his apartment to bathe, dress, and meet Carol at her apartment for dinner. She had spent the day shopping, had lunch with Charlotte in town, browsed through McClurg's for some books on merchandising and marketing. Russ listened, but could not bring himself to tell her of eighteen-year-old Nancy Jackson whose life had come to an end in violent attack, her killer on the loose, perhaps seeking another victim.

"Russ?" she said suddenly.

"What?"

"You weren't listening, tuned out. Are you tired? Would you rather stay in than go over to Gloria's?"

"Would you mind very much?"

"No-o. It'll probably be dull, anyway. You do look awfully tired. Would you like to take a nap?"

"With you?"

"If you think that will refresh you."

"Let's see if it will."

They went to bed and made love, Carol with Russ, Russ with an eighteen-year-old cinnamon-brown girl whose nude body he couldn't shake loose from his mind.

On Sunday, Carol had planned to spend the day with a girl from Evanston with whom she had spent that long-ago summer in Europe. Russ, after she left for her appointment, got into his car and began to cruise the rape-murder location in hope of finding the missing boy. He widened his circle a few blocks at a time, examining the face of every small boy on the streets who was of the elusive one's height and slender build. He came to a small park about two miles from the scene, circled it, parked, and sauntered through it and the dozens of children playing there.

And saw him, recognizing the face and the clothes he had worn on the day before. The boy was walking along a path, a slim branch in one hand, whipping it back and forth. He followed the youngster until they were on the outer edge of the park, then stepped up his pace and caught him by his arm.

"Hold it, son. I want to talk to you."

"Who, me? What for, man? I don't know you."

"Yesterday. You came running out of that house, the one where the girl was killed."

The whites of the boy's eyes grew larger. "You crazy, man. I don' know no house, no girl killed."

"I was in the police car you stopped. I was in uniform. I saw you, talked to you. You pointed to the house, and we found the girl."

The boy's face was ashen with fear. "I didn' do it. I didn' touch her. I was scared an' run."

"Okay. What's your name?"

"Eddie."

"Eddie what?"

"Mercer. Eddie Mercer."

"All right, Eddie. I know you didn't do it, so don't be afraid. Just answer my questions. What happened? How did you happen to be in that house and find her?"

"Jus' found her, that's all."

"How, Eddie? How did you get into that house?"

"I—you goin'a put me in jail?"

"No, Eddie, I'm not going to put you in jail if you tell me the truth, all of it."

Eddie looked around from side to side, then said, "I'm walkin' along the street, an' I see this man come out of the house, leave the door open jus' a little. So I go on up an' ring the bell to see if anybody home. No one come to the door, so I go in, look aroun'. Then I go upstairs an'—an' I seen the open door, an' I look in an' see her on the bed. Man, I was scared. I run out—"

"Okay, Eddie, you're doing fine. Now think hard. The man you saw coming out of the house. Have you ever seen him before?"

"I seen him. I don' know him, but I seen him aroun'."

"Around where?"

" 'Roun' Felix place."

"Felix?"

"Felix place. You know, the bar a couple blocks away, poolroom. They take numbers there, too."

"Can you tell me what he looks like?"

"Sure. He about big as you, real black, short hair, ugly cat. He got a cut on his face here." With a finger, Eddie drew a line from the left side of his mouth down to his chin. "A bad cut, looks like a razor job."

"What was he wearing?"

"Oh, gray coat, black pants, gray shirt, li'l ol' hat. He do it to the girl, mister?"

"Maybe. I don't know for sure."

"He do, he's a real bad man."

"Yes, real bad. Eddie, would you like to come down to the precinct and look at some pictures with me?"

"What kinda pictures?"

"Pictures of men. We'll play a little game. You look at the pictures and try to find that man you saw. If you do, you'll win some ice cream and a dollar."

Eddie grinned. "Shu 'nuf? Jus' to look at some pictures?"

"That's all, Eddie. Look at the pictures, and see if you can find that man."

"Hey, le's go, man."

The detectives on duty listened to Russ and stared at Eddie in slight awe; an off-duty rookie and a black kid who wanted to play games on a Sunday. Sergeant Kaminsky said, "Look—uh—what's your name again?"

"McNeely. Russ McNeely."

"McNeely? You related to the captain down in the Ninth?"

"He's my father," Russ admitted reluctantly.

"Well, we're kind of busy on the usual weekend paperwork right now. Shorthanded, too. We've got some men in the area questioning the family and neighbors. You can leave the kid here till some of 'em come in—"

"If I could let him go through the books—"

Kaminsky shrugged. "Okay, but I think you're wasting your time."

By about four thirty, Eddie Mercer had gone through four ice-cream cones, two bottles of soda pop, and two large books of mug shots, enjoying the game he was playing. He had paused over half a dozen shots of male blacks with scars and markings in varying shapes and sizes, all on the left side of their faces, but none was exactly as he had described it to Russ.

The other detective, Chambers, came by to watch for a moment, then said, "McNeely, you're being conned. Long as you keep contributing to the delinquency of this minor by bribing him with ice cream and sodas, he'll keep going through those mug shots until hell freezes over."

"Don't let it worry you, Chambers," Russ replied. "It's my time and my money, and I don't mind one bit."

"Look, kid, she isn't the first spade broad who got raped, and she won't be the last."

"You're right, but she was a living, breathing human being."

"Your first homicide?"

"Yes. I feel a sense of responsibility toward her."

Chambers stared and muttered, "Well, I'll be goddamned," and went back to his desk.

A little after five o'clock, Eddie turned a page, then went back to it. A few moments later, he said, "You owe me a dolla', man."

Russ followed the small index finger that was pressed tightly below the mug shot of one Willie Coleman, alias William Cole, alias Willie Keene. The healed scar that ran from the left corner of his mouth down to his jawline in a half circle was barely discernible, but it was there, and it fit Eddie's description.

The file on Willie Coleman showed six convictions on charges ranging from assault and battery, rape, armed robbery, and auto theft to narcotics use. Nine other arrests were logged and dismissed for either lack of sufficient evidence or the failure of witnesses to appear. He was forty-two years old, six-one, 220 pounds.

"You're sure, Eddie?" Russ asked with rising excitement in his voice.

"It's him! It's him! You owe me a dolla'."

"And you've seen him at Felix's bar?"

"Sure, man, tha's him. Gimme my dolla'."

Russ gave him two. Kaminsky and Chambers, overhearing the exchange, came over to examine the mug shot and file. "Could be," Kaminsky finally admitted. "The sonofabitch spent more than half his life behind bars, a tough customer." After a moment, he said, "Okay, McNeely, it's something to go on. We'll take it from here."

Next morning, Canady was both pleased and upset. "That was a damned good piece of detective work, Russ. Only thing is, you'll never get credit for it. The dicks'll take him and never mention you."

"What difference does it make, Walt, as long as they get Coleman and put him away for good?"

"Jesus, Russ, it makes all the difference in the world. Didn't you ever learn anything from your father? Something like this is what every cop works for? A job like this rates a top commendation in your record, and that looks mighty big when you're up for a promotion."

"As long as they get the bastard, I'll be happy, Walt."

"Well, goddamn it, I'm not. Christ, we could've kept an eye on Felix's and taken him ourselves."

But Russ felt a sense of personal satisfaction nevertheless. If the Homicide dicks took Coleman, which was their job, well and good.

Four days later, they brought Willie Coleman in. An informant who had been contacted gave Detective Sergeant Will Brady an address. Brady and three detectives broke into Willie Coleman's room and took him without firing a shot. They also found two guns and a knife. The dried bloodstain on the knife was Nancy Jackson's type, B. The semen test matched Coleman's specimen. Test firings from one of the two handguns turned up a bullet with markings similar to two taken from the body of a service-station attendant who had been shot during a holdup a little over a month earlier.

The case made headlines, and as Walt Canady had predicted, the detectives took all the credit for "intensive and intelligent investigation that led to the arrest of the rapist-killer."

Walt Canady was irked. With his copy of the *Tribune* in hand, he told the story to Lieutenant Andersley, who checked it out with Russ, then took the matter up with Captain Braden. Braden took it to Captain Martin in the Detective Division and threatened to go higher, even to the press. After a lengthy discussion, a compromise was reached. A congratulatory letter was sent to Braden, and letters of commendation placed in the files of Patrolmen Russell McNeely and Walter Canady.

On that afternoon Russ received a phone call from Peter. The grapevine was working well. Peter complimented him on his commendation and suggested they have dinner together that night. When he came off duty that afternoon, Russ drove to the 9th and enjoyed the reunion with the precinct men he hadn't seen since he began his training at the academy. When Peter was free, they had dinner at a nearby restaurant and effected a somewhat halfhearted reconciliation. At no time was the name of Elizabeth Frazier brought into the conversation.

"How are you making out otherwise?" Peter asked.

"Fine, Dad. No problems. There are some things I see that I don't like, but I enjoy what I'm doing."

Peter did not inquire into those things Russ didn't like. "And Carol?"

"We're good friends."

"No more than that?"

"Perhaps. If it develops into something serious, you'll hear about it from me."

"Ah— It's possible Charlotte wouldn't look kindly on her daughter marrying a cop. A captain or inspector, maybe, but not a patrolman," he said with a smile.

"I won't worry about that right now, Dad. What is between Carol and myself is between us and not her parents."

"Well, that may be. On the other hand, Ralph suggested that Carol's husband, whoever he might be, could always find a good place in his firm if he was so inclined."

"Would you want to see me resign and take a desk job with Ralph Simon?"

"I told you once, Russ, you're your own man, able to make your own decisions. Mistakes, too, as well as successes. I meant it then, I mean it now, although I would like to see you move up in the department. We're father and son, Russ. If you'll let me, I can help—"

"Please, Dad—"

"I won't interfere, now or ever."

"Thank you. I'd like it that way."

"One more question. Are you getting along financially."

"For my single status, yes."

"Russ, if you ever need—" and as Russ began to protest—"wait, hear me out. I'm not a poor man, son. I've made investments with Ralph in the past that have turned out very well. At my time of life, I have more than I need. Keep it in mind."

"I'll remember that, Dad, and thank you."

It was the first such conversation they had had as adults, and apart from his earlier puritanical feelings about Peter's private life and women, his association with Elizabeth Frazier now, he had never felt closer or warmer toward Peter. As his father had said, he was his own man with his own decisions to make, his own life to lead.

If the subject of marriage had ever come up between Russ and Carol, it had been only in the vaguest of terms, in the context of Scotty Ryner's marriage to Ellen Blanchard, an important social event that they had attended, and that of one or two others of their friends. But as the year 1957 began, Russ hinted at it in several ways; the inconveniences of living apart, the certainty that the Simons were aware of their intimacy, the problems that occurred when he moved to a different duty shift, when it was impossible for their hours to match up with. Then, one cold night when they were driving back to Carol's apartment after the theater, he said with a suddenness that startled her, "Why don't we get married?"

"I don't know," she said.

"Why don't you know? How can you not know?"

"I just don't know?"

"You don't know what?"

"About getting married."

"What is there to know other than you do or don't?"

"It's so—so permanent."

"That's what it's supposed to be, isn't it?"

"I don't know."

"Why is it you know so much about so many things and nothing about this?"

She fell silent for a while, then said, "We're such good friends as we are. I'd hate to see that spoiled."

"Because we'd be married and living together?"

"It happens all the time."

"How about the millions of happily married couples?"

"Happy on the surface, but deep down—"

"Oh, for God's sake, Carol!"

"No. I mean it. I know married people, friends out of college, people at the office. Most of them live with irritations they'd have walked away from if they weren't married. Look, Russ, you're a very serious person, sensitive about your work and career. I wouldn't want to upset that, and I would, probably, if we were married. Then we'd be in trouble."

"That's about as infantile as anything I've ever heard. We're what counts, and if we love each other, the rest of it is of minor importance."

"Oh, Russ. I've thought about it a lot, and my mature, considered opinion is that love isn't enough. We've got to respect each other in other things, the work we do, the other things we share."

"Then let's get married and give it a try. How else will we ever know. If it doesn't work, there's always a way out."

"Divorce. I hate the thought of divorce. It turns two otherwise nice people into vengeful haters trying to destroy each other. I don't want to become bitter about life."

They had reached her apartment. Carol removed her outer coat, gloves, and suit jacket while he stood in the tiny foyer watching her. She turned and said, "Aren't you staying?"

"Should I?"

"Why not, for heaven's sake? You aren't angry about this, are you?"

"I don't really know. I think I am."

She laughed. "Let me fix you a drink. I need one, too."

He gave in and took off his overcoat. She brought the drinks to the living room, and he gulped half of his down while she sat close to him on the sofa, knees drawn up under her. "It isn't that I don't love you, Russ," she said.

"Then what is it?"

"I suppose it's this flaw in my character." When he stared at her, waiting for the rest of it, she said, "I'm a damned snob."

"Funny I hadn't noticed it before this, and I'm very good at noticing things."

"You would if we were married. It would show up when you'd invite your cop friends to our home. When we'd accidentally mix your associates with mine from A C & D. The contrasts would show up, and I'd feel it, and you'd notice it then."

"Okay, so you're an admitted snob. So am I, and so is everybody in the world in one way or another. I don't have to love all the people I work with. There are any number I dislike. Some I like very much. How different is that from everyone else in school, on the team, at work?"

"It becomes a lot more important in a marriage."

"Oh, bullshit."

"It's true, Russ."

"Is it because your mother doesn't approve of cops at my level?"

"That has nothing to do with it, even if some phases of your work do have an effect on me. The uncertainty of so much about it. Your gun is a symbol of that. You're hardly ever without it. We could be out somewhere when you'd be called on to use it and I'd be there to see it. Or you could leave for work one morning and I'd get a call at my office telling me you'd been shot. Even killed. I don't know if I can live with that."

He was annoyed, and his tone showed it. "Are you suggesting we break it off?"

"Oh, no. No, Russ. I didn't suggest that at all—"

"So we go on this way, living apart? On which day will you say to me, 'Russ, I want to get married, but not to you because you're a cop.' What about living with that uncertainty hanging over my head?"

"I don't know. I'm as confused as you are."

"Well, we don't seem to be getting anywhere. It's late, and you've got to be at work in the morning."

"Aren't you staying?"

"No. Neither of us will get any sleep if I do."

"And if you don't, I won't get any at all."

He stayed.

In her work, now assistant to Warren Deland, she began to travel in order to observe the results of her staff planning in the field. Summer overtook spring while she traveled to various test markets through the Midwest, East, South, and far West, sometimes alone, sometimes with other members of the marketing-merchandising staff. Then, late in August, she returned to Chicago, shadows of weariness under her eyes. She had lost some weight and began talking about the possibility of giving up her job.

Then it was September, and she sprang back to life. She and Russ made love hungrily, as though for the first time, and the world was beautiful again. In midmonth he proposed again, and with her acquiescence, Russ phoned Peter and asked him to meet them at the Simon home. On that Sunday they announced their engagement and their intention to be married the following week.

It was a small, private wedding, only their closest friends and family members present. They were married in the Simon home by Father Mulcahy of St. Anthony's. Because of their work, there would be no immediate honeymoon, but the announcement of their marriage appeared in the press, and they were flooded with gifts of silver, china, glassware, linens, and appliances from friends and close associates of the Simons and Peter.

From Ralph and Charlotte they received a check for twenty-five thousand dollars, "no more than a formal wedding would have cost us." Not to be outdone, Peter presented them with a check for a similar amount and a new Buick sedan. They moved into a larger apartment in Carol's building, and Charlotte spent the next month furnishing and decorating it. The reconciliation between Carol and her parents, between Russ and Peter, in their moment of happiness, seemed complete.

In November, Russ was transferred to the Detective division, Intelligence Branch, and moved over to police headquarters. It was a move, he felt sure, that had been quietly engineered by Peter, but lacking evidence, he accepted the change from uniform to plainclothes gratefully, hoping it had come as a result of his investigative work in the Nancy Jackson case. Now his working hours were more compatible with Carol's.

In December, Russ took his acquired leave, Carol the vacation she had postponed the previous summer. They flew off to the Bahamas for a belated honeymoon, a gift from Peter. On their return, they stepped into a family problem that affected both.

Captain Peter McNeely was under fire, attacked by a disgruntled political aspirant whose opponent had won the support and endorsement of Captain McNeely and a huge campaign contribution from Ralph Simon. Also, his opponent had won the seat on the city council.

The loser, an attorney named Dion Cloyne, went to the District Attorney with "evidence" that McNeely's Ninth Precinct was one of the most corrupt in the city, that his men at all levels were on the take from operators of gambling joints, houses of prostitution, bookmakers, narcotics dealers, and were permitting certain bars to operate after hours.

Further, Cloyne charged that Captain McNeely and his good friend, Ralph Simon, were partners in real estate, much of it in houses leased or rented to operators of bordellos at extremely high rentals, which included police protection; that in most instances, they used front men, or women, to hide their ownership of such houses.

The story made big headlines despite the fact that these same charges were old news to the citizens of Chicago. The D.A. replied that his investigators were looking into the charges. The chief of police asserted that Internal Affairs was conducting an investigation of its own. Ralph Simon filed a five-million-dollar lawsuit against Dion Cloyne. Captain McNeely stated he would withhold his lawsuit pending the outcome of the investigations, which, he declared, would prove him and Ralph Simon innocent of the charges. The mayor was drawn into the controversy and promised to take stern action against any officer, regardless of rank, found guilty of accepting bribes to protect gambler, madam, etc., and reiterated his complete confidence in the police department as one of the nation's finest.

Russ at once went to see Peter, who charged Cloyne with seeking personal revenge for his own political ineptitude and failure. Weeks later, the D.A.'s office refused to present the case to the grand jury by reason of the fact that Cloyne's purported evidence amounted to the unsupported statements of a group of known convicted criminals whom Cloyne had once defended. The media, however, charged the D.A. with protecting a "fraternity brother" and editorially called for a "serious investigation in depth," charging further that a considerable amount of political pressure was being brought to bear on Cloyne to admit that his evidence was faulty and tainted.

Which Cloyne, shortly thereafter, did admit, withdrawing the charges as having been hastily made without having been carefully thought out; but without apology. Subsequently, Ralph Simon dropped his lawsuit against Cloyne, and Peter McNeely took no action in the matter of his own suit. The media, after charging that the investigation appeared to have been slanted in favor of those accused, discontinued the follow-up stories by their investigative reporters.

Numerous changes and transfers were made in the Ninth Precinct, but Captain McNeely retained his command. There were rumors downtown that McNeely would probably be retired as soon as the situation cleared up, but those in positions of authority discounted the rumors as wishful thinking. McNeely was a powerful force in Bridgeport, and his presence there was vital to the Party.

In Intelligence, the subject was never mentioned in the presence of Russell McNeely, but he felt invisible eyes staring at his back. There were whispers that Captain McNeely was "in it up to his neck," and Russ felt himself excluded from the general rap sessions and discussions on the subjects of internal graft and bribery. Within a short time he was removed from active investigative work and assigned to Crime Statistics, a clerical operation he found oppressive, degrading, and far beneath his talents.

Carol had taken the charges against Ralph with the equanimity of one who recognized graft and corruption as "the American business way of life." She neither accused nor defended, but accepted. However, she realized that Russ's distress was genuine, that the badge he wore no longer was as glitteringly bright as it had been when Peter proudly pinned it on him at his graduation exercises. He slept badly—on many nights, not at all.

In February of '58, one of the coldest months in Chicago history, Russ began talking of moving to a more clement part of the country. Carol, doing well in her role of minor executive at Anderson, Campbell & Deland, was at first strongly resistant to the idea. Without discussing the matter, she knew it stemmed from his feelings about the corruption factor throughout the ranks of the department, brought to a head by the whitewashing of the charges against his father and father-in-law. Russ persisted, pointing out that she could do her job anywhere in the country where advertising agencies flourished.

When, after several months of persuasion, the subject of "where" arose, they ruled out New York at once, its police department larger but no better than Chicago's. Eventually it came down to Los Angeles, where Carol had visited on two business trips, its police reputation often cited as the best and, for its size, least corruptible in the nation.

In July, Russ resigned from the department, citing as his reason a desire to escape the hardships of Chicago's severe winter weather. Peter's reaction to Russ's decision was decidedly cool. He, like Carol, saw beneath Russ's desire for a change of climate. The Cloyne accusations were still well remembered, and the rumors persisted, and although Peter had been officially cleared and was in a strong position to withstand such heat, Russ was not. The sins of the father had passed on to the innocent son.

"It's your life, son," Peter said finally. "I can't tell you how to live it. Go with God's hand on your shoulder and my best wishes."

The Simons took Carol's decision much harder, but it was a useless struggle against their daughter's strong will. By now, she was eager for the adventure the change would bring, yet when the time came to hand in her resignation, she did so with ambivalent feelings and the regrets of Warren Deland. She came away with highly commendatory letters of introduction to the top advertising agencies in Los Angeles with which Warren Deland had had some contact in the past.

In August, they stored part of their furniture and arranged to have enough shipped to give them a start in a small apartment. Fortunately, there were no money problems, and the natural excitement of beginning a new life in new surroundings gave them little time for regrets they may have felt earlier. They drove cross-country in the Buick, taking their time, enjoying the trip as a second honeymoon.

In Los Angeles, they stayed at a hotel for three weeks before they found a clean apartment in the Silverlake district, perched on a hillside with a spectacular view. When their furniture arrived shortly thereafter, they busied themselves settling in, found congenial neighbors who helped make the transition a pleasant one, and soon learned where they could shop conveniently.

During the month of September they explored the city, its nearby beaches, drove through mountain and desert country, to San Diego to the south, San Francisco to the north, and to Las Vegas to the east, all special delights. Back home, wearied of travel for the moment, it was a time to make decisions. Carol took her letters of introduction to the agencies recommended by Warren Deland, but found no present openings for her particular specialty in marketing and merchandising research. She left résumés, made up a list of other agencies, and began making rounds, sitting through interviews, filing applications. And hoping.

Russ made contact with the L.A.P.D. and sheriff's department, talked with personnel directors, sought out various uniformed officers and deputies to discuss their work with, brought home pamphlets and booklets to examine. He visited their training centers and found them far superior to anything he had known in Chicago and sensed a certain strong pride and spirit in the sheriff's men that, in the end, drew him to that organization. He filed his application and, after a thorough check into his character references and police background, was notified of his acceptance and assignment to the next class at the training academy.

Carol, disappointed in her efforts to find exactly what she wanted, began to lose interest. To lessen her chagrin, Russ bought her a sports convertible since he would be using the Buick for daily transportation to and from Biscailuz Center. When it was delivered, his next purchase was a beautiful red setter puppy to keep Carol company that they named Copper.

Russ found the academic courses not too onerous, took the strenuous physical training in stride, and excelled on the firing range, better prepared by experience than most in the class, which numbered several veterans from out-of-state police departments, trainees from nearby P.D.'s, and a dozen or more former army and marine corps men, all gung ho. He applied himself diligently to the criminal law and criminal justice codes, which were different from those of Illinois, rode patrol as a cadet on weekends, memorized new radio codes, practices, and procedures with a sense of *déjà vu,* and passed his exams with ease. On graduation day, Carol was present to pin the six-pointed star on his shirt, just as Peter had once performed that proud honor.

His first tour of duty, he knew, would be in a correctional facility, and he was fortunate to draw central jail in the city proper instead of one of the detention centers distant from home. During this tour, Carol took Copper to Chicago for a visit, and Russ felt his first taste of loneliness. Luckily, his orientation in the largest jail of its kind in the country kept him fully occupied, a phase that came as an entirely new experience.

Working beside veterans, he began to study the psychology of the criminal mind, trying to understand the hard-core recidivists, the violent, the passive, the common thieves, burglars, robbers, drug pushers, white-collar embezzlers, con men. They came in all colors and sizes, from ghetto slums to affluent homes. They were stoic, aggressive, bold, tough, angry, calm, complaining, whining, submissive. All had two things in common: They were unlucky and had been caught.

The psychology factor was too much to undertake, and with a sense of despair, he gave up trying to understand these men. But the months he spent here, Russ knew, would one day prove valuable in recognizing these same faces on the streets. So he concentrated on those faces, their way of walking or shuffling, distinguishing marks of identification such as scars, tattoos, names, nicknames, aliases, and various manners of speech.

He saw them as they arrived in buses from the fourteen sheriff's stations throughout the county where they had been arrested and booked, saw them in the showers, dispensary, and chow lines, in their cells, at exercise, in chapel, at movies, in the recreation room watching television, poring over law books in the jail's library searching for means of appeal or release. In order to better communicate with the great number of Mexican-Americans he came in contact with, he began to study Spanish.

When Carol and Copper returned, home life was renewed. In off-duty hours and free weekends, they roamed the beaches, Carol's favorite haunt. And as time passed, they began talking of finding a home on the beach, but Russ was due for transfer into Patrol, which he awaited eagerly, and held off on that decision until he would get his first assignment.

Meanwhile, they had learned much about Los Angeles County from personal exploration, maps, and pertinent material found in Russ's manuals. Some of what they learned was interesting and exciting, some appalling in statistics. Covering some four thousand square miles, the county was larger in population than all but seven states in the nation. With a low point of nine feet below sea level and a high point of ten thousand feet, there were 1,740 square miles of flat land, 1,875 that were mountainous, 250 hilly, 60 in mountain valleys, 30 in marshland, 130 in offshore islands, and over 50 miles of seashore. It had the largest Mexican, Japanese, and Samoan colonies outside of Mexico, Japan, and Samoa. Daily, approximately eight million people drove more than five million cars and other vehicles over its network of freeways, roads, and streets.

Of its fourteen sheriff's stations, Deputy Russell Dennis McNeely was assigned to its first and oldest, Firestone, in South Los Angeles.

2•

Firestone station.

From the very first day he reported for Patrol duty, Russ felt he was in his proper element. He learned quickly that Firestone, officially designated Sheriff's Station Number One, was also ranked number one in the seven major crime categories of willful homicide, forcible rape, aggravated assault, burglary, robbery, grand theft, and grand theft auto, much of it dope-related.

Firestone was comprised of ten unincorporated cities and two contract cities, Carson and Cudahy. It was an area of forty square miles with over five hundred miles of streets and roads to patrol, a highly violatile district made up of low- and middle-income workers, with a high percentage of welfare families; an almost equal number of whites, blacks, and Mexican-Americans who preferred to keep within their own ethnic groups and strongly resisted intrusion from outsiders. The unemployment rate was high, street fights and youth-gang wars common daily and nightly occurrences, in and out of school, which promised action around the clock.

In the six-month probation period that followed, riding with experienced training officers, Russ studied the reporting districts to which he was assigned, learned the hot spots where trouble could be expected to erupt at any given moment. He became totally absorbed, and time passed quickly. His first partner after probation was Lee Davidson, a Deputy III, two grades above Russ's Deputy I, who took everything at its face value; the philosophical stride of a man who had seen everything good and evil in the streets and accepted it with tolerant understanding of the human frailties. He was gentle and sympathetic toward the unfortunate victim, cool, tough, and unyielding when the situation demanded.

Within four hours of their first time out, Russ felt a sense of comfortable security with Davidson beside him, an inner knowledge that in a pinch, he could be depended on, and hoped Davidson felt the same way about his rookie colleague. Nothing untoward occurred that Monday morning, but after lunch, Davidson braked the black-and-white toward the curb and said, "Let's talk to that dude."

There were a number of men, women, and youths walking in both directions on the busy street, and Russ said, "Which dude?"

"The one in the brown leather jacket, red shirt, Afro." Russ saw him then, a lean man of about twenty, shuffling briskly in a jive manner, hands dangling at his sides. The car pulled up beside him, and Davidson called out, "Hey, Shoeshine. Hold it a minute."

Shoeshine turned, frowned at the car, then broke into a smile as Davidson got out of the car and accosted him, Russ bracketing him on the other side of the youth. "Hey, man," Shoeshine called out in immediate recognition, "what's doin'?"

"That's just what I was about to ask you," Davidson said. "Where you been keeping yourself?"

"Oh, aroun', just aroun'."

"When'd you get out, Shoeshine?"

"Maybe ten days ago."

"You working?"

"No, man. Just lookin'."

"You seen Buck Tolin lately?"

Shoeshine's forehead furrowed into a frown. "Ol' Buck? No. No sir. Ain't seen ol' Buck since I got out."

"Where are you staying?"

Shoeshine grinned. "Oh, aroun', here, there."

"Let me see your left wrist, Shoeshine."

Reflexively, Shoeshine drew his left arm back in a sudden move, the grin fading from his face. "What for, man? I ain't usin'."

"I didn't say you were. Just hold out your left wrist. We don't want a fuss now, do we?"

He held out his left arm reluctantly. Davidson pushed the sleeve back only far enough to expose his wrist and examined the gold watch and matching band on it. "Thought I saw something bright and shiny while you were walking along. Where'd you get it, Shoeshine?"

"This? This watch? Man, I had that a long time. Like maybe two-three years."

"That's funny," Davidson said. "When I busted you last July on that two forty-two, you were wearing one that wouldn't go for more than ten or twelve dollars. This one, I'd guess it would go for more like a hundred and fifty, even two hundred. Also, it looks like one that was listed in the Curtiss Jewelry ripoff last week. Funny coincidence, Shoeshine?"

His shiny black face turned somewhat grayish. "Look, man, I don' know nothin' about no ripoff. I'm clean."

"Then where did you get this?"

Sheepishly, "Bought it off'n a dude th' other day."

"What dude? He got a name? You know where he lives?"

"Name of Willie somethin' is all I know. Met him in a bar, the Golden Rooster, you know? He hustled me for a twenty, give me the watch."

"Twenty? Where'd you get the twenty? And if this wasn't hot, he could hock it for at least forty or fifty."

"I don' know nothin' about that, Mist' Davi'son." Shoeshine was sweating now, his tone serious, the former light, airy manner turned sober and polite.

"Tell you what, Shoeshine. Let's you and us take a ride to

the station and talk to some detectives. Maybe they'll help your memory come back, huh?"

They brought him in and interrogated him. The watch was on the list of items taken from the Curtiss Jewelry store burglary less than a week earlier. The detectives on the case took over. When their patrol shift ended, Russ and Lee Davidson learned that Shoeshine had confessed to participation in the burglary with Nickey Johnson and Buck Tolin, both picked up a few hours later at the address Shoeshine had furnished.

"Hey, smooth work, Lee," Russ commented.

"All in a day's work, Russ," Davidson said. "You get to know 'em after a while by sight, feel, or smell. Little things you notice. Ordinarily, Shoeshine would be dragging his ass along, looking for somebody or something to hustle. The way he was walking, something told me he was high on something, had a thing going. I saw that gold band, and it didn't fit Shoeshine, not ten days out of the slammer, and remembered the Curtiss job. Just luck."

But Russ knew it was more than "just luck." Alert observation. Know your area and its people. Each is an individual. Each is different in his own way. Rely on instinct. Something out of the ordinary that doesn't fit the normal pattern or picture. To the knowledgeable cop, there is meaning everywhere. You ride, you see, you remember. Memory can often be more important than your gun.

"You take it for what it's worth, Russ," Davidson went on. "Things, people. They can call me 'pig,' 'honky,' 'motherfucker,' even resist a little, it's all in the game. The one thing I won't take is an asshole spitting on me."

They divided their driving time equally and took their calls as they came, rolled on almost every type of crime listed in the book from minor disturbances to major gang and bar fights. They patroled the streets and alleys in their reporting district and kept moving, making themselves highly visible. They made their share of arrests and, after their initial "break-in" period, were soon working in near-perfect harmony as partners, enjoying their successes, grousing over their failures.

They were fully conscious of the covert, often overt, hostility they encountered on the streets, somewhat softened by the welcome received from those to whom assistance had been rendered in the past. They became involved in the usual number of family disputes, which were numerous and often repeats, and rolled on countless "burglary in progress" calls and those in which the burglary had been discovered too late to do more than take the tedious report from the disconsolate victims. They answered back-up calls and, in turn, were backed up by others as needed.

What delighted Russ as much as anything else was the discovery that no one seemed to be on the take; there were no signs of the inborn corruption he had known in Chicago. There were no "bag men" collectors in exchange for protection or special privileges. No bar reported to be operating illegally after hours, no house of prostitution; no suspended gambling house or doper's pad was exempt from investigation or arrest. The teamwork he saw and became a part of was refreshing, in many ways a distinct change from his experiences in Chicago.

Shortly after a 211, holdup in progress, Russ's first, in which Lee Davidson shot and killed a rifle-wielding man and wounded his accomplice, they began visiting each other in their homes on a social basis, enjoying an outing with Claire and Carol at the beach, a dinner out, a fishing trip one weekend, skiing on another. But after a year, Lee made Deputy IV and was transferred to Newhall station.

A friend made, a friend gone. A new partner to break in with.

3 ●

Life at home varied with Russ's duty schedules and Carol's moods. Unsuccessful in her efforts to find the particular job she wanted, unwilling to settle for less, Carol seemed to give up all hope and turned to housekeeping and the care of Copper. On Russ's eight-to-four day shift they enjoyed normal companionship together with their new friends in the neighborhood and a limited few in the department. On his four-to-midnight and midnight-to-eight A.M. schedules, life became more complicated and disruptive. When the strain began to show on both, Carol took a trip to Chicago; and as these trips increased in number, so did they increase in length of time.

During the following year, they vacationed in Chicago together for the first time, but it was not a pleasant trip for Russ. Charlotte and Ralph complained that Carol, as on her previous visits alone, spent hardly any time at all with them, and Russ began to wonder with whom she had spent that time. His own meetings with Peter, always at the precinct station in order to avoid meeting with Mrs. Frazier, were depressing.

In their second week there, tragedy struck when Copper slipped his leash during a morning walk with Russ and was killed by a delivery truck. Carol was inconsolable and refused the replacement he offered her. Dampened thus, they cut their vacation short by several days, and for the remainder of Russ's vacation they scarcely spoke to each other.

In the two years that followed, the situation between them worsened, and they had several talks that bordered on separation and possible divorce. But neither seemed to want to take that extreme step, and after each outburst, both tried to reconcile their differences. Carol would then become moody, resentful at other times, unable to spell out exactly what she wanted. Minor incidents had a way of exploding into heated arguments that left both of them dispirited and often on the brink of crisis, then faded. Lovemaking, once seemingly inexhaustible, became an infrequent, occasional act of physical necessity, satisfying neither of them.

In January of 1965 Russ received his second promotion. On his way home that evening he stopped at a pet shop and bought a male red setter that so closely resembled Copper as a puppy that Carol fell in love with it on sight. They named him Copper II. The affectionate puppy somehow brought a change for the better, and Carol's spirits picked up.

She began now to look for a house in earnest, taking Copper II along to scour the beach cities week after week. In March, she found the one she wanted in Manhattan Beach. It had been built ten years earlier by a retired architect who had died less than four months before. It faced the beach from across the highway, sitting up on a small rise among other expensive private homes. The price asked by the broker was seventy thousand dollars, brought down to sixty thousand after considerable negotiating. Even that figure was far more than Russ had expected to pay for a house, but Carol's infatuation with the house won Russ over, and he wrote a check for five thousand as a deposit, later added another twenty as the down payment, and took a thirty-five-thousand-dollar mortgage. It was the first use they had made of Peter's and Ralph's wedding checks.

They moved in and ordered the balance of their household goods shipped in from Chicago. Charlotte and Ralph flew out to spend a weekend with them, and Charlotte stayed on to help Carol get settled in. When she left, having bought several paintings and an expensive bronze as her "new house gift," Carol showed Russ a check for thirty-five thousand dollars that Charlotte had left with her to take care of the mort-gage "or anything else you want to use it for." Russ insisted that Carol return the check, but she refused and deposited it in their bank account, much to Russ's resentment. Shortly afterward, they received a check for twenty thousand from Peter, also a "new house gift." Russ deposited that check, too, and the subject was dropped.

They became a part of the beach community quickly and made friends easily. On their left were Bob and Sandra Wright, Bob a stockbroker; on their right, Dick Jaynes, an airline pilot who was living with Angela Gordon, a personnel administrator with the same airline. There were engineers, lawyers, doctors, store and shop owners, and retired couples who seemed to have open house most nights and every weekend. Nearby, they met two members of the department; Steve and Joy Barrett and Perry and Jo-Ann Roberts, Steve and Perry deputies working out of Lennox Station in Inglewood.

Life became very social. There was much entertaining and back and forth visiting among them, often forced by visitors from the city who dropped by for a swim and stayed on for drinks and dinner. They explored and found restaurants locally and in nearby beach cities and soon developed a taste for seafood and Oriental cuisine.

The distance to Firestone was considerable, and Russ made the best of it. At best, he and Carol were back on excellent terms, lovers again.

It had been a year of campus unrest, protest marches, increasing militant-minority demands, and general dissension that erupted into rioting and looting in major cities across the nation. In Los Angeles, apprehensive law-enforcement agencies began training personnel in riot-control tactics and stood ready for an outbreak, but the consensus was almost unanimous among city leaders that "it can't happen here." Police authorities were not that optimistic.

And they were correct. It happened in August when the Watts riot began on Wednesday the eleventh and lasted until the curfew was lifted on the following Tuesday, although the National Guard remained on hand until withdrawn on the twenty-second. The twelve-hour shifts were eliminated and a quasi-normalcy returned, yet the city, expecting further outbreaks, remained nervously on edge. The destruction left behind was monumental.

Russ, along with most of the Firestone personnel, had been

on constant patrol in the midst of the sniping, fires, and looting, sleeping at the station or napping in a black-and-white, eating on the run, on alert to roll as the continuing flareups broke out, rushing the injured and wounded to overcrowded hospitals. When he had the time, he phoned Carol, found her on the verge of hysteria with fright and anxiety, several times incoherent with drink. When it was over finally, both were on edge, and when Carol decided to take a month-long trip to Chicago, Russ agreed at once that she should.

A major change in street attitudes took place following the riot, which had left the area in a state of devastation, its blacks—there and elsewhere, with militant Mexican-Americans joining in—expressing open anger and hostility with the Establishment: men, women, and youth alike. It was reflected in their faces, posture, walk, and behavior; on the streets, in schoolrooms, at work. Looting and vandalism, it appeared, was translated into an expression of revolt. They continued to hang around street corners as before, except that now, by stance and attitude, they dared any cop to tell them to "break it up" or "move on," as though hoping that one would and thus give them an excuse to attack the hated pigs, overturn their car, smash its glass, and set it afire. It was a newly acquired sense of personal and group freedom, and they were eager to test its strength.

During Carol's absence, Russ found little cheer in the empty house. After his shift, he fell in with a group that generally stopped at a nearby bar to unwind tensions. Later, he would drop in at Bonnie's at the beach for a meal and a drink or two before going home. At other times he was invited for drinks and dinner with the Wrights or Dick Jaynes. Then he began feeling a certain sense of freedom in their homes and at various beach bars where there were a number of attractive women who were not only plentiful and agreeable, but available.

His first extramarital adventure was with an airline stewardess whom he took home with him for an overnight stay. She, in turn, introduced him to her roommate, which led to a series of sexual bouts that lasted until Carol phoned she was returning, asking him to meet her at the airport. He welcomed her and Copper II back, but from that time on missed in Carol the excitement he had found in his recent adulterous fling; but inherent guilt led him back to a life of normalcy. Or monotony, which had again become synonymous with their way of life.

With his newest partner, Greg Burnham, he rolled on a 459, a burglary in progress, one December day, and on approach, the burglar, a husky young black, ran. Burnham leaped out of the still-moving vehicle, chased the man through an alley into an open field, and at the moment when he leaped on the suspect, broke his right leg in the fall. Russ came on the scene only seconds behind Greg and subdued the burglar, then cuffed him. But Burnham would be hospitalized for weeks, hobbling in a cast for weeks more, and Russ drew as his partner a bright young Mexican-American, Ramon Ycaza, who had just completed his patrol probation, a Vietnam veteran who had been top man on the firing range at the training academy, a valuable side asset.

Slowly, yet easily, they moved into a close working relationship that, once it reached that point of respect for each other, began to ripen into friendship, although it hadn't reached the point of social meeting between Carol and Ycaza's wife, Yolanda. Ray often spoke of his Vietnam experiences, just as Russ related some of his own life with the Chicago P.D., but neither talked much about their personal lives beneath the surface.

Ray claimed Yolanda was a superb cook and occasionally brought tempting samples of her culinary prowess for their lunches and more for Russ to take home to Carol.

Then came the 415-F in which Russ was shot, and Ray killed the man behind the gun, who had murdered his wife. During his hospitalization and recuperation at home, the situation became more tense than ever. Carol began drinking more heavily, and Russ often heard her pacing the outside deck when she believed him asleep. When, three months later, he returned to active duty, they had lapsed into a state of indifference, living as strangers in the same house. Whether Russ came home in time for meals or missed them entirely seemed to matter not at all to Carol.

The strain on both became almost unbearable. The silences between them grew; they ignored each other for the sake of peace, disagreeable as that came to be. For the next two months they lived on the brink of marital disaster, with frequent outbreaks of uncontrollable fury over imagined slights and the increase in Carol's drinking.

Finally, it was Carol who brought it to an end. Early in 1967, two months after Russ had, at his own request, been transferred to the Detective division, she left one morning shortly after he had gone to work. The note he found on his return that night, after discovering that Copper II, her clothing, jewelry, cosmetics, and other personal objects were missing, was a simple, explicit summation of her discontent:

> *I'm leaving for good, Russ. We can't go on like this. I won't bore you with the reasons. You've heard them all. I'm sorry, but I want more out of life than this and can't find it here, or with you. Good-by.* CAROL.

So ended their six-year marriage.

By what he thought of as Carol's defection, he felt cruelly hurt, humiliated over the personal defeat as a husband and as a man. Later, he began to understand the part, however innocently or unwisely, he had played in the catastrophe.

He realized now that despite her expressed willingness to move to California, Carol hadn't really wanted to leave her job at A C & D, the familiar comforts of Chicago, her friends, even the security of her parents. It had been his own desperate effort to escape from under the shadow of his father and remove the blanket of suspicion he felt had fallen from Peter's shoulders to his own. His need for flight had overcome Carol's desire to stay; but they were younger then, very much in love, and his need greater than hers.

Unhappily, he packed and crated those things in the house that he thought Carol would want, the bronze and paintings Charlotte had bought for the house, other items of silver, china, and glass she had been particularly fond of, and shipped them back to her in Chicago without explanation. He received no acknowledgment from her, and a year and four months later they were divorced.

Russ began his new assignment in Vice and before long came to hate the enforced association with whores, gamblers, pimps, and homosexuals. The public seemed not to give the slightest damn who slept with whom for pay, who gambled his money away to whom by honest or crooked means, which males did what with other consenting males, and which prostitutes plied their trade with the assistance of a pimp. Vice was universally accepted as crime without a victim.

Despite foot-long rap sheets, whores brought in were bailed out even before an officer's report could be concluded, fined lightly, and returned to the streets. Even among cops, the detail was known derisively as the Pussy Posse. Evidently, judges felt the way most of the unaffected public did, and gamblers and bet takers, convicted for the fifth, tenth, even twentieth time, received a nominal, easily affordable fine and were back in business within hours of their arrest or trial.

His interest, however, was entrapped by the horrors he saw in the use of narcotics, particularly among the young: the pain and agony they suffered when unable to get that vitally necessary "fix" and the ends to which the addict would go to obtain the money to make his or her next buy from their friendly pusher-for-profit. After a year, he applied for a transfer to the Narcotics Bureau. His application was approved, and after a period of special training, he moved into that field.

Within a year of concentrated investigative work, he received his promotion to sergeant and was assigned to the Major Violator section in Zone II under Lieutenant Bob Barker. Because of his special investigative abilities, he was later placed in charge of the M.V. crew of Zone II and began operating out of Lennox station in Inglewood, although his operating theater took in the Firestone and West Hollywood stations as well as Lennox.

There, he was delighted to find two friendly faces, the two deputies who lived in Manhattan Beach, Steve Barrett and Perry Roberts. In time, he urged them to come into Narcotics. They applied and with recommendations from Russ, their applications were approved. Six months later they were working together. The MV Crew now consisted of Russ, Harry Deliso, Steve Barrett, Perry Roberts, and a transferee from downtown undercover, Joe Paul.

It was 0400 before Russ began to feel drowsy enough to turn off the past and allow sleep to overcome him. He nestled his head into the pillow and drifted off.

Chapter Three

1●

In his office in the fifty-year-old Hall of Justice Building on
Temple Street and Broadway in downtown Los Angeles, Captain John Esau, head of the sheriff's Narcotic Bureau, leaned
back in his chair and listened while his four field lieutenants
read off the net result of the previous week's activities; number of arrests, amounts of various illegal drugs taken, pending activities, current street prices, the names of any upper-
echelon dealers apprehended, and other data thought to be of
importance.

Most of what Esau heard was not entirely new to him.
During the week, he maintained close day-to-day, sometimes
hour-to-hour contact with field operations, either personally
or through his administrative aide, Lieutenant John Rivera,
and his understaffed intelligence unit, headed by Sergeant
Billy Sorensen. Thus, Esau was not as deeply interested in
these ritual recitations as he was in observing the attitudes of
the reciters, watching closely for any changes in their interest
in their work.

When Lieutenant Glenn Toland, Zone IV, completed his
report, Esau said automatically, "Nice going, Glenn. Jack?"

Lieutenant Jack Marcus, Zone I, the junior officer present,
took over and began his verbal account.

If a passerby had seen Esau walking along any street, mowing his lawn, or pushing a cart behind his wife in his neighborhood supermarket on a Saturday, he would have taken him to be an accountant, neighborhood bank manager, or the owner of a small business; probably nearing retirement and enjoying what he was doing. And except for a pair of extraordinarily alert, inquisitive eyes, that was what he appeared to be.

In his late fifties, his hair showing as much gray as it did its original brown, an almost perpetual half smile on his lips, Captain Esau stood just under the six-foot mark, erect, with only the slightest sign of some thickening at the waist, suntanned by exposure to California's beaches when opportunity permitted. Every working day found him at his desk at 0700, being briefed on the narcotics activity and arrests in the county's four zones during the hours since leaving his headquarters the evening before.

In the nearly thirty years since he had joined the department, Esau had served in most of the line branches; Patrol, Vice, Burglary, Robbery, Homicide, and finally, Narcotics. He had seen the old methods go out with the old sheriff, the new efficiency and spirit infused when the new sheriff was elected to take the place of the old. He witnessed the improvements in the training program, in the men chosen to head the various divisions and bureaus, and had approved of what he saw.

Esau had made an enviable reputation in Homicide and within a few years was promoted to captain and became its head. Under his direction the bureau achieved notable results and had broken many spectacular cases. Thus, it came as a shock when, after a few years, he asked the newly appointed chief of detectives, John Traynor, to be relieved of his command and move into the Narcotics Bureau as assistant to Dan Regan, who was due for retirement within a year.

His reasons had been well thought out. To the sheriff, who had been surprised by the request, he said, "I've been in every important bureau in the department except Narcotics, Sheriff. We do our job in Homicide and a good one, if I can be immodest about it, but I haven't yet been able to come up with any means to *prevent* murder.

"Planned secretly or on the spur of the moment, murder is an almost totally unpredictable crime. A man will kill his wife, girl friend, or mistress, sometimes the other way around. Business partners will kill each other in anger or in heat of argument. A neighbor kills another for no more reason than a dispute over leaves that fall across a property line. Revenge killings, holdup killings, cop killings, most without sense or reason, the majority by people who know each other.

"I see the increase in the use of narcotics, the scum who peddle slow death, infect the young who become the scum of tomorrow, a form of delayed murder. We see men and women, even children, become thieves and whores in order to buy drugs, lying, cheating, mugging, robbing, even killing for it, wrecking whole families. Rehabilitation, as we know it, doesn't work.

"I feel that a lot of it is preventable. Dan Regan is doing a good job. When he leaves, I'd like to take over and see what I can do with it."

The sheriff and chief of detectives considered Esau's request. He had a good fifteen years of active service left before his retirement would come up, and he had one of the best records of achievement in the department. Within two months, Esau moved from Homicide into Narcotics and took over on Regan's retirement. The Department saw no reason to regret that move.

When Lieutenant Jack Marcus finished his report, Esau said, "Very good, gentlemen, very interesting. The statistics are impressive. They'll look beautiful on paper for me to turn over to the chief of detectives at his captains' meeting." He paused with a half smile and added, "It's just that the situation is very lousy."

"Jesus, Cap," Marcus protested, "we've been working our crews like dogs as it is. The overtime they've been putting in, the results we've been showing—"

"Jack," Esau said, "I'm not complaining about the results we're getting with the manpower we have to do the job with. Sure, we're taking in more dope, arresting more pushers, but what it indicates to me is that more of the goddamned junk is coming into the County, more pushers are at work, and more addicts are roaming the streets boosting the crime rate to get the money to make their buys."

Bob Barker grinned and said nothing. He had heard it many times before and would hear it again, but Jack Marcus was new at his job, and this was part of his education as a field lieutenant. But, he reflected, he wouldn't be hearing it much longer. Holding a master's degree in police science and administration, he was black, handsome, and a dedicated cop. He had passed his captain's examination and was on the promotion list, waiting for an opening; but the list was long. A few months earlier he had been contacted by the mayor of a sizable community in Northern California and invited to take over its police department as chief. Barker had listened, visited the city, and liked what he saw, then told the mayor and police commissioner, "Could be. I'll consider your offer and let you know."

Esau was saying, "—and the other factor, Jack, is the Intelligence report I circulated recently. Street prices for weed, hash, pills, smack, and coke have been stabilized for months. That tells us there are no shortages anywhere. Plenty of product, plenty of dealers, plenty of buyers despite our hauls and arrest records."

Glenn Toland, the quiet man of the four who generally let his record speak for him, listened and said nothing.

Don Dickerson, Zone III, stubbed out his cigarette in his coffee cup, and Easu said, "Don't do that, Dick. Use the ashtray. That's what they're for, or hasn't your wife hit you with one recently?"

They all laughed, recognizing Esau's way of relieving Jack Marcus's growing tension. "Now what was it you wanted to bitch about, Dick?"

"Only this. We're out on the streets making buys and busts. We're out there following up tips, leads, information that comes in over the transom. We've pulled in tons of weed, tens of thousands of pills, and cocaine and heroin in larger quantities than ever before. Question: What more can we do with what we've got to work with?"

"I'm not complaining about you or your people, Dick, only about the general situation. I can't give you more manpower. All I did was make a commentary on conditions as they are." He smiled and said, "You're not getting too sensitive about all this, are you?"

Again they laughed, knowing the meeting was over. Esau said, "Thank you, gentlemen. Let's get back to work." And as the four lieutenants rose to leave, "Wait a second, Bob. I want to take something up with you."

"Sure, Cap." Barker sat down again and said to John Rivera, "Hey, John, send some more coffee in, will you?"

The door closed, and Barker, still grinning, said, "What's up, Cap?"

"The grapevine's working. I hear your upstate mayor is pushing you for a decision."

"Where'd that come from?"

"A little bird in Personnel. He's asked for more information on your eligibility on the Captain's List."

"He's got no problems there. I've got a whole parade in front of me."

"Well, are you going to take the job?"

"I think so, Cap. It's just a matter of convincing Lorna and three kids that black in Northern California is just as beautiful as black in L.A. They're practically sold on having a chief of police in the family."

They were interrupted by a secretary who brought in the fresh coffee Barker had asked for. "Well," Esau continued, "you know how I feel about it, Bob. You'll make a damned good chief even though I hate the thought of losing you."

"You've got some pretty good men who can take over, Cap. You know that."

"Anybody specific in mind?"

"Yeah, one positive. McNeely. He passed his lieutenant's exams months ago, and he's one of the best narcotics men in the whole bureau."

"I know. I know, Bob, but that would mean jumping him over some other good men on the list."

"Good men, sure, Cap, but not any really good narcotics men. Hell, it's been done before."

"In cases of extreme emergency, yes."

"Don't con me, Cap. All it takes is some muscle downstairs, and you've got more than most."

"Well, we'll see. At least I know where you stand. When does the deal go down?"

Barker exploded into laughter at Esau's street expression. "Hey, this isn't a dope deal, it's a job." He said soberly, "Their chief is retiring in about four months. I'm going to put my letter of intention through at the end of this month."

"Then good luck, Bob. It's been great having you here."

"Thanks, Cap, for everything you've taught me. I'm grateful. It's been a beautiful, profitable experience."

When Barker went out, Esau dialed Rivera's number. "John, get Russ McNeely's file and bring it to me, please."

"Right away, sir."

2●

The fifteen-story Hall of Justice Building, a proud structure when it was built in 1925 to house the Los Angeles County's much-needed courtrooms, its upper five floors comprising a jail, is the headquarters of the county sheriff, an elected official.

Under his jurisdiction are fourteen stations, each a complete police department, spread over a vast area of the county's four thousand square miles. Each station is headed by a captain, with a full complement of patrol deputies, detectives, staff deputies, and civilian personnel. Each has a jail in which to hold prisoners in custody until they can be transported to the huge central jail on Bauchet Street in downtown Los Angeles for further processing, hearings, trial, and detention for up to one year. Elsewhere, the department operates six other detention camps, the Mira Loma facility, Wayside Honor Ranch, and the Sybil Brand Institute which houses female prisoners. It also maintains the sheriff's academy and firing ranges at Biscailuz Center and a substation in the city of Avalon on Catalina Island, out in the Pacific Ocean.

The Hall is also the headquarters for the undersheriff, assistant sheriffs, chiefs of patrol east-west, detectives, administration, personnel, and other branches.

Under the chief of detectives is the Narcotics Bureau, which divides the fourteen stations into four zones. Each station supports its own Narcotics crew, but for each zone there is a small group of experienced agents known as the Major Violator crew and which concerns itself with the more important narcotics cases that are discovered in that particular zone. In the case of Zone II, which covers the Firestone, Lennox, and West Hollywood stations, the Major Violator crew of five is headed by Sergeant Russ McNeely and supervised by Lieutenant Robert Barker.

Narcotics investigators, like Homicide detectives, do not report directly to the station commander, but to the chief of their bureau, Captain John Esau. The undercover men and women, all sworn deputies, work out of bureau headquarters and are assigned on a per-job basis as required by each zone supervisor.

For reasons of convenience, the Major Violator crews may operate out of their headquarters at the Hall or any station within their zone of operations. Working with or without undercover agents, the crews know no regular hours, but follow the work patterns of their quarry.

Narcotics is a crime that pays, and pays fantastically well; a crime in which the customer-addict eagerly seeks out his pusher and, very often, supports more than one, a precaution in the event one of his pushers is caught and taken out of the action. At the lowest level, pusher to addict, business is conducted on the street, in alleys, cars, rooming houses, roadsides, doorways, bars, restaurants, parks, motels, schools, in darkened movie theaters, or anywhere else they believe themselves safe from observation; all at high risk and at a very substantial profit, with the added fringe benefit of having no taxes to pay.

The Major Violator crew, known as the Majors, or simply the Crew, are more concerned with the upper-echelon operators in the dope hierarchy, the dealers who supply the street pusher, the wholesaler-distributor who supplies the dealer, the importer who supplies the wholesaler-distributor. He is their prime target, the man farthest removed, and insulated, from the street.

The Narcotics agent, unlike his colleague in Homicide, who must necessarily wait until a murder is committed before he becomes involved, is at work trying to prevent a narcotics crime that is about to occur, is in actual progress, or will occur in the near future. In order to accomplish an arrest he is almost always compelled to be on the scene, witness the exchange of cash for product, or have knowledge that the suspect is in physical possession of the dope he expects to sell; knowledge sufficient to obtain a complaint from the district attorney's office.

And as the dealers and pushers work under cover to avoid detection and arrest, so must the agents work similarly to discover the lawbreakers. Most of the arrests are made through information received in a variety of ways and sources: the wife of an addict who hopes to restore her husband to a state of normal living; the discarded mistress or girl friend rejected by a dealer or pusher; an addict "burned" by a pusher who palms off a useless powder in place of the heroin paid for; anonymous phone calls from pushers or dealers themselves in an effort to have the agents of the law remove a competitor and expand his own operations.

Some informants are simply police "buffs" who take great satisfaction in exposing a dealer for the kicks or thrill of it, while others inform for an occasional cash reward. By far, the greatest source of effective information comes from those who fall into an agent's hands for dealing, or using, and face a jail or prison term, in which case, most will offer to "cooperate" in the hope of reducing a felony charge to a misdemeanor, a misdemeanor to possible probation.

The Narcotics office, therefore, is always in a state of constant movement from early morning until well into the night or following morning: interrogating "in custody" prisoners picked up the night before; bringing reports and logs up to date; on the phone with complaints, attorneys, informants;

checking with deputy or assistant district attorneys on up-coming cases; securing complaints or search warrants; testifying in court; setting up undercover buys; discussing an arrest with an irate or anxiety-ridden parent.

Only those with the stamina to withstand the pressures of the job, the emotional strain, the dangers that are ever-present, remain in the bureau. Those who can't are generally transferred out into another branch or division. It is a very tough service.

3•

That weekend in the county area of Firestone, East Los Angeles, and Lennox, the No. 1, 2, and 3 stations alone, there were reported five homicides, 36 robberies, 167 burglaries, 5 rapes, 30 felonious assaults, 26 grand thefts, 58 auto thefts, and 103 narcotics arrests in those 8 categories. A total of 720 persons were booked for all crimes in those areas, among them 534 adults and 186 juveniles, the latter represented in every category, with heavier emphasis on gang activities, in which the homicides and felony assaults were involved.

In East Los Angeles, an elderly woman was permanently blinded and paralyzed after being shot by one of two teen-aged purse snatchers when she refused to give up her purse. A fifteen-year old Garfield High student was raped within a block of her house. Two members of the White Fence gang fired shotguns at four Arizona gang members in a moving car, seriously injuring the four occupants.

In the Firestone area, two car thieves, driving a stolen car, shot it out with two sheriff's deputies, resulting in the death of one seventeen-year-old and the wounding of one of the deputies. A man was killed instantly while walking from his car to his house carrying two sacks of groceries. It was later disclosed that the man had no connection with his slayers. Another youth who fired at a man who was quietly clipping the hedges in front of his house fled, and the one adult witness to the crime could not, or would not, give a description of the car or its occupant. A woman, driving her car while under the influence of alcohol or drugs, or both, plowed into a parked camper, bounced off, and slammed into seven pedestrians in a crosswalk, sending all to the hospital. A gun-man, in the act of an armed robbery, was shot and removed to the hospital in critical condition.

In Lennox, a war between the Cripps gang and their ancient enemy, the Espantos, resulted in one death, six injuries by birdshot, one by stabbing, leaving one boy blinded. Burglaries were reported so closely together that units from Special Enforcement had to be called in to back up normal patrol units assigned to those reporting districts. Elsewhere, meanwhile, units reported to an unprecedented number of 415-Fs, family disturbances, throughout the day and night.

Narcotic crews worked around the clock, setting up buys, talking with informants, making buys and arrests. The booking areas and holding cells in each station were filled to capacity, and Transportation was hard pressed to move the suspects to county jail.

The media had a rare plenitude of crime news to publish for its Monday morning readers. And, as the undersheriff remarked to the sheriff that morning, "It's been rather a hell of a busy weekend."

McNeely arrived at the Narcotics office in Lennox at ten minutes past ten and found his crew busily engaged. Perry Roberts was in the jail section interrogating "in custodies." Steve Barrett was on the phone with a deputy district attorney, Harry Deliso was talking to an informant who had phoned him about a truckload of marijuana known to have been driven into the Carson area on the night before, and Joe Paul was in the private booth trying to set up a buy with a dealer for twelve ounces of cocaine.

The Major Violator crew's quarters were separated from the larger area occupied by the station crew of seven, headed by Sergeant Bill Hamlin. Two of Hamlin's crew were testifying in court, the others busy with endless paperwork and similarly occupied with phone calls.

As Russ entered, he called out a general "Hi, men" greeting, which was less a greeting and more an announcement of his arrival. On his desk lay a few memos from Laurie Kelly, the catchall secretary, telephone messages waiting for call backs.

Deliso cradled the receiver and spun his chair around, grimacing with disappointment. "Sonofabitch," he mouthed.

McNeely said, "What's doing, Supermouth?"

"Dominic Delterro."

"What's with D.D., no go?"

Deliso shook his head negatively. "No. The bastard's gone hinky on me."

"What went wrong? I thought you were wired in tight."

"That paranoid creep. L.A.P.D. busted his partner last night, delivering two keys of weed in the Valley, and Dom is very very nervous. Wants me to call him Friday. Maybe he'll be ready then. Maybe."

"So it goes. What else is doing?"

One of the booth phones rang, and Bill Hamlin, closest to it, checked the light button and said to Laurie, "Get it on 7742, will you?"

She entered the booth, closed the door, and picked up the receiver. "Six-seven-eight-seven-seven-four-two."

"Hey, mama, Bobby there?"

"Just a moment." She came out of the booth and pointed a finger at Perry Roberts. He signaled to McNeely, and both crowded into the booth. Perry activated the recorder and picked up the receiver, McNeely holding his ear close to it. "Hello."

"Hey, Bobby?"

"Yeah. Who's this?"

"Pete."

"Hey, Pete, what's doin', man?"

"How you fixed, Bobby?"

"Okay. What's up?"

"Man, I'm low, way down. I need a friend."

"Hell, you got one, friend. What's your problem, Pete?"

"I gotta raise a bill by six o'clock tonight, else I'm liable to get an arm an' a leg busted."

"Well, Pete, a whole hundred—"

"Look, this ain't for nothin', Bobby. I got somethin' to swap for it. Worth a bill, easy."

"Let's hear it, Pete. What you got?"

"Okay. You know ol' Sylvester?"

"Sylvester Tripp?"

"Yeah, that's the cat."

"What about Sylvester?"

"Sat'dy night, he ast me do I wanna drive a car they gonna boost. Gonna rip off Miles Hardy for his stash. One of Miles's dudes went over to Sylvester an' set 'im up, wantsa take over the territory for hisself. Sylvester wants me to be the wheelman."

"When's this deal going down, Pete?"

"Tomorrow night, 'bout eleven o'clock. Onliest thing is, I'm into Benny Garcia for the hundred, an' he wants his bread by six o'clock tonight or else."

"Sylvester won't front you the bill?"

"Shit, man, you know Sylvester. Cheap bastard wouldn'

front a dime to his mother. I do the job an' I get a bill an' a half, on'y by then I'll be too late."

"Hold it, Pete. Just a minute. Lemme see if I got a hundred on me." Roberts palmed the mouthpiece and said to McNeely, "How about it, Russ? Do we front the hundred to get Sylvester, or do I spin Pete off and maybe lose myself a good snitch?"

McNeely took a moment to think about it. Tripp was a good-sized dealer in the Carson area with a past record of violence: armed robbery, assault with a deadly weapon, car theft, more recently deep in narcotics. "You think your snitch is leveling, Perry?"

"I think so, Russ. He's a hot wheelman, and he owes me. He never let me down before."

"Okay. Tell him to set up a meet with you and Steve for two o'clock. If he isn't giving us a hand job, I'd like to take Tripp off the streets for a few years and pick up Hardy along with him."

"Right on." Into the receiver, "Okay, Pete, I can make it. Here's what we'll do—"

Back at his desk, McNeely picked up a copy of the weekly digest of crimes committed in the county. He put it aside after a quick glance and would take it home with him to examine more critically, his thoughts turning back to Whitey Lloyd.

"Russ?" Barrett called from his desk.

McNeely looked around and saw a well-dressed man of about fifty, gray sprinkled through his brown hair at the temples, eyes showing the strain of anxiety behind heavily rimmed glasses, obviously not comfortable in alien surroundings. Russ went to the railing that screened outsiders from the two crews at work.

"Sergeant McNeely?"

"Yes. What can I do for you?"

"I'm Sanford Rice, Sergeant."

"Yes, Mr. Rice. Won't you come in, please. We've been trying to reach you or Mrs. Rice since Friday night. Saturday morning, rather."

"I'm sorry. The other officer told me when he reached me at my home this morning. Mrs. Rice and I returned from Acapulco only two hours ago, and I hurried right down. Where is David?"

"At the moment he's being held at the county jail on Bauchet Street in Los Angeles for his preliminary hearing in South Bay Municipal Court on Thursday morning."

"I phoned my attorney before coming to see you to arrange for bail. That will be possible, won't it?"

"I'm sure it will. Of course, David was given the opportunity to call an attorney after he was booked here, but he chose not to."

"I can't understand it. I just can't understand the whole thing."

"There's really nothing more we can do here, Mr. Rice," McNeely said, and noticing the increasing pallor in Rice's face, added, "Wouldn't you like to sit down, sir. How about a cup of coffee?"

Rice sat down. "I'd be grateful." McNeely signaled to Deliso, who went to the table behind Laurie's desk to get the coffee. Rice said, "My wife and I are terribly upset, distraught—" He withdrew a handkerchief, removed his glasses, and wiped his eyes and forehead.

"I can appreciate how you and Mrs. Rice feel, and I sympathize with you."

"Oh, God. That boy—the devotion and love we've given him. I don't even know what exactly happened. The officer would only say that he was in jail on a narcotics charge. Can you tell me what, how it happened, Sergeant? I'd like to know something more about it before I see David."

"I can only give you the facts, Mr. Rice. We didn't make the arrest—that is, none of us in the office here made it. He was stopped by a patrol unit—let me check the report again." He found the Xerox copy and referred to it. "At zero three ten on Saturday morning, Deputies Zerba and Pakula attempted to stop his car on the San Diego Freeway, traveling north, for erratic driving and weaving across several lanes. He refused to obey their red lights and siren and took off at speeds upward of eighty miles an hour. They managed to cut him off at one of the off-ramps.

"David was belligerent and refused to get out of the car. Pakula and Zerba removed him physically, with some resistance on David's part, but once out of the car, he was unable to stand up. There was no odor of alcohol on his breath, but he seemed to be unable to focus properly, his speech was thick and slurred, and he kept stumbling, falling against the car.

"Zerba then checked the car and found an envelope with seventeen Methedrine pills in it. In the glove compartment, he found a hypodermic kit and part of a spoon of heroin—a spoon, Mr. Rice, is about two and one-half grams, enough

106

for about fifteen or more caps, or fixes. In his jacket pocket was a cigarette pack with nine hand-rolled joints of marijuana.

"He was then brought in here to Lennox and booked for possession, reckless driving, speeding, and driving with an expired license. Because narcotics were involved, we talked with him, but he refused to say anything. We ran the license tags through DMV and learned the car was in your name."

"That boy—" Rice said again, his voice reflecting hopelessness.

"According to his expired driver's license, he is now eighteen years old and will have to stand trial as an adult."

Rice didn't seem to hear this last. The coffee brought to him by Harry Deliso remained untouched. "Also," McNeely continued, "when we checked his arms during our interrogation, they showed old tracks. You'll have to face it, Mr. Rice—"

"That—that's impossible!"

"—David is an addict, a junkie, and not a recent one."

Rice, hearing the words spoken softly, yet bluntly, dropped deeper into dejection. "Where—where in the world—where would he get it, for God's sake?" he said in a quavering whisper.

"Where they all get it. From pushers who are in business purely for profit. Unfortunately, that's how it is."

"My God, Sergeant, where does one go for help?"

"I'm afraid that's out of our hands. Here we see only the pitiful end results of the dirty trade. We do our best to hold it down, keep it from coming in, but—"

Tears welled up in Rice's eyes. McNeely said, "Believe me, Mr. Rice, I'm sorry. I wish I could be of more help to you. There are rehabilitation programs, but just as in the case of psychiatry, the addict must be willing to accept help."

Rice didn't move, but sat quietly staring down at his hands, holding the untouched cup of coffee to keep them from trembling. "We interrogated David, trying to learn the names of the people he was copping—buying from, but he refused to tell us anything."

"I'll talk to him, try—" Rice's voice trailed off.

"If he will, it can help us, but—anyway, I wish you luck."

Rice stood up. "Thank you, Sergeant. I appreciate the time you've given me. I know you must be busy."

"That's one of the things we're here for, sir. If I can help you in any way, I hope you'll call on me."

As Rice went out, Deliso said, "Poor, sad bastard."

McNeely said, "When they're like him, this is the one god-damned part of this job I hate."

Steve Barrett was on the phone with a woman who claimed she had found three marijuana cigarettes in her fifteen-year-old daughter's dresser drawer. "I understand, Mrs. Keller, but what do you want us to do?"

"Do? *Do?* I want you to put a stop to it, that's what I want you to do," Mrs. Keller demanded.

"Let me explain it to you again," Steve said patiently. "If we send someone out to check it and find it's marijuana—"

"It's marijuana, all right."

"—and we arrest Penny for possession—"

"Ar*rest* her? What for?"

"Will you sign the complaint and appear as a witness against her?"

"Of course *not!* I'm trying to keep Penny out of jail, not put her in it, for God's sake!"

Steve's eyes rolled upward in supplication. "That's all I *can* do, Mrs. Keller, by law. We can't raise your daughter for you, control where she goes, whom she sees, what she does."

"It's her boy friend. He gives them to her."

"Do you have any proof we can use as evidence in court, Mrs. Keller?"

"Proof? Of course not. He wouldn't give them to her in my presence."

"Has Penny told you he furnishes it to her?"

"Penny? Hah! She won't even *talk* to me. We haven't talked to each other in three months except when she needs money to buy things."

Steve sighed softly. "Mrs. Keller, may I suggest you have a serious talk with Penny or have her talk to her priest or pastor? Perhaps Mr. Keller can—"

"Oh, for God's sake! Can't you people do *any*thing right?" The receiver slammed, and contact was cut off.

"Hey," Steve called to Perry Roberts, whose desk faced his, "you want a job babysitting a fifteen-year-old weed-head?"

"No," Perry said. "Keep her on ice until she's eighteen, then let me see some pictures of her."

"Man, you're all heart."

McNeely made his call backs quickly, then began rereading the reports on Whitey Lloyd again. Bill Hamlin's crew, like his own, was busy getting the morning's work out of the way in order to get out on the street, make the scene where the action was. They worked, joked, drank coffee, kidded Laurie, each with his mind moving ahead to where the next job was and what might await him there.

McNeely looked across his desk to the four that faced each other in their tightly cramped section of the room. Deliso, Barrett, Roberts, and Paul. The Zone II Majors. A damned good crew, he thought with chauvinistic pride, the best in the Bureau.

Harry Deliso, a Deputy IV, thirty-two, tall and dark, eight years in the department, five in Narcotics, two commendations in Patrol, four in his present job. Harry had dropped out of college after two years to come to Los Angeles to become a movie actor and, failing, went into the department. In his car, he always carried an assortment of clothing oddments, wigs, and a makeup kit, ready to change his appearance or manner as needed in his job. The father of two sons, both in his former wife's custody, he never missed a weekly or vacation visit to the boys unless he was tied up on an important case.

Perry Roberts, Deputy IV, twenty-eight, married to Jo-Ann, a former secretary. Seven years in the department, two in Patrol, one in Vice, three in Narcotics. Perry was expert in street language, dress, and mannerisms and could mimic the part of addict, pusher, or dealer as required. An amateur boxer and a black belt in karate, Roberts seldom found it necessary to flash or use his gun.

Steve Barrett, Deputy III, twenty-eight, married to the daughter of a wealthy real-estate operator, Joy, whom he had met at Cal State in Long Beach. Joy's father had given them their Manhattan Beach home completely furnished as a wedding gift, with Steve complaining about the cost of its upkeep on his salary of $14,000 a year. All in good fun. Graduated at twenty-one, Steve spent two years in the army, one of those in Vietnam, and decided against returning to law school. Having seen the deleterious effects of drugs in Vietnam, he had applied for his present job in Narcotics as soon as his first year in Patrol ended.

Joe Paul, Deputy III, twenty-eight, six years in the department, two in Narcotics undercover work, three in investigation, the most recent addition to the Major crew. Swarthy, mustached, long-haired, Joe could blend into the street scene with little problem. He was single, quiet, and unassuming and worked long hours without complaint, volunteering to take on any job in the works. He was a man with a mission; back home in Baltimore, his younger brother had become addicted to heroin at sixteen and died in the school gymnasium locker room the following year from an overdose of the drug.

The phone rang, and Perry picked it up. He said, "Hold it," and turned to McNeely. "Jailer downtown. Your buddy Whitey Lloyd is getting lonesome for company. Wants to talk to you. In private."

Quietly elated, Russ took the call, spoke with the jailer, and made arrangements to see Lloyd at two that afternoon. Routine matters took up the rest of the morning. After a quick sandwich with Roberts and Barrett and a final discussion on the matter of Pete, the snitch, Russ took off for Bauchet Street and the appointment with Lloyd.

Stripped of his civilian clothes and wearing jailhouse blues, Lloyd shuffled into the interrogation room. He appeared far more subdued and discomfited after several days behind bars, reduced to certain anonymity in the world's largest jail facility. His eyes brightened at the sight of McNeely. "Hey, man," he greeted, "glad to see you."

Russ sat down across the table from Lloyd and offered him a cigarette, then placed the pack on the table between them.

"Thanks," Lloyd said, lighting up.

"What's on your mind, Whitey?"

"Well—" hesitantly, exploring McNeely's face carefully, "I thought we could have a talk."

"Okay, let's talk. How's everything?"

He turned caustic. "Okay. Great. I just feel goddamned lousy, that's all." He glanced around the small interrogation room cautiously, suspicion in his expression.

McNeely said, "We're private here, Whitey. No bugs, if that's what's bothering you. You had your lunch?"

"Such as it was."

"Well, it's not Perino's or Scandia, but it's not all that bad, considering."

"I'm not bitching. I've had worse."

"Then let's knock off the chit-chat and get down to it. What do you want to talk about?"

"I've been thinking a lot, four days of it. I'd like to buy a deal."

"What kind of a deal?"

"Look, I know I'm up for a heavy fall. I know I can't get a free ride, either, but I'd like to buy as much as I can."

"I understand, Whitey, but you know it's not up to me. All I can do is talk to the D.A. and tell him to what extent you're willing to cooperate."

"You don't have to lean the muscle on me, man. I know

110

the drill. What I want to know is, how far will you guys go for me?"

"If you know the drill, you know it all depends on how far you'll go for us. This is no small rap, Whitey, you know that."

"Okay, so I know it. I'll lay it on the line for you. I can give you a pair of heavy dudes, and I really mean heavy. They deal all the way across the board. High-test smack and coke. But big. They don't even fool with weed, hash, pills, or the other little shit."

McNeely looked unimpressed. "That'll do for starters, but it's not enough to water down the rap you're facing, Whitey."

"Not *enough*?" Whitey was clearly outraged. "For Christ's holy sake, man, what the hell more do you want? These guys deal *heavy,* I told you. Pounds, kilos. Jesus, they're probably a couple of the biggest dealers in Southern California, maybe in the whole goddamned state."

"As I said, they'll do for starters. What I want is the dude on top of them, the chief honcho."

Lloyd waggled his head from side to side, simulating despair. He jabbed out his cigarette in the tinny ashtray with vicious stabs. "Man, I'm not high enough up there to know that. Whoever the hell he is, he's too out of sight for me."

"How high?"

"Nowhere, man. I never saw him or heard a name. All I know is these two dudes who deal to me."

"Come on, Whitey, cut the bullshitting. You've got more than one connection."

"I had more, sure, but for the last couple of years or so, all I've used is this one outfit because their stuff is the best quality around."

"But you do know others, don't you?"

"I know Dusty Parker out in the Valley, Phil Sutton—"

"You're just jiving me, giving me dudes who are in the slammer already. You're not giving me a damned thing I don't already know. If that's how you're going to cooperate—"

"Okay, okay. I know Ernie and George Ruiz in East L.A., Jimmie Tice and Willie Acheson in Carson, but I haven't scored off them in a long time. That's the God's honest truth, McNeely. I'm bleeding for you."

"You'll have to bleed just a little harder if you want to do business with me, Whitey."

"I can't. All I can deal you is my connection, and like I told you, they're big."

"Well, let's see how big it is. Give me some names."

Lloyd wet his lips. "Look, you'll keep me under wraps, won't you? They find out I turned them, I'm stone dead."

"If they find out, you can bet your last dime it won't be from me or my people."

He shook another cigarette loose from the pack and lighted it with trembling hands. McNeely said, "Let's have it, Whitey. I haven't got all day to spend rapping over nothing."

Lloyd sighed deeply, exhaling a cloud of smoke. "Okay. All I have is these two dudes. They front for a honcho, I'm sure, but I don't know anything about him, whether he's black, brown, green, purple, or white."

"Let's have some names."

"Eddie Butler. A dude about five-eleven, maybe one-fifty or -sixty pounds, a thin hatchet face, brown eyes, clean shave, a kind of broken nose, maybe from a fight. The other dude is Moose Peterson, big, goes around six-one or -two, maybe two-fifty or -sixty pounds. Light hair, a little thin in front, gray eyes. Looks like a pro linebacker. A cold sonofabitch, must have ice water in his veins."

Neither name nor descriptions struck a responsive chord in McNeely's memory as he tried to isolate them from the many hundreds he had encountered since joining the Narcotics Bureau. "Where do they live or hang out?"

Lloyd held back on the question, keeping it in reserve for some possible leverage later in the game. "I don't know. We do business by phone. I don't pick up. They deliver to me."

"How do you make contact?"

"All I've got is a number. A Valley phone."

"San Fernando? San Gabriel?"

"San Fernando. A seven-eight-five number. I don't know the address. You can check it out. It's a drop."

"How does it work?"

"I put in the call. It rings three times, then a broad's voice comes on. 'I'm sorry I'm not in to take your call. When you hear the beep, please leave a message. Be sure to leave a number where I can contact you. Thank you.' Then I leave the message, how much of what kind of stuff I want. We use a number code. Three is coke, eight is smack. I leave my name, just Whitey, and hang up."

"She have a name, this broad at the drop?"

"If it's the same one I've been dealing with right along, it's Connie. That was before they put in this taped-message deal, when she used to answer the phone in person."

"Connie what?"

"That's all I know, except she's a Chicano. Talks with a

slight Mex accent, you know? Like the way they say 'chure' for 'sure.' "

"So you leave a message. What happens next?"

Lloyd took a deep breath and exhaled slowly. "I guess she relays the message to Eddie or Moose. Anyway, it's usually for a little smack or coke. It's got to come to at least a grand or they won't handle it."

"How does the delivery system work?"

"There's this little shopping center and service station on Hawthorne and Palos Verdes Drive, West. A public telephone booth next to the Gulf station. The number is 377-9172. Once I pass the message on to Connie, I go to that booth on Monday, Wednesday, or Friday, always the night closest to the day I call in. I park next to the booth and wait. If it rings exactly at seven thirty, I answer. It'll be Eddie; once in a while it'll be Moose. If there's no ring, I take off and come back on the next scheduled night."

"Then what?"

"If it rings, we make the contact. He confirms the deal, sets the price, and lays out the meet. A different place every time. Like maybe a shopping center in West L.A., a spot in the Valley, maybe the pier at Redondo, or Marina del Rey, once or twice in San Pedro somewhere, a bar or parking lot. Always at night and when there's some traffic action."

"They deliver in person?"

"Yeah. Mostly it's Eddie; sometimes Moose is along with him riding shotgun. Sometimes it's Moose all by himself."

"You ever get a license number on the car they use?"

"No, but mostly it's a Caddy, maybe a '70 or '71. They always make sure I'm there first, then park somewhere behind me and a couple of rows or yards back. Generally, Eddie comes over to my car and picks up the bread. He goes back to the car and counts it. Then the shotgun comes over and drops the package off to me and tells me to take off."

"What's the most you've ever scored off these dudes?"

"The last deal I got ripped off for. The pound."

"You laid out the bread for the buy?"

"No. I didn't have that much handy, so they fronted it for me."

"So now they're stuck for their money and the junk, too. Looks like you didn't make any brownie points with your buddies this time, did you?"

"I sure as hell didn't and made myself a couple of real good enemies."

"Who else do these dudes deal to?"

"No way, man. They're not stupid enough to let anybody know that. Absolutely no way. These guys are too cagey for that. I don't know anything else, where they get their stuff, where they mill it down, or who else they deal to. That's level."

"You must have a pretty good client list yourself."

Lloyd's mouth opened, then clamped shut, merely shaking his head. "Look, McNeely, you know what street dudes are. They're ghosts. To me, they're just nicknames. They come and go."

"How come the stuff you deal is as heavy as it is? They ever tell you about that?"

"Well, once when they started dealing to me, way back, I asked the same question. Eddie claims it comes in damn near pure, so they can afford to let it go out heavier than the others do. Gives their dealers some room to put an extra cut or two in it. Keeps everybody happy and their dealers coming back to them. They're good business people that way."

"All right, Whitey. Is that all for now?"

"All? Hell, man, you're miles out in front of me now. When does our deal go down?"

"I'll put it in the works today, but it will all depend on what we get out of this little talk."

"Okay, McNeely. I'm playing ball with you, putting my neck on the line. Just don't fuck me around, huh?"

McNeely simply stared at him, then stood up. Lloyd said, "Look, man, this isn't my bag, the slammer. I'm hurting. I laid it all out for you. Everything."

"Relax, Whitey. Let's see what we can get out of this. You'll hear something soon."

"Will I get out on bail, at least?"

"I think I can promise we won't ask for excessive bail. I'll see you at your hearing."

"Just remember, I'm waiting."

"I'll remember."

4●

The telephone number Lloyd had given McNeely, 785-6438, turned up a small, neat house in the 13000 block of Sylvan Street in Van Nuys, a suburban community in the San Fernando Valley. A further check revealed that the house was owned by a man who lived in Thousand Oaks and was rented by a Mrs. Consuela Moya, who had lived there for four years and three months. A credit check showed her to be prompt in payment of all utility bills and charge accounts with gasoline companies and three department stores. She owned a Chevrolet sedan and a Toyota, had a son, Raul, seventeen, a student at Van Nuys High School, a daughter, Carmela, fifteen, who attended the same school. Mrs. Moya had been a widow for a little over five years.

The personal report on Mrs. Moya had come from an agent who had represented himself as a repairman from the gas company searching for a leak that had been reported by a neighbor. He described her as female, Latin, five-three, about 115 pounds, black hair, brown eyes, regular features. Mrs. Moya had been reluctant to admit him until he produced proper credentials, with which he had been furnished. The house, he further reported, was modest in cost, in a modest neighborhood, but its interior was furnished with a number of expensive items of furniture, a large color television set, and wall-sized hi-fi equipment. The Chevvy sedan in the driveway was a recent model, the grounds well tended, with an 18 x 36 pool at the rear, surrounded by a six-foot-high chain-link fence.

There was no evidence to show that Mrs. Consuela Moya was gainfully employed or that she had a police record. Her checking account in a Van Nuys bank showed a current balance of $1,227.69.

A search in Records turned up rap sheets on both Butler and Peterson. Butler's record showed two arrests as a juvenile, no time served. As an adult he had one misdemeanor conviction, possession of marijuana, probation granted; one grand theft auto at the age of twenty, convicted and served eighteen months in Chino; one possession of heroin for sale conviction, two years in Soledad Prison. Butler had also been arrested and convicted on another narcotics charge, but the verdict had been reversed on appeal to the California Supreme Court by reason of illegal search and seizure, the charges against him and his woman companion dismissed.

Peterson's record began in New York where he served three years of a five-year sentence for armed robbery, another two years for assault with a deady weapon. His next conviction was in San Francisco for possession and sale of heroin, for which he served two years of a five-year sentence in Soledad Prison.

Both Butler and Peterson had been in Soledad at the same time, Peterson released three months after Butler's time was up. Obviously, their friendship had begun there and endured.

After consultation with Bob Barker, McNeely suggested a surveillance on the Sylvan Street house, and it was authorized, undertaken by the Metropolitan Bureau. An information-wanted bulletin, showing mug shots and descriptions of both men, was circulated among all Narcotics crews and station detectives, informants contacted and questioned.

Chapter Four

1●

At ten o'clock that morning the man in the solid brown sports jacket and dark brown slacks had been waiting for approximately forty minutes under the hot September sun that beat down on the metal roof of his Dodge sedan. From where he sat near the bus stop he could see the gateway leading into the Chino State Prison. It would have been far more comfortable, he knew, for him to wait in the air-conditioned reception room beyond the gate, but he did not want to be identified with the man for whom he waited.

He squirmed in his seat behind the wheel, feeling the discomfort of the moisture that glued his shirt to his body and the weight of the .38 he carried in a leather holster under his left arm. He moved forward, dug a pack of cigarettes from his jacket pocket, and depressed the dashboard lighter, more to have something to do than for the cigarette itself. Smoking provided some action, but no relief whatever from the heat.

He was a man of average height and build, with rich black hair cut in the manner called "straight," without shaggy ends or long sideburns; a thin-faced man with a rise to the bridge of his nose, which was somewhat prominent, generous lips, dark-complexioned, heavy black eyebrows over a pair of deep black eyes that seemed to smile even when the rest of his face remained immobile. He looked to be older than his thirty-two years, but had seen much in his lifetime, enough to give him a deep feeling of concern for those with whom he came in contact, generally in adverse circumstances.

At 10:20, he stirred, coming alert as he saw his man come walking through the gate; short, slender, hatless, sundarkened by exposure to the elements, lithe. Carrying a small canvas bag in his left hand, squinting against the bright sun. He was wearing the same clothes he had worn on the day he was transported to Chino two years earlier: faded blue-jean trousers, waist-length army-style fatigue jacket over a tan shirt, open collar, brown army shoes. At the gate, the young man looked to his left, then right, saw the bus stop kiosk, and walked toward it. As he passed the Dodge, he glanced at the man behind the wheel, a Mexican-American like himself, with casual disinterest, then stopped as he heard the man call his name.

"Rudy?"

The younger man turned and stared hard into the car, hesitated for a moment, then took a tentative step forward and stopped again. The man in the car said, "Get in, Rudy."

"What for?"

"To save you a fifty-mile bus ride back to L.A."

"Somebody send you for me?" Rudy asked cautiously.

"Nobody sent me. I came on my own."

Rudy frowned. "I know you?" he asked.

"You know me. You just don't remember me. It's been two whole years."

Rudy stood stock still for a moment, indecisively, then took another step forward, peering harder at the man. Sitting behind the wheel in the interior shadows, he could see no resemblance to anyone he knew. "Look, man," he said, "I don't know you. Just bug off an' lemme alone. I don't want no trouble."

The man reached inside his jacket pocket and removed a flat wallet. When he flipped it open, Rudy saw a too-familiar gold-colored six-pointed star on the upper half, an I.D. card on the lower half. The man said, "Ramon Ycaza. Okay?"

Recognition came quickly then, and Rudy Arboleya exhaled with relief. "Hey, sure," he said slowly through a small, tight smile, as though he hadn't smiled in a long time.

"Get in, will you? It's hotter'n the brass handles on the front door to hell."

Rudy walked around to the passenger side and got in.

When he was settled in his seat, Ray Ycaza started the motor and hit the air-conditioner lever all the way up. As they drove away, the bus to Los Angeles pulled up and wheezed to a stop. Rudy stared back at it and said, "Hey, thanks. This is a lot better than that."

Ycaza pulled out his cigarette pack and offered it to Rudy, who took one. Puffing it alive, he asked, "How come? I thought I was all through with you guys. I done my time. This a new service by the sheriff?"

Ycaza smiled. "No, Rudy. I took the day off to do this. And you're not in the clear yet. You were released on parole, you know."

"Yeah," Arboleya said with a touch of bitterness in his voice. "I've got the paper in my pocket. Who I report to, where and when. What I can do, what I can't do, who I can be seen with, no drinking, who I can't consort with. It spells out my whole life for the next three years."

"Par for the course, Rudy, but it's a hell of a lot better being on the outside than inside, right? You killed a guy and pleaded self-defense, and the judge gave you two-to-five on manslaughter. You started that fight in the bar with Richie Obregon, and you were damned lucky we were later able to come up with two witnesses who testified that Richie pulled the knife you killed him with."

"Yeah," Rudy said. "I got you to thank for that. You went to bat for me. My lawyer and Isobel told me you talked up for me at the parole hearing."

"Okay, Rudy. I'm not looking for any thanks or medals. Between you and me, Obregon got what he deserved. I wish I could have gotten you off on probation, but— Anyway, I've been talking to your parole officer—"

Rudy turned suddenly, staring at Ycaza with disbelief. "Jesus, man, you give this service to all cons?"

Ycaza sighed deeply. "Listen, Rudy. Forget that con bit. Start now to get it the hell out of your mind. Something else. In spite of what a lot of people say or think, we're not a lot of vindictive bastards who want to keep our jails and prisons filled. There are criminals who deserve it, but there are a lot of guys like you who got a lousy break. Your record in Vietnam helped. You're not a street hood, and I'd like to see you stay clean. I didn't know your brother, but I knew Isobel's family. Good people."

"Okay. I appreciate everything you did for me. How come Isobel didn't come to meet me like she wrote me she would?"

"She wanted to, but I asked her to let me come instead. It would mean a long ride on the bus, and she'd lose a day's pay at the theater, which she can't afford. She wouldn't have minded that, but I wanted to talk to you before you got back to L.A."

"Yeah, well—okay, deputy, what's on your mind? And how come you're not in uniform? That's what threw me back there when you called to me. I didn't recognize you in civvie threads."

"I don't wear uniforms these days. I was transferred to the Detective Bureau about three months after you were sentenced."

For a few moments they rode in silence along the Pomona Freeway, Rudy's eyes eager to take in the world he had missed during the past two years. Then he said, "How is she?"

"Isobel? Fine. How come you never let her come to visit you on her days off? She wanted to, you know."

"Ah, hell. I didn't want her to see me in my con clothes, with all the other cons around. Last time she saw me was at my trial, when I was wearing my army uniform. Besides, she's Joey's wife—widow—with a two-and-a-half-year-old kid to look after. Chino ain't no place for a girl like her to come visitin'. You seen Robert lately?"

"Yeah. He's doing fine. I've got one of my own named Robert. My oldest. He's six now." He paused and added, "And two younger ones."

"Sounds like you got it made. Hey, who looks after the kid while Isobel is working in that movie house from three to ten at night?"

"Her next door neighbor, a nice old lady. Okay, let's talk some more about you. Your job is all set up with Rodriguez's Garage. Tune-up man. You can handle that, can't you?"

"Hell, yeah, no sweat. That's all I been doing at Chino, keeping cars and trucks in shape."

"So no problems there, then. You take a couple of weeks off to get organized, get your tools together, and go to work. You got enough money to handle that?"

"Yeah. I got almost nine hundred of the fifteen I brought home from Vietnam. Isobel is keeping it for me." He paused, then said, "What about those dudes Obregon hung out with, the bastards who hot-lined Joey? Lucero, Mendenez, Peludo, Rojas—"

"Forget about them, Rudy. Drop it. Most of 'em are in the joint or split. The gang busted up after Obregon died."

"All of 'em?"

"Well, not all. Some are still around, but they've got the word. You keep clear of them, they'll stay away from you."

"Yeah," Rudy said bitterly. "Joey's dead, Isobel's a widow, I threw away two years of my life in a goddamn prison, and those lousy bastards are still out there pushing junk."

"Listen to me, boy," Ycaza said without heat, "knock it off. Forget it, the revenge business. That's what got you in trouble in the first place."

"Forget it? Man, I been dreaming about it every night for two whole years. Every goddamn night."

"So. You want to go out and get caught up in it again? A murder-one rap next time and spend the rest of your life behind bars? Think, boy. Let the law handle your revenge for you."

"The law?" Rudy snorted with contempt. "What did the law do for Joey?"

"Goddamn it, Rudy, get your head screwed on straight. The law didn't make a junkie out of Joey, get him mixed up with pushers like Richie Obregon and those other assholes. He was three years older than you, old enough to know the score. And like it or not, Rudy, he had a choice, the same choice we all have. Go bad or stay clean. He lost his job, had a baby on the way. He stole and robbed to pay for the junk he was shooting. When he couldn't do that anymore, he begged the stuff, threatened to turn his pusher in if they didn't supply him. So they ripped him off. I don't want to see you blow the chance you've got. You're twenty-four. Isobel's twenty-three. Robert is two and a half. You can do a lot to help them, too."

Rudy twisted in his seat, prodded by irritation at Ycaza's words. "What the hell are you," he said, "a priest or something?"

"Oh, man, man. No, I'm not a priest. I'm a cop. Just a guy who once stood in your shoes and made a right move. I did four whole years in the army, two in Nam when it got started. I'm thirty-two, I've got a house, a wife and three kids. I could have wound up like the Joeys in the world. Or out of it. That was my choice, the same choice you can make now."

"Okay, okay. I know you're right. I know it. But two years back there, thinking about it all the time— Goddamn it, it's not right he should die like a dog and they should go on killing other guys."

"Rudy, it's not right and we do our best with what we've

got. Just forget the revenge bit. The only revenge is to outlive your enemies. You're out and you're clean. For Christ's sake, stay that way."

Again the silence, then, "I'll try, Mr. Ycaza. I'll try. I promise."

"Then don't call me 'mister.' I'm not that much older than you."

They were getting closer to the city, the landscape growing more familiar. Rudy kept looking out to his right, then left, watching the steady stream of traffic rolling toward them, past them, the mountains, the blue sky above. Ycaza said, "You figure out where you're going to live, Rudy?"

"I been thinking about it. Isobel wants me to stay there at the house on Andreo Avenue. It belonged to my mother after my old man died. She left it to Joey and me. I lived there with him and Isobel until I got drafted. She told me it's okay if I want to live there with her and Robert."

"Robert could do pretty good with an uncle around."

Rudy smiled for the first time. "Hey, yeah. How about that? Be like raising my own son."

"Sure, Papa. It's a good feeling, huh? Just remember, Rudy, a man is what happens to a boy. You had a good father and mother, and that could do a lot for Robert."

"Yeah." A long pause, then, "So how did Joey get to be a hype and get himself O.D.'d by a lousy pusher like Obregon?"

"Who the hell knows, Rudy? Even with a wife like Isobel, it can happen when a guy is weak, feels sorry for himself, blames the world for his problems, and looks for an easy way out." He sighed and added, "That's all over now. Start forgetting it."

"You think Isobel can forget she's a twenty-three-year-old widow with a son to support?"

"In time, she will. She's trying, but it's not easy. Maybe you can help her."

"Yeah," Rudy said softly, "maybe."

Ycaza said, "You ever run into Ernie or George Ruiz down there in Carson?"

"Ruiz? The big wheel?"

"That's the one."

"I used to see him and his brother George around, but I never knew either one of 'em too well."

"You know about him, though, don't you?"

"Hell, everybody down there knows Ernie Ruiz. Owns the Dos Hermanos Bar and Poolroom, gambling in the back room after hours, whores, loan sharking, everything."

"And dope."

"Yeah, dope. Also, he can come up with a hit guy for a price."

"Yeah, you know him."

"You working dope?"

"No. Homicide."

"Jesus." Rudy took a deep breath. "You asking me for something?"

Ycaza laughed lightly. "No, Rudy. Just stay the hell away from the Dos Hermanos and keep your nose clean. It's close to the Rodriguez Garage, and there's a lot of stuff going on there that you ought to bypass. It's one of Pete Rojas's hangouts and he was buddy-buddy with Richie Obregon."

"Look, if you want me to do something for you, I owe you."

"You don't owe me a damned thing, Rudy. When I drop you at Isobel's, that's it. I'll leave you my card. If I can help you with anything, call me. Okay?"

"Okay, Mr. Ycaza. And thanks for everything. I know you didn't have to do all the things you done for me."

"Not 'mister,' I told you. It's Ray."

"Thanks again, Ray."

2●

It was early afternoon when Ycaza dropped Rudy Arboleya at the house on Andreo Avenue in Carson, one of many houses so similar in construction: small, varicolored stucco, some with tiled roofs, others wood-shingled. It was an area of low-income workers and many welfare families, a mixture of whites and a few blacks, but predominantly Mexican-American; of old model cars, a few pickup trucks. Small stores and shops nearby, a large shopping center at 228th Street and Avalon Boulevard, all spelling deterioration and spoiled air. Ray shook hands with Rudy at curbside. "Hey, come on in," Rudy invited.

"No," Ray said, "not now. Some other time. Reunions should be private."

Ycaza drove along for a while, then stopped for a sandwich before he hit the Harbor Freeway, spun off into the Hollywood, then into the Ventura, and breathed with relief when he reached his hillside home in Sherman Oaks, remembering the Bakersfield *barrio* where he had been born.

Yolanda was home with Johnny, who was four, and Rosa, just two. Robert, six, was in school, the envy of Johnny and

Rosa. Ray embraced and kissed Yolanda, who was busy in the kitchen. "Any calls?" he asked.

"No, nothing. You had lunch?"

"I stopped on the way home."

He went into the den for the children's welcome, interrupting a television movie. Yolanda brought him a glass of iced tea, and he took it out to the shaded sundeck. "You want to take a nap?" Yolanda asked.

"No. I'd just like to sit here for a while and relax."

"Good. I have some work to do, then pick Robert up."

Alone, his thoughts turned back to Rudy and the one question he had asked. *"What are you, a priest or something?"*

A long way from it, Rudy. Just a barrio kid like you. Except that you went one route, and I went the other. And maybe if I'd had an older brother who became a junkie and got himself O.D.'d while I was in Nam, I might have been standing in your shoes when you ripped Richie Obregon off. And I would have.

There was much in his thirty-two-year life that Ramon Ycaza did not enjoy recalling of those early days in Bakersfield, but he had come to realize that in order to forget the past and count one's blessings, one must first remember. And remember well.

Of his father, who had walked out on his wife when Ramon was two, he remembered nothing. He grew up in a two-room rented *barrio* hovel with his mother, Amalia, who worked in the houses of the Anglos as a cleaning woman and laundress, later as a waitress in Chavez's restaurant, barely able to support herself and her son, leaving him in the care of their next-door neighbors, the Maldonados, who had seven children of their own.

What he remembered best and most clearly were the early morning hours when Amalia would return from Chavez's and slip into the bed they shared, feeling her warmth, smelling the perfume of her hair, accepting her love and tenderness, soothing away the hurts and anxieties of the long hours when they were apart.

As he grew, he became a part of the *barrio* street life. At twelve, in school, he became a member of the Bakersfield Bravatos and participated in their "wars" with the Halcón, Matador, and Liberador gangs. With his Bravatos, he became an accomplished petty thief, shoplifter, car stripper, and later, a member of a foursome who specialized in purse snatching, rolling drunks, and muggings. By the time he was

124

fourteen, he had been smoking marijuana for two years, pushing joints and pills for the Coloma brothers, who were in their twenties. And at sixteen, he had burglarized several houses, a drug store, and a radio and appliance shop, the stolen goods fenced off to the Colomas in exchange for drugs to sell for himself.

By that time, he had been expelled from school for truancy several times and once for an act of senseless vandalism, taken back after tearful pleas by Amalia. Later, he was picked up as a suspect on a burglary complaint, but was released when the complaining witness failed to identify him.

Ramon had very early been exposed to sex among the girls who tagged along with the *Bravatos* and immersed himself in the act as though it had been created for himself alone, even to feeling an intense physical desire for Amalia. He still shared the same bed and came to know her voluptuous body by sight; and by touch while she slept beside him, often embracing him, driving him to secret masturbation when he could no longer contain himself.

In his sixteenth year, he made another discovery that almost drove him to committing violence. He awoke early one morning when he heard a car stop in front of the house, expecting that Amalia would come in shortly. He lay there thinking about her, visualizing her shadowy form undressing, getting into bed with him, the feel of her warm, sensual body next to his own. When he heard nothing, he was puzzled and got out of bed, came to the window, and looked out. The car was still there, but he could make nothing out in the darkness. Wearing only his shorts, he went to the front door and opened it, then walked barefoot down the short cement path and peered into the car. He saw her and Juan Chavez on the rear seat of the Cadillac, her dress hiked up above her waist, straps down over her shoulders exposing her breasts, Chavez lying atop her in the most intimate of acts between man and woman.

Voiceless with rage, wild with anger, he looked around and found half a brick lying on the street beside the car. He picked it up and hurled it through the window, shattering it, then found his voice and screamed, *"Bastardo! Puta!"* and ran into the house, weeping bitterly, throwing over chairs, the table, sweeping the bric-a-brac from the cheap sideboard, smashing a mirror, then falling helplessly upon the bed, beating it with his fists.

Some time later, he heard the Cadillac's motor turn over and waited. But Amalia did not come into the house. When

125

he went to the window again, the car was gone. That night, what was left of it, Ramon remained awake. Nor did Amalia return when daylight came and it was time for him to leave for school. When he was free, he went home. He found the debris of his anger swept clean, the two rooms in order, but no sign of Amalia. Late that night, she returned. He lay in bed feigning sleep. He did not move when she got into bed. Later, when he knew she was asleep by her steady breathing, he got up and went into the other room and lay down on the small sofa. When daylight came, he got up, dressed, and left the house.

He did not return for six days, sleeping in an abandoned truck in Dacosta's Wrecking Yard until George Maldonado found him and convinced him to return to his distraught mother. From that day on, Ramon and Amalia lived in silent hostility, he occupying the dilapidated sofa in the living room, unable to look at her without accusation in his eyes, Amalia unable, or unwilling, to speak to him about her fall from grace. He understood now that they would live their lives together, yet separately, asking no questions of the other.

Then he was eighteen, and school was over. He dropped out of the youthful *Bravatos*, concentrated on pushing marijuana and pills in the school area, and later organized a group of four willing students to push for him. He also began taking notice of Yolanda Maldonado, blossoming beautifully into young womanhood, taking her to an occasional movie, for hamburgers, tacos, Cokes, buying small gifts for her, all of which he was well able to afford.

In order to gain a cover for his drug pushing, he persuaded Bernardo Dacosta to give him a job in his parts department, but the work was wearisome and boring. He quit and went back to full-time pushing for the Colomas. This went on for a whole year until the night the Colomas were arrested with a load of marijuana they had trucked up from Los Angeles. The next day, the police picked up Hernando Robles and Mike Vega, two of Coloma's key pushers. Fearful that he would be next, Ramon gathered up his money stash of two hundred and forty dollars, said good-by to Yolanda with a promise to write, and caught the next bus to Los Angeles.

When he found that the Mexican-American community there was only larger, but no better, than the Bakersfield *barrio*, feeling desperately alone and fearful, he waited until his funds dwindled down to ten dollars, then walked into an army recruiting office and enlisted for a four-year period. He was in his twentieth year.

126

When he found time to think about it, all Ramon could recall of his army training was the exhaustion he had endured. Everything else was lost under its tremendous weight except the pity he felt for himself and those who were not as well equipped physically as he, envious of those who showed superior stamina.

He had thought airborne training would be glamorous and applied for it swaggeringly, then soon learned that everyone, regardless of rank, took it with deadly seriousness, particularly the training officers and non-coms. Early-morning calisthenics and drill periods were tough, hand-to-hand combat practice brutal, jump school the most frightening punishment of all. There were the aches and pains, bruises, broken bones, the fears, the burden of eighty pounds of gear to carry; front and back chutes, weapons, entrenching tools, jump helmets; getting out on the flight line, sweating from heat and tension, waiting nervously for the transports that first time, listening to the chatter on every side of him.

"Scared?"

"You fuckin' well right I'm scared."

"Me, too."

"You bet. But *scared*."

"Oh, man. Only the laundryman'll know how scared I am. I'm fluttering."

"What the hell'd you volunteer for?"

"Christ, I don't know. Musta been outta my goddamned stupid skull. You?"

"Don't ask me, friend. If I could remember, I'd use it as an excuse to get myself reclassified insane and go to officer candidate school."

Airborne, Ramon fell victim to the inner panic that surrounded him. The roar of the plane's motors, the vibration, the raucous voice of the jumpmaster, the shouts of the men in response, all were lost on him. He was numb in body and brain. There was no shield he could erect to protect himself from the abject loneliness he felt. And only one way out—down.

Mechanically, he hooked his clip into the overhead line, moved forward to the open door, dry-mouthed. The wind tore across his face like a dull razor as he leaned out, then felt himself being shoved from behind. Whatever he did, he did automatically, by pure instinct and without thinking or remembering. What surprised him more than anything else was to find himself on the ground in one piece, shaken up, scratched and bruised. But alive. And exhilarated.

He made two more jumps and began to think of himself as fully qualified. Then, on his fourth jump, he broke his left arm and cracked three ribs. When he was released from the hospital, he was sent to Infantry. In time, he again went through the monotony of physical training, survival tactics, jungle warfare, jumping, crawling, running. What he enjoyed most was the rifle and pistol range, shooting with surprisingly deadly accuracy, coming off the range among the top marksmen in the battalion. Weapons had become his security.

Hardened, experienced, and well trained, he was chosen to become a drill instructor, enjoying his personal victory over earlier doubts of his ability to survive. Not that it grew any easier, because he was now called on to teach and instruct by demonstrating to others how to do everything they must be taught—over and over again. Taking the heat and cold, the rain and sleet, sleeping in the open on hard ground, eating nondescript food. And then he was far into his second year, and Vietnam began to loom larger than life in the minds of everyone. It was there. Soon, trained men would be at a premium.

He had won his third stripe now, and with it came Vietnam in full flower; yet he felt the greatest confidence in himself. When the order finally came to ship out, he found himself actually looking forward to whatever lay ahead.

After several months there, moving up to meet the enemy, being thrown back, retaking a village they had fought for bitterly only a few days before, it all became dreary replay. In R & R, he was too tired to do more than be grateful his life had been spared up on the line. He spent his time resting, writing to Yolanda, who wrote him lengthy letters in Spanish, never replying to his questions about Amalia, from whom he heard nothing.

Back in action, he took his men out on patrol, herded them through one encounter after another, losing a man here and there, suffering through the problems of breaking in inexperienced replacements who had begun pouring in from the States. He soon learned not to get too personally involved with any man, knowing that the loss of a friend was too dreadful an experience to endure.

He would come out of the lines to find batches of letters from Yolanda and would answer each in turn, assuring her that he was far away from combat and out of harm's way. A lie, but lies, he felt, were necessary. But mostly he was over-come by the weariness of action, then depressed by inaction. He took up with a succession of women, then would go into periods of abstinence, neither of which was satisfactory or comforting to him. For a while, he drank rather heavily, then gave it up when it failed to fill whatever need he felt at the moment. He avoided the temptations of heroin, which was in good supply all around him, knowing well the effects, despis-ing what he saw happening to others.

So, time passed. Move up, take a position, drop back, move up and retake an area they had occupied only days be-fore. They lived with the paranoia of suspicion, trusted no one, man, woman, or child. Death was never farther away than the innocent civilian one encountered on a road, in a village.

Captain Andrews, a veteran of the last days of World War II and Korea, said one rainy day, "This goddamned, useless, fucked-up war is absolutely insane. In the big one, at least, you knew who the hell the goddamned enemy was. Here, it's anybody, everybody. I only wish to Christ my congressman and senator were here, just two paces in front of us."

"Shit, Cap," Bobby Conwell, the huge black sergeant from Georgia said, "I ever saw my congressman or senator two paces in front of me, I'd frag the bastards."

"Bobby, for the first time since I've known you, you're making sense. Let's go. Move 'em out, Ray."

In July of that year there were only seventy-five thousand American troops in Vietnam, trying to stem the tide of NVA moving south, the Cong in the south moving north, and only God knew who or what combinations coming out of the west. In September, when he had been in the army for three years and ten months, those last sixteen in Asia, Ramon Ycaza bought his Purple Heart.

What he remembered first was that it had been daylight, about 1400, and he had been checking the radio out with Rollie Brubeck, his RTO. For some reason unknown to both, the radio had suddenly gone dead in the middle of contact with their base.

Ramon's concern became the concern of everyone in the ten-man patrol. Johnny Phillips drifted over to watch Ramon tinker with the dead radio. Up ahead in the dense growth, they heard Willy Bernstein's low voice. "I hear some move-ment over to my right."

Ramon said, "Johnny, see if you can find the Polack. He's worked with these goddamned things before. Keep your head and ass down."

"Okay, Ray." Two others looked on intently, anxiously. Having worked as a team for several months, all felt the same total reliance on that radio, their only communications link with base and the additional firepower they could call on from Artillery; or gunships, air strikes, slicks, or med-evac choppers to take out their wounded and dead.

Ramon lit a cigarette and shook another loose for Brubeck, who had extended a hand for one. Even before he could take it, they heard the AK rounds coming in from two sides and the shouts, "Dig in! Dig in! Incoming!"

They dropped flat, trying to bury themselves beneath the foliage. Those on the edges returned fire without even seeing the hidden enemy. Ramon, considering the priorities, left the men to their known tasks and tinkered feverishly with the radio, talking, pleading, cursing while the AK rounds tore at the growth around them. Then the first mortar round came in, about sixty meters off to their left. Another round hit closer.

Ramon called out, "Kaminski! Where the hell is the Polack?"

Phillips crawled back, breathing heavily. "You find Kaminski? Where the hell is he?"

"I don't know, Ray. Out there somewhere. All's I know is where I and Durkin are at, and I ain't too sure about that." Phillips hugged the tight circle, not wanting to get too far from this patch of as yet untouched ground. "Find him, goddamn it!" Ramon shouted.

Phillips belly-crawled away. A few moments later, he found Kaminski, his face almost entirely blown away. He crawled back to report to Ramon. "Kaminski's bought it. Dead."

"Anybody else?"

"I don't know about anybody else. Only Kaminski."

The radio began to sputter then, and Ramon grabbed for the mike. "4/32, 4/32."

"32/4," the radio responded.

"4/32, we're under heavy ground attack, one known dead so far."

"32/4, give us your coordinates. We have a gun ship ready to deliver."

"They're too goddamned close to us, on top and two sides. How about some manpower?"

The radio went silent, then sputtered again. "32/4, we've got a slick loading and ready to go."

Ramon gave his position, then called out, "Let's hit the bastards with everything we've got before they try to rush us. We've got a slick coming in."

The firing continued, coming closer as the NVA moved up relentlessly, yet cautiously. Ramon saw Artie Collins rise up to try to move into a more effective firing position. As he shouted, "Down, Artie, down!" he saw Collins's body pitch to one side. Ramon crawled forward to drag Artie back. Within two feet of his goal, he felt as though someone had slammed a baseball bat into his right shoulder. Stunned by the impact, he froze in midair for a split second and took his second hit somewhere along the base of his neck.

4•

When he regained consciousness, it was night. And quiet. He was in a long, narrow room. In a bed among other beds. His head and shoulders were sending shock waves of pain up and down his upper body, which was tightly encased in bandages. His left hand began an exploratory search, but the movement increased the knifelike stabbing. He assumed he was in a field hospital and called out, "Medic!"

Someone at the far end of the room shouted, "Shut up, f' Chrissakes!"

Another voice, closer to him, said, "Hey, soldier, you hurt-in'?"

Ramon's mouth clamped shut, as if opening it to reply would increase his agony. The last voice he had heard called out, "Nurse! New boy's hurtin' here."

She was at his side a moment later, a flashlight in her hand playing its beam over him. He heard her give instructions to someone else he couldn't see, then felt the wet cold of alcohol swabbing his arm and the sting of a needle as morphine flowed into him. In the few moments it took to hit him, the nurse had turned on a light on the stand beside his bed and was examining his chart. Blonde, about twenty-six, tired face and weary eyes. Then the pain began to lessen, and he felt the comfort wash over him.

"Hey," he said softly.

"Hi," she replied. "Feel better now?"

"Yeah. Thanks."

"Ramon Ycaza?" She pronounced it "Why-caza."

"Ee-caza," he corrected.

She smiled and said, "You'll be all right, Ramon."

"Where am I? Saigon?"

"No. Japan. You came in from the casualty staging area at Yokata this afternoon."

"How bad is it?"

"Not too bad. The doctor will see you in the morning. You're in pretty good shape. We'll take good care of you."

"How long ago—you know—"

She glanced at the chart again. "Three days."

"Jesus." Then, "They bring in anybody else from my outfit?"

"I wouldn't know that. Would you like something to drink, ease your throat a little? You sound hoarse."

"Coffee?"

"Well, I don't know why not. I'll be right back. How do you like it?"

"Natural."

She returned a few minutes later. The coffee was strong, but hot. She put an angled glass sipper in the cup so that he wouldn't have to raise his head to get it. "Where are you from, Ramon?" she asked, holding the cup for him.

"It's Ray. Nobody calls me Ramon. From California. What's your name?"

"I'm Lieutenant Noonan, officially, but it's Bernie here. Short for Bernice."

"Listen—"

"You listen, Ray. I want you to swallow this pill and go to sleep. You need all the rest you can get right now. Okay?"

"Okay, Bernie. Thanks."

He put the capsule in his mouth and washed it down with the last of the coffee. Bernie Noonan turned the light off and glided away silently. He started to think of Johnny Phillips, Rollie Brubeck, Joe Catlett, Willie Bernstein. Ben Kinder. And last, he thought of Caz Kaminski, the Polack. Caz had shown him pictures of his wife and two children.

It was daylight when he woke again to find a doctor probing his wounds, a different nurse standing beside the surgical cart. The doctor began taping fresh bandages on his neck and shoulders, seemingly satisfied with what he had found.

"Hi," Ray said, wincing.

"Lo, Sergeant," Major Richardson said. He finished the taping chore and said, "Not too bad. You'll be out of here in a few weeks. You've earned the rest. You in any pain?"

"Yeah. Hurts like a bastard."

Richardson gave the nurse some instructions and returned to Ray. "We'll take care of that for you. How long have you been in Nam?"

"Sixteen months. Three years and ten months in the army."

Richardson nodded. "Good enough. You won't be going back there. Soon as you're able, you'll be heading for home."

Ray said nothing. The doctor said, "You don't look too happy about it."

"Did they bring anybody else in from my outfit when I came in, Doc?"

"I don't know. We take 'em as they come, a few or a few hundred, from wherever they come. Can't keep tabs on everybody. When you're up and around, you can inquire at the admissions office. Hell, they might even be able to tell you."

He never found out. Ten days later he was moved into another ward, able to move around now. Three weeks after that, the healing process going well, he was flown back to Okinawa, then on to Honolulu. After another ten days, the bandages were finally removed, leaving a red, raw-looking scar reaching across his shoulder, another at the base of his neck. His next stop was Travis Air Force Base and after two weeks there, during which he held off getting in touch with anyone in Bakersfield, he received his discharge. It was December 30, 1965.

For the four years he had spent in the army, he had eighteen hundred dollars, much of it won gambling; a Purple Heart medal; some miscellaneous army clothing; an honorable discharge. A shoulder and neck scar.

And a future about which he had serious doubts.

5•

The army provided him with his last official transportation, a bus ride to San Francisco and a travel voucher to the point of enlistment, Los Angeles. He checked into a modest hotel in the Golden Gate city and went out immediately to outfit himself for civilian life; a sports jacket, slacks, sports and dress shirts, two ties, shoes, and underwear. He had a gargantuan meal in a nearby restaurant, then returned to his hotel and put in a call to Amalia. He was told the number had been disconnected, that there was none in the name of Amalia Ycaza.

Alarmed, he phoned the Maldonado home and learned

from Felipe that Yolanda was out shopping with her mother. Later that night, he called again, and Yolanda was home, waiting.

"It's Ramon, Yolanda."

"I know. I know. Felipe told me. Where are you?"

"San Francisco."

"When will you be here?"

"Tomorrow morning, eleven thirty. I'm flying in."

"Juan and I will meet you in his truck. I miss you."

"I miss you, too. Where is my mother, Yolanda? Her number is disconnected, and there's no listing for her."

She hesitated, then told him, stumbling over the words. "I don't know, Ramon. Nobody knows. Five months now, she left Bakersfield. With a man. A guitar player who worked for Chavez. We haven't heard from her. She left a box with your things for us to keep for you."

He took it hard, unable to reply.

"Ramon?"

"Yes. I'm still here."

"Tomorrow morning, eleven-thirty?"

"Yes."

"Listen. I love you."

"I love you."

He sat between Juan and Yolanda, his collar hiked up over the neck scar so that he wouldn't have to answer questions now. Yolanda had grown even more beautiful, so mature at twenty-three, so womanly that he was overwhelmed, almost speechless. They drove him to a motel where he checked in, left his bag, and went to the Maldonado house next to the one in which he had been born, now occupied by a slattern of a woman with four filthy children.

Chavez's restaurant had burned down over a year ago, Chavez now retired and living elsewhere. As were many of his contemporaries. Moved, in the service, working in the fields or as bus boys, waiters, laborers. Or on the streets, in trouble, in and out of jail.

Mama and Papa Maldonado had prepared a huge meal, totally Mexican. Tequila flowed, Papa and George played their guitars, Angela sang, and the few neighbors he remembered danced; but Ramon's eyes were for Yolanda alone, his concern for Amalia somewhere in the back of his mind. He talked very little of his Vietnam experience, but they had seen the neck scar and did not embarrass him with questions.

At nine that evening, Yolanda drove him back to the motel in George's Volkswagen van. In his room, he told her some of what had happened, then gave her the Purple Heart medal to keep for him. And that night, the fantasies that had been with him during so many nights in Vietnam became reality. In the darkness, they undressed and ended a hunger both had longed to satisfy.

Three days later, Ramon left for Los Angeles, determined to find a job, marry Yolanda, and begin a new life away from the one he had known from earliest memory. And despised. He took a cheap room in an East Los Angeles rooming house in order to husband the remaining thirteen hundred dollars of his cash hoard. After two weeks of careful study of job opportunities in the local *Times* and *Herald-Examiner,* registering with employment agencies, replying to box numbers and being interviewed, there was nothing he wanted or was really suited for. In fact, nothing he saw or heard from the Chicanos he met and talked with on the streets and in bars gave him the feeling that he belonged in civilian life.

He felt weary and disheartened that his once-hardened body was growing soft from hospitalization and recuperation, would soon fall into disuse, and began a too-early mourning for the sense of loss it gave him. Then he began wondering if perhaps he had made a mistake in leaving the army; yet he felt a bitterness toward a war he knew could not be won by either side. As Captain Andrews had classified it, useless and insane. Wounding, killing, destroying a country and its people who couldn't care less who ruled as long as it would bring an end to the massive, conscienceless slaughter. He had a craving for something that would answer his growing need for movement, action, something physical. But what, at twenty-four, could satisfy that urge?

Others were restless, too, the media told him. Militancy was on the rise, public rioting and looting, vandalism in schools was spreading, the crime rate rising in every category, involving blacks, whites, Chicanos. The increase in hard-drug use, which he had seen in Nam, was proliferating into epidemic proportions, with Los Angeles ranking close to the top in use.

Cops?

His only contact with police, as with most citizens, had been on the negative side. Yet they were out there, twenty-four hours every day, holding the line against crime. A comparative handful to protect millions against crime of all kinds. Slowly, this thinking began to take hold. And still there remained the old virulence for the blue uniform that represented establishment authority. Blue was somehow identified with the blue uniforms of Bakersfield, a youthful resentment now become adult.

Another two weeks passed. He called Yolanda when the loneliness of his room became overpowering, longing to see and touch her, but not before he was committed to a definite job and purpose; seeing men his own age on the streets, unemployed, in the bars and poolrooms, hustling the days away on the periphery of poverty or crime.

After much soul-searching and self-debate, Ramon walked into the Hall of Justice one morning and was directed to the personnel department of the county sheriff. He asked questions, received answers, and took away pamphlets and folders to study. He was agreeably surprised to discover that at the age of twenty-four, with no special civilian skills, the starting pay, even during the training period, was much higher than he could hope for in the open labor market elsewhere; with appreciable raises as time passed, possible promotions, paid vacations and overtime, plus health and retirement benefits. And in the more familiar khaki instead of blue.

That night he phoned Yolanda, excited, and told her of his plan. "Is it what you want to do, Ramon?" she asked.

"Yes. I want to do it very much, Yolanda."

"Then do it."

On the following morning he returned and applied for admission to the sheriff's training academy.

While his application was being processed, citizenship checked, fingerprints run through local, state, and national files, references (the Maldonados, the army) examined, Ramon returned to Bakersfield to make his decision known to Yolanda's family. Receiving their approval, he and Yolanda announced their intention to be married as soon as he was graduated.

Notified that his application had been approved, Ramon returned to Los Angeles, passed his oral and physical examinations and was assigned to a cadet class starting within ten days. His next move was to buy a cheap used car and move into a room that would give him easier access to the academy and more privacy for study.

6●

The atmosphere, he found, was in some ways remotely reminiscent of the army, but only in appearance and without its stonelike rigidity. The sixty-two men and four women were in the class because they wanted to be. Two previous classes were in more advanced stages of training and, from Ramon's point of view, did not seem to be hurting. After a day or two of familiarization, the classwork began. So far, no problems. Regardless of background, experience, or race, they were equals. Rookie cadets all.

Three days later, while Lieutenant Capper was lecturing on the subject of Introduction to Law Enforcement, he suddenly broke off in midsentence, looking over the heads of the class toward the back of the large room. Most of the students turned in that direction and saw a tall, strongly built man in civilian clothes striding lithely toward the platform.

Capper said, "I see Captain Wade is joining us, either to refresh his memory or to simply say 'hello' informally. Ladies and gentlemen, Captain Ben Wade, commander of the training academy."

Smiling, Wade mounted the platform and said, "Good morning, Walt."

It was a familiar routine to the lecturers and instructors to introduce the class to visiting brass: captains, inspectors, division chiefs, or visitors from outside law-enforcement agencies throughout the country and world who were interested in L.A.S.D.'s progressive training programs.

Sixty-six pairs of eyes were on Captain Wade as he turned to face them. "Thank you, Lieutenant Capper," he said through a warm smile to the sea of white faces with a sprinkling of brown and black among them. "This isn't an official, nor a snooping visit. I like as much as possible to get to know and recognize every trainee who passes through the academy. Sometimes I get the feeling that if you recognize me, I will somehow recognize you later on when you are out in the field.

"I won't add to your academic load by any additional curricula, and you needn't take notes on what I am going to say to you now. However, it occurred to me that you might find a few facts interesting enough to keep loosely in the back of your minds, if there's still room.

"This week, your first, has been a busy one, your minds preoccupied with getting acquainted with each other and your basic studies and training courses. Let me tell you what has been happening in the world outside during that time, events in which you will one day participate, become part of.

"Before this week is over, at least four people will have been murdered in Los Angeles County, hopefully no more; one hundred forty-four citizens will have been feloniously as-

137

saulted; sixteen women and girls will have been raped; three hundred fifty-eight homes will have been burglarized; two hundred forty-three vehicles will have been stolen; sixty-six persons will have been held up and robbed; ninety-three grand thefts will have taken place. There will be approximately four hundred other felonies in which the sheriff's department will be involved. One million seven hundred fifty thousand dollars' worth of property will have been stolen, twenty-two hundred thirty family disputes settled one way or another. There will be an estimated fifteen hundred and sixty-five arrests made, sixty-four thousand eight hundred ninety prisoners fed and housed, ten thousand four hundred fifty transported to court for trial, four thousand seven hundred and fifty sent to penal or correctional institutions, and four hundred fifty-five hospitalized for various reasons. And that isn't the total picture, but it is all in a week's work. Yours, mine, ours together, to hold back the line of crime and violence in the areas under our jurisdiction.

"This will involve over five thousand men and women of the L.A.S.D. who perform their duties and services in the field within the thirty-one hundred ninety-one square miles of the four thousand eighty-three square miles of Los Angeles County for whose protection the sheriff of Los Angeles County is responsible, an area with an awesome population that increases in numbers every day. In that week, those members of L.A.S.D. will cover over four hundred twenty-five thousand three hundred sixty-five county road miles, fly over twenty thousand air miles by helicopter, operate a transportation system that could support many major cities, not to mention a countywide communications system and the supply of food, housing, and medical facilities on a daily basis.

"We are the nation's sixth largest law-enforcement agency and operate the fifth largest penal and correctional system— all of this in one of the largest and most populated counties in the country, which is larger than all but eight of our fifty states.

"Apart from this, we cooperate with other law-enforcement agencies in the matter of narcotics, smuggling, wanted fugitives from elsewhere who find L.A. County a rich area and source of operations."

Wade paused and scanned the faces of the deeply interested rookies, saw the awe expressed in most of them. "These, of course, are mere statistics," he continued, "and we have many more of them. But statistics are for hearing and reading. They will come alive for you only when you have worked our jail system, ridden in our patrol cars, flown in our helicopters, taken part in the specific crimes that occur around the clock.

"You will see, feel, and smell crime, perhaps for the first time in your lives. You will be shocked and shaken by what you see, feel, and smell. But you will become the backbone of L.A.S.D. by your experience and see another side of the coin, one seldom seen by the majority of citizens you will be protecting.

"We will teach you the professionalism you need in order to do your job with skill and pride. And to stay alive." He paused for dramatic effect, then went on. "Pride is something that will come from inside you, something you will get from each other as your professionalism grows, and you grow with it.

"Let me caution you not to become emotionally or morally hardened by what you will see out on our streets and roadways. There will be temptations, too, placed before you, but we hope your own individual consciences and our training program will show you—prove to you beyond any doubt—that these temptations pay poor rewards, if any. You will, I am certain, soon learn that a temptable officer is a contemptible officer.

"I won't take up any more of your time now, but during the balance of your training period, you will see me around from time to time. Remember this: I am available. If you have a particular problem, I invite you to discuss it with me informally and in private. Thank you, and the best of luck to each of you."

So the weeks passed, and the class became deeply involved in its work and with each other. Seven cadets dropped out; a few others were borderline, but lasted. The six Vietnam vets and four members who were former police officers in smaller upstate departments breezed through the physical training and worked together in after-class rap sessions to help each other with their academic problems. Ramon remained barely in the upper half of the class academically, in the top ten in physical training, earning the name "Shooter" for his skill on the pistol range and with heavier weapons.

Eventually, they were graduated with few casualties. The entire Maldonado family, now numbering seventeen strong, came from Bakersfield to attend the ceremony. The sheriff, undersheriff, department chiefs, and other county officials were present to witness the event and congratulate the graduates. Later on that Friday afternoon, Ramon returned to Bakersfield, Yolanda beside him in his car, trailing behind her family in the Volkswagen van.

On Sunday morning, in the presence of her family and relatives, Yolanda and Ramon were married. After a noisy celebration at the Maldonado home, the couple slipped away in Ramon's car and drove back to Los Angeles.

When Ramon reported for his first assignment at the county jail, Yolanda found a small, unfurnished apartment on Verde Avenue, within a reasonable distance of the Bauchet Street jail. Within two weeks, the Maldonados had made two trips in the van, bringing a bed, mattress, and box spring, Yolanda's bureau, a new sofa, chairs, tables, dishes, and silverware. Mama Maldonado brought materials and stayed on to sew curtains and help Yolanda put the apartment in order. Ten days later, Yolanda and Ramon moved from his room and were settled in their first home.

The vastness of the county jail complex where Ramon would spend the next year was, for someone who had wanted action, a keen disappointment. He found the routine monotonous. His first contact with convicted criminals, new arrivals, and those awaiting trial was depressing; awed by the numbers in residence and those arriving daily in transportation vans from the fourteen sheriff's stations for processing.

In time, he came to differentiate between the con-hardened burglars, robbers, murderers with long records, and trauma-stricken first offenders; the former accepting county jail as a brief stopover on their way to a state prison, the latter sunk deeply in fear or remorse, many charged with nonviolent crimes. His curiosity was aroused by the recidivists: habitual drunks, drug pushers, car thieves, rapists, embezzlers, and fugitives wanted in other parts of the state, in other states. Most, he found, were easy to talk to; in fact they were eager to talk, to proclaim their innocence, victims of "the system." They came in all sizes, shapes, and colors, and he found it difficult not to feel some sympathy for those he considered stupid and childish, until he began remembering that for every man inside, there were victims on the outside who had been injured, cheated, or robbed.

The apartment and world outside had a tremendous restorative effect on Ramon. Their quarters were colorful and cheerful; and, he discovered, Yolanda was a superlative cook. Whenever they could, they explored the Mexican quarter in East Los Angeles, drove south across the border into Mexico, bathed in the ocean, and fished from various piers. And made

140

friends with their neighbors and some of the students who had been in Ramon's class.

"Do you miss Bakersfield?" Ramon asked after their third month in Los Angeles.

"I miss things, yes. My family, relatives, a few friends, the things that were comfortable for me."

"Would you want to go back?"

She replied quickly, "Only if you want to go back."

"I can't, Yolanda. It has nothing for me, nothing I miss or want or need. I am happy here with you."

"Then I am happy here, too. Only—"

"Only what, *querida?*"

"Only, I want you to be careful. You came through a bad war with a few scars. I don't want to lose you because of some frightened or crazy animal in the streets."

"Don't worry about that. Don't even think of it."

"I can't help thinking of it. I read in the papers—"

"Try not to apply what you read to me. There's too much in life to be living in fear. Just remember this. I was trained by the army to be a soldier, in the academy as a law-enforcement officer. When I'm out on the street, I'll be better equipped than any crook out there."

His words were no great consolation to Yolanda, yet she smiled and hoped he believed she was reassured.

7●

Ycaza's first assignment to a station was Firestone. During his training period at the academy and tour of duty at central jail he had heard much about Firestone, a "hot" one where there was never a lack of activity around the clock. Feeling his newness, he rose bright and early that morning to make sure his uniform was immaculate, shoes, holster, and belt glittering with polish, gun cleaned. He passed Yolanda's critical inspection and set out for South Compton Avenue, arriving a good hour before he was due to report.

He checked in with the watch sergeant and was introduced to the watch lieutenant, who happened to be passing by at that moment. The lieutenant welcomed him into the official family and turned him over to an administrative deputy, who showed him to the locker room, assigned him a locker, then gave him a quick tour of the station. He met several of the inside working personnel briefly, struggling to remember their names. Returning to the lieutenant's office, they encountered the station commander, Captain Meade, who was discussing a matter with Lieutenant Lesko. The captain's glance seemed to be one of approval, and a bare minimum of words was exchanged between them.

After a short wait, Ycaza was turned over to the training officer who, after fifteen minutes of general discussion concerning his first patrol duties, introduced him to Deputy Greg Canning, with whom he would ride during his six-month probation period.

Canning's attitude toward his new charge was one of cool reserve. Experience had taught him that he was dealing with an unskilled rookie, an unknown quantity. No matter what his academy or jail record of performance showed, his exposure to the street scene was what would count; how he would react to situations that required diplomatic handling or conditions of extreme stress; how much his partner could count on him in an emergency. In the end, Canning's judgment as to Ycaza's fitness would decide his ultimate fate.

After a brief indoctrination into station routine, rules and regulations, Canning took him on a tour of the area he knew only from studying the station maps; the physical survey was awesome. Firestone's jurisdiction encompassed approximately forty square miles and took in the unincorporated areas of Malabar, Walnut Park, Florence-Firestone, Willowbrook, Athens, West Compton, Keystone, Dominguez, East Compton, Lynwood, and furnished contract police service to the incorporated cities of Carson and Cudahy. A lot to learn.

He learned much at roll call and briefing prior to going on patrol. Faces and names of the deputies on his duty tour began to match up. The formality of the academy was dropped here, the atmosphere far more relaxed, yet businesslike and totally professional. The makeup of deputies was much the same as the structure of the area population: whites, blacks, and Chicanos, but with a spirit of brotherhood unlike that on the streets where ethnic groups hewed closely to their own, suspicious, apprehensive, and hostile to outsiders.

"If you have any spirit of adventure," Canning told him, "you're in the right spot. You start every tour without knowing what you'll be running into, and you won't have any control over what you'll be called on to do next. The thing you've got to learn first is to play it cool, take it as it comes."

Ycaza nodded his acceptance. "People will ask you from time to time why you're in this business," Canning continued. "Good question. It can be answered a dozen different ways, but basically, it's the unexpected that can happen ten seconds from now that keeps you on your toes and overcomes the monotony of riding, observing, and being visible. You're out

142

there where it happens, where you're in a position to either prevent a crime or be on it moments after it happens. You'll be helping somebody, saving a life, perhaps, and that's what it's all about."

Ycaza learned much more by listening to the briefing sergeant. Restricted to patroling a single reporting district, the briefings kept him informed of what was happening in other R.D.'s as well as in his own during tours when he was off duty. Normally, the work pattern was routine, but there were items to be called to their attention that must be written down, checked out during the tour: "hot sheets" listing stolen vehicles; suspects in burglaries that took place on the night before; a certain car used in a holdup; an anonymous tip phoned in on a wanted dope dealer who had been seen emerging from a certain house; the wife of a heavy loser reporting a gambling operation in the back room of a poolroom; a jeweler with a tip on two male Caucasians attempting to sell a very expensive diamond ring; a merchant offering a dozen brand-new television sets at less than half price, tying in with the reported hijacking of a delivery truck a week earlier in San Fernando.

Gang activity had stepped up at two neighboring schools and must be kept under close observation. A dance at another school might explode into juvenile warfare. A basketball game between heated rivals could very well erupt into a general battle scene. Burglars had been active here, car strippers there, purse-snatchers at this or that shopping center. "Bugs" Londres was out of jail and loose on the streets. Keep your eyes out for him and any associates. "Bugs" is a heavy dealer in guns and could be armed and dangerous.

So it went. Canning was inordinately streetwise and every bit as GI as any drill instructor Ycaza had known in the army, as he himself had once been; but he understood the necessity for keeping a rookie on his toes while classroom theory was translated into the actualities and practicalities of the street.

He learned other things. For all the emphasis that had been placed on police-community relations, he soon discovered the realities of the public image versus private attitudes. Almost at once, he became aware of public hostility even while in the act of preventing a crime or assisting a sick or injured person. The black-and-white patrol car was the symbol of establishment authority and was hated on sight; the uniform became the flag of the enemy. Crimes in every category were committed against innocent victims who were afraid to complain or identify the criminals in fear of retaliation. The homes of hard-working people were burglarized, and a certain amount of blame was placed on the police for not having been present at the time the incident occurred.

In the briefing room, prior to going on patrol, the language was far less polite than on the outside. Here, it became "them" and "us." Within the family, the lawbreakers were "crooks" and "assholes." Even among the Mexican-American and black deputies it was common to hear an adversary called "spic," "spook," "spade," or whatever derogatory term came to mind, the hard-core militant an abomination to all. Yet the victim, regardless of status, race, or color, met with total sympathy for his injury, damage, or loss.

At the start, Canning drove while Ycaza recorded their calls on the log, experiencing the difficulty of listening to the radio while trying to familiarize himself with the streets, alleys, homes, and commercial establishments in their reporting district. He was palpably annoyed when the calls came with such rapidity that he failed to catch their unit number occasionally and had to be reminded by Canning.

Eager, even overeager, to perform by the book, he soon learned how very different was the live action of the street from the classroom and role-playing exercises where every situation had its concise, logical solution. An entirely different world that left little room for indecision or error.

Canning was a cool, businesslike observer, and Ycaza knew that every move he made, wrong or right, was being meticulously filed in Canning's mind and would no doubt become a part of his official progress report; yet they seemed to work well together despite an absence of warmth between them. They responded to innumerable family disputes, rolled on burglary calls, recovered stolen vehicles, picked up obstreperous drunks, searched for missing children, became involved in gang fights, acted as crowd control at fires, as backup to other patrol units in need of assistance.

The most exciting incident in that month was when they caught a 417, man with a gun, and Canning coolly talked the man into handing over a fully loaded .45 with which he had been threatening several neighbors outside his house, this without the use or threat of force. Ycaza stood beside and behind Canning, his hand ready to draw his own weapon, but Canning's voice calmed the man into submission. Ycaza learned a valuable lesson that day in the importance of keeping one's head in the face of danger.

144

Later, he was involved in a situation and forgot that lesson, which almost caused him to take a life.

It came in their third month together, when he was being given more responsibility in handling their calls. They responded to a "possible 261 in progress, there now. You have a Code Two" and came upon a Latin male in the act of raping a twelve-year-old schoolgirl who had returned to her empty house at the moment when the man was engaged in the act of burglarizing it. The woman neighbor who had heard the girl's first cries ran to a phone and called in to Firestone, and the message at once flashed to 17-David. Canning was driving, and as the car rolled up to the location, the neighbor emerged from the side of her house and pointed excitedly.

First inside, Ycaza heard muted cries coming from a rear room, its door partially open. He pushed through and came upon the scene; the child struggling to escape the hulking man, so passionately engaged in his evil, unaware of an outside presence, driving into the slender body with animal frenzy, one hand clamped over the girl's mouth to prevent her from screaming her painful agony.

Enraged, Ycaza hurled himself on the man, cursing him in Spanish. With a choke hold, he brought him to his feet, slammed him against the wall, driving his fists into the man's face and protruding belly. The man crouched, then drew up a knee and rammed it into Ycaza's groin, missed, but threw Ycaza off balance. Recovering, Ycaza drew his .38, thumbed the hammer back, then heard Canning's voice in his ear. "Hold it! Don't shoot!"

But Ycaza, adrenalin-charged, shouted, "That sonofabitch! Rotten bastard!" and pushed Canning's arm aside, leaped forward, and whipped his gun barrel across the rapist's left cheek, opening a deep wound, then backhanded a slash on his right temple. The man crumpled to his hands and knees on the floor, gasping.

Canning pulled Ycaza back, turned him around. "Get the hell on the radio and get an ambulance here. Move, goddamn it! Now!"

His composure partially restored once the call was put through, he returned to the bedroom. The girl lay on the bed, weeping, knees drawn up, hands between her thin thighs. The bleeding rapist lay moaning on the floor, face down, Canning in the act of cuffing his hands behind him. Ycaza went to the girl, covered her with a blanket, held and soothed her. Canning went outside, brought the neighbor woman in to take charge of the girl, questioned her.

A back-up unit arrived first, then the ambulance. The girl was sent off to the hospital and her parents summoned from their jobs, advised to go to the hospital. Once the culprit was stitched up and removed to Firestone for booking, Canning found Ycaza in the locker room sitting on a bench, head between his hands, elbows on his knees. There was no one else in the room.

Canning stood in front of him, but Ycaza didn't look up. The senior deputy said, "Ycaza, I don't know what in hell to do about this."

And Ycaza, in the same position, replied, "Do what you have to. You saw it, the same as I did. That big bastard, a little girl, a kid—"

"You're a deputy, damn it, trained to keep your cool. The minute you pull that trigger, you become judge, jury, and executioner, and that's not your province or function, no matter what your emotions or feelings are."

"All right. I blew it. Turn in your report and bust me out."

"If you'd shot him, I'd do it without even considering any other course. As it is, I don't know."

Ycaza looked up then, and Canning saw the haunting look in his face, the tears in his eyes; a face of pride, unable to beg for mercy. "All right, Ray, I'm going to give you a break this time. Just remember this: There won't be a second time."

It was the first time that Canning had called him by his first name, and despite the seriousness of his position, Ycaza was forced to smile. "Thanks, Greg. I couldn't help myself, but I'll know better next time."

"Okay." Canning held out a hand, and Ycaza shook it firmly, happily. "He put up a fight. We had to use reasonable force to restrain him. Write the report." He started toward the door, then turned back. "Just in case you think I don't feel it the same way you do, Ray, I've got a twelve-year-old daughter of my own."

"Yeah."

At the end of his fifth month, because of increasing demands for manpower, Ycaza's probation period was ended, and he was placed on regular assignment. By now he knew most of the deputies on his schedule and felt a sense of ease among them. At his first roll call and briefing that followed the end of his probation, he tightened up when he heard his name paired with his new partner. Russ McNeely, a Deputy IV, whose partner, John Burnham, in foot pursuit of a burglary suspect the day before, had been hospitalized with a broken leg. The briefing over, Ycaza looked up to find McNeely standing beside his chair, a light smile playing over his lips. "All set, partner?"

"Set as I'll ever be," Ycaza replied.

He held out his hand and said, "I'm Russ McNeely."

"I know. Ray Ycaza."

"Well, let's go, Ray."

On the parking lot they found their black-and-white, 12/Boy, assigned to the low part of Carson in Reporting District 125, which would take in the area between Lomita Boulevard and 223rd Street north and south, Harbor Freeway and Avalon Boulevard east and west, sharing the adjacent areas with cars 13/Adam to the north, 12/David east.

It was a Monday, the 0800 to 1600 shift. McNeely drove, while Ray rode the passenger seat to handle the log and keep alert for radio calls. Their first stop was at a small house on 237th Street where they would notify the parents of Albert Huerta that their son, victim of an automobile accident two days earlier, had expired at 0744 that morning at the Martin Luther King Hospital. The Huertas, a welfare family, had no telephone, no car. Ray handled that sad chore.

That accomplished, they cruised for an hour without incident. And then, at 1004, they responded to a possible 459, burglary, at a house on Atmore, called in by a neighbor who had seen two men exiting the home of Henry Ortega. Both Mr. and Mrs. Ortega were away at work, their two children in school. The rear door to the Ortega house had been forced open, a television set and radio gone, bedrooms ransacked, drawers emptied on the floors, clothing strewn about. McNeely radioed the description of the suspect and vehicle, a small white pickup truck, gotten from the neighbor who had called in. Ray phoned the victim's employer and notified Henry Ortega, who met them at the house some twenty minutes later.

Ortega walked through the debris for a quick assessment of his loss, pointing to the loose wiring that had been ripped away from the new color television set, muttering angry curses in Spanish at the sight of personal possessions heaped on the floor: letters, papers, family photographs scattered around; a tin box, its top forced open, $360 in cash missing;

articles of his wife's costume jewelry missing along with a food mixer, toaster, and electric grill from the kitchen; his prized leather jacket, some slacks, his wife's suede coat.

Ray listed the items while Russ advised Ortega to touch nothing that might possibly show finger or palm prints for the print man to lift. It was all routine, but both felt Ortega's anguish over the loss of the cherished possessions he and his wife had worked hard to buy. The TV set was new, only four payments made, and Ortega envisioned two more years of paying for something the family could no longer enjoy and that must be replaced.

And then, as they were concluding their report at the scene, they were called on the radio by the dispatcher; 12/Adam, the description of the white pickup truck fresh in mind, had stopped a similar vehicle on Del Amo Boulevard and discovered a new television set, some kitchen appliances, and articles of clothing beneath a canvas tarpaulin. McNeely and Ycaza drove Ortega to the location, where he identified his property, even the leather jacket one of the two men in the vehicle was wearing. The other had a wad of currency amounting to exactly $360 in his trouser pocket. The arrest gave Ycaza more satisfaction than any he had been involved in up to that time.

Disposed of, 12/Boy answered a 415, disturbing the peace, and arrested a belligerent drunk, then responded to another 459 in which the burglar had made a safe escape. The rest of the tour was without notable incident.

McNeely and Ycaza rode together, ate together, worked together, and soon reached that point where Ray felt they were even thinking together. McNeely, more familiar with the area, pointed out known trouble spots, identified numerous gamblers, narcotics addicts, prostitutes, and car thieves, most of them well-known repeaters; identified them by name, nickname, and aliases, pointed out their pads and hangouts.

Weekends were tumultuous, and arresting an offender while surrounded by hostile onlookers could be adventurous, even dangerous; but Ray felt a sense of security in McNeely's smooth, calm professionalism and expertise in handling street situations. Yet Russ could be firm and tough when necessary.

"In a way," McNeely explained, "they're like kids flexing their muscles to see just how much they can get away with. Back down and you're in trouble. Get too hard-nosed, you're in worse trouble. You get in, size up the situation quickly, make a firm decision, get the asshole out of there as fast as you can."

Easily said, not easily done, Ycaza thought. In the Firestone area, that required no small talent. And there was the other side of the coin: the residents, store owners, even street people who waved and smiled and came over to 12/Boy to exchange a pleasant word with McNeely, responding to his "Hey, what's doing?" with five or ten minutes of small talk.

The street scene was by no means strange to Ycaza. He had seen much of it in the *barrios* and bleak ghettos of Bakersfield: the world of unemployment, welfare, the filth, the pimps and the girls they hustled for, the women who continued to bring children into their world, unable to care for them; and the honest poor who depended on government support as their only means of survival in a world in which increasing inflation reduced the value of their checks each month; always in fear of the possibility of being robbed of their money soon after cashing their checks; despising, yet dependent on grasping shop owners who cheated them with inferior foodstuffs and other goods, charging hidden, usurious interest rates, conned them into buying furniture beyond their means to pay and that very likely in the near future might be repossessed and sold again.

And there were explicit dangers. Men and women with hidden guns and knives either for self-protection or to use on someone else. The partners answered a 415-F, family disturbance, on a Saturday night and returned to their car to find a dead dog on the front seat, its throat cut, belly slashed open, blood everywhere. They responded to a bar brawl, and during the fracas inside, someone set their car on fire. Once, driving through an otherwise quiet residential street, a hidden sniper opened fire on their gas tank with a rifle. In another incident, a black man was stabbed fourteen times on a busy street in full view of perhaps twenty or thirty witnesses; but when 12/Boy responded to the scene, no one had seen or heard anything. The viewers merely stood and shook their heads negatively in response to their questions.

And soon, to Ramon Ycaza, the deputy in uniform, it had also become "them" and "us," and he began to question his inner feelings of growing animosity toward the public attitude of resentment for what he represented, establishment authority. Or was it creeping bigotry on his part for the crooks of all ages, all races, all colors?

Testifying in court, he experienced outrage and frustration at the behavior of lawyers who depended on legal trickery to

149

win favor for their guilty clients, asking questions designed to trap him into answers that would not only throw doubt on his testimony, but reflect on his personal integrity and that of the department as a whole. He began to resent judges who handed down extraordinarily mild sentences, even probation, to vicious hoodlums and vandals with previous records, returning them to the streets to commit more crimes; or who set small bail for a burglar or dope dealer who at once would begin burglarizing and dealing dope in order to pay his lawyer and bail bondsman.

"Relax, buddy," Russ cautioned. "Take it easy. So the crook got off this time. We'll have him again soon. Maybe next time we'll get him before a different judge who'll put him away for a long time."

There was the ever-present chance of sudden attack in entering a home to settle a family dispute, approaching a car they had stopped for a traffic violation, in pursuit of a stolen car, arresting a pusher making a sale in a doorway, walking into a store holdup, or coming on a mugging in progress; but the experience and coolness of McNeely, who was sure of every move he made, helped minimize the odds. Each time out, they dealt with brutal men and women, with juveniles banded together to do violence to others, to property, often to each other, needing an outlet to express their rage and frustration in senseless vandalism. And Ycaza, all too familiar with the restlessness of the young, marveled at McNeely's patience and learned to curb his own instinct to crack heads together.

With John Burnham still on crutches and due for temporary assignment to an inside desk job until fully recovered, McNeely and Ycaza continued as partners. As the days stretched into weeks, the weeks into their third month, it seemed, to Ycaza, as though they had been partners for years, a true partnership in every sense of the word. During those times of inaction and monotony, there was little of the impatience he had felt with Greg Canning, who spoke only when it became necessary. At the station, in conversation with other deputies, in briefings, McNeely and Ycaza were recognized as partners and both included in discussions as equals. Which, thought Ray, was how they told us at the academy it would be.

And then Ray was dismayed to learn from McNeely that he was due for promotion to sergeant and transfer to Detectives; genuinely pleased about the promotion, but unhappy at the thought of losing a partner who had given him a tremendous sense of confidence, able now to accept the heavier responsibilities Russ had been placing on his shoulders. The news bothered him, reducing him to frequent silences, even to brooding.

It was their fourteenth week together, working the four P.M. to midnight shift, when they caught the 415-F, family disturbance, one of the many similar they had rolled on during the past week: husband-wife, parent-child, boy friend-girl friend, tenant-landlord. It came at night, a Friday, at ten forty, catching them less than a mile from the location.

"12/Boy, a 415-F, two-three-two-nine Two hundred twenty-ninth."

"12/Boy, roger," McNeely replied.

Ycaza was at the wheel and had tooled into a clear lane, moving toward the location with increased speed, trying to anticipate what would be waiting for them at the other end. And then came the added, ominous information. "12/Boy, on that 415-F, shots fired. You have a Code Three."

McNeely rogered the call with, "12/Boy, rolling."

Red lights on, siren whining, accelerator floored, they tore through deserted streets toward 2329 229th Street. As they turned into 229th, McNeely was on the radio again. "12/Boy is 10-97 at two-three-two-nine Two twenty-ninth," and took up the shotgun that lay cradled beneath the front seat. Even before Ray braked the car and cut his siren Russ was out of the car, moving toward the house, a shell pumped into the chamber, safety off and ready.

As he crossed the narrow pavement and patch of lawn to the three wooden steps that led to a rickety porch, he felt, rather than saw, the presence of people, neighbors, on the opposite side of the street, men, women, and children peering from behind parked cars, house windows, and from the narrow spaces between the houses, heard their muffled, excited voices, the shrill cries and calls of several youngsters.

Normally, a family dispute would have brought them out in the open, within a few feet of the fighting, arguing participants, but with "shots fired," they remained at a cautious distance, waiting expectantly to see what would happen next.

Approaching from the right side, Russ instinctively motioned Ray to the left, both coming in toward the porch from opposite angles. The house was in total darkness, and Ray, revolver in his right hand, flashlight in his left, moved quickly as though to pass Russ and be ready to furnish light. But Russ was already on the steps, then on the porch and at the partially opened front door.

With the muzzle of the shotgun he touched the door, then pushed it wide open. From inside, only silence.

"Police," he called out. "Come out with your hands over your head." There was no response from inside, but from across the street a woman's shrill voice called out, "He's in theah! Watch out! He done kill his woman!"

Ray, directly behind and to the left of Russ, turned on his flashlight and aimed it into the doorway as McNeely started to enter, his back pressed against the door jamb to present the smallest possible target. And as he turned to crouch and move in, the first bullet slammed into his upper left shoulder, spinning him almost completely around; then, in rapid succession, the second bullet hit him lower down as he fell to the porch face down.

At the roar of the second shot, Ycaza leaped over Russ and, crouching, got off two shots, aiming at the flashes he had seen coming from the rear of the hallway. He heard a gasping "ah-h-h-" from inside and bent down for a quick look at McNeely, lying at his feet, bleeding profusely, unable to tell if he was alive or dead. As he turned back into the doorway, a bullet crashed into the door jamb sending splinters flying, then another that slammed into the plaster high above his head.

Ycaza bent and retrieved his flashlight, dropped when Russ fell. He turned it into the hallway, now hearing the sirens of back-up cars wailing into 229th Street from opposite ends. And in that beam of light he saw the gunman, a huge figure, his bulk almost blocking the narrow hallway. Immense, heavy, bleeding from a chest wound and dangling left arm, he came toward Ycaza like a monster out of a movie thriller, wild-eyed, breathing heavily, the "ah-h-h-" rasping in his throat, bumping along the wall from side to side as he came on.

In his right hand he held a revolver that looked as large as a cannon. He raised it, pulled the trigger, and got off a shot that went into the wall well above Ycaza's head. "Drop it!" Ycaza shouted. "Drop it and stand where you are!"

But the puffing, heaving man with insane eyes came on, one staggering step at a time, still on his feet, his knees buckling. Then Ycaza let go with one more shot that thudded into his overhanging belly. Still the man did not fall, clutching for the wall with his gun hand for support. Then, glaring at his tormentor, slipping in his own blood, he moved forward another halting step, emitting horrible noises from his throat.

Deputies were swarming up on the porch, others racing toward the rear along the sides of the house. Windows were broken, and men entered from the rear hall, from the side room. Lights were turned on in the hall. And the gunman, black, six-five and weighing close to three hundred pounds, bleeding from four wounds, still stood there leaning against the wall, chest heaving with a desperate effort to draw air into his lungs, menacing his attackers with an ancient .44 Western-type frontier revolver that was empty.

"Jesus H. Christ!" Gil Davis, immediately behind Ycaza, muttered. "I don't believe it."

"Believe it," Ycaza replied, and as he began to approach the man, wary of some hidden exotic strength he might still possess, the huge figure slipped to the floor in a crumpled heap and died. In the rear bedroom, they found his common-law wife with a bullet hole in her head, her throat slashed.

Ycaza, as the huge man fell to the floor, had turned and gone to the porch where McNeely lay unconscious. Two deputies were administering first aid from their kit, others were keeping the curious neighbors back from the house, and there seemed to be hundreds trying to move in for a closer look.

"Is he alive?" Ycaza said, kneeling beside the two deputies.

"Yeah. Ambulance on the way. Your partner?"

"Yeah." He checked and saw the wounds had been covered and bound, felt McNeely's pulse, listened to his shallow breathing, touched his paled cheek. "He's in shock."

"He'll make it fine," the strange deputy said. "I've seen a lot worse."

So had Ycaza, but he took little comfort in that thought. The whole incident had taken a matter of seconds, yet there were five units besides his own on the street. *And where's that goddamned ambulance with the goddamned doctor? Come on. Come on.* He heard it then, saw its red lights as it made its way through the police units. Doctor, attendants, stretcher. Then Patrol Sergeant Tom Albee, who had been the third car on the scene, said, "Let's get back to the station, Ray. I'll take your report on the way in, then you can go to the hospital." And to Lieutenant Lesko, just arrived, "Okay, Lieutenant?"

"Yes, sure. Go ahead."

En route, Ycaza said, "Was there anybody else in there? Did he really kill somebody?"

"His wife. Or common law," Albee told him. "Beat hell out of her, smashed her skull with the butt of that antique gun, slashed her throat. Never saw one like it before. Octagonal barrel, a .44."

"One time's enough," Ray said. "I hope to God I never see one like it again."

By the time they reached Firestone, Albee had Ray's version. A deputy drove him to the hospital where McNeely was still in the operating room, the place swarming with deputies, reporters, and radio men, all asking questions when they learned Ray and McNeely had taken the initial call. He was saved from that ordeal by the arrival of Captain Ericson and Lieutenant Bell, who took over. He found a phone book at the end of the hall and phoned Yolanda to tell her of the shooting.

"I'm at the hospital, Yo. I don't know yet. Soon as I know what the story is, I'm going out to Manhattan Beach to see his wife. I don't know when I'll get home."

Captain Ericson found him outside the booth. "We've tried to reach Mrs. McNeely, but she's not home."

"I'll drive out and see her, Captain, as soon as we get some word from the doctors. It might be better coming from his partner."

"You know Mrs. McNeely?"

"No, sir, just from conversations with Russ."

"Okay, Ycaza. Take it easy with her."

"I'll do my best, sir. I think I can handle it."

"Yes—well—"

They waited together, a dozen or more, smoking, drinking coffee, talking. Most of them, like Ycaza, were off duty now, anxious to know what the surgical story would be. The reporters were gone, and Ray heard some confusing accounts of the affair from several of the deputies who had answered the call on back-up. He was too concerned with thoughts of Russ and Carol to correct those accounts.

Then a surgeon came into the waiting room and seemed to sense that Ericson, the only man wearing civilian clothes, was in command. The others gathered around in a semicircle to listen. "Let me assure you," the doctor said, "your deputy is in fairly good condition. The shoulder wound is not serious. The other was more complicated, as most chest wounds are, but the repairs have been made, and the prognosis is excellent. He will be taken down to Intensive Care in a short while, under postoperative sedation. He won't come out of it for some hours, so I'd suggest you all leave now and return late tomorrow—uh, later this afternoon—"

It was 0410 when Ray reached the McNeely house in Manhattan Beach. He knocked on the door, got no response, then knocked again and heard Carol's voice call out, "Russ?"

"It's Ray Ycaza, Mrs. McNeely. Russ's partner."

Thus they met for the first time as the door opened a few inches. He saw her eyes examine his uniform; then she opened the door wider to admit him. "What—what's happened?" she said. "Is he—? Oh, God, he isn't dead, is he?"

"He's okay, Mrs. McNeely. I swear it. He's in the hospital resting comfortably, sleeping. The doctor says he'll be fine."

"Where—what happened?"

He told her, not as it had actually happened, but the way he thought would be easier for her to accept, hearing her whisper frequently, "Oh, God! Oh, God!"

"It was a freak thing," Ray concluded lamely, witnessing her distress painfully.

Then anger overtook anxiety. "They're all freak things, aren't they? What else in the world of freaks he works with, is so damned obsessed with, as though he can put an end to all the crime in the world. My God, I can't take any more of this. I can't! I won't!"

He felt helpless, embarrassed, stricken dumb by her sudden outburst. Then, recovering, "Look, Mrs. McNeely, can I fix you a drink?"

"No, no. It doesn't help. Not a damned bit."

"If you'd like, I'll drive you to the hospital, but he won't come out of it until sometime this afternoon."

She said bitterly, "I may never see him again."

"Please don't take it so hard. I swear he's okay. In a couple of weeks, maybe three, you'll have him home—"

"In three weeks, Mr. Deputy," she said stonily, "I may not even be here."

Now Ray became angry, and despite his firm intention not to let her attitude get to him, he snapped, "For Christ's sake, lady, he's your husband, and he was shot in the line of duty, doing his job. Can't you get that through your head? He's okay. He needs you—"

She said coldly, "Thank you, Mr. Deputy. Thank you very much and good night. You can report to your captain that you've done your duty."

He turned away without another word, thinking, *"Jesus*

Christ! Good Jesus Christ! A guy like Russ married to a screwed-up bitch like that!"

While he was home recuperating, the house overflowed with visitors; neighbors all day long, deputies and their wives at night, Captain Ericson, Lieutenants Bell and Lesko, Sergeants Albee, Case, and Michaels, men from other stations whom he had met over the years. Flowers flooded the rooms, get-well cards arrived in bundles. Ray came, bringing Yolanda with him, now pregnant with their first child. Yolanda brought with her a basket of home-made tacos, chiles rillenos, enchiladas and burritos, which she heated and Carol served. A very different Carol, Ray observed, with Russ at home for three weeks. And later, when he was able to get out, Carol drove him to the Ycaza apartment for another special home-cooked meal. During Russ's convalescent period, they exchanged visits and dinners three times, and Ray finally forgave Carol for her outburst on that first night.

McNeely went back to Firestone, on light duty, and Ycaza rode with Arnie Eckstrom, an older, garrulous man with sixteen years in the department, regarded as an authority in historical matters concerning the sheriff's office. He regaled Ray with stories that went back to the nineteenth century, the legendary days of Sheriff Eugene Biscailuz and the present occupant of that office, a former FBI man who had moved the department into its present-day position as a model of efficiency.

Later, he rode with Henry Noriega, to whom he felt a closeness he could not share with Eckstrom, but to whom he could never feel as close as he had been to Russ McNeely. Then the word came through that McNeely was back on full duty and had been transferred to Detectives, moving him out of Firestone to the Hall of Justice. He called Russ and invited him to dinner, but was put off by the pressures of his new assignment in Vice. And in September of that year, Henry Noriega told him casually that Carol McNeely had left Russ to return to Chicago. Permanently.

Ycaza mourned for his former partner, but could find no words to let him know his feelings. And he recalled two lines from Gilbert and Sullivan he had heard at the station when times were roughest: *Ah, take one consideration with another/ A policeman's lot is not a happy one.*

Time passed. Robert was born, and Ray had more personal and immediate problems to be concerned with along with his duties. He tried his best to leave his work at the station when he came off duty, but the presence of his gun and badge were constant reminders to Yolanda that he was out on the firing line eight hours each day or night; often longer as the need required. And Yolanda, knowing how much his work meant to him, remembering far back to the *barrio* days in Bakersfield, never brought the subject of personal danger up; yet it was there in her eyes, the concern she felt when he kissed her and his son on leaving the house, the joy at his safe return.

From Firestone, Ray was transferred to West Hollywood Station, and there he received his first promotion. Working the midnight-to-eight shift, he became involved in many burglaries in this more affluent area and developed a reputation not only for meticulous investigation but for apprehensions and convictions. He worked well with the detectives, and before long, his investigative talents came to the attention of those whose job it was to seek out deputies with special abilities. A year later, he moved to Detectives and was assigned to Vice detail.

By that time, Russ McNeely had gone from Vice to Narcotics and was working out of Lennox Station.

He stirred in his deck chair, heard Yolanda's voice from the kitchen. "I'm going to pick Robert up, Ray," and was gone. In the den, Johnnie and Rosa were squabbling over which program to watch, a normal daily happening. He remembered how, all during those early years, he had searched for Amalia in every restaurant and bar he entered that was patronized by the Mexican-American community. A hopeless search. He never found her.

Chapter Five

1 •

Based on information from a reliable source and having sworn that there was probable and reasonable cause to believe that a quantity of illegal drugs was on the premises, structures and rooms situated at 2613 252nd Street in the city of Lomita, Los Angeles County, Municipal Court Judge Arnold H. Guymon issued a search warrant to Sheriff's Deputy Perry Roberts of Narcotics. The occupant of the house in question was one Miles Hardy, male, black, thirty-four, five-ten, 165 pounds, black hair, brown eyes, light-brown complexion, an ex-felon with two previous narcotics convictions. The warrant was endorsed for night service.

At 9:45, that same night, two unmarked sheriff's cars drove to 252nd Street and, seeing that the blue Ford sedan registered to Miles Hardy was sitting in the driveway, parked among the other cars on the quiet street. Two black-and-white patrol units out of Lennox Station, each with two deputies, were parked nearby in a manner to bracket the house and be ready to act as back-up if needed.

There were lights showing in 2612, and as previously planned from an earlier surveillance run-by, Harry Deliso and Steve Barrett walked to the end of the street, came around to the back of the house, and waited.

When they were in position, Russ McNeely and Perry

Roberts got out of their car and went to the front door of 2612. I.D. wallet in left hand, McNeely knocked on the door and moved to one side. An attractive, slender woman who looked to be about twenty, reacted quickly at the sight of two white men by trying to slam the door shut. McNeely, blocking that move with his foot, said, "Police, miss. We—"

The woman turned back into the house, calling out, "Miles! Miles! The Man! It's the Man!"

But McNeely had pushed his way inside, Roberts with him, both with guns drawn, but held at their sides. At that moment, they heard a commotion at the rear of the house, then Deliso's voice, "Freeze, Hardy! Hold it! Sheriff's Narcotics. Get your hands up over your head!"

In the kitchen, through which he had attempted to escape, Hardy stood at the open door staring into Deliso's .38, then backed into the center of the room. He turned and saw McNeely and Roberts. His shoulders sagged in defeat, his facial features dissolved into helplessness. McNeely said, "Are you Miles Hardy?"

"You know it, man," Hardy replied sullenly. "You busted me back in seventy-two."

"All right, Miles. Get your hands down on the sink and your feet spread out." When he assumed that familiar pose, Steve Barrett patted him down carefully and nodded to McNeely, signifying that he had found no weapons. McNeely then handed Hardy the folded document. "This is a search warrant, Miles. Look it over."

Hardy unfolded the document and merely scanned the print at the top. "What the hell's the roust for this time?" he asked.

"The warrant tells you why. Reason to believe you have a quantity of illegal drugs and narcotics on the premises."

"Oh, bullshit, man. You honkies just jivin'."

"Make it easy on yourself, Miles. That paper gives us the right to search this house from top to bottom, from front to back. You can save us a lot of trouble and yourself a lot of mess getting things back together in place. We know it's here, and we're going to find it if it takes us all night. We want to be reasonable about this, but we can do it the hard way if you force us."

Hardy looked around in frustrated anger, then saw his wife in the doorway, her face reflecting mounting terror. He nodded finally, indicating the hopelessness of his situation. Dejectedly, he said, "Okay. Bottom of the bedroom closet."

"Lead the way."

160

In the larger of the two bedrooms, they found a shotgun leaning against the wall beside the bed, a .38 revolver in the top drawer of the night table, loaded and ready for use. In the closet they found another .38, a sawed-off shotgun, four boxes of 12-gauge shells, and two of .38 cartridges. In a locked suitcase, which Hardy opened on the bed, they found twelve kilo bricks of marijuana, a Pliofilm bag with approximately six ounces of heroin, another with four ounces of cocaine, a carton containing methedrine pills, and a wooden cigarete box filled with about two hundred rolled marijuana joints. In a paper bag were two rubber-banded rolls of U.S. currency that totaled sixty-five hundred dollars.

"Listen," Hardy pleaded, "don't take my wife in. She got nothin' to do with this, nothin'. She don't know nothin' about any of it."

McNeely said, "You know the law, Miles. She's living in a house being used to deal dope and has knowledge. She goes, too."

"Oh, man, you motherfuckers never believe nobody about nothin'. I'm tellin' you—"

"Just hold it, Miles. We'll do the talking for now. You listen carefully, and we'll see what we can do about making it easy on your wife."

A flicker of hope sprang into Hardy's eyes, the possibility of a deal to exchange freedom for the narcotics and the cash. A hard blow, but far better than a bust and prison. "Listen, man," he said eagerly, "you can have it all, the shit an' the bread. Do what you want with it. I won't say a word to nobody, you can—"

"Forget it, Hardy," Roberts snapped, "or we'll slap an attempted bribery charge on you. Now you listen to what we're going to tell you. We're doing you a favor."

"Oh, man. Some favor."

"Shut up and listen. We haven't got any time to waste."

Hardy fell silent, hunched over in dismay. Timorously, his wife asked Barrett for a cigarette, and he gave her one and lit it; her nerves steadied a little more now.

McNeely said, "Sometime around eleven o'clock tonight, you're going to get some visitors. It's a ripoff. Sylvester Tripp is on his way here with a couple of his dudes."

Hardy's astonishment was genuine, else he was a superb actor. "*Sylvester?* Jesus, man, you out of your mind. He's my *friend.* All this shit you see here, he put me into his connection to buy it. You sayin' he gonna rip me off for it an' my bread?"

McNeely nodded. "You'd better believe it, Miles. And we'd find you and your wife with your throats cut sometime along about tomorrow."

Hardy's wife uttered a squeal of fright. "Oh, man, you jivin' us, just honky jive," Hardy said, but the gray pallor spreading over his face indicated he believed McNeely even if his words protested that belief. His wife's hands were trembling so badly that she dropped her cigarette on the carpet. Barrett bent to recover it for her.

"It's true, Miles. It's us or Tripp."

"That sonofabitch. That motherin' black bastard."

"Okay, here's the deal. We're going to put two men outside in the back of the house. Two of us will be inside here, one in this bedroom, the other in the one next to it. You and your wife are going to be in the living room watching television. When Tripp gets here and knocks, your wife will let them in—"

Barrett and Deliso went out to the cars and returned with four short-barreled 12-gauge pump guns wrapped in a blanket. Double-O buckshot shells were pumped into their chambers and were ready. Hardy and his wife returned to the living room, McNeely and Roberts watching from the hallway door. Outside, Deliso contacted the two black-and-white units and alerted them.

At eleven ten, the knock came. McNeely and Roberts closed the hallway door to the merest crack. Lydia, Hardy's wife, went to the door.

"Hi, Mama," Sylvester Tripp said with a broad, ingratiating smile, "Miles home?" and seeing him in his lounge chair in front of the television set, called out, "Hey, brother—"

The door was suddenly flung open, knocking Lydia aside, and Sylvester was inside the room. Behind him came two black men, revolvers waving in their hands. Hardy leaped to his feet and shouted, "What the fuck you think you doin', Sylvester? What—?"

Tripp, still grinning, said, "Okay, Miles, we don' want no shit or hassle. Where's it at?"

"You bastard, settin' me up for a ripoff—"

"You got like five seconds, Miles, or it's your black ass. An' hers, too, once I get through with her. You come up with it, an' fast, or you're dead, both of you."

Hardy looked from Tripp to the two men with the guns, which he knew would not be used in this crowded neighborhood and thus sound the alarm. Knives. They'd use knives, cut his and Lydia's throats, then search for the stash and

162

make off with it. "All right, Sylvester. You'll just take it an' go?"

"Sure, man, you know it. Where's it at?"

"In the bedroom, the closet."

"Show us."

One of the gunmen waved Lydia toward the bedroom. Side by side, she and Miles walked the twelve feet toward the short hallway that led to the two bedrooms. Miles opened the door and allowed Lydia to enter first, he right behind her. The moment Tripp crossed the threshold into the darkened room, Hardy reached for the wall switch. As the ceiling light came on, Miles pushed Lydia ahead of him and flung himself headlong on the floor. Tripp stood there open-mouthed, staring into the barrel of McNeely's shotgun. At that moment, Perry Roberts stepped out of the second bedroom, his shotgun aimed at the backs of the two gunmen who were still in the hallway.

"Hold it, everybody!" Roberts shouted. "One move and it's all over! Drop those guns, goddamn it!"

There was no hesitation. The two guns hit the carpet. "Get your hands up over your heads and grab the wall. *Move!*"

They moved.

Barrett and Deliso had entered from the back. Steve went to the front and returned with Pete Jacks, who had been sitting outside in the car, its motor running. The four men were patted down, two wicked-bladed eight-inch knives removed from under their jackets; then all were cuffed behind their backs. Barrett went out to his radio car and contacted the two black-and-white units that were parked in alleys behind Eshelman and Walnut streets. Within minutes the prisoners, except for Lydia, were on their way to be booked at Lennox Station. The informant, Pete Jacks, would of course be turned loose later.

And as Perry Roberts remarked to McNeely, "Best goddamned hundred bucks we ever spent."

"Considering the load of dope plus sixty-five hundred in cash we took in, I'd say it was a very profitable night," McNeely agreed.

2●

Three days later in Inglewood Municipal Court, Whitey Lloyd, represented by a court-appointed attorney, had his preliminary hearing. Douglas Sherwood, for the State of California, presented his case and four members of Narcotics who testified as to the circumstances of Lloyd's arrest, identified the drugs taken, the money used to make the purchase, the details of his booking at Lennox Station. Undercover agent Sharon Freeman did not appear.

Lloyd's counsel, Jerome Platt, asked that the undercover agent be produced to testify, a request, considering the overwhelming evidence at hand, that was denied in order to prevent public disclosure of her identity. Platt then made a motion that all charges against his client be dismissed, alleging entrapment. Judge Louise Sarabian heard arguments against the motion from Sherwood and denied the motion. She then ruled that a clear case had been made against the defendant and ordered Whitey Lloyd bound over for trial in Superior Court, setting the date for six weeks ahead, and bail at fifteen thousand dollars.

Counsel Platt then made a motion that Lloyd's bail be reduced to one thousand dollars. Sherwood offered a mild objection on the grounds that Lloyd was a known narcotics dealer with two prior felony convictions. Judge Sarabian then considered arguments and ordered bail reduced to twenty-five hundred dollars. Within four hours, a bail bondsman appeared and posted the required bond, whereupon Whitey Lloyd was released pending trial.

Later that afternoon, with nothing special or important scheduled for the Major crew, Steve Barrett said, "Russ, if you're not tied up, how about you and Rachel coming over for dinner. I'm barbecuing."

Russ looked up from his daily log and said, "I don't think we can make it, Steve, but thank Joy for us. I called the shop, and Rachel is due back from New York late this afternoon, and I imagine she'll be tired. How about a raincheck?"

Deliso said, "Hey, Steve, does that include me?"

"You and Perry and Jo-Ann. Been a long time since we all had the same night off together. How about it, Perry?"

But Perry was forced to beg off. "Got a dinner date with Jo-Ann's mother in west L.A., but I'll take a raincheck along with Russ."

"Okay, damn it, don't say I didn't try. You can make it, can't you, Harry?"

"Sure, man. Got a new gal I need to get Joy's approval on."

"What does she fly, American, United, TWA, or a broom?" Steve needled. Harry's penchant for airline stewardesses was well known to all.

"Western, and let your tongue hang out. Next weekend I'm off, we're going down to Acapulco and live with the feelthy reech." McNeely tuned out, picked up his receiver, and dialed a number, heard the high-pitched voice sing out, "Rachel's Casuals. May I help you?"

"Did Rachel get in, Vicki?"

"Oh, hi, Russ. She came in a little while ago, but you missed her by ten minutes. She went home for a dunk in the drink. Try her there."

"Thanks, Vicki." He dialed Rachel's home number, and she picked it up on the third ring. "Rachel?"

"Hi, darling, how are you?"

"Fine. And you?"

"Weary and happy to be home again. I'm just squeezing into something indecent for a quick swim. So good to hear your voice. I've missed you."

"And I, you. How was New York?"

"Horrid as usual, but necessary. I made enough buys to last three months."

"How about dinner?"

"Love to, if we can make it a late one. They fed us too well on the plane."

"Then we can have a drink or two and have something at Bonnie's when you feel up to it. Okay?"

"You'll be home first to change?"

"Yes. Nothing important on the schedule for tonight. See you around six?"

"Mm-m-m, sounds delicious. I'll look in on you."

She had been gone for ten days, and Russ realized how much he had missed her. Their relationship, from the very start, had been one of mutual attraction and respect for each other's work, no questions asked when one was forced to break a date, and in the latter, he was more often the offender.

Desk, log, and calendar reasonably cleared, Russ took off shortly after five and was home in less than thirty minutes. He went out on the deck that overlooked the beach drive below, the beach and ocean, then went to the extreme right edge and looked across the thirty feet that separated his house from the rented one Rachel lived in. She was not on the deck, and he assumed she was in her bedroom napping.

Inside again, he fixed himself a light Scotch over ice, sipped at it, then went in to shower. Lying on the bed as the day came to its end, he felt relaxed and cool, happy that Rachel was home again. The house was still and quiet, the only sounds coming up from the surf and the occasional *swish!* of automobile tires along the asphalt drive below.

It was a comfortable house, and he remembered vividly the excitement in Carol's voice the day she had found it and called him at Firestone to insist he meet her there the moment he came off duty; and when he walked in and found her there with the broker, he knew at once that this would be their new home even though it would mean rising an hour earlier to report to the station.

It had been built with loving care and attention to detail by a retired architect and his wife who had come from Connecticut and had lived it in for nine years until he died and his widow moved back East to be with her family. The house had been designed around its large cathedral-ceilinged living room; kitchen and dining area on the left, master and guest bedrooms on the right, a broad sundeck across the entire rear that faced the ocean. Below, a two-car garage and dressing rooms fronting the beach, now used for storage.

It had always seemed ironic that in this house that Carol had found and loved so much, their marriage had come apart.

3●

Promptly at six, Russ heard Rachel's footsteps on the outside stairway and went to the door even before she could tap out her familiar signal.

"Hello, beautiful."

"Hi, darling." She examined his face for a moment, then stepped into his outstretched arms. "You haven't been getting much sleep lately, have you?"

"Busy days, busy nights, honey. Our customers don't keep the regular business hours yours do."

"I wish I had your stamina. Ten days of running from showroom to showroom, from shop to shop, spying and buying, can do a person in." She kissed him again. "Martinis ready?"

"When you are." He felt her sleek body through the thin minishift she wore over complete nakedness and the surge of blood raced through him in anticipation. He poured their drinks, and they had the first one at the bar, quietly renewing their last physical contact with small, nonessential talk across the counter that separated them, eyes devouring each other.

"If you're very tired," he said, "I can throw something together here—"

She laughed and said, "I'm not *that* tired, darling. No, I'm not really that hungry. Let's stay with the game plan, shall we?"

"Fine. I'm looking forward to a decent meal for a change. What else did you find new in New York?"

"Oh, a few shows, nothing to rave about, a lot of too-rich food, and oh, yes, an offer."

He looked up with an impish grin. "Who offered you what in exchange for what?"

"Not that, you filthy-minded man. The head of the Delta chain called me at my hotel one day—"

"They make tools, don't they?"

"This is another chain, idiot. They specialize in shops like mine all over the country, in suburban shopping centers, resort towns, et cetera. He wanted to know if I would be interested in a proposition—"

"I knew it!"

"Do you want to hear the rest of this, or do you want to sit there and make snide remarks?"

"Go ahead. What kind of a proposition?"

"To buy me out. A very interesting offer. I could make myself a nice piece of loot."

"And what would you do with it, sit around all day and count it? You'd be lost without the shop."

"You must be clairvoyant. That's exactly what I told him. He just smiled and said, 'Think about it. Anytime you change your mind, or decide to get married and quit, we'll still be interested.'"

"A good decision," Russ said. "I approve."

Vividly, he recalled the first time he had seen her, the weekend three years ago when she moved into the house she had rented next door, the one once occupied by Dick Jaynes and his girl, transferred to another flying route by his airline; saw her from sundeck to sundeck, wearing brief pants and halter, struggling to put together a new outdoor barbecue, loose parts spilled out of the carton and scattered over the deck. With eyes trained to immediately record physical statistics, Russ at once categorized her in police terms: female, Caucasian; five-six, 125 to 130; eyes: possibly green; hair: blonde; about twenty-five/twenty-six; complexion: fair, tanned; no visible scars or markings.

She stood up and stared around her in a gesture of helplessness, and he called out across the thirty feet, "Can I help you with that?"

She turned and saw him. "If somebody doesn't, I'll never get this any-child-can-do-it monster together."

So it began, and he soon discovered that Rachel Nugent

167

went far beyond initial statistics. She was nearing thirty, but somewhere in her late teens or early twenties her aging process must have come to a complete halt. Her skin was flawless, hair the color of ripened wheat, cut boyishly short. Wearing blue-trimmed white tennis shorts and matching halter, her well-tanned legs were long and spectacularly shapely, moving with the grace of a dancer. Her slender waist gave emphasis to tempting breasts that the scanty halter could scarcely contain. Her eyes were the color of fresh leaves in springtime, well spaced over a patrician nose, lips full and generous.

She was ready for the second martini, and he poured it for her, another for himself, which they took into the bedroom. Russ drew the draperies across the door-wall glass and turned to be rewarded with the most delightful sight he knew, of Rachel drawing the shift up and over her blonde head.

They made love easily, unhurriedly, savoring each other until they reached that moment when nothing else in the world mattered, passion fully awakened, driving toward the ultimate in human pleasure, locked together and unwilling to have it end.

"God, how I've missed you," he breathed.

"You'll never know how much thought I gave to getting home to this moment," she said.

"I love you, Rachel."

He could say those words, feel and mean them as he could hardly remember speaking them to Carol with the same depth; perhaps because he and Carol had known each other since childhood; in their later years of discontent, the words had become stilted and without meaning.

There were other things about Rachel's rented house that Dick Jaynes had been too lazy or preoccupied about fixing. Russ brought in a man to repair the electronic garage-door opener; then he and Harry Deliso had torn out some of the crumbled bricks in the fireplace and replaced them, built some bookshelves in the small second bedroom, which she had converted into a den. He recommended his own garage mechanic to take care of her car, the best restaurants along the coast, introduced her to his doctor and dentist. In time, Rachel met Steve and Joy Barrett, Perry and Jo-Ann Roberts, and Harry Deliso who, separated from his wife, came down frequently to share Russ's hospitality and the beach.

New to Manhattan Beach, Joy and Jo-Ann took Rachel on

shopping trips to furniture, drapery, housewares and appliance stores where liberal discounts were offered the wives of law-enforcement officers. Within a short time, Rachel had become a permanent member of their group.

As time passed, Russ learned much about Rachel without revealing too much about himself.

She had come from Portland, Oregon, to California in 1969, a year after she learned that her husband, an army first lieutenant, had been shot down in the Mekong Delta in his helicopter. Widowed and now without a family of her own, she visited Bill Nugent's parents in Charlottesville, Virginia, then returned to Portland, sold the dress shop she had been operating since leaving college, sold their house, added the money to Bill's insurance, and opened a dress shop in Los Angeles, far away from all memories of the past.

The new shop was a struggle in a larger city where she was unknown. When her lease was up, her longing for the ocean took her to Manhattan Beach where she found the defunct Sea & Ski Shop that perfectly suited her needs. She signed a two-year lease early in January, 1971, and alive with a new challenge and her exquisite sense of style, the shop attracted attention from the start, winning her a loyal clientele. She hired a young divorcée, Vicki Stratton, and soon found it necessary to employ another girl, Lilith Jansen, to fill in as needed. At which point, she moved from the motel where she had been staying temporarily into the house Dick Jaynes had given up a month before.

When she first learned soon after their first meeting that Russ was a deputy sheriff she showed surprised amusement. "I've never known a cop before," she said. "You're my first."

"Does it bother you?" he asked.

"No-o. I-I guess it's that I don't like the guns that go with the job. My father used to go hunting in Oregon, and I always felt a little sick at the sight of the dead things he brought back, ducks, birds, rabbits, and one time, a deer. I got so I couldn't eat things he killed. My husband had a thing about guns, too. Shotguns, rifles, pistols, always oiling them, polishing the wood. Like a fetish."

"I don't like killing things, either," Russ said. "My gun is for self-defense. I've never killed anyone with it. I hope I never have to."

"That's comforting to know," Rachel said.

And later, as they began seeing each other more frequently, "I'm curious, Russ."

"About what?"

"You, of course. Like, how a man with your education, intelligence, interest in good music and world affairs ever became a cop?"

"Rachel, please. I don't mean to be abrupt or evasive, but I've heard that line a hundred, five hundred times. From my ex-wife, her father and mother, noncop friends—"

"But I'm really interested, Russ. Why, when there are so many others—"

"Better suited for police work? Just as there are soldiers, sailors, garbage men who are particularly qualified to do what they do?"

"You're making me out a bigot or a snob."

"No, but the subtle connotation, conscious or unconscious, is there. Let me see if I can make it more clear. I'm a cop not so much because I've been programmed for it, perhaps, but more because I think it's a very necessary job, one that I know and do better than any other I can think of. And not because my grandfather and father were cops before me, which I can't deny had a considerable effect on my decision to become one. I happen to honestly believe that what I do is important, and I enjoy doing it."

"And yet the way you mentioned your ex-wife, I have the feeling that being a cop had something to do with—"

"Our divorce? Practically everything, Rachel." He paused as though he had tired of the subject, then said, "It takes a very understanding woman to be a cop's wife, something both of us probably hadn't realized. The element of uncertainty, the irregular hours, the tendency to bring home the filth and evil a cop sees on the streets every day and night."

"And the dangers, living so close to death?"

"And that possibility, of course. But where would the public be without police protection, protection they often get without realizing it? There's so much you're shielded from in a community like this and in other areas, so much you'll never see unless you're out on the streets in a high-crime area. That's what the police are for, what we do, the best we can with what the citizens give us to work with."

"I suppose you're right, but I can't equate you with old Mr. Simmons who used to watch out for us kids at our street crossing on the way to school."

"That was old Mr. Simmons's job, Rachel. This is mine."

It was left there for the time being, but would crop up at times when the police were accused of brutality and repressive tactics, until she began to understand that police, like all humans, were subject to the same stresses, strains, and pressures, to feelings of personal honesty and dishonesty, to inherent tolerance and intolerance, and could react to violence with violence; that while lawbreakers spoke out for their civil rights and were listened to, few seemed to realize that law-enforcement officers were entitled to those same rights.

There were, of course, occasional grievous errors committed by the police, and these were broadcast across the pages of newspapers and over radio and television channels; yet when those charges were proved faulty, retractions were seldom given equal prominence. It was something the police had to learn to live with.

The public contact with law enforcement was generally negative; a ticket for illegal parking, a speeder or reckless driver arrested, a drunken driver taken off the streets, all became breeders of resentment. The man mugged, the woman whose purse had been snatched, the car owner victimized by theft of his means of transportation, the burglarized householder, the store owner held up at pistol point and robbed, all these stored up anger because the police were not present to witness and prevent the crime. Also something every cop had to live with.

And while pushers of marijuana, pills, and hard narcotics plied their profitable trade, parents complained that their user-children were being harassed by police. Youth gangs proliferated, and the public closed its eyes to the lack of jobs and playgrounds to direct their energies elsewhere; yet blamed the police for bringing young vandals, thieves, and burglars into juvenile court, thus increasing the work of probation and parole officers, clogging the courts and jails, all at the taxpayers' expense.

Rachel saw Russ in his different moods: exultant over a big dope bust, tired and weary when a big pusher was freed on a legal technicality. All in a day's work, Russ told her, but she could see now how it might have been with Carol—living from day to day with unpredictable disaster that might come with any ring of the phone. *"Mrs. McNeely, this is John, Russ's partner. I'm calling from the hospital—"*

4•

They had moved rapidly from casual neighbor acquaintanceship into friendship and dating that soon reached the halfway point between personal attachment and intimacy when Russ casually invited Rachel to Las Vegas for a weekend. With Vicki and Lilith on hand to take care of the shop, they left on a Friday at noon, took the hour-long flight, and checked into adjoining rooms at the Desert Inn. After a drink at the bar, Russ said, "How much money did you bring with you?"

She looked up in mild surprise and said, "About fifty or sixty dollars."

"Let me have a dollar."

Perplexed, she took a dollar bill from her purse and handed it to him. "From now until we leave," Russ told her, "we're in business together. Partners. Okay?"

"Okay, but what kind of business are we in?"

"Let's go to the crap tables and find out."

At the table, he placed the two dollars on the pass line. The shooter was a grim-faced man who rolled an eleven, and the partnership was ahead by two dollars. Russ let it ride, and the man rolled a four and after two more numbers came back with a four, doubling their bet to eight dollars. Russ drew down six and began again with the original two.

"Lordy," Rachel said, "I can't double my money that easily in a whole year of hard work."

"All right, sweetie," Russ said when the dice finally came to him, "now I'll show you what hard work is like."

An hour later, they went to the bar with a hundred and twenty dollars in Desert Inn chips. Over a drink, Russ undertook Rachel's education in crap-shooting; the intricacies of playing the line, behind the line for more favorable odds, how to place bets on the boxed numbers above the COME slot; to avoid the sucker bets: the FIELD, the BIG six and eight, HARDWAYS, and ANY CRAPS, where the odds strongly slanted toward the house.

They returned to the tables, lost and won, had dinner, saw a magnificent show, then gambled late into the morning hours, and, joyously, won again. Saturday was a repeat of Friday, except for location, gambling at other Strip hotels, dining well, attending a late show. And, at two o'clock on Sunday morning, back at the Desert Inn, Rachel turned to Russ at the crap table and said, "I've got to quit. I'm dying on my feet."

"While we're ahead?" he asked with incredulity.

"Win, lose, or draw, I've had it. Why don't you stay? I'll slip away to my room and go to bed."

"I hate to quit while the dice are still hot. I'll play on for a while until they cool off."

Gathering her own small stack of chips she had been

playing with, Rachel said, "If you win a fortune, knock on my door. I'll help you count it."

The dice were indeed hot, and in the hands of a shouting Texas high-roller whose winner's voice boomed through the casino, the crowds urging him on, the play continued. The Texan was well into a long roll, and Russ had two twenty-five-dollar chips on the pass line, two more behind the line. The point was eight and the roll went on. Russ placed fifty dollars on the boxed six. The eight came in, and the new point was a five. Russ placed another fifty on the nine, and as the roll continued without a seven showing up, he placed similar fifty-dollar bets on the four, ten, six, and eight, his line bet covering the five.

Repeatedly, as those numbers came up, Russ pressed each bet, doubling and tripling their values, then as they hit again, he began drawing down his winnings. The Texan made five straight passes, and the new point became a ten. The shooter, calling on God, the Alamo, the spirits of ancestors long gone, made the ten. Russ withdrew all bets and began again with a single fifty-dollar bet on the pass line. The Texan hit an eleven. His next number was a four and after two more rolls, sevened out.

The next shooter was a woman whose voice was equal in volume to the Texan's, and the crowd was vociferous in their encouragement, crooning, shouting, whispering, praying. Russ backed her fully on the line, behind it, and in the boxed numbers. When she finally relinquished the dice, he estimated that there were close to three thousand dollars in his chip rack.

At four o'clock, the dice cooled off. Three shooters in a row failed beyond a first roll. The dice came to Russ, and he half-heartedly put four twenty-five-dollar chips on the line, rolled a ten, made it, let the two hundred dollars ride, came out with a nine, then a seven right behind it. And quit. Pockets bulging with chips, he went to the elevator and rode up to his floor. In his room, he knocked on the communicating door. There was no answer. He knocked once more, lightly, deciding he would let Rachel sleep and do her chip counting in the late morning. Then he heard her soft, sleepy voice call out. "Russ?"

"It's me. With the fortune."

He heard her squeal with delight and excitement. "Wait, wait." Then the lock turned, and the door opened. "Come in."

He caught a brief glimpse of her as she scurried back to her bed and pulled the covers up over her short nightgown, lime-green eyes bright with anticipation. "How much?" she asked with glee.

"I don't know. I made it, but I brought it to my partner to count." He stood over her, dripping handfuls of twenty-five-dollar chips from his jacket pockets onto the blanket and through her outstretched fingers.

"My God! How beautiful!" Rachel chanted. "What happened? Did you break the bank or just rob it?"

"Pure luck. Never happened to me before like this. It's you, Rachel. You're my lucky piece."

She got out of bed, slipped into a thin robe, and began piling the chips in fours, a hundred dollars to each stack. The row began stretching across the dresser while Russ poured some Scotch into two glasses; but Rachel refused her drink until she had counted thirty-eight stacks with two single chips left over.

"Thirty-eight hundred and fifty dollars!" she announced with a shriek. "It can't be legal!"

"It is, and unless you report it, tax-free. And half of it is yours."

"You're insane. You won it. It's yours."

"We're partners, remember?"

"Russ, I can't take it. It's too much."

"Okay, then I'll leave your half for the maid."

She threw her arms around him and kissed him soundly. "Oh, Russ! It's the loveliest, easiest money I've ever had."

"Easy, hell!" he exclaimed with mock outrage. "I worked damned hard for every dollar of it."

"Such nice, clean work."

"Hey, your drink."

They drank the Scotch, and another; then Rachel removed her robe and got into bed. His eyes followed her every move hungrily, inflamed by the total excitement of the evening and her elegant body. As she drew the light cover up over her breasts, Russ said, "Are you going to leave all that loot lying there on the dresser?"

"You bet I am. I want to see it when I wake up. If I don't, I'll know it was only a dream, and I couldn't stand that. Come here."

He sat on the edge of the bed and took her extended hand, then drew her close to him and kissed her. It wasn't the first kiss they had shared, but much more than the casual "good night" or "hello" kisses that had passed between them; now deep, all-consuming. And when she finally drew back, gasping for breath, he said, "Okay, Rachel?"

She looked up at him through half-closed eyes and replied, "Yes, Russ. Yes."

He undressed with a sense of sudden urgency and slipped in beside her, took her into his arms, feeling her warm sensuality and his own overwhelming need for her. She responded, alive to his touch, eager and tense. His lips closed down on hers, and they moved to adjust to each other, hands moving in intimate exploration and discovery.

He could sense readiness in the tempo of her breathing, saw it in her slightly disoriented eyes as she looked dreamily at him, trying to focus on his face, felt it in the movement of her as he covered her body with his own. He entered slowly, heard her first gasp of indrawn breath, felt her legs tighten around him. He stroked easily, gently, and she began to respond to each thrust with an upward counterthrust until they achieved smooth rhythm; then he drove with almost uncontrolled passion.

She was at the peak fringe, crying, "Russ—Russ—darling—oh, my *God!*" clamping him viselike, clinging, wet with their mingled perspiration, receiving, giving, then moving into total orgasm just as Russ, fully expended, achieved his own explosive climax.

He held her tightly, kissing her open mouth, feeling her shuddering body in release as she fell back limply in postcoital euphoria. And then, withdrawing, they lay face to face in each other's arms, unwilling to part.

She was asleep. Russ, momentarily exhausted, lay drowsily, his arms cradling her. It had been a long time—years—since he had given himself so completely to the sex act, had received so much from it. Not from Carol in the latter years of their marriage, when love had become a token, mechanical thing; and surely not from those who had followed her in a succession of one-night bouts of sexual acrobatics. On this night he had possessed, and been possessed by, the loveliest woman he had ever known, and this, he knew now, as though it were a first discovery, was how it should be between a man and woman in love.

And, in that revelatory moment, he found himself erect again, but Rachel, lying peacefully in his arms, was deeply asleep, and he could not bring himself to waken her. He slipped away and showered, then returned to lie beside her again; soon, he began to see light at the edges of the drawn draperies as the bronze dawn drove the night away. Then he, too, slept.

5●

Now, in his own home, as he lay beside Rachel in half sleep, she woke and said, "What time is it?"

"Seven forty-five."

She sat up. "I'd better get into something more presentable, don't you think?"

"I like you just the way you are."

"And you are a greedy pig, Sergeant."

"Watch it, girl. That's a dirty three-letter word in my league."

"We're not talking about the same kind of pig." She scurried away from his playful slap, slipped into the minishift, into her cork-platformed shoes. "Pick me up in thirty?"

"Ten-four."

At the door, she turned and laughed. "Pig!" and was gone.

At eight thirty, he parked in the lot behind Bonnie's, a popular bar-restaurant near the pier. The dining room was almost full, but Bonnie, co-owner with her husband Chuck Nelson, who ruled over the bar, had a booth at the rear waiting for them. They ordered a drink, then a second. Bonnie returned with menus and said, "Chuck has something for you, Russ. See him before you leave."

"Sure, Bonnie, thanks."

"Always business," Rachel commented.

"Nature of the beast, darling. It's all around us."

They ate leisurely, interrupted occasionally by local residents they knew, Rachel elaborating on her experience in New York. It was past ten when the patrons at the bar began to thin out, enough to give Chuck a breather. Russ excused himself and went to the near end of the bar where they could talk without being overheard.

Chuck, an ex-navy man, had been a member of the Manhattan Beach community for over twenty years. A large man, hitting close to the 240-pound mark, he and his diminutive wife, Bonnie, had begun the bar-restaurant after Chuck's retirement from the navy on disability. Bonnie's served excellent food and liberal drinks, making it a favorite beach hangout.

Like many bartenders, Chuck was very cooperative with

the local police and sheriff's officers who patronized the place, which had the residual effect of warning would-be burglars and holdup artists that this was protected property and was a narc, a piece of information he and Bonnie kept off limits. Chuck was fully aware, of course, that McNeely strictly to themselves since public knowledge might offend or inhibit some of their customers.

"Hey, Russ, what's doin'?" Chuck greeted.

"Not too much, Chuck. Bonnie said—"

"Yeah. Have one on the house?"

"Would you believe coffee?"

"Sure, why the hell not? All kinds of crazy things happen around here. Even had a guy the other night come up to the bar and order a glass of milk." He poured the coffee, and Russ saw Bonnie at the table in conversation with Rachel. Chuck said, "Ain't seen you or the boys around lately. Busy?"

"We've been having our hands full."

"Yeah, I'll bet. Damn stuff's all around everywhere these days."

"See much of it around here?"

"Some. Mostly it's garbage, weed and some hash. No real hard stuff, but I know it's around."

"So what else is new?"

"Got somethin' might be interesting."

"If it's local, why not the M.B.P.D.?"

"That's just it. It's more in your line."

"What've you got, Chuck?"

"You know Chris, don't you? Chris Corman?"

"Of course." Chris was one of Bonnie's waitresses, had been working there steadily for three years. A former addict, she had gone through a rehabilitation program, kicked the habit, and remained straight. She was twenty-four now, engaged to a mechanic at Borden's Bike Shop, a motorcycle agency in Redondo Beach a few miles south. Russ looked around. "I didn't see her around. She off tonight?"

"No. She's in the office lying down."

"What's her problem?"

"Some creep she knew from the old days, he walked in one night and spotted her. Been hanging around lately, and she's scared."

"Dealer?"

Chuck nodded. "Used to cop off him, but from what she told me, he's into something bigger now. She didn't tell me too much about it, but he was in again earlier tonight. She spotted him before he saw her and ducked back into the office, kinda shook up. Bonnie talked to her after you called in for a reservation, and Chris said she'd talk to you about it."

"Okay. This dude have a name?"

"I don't know it. She's real uptight, afraid to get involved with him."

"I'll go back and talk to her. Thanks for the coffee."

Russ went back to the table and learned that Bonnie had already briefed Rachel. With a nod and "I won't be too long, wait for me," he went to the rear door, knocked, and opened it. The small cluttered office was in darkness.

"Chris? You in here?"

"Here, Russ. Turn the light on, will you, please?"

He found the wall switch, and a desk lamp came on. Chris was lying on the somewhat battered sofa beside Bonnie's littered desk, blinking as the light hit her eyes. He sat in the desk chair, lit two cigarettes, and handed her one. "What is it, Chris?"

"Trouble, trouble, toil and trouble, or something like that," she chanted. "Christ, I thought I was all through with it."

"Tell me about it."

She sat up, sucking deeply on the cigarette. "This guy, I used to score off him a long time ago. I hadn't seen him since I got busted and went on the rehab program. Then about two weeks ago he wanders in, just like that, and sees me."

"He wanted to deal to you?"

"No, not exactly. I told him right off I was clean and was going to stay that way. He bought that, but then he started talking. It was funny because he didn't need me to pimp a stew for him, for God's sake. Then he got down to what he wanted, asking me if I knew any stews around who'd like to make a few fast, easy bucks. Like for what? I asked. For practically nothing, he said, just what they normally do, fly. Except that they had to be on the Mexican run, Western, Mexicana, or Mex-Am. You know, Mexico City, Guadalajara, Puerto Vallarta, Acapulco."

"You know why, don't you, Chris?"

"Sure. I'm not all that stupid. He's recruiting mules. Somebody to fly a key of heroin or coke in for like a thousand dollars a trip. That's the going rate, isn't it?"

"Yes. Where does it stand now?"

"I told him I'd look around and see, but I didn't, and I won't, but he keeps coming around, bugging me. Three times now, but I saw him coming in tonight and ducked out on him."

"Then he'll be back, won't he?"

"Yes, and I'm scared, Russ. I don't want to tell Roger and get him involved with these animals. Roger knows all about me, has been helping me right along. If I tell him about this, he'd just as soon kill the creep."

"What's his name, this dude?"

"Eddie."

"No last name?"

"When I first knew him, he was Eddie Blake. Later on it was Harris. The time I lived with him, the couple of months when I was scoring off him, he was using the name Masterson. It could be any one of those, or something else, but it was always Eddie up front."

"Give me as good a description as you can, Chris."

"That won't be too hard. He's twenty-eight, maybe thirty, a skinny dude, maybe five-ten or -eleven, about a hundred fifty-five or sixty pounds at the most. Black hair, kind of longish but not hippie, no mustache or beard. He dresses pretty good, flashes a solid roll, so I guess he does okay. Nothing real special about his looks, just ordinary, I guess you'd call it."

"No scars or other identifiable marks on him?"

"No-o, none I can think of, nothing special."

"What kind of a deal did he make you, your end of it?"

"Two hundred for every girl I connect with him if she goes through with it. A finder's fee, he called it."

As she talked, McNeely's mind was fixed on the description. "Did he ever use the name Butler when you were living with him?"

"Could be. He used so many, I stopped paying attention. It was like he used a different one with every pusher he was working with, you know?"

"Okay, Chris—"

"Listen, can you get him off my back, Russ?"

"Well, I can't just pick him up for no reason at all, Chris. Without something to go on that a D.A. or judge will buy, we're dead, but if you're willing to go along with this thing and help me, I think we can handle it."

"Just tell me what you want me to do."

"All right. The next time Eddie shows, don't get nervous or be afraid. Talk to him. Tell him you've found a stew for him, a girl who needs money to keep a kid brother in college or help her folks back home out of a temporary financial jam and is willing to go the route for a thousand a trip."

"Which airline?"

"Make it Mex-Am."

"Okay. How long do you think it will take?"

"Not too long. Stall him. Tell him the girl needs a little time to come around. A couple of days at the most, enough to give me the time I need to set it up."

"I'm worried, Russ. This ape can play rough. I know. I've seen him that way."

"Don't worry about that, Chris. Just play along with him. I'll be in touch with you as soon as we're set. Why don't you run along home now and try to get some rest."

"I will later. Rog is picking me up around eleven."

"Good. You feed it to Eddie, and we'll furnish the stew. And trust me, will you, Chris?"

"What else can I do, Russ?"

On the way home later, Rachel know from past experience and without Russ having told her anything about his conversation with Chris that he was deeply involved, his mind busily engaged. She knew by his slow responses, the way his hands gripped the wheel of his Thunderbird. Later, on her sundeck, after a stiff Scotch she had poured for him, she knew he had worked out some partial solution to his problem, or Chris's. He was actually in a high mood, and their lovemaking this time was smoother, longer lasting.

They slept together until Rachel's alarm went off at eight, had breakfast, then Russ went next door to change for work, his memory nagging at him, trying to bring one name to the surface; one name out of the many hundreds he had dealt with over the past few years. A name that had a significant bearing on the matter he had discussed with Chris Corman, but with which the name of Eddie Butler had no association or meaning.

Before he reached Lennox, the name floated to the top of the others, giving him a sense of exhilaration.

Ann Stennis, who had been a stewardess.

6•

In his home on Caribou Road in the hills overlooking the Malibu coastline, Don Reed had awakened early after a restless night. He went to the kitchen and put on a pot of coffee, walked down to the hedge-lined driveway to pick up the morning *Times*. He returned and scanned its pages until the coffee was ready. One cup was enough to drive away some of the weariness he felt, but not the irritability brought on by his telephone conversation with Eddie Butler on his return from Mexico late the night before.

He went to the bathroom and showered, shaved, then dressed in a casual sports shirt and went out on the sundeck for a second cup of coffee and a closer reading of the paper. Far below, looking across an occasional Spanish tile rooftop, he could see a steady stream of toy automobiles heading toward the city, the gray-blue Pacific beyond. Later, the sun would slice through the mist and create the wondrous day for which the beaches of Southern California were justly famous.

Don Reed was forty-one, an even six feet tall, his 185 pounds well distributed. Dark blond hair framed an oval, now serious face with deep blue eyes, slightly hooked nose, and a mouth that was perhaps too wide, yet not unattractive. His clothes were expensively tailored, linen immaculate, hair neatly trimmed, nails manicured, shoes carefully polished; a man who took great pride in his appearance and could be taken for what he privately considered himself to be, a successful businessman.

He checked his watch. Ten o'clock. The traffic below was thinning out. He went inside, slipped on a tie and jacket, then headed his Mercedes down to the Pacific Coast Highway and toward the city. As usual, he drove at a modest pace, yet feeling a sense of strength in the quiet power of the machine he controlled, knowing that by need or whim, he could call it up by a slight movement of his right foot. He enjoyed that kind of hidden, under surface energy not only in driving, but in dealing with people.

Reed had come a long way from the humble surroundings in which he had been born David Rhodes in Boston. His mother had died when he was eleven, leaving him in the hands of a bewildered father who operated a dry-cleaning and pressing store on the ground floor of their home. Albert Rhodes was then in his early fifties, a gentle man who had no idea how to cope with the responsibility of raising a young son. Thus, David spent much of his time in the streets where he began to learn about life.

He was a somewhat undistinguished student in high school, but eventually made it to Boston College when he began to pick up an interest in mathematics, which fascinated him. In his junior year, Albert Rhodes died, and when the store and house were sold, there was little more than a thousand dollars left after doctor's bills, hospital and funeral expenses, taxes, and the lawyer's fees were paid.

David's last two years in college were financed by gambling. Poker and bridge came natural to him, but could not carry the entire burden. Whereupon, he organized and operated a widespread football lottery, ordered the cards printed, hired student salesmen on commission, and got his first taste of what was then big money for him. Successful, his operation attracted an off-campus syndicate that offered to buy him out for a good profit. He took the offer, was retained to manage the lottery, and used his agents to accept bets for the syndicate's numbers and bookmaking operations. In his senior year he became a partner in an off-campus prostitution ring.

Prior to graduation, vice officers broke up his latest venture and David, in order to avoid arrest, hastily gathered up his cash assets, close to forty thousand dollars, and fled Boston. In New York, he sold his car to a used-car dealer, caught a train to Washington, D.C., where he bought a new car in the name of Donald Reed. He remained there long enough to acquire a driver's license, gasoline credit cards, and other items of identification to support his new name.

Thus armed, he drove to Miami Beach; there he soon learned that this happy playground of the rich was in the firm grip of well-organized syndicates that frowned on unaligned opportunists. After a month or two of discouraging experiences, he moved west to Las Vegas where the opportunities for free-wheeling entrepreneurs were even more restricted. He watched the gambling operations, took a fling at the tables, won a few thousand dollars, but the action was too slow on his side of the table. When his luck began to run cold, he suspected that there was less honesty in Las Vegas than was being advertised and decided to push on to Southern California. He was then four months away from his twenty-second birthday.

Attractive, glib, personable, and with the right amount of street cunning, he made contacts with a few restless women and willing girls who led him to equally restless men in search of action. Within six months, he rented a large house in the Hollywood Hills and established a private gambling casino complete with knowledgeable dealers and handsomely endowed, willing hostesses who served good drinks, excellent food, and encouraged the play both at the tables and in the upstairs private rooms.

The operation lasted for almost two years when vice detectives raided it and arrested Reed. One of his more consistent patrons, a lawyer named Paul Landis, handled his case, pleaded him guilty, after effective bargaining with the district attorney, and won him a one-year sentence in county jail. He was out in eight months, most of his profits intact.

That unhappy experience turned him in another direction. In county jail he had come in contact with a narcotics dealer, George Ruiz, whose brother Ernie was a kingpin of sorts in the heroin trade in East Los Angeles. Because of his curiosity in most sources of high profits, David quietly solicited George Ruiz's friendship and, on release, won an introduction to Ernie, who, after considerable negotiation, became not only his supplier, but instructor in successful dealing of drugs.

In time, he learned its dangers as well as its financial rewards. In the former category, the greatest peril lay in dealing directly to the consumer, the user, thus placing himself within easier reach of the dreaded narc undercover agents. He began then to organize his own pushers in order to insulate himself from the users.

Eventually, he had a dozen men and two women looking to him for heroin and discovered that he was still on the borderline of arrest since his pushers, if arrested, could bargain with the law by pointing a finger at him. He then chose two men and one woman to act as his principal dealers, which moved him up to a higher level of safety. It was not high enough. One of his three dealers, the woman, was arrested and turned informer. A week later, in the act of delivering a quantity of heroin to that very same informer, Reed was busted by four sheriff's narcotics deputies. Paul Landis again represented him on the charge of possession for sale and could do no better for his client than a three-year term in Soledad State Prison.

Three years gave him many nights to think and plan. He reviewed the weak points of his operation and worked out dozens of ways to overcome them, then spent hours discovering the weaknesses in his schemes he had come to believe were foolproof. There was no way, he finally determined, to operate with complete secrecy. Then, how to minimize the risks?

In Soledad, there were many narcotics offenders who had operated at various levels: distributors, major and lesser dealers, pushers. In rap sessions, he listened carefully to their exploits, boastings of big deals, unnamed connections, and rewards, but came away from those seminars with one explicit piece of valuable knowledge: All had been caught and imprisoned; all were losers like himself. There had to be a way, and it could only work if one operated at the top level. For that, he would need a top connection with greater financial resources than he had.

Freed in 1965, Reed returned to Los Angeles, which he now considered to be his home, a city with a vastness and wealth opportunity than any other he had known, a city hardly as complicated as syndicate-controlled New York, Chicago, Detroit, Miami, New Orleans, and others. Here was an abundance of money that flowed loosely in the hands of willing spenders, people who moved around looking for action. Somewhere in that city was what he was looking for and had not yet found.

On his return to Los Angeles, he checked into a Hollywood motel and immediately placed a call to Paul Landis. Two hours later, Landis picked him up and drove to a quiet Beverly Hills restaurant where Reed enjoyed his first excellent meal in three years. Landis, a man in his middle forties, balding and plumpish, smiled quietly and nodded knowingly as Reed recounted his Soledad experience.

At the conclusion of the meal, Landis said, "I know you're anxious to get the envelopes you left with me. They're in my office safe. Let's go back and I'll turn them over to you. I'm sure you'll need them for whatever you have in mind."

"Yes, Paul. All I have on me is about a hundred."

Landis signed the check. They drove to the Wilshire Boulevard offices of Landis & Wharton, and as they entered the plush, high-ceilinged private office that overlooked the city through an entire wall of glass panels, Landis said to his secretary, who had followed them in, "Hold all my calls for an hour, Rena."

She handed him several pink message slips, smiled, and went out. Landis crossed the room to a Miró painting, swung it away from the wall, turned the dial of the safe behind it. He removed three small envelopes from a larger one, brought them back to the desk, and handed them to Reed, who broke the wax seals and removed a tagged key from each envelope. Landis said, "The rent on the boxes has been paid to the end of the year."

"Thanks, Paul. I'll empty them out long before then."

"Out of curiosity, how much do those three keys represent, Don?" Landis asked.

"Exactly one hundred and fifty thousand." Then he added, "Hardly worth three years in Soledad."

"Yes, well—what are your plans now?"

"I don't know. I've probably made a thousand ninety-five

184

plans, one for every night I spent up there." He grinned and said, "I came to only one conclusion. I don't want any more Soledads by that or any other name."

"Then you're planning to get into something legitimate, I take it."

Again the slow smile as Reed said, "Let's face it, Paul. I'm not cut out for the straight life. I was born to be what I am, a hustler, but it's taken me this long to discover that I'm doing something wrong, going at it the wrong way."

It was Landis's turn to smile. "At least, you're honest about it, unlike most of my clients, past and present." He paused, still smiling, then said, "You interest me, Don. Tell me about yourself. I mean before we met that first time. Your background, school, the works."

For half an hour Don talked, and Paul Landis listened with deep interest. When Reed had brought him up to the moment of their first meeting, he said, "That's about it, Paul. You know as much about me as I do, more than I've ever told any man or woman."

Landis said, "I appreciate what you've told me, Don, and you can rest assured it won't go any further than these walls. If you'd care for a bit of advice—?"

"I'll listen."

"You're in the wrong end of this thing, Don."

"Where have I missed?"

"That's easy to define. You've been working at the wrong level. You belong nearer the top where your mind and skills would be managing an operation rather than at the operational level itself."

"That's a conclusion I reached up in Soledad. The question is, how do I get there?"

"By reaching the power structure."

"You're talking in riddles. I don't know what the power structure is or how to reach it."

"All right, let me explain. There are men with money, lots of it, who are always looking for a quick profit, legally, on the fringes, even illegally, particularly when the profit is tax-free. Generally, they employ a man who knows the art and is able to put together certain deals for them while they, the money men, remain behind the scenes. The front man gathers together the money and puts it to work for these shadow clients. The faster the turnover, the greater the rewards."

"I understand, but how do I fit into that kind of setup?"

"Like those shadow clients, I can't afford to get involved

except from the legal angle. However, I can arrange for you to meet a man who may be interested in your ability and talents. Let's say he is a fund manager, the front man. I've represented him on numerous occasions, and I think you two may get along very well together. If you're willing, of course."

"I'm willing, Paul." Reed paused, then asked, "How do you fit into this as far as I'm concerned?"

"Simply this. You retain me as your personal attorney, for which I take an annual ten per cent of your action."

"Fair enough, Paul. Will you set it up for me?"

"Within a week or ten days. Why don't you disappear for a while, go down to Laguna and soak up some sun, good food, a little feminine companionship, eh? Call me in about ten days and I'll have some word for you."

Reed left exhilarated. He removed five thousand dollars from one of his three safety-deposit boxes, rented a small furnished apartment on Shoreham Terrace, then shopped for a completely new wardrobe. He drew out more money for a sports car and took Paul's advice. Laguna Beach was exactly what he needed to remove the final traces of prison from his mind.

Ten days later, they met for lunch at Scandia where Paul introduced Don Reed to Charles Valentine, a finance consultant, according to his business card and a former air force fighter pilot in Korea. Landis stayed for lunch, during which Reed and Valentine exchanged pleasantries without touching on the purpose of their meeting. Landis left after the meal had been consumed to allow his two guests to become better acquainted and, if Valentine saw fit, to get down to business. After a few drinks, Valentine invited Reed to his Wilshire Boulevard condominium to meet his wife Margaret for drinks and dinner. Reed was tremendously impressed with Valentine's suave manner and his obviously affluent, easy way of life. Thus far, there was no commitment on either side.

They met again two days later, and Valentine laid out his plan. He had a contact in Texas for the importation of heroin and cocaine, a Mexican connection who had solid connections in South America. Overall, the organization distributed in the Midwest and East. Valentine operated solely in other parts of the country. What he wanted was a man who could step in and expand the operation on a broader scale and operate it at the highest possible level on the West Coast.

Valentine had the local financial backers and a small distributing organization. Reed would move into that top spot, organize and take over the distributors, set up a cutting mill, handle the receipts, which he would turn over to Valentine.

Reed's investment? Not a penny.

His income? Incalculable.

It took six months to set the deal up. Don Reed now knew everything he needed to know except the names of Valentine's financial backers. When they were ready to start operations, Valentine and Reed flew to Texas to meet Royal Chase and Alan DeWitt. From there, DeWitt flew them to Guadalajara in their private twin Beechcraft to meet Hector Villanueva.

What Valentine, Chase, DeWitt, and Villanueva had in common was their Korean wartime service, flying fighter planes in the same wing command. Villanueva, a second-generation American of Mexican descent, had been shot down in combat, rescued by helicopter, hospitalized, and later retired for disability. Back home, he felt it economically prudent to live in Mexico on his retirement pay. Later, he married a Mexican girl and fathered two children.

Chase, the original Texan, and Valentine, the smooth financial manipulator, had put the smuggling deal together. DeWitt, from Ohio, had been brought into it, bored with his postwar job in an insurance agency. Villanueva became the supply contact. It looked very sweet indeed to Don Reed.

Back in Los Angeles, Reed looked up Eddie Butler, whom he had known in Soledad, and whose quiet manner had impressed him greatly. Eddie had been turned in by an informer and taken a full five-year fall. Con-wise from previous jail terms, he, too, had felt a lack of proper organization and protection. Reed invited Butler to join him, to act as a recruiter of dealers. In turn, Butler brought in Moose Peterson, also a graduate of Soledad, as his operational partner and muscle man.

While Butler and Peterson began making a careful search for nonuser dealers, Reed sought a cover where the heroin and cocaine shipped in from Chase's Texas ranch could be safely adulterated, repackaged in varying amounts, warehoused, and distributed. He found it through a lead in Simon Hernandez, who owned and operated in San Pedro an auto and truck wrecking yard that specialized in rebuilt auto parts, body repair, and painting under the name of Tri-City Auto Works, and which was in financial difficulty.

Most important, Butler and Peterson would market the final product through distributors and dealers who would have no contact with, nor even suspect the existence of Don Reed. This became Reed's measure of security.

Within a year, the operation became unbelievably successful, with product flowing in from Texas at regular intervals. When cocaine fell into short supply, Butler recruited "mules," or couriers, to bring the powder in from his own Mexico City contact, using airline stewardesses to whom he paid a thousand dollars a trip for the service. Reed frowned on that practice, but Butler, upon whom he had come to rely more and more, insisted that if Reed refused to permit him to continue, he would quit and go it alone. Reed gave in on that point when cocaine use began proliferating, became the "in" drug among entertainment personalities, and Texas was hard pressed to fill their demands.

Business boomed. Rock singing stars, actors, writers, hip young executives bought into the cocaine scene, popular among those who, from childhood, had a natural aversion to the needle. To others, it removed the need to carry incriminating "works" for a hit. More important, sniffing cocaine by nostril eliminated telltale track marks in the arm, required with heroin use, and a dead giveaway to family, friends, associates, and the police.

For greater security, now obsessed with its need, Don Reed quietly bought the Caribou Road house in the name of David Rhodes. His Mercedes was licensed and registered in that name at the address of his new apartment on Alicante Drive in West Hollywood, leased as an accommodation to the need for conferences with his two principal subordinates and for occasional social encounters with female acquaintances. The Caribou Road address had never been revealed to either Butler, Peterson, or Valentine.

And now, Eddie Butler and Moose Peterson had committed a gross error by breaking one of his most rigid rules of business conduct, extending credit to a dealer, Whitey Lloyd, a matter that required immediate attention and correction.

7●

Reed reached the apartment on Alicante Drive at eleven o'clock. Twenty minutes later, Butler and Peterson arrived, contrite and apologetic as they related the detailed events of the Whitey Lloyd fiasco.

"How, for God's sake, did he find out where you lived?" Reed demanded.

Butler told him, just as Lloyd had given it to them.

"Where is he now?"

"Out on bail, as of yesterday."

"Where?"

"Inglewood Municipal Court."

"How much?"

"Twenty-five hundred. He had a lawyer, a dude named Jerry Platt."

Reed's lips tightened into a grim line. "Two prior convictions caught with a whole pound of cocaine and a gun, and he's out on only twenty-five hundred?"

"That's it."

"He must have given his brain a total enema to make a deal like that," Reed commented.

"There's always that possibility," Butler agreed.

"And he can not only name you, but knows where you live. That makes him a definite problem, one we can't afford," Reed said. When neither Butler nor Peterson disputed that statement, he continued. "He knows Connie's number and her part in the operation. He knows our contact system, our delivery—"

"It's only his word—" Butler began.

"His word, as you call it, Eddie, can turn every narc in Southern California loose on your tails. If they pick up one or both of you for questioning, Lloyd's word can become sworn testimony in court. That's what comes of letting a two-bit dealer handle a pound deal without arousing your suspicions."

"Okay, Don," Butler said, "we took a chance because we were sold that he was moving up into the big time. Even if he'd laid out the whole bundle in cash and got himself busted, he'd still be telling everything he knows to buy a deal. If it's the money, hell, Moose and I'll—"

"It's not the money, Eddie, as much as the idea that you both swallowed, that a balloon and ounce man becomes a pound dealer overnight. It sounds phony and turned out that way."

"I know, but—"

"But we're sitting here crying over spilt milk. When does he come up for trial?"

"In six weeks. Question is, what do we do, cut Connie's phone off and lose a lot of business?"

"No, not for a punk like Lloyd."

"You got any ideas, Don?"

"I spent most of last night thinking about it."

"Okay. Moose and I got us into it. You lay it out, we'll take care of it."

"Moose?"

"Like Eddie said, Don. You want him taken care of?"

"Maybe. Let me think about it some more."

"Okay." For a few minutes there was silence, each man deep in his own thoughts, then Butler said, "Our inventory is down pretty low, particularly on coke, not much better on smack."

"I know. I talked to Hernandez last week before I took off for Mexico."

"We got anything coming in soon?"

"There are a few problems to clear up first. I flew down to Guadalajara to see the contact man there. His main connection in Caracas got mixed up in some kind of gun deal for some Chileans and hasn't been heard from in over two months. He was trying to reach his guy in Bogotá, but couldn't make contact. That's what held me up down there."

"I told Hernandez to repackage what we've got in smaller quantities in case we have to start rationing if we can't get more product."

"It should be opening up soon. Our Mexican guy will start putting the pressure on. What about your Mexico City connection on coke? Anything there we can pick up to hold us over?"

Butler said, "It's still there, but we're short on mules. Until last month, I had two, but one got herself transferred to the Hawaii run, and the other got married and quit."

"Anybody else in sight?"

"I've got this broad who used to score off me down in Manhattan Beach, a waitress, bird-dogging for me. Says she's got a possible, a Mex-Am stew. I'm supposed to call her tonight. I'll talk to her, and if she sounds okay, I'll set up a meet and look her over."

"Good. Right now we need her. See if you can pick up a couple more through her. Until Guadalajara re-establishes contact, we'll have to go light with what we've got."

"Unless we have Simon put an extra cut into what he's got down there," Peterson suggested.

Reed frowned and said, "No, Moose. We've built up a reputation for quality, let's keep it that way. Eddie, keep on that courier thing."

"Okay," Butler said, "I'll set this one up tonight."

"Then let's leave it there for now. I'll talk to you later about the Lloyd thing."

Chapter Six

1•

At 0915 Russ McNeely phoned Homicide and reached Ray
Ycaza as he was about to leave his office with his partner,
Danny Geiger. "Hey, old buddy," Ycaza exclaimed with delight, "like a voice out of the dark past. How the hell are
you?"

"Fine, *amigo*. How are Yolanda and the brood?"

"Great, Russ. Asks for you all the time. What's doing?"

"Got a few minutes to spare?"

"I'm on my way out with my partner. Got an autopsy to
witness. Is it important?"

"Could be. Remember the Ann Stennis case about two
years ago, the Mex-Am stewardess? That was yours, wasn't
it?"

"Jesus, yes. You have something on it?"

"Something I ran across that jiggled my memory, but I
need a few things to put it all together. What was the name
of the security chief at Mex-Am?"

"Bill Willard. Used to be a lieutenant in the department
until he retired and took the Mex-Am job."

"He's still there?"

"I'm sure he is. I ran into him, oh, about a month or so
ago at a retirement party. What's up, Russ?"

"It'll take too long to detail it over the phone if you're in a hurry. How about meeting me here at Lennox when you're through with your autopsy?"

"I'll be there. I'd sure like to close the book on that one."

Ycaza replaced the receiver thoughtfully. Danny Geiger, a recent addition to Homicide assigned to Ycaza for investigative indoctrination, closed his attaché case and nested the .38 detective special in his holster. "Ready, Ray," he said.

"Yeah. Let's go."

"Was that something we're working on?"

"No. An old case, but still open. Happened about two years ago."

Twenty minutes later, standing in the room where he had attended his first autopsy only two weeks after joining Homicide, Ycaza experienced some of the same uncertain feeling even after the many that had followed. Except for the victims, each visit had been a depressing replay of the one before. This was Geiger's first autopsy, and as the body was undraped by the two white-coated examiners, he caught the younger man's shuddering response and saw him turn away from the nineteen-year-old corpse, the right half of his head shattered by a shotgun blast.

"Easy, Danny," he said softly.

Geiger looked at Ycaza, then forced himself to stare at the victim whose life had been taken in so brutal a manner, dead before he had even begun to live; a student on his way home from night school, cut down by someone in a car that sped out of sight before anyone could get a description or license number. The victim had no known police record, and neighbors had spoken of him as a quiet, studious boy who had a job and had never been in trouble, an only son, the sole support of his widowed mother and younger sister.

"Christ, Ray," Geiger said, "this is the one part of this job I'll probably never get used to."

"You stay with it long enough, you will." These were the very same words his first partner in Homicide, Frank Gray, had said to him, but Ray hadn't believed him then. Nor did he today.

Watching the two pathologists as they examined the corpse, making notes as they went along, Ycaza thought back to his own first homicide victim when the body of Ann Stennis lay on a stainless-steel table exactly like this one, he expecting to disgorge the meal he had eaten an hour earlier.

The room was wide and long, lighted by overhead fluorescent tubes, eerie in silence, banks of slide-out compartments against the walls resembling oversized filing cabinets. Two white-coated men were examining the cold body of Ann Stennis, picked up beside the road at Playa del Rey at five o'clock in the morning, her airline jacket and purse beside her, naked to the waist, one stocking on, one off.

Photographs had been taken of the strangulation marks on her neck, the nylon stocking used by the murderer to kill her; right, left, front, and back views. Turning the naked body to photograph the snakelike imprint around her waist up to her smallish breasts, the impression of a tight undergarment she had worn and was now missing.

Ycaza had kept his eyes averted, but Frank Gray, his senior partner, followed every move with professional interest; and all Ray felt was that growing depression that death by violence gave him in these solemn, barren, sterile surroundings; grateful when Frank said, "Okay, Ray, let's go."

In the glass-walled room next to the autopsy room, they checked through Ann Stennis's personal effects. Shoulder bag, shoes, skirt, jacket, panty girdle, stockings, uniform cap with the Mex-Am Airlines insignia that matched the one on her jacket.

Frank Gray spilled the contents of the bag onto the table for inventory, calling the items off as Ycaza recorded them on the official form. Two lipstick containers, compact, wallet with airline I.D., credit cards, several snapshots, probably of members of her family, driver's license, $43.00 in bills, 87 cents in coins, two Mexican pesos, checkbook with a balance of $130.79, car keys, apartment keys, address book, ballpoint pen, one package of Dentyne, one of Pall Mall filter-tip cigarettes, a tin of aspirin, plastic container of unidentified pills, non-prescription, eye-makeup kit, gold-colored Zippo lighter, gold wristwatch with flexible band, two books of matches, one from Mexico City, one from Acapulco.

One of the pathologists came in from the autopsy room. "We found another item to add to the report," he said. "The deceased was in the early stages of pregnancy, twelve to fourteen weeks." He went out, and Gray said, "At least, she wasn't raped."

And Ray thought, "That ought to be one hell of a great comfort to her."

The investigation into the murder of Ann Stennis was fruitless, traumatic to Ray, perhaps because it was his first homicide. Or because he couldn't forget the tormented expression on Ann Stennis's face.

The investigation had taken them from the office of Bill

Willard, the former deputy who was now Mex-Am's security chief, to the apartment she shared with three other stewardesses. They had checked out the names in her address book, notified her parents in Racine, Wisconsin, talked with her father who had flown to Los Angeles to claim her body. Everything pointed to the conclusion that Ann Stennis, from the imprint of the missing undergarment on her body, had been a mule for an unknown dope importer and had probably been killed in a dispute over the payment of cash to her. Months later, after Frank Gray had retired from the department and gone to Oregon to live, the case was still open on the books without a single clue to follow up. And still open in Ray Ycaza's mind.

Now there was a possible lead, and Ycaza's interest was reawakened. Before he drove to Lennox to meet McNeely, he got out the book on the Stennis case and reviewed it page by page: initial reports, supplementaries, medical examiner and autopsy reports, photographs, every interview that had been made.

After being introduced to the MV crew by McNeely, he said, "Give me the drill, Russ."

McNeely related the details except for the names of his informants, Chuck Nelson and Chris Corman. "This crook, Eddie Butler, is a dope dealer we ran across through another dealer we've got on a heavy deal. According to our informant, he's looking for mules to carry the stuff in from Mexico. There's always a shortage. After a while, they get hinky and quit or get transferred to other runs, so Butler is out recruiting replacements. Our informant used to score off him and looks like a natural source for him. She was on rehab and is clean, engaged to a nice kid with a job and wants to keep it that way.

"She's scared of this dude, knows he can get rough and wants no part of the deal. She begins to show the pressure when Butler contacts her, and her boss asks, 'What the hell?' She begins to cry and lays it on him. He happens to be a friend and talks her into spelling it out for me. Because it involved dope, I remembered the case you and Frank Gray worked on, and here we are."

"Yeah," Ycaza said. "Hell, yeah, Russ, it could be the same deal, the same M.O., the same dude. I've got a feeling about it."

"So do I."

"How can we set this crook up?"

"We've got it rolling now. One of our undercover girl deputies did two years as a stewardess for Western and PSA before she came into the department. Sharon Freeman. Young, fresh-looking, three years in Narcotics. I'm sure we can get Bill Willard to put her in a Mex-Am uniform to take the ride. I think I can put her up with a friend of mine at the beach to give her an authentic cover, and we'll have a tail on her at all times. Our informant wires her into this Eddie dude, and she agrees to mule the junk in from Mexico. He meets her on arrival here, she turns the stuff over to him, and we take him. How does it sound?"

"Great. You lay this on your—what's her name?—Sharon, yet?"

"Not yet. I'll have to clear it through Barker and the captain first. I don't know how they'll feel about putting Sherry in a jeopardy situation. One slip and—"

"When are you going to talk to Barker and Esau?"

"I've got to go downtown this afternoon on another matter. I'll see Barker then."

"Okay, Russ. If they put their blessing on it, I'll talk to Captain Sawyer. I know he'll want in on this one."

"You'll be welcome, *amigo*."

"Thanks. I'll owe you a big one."

"Forget it. I still owe you one for Firestone."

"Blow it, man. I wrote that one off long ago."

"Maybe, but it's still on my payoff list."

2•

In his office that morning, Captain John Esau sat puffing on his cigarette as he listened to John Rivera's briefing on narcotics operations in the county during the past twelve hours. He concluded with a raid made at 0330 in the Topanga Canyon area by the Malibu station crew, a house that had been under surveillance for over three months. They had arrested Milton Lockman, a dealer with four misdemeanors and two prior felonies, along with two women and three males, and taken nine kilos of marijuana, an ounce of hash oil, one of heroin, and two of cocaine.

Esau looked up and smiled. "Good bust, John."

"Yes, sir. Lockman had them running in circles for a long time. Now if some fatheaded judge doesn't become overwhelmed with an overdose of good will and the milk of human kindness, Milton ought to be fifteen years older by the time he's out dealing again."

Esau sighed and stubbed out his cigarette. "Yes, well, we

do the best we can with what the good Lord provides. Time for a cup of coffee before the chief's meeting, John?"

"Yes, sir." The administrative lieutenant went to the door and spoke to one of the clerks on the early shift. Moments later, she appeared with the captain's coffee. Rivera gathered up his abbreviated notes and placed them in front of Esau, all cases in which the chief of detectives might show particular interest.

"This thing with Lloyd," Esau said.

"Yes, sir?"

"The deal McNeely mentioned in his report to Barker, the one in Manhattan Beach. McNeely believes the dealer involved is the same one Lloyd gave him. Eddie Butler."

"Yes, sir."

The Butler case of five years ago. Eddie Butler had been stopped for a routine traffic violation in West Hollywood. During his questioning at curbside, the deputy's partner, standing on the right side of the vehicle and slightly to the rear, saw Butler's woman companion remove a small package from her purse and conceal it between the bucket seats. He flashed his light inside and asked her what was in the package. When she refused to reply, he reached across her and took the package from its place of concealment. The package, a brown sack, contained a Pliofilm bag with a half ounce of brownish powder that the deputies took to be Mexican heroin. A test proved the powder to be just that.

Butler and the woman, Felice Thorne, were arrested and booked at West Hollywood station. At their preliminary hearing before a municipal court judge, their defense attorney sought to suppress the contraband by reason of illegal search and seizure. The judge admitted the evidence, and the case was tried in superior court where the co-defendants were found guilty. Whereupon, Butler's attorney filed an appeal. A three-judge intermediate appellate court reviewed the transcripts and wrote an opinion declaring the police conduct to be unreasonable and ordered the evidence excluded.

The prosecution then appealed the decision to the California Supreme Court, which, in a four to three decision, found that the officers had acted unconstitutionally and without probable cause. Thus, Eddie Butler and Felice Thorne, free on bail during more than a year of legal maneuvering, were declared innocent and the charges dismissed.

"What do you think, John?" Esau asked.

"I think we've got a good chance at him. I'd like to see it stick this time."

196

"Yes. So would I."

Outside, the people on the 0800 shift were arriving. Sergeant Billy Sorensen, Intelligence, with a handful of teletypes to study; the four field lieutenants arranging their activities for the day; civilian clerks and typists, teletype and communications operators, switchboard relief deputy; undercover agents, both male and female sworn deputies dressed in business suits, miniskirts, denims, and slacks, all relating to the section of the county in which they would be working: suburbs, cities, beach towns, schools, slums, ghettos, bars, poolrooms, or out on the open street.

They were white, black, brown, and two were Orientals, and apart from their specialized training, all had been through the academy, wore the badge, and when necessary, the gun. And had one thing in common: their dedication to the job of holding back the narcotics line.

It was 0750 when Esau crushed his paper cup and threw it into the wastepaper basket, gathered up his notes, and started toward the elevators to the chief of detectives' office for his captain's meeting. As he left the office, he said to Rivera, "I'd like to see Bob Barker and McNeely on that Butler thing, John."

"I'll arrange it, sir," Rivera replied.

At 1400, Captain Esau sat at his desk listening as Russ McNeely outlined the situation concerning the man he now knew was Butler. Chris Corman had made a positive identification of his mug shots. The captain listened and allowed what he heard to sift through the thousand and one other matters he had on his mind. When McNeely concluded with "That's it, sir," Esau turned to Lieutenant Barker and said, "How do you feel about it, Bob?"

Barker's smile indicated his mind was already made up. "I say we go with it and give this crook a nice, long vacation. I had a talk with the guys in Homicide, Lieutenant Kelleher and Captain Sawyer, and with that M.O. shaping up, he's almost got to have some tie-up with the Stennis murder. At least, it's as close as anybody's been able to come up with one."

"It would certainly look that way," Esau agreed. "Too close not to be related. But we've got to consider Sharon."

"Cap, if I know Sherry, she'll jump at it the minute we clue her in. She's the only gal we've got with an airline background, and that's the key to the whole deal."

"Russ?"

"I agree," McNeely said, "but if Sharon says no, and I wouldn't blame her if she backs off, it's out, and we'll have to go another route."

Barker said, "Eight to five she buys it."

"Do we call her in and put it to her?" Russ asked.

"Not yet," Esau countered. "This is a jurisdictional matter, and I'll have to clear it topside. I'll have an answer no later than 1800."

Back at Lennox, McNeely waited, scanning through his file of pending operations; the Lloyd and Tripp-Hardy cases; court appearances coming up; a considerable and never-ending backlog.

He made several call backs to deputy D.A.s at South Bay and Inglewood who had phoned him during his absence and at 1740 took the call from Barker. "It's your baby, Russ. Okayed from the top down."

"Have you talked with Sharon?"

"No. She's out working a deal with the Antelope Valley crew. I checked with Dickerson out there, and he tells me the deal went down and she's on her way back. I'm leaving a note for her to report to you at Lennox tomorrow at 0930. I'll be there, too."

"That's great, Bob. I'll give Ycaza the drill. He wants in on it, you know."

"Okay, but it will all be up to Sherry."

At 0930 the following morning, they gathered in a private consultation room. Sharon Freeman, McNeely, Perry Roberts, Ycaza, and Barker, who indicated to Russ to start the meeting going. Roberts brought in a tray of coffee; cigarettes were lighted.

"Sherry," Russ said, "we've got this deal in the making and want you to listen carefully. First of all, if you don't want in on it, simply tell us, and it won't go any farther than this room and the five of us, and without prejudice."

"For starters," Sharon said, "it sounds pretty heavy."

"That's a strong possibility. I'm going to lay it out as best I can, then you can take your time to give us your decision either way. We can give you until tomorrow, but no longer than that."

She glanced around the table at their faces, smiling uncertainly, then back to McNeely; without any knowledge of what it was about, she knew that no matter what was involved, their first consideration would be for her safety. In three years, working with every crew in the department, she had found herself in dangerous and bizarre, even exotic situations, but above all other considerations, her safety had come first, more important than the case they were working on at the time. Male undercover agents she had teamed up with had that same regard for the female agents. She had worked with McNeely's crew many times and knew there was none better in the entire department.

She listened to the story of the murder of Ann Stennis, only vaguely familiar to her, grimacing at the details as Ycaza related them. That established, McNeely took up the story and outlined the case at hand: the plan to wire her into the man known as Eddie, now known to be Eddie Butler, as a Mex-Am stewardess, relocating her in Rachel Nugent's home temporarily; the flight down; the pickup in Mexico; the return and meet with Butler to hand the junk over; the ultimate bust.

Sharon nodded her understanding, but not her consent.

"We won't take any unnecessary chances, Sherry," Barker broke in, "but we can't anticipate every move in advance. Some of it will have to be played by ear. Your ear. We don't know how they work, whether they'll send somebody along to keep an eye on you at all times, but we'll have someone along to keep an eye on you just in case." And then, "That's it, unless anyone else has something."

No one had anything to add, and it now rested with Sharon. She sipped the last of her coffee, crushed the paper cup, and said, "Okay, I can give you my answer now. I'll buy it."

"You're sure you don't want to sleep on it, Sherry?" Russ said.

"No, I think not. It'll only keep me awake trying to decide. Besides, this sounds bigger than anything I've ever worked on. Spoons, balloons, ounces, sure, but this puts me into the big-time trade. Count me in."

"Okay," McNeely said with a smile at Barker. "Ray and I will run over and see Bill Willard at Mex-Am and start the ball rolling. Sherry, you pack a bag and meet me back here at seventeen hundred so I can take you to Rachel Nugent's house. You'll have to get fitted for uniforms and back into thinking like a stew."

"No problems there."

"This afternoon, I'll contact our informant and have her set up the meet with Butler."

"One thing," Sharon said. "Does this crook carry a gun?"

"That's something we don't know, but we'll have to assume

he does. On the trip down and back, of course, you'll be carrying yours. Keep in mind that we don't know just how he will arrange the meet with you, but we'll be somewhere close by and within reach."

"I copy you loud and clear," Sharon said.

3•

On the following Friday, as dusk began turning into early nightfall, Sharon Freeman drove the '72 Mustang along Victory Boulevard in North Hollywood exactly as directed by the man to whom she had been introduced on the phone by Chris Corman two nights earlier, given only the name Eddie. As she crossed Lankershim Boulevard, she knew she had picked up the tail and felt a momentary rush of excitement, or anxiety. She made two lane changes within two blocks and noted that the car behind her followed both changes. *It's him*, she decided, and continued west in the right lane.

At Laurel Canyon Boulevard, she hit the crossing just as the traffic lights changed from yellow to red and shot across. The tail car followed closely behind her despite oncoming traffic from south and north; and now there was no doubt left in her mind. Approaching the billboard sign, the neon came on: VICTORY DRIVE-IN MOVIE; she checked her rearview mirror again and saw the right-turn indicator flashing on the car behind.

She turned into the driveway into a rank of cars waiting to pay the admission fee. The file moved slowly; then she was at the box office, handed the woman a five-dollar bill, received her change, and moved ahead into the open-air theater arena. She passed two rows and turned left into the third, saw the parked Plymouth with a sigh of relief, and pulled into the vacant space on its right, leaving two empty spaces next to her car. A moment later, the tail car, a maroon Mercury sedan, pulled in beside her with the single male passenger.

Sharon lifted the speaker from the stand on her left and hung it inside the Mustang, adjusted the volume to the cartoon being shown on the huge outdoor screen. In doing so, she glanced at the Plymouth and saw Joe Paul slumped behind the wheel, looking straight ahead at the screen. The blonde girl with him was busy dipping a hand into a carton of popcorn. Up ahead, patrons were moving toward and coming from the refreshment stand, preparing for the double feature scheduled after the cartoon. And in the Mercury, the

...going through the *same* motions of adjusting his loudspeaker.

...artoon came to an end. The music changed tempo to ...nce two coming attractions. A plane floated across at a ...i level, its lights blinking. Then the first feature of the ...ening began, a police epic titled, *Badge and Gun*, exploding into a pursuit and shootout between a black-and-white and a black sedan with four mobsters in it, three of them firing handguns.

Sharon's eyes were on the screen when the door on her right side opened and the man from the Mercury got in beside her. "Terry Wilson?" he said.

"Yes. You're Eddie?"

"That's right." He settled back in the seat. "Don't look at me," he said. "Watch the screen."

She turned away, then touched the amplifier knob and lowered the sound. And waited. He said, "Our friend tells me you can use some extra money."

"Who can't?" Sharon replied.

"Okay. You look like a bright girl who knows how to keep her mouth shut. Did our friend explain the deal to you?"

"Yes. Chris told me—"

"Let's not start mentioning names, okay? The question is, Are you all set to go?"

"I guess so."

"No guesses, baby. You're in, or you're out. Make up your mind. Which is it?"

"All right. I'm in."

"Good girl. What's your schedule for this weekend?"

"I'm due out tomorrow morning on Flight Sixty-two at eight twenty. Mexico City, Guadalajara, Mazatlán, Acapulco, return to Mexico City. We lay over Saturday night, pick up the return to L.A., due in at eleven fifty-five P.M. Sunday."

"That's fine." He reached into his jacket pocket, removed a credit-card wallet, and extracted a slip of paper. "When you get to Mexico City on your way down, call this number from a public phone at the airport. A woman named Lucia will answer. Ask her how her Aunt Bettina is. She'll tell you she's much better and would like to see you. You'll then give her your bust and waist sizes and your arrival time back in Mexico City from Acapulco. When you get back, call her from a public phone. She'll give you an address. Take a taxi there. She'll put a rig on you that won't show through your uniform.

201

"Back in L.A. I'll be waiting at the curb at ~~Mex-Am. It~~ won't be this car. A blue Ford sedan with a white ~~ness-card~~ size, under each windshield wiper. Walk ~~up~~ and get in, and we'll take off. Act natural and no ~~tricks~~ you can get yourself blown up. Understand?"

Her mouth was too dry to reply. She nodded. He removed some bills from an interior section of the wallet. "About the money. You get this two hundred and fifty now." He shoved the three bills toward her, and she took them. "You get the other seven fifty when you deliver the goods. Okay?"

She wet her lips and said, "Yes. Okay."

"Relax. Enjoy the picture."

"Do I have to stay? I've seen better movies on TV."

"Stay and see both pictures. I'll leave at the end of the first one."

"If I have to, can I reach you at the same phone number?"

"No way, baby. That was a public phone. I never use the same one twice. And don't worry, I'll be in touch with you if necessary." He turned, put his hand under her chin, and turned her head toward him. "You're a very pretty chick. If this thing works out okay, there'll be a lot more of them." He leaned toward her and instead of the kiss she expected, turned his lips toward her ear and said in a low voice, "Don't get any funny ideas about talking to anybody about this. If you do, you won't look very pretty when I'm done with you."

Before she could answer, he was out of the Mustang and back into the Mercury. Sharon put the money and slip of paper into her purse and watched the picture on the screen through a blur. She then lit a cigarette, the signal to Joe Paul that the contact had been made and concluded.

When the first feature ended, the man in the Mercury backed out and drove away. Sharon was tempted to get out and go to Joe and the girl in the Plymouth, but decided against it. Eddie Butler could very well have circled to a rear row to watch for just such a move. Nor, for the same reason, did Joe Paul show any signs of making contact with her, under orders to take any and all cues from Sharon. The intermission ended, and she sat through the entire second feature, equally violent and unreal, the opposite of the first, in which a black superhero in the James Bond tradition, single-handedly decimated white gangster mobs on two continents.

When it came to its final explosion, Sharon pulled out in the mass exodus. The Plymouth followed her out, keeping a reasonable distance behind her. To throw off any possibility of a tail left behind by Butler, she crossed the Santa Monica mountain at Beverly Glen, turned right on Sunset to the San Diego Freeway, and headed south to the Century off-ramp and east to Lennox Station. Joe Paul pulled up beside her on the parking lot and introduced her to Deputy Lisa Cross, borrowed for the occasion from Lennox. McNeely was waiting for them in the Narcotics office, where the $250 was marked and placed in an evidence envelope while she and Joe dictated their reports into a tape recorder.

Sharon made the call to Lucia in Mexico City as directed, properly identified herself, and passed on the required information regarding her bust and waist sizes. On the plane with her was Perry Roberts, a tourist traveler. En route, they made it a point not to be seen together in conversation beyond that which her duties as a stewardess required. When they boarded in Acapulco for the return trip to Mexico City, Perry was wearing an entirely different character; wigged, false beard and mustache, faded denims, and sunglasses.

In Mexico City, following Lucia's directions, Sharon taxied to the residential address given her on the phone that she had passed to Perry inside a book match cover. It was in a small, elegant house on Rio Duero off the Paseo de la Reforma in a quiet, well-kept neighborhood. She saw Perry's rented car as it passed by and parked at the end of the block while she paid the taxi driver.

Inside, Lucia, an attractively dressed woman in her mid-forties, greeted her with a minimum of conversation and led her to a second-floor bedroom. In halting English, she ordered Sharon to remove her skirt, blouse, jacket, and bra, then fitted her into a body harness that hugged her tightly from the lower waist to just beneath her breasts. There was a certain unfamiliar thickness that made her feel uncomfortable, but Lucia assured her she would get used to it within a short time and cautioned her to sleep with it on that night.

She found that the uniform adequately covered the harness, which was designed in a series of pockets sewn together into one piece; and as Sharon examined herself closely in the full-length mirror, she admired the workmanship despite the fact that she was 2.2 pounds heavier, yet hardly looked plumper.

The task completed, they went downstairs where a man waited to drive her back to her hotel, Perry following in his car. Thus far, there was no cause for alarm or suspicion. The crunch would come in Los Angeles when it would be time to deliver the harness to Eddie and collect the $750 due her. If all went well.

The plane was on time, putting down at eleven fifty-five P.M. Sharon was pleased that she had carried her duties as a stewardess off so well after an absence of three years and with only two days of crash orientation and without giving the other stewardesses any cause to believe she was anything other than what she appeared to be, a recent transfer from TWA. She went through customs with the flight crew, and as she exited at curbside, one of the other girls said, "If you don't have a ride, Terry, my car is in the parking lot."

"No, thanks, Andrea. My boy friend is picking me up."

"Lucky you. See you."

"Good night. Nice flying with you."

She saw the blue Ford sedan at the curb, the small white cards under the windshield wipers. Its lights came on and began moving toward her. She glanced back casually and saw Perry Roberts as he crossed the pavement, walking to his left where McNeely and the other men should be parked, ready to tail the Ford as soon as she got into it. As she reached the Ford, Eddie leaned over, raised the lock button, and opened the door for her. "Get in and let's get moving," he said brusquely.

She got in and felt a wave of apprehension engulf her, unable to speak, only obey. And pray silently. There was no exchange of conversation until Eddie pulled out into the heavy traffic pattern, reached Sepulveda, then turned off onto Manchester Avenue.

"Everything okay, beautiful?" he said then.

"No problems," Sharon replied. "It was a breeze, but I'd like to get out of this damned rig. I feel like a packhorse."

Eddie laughed briefly, guiding the car smoothly, carefully, through traffic. "Not packhorse, baby. The terminology is mule."

"Whatever it is, I'll be glad to be out of it."

"Pretty soon now. Relax. The toughest part is over."

And Sharon thought, *How would you like to place a big, fat bet on that, Eddie boy?*

Her shoulder bag, with the two-inch detective special, was on her left side next to Eddie. She removed it casually and switched it to her right shoulder and unfastened the catch with her right hand. Eddie didn't appear to notice, his eyes on the road ahead, aware of the traffic. She wanted desperately to look back through the rear window to see if she could pick up one of the tail cars, but decided that the move might divert his attention from his meticulous handling of the car. Up ahead, he grew momentarily tense when they saw an L.A.P.D. black-and-white patrol car cruising along, but it turned right into Pershing and was out of sight by the time they reached that corner. A few blocks beyond, they came to Vista del Mar and were heading into Playa del Rey, where Eddie turned left, the ocean now on their right.

"Where are we going to do this?" Sharon asked.

"I've got just the right spot picked out. It's close by."

"Out in the open? For God's sake, Eddie, I've got to strip to get this thing off," she protested indignantly.

Eddie grinned owlishly. "It'll be dark enough. Nobody but you and me'll know about it."

"Oh, man. You don't make it easy for a girl, do you?"

"Come on, Terry, what's the hassle? It won't be the first time you stripped down in front of a dude."

"I know, but never in public."

"Don't let it bother you. I'm only interested in what you're carrying, not what's under it. You can do it in the back. I'll be sitting right here behind the wheel. Hey, here we are." He made a left turn into Sandpiper, drove half a block, and parked, turned the lights off. There was only one light at the corner of Trask, ahead of them, the rest of the street and houses on either side dark, cars parked intermittently on both sides of Sandpiper. "Get in the back and get the rig off fast as you can. Let's go."

Expertly, the three tail cars had proceeded from Los Angeles International into Manchester, in visual contact with the blue Ford and by car radio with each other when voice contact was necessary. Russ McNeely, in unit David-6-Mary-2-Sam, with Steve Barrett, Perry Roberts, and Harry Deliso in David-6-Mary-3, Joe Paul and Ray Ycaza in Ycaza's David-3-Adam-7. As they reached Vista del Mar, McNeely contacted Ray and suggested that he pass the Ford and maintain a six-car-length distance in front to watch for a turnoff, in which case, David-3-Adam-7 would make a similar turn on the street next to that one and parallel it. Ray complied and passed the Ford without glancing at it.

At Sandpiper, the Ford braked and made a left turn. McNeely flashed the word to Deliso and Ycaza, then passed the corner slowly, saw the Ford's lights go off. He then pulled to the extreme left side of Vista del Mar, parked, and got out, Barrett on his heels.

Deliso had turned up Bolt to the next cross street, Trask, parked at Trask and Sandpiper out of view of the Ford. Ycaza turned left into Ivalee, then left again on Trask within a few feet of Sandpiper. The six men, in their locations, looked for and found shadows, then began to move in on foot, crouching behind the cars parked at the curbs.

In the rear section of the Ford, Sharon began removing her uniform jacket, then unbuttoned her blouse. Before removing it, she reached back and pulled the harness zipper down, uttering a sigh of relief to escape its confinement. She slipped the blouse off and began to remove the harness over her shoulders, then looked up and saw Eddie had turned to watch her. "Hey, you're cheating," she exclaimed.

He grinned and said, "For a thousand bucks, baby, I'm entitled to a look."

"Okay," Sharon said, "take a good look and let your tongue hang out."

"Don't let it bother you, baby. I've got my own thing, and you're not it."

She had the harness over her head now, moving slowly, allowing Eddie his thousand-dollar look at her firm, round breasts, looking beyond him through the windshield, hoping to catch a glimpse of someone, anyone, coming down on them to take Eddie out, unable to see the crouching figures behind the parked cars. She had Eddie made as a fag now, that part of little concern to her, and then she had the harness off and placed it beside her on the seat while she slipped the blouse on and slowly began buttoning it, killing more time.

"Hand it to me," Eddie said, and she folded the harness over twice and passed it to him. He took it, felt its weight, then shoved it into the opening beneath the driver's seat. She was halfway through the buttoning process then and said, "How about the rest of the loot, Eddie?"

"Sure." He reached into his jacket pocket and withdrew his wallet, saying, "Come up front and get it."

She picked up her uniform jacket and slung it over her left arm, then opened the rear door and got out, reaching into her purse to feel the comfort of the pistol grip that lay inside. At that moment, she saw McNeely and Barrett crouching behind her at the rear of the Ford, guns in hand, motioning her out of the line of possible fire. She turned, opened the front door and leaped aside as McNeely rose up and pushed his way inside and onto the front seat, his .38 barrel leveled at Eddie's chest. "Sheriff's Narcotics! Freeze! You're under arrest!"

Eddie turned toward the left door in alarm, only to come face to face with Harry Deliso's gun, aimed at the side of his head. "Hands on top of your head where I can see 'em, Eddie," Deliso ordered. "Come out slowly and don't make any sudden moves. This little thing makes big holes."

Eddie slumped back into his seat and slowly placed his hands on top of his head. "Come on, move it," Deliso ordered. Eddie slid out on the left side, lips drawn in a tight, grim line, eyes flashing with pure venom. Sharon looked on from the opposite side of the car. "You lousy whore bitch!" he exclaimed in a sudden outburst of fury.

Deliso slammed him up against the car and held him there. "Get your hands up on top of the car, feet spread apart and out."

There were seven against him, and any action on his part, he knew, would be senseless. Then Roberts was patting him down, found no other weapons. Ycaza put his cuffs on Eddie's wrists behind him and led him to McNeely's car. "You want to ride with me, Ray?" McNeely asked.

"No. We'll follow you in. I'll talk to him at the station."

"Sherry?"

"I'll ride in with Perry," she said, unwilling to be close to Butler, even with cuffs on and separated by a full seat.

At the station, before talking with Butler, McNeely took her aside. "How do you feel, Sherry?"

"I don't think you'd believe me if I told you," she said.

"How would you like a few days off, relaxing at the beach?"

"Oh, man, you've just won a permanent place in my heart."

"You've earned it. I'll square it with Barker and the captain. And Rachel. Okay?"

"Double okay."

4●

During two hours of interrogation, Butler refused to talk, even to admitting what they had already learned: his name, address, prior record, involvement in this most recent misadventure. A check on his telephone bills over the past four months showed no toll or long-distance calls, nor had they expected any would show up. In Butler's business, such calls would have been made from public telephone booths.

They had obtained a search warrant, gone through the house on Warren Canyon Drive, and come up empty-handed. There was no sign that anyone other than Butler occupied the premises, male or female. If Peterson lived there with him, he had obviously removed every trace of his personal belongings and presence. Information from neighbors elicited little more than surprise and descriptions; the two men had been seen coming and going from the residence, but at odd and irregular hours. They were quiet, kept to themselves, had no known visitors, made no effort to be friendly, held no parties, and were, in fact, seldom seen. One man suggested that they were homosexuals in need of the kind of privacy they sought.

"What about your buddy?" Ycaza asked on the third day of questioning at the County Jail.

"What buddy?" Butler asked.

"The guy you've been living with."

"I live alone, man."

"Come on, Eddie. I mean the big dude. Moose Peterson."

Butler smiled and said calmly, "I don't know any Mooses. Or is the plural Meese?"

"You did time together in Soledad. He got out three months after you and came to L.A. where you wired in together, lived together up on Warren Canyon Drive."

"Prove it."

"We will, Eddie. We'll have plenty of time to do that while you're on ice."

"You finished with me now?"

"Not yet. I want to give you a name to think about while you're relaxing in our little country club here." He paused, then said, "Ann Stennis." He watched Butler's face closely for some reaction, missed it when Butler suddenly looked away and reached for a cigarette.

"Never heard of her," he said.

"You're very sure about that?"

"Damn sure. I don't know the name at all."

Ycaza waited, watching him. Butler was devoting an uncommon amount of attention to his cigarette, examining it, rolling it between his fingers, avoiding the eyes of the detective.

"Okay, Eddie," Ycaza said, "you're in deep this time, and we've got you cold on the narcotics rap. If you get out in under fifteen years, that will be a red-letter day in your life. Meanwhile, if you feel in a talking mood, get in touch."

Butler smiled.

"You got a reversal five years ago, compliments of the state of California," Ycaza continued, "but the circumstances are a lot different this time. Think about it."

208

Butler assumed an air of indifference. "You're wasting your time and mine, man. I beat that rap, and I'll beat this one."

On their way back to headquarters, Ycaza said, "That skinny bastard is in with the same crew that killed Ann Stennis. I know it. I can feel it."

"Maybe," McNeely said, "but just try to get a murder complaint on a hunch, and some assistant D.A. will laugh you out of his office."

"Yeah, but—"

"But what?"

"Screw the assistant D.A. I'm staying with it. He's all I've got to go on."

"Sure, Ray. Meanwhile, we've got him on the dope rap, and he's not going anywhere until his hearing; then he'll probably go out on bail."

"When he does, I won't be too far away from him."

"Well, on a good 11501-C, he's good for up to fifty thousand bail. If we could find Peterson and tie him into Butler, that could be something else again."

"Look, I'm just as hot for Peterson as you are. Could be we could squeeze him if he and Butler are as cozy as I think they are."

"Sure. If we come up with anything on our end, I'll let you know."

"Okay. Let's keep in touch."

Back at Lennox later, there were other matters to occupy McNeely's time and thoughts—an accumulation of paperwork, neglected over the past few days. Deliso and Roberts were out setting up a buy from a doctor who specialized in weight-control reduction problems and had been selling an inordinate amount of pills to men and women, many of whom had no weight problem at all. Joe Paul was talking to an informant in his one-room apartment on Ravenna Avenue in Carson who wanted to turn in his ex-wife, a pusher, now living with a former friend. Steve Barrett was discussing a case with an assistant D.A. in Inglewood. It was nearing five o'clock, and McNeely decided to check out for the day.

On his way home, he dropped in at Bonnie's and had a drink with Chuck Nelson and learned that Chris Corman had taken his advice and gone home to Denver to visit her family for a month, a security measure against retaliation from Butler or any of his possible associates, whoever they might be. Chris's fiancé, Roger Lamb, had gone with her. McNeely had the one drink with Chuck, then stopped by Rachel's shop and persuaded her to have dinner with him at the Skylark in Redondo Beach.

5●

In Don Reed's apartment on Alicante Drive in West Hollywood, Moose Peterson sat dejectedly in a leather swivel chair, a drink in one hand, watching a daytime-television game show with little interest. The comfortable sofa was open, sheets rumpled, pillows askew. On the floor in one corner was an open suitcase jumbled with an assortment of clothing and personal belongings he had hastily removed from the Warren Canyon house the moment he received the phone call from Eddie Butler advising him of his arrest, asking him to notify Reed. The '71 Cadillac was stored in the Tri-City yard in San Pedro, its tags removed, hidden among a dozen or more wrecked carcasses.

He looked up when he heard movement at the door, a key being inserted in the lock. He stood up quickly and moved behind it. The door opened about three inches, held by the chain guard, then he heard Reed's voice. "Moose?"

"Yeah." Peterson closed the door, removed the chain guard, and admitted Don Reed, who stared at the unmade sofa bed, the stub-filled ashtray, and whiskey bottle and glasses.

"For Christ's sake, Moose, are you afraid of a little fresh-air poisoning? Open some windows and let a little of this stink out. And make up the bed after you sleep in it, can't you?"

"Christ, Don," Peterson complained, "I've been cooped up here for almost a goddamn week. Eddie's in jail; you haven't been around—"

"That's no excuse for turning this place into a pigsty, is it?" Reed went to the television set and turned it off. "And keep off the booze—" He stopped in mid-sentence, dropped into a chair, and said in a more even voice, "Sit down, Moose. Let me bring you up to date on what's going on, why I haven't been around." When Moose was seated, he continued, "I've got Paul Landis working on Eddie's case. The D.A. is going to ask the limit on his bail, fifty thousand. What's more, Paul tells me the sheriff's people are looking for you as an accessory, which means the L.A.P.D. will be cooperating with them. You've got to get out of here, hole up somewhere else, a safe place to lay low until things cool off."

"That won't be too hard, but I miss Eddie—"

"For now, you'll have to forget Eddie until he's out on

bail. In the meantime, I've got Anse Talbot to turn his operation over to his number-two man, Del Foreman. Anse is coming up from Orange County to take over contact with our distributors here until Eddie is out of the woods."

Peterson stared open-eyed at Reed. "Landis thinks he can get Eddie off on this rap?" he asked with incredulity.

"Not entirely. Eddie will have to take some kind of a fall, he thinks, but we'll get him out on bail first, then stall the case until he can get it before a friendly judge who'll give him the minimum. If we can work a deal with the D.A., Eddie will cop a plea on a lesser charge."

"What'll that get him?"

Reed shrugged. "A year in county, maybe less if—"

"If what?"

"The problem is Whitey Lloyd. If Lloyd testifies, they'll have him on that rap as well, and the D.A. will throw the book at him."

"What about the broad who set Eddie up?"

"The girl in Manhattan Beach? Don't worry about her. She's an ex-hype, and Landis can handle her. He has an idea he can convince a judge that there was entrapment involved. But right now, Whitey is the guy we've got to concern ourselves with. His is the testimony that can hurt."

"Yeah," Peterson agreed.

"So—'"

Peterson stared at Reed for a moment while the message got to him slowly. "You want him taken out?"

"It would help one hell of a lot to get Eddie out of this bind."

"Okay. I know where his pad is. I could tail him and—"

"Not you, Moose. You're into this too deep as it is, and you're too identifiable. I don't want anything as obvious as a hit on the street, in a telephone booth, or in a barber chair. If we can make it look like a dope ripoff, some pusher looking for his dope stash—"

"Yeah. Sure. You're right. I know a dude who can pull off a deal like this."

"Can you get in touch with him quickly?"

"Sure. A real pro. A black dude."

"Where?"

"Works anywhere, lives in Vegas. Name's—"

"I don't want to know his name. Is he safe?"

"Sure. Told you, he's a pro, a real hit man. But he don't work cheap."

"How much?"

"Twenty-five hundred ought to do it for a job like this."

"Okay. You'll need a car. I'll have Hernandez get one for you. Get your things together. Late tonight, I'll drive you down to San Pedro and get you the car. You'll have to find yourself a safe place to hole up, then get in touch with your man, meet him, and lay it out for him. I'll get the twenty-five hundred for you. Give him half in advance, the other half when the job is done. All right?"

"Yeah, sure."

"Okay. I've checked out Lloyd's apartment house. There are two units available for rent at Rolling Hills Villa, and there are at least two black families living there, so that won't be a problem. I've seen them coming and going, which makes the setup perfect, the way I have it figured out. Listen carefully, Moose.

"Your man should be dressed like a straight, a business executive recently moved to the area from the East looking for an apartment. Call Cora Thomas at the Newton Street drop and get her to put him up there until the job is done. Have her rent a car for him—"

6●

Two nights later, at 9:30, Moose Peterson lay on the pull-down bed in the furnished efficiency apartment on Loma Vista Avenue in Lakewood. Since Eddie Butler's arrest, he had not shaved and had darkened his hair, newly grown beard, and mustache by several shades with a commerical lotion. Outside on the parking lot stood the gray '69 Dodge two-door that Simon Hernandez had furnished from the Tri-City wrecking yard where the '71 Cadillac lay hidden. The tags on the Dodge had been removed from an abandoned Chrysler and not turned in to MVD.

Under the name of Norman Abbott, he had rented the small apartment, one of twelve units, in a crowded section near a large shopping center, where he felt he could shop for food and other necessities without too much danger of being recognized. The telephone had been installed under his alias, to be used only for incoming calls.

It had taken two days to reach Walt Dyer at his apartment in Las Vegas, and now he waited for Dyer to make an appearance, somewhat nervous and apprehensive. In all the time he and Eddie had shared the Warren Canyon house, this was the first time they had been separated longer than overnight, and only now did he realize how much he had relied on Eddie.

He got up off the bed and tried to move about, but the single bed–living room, small bathroom, and tiny kitchen hardly permitted pacing room for the big man. The small black-and-white television set that was bolted to the wall gave poor reception, but he could not afford to complain to the aging manager of the Loma Vista Apartments and thus call undue attention to himself.

At 9:50 he heard steps in the hallway and paused, waiting. The steps came to a halt at his door. He went to it expectantly. On the first knock, his hand was on the grip of the .38 in his shoulder holster. "Who is it?" he asked in a low voice.

"Walt," came the reply, and Peterson opened the door.

Walt Dyer came into the room cautiously, eyes alert, moving to take in the whole scene in a single glance. He was just over chest-high to Peterson's bulk, about twenty-seven years old, a slender, cinnamon-colored man with straight black hair, thin features, and piercing black eyes. He was clean-shaven except for a thin mustache over thin lips, and his clothes, casual jacket, flare-bottomed slacks, and sports shirt, were neat and well fitted to his body.

"Hey, Moose," he greeted without smiling, "what's with the heat?," indicating the .38 he was holding at his side.

"Not for you, Walt. That's for uninvited guests."

"Yeah, well, put it away, man. Those things make me nervous."

"Sure." Peterson holstered the gun. "You want a drink?"

"Not now. After we talk, maybe. What's doin'? Didn' get much from you on the phone."

"Sit down. The chair. I'll take the bed."

Dyer sat down and looked around him, then back to Peterson. "Okay, Moose, what you got goin'?"

"Something in your line, Walt. I need a good clean job with a good setup."

"Yeah? Lay it on me an' I'll tell you how good the setup is."

"Okay." Peterson gave him the details exactly as Don Reed had outlined them: Lloyd's name, description, and address; Cora Thomas's rented house, within a mile of Lloyd's apartment, where he could stay during the operation; then the method.

It was the method that gave Dyer cause for the most

thought, and after many questions, he decided in its favor. "What about the pad, the broad, and the car?" he asked.

"It's a small house, 4717 Newton Street, one of the telephone drops we use. The broad's name is Cora Thomas—"

"Black, brown, or paddy?"

"White, but don't let that throw you, Walt. A good-looking chick who's been through the mill. She'll rent the car for you with a phony credit card and return it after the hit goes down."

Dyer nodded approval. "I want the bread up front."

"What are you talking about?"

"Three big ones."

Peterson shook his head. "Twenty-five hundred, Walt. That's all I've got for the job. That's it."

"Three."

"Can't make it, Walt. I can give you twelve-fifty on the handshake, the other half when I read in the *Times* he's been totaled. That's the way the man laid it out."

"Fifteen an' fifteen or I walk, Moose."

Peterson shrugged. "Then walk. Glad to hear you're doing so good you can turn up your nose at twenty-five hundred."

Dyer laughed then, not with humor, but evilly. "Okay, paddy, long's I'm here, I'll take this one. Next time, you can't come up with three, don't call me, okay?"

Gratified with success, Peterson smiled. "Sure, Walt." He pulled out a wad of bills and handed it over. Dyer counted out the twelve hundred-dollar bills and one fifty. They shook hands, and Peterson gave him the slip with Cora Thomas's address and instructions how to get there from Lakewood, another with Whitey Lloyd's address, then a small package of business cards. "Stash those in your car. Take a taxi over to Cora's pad sometime tomorrow after you put yours in a garage somewhere. Get on it as fast as you can. The man wants it closed out by the end of the week. Make sure it looks like a dope ripoff—"

"I got it, Moose. Don't tell me how to do my job, man."

"Okay. The minute it shows up in the paper, come back and pick up the other half."

"Don't worry about that part of it. Just you be here with it. I'll see you."

Dressed to Peterson's specifications in a neat business suit, hat, and carrying a slim attaché case, Walt Dyer fit his assumed role adequately, that of an upcoming business executive. In the yellow Torino rented for him by Cora Thomas,

Dyer had spent two whole days and nights in the vicinity of Whitey Lloyd's apartment house, checking him out in the morning, back in at night, studying his pattern of movement. He made no effort to tail Lloyd to see where he was going, interested only in when he returned, usually around midnight.

On the third morning, when Lloyd drove away in the '72 Chevvy sedan he was currently using, Dyer pulled into the apartment complex, parked, and walked to the small office of the manager, Harold Lawton. Mr. Lawton was pleased and eager to show the vacant apartments to the gentleman whose business card read: WATERS HYDRAULIC EQUIPMENT, 1780 Broadway, New York, N.Y. 10019, (212) 265-7330. In the lower left corner, the name: John Hall Ellison, *Director of Sales, West Coast.*

Mr. Ellison rejected the one-bedroom apartment, but reacted favorably on 242, a two-bedroom affair at three seventy-five per month on a one-year lease, first and last month's rent in advance. He was, in fact, very impressed and delighted with the lush gardens, pool, recreation room, and ample parking space. He had, he informed Mr. Lawton, been transferred to Southern California to take over the Western region sales organization and would be joined by his wife early next month when his furniture was due to arrive. No, no children, no pets.

At exactly noon, as preplanned with Cora Thomas, Mr. Lawton was summoned to the telephone by his wife to take a call from a woman who said she was calling for the city attorney on an important matter. Mr. Lawton apologized for the interruption and went to his office to take the call. Leaving Dyer alone in 242. And the master key in the lock. Swiftly, Dyer removed an oblong block of plasticene clay from his jacket pocket, then removed the key and made an impression of it on one side of the clay block, a second on the other side. He then replaced the key in the lock.

When Lawton returned, complaining of the "idiot who hung up the moment I answered the phone," Dyer agreed to take the two-bedroom apartment and handed Lawton a one-hundred-dollar bill as a deposit until the following day when he would return to sign the required one-year lease that was to be prepared for his signature.

By ten-thirty that night, Dyer was in possession of a replica of the master key to every apartment at Rolling Hills Villa.

More pertinently, to Whitey Lloyd's apartment, 200.

Chapter Seven

1•

The day had begun warm and by midafternoon turned hot and humid. Ramon Ycaza and Danny Geiger had spent fruitless hours questioning a list of people who lived near the small Fix-It Shop of Carlos Mena, Mexican-American, 68, five-seven, 145 pounds, gray hair, brown eyes, who had been stabbed and bludgeoned to death two nights before in the back room of his shop where he lived. A customer, calling for a toaster she had left to be repaired the day before, thought it strange that the shop was not open at its normal time, eight thirty A.M. Even stranger that it was still closed when she returned two hours later.

Thinking that Carlos might have been taken ill, she started toward the rear of the store when she saw a black-and-white coming down Avalon Boulevard and hailed it. The deputies, who knew Carlos Mena, investigated and found his body in the back room. In the shop, the lock on a glass-enclosed wall case had been ripped off, one entire shelf swept clean. From store owners on either side of the Fix-It-Shop, the deputies learned that the shelf had held a number of handguns that had been left to be repaired. A record book showed the number of missing weapons to be four.

The case was assigned to Ycaza and Geiger. There were

no fingerprints, only several bloodied footprints leading from the back room to the store proper, but these were blurred and not clearly distinguishable, as though the murderer had dragged something across them to wipe the blood away. They found a towel in a trash barrel that had been used for that purpose. Time of death was set between eleven P.M. and two A.M.

Lab men had photographed the small, thin body from every angle, showing each stab wound, each blow that had landed on his skull. They took dust particles and small pieces of debris from various parts of the rooms, the lock still attached to its hasp, the dirt from beneath Mena's fingernails, and chalked the outline of his body where it lay crumpled on the floor.

Detectives had fanned out from the shop to talk to people, but learned nothing. The murder of Carlos Mena was now the responsibility of Ycaza and Geiger, to be added to their backlog of pending cases.

It was, of course, a ripoff by someone in need of guns, a valuable commodity either for sale, personal use, or to be traded for narcotics, and it was believed that the break-in had been committed by more than one perpetrator. Ycaza had the strong feeling that it was a gang-oriented job since only the guns had been taken, other usable items left behind. Over the past few months there had been an increase in youth-gang crimes, and Patrol had been gathering up guns, knives, homemade blackjacks, chains, and other weapons from students and street hoodlums. The ensuing shortage marked the Fix-It Shop for burglary and, incidentally, murder, evidenced by the signs of struggle in the back room.

They had parked the car just around the corner from the shop and were about to get into it to return to the Hall of Justice when a voice called out, "Hey! Mr. Ycaza!"

Ray turned and saw Rudy Arboleya dressed in tan mechanic's coveralls approaching from Carson Street. "Hey, Rudy. Long time, eh? How are you?"

"Okay. What you doin' down here, slumming?"

"Business. How's the job?"

"Okay," and with a widening grin, "I'm on top of it."

"How are Isobel and Robert?"

"Both great, man."

"Shake hands with my partner, Danny Geiger. Danny, this is an old friend, Rudy Arboleya."

The two shook hands perfunctorily and with no particular display of enthusiasm, acknowledging each other with mild

218

disinterest. To Geiger, "friend" could mean bare acquaintance or a snitch. Rudy said, "Can I talk to you a minute, Mr. Ycaza?"

"Sure, Rudy, but not until you knock off the 'mister' and call me Ray."

Rudy grinned boyishly. "Okay, Ray." He glanced at Geiger again and said, "Private?"

Geiger was certain now that Rudy was an informant; probably for a few dollars he could work out of Ycaza. He unlocked the car, got in behind the wheel, started the motor, then turned on the radio and air conditioner.

Ycaza moved a few steps away from the car. "What's on your mind, Rudy?"

"Hey, listen. I was goin'a call you. I only been out a little while now, you know, workin' steady, even got a savings account goin'."

"That's fine, Rudy. Glad to hear everything's going so well for you."

"Not everything. Like, Isobel, Robert, an' me livin' in the same house, you know? Well, we been talkin' it over, an' we want to get married, make it legal, you know, but my parole guy Tom Lopata, he don't think it's such a good idea, all my parole time left to do."

"Are you telling me you have to get married, Rudy? Isobel isn't pregnant, is she?"

Rudy flushed. "No. Hell, no, man, nothin' like that. Yeah, we been, you know, but she's not pregnant. Thing is, she had a strict old man an' old lady, religious an'— Hell, you know Isobel better'n me. It's kinda tough on her livin' this way."

"You want me to talk to Lopata for you, try to work it out with him, is that it?"

"Well, you know him. I thought maybe if you—"

"I'll call him in the morning and have a talk with him. Okay?"

"Hey, thanks, man. It'll make Isobel happy. Me, too."

"Don't spring anything on her yet. Give me a chance to talk to Tom first."

"Sure, Ray. I appreciate it."

"Okay. You're a lucky dude. Isobel is a fine girl."

"Yeah, I know it. I owe you."

"Forget it." Ycaza started his hand up in a "good-bye" wave, then checked it. "Rudy, you hear anything about the ripoff down here the night before last, anybody talking—"

"You mean old Carlos?"

"Yes."

"Hell, everybody's talkin' about it. I didn't know him, but they say he was a nice old guy. Lived and worked here most of his life. Moved in back of the store when his old lady died about six years ago."

"I know. We got that from his neighbors. You hear anything else?"

"Well, like the guys in the shop are always talkin'. Most of 'em knew the old guy, but I don't know how much of it is straight, you know?"

"Like what, Rudy?"

"Well, like they figure it was some of the Duke gang down on Piru Street. They seen a couple of the Dukes around here lately, way off their own turf. Figure they ripped Mena off for them guns."

"The Dukes, up here?"

"Yeah. Cruisin' aroun', you know, like they're casin' a job. They were aroun' a couple of times, but nobody seen 'em since the ripoff."

The Dukes. Like the Cripps. Like any of a dozen similar gangs in the area. "They see anybody they could put a name to, Rudy?"

"They mentioned one, Robbie James, goes by the name Jesse. I seen that one myself. Big ugly kid, maybe seventeen or eighteen, got a face looks like meat loaf."

"Jesse James. The name's familiar." Then as an afterthought, "Goddamn it, Rudy, we've had a dozen or more of our people talking to everybody down here and couldn't get a word out of them about the Dukes being in the neighborhood."

"Hell, Ray," Rudy said, "you expect people down here to talk to cops about gangs? You think they want to get a gasoline bomb tossed in their car? Anyway, they probably figure to take a trip down to Piru and blow up the Dukes and their clubhouse. These honchos around here'll do it too, unless you guys beat 'em to it."

"Okay, Rudy, thanks. When do you have to see Tom again?"

"Regular day, next week, Thursday."

"Okay. By then he'll have something to tell you, one way or another."

"Sure. Thanks, Ray."

In the car, Geiger said petulantly, "Can we head for the barn now? We're on call tonight, and I'd like to sack in early. We've been on this one two days, and I'm bushed. I'll lay you ten to one we get called out tonight."

Ycaza said, "It isn't three o'clock yet. We've got time to take a run down to Piru Street."

"What's down there?"

"The Dukes. And the Dukes' clubhouse." He picked up the microphone and called in, requesting a back-up team to meet them near the location and a two-man black-and-white to stand by.

At 3:40, they had met Bob Timmins and George Fields, discussed the situation, and advised the black-and-white, 14/Edward, where to cruise so as not to raise any suspicions. They had then cruised the Piru Street area and located the clubhouse, an abandoned shacklike structure easily recognizable by the decorations on the once-white plastered front in bright colors that had been sprayed on in enamel: individual names, the club name, obscene references to all lawmen, examples of lewd art. Our turf. Outsiders keep off.

In passing separately in their cars, they had heard radio music playing and voices, both male and female. Outside, the ground was strewn with beer cans and a litter of paper and refuse. The front door hung loosely on one upper hinge, and one of the two front windows was boarded up, the other without its original frame or glass.

At four o'clock, Ycaza passed the word. Timmins and Fields came down the alley behind the house, and Geiger ran his car up on the pavement in front, stopping short of the bottom step. Behind them, the black-and-white rolled up. With one shotgun and three revolvers ready, they kicked the front door aside and entered.

Inside were seven black males ranging in age from fifteen to nineteen. The four black girls were younger, from thirteen to fifteen. Four were dancing in the center of the barren room, the others seated on the floor, backs to the wall, listening and watching. The only furniture in the room was several wooden crates, one of which held the small transistorized radio, another with three six-packs of beer.

In the back room, when Timmins and Fields entered from the rear, one couple lay on a thin straw mat copulating; as the officers intruded, they parted, with shrieks from the girl and curses from the boy. Timmins ordered the pair to dress, then took them into the front room.

"Everybody," Ycaza ordered, "up on your feet, face the wall." The Dukes and their duchesses obeyed slowly and sullenly, cursing, muttering obscenities. The boys were patted down quickly, the girls scanned. From the tallest, heaviest male, about seventeen, Geiger took a .32 automatic. From another, about sixteen, a double length of chain that was wrapped around his waist and a switchblade knife. The automatic was, according to his record book, on the list of guns taken from the Mena Fix-It Shop.

Ycaza handcuffed the boy from whom Geiger had taken the automatic and removed him to the back room. His description fit the one given him by Rudy: one side of his dark brown face was deeply pitted—"a face looks like meat loaf." He had nothing on him with a name that could identify him.

"What's your name?" Ycaza asked.

"None of your fuckin' business."

"Okay. You want to get tough, we'll show you how tough we can make it for you, Mr. Robbie James, alias Jesse James." The name hit home. Ycaza saw it in his eyes. "You're under arrest for the murder of Carlos Mena. That's premeditated murder, Murder One, the Big Casino, smartass, committed during an act of planned burglary to obtain guns. I'm going to read your rights to you."

"Skip the bullshit, pig."

"You'll listen whether you like it or not. You have a right to remain silent. Anything you say can and will be used against you in a court of law. You have the right to talk to a lawyer before we talk to you and to have him present while we talk to you. If you cannot afford to hire a lawyer, one will be appointed to represent you before any questioning, free of charge. Do you understand each of the rights explained to you?"

There was no response.

"Do you want to talk about this case or not?"

Sullen silence.

"Do you want a lawyer or not?"

"Shove it, man."

"Okay, big man. That .32 we took off you came from Carlos Mena's shop. Where's the rest of it?"

"No way, pig."

Geiger came in. "Anything, Ray?"

"Yeah. Let's take this dump apart."

Timmins and Fields came in then, leaving the two uniformed deputies to guard the others in the front room. They began the search in the back room, Jesse James looking on. Then Fields, in the sinkless, stoveless kitchen, found the loose board in what was once a closet. He pulled it up and saw the open wooden box with the rest of the handguns, plus a sawed-off shotgun, two zip guns, an assortment of knives, a

Marlin .30-.30 rifle, and a store of shotgun shells, .22s, .38s, and .45s.

The suspects were transported to Firestone station to be booked, and Ycaza and Geiger returned to the Hall of Justice at 7:10. As they were leaving for their respective homes, Geiger said, "I'll still lay you ten to one we get called out tonight."

"That's what we get paid to do, Danny boy," Ycaza replied. Then, "If there's one thing I love about a good partner, Danny, it's his unflagging optimistic outlook toward life and his job."

2●

It had been six days since Whitey Lloyd had been released on bail. He had made one attempt to contact Eddie Butler before making his deal with McNeely, but Connie had insisted that Butler was "out of town on business." There was no use talking with Moose, who was without Butler's authority. Then, convinced that Butler, angry at getting burned for the cocaine and money, had cut him loose, he had placed the call to McNeely.

At his preliminary hearing, bound over for trial in Superior Court, he discovered that McNeely had come through for him and bail was set at twenty-five hundred dollars, which meant a bondsman's fee of only two hundred and fifty, easy enough to raise. But there was still the risk that at his trial in Superior, some heavy-handed judge could slap a ten on him, maybe even a fifteen. After all, once he had served his purpose, why in hell should he trust McNeely, the D.A., the judge, or the whole lousy system?

Now, as he drove away from his apartment in the car borrowed from Lee Michele, his mind blurred with thoughts of some way out of his difficulty. Butler, the best connection he had ever had, was lost to him. So was his prized Stingray, impounded by the narcs. He had a stash of about four thousand in cash and about fifteen hundred worth of marijuana and heroin. He considered an alternative to hanging around waiting for his trial date, an idea that had been rustling around in his mind for several days: jump bail and take off for Mexico.

He could push the weed and smack in his stash and add another fifteen hundred to his cash hoard. With over five grand, he could last a year below the border, try to get into something there, maybe set up a deal to move stuff north without having to cross the border himself. Use mules. He had a fair working knowledge of the language. That, or take the carrot McNeely dangled in front of his nose—a year in county jail—if he could believe a narc. But even in jail, Butler's long arm could reach him, find some way to rip him off.

He drove aimlessly and without direction, found himself in Santa Monica where he stopped for lunch at a drive-in, then hit a bar and consumed several glasses of beer. Later, he had his tank filled and followed the coastline south, loafing along. He thought bitterly of "Terry Dunn," the bitch who had set him up for the bust, and what might have been if she had been what he had naïvely, stupidly, believed her to be instead of an undercover narc. That face. That body. Jesus. The "in" he had dreamed of for so long, to become a really top operator. Somehow, he should have known it was too good to be true, but she had conned him good, and he had bought it.

He began again to think seriously about taking off for Mexico. Why the hell not? Loaded with Americans. Army vets living on pensions. Rich tourists. Hypes. Hippies. Runaways. Somewhere down there, he was sure he could come up with a good connection. No weed. Too damned bulky. Heroin. Coke. Smaller packages, easier to mule across the border.

He stopped for dinner at a Mexican restaurant in San Pedro to heighten his mood, and after his fourth Carta Blanca, he came to a firm decision. Tonight he would sell off the weed and smack in his stash. Tomorrow he would pack his belongings, take Lee's car, and head for Mexico. Lee could keep his furniture in exchange for his car.

San Diego, El Centro, Yuma, Tucson, Nogales, then south to wherever the roads led him. He could visualize places he had never seen before by their names. Hermosillo, Mazatlán, Guadalajara, Mexico City. Lay low for a couple of months. Find a broad to shack up with, one who could help him find the connection he wanted— He was with it now, getting high on it, and wanted action.

He drove to the Green Parrot on Pacific Avenue where he found Otts Kinney, not his best pusher acquaintance, but who would do in a pinch. And made a deal, after some bargaining, for an even thousand dollars if Otts could come up with the cash that night. Otts said it would take a few hours to put that kind of bread together, and they agreed to meet back at the Green Parrot at the two A.M. closing hour. Whitey knew that Otts was an untrustworthy thief and warned him. "No tricks, Otts. I'll be carrying my gun."

And Otts grinned and said, "Makes us even, Whitey boy. I'll be carrying mine, too."

They sat for a while drinking beer; then Otts left to start putting the thousand together. Whitey stayed behind and shot a few games of pool by himself, drank a few more beers, and shortly after midnight left to empty out his cache of dope and get back to San Pedro to meet Otts.

Whitey Lloyd never kept his appointment.

3 •

By the time he had eaten the dinner Yolanda had warmed up for him, the children had been bathed and sent to bed, the television set in the den turned off. Ray helped Yolanda clear the kitchen table, and standing at the kitchen sink drying the dishes as he handed them to her, she said, "Your son."

Ycaza grinned, wondering what *his* son had been up to. "Which one of our two beautiful sons are you talking about, Yo?"

"Robert, who else?"

"Let's have it. What did he do today, burn down the Fulton Avenue School or rip you off for some extra candy money?"

"No, but you'd better have a good talk with him."

"He's only six, Yo. He's not into *that* already, is he?"

"No, not *that*, but you'd better put your code book where he can't find it."

"My code book?"

"Yes, your code book." She began laughing and said, "We've got a genius on our hands. Six years old and he not only reads, he spells."

"Okay, come on. What's it all about?"

"He brought home a note from his teacher yesterday asking me to come see her. Today, I went." Yolanda began laughing harder, infecting Ray with it.

"So what's so terrible if you can laugh about it that way?"

"Oh, Ray." She took the towel from him and wiped her eyes with an edge. "Kids today, they're something. Robert got hold of your code book and learned a whole new alphabet. Adam, Boy, Charlie, David—"

"I know the code, Yo. What happened?"

"He got angry at a boy in his class who was teasing him and said, 'You get away from me, you Sam-Henry-Ida-Tom.' When the other boy called him a dirty Mex, Robert got furious and yelled, 'Frank-Union-Charlie-King, you, you stinking paddy!' The teacher heard it all and broke up the fight before it got started. Later, she began to think the Frank-Union thing over. It didn't take her long to figure out what Robert had called the boy. So, the note—"

Ray was laughing uncontrollably. "Hey, did you fix the rap, maybe get him off on probation?"

"This time, yes. The next time it happens, *you* will go to see her."

"Okay, I'll have a talk with *el hijo* and throw the code book away." He put the towel down and kissed her. "Hey, did she at least give Robert an A in Spelling?"

"Oh, you! Go on, get to bed. You're on call tonight."

"Hey, another half hour won't make any difference, call or no call."

She grinned at him and said, "Why is it you always get that way when you're on call?"

"I don't know. It's the homicidal tendency in me."

"All right, but—"

"No buts. Go get undressed, huh?"

It was a little past ten when they had finished making love, and regretfully, Ray got out of bed, put on his pajamas, and returned to the living room. On those nights when he was on call, the bedroom phone was turned down, the second phone plugged in beside the sofa bed in the living room so that Yolanda and the children would not be awakened if he were to be called out on an emergency.

He was in his third hour of sleep when the telephone began to shrill him awake at 0223. Reflexively, he reached for the receiver and lifted it on the first ring, held it to his chest while struggling to bring some sense of order to his sleep-confused mind. As he raised the instrument closer to his ear, he heard the voice of Burr Grant saying, "Come on, Ray. Hey, *amigo*, let's hear your melodious voice. I know you're there."

"Up yours, Burr," Ray grunted. "What's your problem?"

"I don't have any, but you've got a dead. Got a pencil handy?"

"Hold it." Ray sat up, turned on the lamp, and found his notepad and pen. "Okay. Let's have it."

"Two-five-nine-two-five Rolling Hills Road, just off Pacific Coast Highway, Rolling Hills. Victim's name, Whitey Lloyd, male, Cauc, twenty-eight, five-eleven, one hundred sixty-five pounds—"

"I'll get it all there. Heart attack?"

"Two slugs in the back of his head."

"Suicide, huh?"

"What else, with the weapon missing. Okay?"

"Yeah. You call Geiger yet?"

"On his way. He'll meet you there."

"Okay, Burr. Go back to your porny magazines. See you."

He shivered in the early-morning chill, then went to the bathroom and threw some cold water on his unshaved face, dressed quickly, and went outside. All about him was quiet, the neighboring houses dark, the world asleep. He backed the Dodge out of the garage, turned on the radio, and removed his battery-operated shaver from the glove compartment. Once on the freeway, he moved into the clear left lane, accelerated speed, and began shaving the stubble from his face. Geiger, who lived closer to the location, would be there before him, doing the preliminary work. Long ago he had given up wondering what awaited him at the scene of a homicide.

There was hardly any traffic at this hour, the night air vigorously cool. He finished shaving, concentrated on his driving and the disc jockey on KMPC, and reached the U-shaped apartment building in under thirty-five minutes. He parked the Dodge beside one of a pair of black-and-white patrol cars that stood near the stairway that led to the second level.

Lights were on in more than half the apartments on both levels. Curious tenants, most of them wearing robes over their nightwear, stood about in small groups talking in low voices, waiting to be interviewed by two uniformed deputies. On the balcony above, another uniformed officer stood guard at the entrance to apartment 200, and as Ycaza mounted the stairs, flashlight in hand, he saw Geiger talking to a robed young woman, making notations in his field book.

Geiger saw him approaching and stopped talking to the woman, but Ycaza waved, stabbing a finger in his direction, telling him silently to continue his questioning procedure while he took a look inside. To the deputy at the door, he said, "Ycaza, Homicide. You the handling crew?"

The deputy stepped aside. "Yeah. Harding, Lennox. My partner Maxwell is down below in the manager's apartment. Sergeant Davis and some of our guys are knocking on doors around here asking questions."

"Anybody been inside?"

"Only to check the body for some I.D. Found his driver's license and called the information in. Your partner went in to have a quick look around. Nobody else."

Ycaza nodded, and Harding opened the door for him. The lights were on. "Were the lights on when you got here?"

"Yes."

"Who found him?"

"The woman your partner's talking to, the victim's next-door neighbor. She was in bed watching a late TV movie. About the time she turned it off, she heard something, some movement, somebody walking around. She got out of bed and came out on the balcony, and all she saw was the head and shoulders of a guy, average size, according to her, going down the stairs, then heard him run down the driveway and outside. A couple of seconds later, she heard a car motor turn over and take off.

"The door was closed, lights on in the victim's apartment, the way they are now. She knocked and got no answer. Tried the door and it was locked, so she went down and knocked on the manager's door, a guy named Lawton. Your partner's talked to him already. He came up, unlocked the door, and they found the place all torn up, the way it is right now, and the victim lying across the bed, the way he's in there now. Lawton went down to his office and called the station. Maxwell and I rolled on it, then Dilworth and Larue, then our patrol sergeant, Wen Davis. They're all out trying to find somebody who may have seen the perpetrator."

"Okay, Harding, thanks. I'll talk to your partner later." Harding went out to take up his post again.

The living room was in a state of disarray, chairs and sofa moved from their original positions, pictures on the wall hanging at odd angles, a chest with its drawers opened, a cabinet with records and tapes strewn about. Similarly, the cabinets in the kitchen had been gone through, boxes of cereals lying on the ledge and floor, grains and flakes poured into the sink.

In the bedroom, the blond male victim lay across the unmade bed, face down, the back of his head a mass of gore, blood pooled on the blanket and sheets. He was fully dressed, shoes, slacks, shirt, jacket, his feet hanging over the near side of the bed. The room itself was in chaos, every drawer in the double dresser open, their contents spilled out on the floor. All but a few of the garments in the single closet had been flung in a pile on the floor, a shelf of books wiped clean, two suitcases open, shoes scattered among the debris. Even the cabinet in the bathroom had not been overlooked.

Then Geiger came in. "One hell of a goddamned mess."

"Yeah," Ycaza agreed. "Sonofabitch was looking for something he wanted to find very much."

"Yeah, man. How do you make it, Ray?"

"I don't, yet. Could have brought the dude home with him, could have been here when the shooter, whom he must have known, knocked on the door. Or the dude was already inside waiting for him to get home. What's with the girl next door?"

Geiger told him substantially what he had already heard from Deputy Harding, adding little else. "What about the manager?"

"Their stories back each other up."

"The tenants?"

"A total blank so far. Nobody but the girl heard or saw anything, not even the manager, who's in Apartment 100, directly below. Two shots and only the girl *thinks* she may have heard them, but can't be sure. She's really shook up."

Ycaza picked up one of the pillows lying on the floor beside the bed. It had two holes, showing powder burns, scorched around the edges. "A pro job," he said musingly, "knew what he was doing. Used that to deaden the noise. Look at the side of his neck, the bruise mark. Must have taken one hell of a chop there. Knocked him out, ransacked the place, then dragged him in here and blew him up. Anything on him?"

"Wallet was empty, watch missing. Just the usual crap left. Keys, change, a couple of loose bills, pen, pencil, cigarettes, lighter. It's all on the table in the living room."

"Looks like we've got us one, Danny boy."

"Sure does."

"You call in yet?"

"I called in to Burr. He said he'd make the necessary notifications."

"Okay. Go out and see what the guys have turned up, if anything."

Ycaza examined the driver's license, recording the statistics in his memory along with the photograph. He found Lloyd's social-security card in the wallet, a faded snapshot, its image unrecognizable, a gasoline credit card, bank credit card, a plain I.D. card with his name, address, and phone number, the item "Notify in case of accident" blank. He took up the key ring and studied the keys. Two were quickly identified as car keys, three smaller ones that evidently fit the two suitcases and a small bag. He tried them and found that they did fit. There were two Yale-type keys. He went to the front door and tried one. It didn't fit the lock. The second key did. He studied the one that didn't fit with some curiosity.

He returned to the bedroom and examined the body of the late Whitey Lloyd more carefully, trying to gauge the angle from which the shots had been fired. Downward. Lloyd had no doubt been unconscious, lying on the bed face down when the triggerman shot him twice, using the pillow to deaden the nóise of the gun. Despite the disarray in every room, there appeared to have been no physical struggle; his shirt and tie were in place, coat and slacks undamaged. A righteous ripoff. Execution.

He went to the phone and dialed Burr Grant. "Anything on this dead yet, Burr?"

"We've got it on the wire to Sacramento, checking the files. Nothing yet. How you doing?"

"Lousy. This dude didn't even have a can of beer in his refrigerator."

"Tough. Just for the record, it's slow as hell here. Kelleher is out on one in East L.A. A multiple."

"You bastard. Why don't you get off your fat ass and come down here and do a little work for a change?"

"Who, me? No way, man. Work is for peasants. Besides, I'm only halfway through this art magazine."

"Art? Shove it. See you, Burr."

The deputy coroner and lab men arrived a few minutes later, and the usual confusion took place. Ycaza remained in the bedroom while Lloyd's body was cursorily examined and officially declared dead, which was hardly news. The rooms, furniture, doorknobs, mirrors, and everything else that might possibly produce a print had been thoroughly dusted. They swarmed over the apartment like locusts, taking measurements, marking the position of the body on the bed with tapes, taking photographs from every possible angle, making sketches for a blowup rendering of the entire scene. Cursing under his breath, an artist drew in the furniture and items heaped about on the floors and kitchen ledges. Another man assisted him by taking meticulous inventory of those items, listing each and its position.

Meanwhile, other men were out on the streets and in the courtyard continuing their efforts to find someone who might have seen anything, heard anything, a human or vehicle in the area at or near the time of the murder.

The body was removed then, and Ycaza went down to the manager's office to talk with him and the girl who tenanted the apartment next to Lloyd's, 201, Lee Michele, a soft-speaking, unprepossessing female, twenty-eight, who was a teller in the Bank of America branch nearby.

Lee Michele repeated her story to Ycaza, unable to add to what she had told Deputy Harding and Danny Geiger. He sent her off to bed, then talked with Harold Lawton, the manager, who seemed to be enjoying his moment in the spotlight. Lawton had seen nothing unusual, had heard nothing

230

until Miss Michele wakened him and his wife by knocking on his door. He described his tenants as "good people, quiet, respectable adults who have never given me a moment's trouble."

"What about Mr. Lloyd?" Ycaza asked.

"No problems with him, either. Look, I don't pry into anyone's private life as long as they behave and pay their rent when it comes due. I don't know what Lloyd does—did—for a living. He didn't have much company, if any, that I know of, came and went quietly— Oh, yes, he did have some problem with his car a few weeks ago, a silver and black Corvette. Expensive. He told me it's been in the shop for repairs.

"This is a good, clean place, Sergeant, integrated, but with business and professional people. Always filled up. Only two apartments out of thirty-six are vacant, 116 and 242, and I've got a deposit on 242." Lawton produced a business card of the man who had inquired about 242. Ycaza recorded the data on the card in his notebook, asked for and received a description of John Hall Ellison, the light brown-complexioned black who, Lawton told him, said he was staying with friends temporarily.

Where? Mr. Ellison hadn't left an address or telephone number, had recently come out from the East, transferred from his New York office.

Yes, Mr. Lawton had noted Mr. Ellison's license number on the back of the card. Ycaza turned it over and saw the penciled notation. 368-SUL.

For any special reason?

No, just a usual business practice. Out of habit.

Ycaza recorded the number for the same reason. Habit.

4•

At 1000, Ycaza and Geiger were in Lieutenant Kelleher's office drinking coffee while the lieutenant, red-eyed and weary, looked over the original complaint report and first supplementary that Ycaza had dictated to a secretary at 0735. Kelleher had responded to a multiple homicide and suicide at 2240 the night before that had kept him busy until 0930. He pushed the papers away, sipped more hot coffee, then said, "Where are we right now?"

"Autopsy's set for 1045. We're waiting for CII to come through with anything they've got on him. Also the lab reports. We talked to as many people as were available last night and have some people canvassing the neighborhood, checking on anybody who might have seen a car leaving about the time of the murder. Somebody on foot, anything unusual. Danny and I are going back to check the place over again, talk to anybody in the unit who may remember something they overlooked or forgot last night."

"I see Burr notified the press. I haven't seen the morning *Times* yet. Anything there?"

"No. They probably got it too late."

"What's it look like to you, Ray?"

Ycaza shrugged. "I'd rather wait until we hear from Sacramento and the lab guys. Offhand it spells out to a goddamn execution, an attempt to make it look like a burglary. It's got a hit man's M.O., could be involved in gambling, dope, some racket. It sure as hell wasn't a burglary. There was a portable television set, a small radio, and a cassette recorder that weren't touched. But somebody was looking for something this guy had. A stash of some kind."

"One man?"

"I'd guess yes. The Michele girl saw the head and shoulders of an average dude disappearing from the scene down the steps. Of course, it's possible a second guy, if there was one, preceded him and was out of sight by that time, maybe waiting outside in a car."

"Yeah, that's possible."

Captain Art Sawyer came into the office and dropped heavily into the chair beside Kelleher's desk. "Ken, Ray, Geiger." He acknowledged their presence individually, then shook his head with a tight smile and said, "Ken, you keep lousy hours. You ought to try getting some sleep for a change. You look like hell. And you need a shave." He clucked his tongue inside his cheek and added, "Chief sees you looking like that, you could draw a reprimand."

Kelleher grinned wearily at Sawyer's homespun humor. "Yeah, sure, Art. I'll take care of it."

"What's happening?"

"Not a hell of a lot," Kelleher said, sliding Complaint and Supplementary across the desk, adding, "yet."

"What was your deal last night in East L.A.?"

Kelleher yawned. "No problems. The guy killed his wife and son, wounded the daughter, and stood off some neighbors with his twenty-two rifle. So damned many people all over the place, we didn't want to go charging in, couldn't use gas because of other people on the second floor who couldn't get out while this dude was behind a brick wall ready to take potshots at anything that moved.

"Patrol guys tried to talk him out of the house, but no

way. By the time we got there, he'd already fired a dozen rounds, but didn't hit anybody. Nobody fired back because they didn't know if there was anybody in there shootable besides the guy. Preston, Dembrow, and I worked our way around the back, climbed in through a window, and were in the hallway when he shot himself through the mouth. We got the girl to the hospital in time. She'll make it."

Sawyer had been scanning the reports and placed them on the desk. "Okay, Ray," he said, "you stay with this one. We don't need any more unsolveds."

"Sure, Cap," Ycaza said with not too much conviction.

"Ken," Sawyer said unnecessarily, "give him everything he needs," and went out.

Geiger, who had been almost unnoticed by the captain, looked very unhappy; the most recent addition, his presence was acknowledged but otherwise ignored. "Okay," Kelleher said, "take it from there, men."

Both stood up, retrieved their reports, and went back to their desks to arrange a schedule for the day.

They attended the autopsy and learned nothing they didn't already know. There was nothing as yet from the lab as far as a ballistics report was concerned. By midafternoon, they had assembled all the available information on Whitey Lloyd: arrest records from L.A.P.D. and sheriff's records, vehicle data, rap sheet from CII in Sacramento, plus one additional piece of information: that Russ McNeely and his MV crew had been involved in Lloyd's most recent bust.

Ray dialed the Lennox number, got the Narcotics office, and asked for McNeely. Perry Roberts took the call and informed him that Russ was out in the field and would not be in for the rest of the day.

"Leave word for him to call me in the morning, will you?"

"Sure. First thing."

"Hey, tell me, how important is a doper named Whitey Lloyd to you guys?"

"Heavy," Roberts told him. "He's out on bail on a deal to wire us into his chief honcho."

"Was," Ycaza said.

"What do you mean, was?"

"I hate to break it to you like this, but you can scratch him off the Red Cross list of possible blood donors. He got himself ripped off last night. Two slugs in the back of his head."

"Oh—Jesus. That blows the hell out of a good one. Where?"

"His pad on Rolling Hills Road. You know it?"

"Yeah, we know it. You got anything on it?"

"Just a dead. So far, nobody who saw anything but the head and shoulders of an unknown suspect—in the dark. We're just starting to dig into it."

"Keep in touch, will you?"

"That's what I'm doing now. And have Russ call me, will you?"

"Sure thing."

5•

He was still feeling an unusual sense of well-being over the arrest of Eddie Butler at dinner with Rachel at the Skylark in Redondo Beach. She was eager to hear the details, particularly the part Sharon Freeman had played in it. This time, because Sherry had stayed with Rachel for several days to lend background and credibility to her role as a Mex-Am stewardess, he filled her in on the details.

Rachel was aghast. "How could you possibly allow Sherry to expose herself that way, Russ? Those awful, ruthless people—"

"We had her covered, Rachel. Perry was with her on the flight, and we were waiting on this end."

"That darling girl. I don't understand it."

"That darling girl, Rachel, is as professional a cop as any man in the department, trained in her job and damned well skilled at it."

"And I suppose if she'd been killed, she'd have had one of those lovely televised buried-with-full-honors funerals?"

"Hey, why so morbid all of a sudden?"

"It's a morbid business. More like a war. When I think of the widows and fatherless children they leave behind, I shudder."

"Come on, let's forget it and concentrate on our food."

Rachel smiled and said, "She really is a lovely girl. Sherry, I mean. I enjoyed her company so much. She has a standing invitation to visit me any time she's free."

Russ laughed. "She's had the same invitation from half the guys in the bureau. Most of them are half in love with her."

The evening took a more relaxed turn, and Rachel expressed no further interest in the case nor in the fate of Eddie Butler. By eleven they were back in Rachel's apartment to listen to the Claudio Arrau recording she had bought that afternoon. Sipping brandy while listening, she said quietly, "Why didn't you and Carol have children?"

The question surprised and annoyed him. Carol was a subject he had never discussed at large with anyone, not even with those who had known her, keeping her locked away in his private memory bank. He said, "We never really talked about it except on the fringes. Never seriously. Why?"

"I thought all couples discussed children a lot, even before they got married. Bill and I did. We'd planned to have at least four after he returned from Vietnam."

There was an awkward silence then, and he knew she was still waiting for an answer to her original question. He said, "To be truthful about it, there never seemed to be a right time. Something was always happening. Carol's job and the difference in our working hours, our move to California, then to the beach. I'm glad now that we didn't."

"Wouldn't you want a son or daughter? Or both?"

"When I look around me, Rachel, and see what's happening to kids these days, the idea shakes me up a little. I'm not talking about ghetto street kids, but those from affluent homes in Bel Air and Beverly Hills, the Valley, here in our beach communities and schools. The peer group, follow-the-leader thing that parents can't control and give in to. I know they're in the minority now, but how long before they become the majority and pass on that same permissiveness to the next generation and those that follow?"

"Isn't that a classical cop exaggeration, Russ?"

"Perhaps. But most people don't see the situation the way we do, on the street, in jail for pushing or using, in the agonies of withdrawal, with parents who are sometimes addicted themselves or so straight they can't believe what they see when it reaches their own kids."

She sighed and said, "I wish you weren't so close to it."

His irritation showed then. "Do you think if I weren't, the situation would disappear by itself? That by trying to put an end to it, we are actually encouraging it?"

"No. I'm only thinking of the effect of it on your general outlook. I think you'd make a wonderful father if you'd allow yourself to think like one."

"Are you thinking of me or us?"

"Maybe both."

"Well, we could get married, and you could start in on a reform program."

"The first part is interesting. I'm not so sure about the second part."

"Then do we continue to go along the way we are?"

"For the present, I suppose that's the best we can do, isn't it?"

"The offer still holds good, Rachel."

"Thank you, Russ. Let's wait and see what happens."

In that sober, reflective mood, his earlier desire to make love to Rachel diminished somewhat, nor did he sense any urge on her part. He left then and returned to his house and slept fitfully.

When he left home early the next morning, his mood matched the foggy mist that hung over the coastline and curtailed his view of the ocean. On his AM radio, KMPC's Dick Whittinghill was cheerily promising sunny warmth with the high in the mid-seventies by early afternoon. Within half a mile of Lennox, dappled sunlight had begun breaking through the overcast, and the steady drone of planes could be heard as they reached for their designated runways approaching Los Angeles International.

The office was bustling with activity when he arrived; on the phones, at their typewriters, preparing to leave for court appearances or to obtain complaints from various D.A. offices. Of his MV crew, only Steve Barrett and Harry Deliso were present. Joe Paul was in the jail section handling the in-custodies, and Perry Roberts was not in. Steve and Harry brought their coffee cups to his desk and began to bring him up to date on a buy they had made the night before.

Russ checked the message blackboard and noted that Perry was due in South Bay Municipal Court, then the notation beneath: *Russ—Call Ray Ycaza, Homicide.*

"You know what that's about?" Russ asked Deliso.

"No. We saw it this morning when we came in."

"Where—?" He broke the question off when Bill Hamlin stopped at his desk and said, "I've just been talking to John Rivera downtown. He gave me a message for you."

"What's up?"

"Not up. Down. Somebody iced your crook, Whitey Lloyd, night before last. Took two in the back of his head. John got it off of yesterday's homicide report."

"Oh, Christ! Anything else on it?"

"No more than a short paragraph. No details."

"Oh, man. That puts a hole in our deal on Butler."

"Could be. Where's Butler now?"

"In county jail, waiting for his hearing."

"That let's him off the suspect list."

The phone rang, and Deliso answered it, looked up, and pointed to McNeely. "On four. Our leader."

Russ picked up the receiver. "Hello, Bob."

"Hi, Russ. You hear about Lloyd?"

"Just heard it. What've you got?"

"Not much, according to Homicide. Took him off in his pad around midnight or thereabouts. Two slugs, like to tore the back of his head off. They figure he was knocked out first, took the place apart, used a pillow to deaden the noise. The shooter spent quite a bit of time there."

"Oh, hell. That really tears our deal on Butler."

"Not altogether, but it doesn't help us any. Anyway, Homicide is sending somebody out to talk to you. See if you can fill him in or whatever you've got in your files on Lloyd."

"I'll be here."

"Okay. We've given him what we've got here, which isn't much. He's on his way there now. Ray Ycaza. Says he know you."

"Sure. I've got a message on my board to call him."

"He just left here for Lennox. Give him everything you've got. And keep in touch, okay?"

"Sure, Bob. See you."

Barrett returned from Laurie's desk with a cup of coffee for McNeely, who took a sip, then relayed the information to Deliso and Barrett. Deliso observed, "Butler must have been working some powerful voodoo from his cell."

"Yeah," Barrett agreed. "For damned sure he couldn't have pulled that trigger himself. We'll play hell trying to tie him into a murder rap."

"Well, let's not speculate," McNeely said. "We'll hear what Ray Ycaza has to say."

Twenty minutes later, Ycaza arrived, a beaming smile and extended hand for McNeely. "Thought I was through with you guys after you took Butler, but here we are again."

"Glad to have you aboard, Ray. What've you got?"

Ycaza told them of the events of that night, how Lloyd was found, of Lee Michele who had heard noises, of her sighting the possible suspect's head and shoulders, of the manager, Harold Lawton.

"Not a hell of a lot to go on, is it?" McNeely said.

"Not yet, but I want to get back to the Michele girl and Lawton. According to her, the quick glance she got of the dude's head and shoulders, average. They're always average. We've had our guys out canvassing, but nobody's come up with anyone who saw or heard anything."

"Well, we can give you our whole package on Lloyd. Too bad our friend Butler's in the slammer, or we could have a possible suspect for you. From the stats we've got on his buddy Moose Peterson, he doesn't fit the 'average' picture, either."

"Can I have a copy of Lloyd's statement to you and the files on Butler and Peterson to take with me? I'll have somebody run a check on them to see if anything else shows up."

"Sure thing. We've got spare copies already Xeroxed. Anything else we can do for you, Ray?"

"Maybe. I'm on my way down to check out Lloyd's pad again and talk to the girl and the manager. There was the usual confusion the other night, you know, too many people around, everybody charged up. My partner Geiger is on his way there right now."

"You think I can be of any help to you?"

"If you can spare the time, I'd appreciate it. Captain Sawyer and Lieutenant Kelleher seemed to think that since it involves a doper, an expert narc like you might just spot something we dumb homicide dicks might have overlooked."

Russ said, "I'm glad the department's elite is beginning to appreciate their lower-echelon brethren. Okay, Ray, let me check it out with Bob Barker. Jurisdictional crap, you know."

"You don't have to do that. Sawyer talked to Captain Esau, and he had Barker phone you on the spot."

"Okay, then, let's go do it."

McNeely checked himself out on the message blackboard, spoke with Deliso and Barrett for a minute or two, then followed Ycaza out to his radio car. Ray said, "I mentioned to Yolanda that I'd run into you again, and she told me to ask you out for dinner. Consider yourself asked."

"Thanks, Ray. Let's do it soon." It was said, but McNeely knew that the chances were slight. Something would come up. Something always came up; and he was somewhat reluctant to introduce Rachel around beyond his own immediate crew.

He looked out at the passing traffic idly, his mind turned back to the conversation he had had with Rachel the night before; marriage and children. The radio, their support system, was turned down low and chattered constantly, so vital a part of their daily lives: advisories to patrol cars in their various reporting districts, dispatching cars to accidents, family disputes, street disturbances, a robbery or burglary in progress—routine matters that no longer concerned them, matters in the modern urban complex that few citizens were aware of as they went about their daily occupations: cars checking out of service to eat, others reporting themselves clear for assignment. Traffic was dense, but there were no delays en route.

Outside Lloyd's apartment, Ray opened the door with the

key he had found on Lloyd's ring. Geiger was inside lying down on the sofa, now back in its normal place. He stood up, young, slender, and acknowledged McNeely's greeting.

"Anything, Danny?" Ycaza asked.

"Nothing new, Ray. The Michele girl is in her apartment next door, still kind of shook. Her boss told her to take the rest of the week off."

"You talk to the manager?"

"Not yet. He went off on some errand earlier. His wife said he'll be back shortly. I'll go down and see if he's back."

"Okay. Tell him I'd like to talk to him later."

Ycaza was staring down at Lloyd's key ring, which he was still holding, then looked up and said, "Let's go see the girl." He and McNeely walked out and at 201 Ray knocked on the door. Lee Michele came to it, asking, "Who is it, please?"

"Ray Ycaza, sheriff's department, Miss Michele."

The door opened, and she saw them across the chain guard. "Oh. Just a minute." The door closed, the chain rattling as she removed it, then opened again. "Come in, please."

"This is Sergeant McNeely, Miss Michele."

She nodded. To Ycaza, she said, "I remember you."

"Yes. I hope we're not disturbing you too much. I'd like you to tell Sergeant McNeely in your own words what you told me."

"Sure," she said wearily, "why not? I've repeated it so many times already, I'm beginning to think I'm a tape recorder." She invited them to sit down and told it to McNeely from the start, which was exactly the way she had told it to Geiger and Ycaza, as Ray had told it to him.

"Did you know Mr. Lloyd other than as a next-door neighbor, Miss Michele?"

She hesitated for a moment, then replied, "Of course, we'd speak in passing, or when we'd meet at poolside and talk once in a while, that kind of thing. Once when I ran out of coffee, I think it was, I borrowed some from him. He was a quiet sort of man, hardly ever had visitors or parties like the rest of the people here."

"Did he ever discuss the kind of work he did?"

"No, never. He didn't volunteer, and I didn't ask."

"Did he ever mention a family, friends, someone close to him?"

She shook her head from side to side. "No, I can't remember that he ever mentioned anyone or where he was from, no place he called home other than this."

"What about the man you saw leaving here just before you found Mr. Lloyd. Would you have any recollection of having ever seen him before?"

Again the negative shake of the head. "No, nothing more than what I've already told you. I'm sure I couldn't recognize him if I saw him again. Just the back of his head, no hat, and his shoulders. It was dark, you know, no light near where he was going down the stairs. I can't even tell you the color of the jacket he wore. By the time I thought to go to the end of the balcony and look down, he was gone. Then all I heard was his footsteps, moving fast, almost as though he was running, and the motor of a car come on."

"Okay. Thank you, Miss Michele," McNeely said. And to Ray, "Unless you have anything more."

"No, not right now. Let's have a look next door again."

Geiger was waiting outside on the balcony. "Lawton's back, having his lunch right now. I told him you wanted to talk to him, to stay put. He'll be there when you're ready for him."

"Fine, Danny. Russ and I are going to go over the apartment again."

"Yeah, sure. I'll slip down to the corner and grab a sandwich. Bring something back for you?"

"No. You go ahead."

The apartment, with the exception of the victim's body tapes and the powder marks left by the print men, was quiet, and other than that the heavier pieces of furniture had been replaced in their proper positions, in the same state of disorder as when Lloyd had been found. Ycaza said, "The bastard went through this place like a goddamn hurricane looking for something, probably a dope stash."

"And cash," McNeely added. "At Whitey's level, they generally keep cash and dope handy to do their wheeling and dealing. He can get a call at midnight or three in the morning to make a buy or a big sale. At that hour, he can't go running to a bank or his safety deposit box."

"Don't prep me, Russ. I know how it works. Take a look, will you, see if we missed anything."

"Okay, but don't expect anything much after your guys went through the place."

"Be my guest."

Ycaza went to the kitchen, and McNeely began his check with the entry guest closet, then the living room and kitchen where Ycaza had put on a pot of coffee, searching meticulously, examining furniture, raising the edges of the carpeting, pawing through bookshelves, cabinets, the sideboard. He paused long enough to take a cup of the coffee Ray offered him, then checked the refrigerator and freezer compartment. In the bathroom, he looked inside and beneath the toilet tank, sink, and medicine chest to see if it could be removed and a space left behind it that could conceal a stash. It couldn't.

In the bedroom, McNeely said, "Last port of call, Ray. If we bomb out here, we've had it. Help me move the bed away from the wall."

The bed was moved, baseboards inspected, moldings tested, carpeting lifted at all four corners and around the edges. Ycaza went back to the kitchen for another cup of coffee. All that remained now was the large walk-in closet that had been emptied when the clothing had been thrown out onto the bedroom floor. Using a chair and his flashlight, McNeely moved along the length of the U-shaped shelves, tapping at the overhead ceiling. He removed the chair and repeated the process along the floor, on his knees, rapping knuckles against wood and plaster every few inches.

The carpet here was held in place by strips of aluminum molding, and as he moved toward his left, closer to the door, the molding ended about three feet short of the left wall. And similarly on the opposite side of the closet. Here the carpet was free. He raised the edges and disclosed the original wooden flooring, then stood up and pressed his right foot down on the boards where they joined the wall, knelt down again, using his flashlight in the dark corner.

And saw that the floorboards ended at the wall, but did not continue across the threshold into the bedroom. He pressed down with both hands, felt the boards give under pressure. Then he stood up and the carpeting fell back into place.

"Ray?" he called.

"Right here. Something?"

"Maybe. Get in here, close to the left wall." When Ycaza was in position, "Press down with one foot, release, then push down again."

Ycaza did so and felt the boards give. "Hey, what do you know—?"

McNeely knelt again, pulled the carpeting back as far as it would go, about eighteen inches, to the point where the aluminum molding began. Against the back wall, his fingers found a narrow space. He reached in and pulled upward, and a section, the full width of the closet and approximately sixteen inches in length, came up in his grip. The space beneath was about eight inches deep between the ceiling of the apartment below and the floor.

Whitey Lloyd's stash.

Inside was a metal fishing-tackle box, beside it two small cardboard boxes containing a U.S. regulation .45 automatic and two boxes of .45 cartridges. "Here's what your hit man was probably looking for," McNeely said.

Under his breath, Ycaza muttered, "Sonofabitch!"

They brought it all into the living room and placed it on the sofa. In the tackle box were six kilos of marijuana in brick form and a heavy manila envelope that contained a sheaf of U.S. currency totaling forty-two hundred dollars in twenties, fifties, and hundreds. One of the small cartons contained a Pliofilm bag with approximately a thousand Methedrine tablets. The other turned up a similar bag with the same number of Seconal capsules and a smaller bag that McNeely identified as Mexican heroin.

Ycaza whistled. "I'll be damned. Crime doesn't pay?"

McNeely said laconically, "Ask Whitey Lloyd the next time you go down to the morgue."

"Next time I make a search, I'm going to peel the goddamned paint and paper off the walls."

"You work dopers long enough, you'll learn to think the way they do. We've found stashes in hollow doors, inside chair legs, bedposts, you name it."

"What do you estimate this shit is worth, Russ?"

"Depends on how much the heroin's been cut and whether you're talking street value or dealer or pusher cost. I'd guess offhand this is worth about sixteen or eighteen hundred on the street. Let's inventory it and take it downtown, let the brass decide where the jurisdiction lies."

"Yeah. We'll want to run that .45 through for wants. Some GI probably walked it off post and sold it to a willing buyer. If it's clean, it's worth a lot to a needy hood."

On the ground floor they met Geiger, just back from his lunch break, a toothpick jutting upward out of his mouth. They went to Lawton's small office where the manager was waiting, an open ledger and a pile of invoices on his desk. He closed the ledger and stood up, smiled effusively, more composed than he had been on the night of the murder. "What can I do for you gentlemen?" he asked, adding, "First time in all the years I've been in this business anything like this has ever happened to me."

Ycaza said, "The man who left the hundred dollars deposit on Apartment 242—"

"Mr. Ellison? I've got the lease made up right here." He picked up the printed form from a letter tray and displayed it for them.

"When did he say he'd be back to sign it?"

"Around noon yesterday. I remember distinctly."

"He's a day and a couple of hours late, isn't he?"

"Well, yes, but I kind of expected he might be. He's new out here, you know, probably tied up on another business matter." But Lawton, suspecting that Ycaza was trying to make a point in another direction, sounded less certain than before.

"Could you give us a clearer description of Mr. Ellison?" Ycaza asked. At which, Geiger had his notebook out, pen poised.

"Well—well, yes. Let me see. He's about five-ten, I'd guess, about a hundred sixty or sixty-five pounds, Black, light-brown complexion, straight black hair, a thin mustache, no beard. He wore a medium-gray suit with a lighter pin-stripe, white shirt, gray and blue tie, black shoes, and a light blue hat, one of those narrow-brimmed things."

"Did you notice any scars or other distinguishing marks, the color of his eyes?" Ycaza pressed.

"Brown eyes, I think, and no, no scars or marks that I can remember." He paused, then said in a perplexed voice, "Why? You don't think *he* had anything to do with this, do you?"

"Do you still have his business card, the one I took the information from the other night?"

"Yes." He detached the card that was clipped to the back of the lease and handed it to Ycaza, who handed it to McNeely. Ycaza said, "I think you'd better forget about the lease, Mr. Lawton. You're probably a hundred dollars ahead. I doubt that your Mr. Ellison will be back."

Again, "Why? Why do you say that?"

"Because we ran a check on his company and him yester-day, and the word came back from New York this morning. There's no such company at that address, no such phone number for a Waters Hydraulic Equipment outfit, and very likely, no such person as John Hall Ellison."

Mouth open in surprise, Lawton sat down. McNeely said, "When you showed this Ellison Apartment 242, you used a key, didn't you?"

"Yes, of course. The master."

"Not the key to 242?"

"No. I used the master because there were two apartments vacant, the one bedroom on the first floor and 242. He wanted the larger one, as it turned out, and I used the master for both apartments."

"May we see the master key, please?"

Lawton swiveled around and removed the master key that hung from the wall hook behind his desk. He handed it to McNeely, who held it by the thin plastic slab to which it was attached.

"Was this out of your sight at any time while Mr. Ellison was in the apartment?" McNeely asked.

"No-o- uh, wait. Yes. Yes, I left it in the lock while I went to answer the office phone."

"And Ellison waited there while you were gone. Alone with the key."

"Yes. Yes, that's right."

McNeely examined the key carefully, turning it from side to side. He reached into his trouser pocket, took out a small penknife, and scraped a small particle of dark matter from the groove on one side. Ycaza, watching him, took a small cellophane envelope from his jacket pocket and held it open while McNeely slid the tiny particle into it from the blade of his knife.

Ycaza said, "Mr. Lawton, you told me that Mr. Lloyd was having a problem with his car, a Corvette, that it was in the shop for some repair work. Is that correct?"

"Yes. That's what he told me."

"He had only that one car?"

"Yes, of course."

"Can you tell me if he had another car available to him while his car was in for repairs? A loaner or a rental car?"

"Yes. He was using Miss Michele's car."

"Miss Michele loaned him her car?"

"Yes, the one sitting out on the parking lot in the back. A '72 Chevrolet sedan. Miss Michele works at the Bank of America only two blocks down the street, and she allowed him to use it."

"Were Lloyd and Miss Michele close friends, Mr. Lawton?"

"Well, yes, I would say so. I've seen them go out together occasionally and at the pool. I can't go beyond that. I don't spy on our tenants, as I told you."

Ycaza took out the key ring that had been found on Lloyd's person and looked at the key to Apartment 200, then at the one, almost identical, next to it, fingered it for a moment, then said, "I think that will be about all for now, Mr. Lawton."

"If Mr. Ellison should come back, shall I—do you want me to call you?"

Ycaza said briefly, "He won't be back. Bet on it. But if by some miracle he does, you have my card."

Outside the office, Ycaza said, "Puts us right up against a pretty blank wall."

"So far," McNeely agreed. "About that '72 Chevy, Ray, you know we impounded Lloyd's Stingray. He was using it the night he sold the coke to Sherry Freeman. He used a '72 Chevy to make an earlier buy from her."

"And he was a hell of a lot cozier with Lee Michele than Lee Michele wants us to know about. Let's go back and rap a little more with her."

When she opened the door this time, her eyes widened with surprise, then narrowed with apprehension at the sight of the two men who had left her a little more than thirty minutes before. "Yes? What is it?"

"We'd like to ask you a few more questions, Miss Michele. May we come in?"

"Y-yes."

McNeely observed her more closely now, trying to think of her in relation to Whitey Lloyd. She appeared to be in her late twenties or early thirties, dull brown hair, brown eyes, and totally undistinguished in looks and appearance—a type his mother would have called "mousy" or "old-maidish." The dress she wore fell well below her knees and fit her body rather loosely. He noticed now that she squinted, as though she wore glasses but preferred to go without them out of some sense of vanity. She was, in fact, not a particularly attractive woman.

Ycaza said, "I understand that Mr. Lloyd had been using your car while his was in the shop for repairs, Miss Michele."

"Yes, that's right. He asked me to allow him to use it, and since it wasn't too great an inconvenience for me, I gave him my permission to do so." Her arched eyebrows seemed to ask, *Is there anything wrong in that?*

"If I may, I'd like to ask you a personal question. The other night, when the murder occurred, you told me you knew Mr. Lloyd only slightly, spoke in passing or if you happened to meet at poolside. You've made that same statement to Sergeant McNeely. Would you like to change that statement now?"

She became flustered and rubbed her hands together nervously. "Why should I? I don't know what you mean," she said.

"I'll try to be more explicit, Miss Michele," Ycaza said. "You seemed at those times to want us to understand that your relationship to Mr. Lloyd was that of casual neighbors, nothing more. We now have reason to believe that you were more than that, that you dated Mr. Lloyd—"

She lowered her head, her face crimsoning. "I don't know what you mean, what you've heard, and I know nothing more about the—the murder—than what I've already told you."

"Miss Michele," Ycaza said with a show of patience, "we are trying to learn as much as we can about Mr. Lloyd in order to find out who murdered him. If you withhold information from us, you are breaking the law. If you refuse to answer our questions, we can take you downtown to Headquarters—"

"Oh," she gasped. "Please. Not that. I'm not a criminal. I haven't done anything wrong. I could lose my job at the bank—"

"We wouldn't want that to happen, of course, but we're going to have to know just what and how much you knew about Mr. Lloyd and any of his friends or associates. I can assure you that anything you tell us will be held in confidence."

"I don't know what else I can tell you."

Ycaza stood up and took the key ring from his pocket. He walked to the front door and opened it, inserted a key into the lock. Lee Michele watched him closely, her face gone pale now. Watching her, Ycaza turned the key. The bolt slid back easily. He withdrew the key and closed the door again, then returned to his chair. "Miss Michele," he said, "the key that unlocked your door was on Mr. Lloyd's key ring. Are you still going to insist that you and he were only nodding acquaintances?"

Seeming to crumple before their eyes, she put her hands up to her face, and began sobbing softly. They waited for a few minutes until her shoulders stopped shuddering. She got up, went to a table and removed several pieces of Kleenex from the box, and wiped her eyes, blew her nose, then returned to the sofa.

"We were friends, of course," she said, "but that was a very personal thing between us and has nothing to do with his death."

"At the moment, Miss Michele," Ycaza said, "everything,

personal or impersonal, has, or may have, something to do with his *murder*." He emphasized the word to impress the difference between natural death and death by violence.

"All right," she said, more composed now. "We were having an affair. Is that what you want to know?"

"Not entirely or particularly," Ycaza said. "What we want to know is anything that will be helpful to us in our investigation. What other friends did Lloyd have?"

"I don't know any. I never met any."

"Did he ever mention the names of any of his friends or associates?"

"No, never."

"Do you know what kind of work Lloyd did, what his source of income was?"

"No, not exactly. He never talked about it."

"You weren't curious about that?"

"I asked him once or twice, but he wouldn't discuss it with me. I imagined that it might be something—something possibly illegal, but he wasn't a violent man, and I had no definite reason to suspect—"

"Did you know that he had been arrested recently on a narcotics violation charge, that his Corvette Stingray had been impounded by the sheriff's people for having been used in transporting dope?"

"Ah—no. I knew he had been arrested, but I didn't know what it was about. He told me he had been picked up for some traffic warrants that had been issued, for failure to appear."

McNeely said, "Miss Michele, someone put up the amount of two hundred and fifty dollars to pay a bail bondsman's fee to get Lloyd out on twenty-five hundred dollars' bail. Do you know who put up that money?"

"I did. I hadn't seen him for about a week, and then he telephoned me one day from the county jail and asked me to do it for him, and I went to the man, the bondsman whose name he gave me, and arranged it."

"Did Lloyd ever give you anything to keep for him, papers of any kind, perhaps a package?"

"No. Never."

There was silence then, and she said, "I've told you everything I know. Look, he wasn't in love with me, I know that. I've never had many friends in my life. I was engaged once, a long time ago, but it never worked out. I left home because of it and came here and got a job, the one I have now. I need it. I can't afford to lose it." She paused, then went on.

"I was lonely, and Whitey was kind to me. That's how it happened. I know he had other friends, women, too, but I—I wasn't in any position to protest. I didn't want to—lose him."

When neither McNeely nor Ycaza responded to that, she asked, "Are you going to arrest me? I'll surely lose my job if you do."

"No," Ycaza said, "we're not going to arrest you, and we'll keep all of this between ourselves. I think that's all for now, but don't leave the city unless you telephone me and let me know where you are going and when you'll be back. I'll leave my card with you. And if you should think of something else that might be helpful to us, call me. We'll be in touch with you."

"Thank you," she said, relieved, and took the card.

Outside, Ray said, "Poor lonely broad. Stupid. For a hundred bucks, if she knew how, she could make herself look a lot more human and appetizing. Goes for a creep like Lloyd."

McNeely said, "Ray, don't ever question the women men fall for or the men women go ape over. That's still the biggest mystery of all times."

"Yeah, you're right. Else, why would Yolanda go for a creep like me. Is that what you're saying?"

McNeely laughed. "No, *amigo*, that's what *you*'re saying." In front of Lloyd's door now, "If we're through here, let's take this stuff downtown and get it checked in."

"Sure. I'll get Danny headed back, too. Nothing else we can gain hanging around here."

They were heading north toward the city when the radio sputtered with a 10-21 for David-6-Adam-7. Call your station by phone, for Ycaza. He took the next off ramp, found a public phone at a service station, and checked in. Lieutenant Kelleher took the call, his voice charged and eager.

"Ray, is McNeely with you?"

"Yup. What's up, Ken?"

"We've got a beauty here. For both of you. I didn't want to put it out on the air."

"What is it?"

"The ballistics report on the Lloyd came in a little while ago. The two slugs they took out of him are .38s, perfect matches with the two they recovered from Cruz Despues's body last July."

"Jesus. We're on our way in, Ken.'"

Chapter Eight

1●

The atmosphere in the office of Captain Sawyer was one of subdued excitement, yet easily discernible in the faces of the men who sat on either side of the long conference table that was centered on the gray-green desk; Sawyer, Kelleher, and Ycaza, of Homicide, Captain John Esau, Lieutenant Barker and McNeely, of Narcotics. On the table before them lay the files of Cruz Despues, Ann Stennis, Whitey Lloyd, and Eddie Butler.

Ycaza and McNeely studied the photographic blowups of the bullets taken from the bodies of Despues and Lloyd and the accompanying ballistics reports from the Criminalistics Lab. Someone had worked for hours to trace the numerous microscopic striations engraved on the bullets while spinning through the barrel of what had been identified as a Colt .38. The very same and identical gun.

Kelleher said, "No question, Ray. Identical lands and grooves, fired from the same weapon."

Ycaza pushed the blowups toward the center of the table. Barker said, "All we're missing now are the gun and the dude who pulled the trigger."

Sawyer said, "Okay. We've got our ident-kit man down there with Harold Lawton getting a description and drawing of our mystery man, John Hall Ellison. As soon as he has something, we'll broadcast it and see what turns up."

Esau turned to McNeely. "What about Butler's partner, the Peterson guy Lloyd gave you, Russ?"

"Nowhere in sight. He probably took off or went underground as soon as he heard Butler was busted. We got his mug shots and stats from his file, and the APB has been broadcast. So far, nothing. From Lawton's description of Ellison, of course, we've got to rule Peterson out as the hit man."

Sawyer said, "What is the status on the Butler case?"

"We've got him cold and no way out except for the possibility of bail. At this moment, the only line still open is our surveillance on the Moya woman's house in Van Nuys, the drop Lloyd was using to contact Butler and Peterson for his buys. Of course, it's very likely they have one, two, or three more similar drops in other areas, but we can't say for sure."

Kelleher said, "What about bringing her in for a talk, put the squeeze on her? She's got a teen-age son and daughter to think about. That could be the leverage we need."

"I don't think I'd move too fast in that direction, Ken," Esau interjected quickly. "She's the only live link we know about, and I'd hate to cut that off at this point. As long as we've got a stakeout sitting on her, there's a possibility, however slight, that Peterson may get in touch with her. Wherever he's hiding right now, he may not know we're looking for him actively, and if he starts feeling secure, he may begin circulating. If we pull Connie Moya in for questioning, he'll know we're on to something and stay buried. Right now, slim as it is, she's our one hope."

Sawyer said, "I'll go along with that for now. We want this crook, or anybody we can tie in with the execution of Despues." He paused to take a sip of coffee. "I know how much this means to your bureau, John, and we'll do anything we can to close this case out."

Included with the lab reports was the analysis of the material McNeely had scraped from the master key used by Lawton to unlock Apartment 242 for John Hall Ellison. It was determined to be oil-based clay, the kind generally used in sculpture, available in most art supply stores, and could easily have been used by Ellison to take an impression of the master key. Which told McNeely and Ycaza nothing more than the method by which the hit man had gained entry into Apartment 200 and waited in darkness until Lloyd came home to his rendezvous with death.

Together, they waited in the conference room next to Sawyer's office next morning, reviewing the material thus far assembled, waiting for their respective captains to return from their meeting with the chief of detectives. The meeting had begun at 0810 and forty minutes later was still in progress. They heard the name of Inspector Barry Walton being paged, and Walton, of Homicide, passed by on his way to the chief's office, carrying a file under one arm. Moments later, Inspector Henry Garland come out of the chief's office and joined them in the conference room with a smile that indicated approval.

"The chief bought it," Garland said. "As of right now, you two are our integrated Homicide-Narcotics crew. We're going to set you up in an office on the eighth floor. Get your stuff together and let's get you squared away."

On the eighth floor, primarily the preserve of Narcotics, McNeely and Ycaza moved into a small room formerly used for special field and communications equipment, file cabinets, and miscellaneous storage. By noon, it had been cleared out, two desks moved in, arrangements made for telephone installations, a portable two-way radio, typewriters, a file cabinet borrowed for the temporary arrangement.

In the midst of reviewing and discussing the case with Barker and Kelleher, assessing their most recent activities, the drawing purported to be the face of John Hall Ellison arrived from the staff artist. They studied it closely along with the additional notes written along the margin, but no one present recognized any identifiable characteristics. McNeely ordered reprints made to be circulated with as complete a description as they were able to put together, marking it for special attention to all Homicide and Narcotic agencies in the state. The number and model of the .45 found in Lloyd's apartment were similarly circulated.

On the streets, locally, detectives and narcotic agents were out contacting informants in a desperate effort to locate Peterson. The auto license noted by Lawton, 368-SUL, had been run through the Motor Vehicles Department in Sacramento and was shown to belong to Econo-Drive, a rental agency near Los Angeles International Airport. The information was turned over to Danny Geiger to check out.

The pretty uniformed clerk at Econo-Drive remembered the woman who had rented the yellow Torino very clearly. The record showed her to be a Mrs. Margaret Dowd, who used her driver's license and several credit cards in that same name for identification, stating that her own car had been in an accident and would be out of commission for about a week. She had paid the deposit in cash, returned the car six days later, and paid her bill, also in cash.

Mrs. Dowd, according to the clerk, was a smartly dressed woman in her early or middle thirties, about five-three or -four, blue eyes with blue-green eye shadow, creamy complexion, and bronze-red hair, probably dyed, but very attractive. Her address was given in a West Hollywood apartment house on Sweetzer Avenue.

At that address, Mrs. Margaret Dowd, who didn't quite fit the clerk's description, turned out to be the wife of a Hollywood insurance salesman who had reported her purse and its contents stolen from her car some four weeks earlier when she left it parked for only a few minutes to run into a shop to pick up a package. The report, she added, could be found at the West Hollywood sheriff's station, and when would her license and credit cards be returned to her? Geiger told her they had not yet been found, that she would be notified when that happy event occurred. He then checked Mrs. Dowd's statement at the West Hollywood Station and found the report that backed up her story.

Captain Esau looked in on McNeely and Ycaza in their new quarters and was brought up to date on what little progress had been made thus far. "I'm not pushing you," he said, "but I thought you ought to know that Chief Traynor got a query from the undersheriff. With the Despues murder involved, he's very much interested."

Of course he would be. So would the sheriff. And every deputy in the field who put his life on the line every time he hit the street.

"If you have any suggestions, Captain—" McNeely began, but Esau waved him off. "No one's being critical, Russ, but in a matter like this, one homicide and two possibles, we're bound to have the brass looking over our shoulders. Just stay with it."

"Yes, sir. We intend to do just that."

2●

Three days passed. The murder of Whitey Lloyd had been reported in the press as a possible narcotics-related matter and had been overshadowed by the printed and electronic media in favor of the more spectacular news that followed: A Beverly Hills actress-socialite accused of the hit-and-run deaths of an elderly couple on a Wilshire Boulevard crosswalk, caught when she ran into a parked car six blocks west of the incident, charged with driving under the influence of alcohol and felony manslaughter; of two children who discovered a partially buried hand in the yard of a nearby vacant house where they had been playing, subsequent investigation of which revealed four missing teen-age bodies; of a series of brush fires that had burned off nine hundred acres, destroyed two houses, threatening others; of the exposure of an assemblyman up for election, accused of accepting a fifteen-thousand-dollar bribe from a convicted embezzler to influence a judge's decision in the matter of probation instead of a prison term.

Under its SOUTHLAND NEWS heading on page 2, the *Times* gave the Lloyd story a mere inch and a half, with an equal amount of space in the afternoon *Examiner*; no mention of the incident was made on evening radio or television.

Ycaza, McNeely, Geiger, and other detectives had gone back to the scene for the fourth time to talk with other tenants, Lawton, Lee Michele, and several neighbors, while still others scoured the neighborhood for six blocks in all directions talking with children, parents, store owners, and drivers of various delivery trucks. No one had seen the yellow Torino or its driver.

Back in their cramped office, McNeely spread out the files once again and reviewed every detail of the case, reread each interview, the reports of each officer who had been on the scene, patrol officers and detectives, the coroner's and lab reports. All dry holes.

On Tuesday morning, when they met again to start a new day together as a two-man crew, it appeared that this would be very much like the day before, and the day before that one. They had coffee with Bob Barker and John Rivera, Esau's administrative aide, then returned to their facing desks and began opening their files to examine them for some elusive, overlooked clue. The phone rang, and Ycaza picked it up on the first ring. "Ycaza here."

"Ray? Tom Crane. Got something going. Is McNeely with you?" Crane was one of the Metro Bureau men assigned to surveillance duty on the Consuela Moya house in Van Nuys.

"Yeah, Tom." Stabbing a finger at McNeely's phone, "Crane, Russ. Something doing." Russ picked up his receiver eagerly. "I'm on, Tom. What've you got?"

Crane's voice, pitched an octave higher than usual, was saying, "Just as Gordy Palmer relieved me here at zero seven thirty, a seventy-two Ford Pinto pulled up at the Moya house. Tag six sixty-three, Ocean-Young-Zebra, brown-over-tan body. A woman got out, went inside, and came out at zero seven forty-three. From the stats on her, Gordy and I both made her as Margaret Dowd, the broad who rented the yellow Torino for the Ellison dude. I left Gordy on Sylvan Street and tailed the Pinto down here to Torrance, forty-seven seventeen Newton Street. En route, I ran a ten-twenty-eight on her tag, and it comes back Cora, that's Charlie-Ocean-Robert-Adam, Thomas, normal spelling, at that address, same description."

"Good make," McNeely said, "perfect. Wait there for us, Tom. We're on our way. If anything happens while we're en route, we'll be on the radio."

"Okay. And hurry it up, will you? I've been on this mother since eleven last night."

"Ten-four."

Both hung up, clipped their guns to their belts, grabbed up their jackets, and hurried out. Traffic was heavy when they hit the Harbor Freeway, but thinned out beyond Century Boulevard. At 0955 they reached the Newton Street address, saw Tom Crane's car half a block away, parked near a service station from which he had phoned, and pulled up behind him.

Crane got into their car and pointed to 4717, a small white stucco with a red-tiled roof. In the narrow driveway next to the house stood the tan Pinto with the dark-brown top. "She's still inside," Crane said. "I walked by not more than ten minutes ago and saw her through the front window."

"Let's go," McNeely said to Ycaza.

"You want me to come along?" Crane asked.

"Why don't you take off, Tom," Ycaza said. "You've done your good deed for today."

On the first knock, the woman opened the door and stared at the two men through the screen door, eyebrows raised in question, eyes wary with suspicion. The screen door, they noted, was locked. "Yes, what is it?" she asked finally.

"Miss Thomas? Cora Thomas?" McNeely asked.

"Yes. If it's something you're selling, I'm not—"

McNeely flipped open his I.D. wallet, displaying the star and I.D. card. "Sheriff's Department, Miss Thomas. I'm Sergeant McNeely. This is my partner, Sergeant Ycaza. We'd like to talk with you for a minute or two. May we come in?"

Miss Thomas's eyes flicked nervously from McNeely to

Ycaza, showing no other reaction, making no move to unlock the screen door. "What is it about?" she asked, making an effort to bring her voice under control.

"We'd prefer to come in rather than talk outside where your neighbors might see or overhear us and become curious."

She hesitated, indecisive, then said, "All right," and unlatched the door. They stepped inside, into a small living room that was somewhat overcrowded with a long, curved sofa, two upholstered side chairs, marble-topped coffee table, a color television set atop a long, low stereo cabinet. Standing there facing them, she said, "What is this all about?"

"Miss Thomas," McNeely said, "we're investigating a case in which a yellow Torino was used to commit a felony. The license number of the car was three-six-eight-SUL, a rental car. The name used by the woman who rented the car was Margaret Dowd."

Miss Thomas turned away and sat down on the sofa. Her green linen dress hiked up, revealing more inches of well-formed thigh covered by flesh-toned nylons. Her face was more attractive now that she had regained some of her composure, and her attitude was a cross between insouciance and disdain as she lighted a cigarette. Her complexion was smoothly pink. High cheekbones and a sensual mouth showed a hint of firmness, perhaps even cruelty. Neither McNeely nor Ycaza felt she would be easy to deal with and would require tough handling.

"I'm sorry I can't help you," she said finally. "I don't know a Margaret Dowd or anything about a yellow—Torino, you said? What's all this got to do with me?"

"This, Miss Thomas. The description furnished us by the auto-rental clerk fits you perfectly. Did you rent that car?"

"No, of course not." She said it with a strong voice and the barest smile. "I'm sure my description will fit thousands or more women in Los Angeles."

"Miss Thomas," McNeely said, "the auto-rental-agency clerk assures us she can positively identify the woman who used Margaret Dowd's driver's license and other identification when she rented that car. We also have the written signature used on the rental form, which our handwriting experts can analyze and match with the signature on your own driver's license. Also, we can obtain a search warrant, if necessary, to go through this house to find the I.D. used to rent the Torino. If you insist you are not that person, we'll have to ask you to accompany us downtown for further questioning. That's up to you."

She thought for a few moments, then said, "Can I call my lawyer?"

"Not just now," McNeely said. "We're still conducting our investigation and haven't placed you under arrest. Yet. Did you rent that car?"

She shrugged and put her cigarette out, then said, "I lose either way, don't I?" When the question went unanswered, she stood up and said, "Okay. I rented the car."

"Do you have in your possession the driver's license and credit cards in the name of Margaret Dowd that were used to identify yourself?"

"Yes." She went to the stereo cabinet, pulled the doors open, reached in behind the stacks of cassette tapes, and removed a small black purse, which she handed to McNeely. He asked her to remove its contents and place them on the coffee table. From the purse, she took out a brown leather wallet, opened it, and laid down several department store and gasoline credit cards and a driver's license, all in the name of Margaret Dowd.

"Miss Thomas," McNeely said, "for the time being, we are placing you under arrest for illegal possession and use of property stolen from a vehicle owned by Mrs. Margaret Dowd. Please listen carefully while I read your rights to you—"

After being searched by a matron at Lennox Station, Cora Thomas was booked, then interrogated by McNeely and Ycaza. Waiving her rights and agreeing to talk, she gave her occupation as an unemployed dancing instructor who had used up her unemployment compensation and was living on her savings until she could find another job.

"Where did you get the credit cards and driver's license belonging to Mrs. Dowd?" McNeely asked.

"They were given to me by a man."

"What man?"

"I really don't know him."

"You're saying that a man, unknown to you, gave you those objects for no reason you know or are willing to state?"

"Well, it's sort of complicated."

"We'll let that pass for the moment, Miss Thomas. Now tell us about the man you rented the car for. Name, address, description, and anything else you know about him."

"I don't—look, he told me his name was Ellison. A light-colored spade. I—uh—met him when I was a dancing instructor, went out with him a few times, off and on. He looked me up recently and paid me fifty dollars to rent the car for him and gave me the license and cards to use for identification. That's it."

"Where does he live? What's his phone number?" Ycaza pressed.

"I don't know where he lives. I was never there. And I never called him. He always called me."

McNeely pulled out several police photographs and showed them to her, one at a time. "Can you identify any of the three men in these mug shots?"

She glanced at each, the photos of Moose Peterson, Whitey Lloyd, and Eddie Butler. "No," she said calmly, "I don't know any of them."

"Okay, Miss Thomas," McNeely said, "let me put this to you. We feel you know more than you want, or intend, to tell us, and we're wasting a lot of time. We're going to hold you on this present charge. We're going to do a thorough check on you, interview everybody in your neighborhood. Someone will have seen your Mr. Ellison or the yellow Torino he drove for five or six days. Meanwhile, you're in for possession of stolen property—"

"I told you!" she snapped angrily. "I didn't steal those credit cards or license, damn it!"

"—and as a possible accomplice in a felony murder—"

"That's ridiculous!"

"—and we're going to make every effort to tie you in with John Hall Ellison unless you stop fooling around and start co-operating. If you're as bright as you seem to be, you should realize how stupid it is to cover for somebody who can put you behind bars for one very long time."

"Oh, for Christ's sake! I—don't—know—any—Ellison!" she shouted, biting off each word separately.

They waited patiently, letting her mind absorb the implied consequences. Ycaza wrote something hurriedly on a scrap of paper and showed it to McNeely. *Connie?* He glanced at the word and shook his head negatively. Ycaza then turned to Cora Thomas and said, "Suppose you tell us what you know about a man named Moose."

They saw her reaction in her eyes and the tightening of her jawline, mouth clamped shut, shaking off the question without replying. McNeely said, "Think about it, Miss Thomas. You're a very attractive woman. We don't know if you have a prior record, but we'll know that before this day is over, tomorrow at the latest. Prison won't be kind to you, and we can make things a lot easier for you if you cooperate with us at this stage. Later, as we develop more information and facts, and you decide to talk then, we may not want to talk to you, in which case you'll have to take the full fall. The choice is up to you."

She sagged in her chair, dejected and weary. "All right," she said, "to hell with it." She moved a hand toward the pictures that were lying on the table and picked them up one by one. "This one is Eddie Butler. This one is Moose Peterson. I don't know this one. Never saw him," she said of the third, Whitey Lloyd.

Ycaza withdrew a folded sheet from his inside jacket pocket and laid it flat on the table, the drawing made from Lawton's description. "What about this one?"

"That's him," she said, "Ellison." Simultaneously, McNeely and Ycaza exhaled with satisfaction.

Ycaza said, "You're doing fine so far, Miss Thomas. Now tell us something about yourself. Where you're from, what you've been working at, where, and how you know Butler, Peterson, and Ellison. Take it from page one."

She had a record. One arrest in Nashville, where she had lived prior to coming to Los Angeles. Three arrests by LAPD for prostitution. One in Las Vegas on extortion, for having enticed a man to a hotel room, threatening to expose him if he didn't pay her five hundred dollars. One arrest by the sheriff's department in West Hollywood for possession of narcotics, dismissed for lack of evidence.

She had been, as claimed originally, a dance instructor for a franchise operator, fired for becoming intimately involved with several of her male students. She had turned to go-go dancing in a topless bar where she picked up her fourth arrest for prostitution.

Upon that release, she met a man who had picked her up in a bar at Marina del Rey. After a weekend trip to Lake Arrowhead with him, he introduced her to another man who put her up in the Newton Street house where she began acting as a message drop. The name the second man gave her was Eddie Rogers, but she learned later that his real name was Butler. Yes, she knew that Butler and his friend Moose Peterson were dealing in narcotics on a large scale, but had never seen any of the stuff nor their contacts. She merely transmitted phone messages between distributors or dealers and Butler, sometimes Peterson, always in code.

258

What was the code?

Cocaine was identified by the number three, heroin by eight. None of the contacts made was for marijuana or other drugs. Only cocaine and heroin.

"What," McNeely asked, "was the name of the man who first introduced you to Eddie Rogers, or Butler?"

"I can't remember."

"You spent a weekend with him at Lake Arrowhead and can't remember his name?"

"I—let me think. It was Harry— No, Howard, I think. Howard Barnett. Or something like that. It was some time ago, and I never saw him again after he introduced me to Eddie."

The license and credit cards belonging to Margaret Dowd, she told them, had been furnished by Butler. She denied ever having intimate relations with Butler and Peterson, even smiled at the question. "Those two? No way. I think they're a pair of homos."

"And John Hall Ellison?" Ycaza asked.

She nodded. "While he was staying here with me, yes."

"Where is Ellison now?"

"I don't know. He left here that last night and never came back. I never saw him before he came to stay for a few days. I haven't seen or heard from him since."

"How about Peterson?"

"I don't know that, either. He phoned me and told me Ellison would be coming over to stay for a short while."

"You weren't curious why? You didn't ask?"

"Look, mister," she said, "I get paid for doing things, not asking questions about why, where, how, when, or who."

McNeely took over again. Now that she was cooperating, he was less reluctant about hitting her with the Moya name. "What was the purpose of your visit this morning to the home of Consuela Moya in Van Nuys?"

She looked up in genuine surprise. "You know about Connie? So that's how you got to me." When this drew no reply, she said, "I got a call at five thirty this morning from some guy who said he was calling for Moose and Eddie—"

"No name?"

"No name, and I don't know where he was calling from. He told me to get to Connie in person and tell her not to take any more calls from anybody until she was contacted by Eddie when he gets out on bail, and not to make any calls to him at three two seven seven six five nine. To cut off the recording machine, and if anybody called, she was to say, 'You have a wrong number. There is no Connie here. She moved,' and hang up."

"Do you know the reason for that message?"

"Only a guess. You guys probably had her phone tapped."

"Did the man ask you to carry those same instructions to anyone else?"

"No. Just Connie. He told me to tell her she would get her monthly money as usual."

"How?"

"The same way I got mine, I suppose. By mail."

"A check?"

She laughed shortly. "No way. Always in cash, wrapped in a blank sheet of paper."

"Was there a return address written or printed on the envelope?"

"No. Always in a plain envelope."

"What about your car, the Pinto?"

"I bought it used, with cash that Eddie gave me."

For the time being, Cora Thomas was sent to Sybil Brand Institute for Women. The phone number, 327-7659, as McNeely had suspected from the method she described, turned out to be a public telephone booth at the corner of Victoria Street and South Broadway in Gardena.

In discussion with Esau, Barker, and Inspectors Walton and Garland, the subject of bringing Connie Moya in was again broached, again put aside on McNeely's objections, giving two reasons: that it was not likely she could tell them more than they had learned from Cora Thomas; and that with Cora out of action, there was the outside chance that Peterson, knowing he was the object of a search, might possibly show up on Sylvan Street in Van Nuys. The surveillance there was ordered maintained around the clock.

The meeting ended on that note. Ycaza radioed the Metro man in Van Nuys, who reported normal activity; the boy and girl were off to school, Connie Moya to a nearby supermarket on Victory Boulevard near Woodman. She had made no attempt to use a public phone, returned thirty-five minutes later with a sack of groceries.

Sergeant Billy Sorensen, the Intelligence man, came in with several teletyped responses to inquiries. "Anything from our cooperating agencies, Billy?" McNeely asked.

"Not much we can use. The .45 Colt automatic was stolen from the Fresno National Guard Armory almost two years ago. Nothing but blanks from any informant contacts."

"What's with Cora Thomas?" Ycaza asked.

"She's having her preliminary a week from Friday. The D.A. won't fight a minimum bail, but considering what happened to Whitey Lloyd, she may decide to stay in protective custody. But if she makes bail, we'll have our guys sitting on her." Sorensen got up to go. "If you come up with something we can help you on, holler."

They broke for lunch at the Dutchman's, and during it Ycaza said, "Christ, I feel like I'm dying on the vine. This damned thing isn't *moving*."

"Got any suggestions for making it move faster?" Russ said.

"Well, maybe we could go back to our original assignments while we're waiting for something to break."

McNeely shook his head from side to side. "When the chief makes an assignment, *amigo*, you take it and keep it until *he* decides to cool it. We've got one here that overlaps Homicide and Narcotics and involves one of our own. The sheriff and undersheriff are interested in it. We're just damn lucky the press isn't riding hard on us, or we'd be working inside a sweatbox."

"I wondered about that. How come they aren't onto it?"

"Just slipped by in the multitude of other crimes. I guess they figure it's a case of crooks killing a crook, and who the hell cares as long as some innocent John Doe didn't get ripped. I don't think they really care that much unless it becomes a big minority thing between 'us' and 'them.' It used to be that way in Chicago during prohibition days. Crooks killing crooks was practically legal then."

"Way before my time," Ycaza commented.

"Mine, too, but in Chicago, old-timers were always talking about those 'good old days.' "

They made several phone calls to informants and phoned in for messages. Ycaza had one, to call Rudy Arboleya. He made the call-back from the office of the Dutchman's. Rudy was in high spirits when he answered the phone in the garage. "Hey, man, I wanted to tell you thanks for talking to my parole guy."

"Good news?"

"Yeah. Well, he wasn't all that happy about it, but we got it squared away. You done a good job on him."

"Glad to hear it, Rudy. I hope you and Isobel are happy about it."

"Yeah, Ray, we sure are. As soon as we can both get a few days off, we're goin'a do it."

"Well, lots of luck and take care."

"Sure, and thanks again. That's another one I owe you."

They walked back to the office, and Ray decided to go over their files and make a few more phone calls. Russ, feeling the need to get out, decided to take a run out to Lennox and see how things were going with his crew.

At Lennox, he found Steve Barrett and Perry Roberts setting up a buy for that evening, using Joe Paul, wearing a false beard, mustache, and a hippie outfit complete with Indian-beaded headband and fringed leather jacket, to make the initial contact. He spent half an hour with them, then rapped with Bill Hamlin and Vic Lopez for a while, feeling a sense of longing to be back in the day-to-day, night-to-night action. He got back into his car and started toward the Hall of Justice when he took a 10-20, asking his location. Advising the dispatcher, he was given a 10-19, return to your station. He speeded up, hoping it was another break in the Lloyd or Despues case and within thirty minutes was standing beside John Rivera's desk. "What's up, John?"

"Captain had me put in the call for you. He's on the phone right now. Be off in a couple of minutes. Coffee?"

"No, thanks. Just left Lennox, and I'm floating with the stuff. You seen Ray around?"

"No. Not since he went out a couple of hours ago."

Russ picked up the phone on Rivera's assistant's desk and dialed Rachel's shop, learned from Lilith that she was busy with a customer. He left word that he would call her later, and as he hung up, Rivera called to him. "He's off the phone now, Russ. Go right in. He's expecting you."

Russ knocked and opened the door. Captain Esau looked up and said, "Come in, Russ. Close the door and sit down. Hope I didn't pull you away from anything important."

"Not a thing, Captain. No problem."

"Yes—well—I'm afraid I've got one for you."

"Sir?"

"Some bad news, Russ. It's hard to know just how to handle a thing like this, but—it's your father, Russ. He's had a heart attack."

Stunned momentarily, "My father?"

"I'm afraid so. You'd better arrange to get out as quickly as you can."

"Yes. Of course." Then, "How did you get the word, Cap?"

"It came up from downstairs. They got it from Chicago P.D. Your father's housekeeper called your home and couldn't get an answer, then called the local P.D. and asked them to try to reach you. They passed the word up here to me."

"I see. I'll check out——"

"I've already taken care of that. If you can make it, you've got an eight o'clock reservation on United. Take off and good luck, Russ. We'll take care of things on this end. Don't think about it. And I hope your dad makes it."

"Thanks. I'll let you know when I'll be back."

"Take all the time you need. Get along now."

Outside, he found Ray beside Rivera's desk and knew at a glance that John had already told him. "Sorry as hell, Russ," Ray said. "Would you like me to run you down to Manhattan Beach?"

"No thanks, Ray. I've got my car here. You run across anything?"

"Nothing worthwhile. Forget about it. I'll stay on top of things while you're gone."

"Okay, Ray. John, I'll phone you from Chicago when I'm ready to come back."

At home, he phoned Rachel at the shop to tell her he was leaving. She insisted on coming at once to help him pack and drive him to the airport. In his pocket was the slip Esau had given him with Elizabeth Frazier's name and phone number, and those of Dr. Micah Morrisey and St. Anthony's Hospital where Peter McNeely was hospitalized. He placed a call to Dr. Morrisey and learned from his exchange that the doctor was out on a call. He then phoned St. Anthony's and was told by the curt desk nurse that Peter was holding his own, that Dr. Morrisey was with him and couldn't take any calls.

Waiting for Rachel, Russ poured a drink, then began to put together the clothes and other necessities for his journey. Feeling guilt. He hadn't heard from nor written to Peter in over three months.

Chapter Nine

1●

On the plane, McNeely settled down in his window seat in the first-class compartment. The one beside him remained vacant, as were half the others in the forward section. Soon after takeoff, he thumbed listlessly through the pages of the afternoon *Examiner* and found nothing to divert him from the thought of what might be awaiting him in Chicago.

The plane reached its turning point somewhere west of Catalina Island, turned, and swept back inland across ocean, beaches, deserts, and mountains toward its destination. A smiling stewardess handed him a menu and took his order for a Scotch over ice. She returned moments later with the drink and asked, "Would you like to order your dinner now, sir?"

"Nothing, thank you," Russ replied, taking the drink, "this will do it."

"There's a lovely selection——" she persisted, but he had no feeling for food. "No, thanks. Another one of these a little later, perhaps."

She left. He turned off the overhead reading light and sipped his drink. It was his first trip home—he still thought of Chicago as home—since the summer before he was shot, a vacation to visit Carol's parents and his father. Carol had flown back at least three times each year, and the Simons had spent the one brief visit with them after they had moved to the beach.

He reflected on the deterioration of his relationship with Peter, dating its beginning to the introduction of Mrs. Frazier into the McNeely household. His attitude toward Peter had been a bone of contention between Carol and himself, she insisting that Peter had every right to live his life in his own way; but then Carol had seen his father only as other outsiders saw him, never through his, Russ's eyes. Nor did she see his deep hurt at the insult to the memory of Nora.

It was late when he deplaned in Chicago, and he went directly to a telephone booth and called the hospital. On identifying himself, his call was transferred to a Doctor Lang, who told him Peter had expired two hours earlier; his body, on orders from Mrs. Frazier, removed to the Comiskey Funeral Home in Bridgeport.

In a state of quiet shock, he claimed his two-suiter and taxied to the Drake, registered, and ordered a rental car for the following morning, then went to his room and to bed. In the morning he telephoned Dr. Morrisey, whose receptionist reported that the doctor was at the hospital making rounds. He dressed and went down to the coffee shop where he read the story of retired Captain Peter Liam McNeely's death at the age of seventy-four, after devoting nearly forty years of service to his city on the police force, a man very active in local politics. There was no mention of the major scandal in which he and his precinct had once come under fire. Back in his room, he phoned John Rivera and told him of Peter's death and that he would probably return immediately after the funeral.

At ten o'clock he drove to the Comiskey Funeral Home and was told that Peter's body was "being prepared." He learned from Charlie Comiskey that all arrangements had been made by Peter himself in a sealed letter left with his attorney, Mark Farrell. Peter would be buried beside "my dear departed and beloved wife, Nora."

From Comiskey's office he phoned Mark Farrell, who told Russ he was due in court and would see him at the funeral next day and arrange for a private talk afterward. Now, reluctantly, he dialed the familiar number on South Lowe Avenue. Mrs. Frazier answered and, after a few moments of hesitant conversation, asked him to "please come home. People are arriving and are asking for you."

He drove there slowly, his mind in a state of confusion, ambivalence, and guilt. Cars were parked on both sides of the street, precinct officers, each wearing a black band on his left arm, on hand to keep the traffic moving. Neighbors stood on their front porches and pavements to watch the unusual amount of movement. Russ recognized Sergeant Reese, who had once been Peter's driver, and who greeted him somberly and ordered the driveway barrier removed to allow parking room, then accompanied Russ to the front door.

Mrs. Frazier, not surprisingly, looked splendid, hardly older than the first time he had met her. Hostess to the flow of visitors, accepting condolences and sympathy, she introduced "Russell, Peter's son, you know, from California." Some of those present, he knew, some were vaguely familiar, still others complete strangers to him. Those he remembered showed their years, older, grayer, saddened by the departure of a contemporary, leaving them behind to wonder who among them would soon follow him to their graves.

He took particular notice of the absence of Ralph and Charlotte Simon and wondered if they had been there earlier and left before he arrived; but they were not present at the funeral on the following afternoon, among the many police officials, political figures, and friends who attended the services, to hear the eulogies spoken over the flower-covered casket.

After the interment, a steady stream of visitors returned to the house, and, somehow, with the help of a caterer and neighbors, directed by Elizabeth Frazier, some sense of order seemed to flow from the human disorder created by friends who had not seen each other for a long time and spent hours visiting and reminiscing among themselves. Telegrams and flowers continued to arrive in profusion, a wreath of white carnations from Rachel Nugent, another from the bureau staff, telegrams from his crew and Ray Ycaza, too late for the funeral and delivered to the house instead.

Then it was over, the callers gone, and only he and Elizabeth Frazier remained. She brought two cups of coffee into the living room, and he accepted one gratefully. Seated facing each other, she said, "Russell, we'll have to talk about things before you go back to California."

"Yes, he replied wearily. "I'm seeing Mr. Farrell in the morning. After that, I'll come back here. We can talk then." He finished his coffee, bade her good night, and left.

At ten the following morning he was at the attorney's office in the Loop. Farrell, a kindly white-haired man in his late sixties, displayed honest sadness for the passing of his old friend and client. "One of the best, Peter was," he stated. "The kind you hate to see go. Of course, losing someone that close to you, in your own age bracket, only brings home thoughts that someone up there is still watching our time cards."

Amenities aside, there was Peter's will to be read and discussed. Apart from charitable bequests and small amounts of cash to some whose names were not familiar to Russ, the house on South Lowe Avenue was left to Mrs. Frazier along with the furniture, the Oldsmobile sedan, two five-thousand-dollar bonds, and stocks valued at fifteen thousand, another ten thousand in cash "in appreciation for her labors of years as my loyal housekeeper and the comfort provided me as a friend."

To "my son, Russell Dennis McNeely, now residing in Manhattan Beach, California, the balance of my estate and worldly possessions."

This, Farrell outlined, consisted of two insurance policies totaling forty thousand dollars, stocks valued at eighty thousand, cash in the bank and savings and loan accounts amounting to forty-two thousand dollars. "Of course, there'll be funeral expenses, taxes, a few outstanding household bills to be deducted. And my fee, you understand."

Farrell waited, as though expecting opposition to the seventy or eighty thousand dollars Mrs. Frazier would receive, and when Russ failed to respond or object, he added, "She was good to him, Russell."

He smiled bleakly. "Mrs. Frazier?"

"Mrs. Frazier. Once he retired, he wasn't the easiest man to live with. She did her best to make him comfortable, even happy."

"I understand, Mr. Farrell, and I have no quarrel with my father's wishes. I wasn't exactly a great comfort to him."

"We talked about you from time to time. He missed you, but he understood that, too, in his own way, and never held it against you. He blamed it on the system he was caught up in, the one you refused to accept. It's all in how one looks at it, opportunity to some, corruption to others. He chose to go along with it because it was there and there wasn't anything he could do about it. But he was big enough of a man to know you were entitled to your own way of life."

The almost one-sided discussion of Peter disturbed Russ,

and he cut his visit short, using his need to return to California that evening as his excuse. He accepted Farrell's estimate
of a final "hundred thousand, maybe a bit more after debts
and taxes" and left.

He drove slowly through the old neighborhood, past the
schools of his youth, recognizing landmarks he hadn't thought
of in years, past the Ninth Precinct, more dilapidated than
before, and put aside the momentary impulse to enter the
building and take a last look at "McNeely's precinct," which
had been a considerable part of his own early days. Now
it was like visiting a foreign city, feeling alienated in these
gloomy surroundings.

He felt less uncomfortable in Elizabeth Frazier's presence
this time, knowing that once he walked out of the house for
the last time, it would be over forever. He would never again
think of the house or the city as "home." She was in a talka-
tive mood, discussing matters he thought should have been
talked of only between his father and himself, yet she seemed
anxious to make him feel at ease. She already knew the details of the provisions made for her in Peter's will, but added
details he was unaware of.

"Your father was very kind and generous to me, Russell,"
she confided. "There were other gifts he made to me in case
there were problems that would come up," which Russ inter-
preted to mean "in case you contested the will."

"Peter gave me a good sum of money a year ago, just before he had his new will made out. I thought you should
know that."

"I've no objections whatever, Mrs. Frazier. It was my father's to do with as he pleased. Understand, I hold no animosity toward you."

"Thank you," she said, then, "There are some personal
things in—his room. A small box of things, jewelry that belonged to your mother, his watch and ring. You'll want those,
of course. Anything else that you'd like, you're at liberty to
take."

Russ took the small box that had been his mother's and
her Bible. He took Peter's watch and ring and several pieces
from his unique collection of handguns, honorary badges,
photographs, and snapshots of the McNeelys, singly or together, his grandfather's key-winder watch and thick gold
chain that held various insignia of Irish societies to which he
had belonged, mementos of a man he had never known or
seen.

These he packed in a cardboard carton and was ready to leave. "What shall I do with his clothes?" Mrs. Frazier asked.

"Give them to any police charity that can make use of them."

"Yes. I'll do that." She followed him to the door and said, "I wish it could have been different between us. Peter loved you so much. He wouldn't marry me because he felt he would have lost you forever."

The softness of her words took him by surprise, and he choked up. Then he said, "He never mentioned it to me. It might have made a difference."

"No, I don't think so. I could see that in you the first time we met."

"I'm sorry," Russ said. "Good-by, Mrs. Frazier," and, remembering a phrase Peter used so often, "Go with God's hand on your shoulder."

On his way back to the Drake, he thought again of Ralph and Charlotte Simon and their failure to put in an appearance at Peter's funeral, although he hadn't expected Carol would come. But Ralph, Peter's oldest friend and political ally, who handled his insurance——? He felt oddly disturbed, then put the matter out of his mind.

At the hotel, crossing the lobby with the carton under his arms, he didn't recognize her as she rose from a chair and came toward him, then followed him to the desk where he got his key.

"Russ?"

He turned and saw her then, unfamiliar in a hat and tweed suit, somehow younger, fresher looking than he remembered her during their last weeks together in California. "Carol——"

"Hello, Russ."

"Carol. How are you?"

"Fine," she smiled lightly. "I wanted so much to come to Peter's funeral, but I knew there would be questions from the curious that might be embarrassing to you."

"It's all right, Carol. I understand. You——"

"I was fond of him, Russ, even though there was a lot I never understood about your relationship. I think it had something to do with us, too."

"I'm sorry about that, too, that I could never really explain it to you." There was an awkward moment of silence, then, "Could we have a drink together?"

She nodded. "Yes. I'd like that."

He handed the carton to a bellboy along with his key, then

guided Carol to the cocktail lounge. Over their drink, she said, "I'm sure you're curious why dad and mother weren't at the funeral or came to call. They're on a month-long trip to the Orient. I haven't any idea where they are at the moment, Tokyo, Hong Kong, Singapore, Taiwan, or wherever."

Russ nodded, accepting her explanation. "And you?" he asked.

"We're happy. Two children. Junior is three now. Betsy is fourteen months."

He felt a sharp inner shock. In none of his father's infrequent letters had he ever mentioned that Carol was the mother of two children, and now he felt even farther removed, totally remote from that part of his past. Peter had written him when Carol married Warren Deland following the divorce, but the subject of Carol had been a closed one between them after that brief note. "Congratulations," he said now, "belated as they are. I wish you and Warren every happiness life can offer."

"Thank you, Russ. Coming from you in this way means a lot to me."

He said, "I've always wanted the best for you, Carol, even though I never knew how to bring it off."

"Please, Russ. I—let's don't start rehashing things. I'm willing to share any blame. I suppose it was because I was never cut out to be a cop's wife, that very special kind of woman who has to compete with the excitement of the street. I never knew that until it was too late."

He had no answer to her correct analysis of their star-crossed marriage, and there was little else they could talk about with any sense of ease. He finished his drink and said, "I should get on with my packing. I'd like to get home tonight." He said "home" with new meaning.

She stood up and held out her hand. He took it, looked into her moistened eyes, and saw something close and familiar there, a memory of the distant past. Then she moved closer, still holding his hand, and kissed his cheek. "Good-by, Russ. All the luck and happiness in the world," and turned swiftly away.

Minutes later in his room, packing, he began the slow process of trying to shut out this last memory, along with others, from his mind, concentrating on *home;* Rachel, his crew, Ray Ycaza, and the case at hand. There were three hours to plane time. He placed a call to John Rivera and asked him to notify Ycaza that he would be back in his office next morning.

"Sure, Russ. Anybody else?"

"Yes, John, one more." He gave him Rachel's number, his flight number and time of arrival.

2 •

On the way to the airport rain began to fall. Massive clouds hung over the city and Russ wondered if operations would be shut down. Then, as though he had actually asked the question, the cab driver gratuitously offered with complete reassurance, "This ain't nothin', mister. They'll take off."

The activity at the airport was, as usual, chaotic. Russ checked his bag through, picked up a copy of the afternoon paper, had a cup of coffee and a sandwich, and killed some of the time by looking at the various exhibits and poking through the gift shops, seeing nothing that he thought would appeal to Rachel. When he heard his flight announced, he joined the throngs waiting to board. Buckled into his seat beside a window, there was a twenty-minute wait, but once the plane broke through the dense overcast, he settled down for the smooth flight to Los Angeles.

Russ opened the paper and scanned through its pages, but found no further mention of Captain Peter Liam McNeely. The press had paid its last respects and filed Captain McNeely's life away in its libraries. He sighed deeply and put the paper aside, then ordered a Scotch from the attractive stewardess and, when it came, sipped it slowly, trying to analyze his feelings, only now beginning to sense the total weariness of these past three days.

He tried not to remember Peter as he had seen him at Comiskey's, but the image came back to him again and again: a man he could hardly remember; old, shrunken, the futile attempts of the mortician's cosmeticians to eradicate the pallor of death and ravages of time from his deeply lined face. He tried to recall the Peter McNeely he had known at the height of his physical powers, moving strongly about the precinct station, striding erect along its streets, the symbol of power and authority. He saw Peter in their home, always gentle in the presence of Nora, showing his deep concern for her.

His eyes grew damp when he recalled those rare times when, between the ages of six and ten, Peter would take him and his mother for a drive in the car, or when they were together on the beach, outings that were often cut short because Nora would become overly tired.

And he wondered now how much Nora had known of the dark side of Peter's outside life, or suspected. In no way, either by manner or hint of words, had she ever, in Russ's presence, indicated that Peter had ever been anything but an upright, decent man, a loyal husband and father. Then why, he thought with a sense of regret, even remorse, could he not have looked to one side, as Nora had, and seen the other side of the man? His needs, the man who, despite their differences, had distributed his wealth generously among charities, old friends, to the woman who had cared for him since Nora's death, and finally, to himself?

And if his feelings about Peter's tainted wealth were great enough to have driven them apart then, how could he now accept more than a hundred thousand dollars from him in death?

Not during the entire flight had he devoted any thought to what lay ahead of him in Los Angeles.

Except for Rachel.

She was waiting there when he deplaned, and he brightened at the sight of her over the heads of those who were preceding him into the waiting lounge. He reached for her, held her and kissed her, feeling that this was his moment of total freedom from the past.

"You didn't get much sleep," she said finally in mild accusation.

"No," he admitted, "it wasn't restful, to say the least."

"I know, Russ. It's something we all have to live through, and it's not pleasant or restful. But it's over now."

He knew it wasn't over, no more than it had been over for Rachel when she received word of the death of her husband. They went silently, arms linked tightly, down the escalator toward BAGGAGE INCOMING.

"I'll get the car and meet you out front," Rachel suggested, but he negated that with a shake of his head.

"No. Wait here with me and we'll get the car together."

So they stood at the turntable's edge, arms still linked, until his bag slid down the chute, separating only when he reached in for it, then crossed the roadway into the huge parking lot. She slid in behind the wheel while he placed the bag in the rear compartment, then got in beside her.

"Relax, darling," Rachel said. "You're home now."

Exhausted, yet restless, he fell asleep in her arms, in his own bed, soothed and comforted by her presence. It was still dark when he felt her hands on his shoulders, calling his name, and was startled awake.

"What—what's wrong—"

"You were turning, tossing and talking, almost shouting—"

"I—I—what—?"

"Let me put some coffee on."

"What time is it?"

"A little past three. Bad dreams?"

"No—no, I can't remember a thing. I'm sorry, Rachel."

"Coffee?"

"My God, it's chilly, and I'm dripping with sweat."

"I know. Change into something dry while I get the coffee started."

Over coffee and apologies, he began talking as though a faucet had been turned on about things he had thought he could never tell anyone. Of his childhood with Nora and Peter, of Bobby Simon's suicide and his attachment to Carol, Nora's death, and his break with Peter over Mrs. Frazier, his marriage and its breakup. And of his ambivalence toward Peter, his remorse over the lost years between them.

Rachel listened without interruption, accepting all of it until he finally emptied himself of his capability for words. Then she said quietly, "Don't take on so much of the guilt, Russ. It wasn't all yours alone. You didn't leave him with emptiness. He had Mrs. Frazier and his memories. You had your own life to live, your wife and future to look to. Regrets, yes. We all have them."

"I have so many, Rachel."

"You're not alone, Russ. Regrets become a part of our memories, and memories grow dim and fade. Remember this: He loved you in his way, just as you loved him in yours. What was done can't be undone, but how you think of him now is what is important. That's what you can live with. Now let's try to get some sleep."

In bed again, they fell asleep almost at once, his arm around her shoulder, lips close to her face.

He awoke at his usual rising hour, alone in bed, smelling the fresh coffee, hearing Rachel moving about in the kitchen. He looked in on her only long enough to call "good morning" and kiss her, then showered and shaved.

They breakfasted together, and she could sense his eagerness to get to his office and the work at hand. And, driving there, Russ thought of Rachel's calming words about regrets and memories and smiled happily at her wisdom. Rachel made everything seem so clear. Everything in its proper place. Rachel. God bless Rachel.

After checking in with Rivera, Barker, and Captain Esau, and welcomed back by the staff, accepting their condolences, Ray arrived. In their office, he placed a call to Lennox and talked with Deliso, Barrett, and Paul. Roberts was in court. The crew had been unusually busy, and he promised to visit soon and be brought up to date on their activities.

When he was finished, Ray returned with two cups of coffee and clued him in on the progress of the case. "Butler is out on fifty thousand, and we're sitting on his pad day and night. He hasn't made a move. The Thomas broad went out on fifteen hundred and we've got men on her pad around the clock. No sign of Peterson anywhere. We've got a dozen or more maybes on him, ran every one of them down. Nothing. And not one damned thing on John Hall Ellison."

"What about Connie Moya?"

"*Nada.* The stakeout is still operative, but she's Mrs. Clean in person. The two kids go off to school, come home, all normal as apple pie. Connie goes out to shop at her favorite supermarket, comes home, stays there. Had one laugh. A neighbor reported a suspicious man loitering in a car. Two Van Nuys cops came down on Lou Burns like John Wayne. Lou identified himself and got a lecture on how to conduct a stakeout. Boy, was he burned good."

"So what else is doing?"

"Well, the weather's been fantastic. Geiger and Harris nailed the hoods who ripped off a couple of dudes in front of their home during a birthday party. The Rams are—"

"That I can read about on the sports pages. Anything on tap we can follow up?"

"Stick around, *amigo.* Maybe the Good Fairy will phone in with another tip."

"Sure. I'll look under my pillow tomorrow morning. She may show up and leave a note for me." In mild disgust, Russ picked up the thickening file and read through the most recent supplementary surveillance reports and saw nothing to excite his interest. He went out and chatted with Bob Barker, about to leave on a buy deal in the Firestone area, then with Sharon, getting ready to drive to West Hollywood to work a deal with the station crew there. Movement, but he no longer felt a part of it, manacled to the Lloyd/Despues/Stennis cases.

The call came in from a member of the Torrance P.D. narcotics team, Jerry Keating, whom Russ knew from previous deals on which they had been involved together. Ycaza flagged him down in the outer office. "A Torrance narc, for you, Russ."

"McNeely here."

"Russ? Jerry Keating."

"What's doing, Jerry?"

"Maybe a line on this Peterson dude you're looking for."

"What've you got?"

"A spade hype-pusher we busted last night. We sprung Peterson's name on him, and this cat's eyes went tilt, but he wasn't too anxious to talk. We hit him with it a few more times, and he came through. Seems he knows your dude from way back, read us a pretty good description of him. Claims he's seen your man around in San Pedro maybe half a dozen times in the past six months. We sweated him for more, but that's all he came up with. He turned two other pushers for us, so I figure he'd come clean if he had anything more on your dude. We're holding him here on possession for sale, if you want to talk to him."

"What's your dude's name?"

"Rafe Jackson, with a few more aliases. Changes names like you change shirts. We've had him before, got a full book on him."

"Thanks, Jerry. I'll drop by later and look him over."

"Okay, any time. I'll leave word here in case I'm out on the street."

It wasn't much to go on, but it provided some needed activity. He and Ycaza made the trip, interviewed Jackson, and came up with no more than Keating had told Russ on the phone. Jackson was too far down the line to be scoring directly from Peterson or Butler, but his description of Peterson had been close, and he had known the name.

They drove to L.A.P.D.'s Harbor Division in San Pedro, talked with the detectives and narcotics men there, left copies of Peterson's mug shots, the Ellison sketch and description with them. On the way back, they checked by radio with the surveillance team on Warren Canyon Road, on the one on Newton Street, the third on Sylvan Street. All reported quiet, normal activity.

"We're sure as hell spinning our wheels on this one," Ycaza commented as he returned the mike to its holder.

"Looks that way, but that's how it goes. Ten minutes from now all hell could break loose."

"The police classroom solution to monotony, the thing that keeps cops on the job, the unexpected. How we depend on it. It's our food, air, and water."

276

McNeely said, "Eventually, all cops become philosophers. And bores."

And thus ended their fruitless day.

3●

Three days passed. Nothing new had developed, nor had there been anything of particular note from the surveillance teams. The only fringe benefit for Ycaza and McNeely was that their night hours continued undisturbed, permitted normal social activities and uninterrupted sleep. Over the weekend, Ray took his family to Bakersfield for a visit with the Maldonados, and Russ and Rachel went fishing with the Camerons, neighbors who owned a thirty-eight-foot Chris Craft.

On their return from Catalina early on Sunday night, Russ and Rachel drove to her house where she put on a pot of coffee and Russ poured brandy for them. Later, they showered and got into night clothes, and watched the Eleven O'clock News, and prepared for bed. And lying in each other's arms, warm and secure, she sensed that the emotional strain of Chicago had diminished, feeling it in his speech, his relaxed body and breathing. In a semidoze, she heard him say, "Rachel, I love you. You believe that, don't you?"

It took a moment or two to realize he had said it, then, "Yes, darling. And I love you. Very much."

She felt his arms tighten around her. "Do you ever think that you might come around to marrying a cop?"

"That," she teased, fully awake now, "would depend on the specific cop."

"Specifically, then, a cop like me."

"No," she said, "not a cop *like* you."

"More specifically, me."

It was beyond teasing now, and she remained silent, burrowing closer, her lips pressed against his shoulder. Russ said, "To put it more formally, Rachel, will you marry me?"

"Oh—Russ—"

"Well, will you? Seriously—"

"I don't know, Russ. I've thought about it, asked myself why I hadn't said yes the first time."

"What answers do you come up with?"

"Yes and no. About even."

He fell silent, confused, waiting. She felt his arms relax and moved away, only inches, but enough so that he withdrew his arms entirely and rolled over on his side, facing her. "We seem to be having a problem again," he said.

"Why can't we go along as we are?" Rachel asked.

"I guess because I think there should be more between us than this. A more stable foundation to build an even closer relationship, one that— Oh, hell, Rachel, don't you want more than this?"

"I—yes—but—"

"But what?"

"I don't know if I can make you see it the way I do, Russ."

"Try me."

"All right. I was young when I married Bill just before he joined the air force. Both of us were so filled with confidence that he would come back and the whole world would belong to us. Bill and me, our children. Neither of us even considered the dangers. His letters were always cheerful, talking about the future. Then, six months later, he was dead. It was so sudden, so shocking, so unbelievable. An air force major at the door to tell me about it, that Bill was dead and wouldn't be coming back. Except for a letter, a certificate of commendation, a medal in a box he never saw or wore, something about his insurance. His body was never found, so I didn't even have him to bury.

"It took me over a year to get things straightened out in my mind. I've told you the rest, how I came here. We met and I was happy again. Then, hearing you, Perry, Steve, Harry, and Joe talking about your work, exposing yourselves to dope dealers, guns, and knives, it seemed to be the same thing happening all over again. Living with insecurity. It made me realize that that was what happened to your marriage to Carol, not knowing when you left in the morning whether by nightfall she would be a wife or a widow. The same thing frightens me, Russ. I really don't know."

He waited until her passionate indictment had passed, knew she was crying softly, silently to herself. Then he put his arms around her again and said, "Rachel, have I made you happy?"

"Yes—oh, yes, Russ—"

"Rachel, listen. Life itself, here, anywhere, is filled with dangers and risk of all kinds. We're surrounded by danger. Driving in a car, walking along a street, a sudden heart attack, a crook with an eye on your purse. They're in the papers every day of our lives. I have a job to do, a necessary job for which I've been trained. There's less chance of my being killed on duty than most people have driving the freeways every day—"

"What about these two scars," she said, running her finger over them.

"What about lightning never striking twice in the same place?" he countered.

"You're rationalizing, Russ, the way Bill and I used to talk about his flying. The thought of going through that again as a wife—"

"Can you honestly say you love me, Rachel?"

"Yes. I do, Russ, honestly."

"Then—let's put it aside for now. But keep on loving me. I need you. I need to know you're here, close to me. I count on it."

She didn't reply, but moved closer to him, kissed him. Minutes later, she was asleep. It took much longer for Russ.

4●

Don Reed pulled into the parking lot at the Harrington Coffee Shop near the Santa Monica Airport, locked his Mercedes, and walked over to Charlie Valentine's Lincoln Continental and got in. Valentine started the car and drove out, heading toward the freeway.

"Where are we going, Charlie?" Reed asked.

"Just for a ride and a quiet talk."

"Sounds like you've got a problem."

"The reason I asked you to meet me is because there *is* a problem. Yours. And I don't want it to become mine."

"Naturally. Let's have it."

"I had lunch with Paul Landis yesterday. He told me all about your man Butler, who'll probably get hit with a fifty-thousand-dollar bail. Also about one of your women operators out on fifteen hundred. And that your number three man is in hiding from the police, who are looking for him in connection with the murder of one of their dealers."

"Okay, Charlie, to use your words, it's my problem, and I'm on top of it. Butler will have to take some kind of a fall. Moose Peterson is staying holed up. A man his size is too easy to spot. Soon as this thing cools a little, I'll get him out of here, across the border into Mexico, until it's over. I'm setting up this deal so that things will run the same as they did before, even with Eddie and Moose out of it."

Valentine took an off-ramp, and they were now driving along the coast road. For some minutes there was silence between them, each man gauging the other, seeking answers in his own mind. Then Valentine said, "This thing is getting too damned risky, Don. I think perhaps we should suspend the whole operation temporarily."

Reed's irritation was apparent. "That's pretty damned infantile, Charlie. It took a hell of a lot of time, effort, and money to put this thing together. We've got a dozen or more major distributors handling our product and relying on us to supply them with high-quality merchandise. Each of them has his own corps of dealers working, and each dealer has his army of pushers hustling to make a hell of a profit for us. Me, you, the guys in Texas, your financial backers. If we suspend operations, we lose our distributors, and it would take years to get back to where we are right now."

"That's all well and good, Don, but your two top men have put the whole show in jeopardy. I have a strong obligation to my friends in Texas and to the men who put up the money—"

"And double their money four to six times a year."

"—and can't afford to become involved in—in *murder*, for God's sake!"

"Hold it, Charlie. You, they, everybody in this thing knows what the risks and dangers are. To make money fast, as we've damn well been doing, there are those risks and dangers. The way we're set up, they've been minimized—"

"Until now," Valentine interjected.

"—and one slip doesn't mean we've got to tuck our heads under our arms and give it all up. Landis is on Butler's case, I've talked to him, too, and he feels he can stall things. Plea bargaining, a sympathetic judge. There's no doubt that Eddie will have to plead guilty and take a short fall, but he'll be well paid for it. He won't talk."

"And the Thomas woman, out on fifteen hundred. You know very well she talked, don't you?"

"It figures, but we can handle that before Eddie comes to trial."

"With another murder, Don?"

Reed said, "Charlie, the success of this operation until now has rested on the one solid fact that each of us has allowed the other to do his job independently. If we start interfering now, it's all over."

"Understand me, Don, I'm not interfering at the operational level, only as far as it affects the security of my friends in Texas and here."

"Then I suggest you let me handle it in my own way and trust me. I've already made arrangements with one of my top distributors down in Orange County to come up and take over Eddie's job and his number two man along with him. Let me worry about Cora Thomas and Moose Peterson. I don't know who your respectable financial backers are, but you can tell them, Roy Chase and Al DeWitt, to relax—"

"As a matter of fact, I haven't told them anything yet."

"Then don't stir up a can of worms. Only you know who your backers are and the Texas people are known to just you and me. You do trust me, don't you, Charlie?" he added with a smile.

"Of course, Don, but I don't underestimate the resources of the police."

"If it makes you feel any better, neither do I. Let's turn around and go back now, shall we? I've got a number of things to do. And keep it cool, Charlie. It will never reach high enough to me, and that's your safety factor."

On the way back, Valentine seemed less tense, and a few minutes later he said, "Don, how much will you need before you quit?"

Reed laughed lightly. "When we first started out together, I set my sights on a million, clear and tax-free. Two years ago, when I had that million salted away safely out of the country, I moved the goal up to two million. I'm almost there, but man's inherent greed, the same disease we all have, you and your backers, is still working on me. The mark is now three. When I hit five, I hope I'll be cured to the extent that I can put it all behind me, move to the Caribbean, South America, or Europe and take the rest of my life to spend it. Every dime of it."

Valentine said, "I hope you make it, but I wouldn't set that high a goal."

"I'll make it. What about our next shipment? We're beginning to hurt."

"It's being set up. Villanueva got in touch with his man in Bogotá finally, who has made all the arrangements with a new source: a Paraguayan revolutionist general who needs the hard cash to buy guns, grenades, and other equipment and has his supplier working overtime. We're setting up the biggest deal yet, a hundred kilos of heroin and a hundred of cocaine for the first trip. If that works out, we'll duplicate it two months later."

Reed whistled in approbation. "Christ, that's one hell of an outlay."

Now, Valentine smiled. "Which is something else you don't have to worry about. Chase is allocating a hefty chunk of it to us. Can we handle a hundred kilos of each?"

"If you can handle the financing, we can handle the merchandise."

"Okay, Don. It's heavy, no doubt about it. My end of the deal will come to two and a half million."

Reed's mind became a computer, equating the outlay with the profits at the distributor level. The street value was incalculable, far into the tens of millions. Valentine interrupted his thoughts. "Chase and DeWitt bought a new Cessna Skymaster, the turbo-charged job. They flew it down to the ranch from Wichita a few weeks ago. When I've put the money together, DeWitt will fly it up here to pick it up."

"We could use the coke right now. We're scraping the bottom of the barrel."

"Ration what you have until this new load comes in."

"When?"

"Within two or three weeks."

"I think we'll just barely squeak through."

"This other thing, Don——'

"Let me handle it, Charlie. It's just a matter of time before I have it all straightened out."

"It's more than that. I think we should lay it on the line to Chase and DeWitt. As a matter of fact, when I spoke to Roy the other night, I suggested that when Al flies up for the money, I might go back to the ranch with him. And bring you along with us."

Which came as another surprise. Until now, and since that first introduction, Valentine had never suggested another face-to-face meeting between Reed and the Texas group.

"Something important?" Reed asked casually.

"Just to discuss the operational setup you're planning with your new people."

Reed thought for a moment, then said, "Okay, count me in."

"Fine. I'll let you know when Al plans to come up."

5•

At noon on Thursday, Rudy Arboleya came out of the corner restaurant, went to the public phone booth on the wall facing the parking lot, and dialed Ray Ycaza's number. Ray was out, but Rudy refused to leave his name or a number. At five-thirty he tried again from the shopping center and was told Ray had left for home.

After eating his dinner, he walked past the cashier's box at the Rialto Theater and spoke with Isobel for a while, then tried Ycaza's home number, and caught him just as he was finishing his dinner. "Ray? It's Rudy."

"Hey, *amigo.* How goes it?"

"Okay, Ray. Pretty soon, soon's Isobel and I can get some time off together, you're goin'a get an invitation to a private wedding. You and your wife."

"That's great, Rudy. We'll be happy to come."

"Something else, Ray—"

"What?"

"Something I heard at the garage, in your line."

"What is it, Rudy?"

"Well, you know how these guys rap about everything, broads, money, dope, you know? Well, I heard one guy mention the name of one of your guys who got iced—"

With heightened interest, "What name, Rudy?"

"Cruz Despues, an undercover dick."

Ycaza tried very hard to suppress the excitement he felt. "Cruz Despues. Who mentioned him, Rudy, in what way?"

"Look, I got to get home an' take over watchin' Robert from the neighbor lady who's babysittin' him. Can we meet somewhere when I get off work tomorrow an' I'll lay it on you?"

"Listen, Rudy, this can be very important. To me and the partner I'm working with. If I can get hold of him, can we make it tonight?"

"He a Chicano or a paddy?"

"A paddy, but he's good people." Ray remembered Rudy's first encounter with Geiger and said, "Not the one I introduced you to that time. This is another partner."

"Yeah, okay, but not here. Somebody spots two straights showing up around here, the word goes out, you know?"

"Set it up any way you want."

"Okay. Isobel gets off like close to nine forty-five, maybe ten. I'll take off soon's she gets home an' meet you—uh—on the corner of Ravenna an' Two twenty-third. I'll park on the corner there around ten-fifteen."

"Right. If you don't get a call from me by eight-thirty, it's on."

"Okay. I'll see you."

Ycaza hung up and dialed McNeely's number. After eight rings, he dialed Rachel's number and found him. It was only necessary to mention the name of Cruz Despues to get McNeely's immediate assent to meet him at the specified location. He arrived at ten o'clock and was joined moments later by Ycaza. A lead—any lead—in the Despues murder had a far deeper emotional pull than that of Whitey Lloyd; and both were tied to a single suspect, the elusive Ellison. In Ycaza's car, the partners had little to discuss for the moment. Rudy Arboleya was the key to whatever they would learn. They sat smoking their cigarettes in silence until both saw the car approach, stop just ahead of them, and park.

"That's him," Ycaza said, and got out on the poorly lighted street and signaled with a wave of his hand. Rudy walked back to the car and got in the front seat beside Ycaza, McNeely now on the rear seat.

"My partner, Russ McNeely, Rudy. Rudy Arboleya, Russ, the friend I told you about."

Rudy acknowledged the introduction with a brief nod. Ycaza said, "What's the story, Rudy? Give it to us from page one, eh?"

"Sure, Ray. It's like this. At the garage—"

Ycaza interrupted for McNeely's benefit. "Excuse me, Rudy. That's the Rodriguez Garage on Two twenty-third, just off Avalon, Russ. Handles most of the repair work in that area. Go ahead, Rudy."

"Okay. Comes noontime, the whole place shuts down for lunch except for emergencies or some guy comes to pick up his car. We got nine mechanics in the shop. We all bring our lunch and eat it there, except once in a while, one or two guys get tired of cold food and go down to the corner to Manuelo's for something hot, or they pick up something from Lazarro's Food Market close by.

"So the guys eatin' in eat together in twos and threes. Artie Lucero, Mike Mendares, and Gil Peludo, always together. Sometimes they eat quick, go up to Two hundred twenty-second Street to Dos Hermanos for a couple beers, and shoot a game of pool.

"Yesterday noon, Artie, Mike, and Gil do that. About ten minutes later, Pete Rojas shows up."

"Tell Russ who Pete Rojas is, Rudy," Ycaza suggested.

"Pete used to work for Rodriguez before I came on the job, used to hang out with a gang along with Richie Obregon, used to be the parts man there. What I hear is, Rodriquez found out Pete was pushing more than parts, an' some strange lookin' cats were showin' up around the place to rap with him—"

"Pushing what besides parts?" McNeely asked.

"Stuff, man, dope. So old man Rodriguez, he don't go for that shit in his place, an' he cans Pete. Next, there's a hassle

284

between the old man an' George Ruiz, the guy I hear Pete's been pushin' for, but the old man tells George he won't take Pete back and George an' his brother Ernie can go screw theirselfs.

"Next thing you know, Pete's workin' for a parts wholesaler down in San Pedro, Tri-City, delivering parts to garages like Rodriguez, so Pete starts comin' around like once a week to deliver the rebuilt parts we order from Tri-City. Also, he drops off the junk he pushes in the neighborhood, right?"

"Where, Rudy?" Ycaza asked.

"Well—" He hesitated. "Maybe to one of the guys in the shop, I don't know for sure, but mostly, he stops at Dos Hermanos Bar, maybe to deliver stuff to the bartender or whoever—"

"Ernie and George Ruiz," Ycaza said to McNeely, "own the Dos Hermanos."

"I know," Russ said. "Our Firestone crews have had them tabbed for some time, but we've never had enough to go on. Go ahead, Rudy. Where does Cruz Despues fit into this?"

"Well," Rudy continued, "Pete shows up around noon, delivers some orders to our parts man, raps a little with a couple guys, then asks where Artie, Gil, and Mike are. Benny Contreras tells him they're over shooting pool. He gets in his panel truck an' takes off. Half an hour later, Artie, Mike, an' Gil come back, an' Mike is bitchin' mad. His stall is next to mine, an' he's blowin' off about Pete, what a thief he is. I just keep workin', an' later on, there's a break, an' Mike is still freaked out about Pete, so I ask him, 'Hey, what's happenin'?'

"Mike says, 'That sonofabitch Rojas. I'm makin' bucks for him, an' he's screwin' me around. Owes me three hundred I put up for some stuff, an' he tells me next time. Next time. Three times now he tells me next time. If he wasn't a goddamn ex-pug, I'd lay a fuckin' bolt cutter on his head.' Well, he goes on like that, an' I say, kiddin' him, you know, 'Whyn't you drop a dime an' blow the whistle on the punk?'

"So Mike says, 'You out of your mind, man. I blow the whistle on one of Ruiz's pushers, I go down the drain. I ain't no goddamn hero like Cruz Despues.'

" 'Like who?' I ask him. 'Cruz Despues. Casey. You didn't know Casey?' 'No,' I say, 'who the hell is Casey Despues?'

" 'Oh, yeah,' Mike says, 'you were up in Chino when it happened.' 'When what happened?' I say.

" 'When they blew his ass up,' he tells me.

"Well, Mike wants to talk, work his burn off, so he says, 'Casey was an undercover cop for the sheriff. He was gettin' a little too close to Ernie an' George Ruiz. They know who Casey is, so they set him up, get a broad to call him an' say she had some info she could give him if he'll meet her at Moreno's Bar late at night. Okay. This Despues kid shows up an' there's this hit man waitin' for him out in the parkin' lot. Bang! Bang! He's ripped off. Clean. Just like that.'

"I ask Mike who done the job for Ruiz, was it Pete Rojas? He says, 'Hell, no, man. Pete don't use guns, only his fists.' Then he tells me he heard it was an out-of-town spook who makes his living hittin' guys who get in somebody's way. A real pro.

"Last night I got to thinkin' about it an' like I owe you a solid for all you done for me. An' Isobel an' Robert. I try to get Mike to talk more about it today, but he's worked off his burn on Pete an' tells me to forget it and don't say nothin' about him talkin' about it. When I got off work this afternoon, I called you. That's it."

For a moment there was silence in the car; then McNeely said, "Where is this Tri-City outfit?"

"I been there a couple of times to pick up parts between regular deliveries. It's on Sixth Street between Reckord Avenue and Mesa Street in San Pedro. A big wrecking yard, body shop, takes up a whole half block."

"What type of vehicle does Pete Rojas use to make his deliveries?"

"It's an old Chevy panel job, about a '68 or '69, solid sides, double doors in the back."

"Can you recall the license plate on it?"

"No. I never noticed."

"How many mechanics you work with are users?" McNeely asked.

"Maybe one or—hey, man, don't go layin' any muscle on those guys. I'm dealin' you heavy on the other thing, that's enough. These guys work for a living. You bust anybody down there, Mike Mendares'll start rememberin' he talked to me."

Ycaza said, "I'ts okay, Rudy. We won't touch your buddies."

"Rodriguez isn't any part of this?" McNeely said.

"No way, man. He's an arrow, real straight. Only reason he even lets Pete deliver is, if he don't, George Ruiz'll get one of his punks to toss a fire bomb in the garage some night. Bloo-ie! Up she goes in smoke. An' if one or two of the guys are users, he for sure don't know nothin' about it, else he'd of fired their ass out of there long ago."

"Okay, Rudy. If any of this works, we owe you, and for the Jesse James thing, too. I promise you your name won't be mentioned in any report we write."

"Thanks, Ray. These cats find out, I'd sure as hell have to start worryin' about Isobel and Robert, you know?"

"Don't worry, we'll keep you out of it."

"Okay. I get anything more, I'll call you again."

"Sure. You do that. Anything else you want to ask, Russ?"

"No, I've got the picture. And thanks, Rudy. I owe you one, too."

"No sweat, man. You finished with me?"

"Yes," Ycaza said, then, "You didn't tell Isobel or anybody else about this, did you?"

"Oh, man, no. I'd have to have garbage for brains to do that."

They were silent for a while after Rudy left them; then Ycaza said, "What do you think, Russ?"

"Another link in a long chain, Ray. A few more to tie together. A spade made the hit on Casey Despues. A spade made the hit on Whitey Lloyd. The bullets in both hits match up. Ellison, whoever the hell he is, is our man, no two ways about that. Rafe Jackson has seen Moose Peterson in the San Pedro area several times. Pete Rojas works for Tri-City in San Pedro and delivers to the Ruiz brothers and may even do some pushing for them on the side. We don't need a calculator to tell us what that adds up to. If we can break this the right way, we can come up with a lot of good-sized fish in our net."

"You make it sound logical, Russ, except for the spade. Chicanos and spades around here are more blood enemies than blood brothers. They don't generally play footsie with each other."

McNeely shrugged. "Unless he was imported. A big-time doper like Ruiz can afford what it takes for a single hit, and an out-of-town hit man couldn't care less who he works for."

"Could be. At least, we're moving in the right direction. Let's sleep on it, Russ. Tomorrow morning we can start fitting some of these new pieces together."

Chapter Ten

1●

On the following morning, in Inglewood Municipal Court, McNeely, Ycaza, Roberts, Barrett, and Deliso were present at Eddie Butler's hearing, at which his attorney's motion to dismiss was denied, his trial date in Superior Court placed on the calendar, with bail at the maximum fifty-thousand dollars. Paul Landis's motion for lower bail was also denied. Within an hour, a bondsman posted the required bond, and Butler was released. He left with Landis, a detective from Metro Bureau tailing behind.

Moments later, the Metro team assigned to maintain a surveillance on Butler's house on Warren Canyon Drive was notified, and shortly thereafter, the team of Scotty Rich and Roland Nelson, having previously checked out the location, were in position, able now to check Butler's comings and goings and those of any visitors. In a quiet residential section such as this, it would become necessary to move from one location to another in order to prevent inquisitive neighbors from phoning to the nearest police station to report suspicious loitering by two possible burglars; therefore they had picked three such spots least likely to cause such suspicions.

In Landis's car, Butler said, "What comes next, Paul?"

"Let me worry about that, Eddie," Landis replied easily. "You're free for the next two months, and I can stretch that out with one or two continuances, if necessary, to give us more breathing room. For the present, I'd guess your house will be under some sort of surveillance, hoping to pick Peterson up, or anybody else among your associates, so be careful."

"That'll never happen. We've never used the house for a meet with anyone except the one time Lloyd got onto us. What about my phone?"

"I doubt they'd try to fool around with that. In order to tap it legally, they've got to get a federal court order, very tough to get these days. Also, after thirty days, they're required to submit transcripts of every conversation recorded to the court and us. However, it would be a good idea to make any necessary calls from public phones. Even if you're being tailed, you'll be safe in a public booth."

Eddie nodded. "No problem. Where are we going now?"

"To my office. You're a client, so there's nothing in that to excite undue interest or suspicion. Don is waiting there for us, so you'll be able to talk in safety. In the future, we can arrange similar meetings without the cops knowing you're meeting Don instead of visiting your attorney."

"Okay. Where is Moose?"

"Don will give you that information. There's a wanted-for-information-and-questioning out on him, so you won't be able to meet in public, of course. At the moment, I can tell you he's safe."

"Can I phone him?"

"I'm sure you can. Once. Then set up a time and place schedule where you can reach each other by public telephone."

In Landis's office, Don Reed was waiting. After initial greetings, he and Eddie moved into a private conference room where Eddie's first question was, "Is Moose all right?"

"He's fine. Here's his new name, address, and phone number down in Lakewood. He's called me at the apartment a few times, getting antsy. You can work out some way to meet him, but make sure there's no tail on you. And no more calls to my apartment except in emergencies, and only through you. Okay?"

"Sure. Who's minding the store?"

"Let's discuss that first. I've brought Anse Talbot in from Orange County and arranged for him and his number-two man, Del Foreman, to handle the contact with our distributors. He's already in operation, and his setup down there is being taken care of. He's met with Simon Hernandez and our key distributors already." Reed, watching Butler closely, noted his reaction and continued.

"There's nothing for you to worry about on that score, Eddie. As soon as you and Moose are in the clear, you'll come back to a much better situation, sitting on top of Talbot and Foreman, directing the operation at a level higher than before and farther out of reach of the narcs."

"There's still the question of what kind of a fall I'm going to have to take, Don."

"All I can tell you, Eddie, is that you're going to have the best that money can buy. Paul has been working on it, wheeling and dealing. He's got an idea that the D.A. isn't as sure of himself as he'd like us to believe, which means there's the best possibility that a deal can be made. How do you feel about doing a year in County, say a total of eight months, maybe nine, with good behavior, and parole?"

"Not too damned good, but it sounds better than a full jolt in the joint."

"If we can buy that, it's like finding gold, Eddie. You won't lose by it financially, you know that. Just your freedom temporarily."

Butler smiled weakly. "It that's the best we can do, I'll have to buy it."

"Good. It's possible we may be able to do better, but for the moment, we're hanging on to this possibility."

"All right. Where do I stand right now?"

"Out of it. Until your trial, no contact with any distributor or Hernandez, and as little as possible with me. The same goes for Moose. If they tie either one of you up with Lloyd, all bets are off."

"What about the dude who did Lloyd?"

"He's a pro. Moose got hold of him. He did his job and collected his fee, twenty-five hundred. He shouldn't be a problem. There's something else. I'm going to have to be out of town for a while, possibly a week. A trip to Texas to help set up the biggest buy we've made yet. Once it's set up, there'll be another one just like it two months later and probably every two or three months after that. If it works out, we'll have the biggest operation going in all of Southern California, maybe spread out north as far as San Francisco."

"Jesus," Butler breathed.

"I'm telling you this for one good reason, Eddie, to let you know what you'll have to look forward to when this is all over and you're in the clear. In a year or two, with this setup going for us, we can call it quits, retire with all the money we'll ever need, free and clear."

Eddie nodded. He had few doubts about Don Reed. His big ace in the hole was that if Reed double-crossed him, he could pull him down, destroy him. Paul Landis and the Texas group with him. His one regret was that Reed's financial backers, the "legitimate" fast-buck businessmen who put up the money and took their tax-free profits, were unknown to him. He thought of them as parasites and despised them. But Reed, Landis, and the Texas people were enough security for the moment. He could afford to wait it out.

2●

The Butler hearing concluded, McNeely and Ycaza returned to the Hall of Justice. Captain Esau was in his office meeting with his four field lieutenants. They went into their own office, got out of their jackets, removed their guns, and prepared to put the pieces of their jigsaw puzzle together.

On the large chart they had made up earlier, they now added the names they had gotten from Rudy Arboleya; those of Tri-City Auto Works, Pete Rojas, Ernie and George Ruiz, Mike Mendares and the other mechanics at Rodriguez Garage. These, they kept separate from Eddie Butler and Moose Peterson, not yet fully connected, but listed on the same chart as possibles. Just _how_ they were related was the imponderable, waiting for some source of information or action to tie them in together.

The phone rang, and McNeely answered it. John Rivera said, "Captain would like to see you and Ray for a few minutes, Russ."

"Be right there." To Ycaza, "Let's go. Esau wants to chat with us."

The meeting was still going on, and Rivera said, "Go on in. You may learn something."

They knocked, entered the inner office, and Esau looked up. "Come in, Russ, Ray. Take a seat. I'll be through here in a minute." Then continuing, "Mm-m—yes, here we are. Out of seventeen hundred and ninety-five narcotics arrests last month, three hundred eighty-five were rejected by the D.A. and one hundred and four released for other reasons, which indicates that there's some sloppy work going on in the field, and I want that tightened up; twenty-one and a third per cent rejections are too high, and I don't want to be sitting in the chief's office trying to explain why. As for the other figures

I've quoted, there's an indication of a bit of drying up in several of our zones, not quite panic level, more like a temporary shortage. The heroin picked up during the last ten days is down as low as three to five percent in quality, and street prices are up as much as twenty-five to thirty-five per cent in some areas. Here—" he picked up a sheet of Xeroxed figures—"burglaries and street crimes in those same areas are up, probably hypes trying to meet the inflated prices."

Lieutenant Marcus said, "That parallels what I've been hearing from some LAPD guys. A few major dealers have been taken out, and the little guys are running short. Maybe the tail is beginning to wag the dog?"

Lieutenant Dickerson snorted audibly. "Don't you believe it. Hell, in nine years, I've seen it happen a dozen times or more. We take out a few big crooks, somebody moves into those slots and take over."

"You're right, Dick," Esau agreed. "We can't get too complacent about a temporary situation. We know we can't stop the flow no matter what the shortage may be at the moment. These figures are six days old. By now they could be dead, so let's not get too optimistic." He stood up and said, "I think that's all for now, gentlemen. Let's get back to work."

As the four lieutenants filed out, Esau said to Bob Barker, "Hold it, Bob. This concerns you, too." Barker resumed his seat. John Rivera ushered Sergeant Sorensen in and closed the door. "Russ," Esau said, "bring us up to date."

McNeely did so, using his field notebook to refresh his memory, outlining his and Ycaza's meeting with their latest informant, unnamed, and the leads they had obtained, concluding, "I've already alerted the MV and station crews at Lennox to Tri-City in San Pedro. We'll be keeping a close eye on the panel Chevy Pete Rojas uses for deliveries, with a camera aboard in case they catch him delivering anything other than auto parts. Also, we're extending our search for Moose Peterson to San Pedro.

"We now have Metro teams sitting on Butler's home as well as those of Connie Moya and Cora Thomas and a tail on Butler since his release on fifty-thousand-dollar bail this morning. Somewhere along the line, we're hoping he tries to establish contact with Peterson, or vice versa. We have a five-state APB out for Ellison, and if nothing happens within another forty-eight hours, we'll put it on nationwide. Meanwhile, we've covered the five-state area with our Special Bulletin with the artist's sketch and full description. That's it for the moment."

"Good," Esau said. "Now I'm going to let you in on something we've been working on that might touch on this case. Last October, at the Drug Enforcement Administration's Western Regional Conference in Denver, I ran into Bert Esmond who used to be my deputy here. He retired and became chief of the Narcotics Bureau in San Antonio, his home town. Bert was telling me about an operation his people have been working on with DEA for about a year, a transmission belt for dope that runs between South America and the United States.

"This operation, he and DEA believe, imports heroin and cocaine and delivers in big lots to major distribution centers, New York, New Jersey, Chicago, Detroit, Gary, etc., and probably to the West Coast. He wondered if we had anything going that could point to Southwest Texas, and at that time I had to tell him we had nothing for him. Bert introduced me to the deputy director of DEA's Dallas office, Willis Ames, who gave me a little more on it and said that if we turned up anything that was even remotely related or useful, he'd appreciate hearing about it.

"We had nothing going to tie into a Texas operation, so I dictated an information memo for Billy Sorensen, who passed it around to our field lieutenants. We got no fallout, and Billy kept the memo in his Intelligence files. Billy?"

Sorensen opened a file, removed a number of Xerox sheets, and handed a set to each man present. "Yesterday, we received this information from Willis Ames out of the DEA office in Dallas. The cover letter is directed to the DEA office here in Los Angeles, with a note to Captain Easu reminding him of their October meeting in Denver. The material attached to it comes from DEA in Washington and tells the story."

Esau said, "Read it and we'll take it from there."

The second letter, long and detailed, was datelined from Washington to Dallas and read:

On 3/May/75, S/A Lee Tenady, DEA, Bogotá Colombia, relayed the following to DEA, Washington, D.C., transmitted herewith for action your office:

25/April/75: Intercepted telephone call made by unknown male, originating Guadalajara, Mexico, phone number unknown, to 561.767 Bogotá, a number under surveillance this office, located in the home of Armando Duprez. Call was taken by a male addressed as "Estaban," identity unknown this office. Discussion followed relating to one hundred (100) kilos *harina* (flour) and one hundred (100) kilos *cereal* (corn), words interchangeable with heroin and cocaine.

26/April/75: Intercepted telephone call from Bogotá, 561.767, made to Guadalajara, Mexico, 25-27-84. Discussion between "Estaban" and male addressed as "Hector," in which Estaban advised that the *harina* and *cereal* would be ready on 15/May/75 at prices previously agreed upon in Guadalajara. Estaban then asked Hector to advise "Bishop" (no further identification). Hector replied he feared "interference" on his telephone line (a tap?) and asked Estaban to make the call.

27/April/75: Telephone call from Bogotá, 561.767, made to (512) 655-6501 (San Antonio, Texas) in which Estaban spoke with unidentified male who took same message, advised he would relay it to "Bishop."

Armando Duprez, Bogotá, suspected to be one of a number of message drops for large narcotics syndicate operating widely in South America. This letter for your information and/or action in San Antonio area.
End message from Washington.

Continuing, Dallas office, DEA, referred above information to San Antonio office and returns the following:

Telephone number (512) 655-6501 is unlisted phone on premises of Excalibur Motel, San Antonio. Excalibur is managed by Lester Varick, owned by Bishop Enterprises, a private holding company in which Royal Chase is majority stockholder, Alan DeWitt, minority stockholder, both residing on Wrayburn Ranch, 28 miles north of Del Rio on U.S. 277.

26/April/75: At 2005 hours, by court-approved telephone tap on (512) 655-6501, intercepted call to (213) 274-8421, conversation re: "flour" and "corn" discussed (as previously noted) between caller, Les (Lester Varick?) and male, identified as "Charlie."

Information referred to deputy director, Los Angeles office.

Above information forwarded for your information and/or action.

Willis Ames
Deputy Director, DEA
Dallas, Texas

When the letters had been read, Esau said, "Two things. First, we know that a hell of a lot of cocaine has been blowing into our area from unknown sources for some time, and very recently, we find that someone has turned off the spigot. We now are thinking that the flow may hape been from a single source and that by taking out that source, the flow has been reduced to a trickle."

"Butler and Peterson?" Barker suggested.

"A possibility we can't afford to overlook," Esau said, "but now we have a name 'CHARLIE' and a phone number as well. Billy, as I am certain the L.A. office of DEA has, checked out the number and came up with Charles T. Valentine, Bradbury Hall, Apartment eight hundred, a condominium on Chatham and Wilshire. The number is unlisted, but we're checking it out against a Charles T. Valentine who *is* listed in the white pages as a tax consultant in the Hamilton National Bank building in the thirty-five-hundred block of Wilshire. By coincidence, that happens to be the address of Paul Landis, the attorney representing Eddie Butler. Billy has one of his people running a check, credit and otherwise, on this Charles T. Valentine to see if he's one and the same as the other."

McNeely glanced at Ycaza. "Could be something, *amigo*," he said.

"Yeah. Could be the deeper we dig into this cesspool, I'm becoming more Narc than Homicide." Barker laughed, and Ycaza said to Esau, "Does Captain Sawyer have any of this?"

Esau grinned. "It was all laid out this morning at the captains' meeting. We've got a full green light from the chief. It's an outside chance, but we all agreed it was worth every effort. After the meeting, I phoned Lyle Carter at the local DEA office. He was out at the moment, so I phoned Willis Ames in Dallas and offered our full cooperation. On his part, he's offering the same. Less than an hour later, I had a call from Lyle Carter. He's assigning a special agent, Eugene Morris, to work with us. Morris is out of the Dallas and San Antonio offices, and he'll be working on this with us. He will also have full authority from Washington and Dallas.

"Also, the sheriff and undersheriff have put their blessings on the case, which makes it top priority." To Barker, "Bob, I can't divorce you from Zone Two, but stay as close to this as you can and give this new crew of ours what support you have available. Coordinate manpower and equipment, everything possible.

"I can only add that Morris already has some information

on this Valentine character, the same as we have, but he's interested in what I told him and Carter about Butler and the Paul Landis coincidence. That's all for now, gentlemen. Gene Morris will be here at thirteen thirty. You'll be here to meet with him and give him everything we've got."

Barker and Sorenson followed McNeely and Ycaza back to their small office. McNeely's first act was to enter the name of Charles T. Valentine on their chart along with the names of Armando Duprez, Estaban and Hector, Roy Chase, Alan DeWitt, and Lester Varick in separate columns. After more discussion, Barker left for Firestone station, Sorensen to his own Intelligence section. McNeely and Ycaza spent the balance of the morning arranging their files and supporting data in sequential order for the benefit and enlightenment of DEA Special Agent Eugene Morris, both wondering privately how he would fit into their official family as a full member of the crew. When they were finished with their chore, they had a complete set of dossiers ready to be Xeroxed for Morris.

After a quick lunch of sandwiches brought in by an office "gopher" and coffee from the office percolator, Eugene Morris appeared promptly at one thirty. He seemed younger than his thirty-two years, dressed in a dark gray suit, white shirt, solemn blue-white tie, black loafers, and carried an attaché case; portrait of a young, upcoming attorney or bank executive. Other than a broken nose that had not quite been properly set, his features were clean, with deep blue—almost black—eyes and smoothly combed dark hair.

At first handshaking, he was soberly correct and unsmiling, but as the three began developing the material each had to offer, formality was swept away. Morris became "Gene" and displayed a sense of humor and keen intelligence.

Barker returned to meet Morris, then left again to supervise a buy with the West Hollywood crew, one involving information concerning half a ton of marijuana on its way north from Mexico. Billy Sorensen dropped in to offer full support of his Intelligence unit. Captain Esau looked in after lunch to welcome Morris, then excused himself to attend a meeting with Chief Traynor. Morris expressed his pleasure at the obvious warmth in their reception. Fully relaxed now, the Butler/Peterson/Ellison system in mind, he began to talk a little more about himself.

He had, he told McNeely and Ycaza, spent three years in Southeast Asia, operating in Burma, Thailand, and South Vietnam, then two years in South America, five months in

Dallas and San Antonio, the last six weeks in Los Angeles, searching for some tie-up with the Texas operation.

"What about this Texas thing, Gene?" McNeely asked.

"Okay," Morris said, "let's get into that end of the deal." He took out a notebook to which he referred from time to time. "About eighteen months ago, a station wagon with Texas plates, driven by a male Caucasian, got into an accident with a private sedan between Arlington and St. James, Missouri, while en route to St. Louis. The woman in the sedan was from St. Louis. She crossed lanes, and the station wagon rammed into her, admittedly her fault. Both drivers required hospital aid. When the two vehicles were towed in, the station wagon was found to be carrying a heavy load, twenty kilos of Mexican heroin and another twenty kilos of cocaine, both cut by about fifty per cent, and undoubtedly on its way to an unknown syndicate in St. Louis. The local cops called us in, and we ran a check on the Texas tags.

"They came up registered to Lester Varick, Excalibur Motel in San Antonio, who claimed the wagon had been stolen several days before, the theft unreported because he had been out of town visiting a brother in La Jolla, California, at the time, driving his other car, a Cadillac.

"The injured driver of the station wagon, Toby Brewer, about twenty-two, was booked and questioned, refused to admit or deny anything, was satisfied to take a five-to-ten fall. He's in prison now. But we weren't entirely satisfied with Varick's story. He does have a brother and sister-in-law living in La Jolla, but no one in the area saw Les Varick or his Cadillac anywhere in or around La Jolla while he was supposed to be there. No hotel or motel or gasoline receipts en route or during his return trip.

"We learned the Excalibur is a part of Bishop Enterprises, a local conglomerate of sorts, which also owns the Wrayburn Ranch on U.S. 277, where the head of Bishop, a man named Royal Chase, lives with his partner, Alan DeWitt. Big place, a lot of acreage, employs a couple hundred people, ranch hands and servants. Also, a landing strip for privately owned planes; an old Stearman biplane crop duster, a twin Beechcraft, a new Cessna Skymaster turbo job that gets good distance and can carry a dependable load.

"Nothing important showed up. Les Varick occasionally drove to the Wrayburn Ranch, but since Excalibur Motel is owned by Chase and DeWitt, a reasonable association. In time, Dallas and San Antonio slacked off. But it was known that narcotics in heavy amounts were flowing into the area, and it was suspected that much of it was being transported to various parts of the country. Dallas had tips galore, but nothing concrete and no mention of the Wrayburn Ranch, Chase, DeWitt, or Varick.

"That is, until the letter you have there from Lee Tenady in our Bogotá office, which opened up a whole new can of worms and tied them together in a neat package. Since I came out of the Texas area, Willis Ames assigned me to the case, working out of San Antonio. Six weeks ago, I came out to L.A. to see if there might be something that we could wire into here. When the L.A. phone number lit up and gave us this new name, Charles T. Valentine, Ames got a jolt of adrenalin and had Lyle Carter and me on the phone for about an hour. Captain Esau filled us in a little on the case you're working now. What makes it interesting is that our people have been quietly investigating Tri-City down in San Pedro."

"On what basis?" McNeely asked.

"A tip. An anonymous phone call from a male, suspected, from his voice, to be black. The message was taped and lasts about twenty seconds. From memory, it goes like this:

You dudes in'trested in a dope deal, whyn't you go down t' San Pedro, look up a place called Tri-City Auto Works. It's a wreckin' yard, sells stripped parts they rebuild, sell to garages. Look close, you find yourselfs what you lookin' for. It's on Sixth Street off'n Harbor.

"That was the entire message. We figured the caller was probably a competitor trying to eliminate competition, maybe somebody who got burned. The call came in less than two weeks ago, and we haven't been able to put much together. Owner is a Simon Hernandez, who inherited the works from his father-in-law, now deceased, and began expanding the operation about five or six years ago until his plant now occupies a half block along Reckord Avenue, the entire block on Sixth, and a half a block along Mesa Street.

"He has eight male Latin employees as mechanics, one in the parts store, two in the warehouse, one driver who handles deliveries, one female Latin in the office. Hernandez lives in a house in Long Beach that would go for about sixty thousand or more, married, two children, both daughters. His credit is good, with no major outstanding debts. That's it for now."

"Okay," McNeely said, "here's what we have." He opened his files on the Butler case, brought in Lloyd, Ann Stennis,

Butler's involvement with Moose Peterson, the missing John Hall Ellison. Concluding those, Ycaza took it up and related their conversation of the night before with Rudy Arboleya. When he mentioned the name of Pete Rojas, he saw recognition in Gene Morris's face, who said, "Hernandez's driver."

"That's right, and that's all we have so far."

"Okay," Morris said. "Here's where we stand. Willis Ames and Lyle Carter, like Captain Esau, believe there may be a solid tie-in between Texas and L.A. You people have a lot at stake, and so do we. Ames has suggested that since you've been on this end of it longer than we and are more familiar with the area, we pool our resources and talents and work together on it. I'd guess that the meeting Captain Esau is having with Chief Traynor right now is to discuss those details and arrange that aspect of it."

McNeely said, "If that's how it is, it's certainly okay with me. Working with the affluent federal-supported DEA can ease our financial burdens a lot and give us the use of some sophisticated equipment we don't have available to us."

"You can count on it, Russ," Morris said. "All the lights on this one have been turned green by Washington."

"Ray?"

Ycaza said, "Sure, man. I'd like to know what it feels like to be a rich cop for once."

3●

On the following morning, McNeely, Ycaza, and Morris began their first full day together as a crew. A new, larger office was found on the eighth floor to accommodate them, a third desk and table brought in, a large blackboard installed on one wall; maps of the United States and a separate one of Texas hung on the opposite wall.

The blackboard was divided into three sections, the first headed: TEXAS SYSTEM. Listed in separate boxes below were the Bishop Enterprises; the Wrayburn Ranch, Excalibur Motel, and other holdings; the names of Royal Chase, Alan DeWitt, and Lester Varick.

The second section, LOS ANGELES SYSTEM, showed every name known to McNeely and Ycaza, with that of Charles T. Valentine its most recent addition, a question mark beside it.

The third section was headed: MEXICO/S.A. SYSTEM. It listed Armando Duprez and Estaban in Bogotá, Hector in Guadalajara.

Working together on a first-name basis, all formality dropped, the newly formed crew introduced Gene Morris to

300

the Dutchman's for lunch, and while each was attacking his food with zest, McNeely asked, "What do you have on Chase and DeWitt aside from the suspicion that they are the chief honchos in this operation, Gene?"

"Enough to support what suspicions we have," Morris said. "Chase is about fifty, give a year or two either way, DeWitt about a year or two younger, and about whom we know less. Chase is a Texan, born and grew up around San Antonio, from a poor family, orphaned at fifteen. Used to hang around the San Antonio airport running errands for the mechanics, infected with the flying bug. He lived nearby with a distant relative who didn't pay much attention to him. Seems as though he fell in with a crop duster named Chip Wrayburn who owned a twelve-hundred-acre spread between Del Rio and Sonora, not worth very much, and who had a Stearman biplane he used to take on crop-dusting jobs. Wrayburn took to Roy Chase, who was apparently a bright kid. The Wrayburns were childless, so they virtually adopted him and gave him a home. The boy was crazy about planes, learned all about the Stearman, kept it clean and in repair, then learned how to fly it. By the time he was seventeen, he was an expert crop duster in his own right, almost as good as Chip Wrayburn.

"By the time the police action in Korea broke out, Roy Chase was twenty-two. He joined the air force and became a hot fighter pilot, made a big name for himself as a double ace and came back in fifty-three with a chestful of medals. By that time, Chip's wife Katie had died, and Wrayburn wasn't in too good shape himself. Brought a niece of his in from Houston to live on the ranch, about Chase's age.

"In fifty-four, Roy married the niece, Libby. Chip Wrayburn died in fifty-five. Roy took over the twelve hundred acres of scrubland and put every cent he owned into it according to our information. Brought in some cattle from Mexico, hired a foreman and some Mexican hands, leased more grazing land, and became a full-time rancher, successful from what we heard. In time, he added the twenty-six-hundred-acre Bishop ranch to the east and made that his headquarters, then added another thirty-two hundred acres, the Del Long spread, to the northeast. About that time, he bought a Beechcraft, and he and Libby began flying around the state and below the border into Mexico.

"Somewhere along the line, Chase picked up Alan DeWitt, who came from Ohio somewhere. Our information on him is skimpy, but we have reason to believe he worked as a real-estate broker in a small agency. As we heard it, Chase talked DeWitt into moving to Texas, and it was he who put the land deals together for Chase, also developed the conglomerate. Incidentally, the old Wrayburn Ranch has now grown to about one hundred thousand acres or more in size, running a considerable herd of cattle, doing well financially. They've built roads, dug a number of additional wells and a landing strip capable of handling the old Beech and the brand-new Cessna. Two years ago, Libby Chase died of cancer. No children. Chase never remarried. To our knowledge, DeWitt has never married, but that's only conjecture."

When they returned to their office, McNeely asked, "Just where is this Wrayburn Ranch?"

Morris went to the wall map of Texas and pinpointed it for him. "Here's Del Rio, about a hundred and fifty miles west of San Antonio, just across the Rio Grande from Villa Acuna, Mexico. Here's U.S. 277 running north and east from Del Rio to Sonora and on to San Angelo. Right about here—" marking the spot with his pencil—"about half the distance to Sonora and about a mile east, is the Wrayburn spread, maybe twenty-eight to thirty miles from Del Rio."

"Within easy access to the Mexican border," Ycaza commented.

"Yes, and by plane, within reach of a lot of Mexico and South America," Morris said. "That's one hell of a long border between Mexico and Texas and not nearly enough manpower to patrol on land or by air, day and night. All kinds of things can happen in any given twenty-four-hour period. And probably do."

"And all of this came out of a simple automobile accident somewhere in Missouri?"

"Well, the Toby Brewer accident started the whole ball of wax. We never did buy Varick's statement about his station wagon being stolen by Brewer. Turned out that Brewer, according to an informant, used to hang around the Excalibur, but wouldn't admit it. Nor would Varick or any of the other motel help. What made it more suspicious was that Brewer, a kid of around twenty-two, was willing to take the fall without admitting or denying anything. A real stonehead.

"So we put a tail on Varick and followed him to the Wrayburn Ranch, which gave us the tie-in to Chase and De-Witt, but little more, until the tapped phone call from Bogotá wired Varick in and gave us the lead on Charles T. Valentine. What really topped things off was when we discovered that there's one hell of a lot of muscle behind Chase, big political muscle at the local, county, state, and even national level, which smells like protection from the top down, and probably bought with heavy campaign donations."

"That takes a real bundle of bread," McNeely said.

"You'd better believe it, but we can't prove a damn thing except that nobody with authority will talk about Chase or cooperate with us. Besides the ranch and Excalibur, there are investments by Bishop Enterprises in other motels in Houston and Galveston, some in oil, a car agency in Dallas, a resort hotel in Acapulco and another in Mazatlán. That gives them reasons for flying across the border on legitimate business, and we don't know who they pay off down there. What else they fly for, or in, is what this is all about.

"We've had our people check out that phone number in Guadalajara. Turns up a public phone and our man Hector becomes a mystery man."

Back in their office, Ycaza, noting the thoughtful look on McNeely's face, said, "What's bugging you, *amigo?*"

"Something that should add up, but hasn't so far."

"Like what?"

"If this Royal Chase was the hot fighter pilot in Korea, and his buddy DeWitt is flying those planes of theirs down in Texas, why hasn't anybody checked into the fact that they may have flown together in Korea. And if so, can we get a roster from the air force and see who else may have been flying with them at that time?"

Gene Morris looked up and said, "Yes. Why not?"

"How fast are your connections in Washington?" McNeely asked.

"I'll get a teletype off right away, urgent."

Ycaza patted McNeely's head. "That's using the old noodle, teacher," he said.

4●

At that moment, Royal Chase cradled the telephone receiver and swiveled around to face Alan DeWitt, who had just entered the ranch office. "That was Les."

"What about?" DeWitt asked.

"He had a call from Val in L.A. He's put his money together and wants to know when you'll be coming up to haul it away."

"I can take off early Monday morning, be back here by late Tuesday."

Chase nodded. "I'll ring Les back and have him pass the word. You'll have a third passenger. I agreed to his bringing along his man, Reed, for the ride. If we're going to expand the West Coast deal, I want another close look at him. Val said something about some problems up there, and I want to hear about that before we go any further."

"Okay. I'll phone Heck in Guadalajara and have him pass the word on to Estaban, get us a firm date in Bogotá with *el general*."

"You'll be carrying a good load. Both ways, Al."

"The Skymaster can handle two hundred kilos. I just hope this General Mendenez doesn't get any bright ideas when he sees six hundred thousand in U.S. cash."

"I doubt it. The way Estaban has it set up, the deal is for a hundred kilos of each every two months. He'd be cutting off his Paraguayan nose to spite his face if he ripped you off for the money. And he needs Estaban to turn the cash into guns and ammo for him, so what would he gain? Just don't get into any kind of a hassle with the bastard. We haven't gone wrong on Estaban's judgment before."

"Always a first time, old buddy. Dealing with a new face, particularly a guy with his own army, sort of gives me a doubt or two."

Chase had moved to the bar now and was pouring bourbon into two glasses. As he returned to his chair and handed a glass to DeWitt, he laughed lightly. "Must be we're getting old, buddy. Time was you'd walk into a lion's cage and spit in his eye without blinking one of your own."

"Salute," DeWitt said, and took a sip of his drink. "Yeah," he said, "I guess age does that to a guy."

They sat facing each other across the huge desk, each in a large leather chair. DeWitt raised one booted foot to the edge of the desk, relaxed now, cigarette in one hand, drink in the other. The afternoon sun began hitting the Venetian blinds in the west wall, and laddered slats of light fell across the imported rug.

"Beginning to catch up with you?" Chase asked.

"Damn. Some of it. Maybe."

Chase's eyes squinted at the amber liquid in his glass. "Comes to all of us sooner or later. Age. Like it came to old Chip. I wish you could have known him, Al. He was a good old boy. When I left here in fifty, he was sound as a bar of solid gold. Came back in fifty-three, he was a dying man. Like Libby, too, the way that cancer ate her away, almost overnight it seemed like."

"I know," DeWitt said, then, "I wish I could have known

Chip too, but Libby was like a sister. I felt closer to her than any of my own."

"Yeah, she was like that." Chase took another long sip. DeWitt said, "The deal with the general that Heck set up, Roy, how do we come out of it?"

"A hundred keys of each. Twenty-five hundred a key for the scag, thirty-five hundred for the coke, comes to an even six hundred thousand dollars on our end. Fifteen thousand for the coke and ten thousand for the scag to Val, comes to two and a half million. Leaves us with a gross profit of a million, nine hundred thousand."

"Nice chunk."

"That's before expenses and splits with Heck and Val, but tax-free."

"Tax-free. Has a nice ring to it."

"Another drink, Al?"

"No, not right now."

For a moment they sat in silence, then Roy Chase said, "Al?"

"What?"

"You ever think of getting the hell out, start living on what we've got piled up?"

DeWitt's foot dropped from the desk edge to the floor. He sat up in his chair and stared at Chase for a moment. "Sounds like you got a real serious case, old buddy."

"Well, I'm sure you must have given it some thought at one time or another while you were flying around over Mexico and South America. Question running through my mind is: How long do we stay in this thing? How much does a man need to be secure for the rest of his life? And what happens if your luck runs out?"

"That's three questions, and I haven't got any answers to any of 'em right off the top of my head. What else is on your mind?"

"Well, we must be worth between ten and fifteen million apiece right now. Who are we going to leave it all to when we go? And once again, what if we make that one slip we've avoided so far and the whole thing goes up in ashes?"

DeWitt frowned, sobered by Chase's words. Roy was still barely under fifty, tall, strong, an attractive man. DeWitt knew that Roy had been spending more and more time in Houston with Catherine Howell, forty-two, charming, graceful, the widow of Lincoln Howell, a former oil-company executive. The ranch, in capable hands, left little for Chase to concern himself with, and the other operation was almost totally in DeWitt's hands, certainly unknown to Catherine.

Other than flying to Houston and back, Chase had little to occupy his time. He did little reading, had no hobbies, his other friends limited to politicians who were, in fact, a dull and greedy lot with only one purpose in life: to perpetuate themselves in office. In recent months, DeWitt noted, Roy hadn't even been near the stables, once his most pleasurable form of exercise. Ergo, DeWitt reasoned, it must be Catherine Howell who had brought on this not too puzzling change in Chase.

"I'd say we're due for some heavy talk," DeWitt said now. "You wouldn't want to give up the ranch, would you, Roy?"

"Hell, no. Never. But I don't want to be tied down to it. I'd want to keep it as a place we could come back to whenever we felt the need."

"What about our key people?"

"What's the problem? There's Val and Heck; both probably have enough to retire on. We could make these next two deals our last, give Excalibur to Les, clean up some of our other holdings, except maybe the places in Acapulco and Mazatlán. Maybe you ought to start thinking about getting married—"

"Hey, let's not go *too* far with this thing, old buddy."

"Hell, you're what? Forty-seven, forty-eight? Settling down time, Al. Cathy's got lots of friends all over Texas."

"Mm-m—. You ever talk to Val or Heck about this, Roy?" DeWitt asked.

"Not Val, but Heck sort of hinted at it the last time I saw him down in Hermosillo. We're all starting to push against time. He's got Magdalena and two kids, one in college, the other on the fringes. Maybe it's time to pack it in, see something of the rest of the world."

"Maybe you're right, Roy. Any of us is entitled to what he wants. Like, I don't want to leave the ranch or give up flying."

"Hell, you don't have to. This place will always be your home, the planes along with it." Chase's eyes crinkled as he added, "Just leave the old Stearman alone. I might want to do a little crop dusting with it some day."

Again, they fell into a silence that was almost audible, then DeWitt went to the bar and brought back two more bourbons. "So we pack it in after these next two trips, Roy?"

Chase clinked his glass against DeWitt's. "I think so. Let's put it up to Val when he comes down. You can talk to Heck when you see him down south. If we're all agreed, we'll get together and make it final. Close it down, bust up the milling operation, pay everybody off, and break clean, keep the ranch operating."

"Okay," DeWitt agreed.

Chase sank deeper into the ponyhide sofa he had moved to. "What would you say if I told you I was thinking of getting married, Al?"

DeWitt grinned broadly. "It blows my mind, old buddy, but I'm for it all the way, long as it's Cathy."

"It's Cathy, and you knew it all the time, you slick bastard. You staying for supper?"

"Not tonight. Got a little thing going for me in town."

"Poker again?"

"For a few hours, then something with a feminine touch to it."

5●

Alone later that night, Royal Chase relaxed in his den in a sense of freedom he hadn't known since his flying days in Korea. And, thinking of those days and times, he inevitably turned the calendar backward as though nothing before then had ever happened.

Royal Chase, Alan DeWitt, Hector Villanueva, Charles T. Valentine.

They had met in 1950 during flight training in Texas, Chase with his six years' experience in crop dusting, Valentine a civilian flight instructor from Santa Monica, California, DeWitt a sophomore out of the University of Missouri, Villanueva from New Mexico and with a burning desire to fly.

In Korea, they had become a fearsome foursome, a four-man gang, somehow knowing each other's mind, able to anticipate and react to every move and flying tactic, Chase their acknowledged leader. They had lived together, played together, hunted and killed the enemy together until Villanueva became their first casualty, shot down by ground fire while flying support for Chase, whose plane was limping back to base with a malfunctioning engine.

Yet Heck had survived, picked up by a rescue chopper called in by Chase, although wounded badly enough to be returned to the States where he was discharged with a disability pension; and promises from Chase, DeWitt, and Valentine that when it was over they would somehow be back together again in a grand reunion.

It was Chase who found the answer that accomplished their reunion.

On his return to Texas, Chase was shocked at his first sight of his benefactor, Chip Wrayburn, now a sickly sixty-five, yet pleased that his niece Libby, whom Chase had never seen before, had been installed at the ranch to care for him. From that very first day, Roy took over, spent his own money and time to try to make Chip's twelve hundred acres of scrubland into a working ranch. He brought in a small herd of Mexican cattle, and after a year of hard labor, it seemed that something might come of his efforts. At that point, he hired a foreman and some Mexican ranch hands, leased some adjacent grazing land, and married Libby. Three months later, they buried Chip. The ranch now belonged to Roy and Libby.

When it began to pay back well-deserved profits, and they could ease up, monotony set in. Restless, Roy overhauled the old Stearman biplane, cleared the overgrown landing strip, and began flying again, child's play after jet fighters. Later, he put in a bid for a moth-balled Grumman in which he and Libby flew on to Santa Monica for a reunion with Charlie Valentine, handsome as ever, now married to a former flying student, Margaret Buckminster.

From Santa Monica, they flew to Guadalajara where Heck Villanueva was living on his air force pension. Almost fully recovered, but left with a slight limp, Heck had married a charming Mexican girl, Magdalena, a positive factor in restoring him to his former health and strength. Returned to the ranch, Chase phoned Al DeWitt in Ohio and invited him to visit, and Al, depressed with his work, eagerly accepted. Charlie and Margaret flew in from California, and Chase flew down to Guadalajara to bring Heck and Magda back to the ranch with him.

It was a magnificent reunion, and toward its end, the four friends drove out one morning to a remote grove of trees and discussed a means to remain in close touch; and it was Roy once more who found the means.

Charlie Valentine, with his California connections, eagerly accepted the role of money man, to put together a group of investors in the new, exotic enterprise. Al DeWitt telephoned his resignation back to Ohio and moved to the ranch to work out the details of the project. Heck Villanueva returned to Guadalajara to make some vital connections. Chase, the leader, organized a distributing system and sought out the men he could trust to make contact with out-of-state buyers and transporters.

Villanueva came up with Estaban Alessandro, an Argentinian whose connections were politically powerful in his native country as well as in Uruguay, Paraguay, Chile, Bolivia, Colombia, and Venezuela. Carrying a diplomatic passport as commercial attaché, Alessandro became the group's most important contact with suppliers in South America.

The operation moved slowly, carefully, starting with small amounts of heroin and cocaine, with DeWitt flying the contraband across the border in the Grumman, using low-level evasive tactics to avoid interception. Chase flew alternate trips with DeWitt until the project began expanding to such a degree that Chase's time was more effectively spent supervising the milling operation, using Mexican labor to dilute the heroin and cocaine to dealer strength, organizing the transporters, and handling the cash in advance of delivery to Chicago, New York, and New Orleans.

And as the operation grew, it became necessary to buy protection, feeding cash into private hands and into campaigns of the politically ambitious, making cash payoffs south of the border to permit takeoffs and landings with a minimum of inspection, and to pay the cost of transporters and guards, legal fees, and bail for those caught on infrequent occasions. In the years that passed, no suspicion had yet been directed to the Wrayburn Ranch or Bishop Enterprises, the cloak for Chase's and DeWitt's other holdings. It had all been so exciting in those days.

Now, Chase reflected as he poured a final glass of bourbon before retiring for the night, is the time to pack it in, get out for good. The excitement was gone. He felt a quiet elation about his talk with DeWitt, at Al's acceptance of his heretofore unspoken desire to be free and clear, to marry into Cathy Howell's circle of respectability. He was certain that Villanueva, with a wife and two teen-age daughters, felt the same way. With a vote of three against one, Chase felt that Valentine would have no alternative but to go along with the majority decision.

That night, Royal Chase slept better, more peacefully than he had in many months. Even years.

6•

Among the names on the air force roster that was received from Washington by teletype were those of Major Royal

Chase, Captain Alan G. DeWitt, and Captain Charles T. Valentine, all members of the same fighting group in Korea. McNeely was first to notice that the name directly below that of Valentine, listed alphabetically, was that of First Lieutenant Hector Villanueva, the first name coinciding with that of the "Hector" first mentioned in Special Agent Lee Tenady's report to DEA, Washington, in the telephone conversation between "Estaban" in Bogotá and "Hector" in Guadalajara on April 26.

As in any case in which a possible lead turns up, the roster generated considerable excitement in the crew. "Christ, what a break," Gene Morris said. "This ties our man Valentine into Chase and DeWitt in Texas and gives us Villanueva as a possible in Guadalajara."

"The question," McNeely said, "is how?"

Morris, busy drawing an arrow from Valentine's box under CALIFORNIA SYSTEM to the section headed TEXAS SYSTEM, remarked, "Another piece to add to our puzzle. If it's all right with you, I'll move one of our men in to keep tabs on Mr. Valentine."

"Okay," McNeely agreed. "I've got a team of our people on Tri-City with cameras to see exactly what Pete Rojas is up to."

Ycaza said, "I'll be hanging in somewhere between Dos Hermanos and the Rodriguez Garage. Rudy tells me today is a usual delivery day for parts from Tri-City."

"Then Gene and I ought to stay close to the phones here to see what comes in. If something breaks, we'll contact you by radio. If you're out of your car, Ray, phone in every hour or so if you can."

"Let's keep to the phones, Russ. My radio car is too easy to make. I'll use my own car. It needs a little work. That'll give Rudy a tune-up job and me a reason to be there."

"Check. But keep in touch."

Ycaza waved and left. Morris was on the phone to check with his office. McNeely made a call to Lennox and found no one to talk with. Both his and Bill Hamlin's crews were hitting the streets. There was nothing for Morris from his office on Dallas or Washington.

The monotony of inactivity, the waiting, set in, both eager to be out, moving around, into something. They discussed the case, talked about past experiences, then walked to the Dutchman's for lunch, returned an hour later. Then Ycaza called in, reporting a blank. An hour passed without any word. Among the surveillance teams all was quiet.

At three o'clock the DEA man sitting on the Valentine condominium at Chatham and Wilshire phoned in a list of license plates belonging to cars that had arrived and parked in the underground garage as opposed to those that stood outside in the visitor parking area. A teletype check to DMV returned the information that a Lincoln Continental, license plate 448-BUR, was registered in the name of Charles T. Valentine at that address. Lambert, due to be relieved by the night man, Ira Dixon, was instructed to advise Dixon that the Lincoln was his objective. At five-thirty, Ycaza phoned in and checked out for home. Moments later, Morris and McNeely wrapped it up for the day.

At eight-thirty, while having dinner at his house with Rachel, the phone rang. It was Harry Deliso, staked out on the Tri-City location with Perry Roberts.

"What's doing, Harry?" Russ asked.

"Thought you'd want to know, Russ. This place is closed down for the day, but lights are still on in the warehouse building, some people still there. We're going to stay with it until they leave or somebody shows up."

"Okay, Harry. Just don't make any move that will give you away. All we're looking for now is information that will lead us to the top."

"Right, Russ. Will do."

At midnight, he walked Rachel across to her house and returned just as the phone was ringing. It was Deliso again. "All right, Russ, for what it's worth, we've got a fix on a Mercedes coupe, license one zero four, King-Lincoln-Xray. Arrival time twenty-one zero five, left at twenty-three ten. I waited here on foot while Perry trailed him. The place emptied out five minutes later. At twenty-three fifty-five Perry came back, lost the Mercedes when a truck cut him off."

"Have you run the tags?"

"Yes, just now. Comes back David Rhodes on Alicante Drive in West Hollywood. Shall we check it out?"

"No use at this point. Wrap it up and I'll pick it up again in the morning, okay?"

"Right on. Call you in the morning."

At the Alicante Apartments in West Hollywood, Deliso and Roberts found the Mercedes 104-KLX in the parking lot at the rear the following morning. In the unattended lobby, the number of Apartment 14 showed the occupant to be David Rhodes. From a phone booth in a service station three blocks away, Deliso relayed the information to McNeely, who advised that he would have one of Billy Sorensen's people run a check on the name, which was unlisted in the phone book.

Meanwhile, he ran the name through Records and CII in Sacramento. David Rhodes was unknown. DMV showed no legal history, abstracts, failures to appear, wants, or warrants. In all respects, David Rhodes was Mr. Clean. But the information did not put McNeely off. Mr. Clean had been in night contact with Tri-City, a blemish that could not be overlooked. David Rhodes was most likely using another identity. Another stakeout was authorized and a request teletyped to DMV in Sacramento asking for a facsimile of David Rhodes's driver's license, which would give the crew a look at his face. The request also asked for a photocopy of the thumb print on Rhodes's application for his driver's license.

Later that afternoon, Metro Bureau's Pat Cross called in with word on Eddie Butler. At 1500, Butler had emerged from his house on Warren Canyon Drive and driven to a service station in Hollywood where he had his gas tank filled and used the public phone booth to make a phone call; he then drove to a coffee shop where he sat at the counter and had a cup of coffee. Shortly thereafter, Butler got into his car and began driving aimlessly northward, then east to Sunset Boulevard. Cross and his partner Gary Marek soon became aware that Butler knew he was being tailed and dropped back about a block or two, allowing other cars to pass and get between them and the suspect's car.

When the two cars were within half a mile of the San Diego Freeway, Butler suddenly speeded up and, with the crush of traffic, was lost to them. At the off ramp into the freeway, Cross decided that Butler had taken it and followed. After several miles, they came to the conclusion that Butler had not taken the freeway and gave up the search, exiting on Washington Boulevard.

After talking it over, they decided to return to the Warren Canyon location and wait for Butler to return. At five-forty, Butler's car pulled into the driveway, and he went into the house.

McNeely hung up and passed the information to Ycaza, who said, "Jesus, we'd better call out the bloodhounds. They'd do a hell of a lot better job than our people."

McNeely laughed and said, "Come on, Ray, how many times have you lost a guy you were tailing?"

"Oh, maybe one or two, but——"

"But they hurt every time, don't they? Let's not lower the boom on Cross and Marek, huh?"

"Yeah, you're right, Russ. For a case that started out with so damned little, we're strung out now from here to Texas, Mexico, and South America. And we still haven't got even a single line on John Hall Ellison."

"At least, we've got something working, and that's better than what we had a little while ago."

"Look, I know you're right, but I want Ellison so damned bad it makes my teeth hurt."

"Don't you think I don't? After all, this crook is tied in to Cruz Despues, and that means as much to us as the rest of this deal."

"Sure, Russ."

"Okay. As long as Butler is loose, we've still got a chance at Peterson, and that could give us a lead to Ellison. *Paciencia, amigo, paciencia.*"

"Patience is what I'm gradually losing, buddy."

"It's one and the same case now, Homicide or Narcotics or both. We're a crew, remember?"

"Okay, teacher, I'll behave," Ycaza said with a grin.

The surveillance on David Rhodes's apartment turned up an oddity. Perry Roberts took a chance and rang the bell at Apartment 1, listed on the house roster in the foyer as MANAGER. A Mrs. Harrison opened the door, and Roberts flashed his badge and I.D. card. Mrs. Harrison invited him in. He told her he was from the West Hollywood station, Burglary division, inquiring into a report from a nearby apartment house on an attempted burglary the night before and asked if she had had any similar problems recently.

"No," Mrs. Harrison said, "not since a month ago when Mr. Jarvis in number 9 had his car trunk broken into and some sample dresses were stolen. But I know there have been problems in the neighborhood."

Mrs. Harrison, graying and widowed, was not only willing to talk, but was eager for someone to talk to: about the problems of keeping help, trying to get a repairman to fix the washer-dryer in 16, replace the broken mirror in 8, etc. etc. etc. She spoke of her tenants, most of them in the "profession," a word taken to mean motion pictures or television, "except for one or two, like Mr. Jarvis and Mr. Rhodes," she added.

"Oh? Mr. Jarvis and Mr. Rhodes aren't writers, actors, directors, or producers?" Roberts asked.

"No, no, not even connected. Mr. Jarvis is with a dress house."

"And Mr. Rhodes?"

"I really don't know about Mr. Rhodes. I think he must be a salesman of some kind."

"He must be pretty lonesome here, out of his element."

"Oh," Mrs. Harrison laughed slyly, "he's not all *that* lonesome. He has company occasionally, a girl once in a while, never the same one twice. Not like the others, who like to have parties now and then. But he pays his rent promptly, and as long as he doesn't disturb anybody else—"

"That's strange, your not knowing what he does, I mean." away for a few days at a time, so I suppose he must do some traveling. But he's a very pleasant man, always quiet and polite when I do run into him."

"Well, then, if you haven't any burglary problems, I'll move along and check some of your neighbors. Thank you, Mrs. Harrison."

Outside, he reported his finding to Harry Deliso. From a public phone, Harry relayed the word to McNeely. "Is his car there now, Harry?" McNeely wanted to know.

"Yup, it's on the lot."

"Stay with it. Let's see what our alleged salesman is selling and to whom."

"Okay. We'll keep in touch."

Twenty minutes later, Roberts spotted the man as he exited the rear of the apartment house and went to the Mercedes, reaching into his trouser pocket for his keys. Roberts nudged Deliso. "Our guy."

It was then six-thirty. Rhodes moved out, and Deliso followed a few seconds later. Thirty minutes later, in very heavy home-going traffic, they were heading north on Pacific Coast Highway. With every lane solid with cars, they continued on past Santa Monica and eventually turned eastward into the hills on to Latigo Canyon. They laid back cautiously so that the taillights of the Mercedes were barely visible, losing sight of it around each curve, catching up, until it turned into Caribou Road, saw it enter a driveway, noted its number, 3622, in passing. A quarter of a mile down the road, they backed into a driveway, turned, and came back. The Mercedes was parked inside the grounds in front of the house, lights now showing on the first and second floors.

The house at 3622 Caribou, like the apartment on Alicante Drive and the Mercedes, was in the name of David Rhodes.

314

The telephone for that address was unlisted. By midmorning, the photograph on the driver's license for David Rhodes was identified by Deliso and Roberts as that of the occupant of the apartment from which they had tailed him to the Caribou Road address.

McNeely sent the copy of Rhodes's thumbprint to Records and Identification to be checked out. In the field lieutenant's office, he dropped the license facsimile on Bob Barker's desk. "Anybody you know, Bob?" he asked.

Barker examined the photograph carefully. "Damn," he said after a few moments, "this dude looks familiar. I've either seen him, or we've had him, but not under that name. I know I've seen him somewhere. Maybe a long time ago."

"I've got Prints checking his application thumbprint. Maybe they'll come up with something."

"Five to one they do. This baby's been in custody at one time or another. Maybe long enough back to've changed him a little since then."

Lieutenant Marcus came over and looked at the small photo and shook his head negatively. Nor did it register with Lieutenant Dickerson, just back from lunch. Lieutenant Toland, who headed Zone IV, which included the Malibu area, thought there was something familiar about Rhodes's face. "But not connected with dope. Maybe while I was working Vice. Rhodes—Rosen—Ross—Reed—Hey! Reed! That's who this dude is, Don Reed. We had him on a gambling and prostitution rap, sure. Check that out with R & I."

Barker grinned broadly. "I think he's got it. By jove, I think he's got it. Thank you, my fair lieutenant."

The data received from Records and Identification on Donald Reed were sufficient to match him with David Rhodes. His stats read: Male, Caucasian/six feet/180 lbs. Hair: Dk. Blnd/Eyes: Blue/Mar.: Single/DOB: 2-8-33. First arrest: 9-16-57, Hollywood Division Vice, L.A.P.D., convicted of operating an illegal gambling house and providing females for purposes of prostitution; served eight months of a one-year sentence, L.A. County Jail. Second arrest, 4-27-62, by L.A. Sheriff's Malibu station narcotics detectives, convicted of possession of dangerous drugs for sale; served three years of a three-to-five sentence, Soledad State Prison.

Donald Reed's mug shots matched the more recent photograph on David Rhodes's driver's license. More conclusively, the thumbprint on his application was identical to that taken at the time of his arrests.

315

"So," McNeely said after he had brought this news back to Morris and Ycaza, "we have Don Reed, alias David Rhodes, tied into Tri-City, and we have Charles T. Valentine wired into the same outfit as well as with the Texas group. It gets more interesting by the hour, by the day."

Morris laughed lightly. "When you consider that we've been on this damned thing for over eighteen months, using God-only-knows how many men, the amount of equipment and money, any little piece we can add to our puzzle is like diamonds."

Ycaza squirmed in his chair, staring at the blackboard. "I'd just like to find one lousy little piece of that puzzle with John Hall Ellison's name on it."

"It'll show up," McNeely predicted. "It all goes back to Whitey Lloyd, and your boy Ellison is in it up to his neck. If we're lucky, you can clear up the Lloyd and Stennis unsolveds and come out smelling like a rose."

"That's a very big IF, amigo," Ycaza said glumly.

That night in Carson, violence erupted between the black Colts and Chicano Cobra gangs. One Colt youth, sixteen, was shot and killed, two Cobras, fifteen and seventeen, were seriously wounded; several others sustained lesser injuries. Responding deputies rounded up nine youths for questioning, but all denied having witnessed, or been near the battle site. For that matter, none claimed membership in either the Colts or Cobra gangs, or any other.

On the same night, sheriff's narcotics deputies, on information supplied by undercover operator Johnny Segura, simultaneously raided two houses and four bars, arrested six men and four women in the houses, three bartenders and five waiters, two waitresses and seven young customers. The total haul amounted to four ounces of heroin, four kilos of marijuana, half an ounce of cocaine, and over a thousand amphetamine capsules.

Later that night in Lennox station's Narcotics office, undercover operator Johnny Segura laid out more of the background for the MV crew, who had been among the twenty-two deputies involved in the raids.

"The Colts are copping from Little Willie's Bar. The Cobras have been in short supply and decided on this rumble to rip off some stuff from the Colts. Here's a list of some of the other Cobras who are involved. Four were in the nine you picked up for questioning. The last two names on the list, Everett and Woody, are Colts dudes. I wasn't there, so I don't know who did the shooting, but I'll keep my ears and eyes open."

"What brought it on, Johnny?" Deliso asked.

"The Cobras. Their supply has dried up some since Louie Lopez and Bunny Martinez got busted, which means they're running short of stuff and bread. If you can't push, you're broke and can't live it up with the chicks or buy gas for the cars. Anyway, it's beginning to look like George Ruiz will start dealing in Carson, and if he does, you'll be looking at a real war between the Ruiz brothers and the Willie Acheson and Jimmie Tice crowd."

"Bet on it," Perry Roberts said. "Tice and Acheson won't stand still if the Ruizes move in on their turf."

"How the hell do you stop a thing like that?" Johnny said.

"I don't know. I'll talk to Russ about it in the morning. Maybe he'll have some answers. At least, we're forewarned. Anyway, stand by, Johnny. Russ and the lieutenant may want to set up a meet with you."

"Just let me know when and where, Perry."

Barker and McNeely had talked with Johnny Segura, then with Captain Esau, who moved quickly to set up a standby task force to move in at the first sign of a war between the Ruiz people in East Los Angeles and the Acheson-Tice faction in Carson. Meanwhile, skilled Narcotics detectives drawn from outlying areas would be sent into both areas to keep a close watch on the movements of all known pushers. Juvenile gang details and Patrol were alerted and detective teams strengthened.

On Saturday morning, Cora Thomas left her house on Newton Street and drove half a mile to the Pacifica Shopping Center. Less than a block behind her Pinto, Metro Bureau's Adam Parrish and Augie Rice, in a dark blue Plymouth radio car, tailed her. At Pacifica, the Pinto moved into the crowded parking lot and took a space that had just been vacated near Ralphs' supermarket. The Plymouth moved past her and found another space about thirty yards beyond.

Cora Thomas locked her car, entered Ralphs', found a shopping cart, and moved toward the fruit and vegetable stands. Parrish remained in the Plymouth while Rice watched Cora from the outside. When she disappeared from his view, he entered the store, got behind a cart, and moved in her direction, remaining far enough behind to keep an eye on her. Occasionally, he examined shelves of cans and cartons, the frozen food items in their refrigerated cases, dropping a few packages into his cart.

In Cora's cart were some apples, oranges, two packages of cheese, two of breakfast cereals, several cans of soup. At the meat counter she chose a prepackaged steak, a ham slice, and a carton of chicken livers. She turned into an aisle and put a loaf of bread and a small package of rolls into the cart, turned, and began looking over some items of paper goods. She reached up and removed two packages of napkins, then, reaching for a roll of paper towels, looked up and across the shelf at the man who was facing her in the opposite aisle: a cinnamon-colored man who wore sunglasses and a modified Afro hairdo. At the moment when their eyes met, the man removed the sunglasses, and despite the Afro, short-sleeved sports shirt with thin blue and white stripes running horizontally, she recognized John Hall Ellison, the only name by which she knew him, and her mouth dropped open in sheer surprise.

"Keep lookin' down, Cora," he said in a low voice as he replaced the sunglasses and began looking over various items on his side of the shelf.

She was startled, and her face showed it. But she obeyed. Removing the paper towels, she inched along the aisle slowly, he moving along with her in the other aisle. When she stopped, he stopped, and she said in a whisper, "You're crazy, John. You've got to be out of your mind. The cops are looking for you everywhere. They've got a drawing of you."

"The way I was, not the way I am," he replied in an equally low voice. "Listen. You got a tail on you. The dude two aisles over, brown suit, tan shirt, brown-striped tie, curly brown hair."

"I know. He and another guy have been sitting on my house for days. They're in a blue sedan, a Plymouth."

"Yeah. Cop car. I know they been on you. I been waitin' for you to come out of the house."

"What do you want, John? You're insane to keep hanging around here. They'll pick both of us up."

"No, they won't. Listen to me. Keep movin' along. Come up this aisle, pick up some things from the shelf behind me. I'll be on the other side of it. Do what I tell you, else you're in real big trouble."

"You're crazy," Cora repeated.

"No, you are. You talked to the cops. Moose an' Eddie knew it the minute you got out on low bail. Now listen to me an' do what I say."

318

"What do you want?"

"Just keep moving along, pick out some more stuff, and listen. Your tail is too far away to hear anything. Keep clear of these people——"

Half an hour later, Cora Thomas went through the checkout counter, then wheeled her cart with three sacks of groceries in it to her car. Augie Rice left his partially filled cart inside the store and walked out empty-handed, went to the Plymouth, and watched as Cora unlocked her car, put the three bags inside. As she turned to wheel her cart back onto the rack in front of the store entrance, Rice got into the car beside Parrish.

"Milk run," he said. Parrish turned back to keep an eye on Cora, but couldn't see her because of the moving traffic behind him.

"Hey, where the hell is she?" he said to Rice. Augie got out of the car and looked in the direction she had taken.

"Gone," he said shortly. "Probably went into one of the other stores. Be back in a minute."

He went in search of her, then signaled to Parrish, who went to the right of Ralphs', Rice to the left, peering into the Sav-on, Chapman's Liquors, Hartman Florists. Amy-Lee Beauty Shop, Carlton Barber, Eagle Varsity, and other shops that flanked the supermarket.

Cora Thomas had vanished.

She had followed his instructions to the letter: put the groceries inside the Pinto, locked it, pushed the cart back to the pavement rack. Then, without looking back, she joined the flow of pedestrian traffic, keeping to the inside of the pavement until she reached Ewalt's Coffee Shop. She went inside quickly, moved to the rear, and exited by the side entrance that faced the parking area and Texaco Station. The gray Oldsmobile 98 was waiting at the side door, its motor running, John Hall Ellison behind the wheel. She got in beside him, and he took off, chuckling lightly to himself at the thought of the consternation of the two duped cops.

There was no conversation between them until they were on the Pacific Coast Highway heading south. When he reduced speed to a normal fifty miles per hour, Cora Thomas lighted a cigarette and said, "Okay, John, what's this all about?"

"Just giving you a helpin' hand, that's all."

"Where are we going?"

"If nobody catches up to us, first Tijuana, then Ensenada."

She turned toward him angrily. "You're out of your mind, flipped. Take me back to my car, you damned fool."

"Cool it, baby. I told you you're in trouble. Big trouble. The minute those cops get off your tail, you're gonna take a hit."

She stared at him in doubt and near terror. "A *hit? Me?*"

"A hit, an' you. Lemme lay it on you righteously. Only three days ago, I got a call from your friend Moose. Seems like he, Eddie, and whoever sits on top of 'em, didn' like the idea of you gettin' a free ride on a lousy fifteen hundred dollars bail. They figure you talked an' put the heat on both the dudes. Right?"

She said, "They busted me for possession of stolen property, property they gave me to use to rent the car for you. I didn't tell them anything about you except that you stayed with me. They pretty much knew that already."

"Well, okay, except they got it from a lawyer man who got it from a friend of his on the inside that you tied Moose an' Eddie into this thing. Cops are out lookin' for Moose for questioning and sure as hell for me, too. Okay. Moose asks me to take a contract. On you." He paused for some reaction, saw her face go pale, mouth open, but wordless.

"On you, baby," he repeated. "They put a three-thousand-dollar price on you, but I told him, No way. Too chancy with a tail on you around the clock."

"Look, John—"

"What?"

"Take me back to my car. Please. Just drop me off a block or two away. I won't say a word about seeing you."

"You think I picked you up to rip you off?" he said with a broad grin.

"I don't know what to think. Just take me back. I'll feel safer with a twenty-four-hour tail on me. If I get the chance, I'll blow town, the state, go East—"

"Now you're talkin' crazy, baby. You even look like you wanna skip town, jump bail, they'll pick you up and throw you back in the slammer. You cross the state line an' the FBI will be on you for fleein' to avoid prosecution. I'm goin'a take you to Mexico where you'll be safe. With me."

"My car—"

"Forget your car, the groceries, the house, your clothes. I'll get you whatever you need—"

"Why? Why, John?"

Staring at the road ahead, smiling with self-satisfaction, "Because I need a coolin' off period, too, an' I don't want to do it all by myself. You're a nice, classy fox, an' we're goin'a have us a real ball."

7•

The disappearance of Cora Thomas, under the circumstances described by Deputies Rice and Parrish, came as a bewildering surprise to the crew. "How in hell," McNeely demanded, "could you lose her? Two of you sitting on her and she simply walks away from her car, leaves her groceries, and disappears in thin air?"

"Well, Sergeant," Parrish said contritely, "you've got the word of both of us. She locked up, pushed the goddamned cart back across two traffic lanes to the pavement. Cars were passing both ways between us, people all over the place. How do we figure she's going to abandon the car and groceries and take off? It's our guess somebody was waiting for her nearby by arrangement. She turns a corner, gets into the car, and she's gone. By the time we got back to our car and circled the area, she was long gone and out of sight."

Rice took it up then. "So we radioed in, but couldn't do more than describe her physically. We saw no car, nobody else. Patrol is on the alert, but without anything more to look for but the broad herself."

"Who's watching the car?"

"Phil Benson's on the car, and Tom Anderson's on the house."

"Well—"

Don Reed was equally astonished when Eddie Butler reported that Cora Thomas was missing. "I cruised the house. No lights, no sign of anything except the cop car with two dudes sitting on it, waiting. Garage door is open, no car in sight all day yesterday, last night, this morning. She's gone."

"What did you get from Moose?"

"Zip. Nothing. He called his man in to do the hit on her, but the dude wouldn't take it. Too close to the Lloyd thing, and he knows there are cops watching the house. Moose had some crazy idea he fell for Cora after shacking up with her for five days. A cool spade with money to splash around, a good-looking, sexy chick. It could be."

"You really think he might have taken off with her?"

Butler shrugged. "I don't know of anybody else she knew who could engineer a thing like that with two dicks on her tail."

"Well," Reed said, "he's a hell of a lot hotter than she is.

If they're together and running, he'll be smart enough to stay under cover and keep her there with him. Maybe it's not as bad as it looks."

"Yeah. Unless he gets careless."

"With a murder rap hanging over his head, he can't afford that luxury. If she's with him, there's no telling where they are. For damned sure, he won't go back to Vegas, and he wouldn't be stupid enough to stick around here." Reed stood up and went to the window, looking down the twisting road that led into Sunset Boulevard. Butler waited.

"Okay," Reed said finally, "we can't afford to waste time playing guessing games. I've got everything squared away between Anse and Del to handle the operation with Hernandez while I'm away. We're leaving here the day after tomorrow for Texas and will probably be gone for three or four days. In the meantime, tell Moose to keep under wraps until he hears from me."

"Okay. I'll call him and lay it out for him."

"Do that. And one more thing. Tell him not to leave his place except for absolute necessities. No bars, no broads, nothing. He's too noticeable. Also, if they get to him and he resists, he's killable. When we get back, we'll talk about getting him out of here, move him down to Mexico for a while."

"Okay, Don. You can count on Moose."

"I hope we can. That's it, then, Eddie. Be careful."

Chapter Eleven

1•

On his private estate several miles northeast of Parano, equidistant between Medellín and the Rio Magdalena and a short distance from Bogotá, General Gerardo Aramis Mendenez entertained his guest, Estaban Alessandro, at supper. Since the occasion was for the purpose of discussing business, Señora Mendenez had supervised the serving of the meal, then quietly retired to spend an hour with her three children before they were put to bed.

The meal concluded, Mendenez and Alessandro went out on the patio where servants brought coffee, cognac, and Havana cigars. Both men relaxed in comfortable lounge chairs, looking over the irregular-shaped pool that shimmered with underwater lighting. Huge rocks and lush growth bordered the pool, giving off the deception of having been formed by nature; it was fed by an artificial waterfall, heated and filtered by modern equipment, all emphasizing its natural appearance.

Overhead, the blackness of the sky at eighty-five-hundred feet above sea level was broken only by brilliant stars and a quarter moon. A hundred yards beyond the sprawling house in every direction, light standards faced outward to provide illumination for a corps of armed guards who patroled their stations with fierce guard dogs.

Alessandro, a slender, olive-skinned man in his middle forties, understood that the protection of the Mendenez estate and its occupants was permitted by the Colombian government because Gerardo Aramis Mendenez, a Paraguayan national, had requested, and been granted, political asylum when, in 1972, he had been deposed as minister of security by a new regime; there had been numerous attempts to assassinate him and kidnap members of his family for alleged crimes against the people of Paraguay.

Mendenez, extremely wealthy, had been permitted to live with his family on the huge estate he had acquired and turned into a veritable fortress, accompanied by several upper-echelon members of his staff who had sought asylum with him; this, provided that he would not engage in political activity in Colombia.

On the surface, Mendenez gave the appearance of having complied with that restriction. He appeared in Bogotá infrequently, always with bodyguards, to attend luncheons with officials in high office. He contributed generously to various hospitals and useful charities, and if privately to certain ranking individuals for other purposes, that fact was either unknown or went unnoticed. But secretly, the general, a physically strong man of heroic military stature beneath exquisite civilian tailoring, was engaged in a program to supply funds and arms to support his revolutionary comrades in Paraguay, with whom he maintained close, clandestine contact, in their desperate efforts to retake control of the government and restore Mendenez to his former eminent position; and quite possibly to the greater glory of the presidency.

Thus, his business with Alessandro, who, as one of his agents and able to travel abroad with impunity, provided the necessary funds and arms to fan the flames of Mendenez's ambitions. For Alessandro, this was no great difficulty. He was a noted trafficker in the profitable narcotics trade, and his expertise lay in his role of middleman between South American syndicates with cocaine and heroin to sell and the *norteamericanos* with money to buy. And Mendenez had both to sell.

On his estate, hidden from prying eyes by thick jungle growth, protected by his own guard corps and officials paid to look in other directions, was as professional a processing laboratory as any in Europe or Asia, staffed by expert chemists who were well paid to convert locally grown poppies into opium, into morphine base, into pure heroin, and dried coca leaves into coca paste, into crystalline cocaine.

To the east of that heavily grown jungle and between one similar to it, workmen had cleared truck roads and a twenty-five hundred-foot-long landing strip where Mendenez's private twin-engine Piper Navajo and others directed there by Alessandro, could land and take off without difficulty or outside interference. At night, peons trucked and back-packed the raw materials in and left with their pay. The final product was sold and the money sent by Alessandro's couriers to the sellers of guns, explosives, ammunition, and vehicles, which were then smuggled into Paraguay and turned over to the revolutionists to carry on their work.

Now that they were comfortably relaxed, their cigars alight, Mendenez said, "Eh, Estaban, what news from the north?"

"Good news, *general*," Alessandro replied. "I have spoken with my people, and it is arranged. A hundred kilos each of heroin and cocaine on this trip and another hundred of each in two months. Or sooner, if it can be arranged. Perhaps even more in the future."

"Ah-h-h-," Mendenez sighed with satisfaction.

"Yes. The *gringo* appetite grows stronger and stronger."

"When?"

"I have arranged for the man, DeWitt, to arrive on the eighteenth. I will meet him in Guadalajara and bring him here."

"Good. We will be ready."

"And please to remember the gasoline to refuel the plane."

"It will be done, Estaban." He sighed happily again. "It will be useful, six hundred thousand dollars." Mentally, he translated the U.S. currency into about thirteen million Colombian pesos, then into eighty million Paraguayan guaranis.

"It will buy a lot of guns and bullets," Alessandro said softly.

"Ah, yes. Yes. I have a list of requirements ready."

"Excellent, *general*. I am sure I will be able to satisfy your needs. There are no problems here?"

Mendenez laughed. "None, none. With cash gifts in the proper hands, we are safe. And you?"

Alessandro shrugged, smiling thinly. "Who will pay attention to a humble Argentinian commercial attaché who travels to perform his modest duties on a diplomatic passport?"

Mendenez chuckled and reached for the cognac decanter.

Don Reed arrived in San Antonio at 2:45 P.M. by United Airlines carrying the current issue of *Time* magazine under his left arm, holding a copy of *Playboy* in his right hand. He claimed his two-suiter and, on his way out to the rank of taxis, was accosted by a deeply sunburned man wearing sunglasses, dressed in casual Texas garb and a cattleman's straw hat.

"Reed?" he said.

"Yes. You're Varick?"

"That's right. This way."

At the curb was a Mercury station wagon. Varick slipped in behind the wheel as Reed tossed his suitcase on the back seat and got in on the curbside. "Nice flight?" Varick asked.

"Not bad."

"Want to stop off for some food?"

"No. I had a good lunch on the plane. I could use some sleep, though. Didn't get much last night."

"Okay, lean back and relax. We've got about a hundred and eighty miles to the ranch. Take a little under three hours. Grab some shuteye if you can."

Varick handled the car expertly through the city traffic to U.S. 90 and settled down to an easy-paced sixty miles per hour. Don Reed slid down in his seat, rested his head against the back of the seat, closed his eyes and slept.

Laying back less than a quarter of a mile and allowing several cars between his Buick and the Mercury station wagon, Special Agent Max Arnold, out of the DEA's San Antonio office, picked up his microphone and radioed in to Special Agent in Charge Jesse Tyler, giving his location and a description of the man Lester Varick had picked up at the airport.

"Okay, Max, stay with them. They're probably heading for the Wrayburn Ranch. I'll pass the word along to Carlos Azuela in Del Rio to keep an eye out, have him pick up the Merc there."

"Roger. I'll call in when Carlos makes contact."

For months, Les Varick and his Excalibur Motel had been under close surveillance by a special group of DEA agents working out of San Antonio. Alternating, the agents had checked into the Excalibur singly for a day or two at a time, giving their home addresses variously as Jackson, Mississippi, Auburn, Florida, Albuquerque, New Mexico, and other cities. In each case, the license plate on the agent's unmarked car matched the state from which he had registered. Other agents maintained surveillance from the outside, changing frequently. Still others worked between Del Rio and Sonora, the towns closest to the Wrayburn Ranch, as well as the back roads bordering the headquarters of Royal Chase and Alan DeWitt, dressed as ranch hands, driving nondescript cars, panel or pickup trucks, on the alert for any unusual movement or activity, particularly on the extreme eastern border of the property where the private airstrip and its barnlike hangar were located but could not be seen from roadside.

In Del Rio and Sonora, the two towns most often visited by the ranch families in the area, still other agents lounged about those stores and shops most likely to be patronized by the Wrayburn people, hoping to overhear something pertinent in their conversations, attempting to engage them in some—any—kind of talk: weather, stock, cost of feed, or to ask directions.

Nothing worked. Wrayburn people kept strictly to themselves, made their purchases together, ate or had a few beers together, shot a game of pool, saw a movie, or on occasion dallied with a street girl, then returned to the ranch.

The agents worked without local assistance, fully aware of the weighted political influence wielded by Chase and DeWitt, all the way up to Austin and perhaps higher. Therefore, they moved cautiously in order not to attract the attention of local lawmen. Their orders were, simply, to observe and report any suspicious or untoward activities that concerned Wrayburn Ranch and its people.

Thus, Agent Max Arnold considered his tail job on the familiar dark blue Mercury station wagon as routine. He paced it through Hondo, Uvalde, and Bracketville into Del Rio. As the Mercury turned northward into U.S. 277, he saw the green-and-white Dodge pickup truck behind him, slowed to allow Agent Carlos Azuela to pass and take over the surveillance. At the next crossroad, Max Arnold made a U-turn and returned to Del Rio where he stopped for gas and to phone in to SAC Jesse Tyler.

Continuing on U.S. 277, Carlos Azuela followed the Mercury for some thirty miles to the entrance of the Wrayburn Ranch, marked by a wooden arch with a sign that read:

W R A Y B U R N

Private Property

NO TRESPASSING!

The station wagon turned in, and two vehicles behind it, Azuela's pickup truck continued on in the direction of Sonora. A few hundred yards north, he made a U-turn and headed back toward Del Rio.

3●

In Los Angeles, Eugene Morris took the call from SAC Jesse Tyler, who gave him a clear description of the man who had arrived in San Antonio to be picked up by Lester Varick and driven to a destination he assumed would be the Wrayburn Ranch. To Russ McNeely and Ray Ycaza, the description spelled out to Reed/Rhodes, heightening the interest of all three.

They discussed this new development with Lieutenant Barker and Sergeant Sorensen, then trooped into Captain Esau's office to bring him up to date. Esau said, "It looks like we've really stepped into the Big Casino."

"A hell of a big one, Cap," Barker agreed, "bigger than anything I've seen yet."

"It could be, Bob. We've got more lines into this thing now than a damned maypole." To Morris, "What's doing on your end, Gene?"

"The usual surveillance at the San Antonio and ranch end, still trying our damndest to get closer to the picture. We've tried to work a man inside as a ranch hand, mechanic, laborer, anything, but nothing was ever accomplished. Unless it's somebody damned well known to them, there's no hiring at all, ever. We sometimes know when their plane takes off, sometimes when it lands again, but that's about it, and we've never had enough to go for a search warrant."

"Reed," Esau mused. "Valentine. We might be getting somewhere close to the top."

"The top," McNeely suggested, "is on that ranch in Texas. They control the input."

"Most likely," Esau agreed, "but my money says that the people behind Valentine, the financial backers, must come from here." He looked up at McNeely and smiled. "You wouldn't be angling for a trip to Texas, would you, Russ?"

"Well, it wouldn't be hard to take. I'd like to see the inside of an international operation for a change of pace."

"I don't think so," Esau countered. "What would our friendly DEA people say if they thought you were trying to muscle in and take the ball out of their hands?"

Morris smiled and said, "If this thing continues to develop

on this end, Captain, it might not be a bad idea at that. I'd like to check it out with Lyle Carter, with your permission, and sound out Willis Ames in Dallas."

"Well, let's not rush things. Suppose we try to find out just why Reed is in Texas and how, exactly, he ties into this Valentine character. Or with Butler and Peterson."

"Or," Ycaza threw in, "our missing John Hall Ellison, not to mention our vanished Cora Thomas."

"Yes," Esau said, "and how it all involves our mysterious Tri-City Auto Works and Mr. Simon Hernandez. For now, let's think about it and meet here around ten hundred tomorrow."

At eight-twenty that night, just before leaving his house to pick up Rachel at her shop and drive to El Sótano, a basement restaurant in Palos Verdes noted for its Mexican food, McNeely phoned the Narcotics night-watch commander for any messages. After the fourth ring, Vic Olds came on the line. "Hey, Russ, I was just ringing your number and got a busy signal. Got a message for you from Metro. Your guy Valentine is missing."

"What do you mean, missing? Lost, strayed, stolen, or kidnaped?"

"Just missing. He was tailed to his Wilshire office this morning. Left for lunch at thirteen-fifteen with his lawyer Paul Landis, back at fifteen-ten. Landis left for the day at seventeen-forty-five. When Valentine didn't show at nineteen-hundred, Ben Guymon went up and found his office dark, the door locked. An elevator man told him Valentine left at about eighteen hundred, but his Lincoln was still parked in the underground garage. Ben sat on the car for a while, hoping he would show up. He called in about five minutes ago with the word."

"Seems like it's becoming par for the course, everybody disappearing from under our noses. Okay, Vic. Get somebody out to his place and sit on it until he shows up. I'll be at El Sótano in Palos Verdes until about twenty-two-thirty, then home. If anything turns up, call me."

4●

At lunch earlier that same day, Paul Landis and Charles Valentine, after their vodka martinis had been served, studied the menus and ordered their meals. Landis said, "Damned busy morning. For a moment, I didn't think I'd be able to get back to the office."

"Well, don't get hung up this afternoon. I've got one hell of a lot of cash locked in my office safe that needs tender, loving care," Valentine said.

"Don't worry, Charlie. That part is all set. When we're ready to go, we'll have it brought down to my car and locked in the trunk. I'll have one of my people sitting on it until you're ready to take off."

"The Ambassador, between six-fifteen and six-thirty. I'll leave my car in the garage until I get back."

"Good. What about Reed?"

"I changed that. He's going to catch an early flight to San Antonio. Varick will meet him and drive him to the ranch. He'll get there before Al and I do."

"I don't get it, Charlie. Why do you need him in Texas?"

"The way things are shaping up, Paul, I'm planning to use him to carry these cash loads to Texas in the future. I'd like to get a little farther away from the line of fire. Reed is reorganizing his setup at the top, moving his top man in Orange County here to take over from Butler. Eddie will have to take some kind of a fall, so we can't count on him, and Peterson is too much of a lightweight to run things without Butler. Reed will use him as a sort of liaison between the new people and Hernandez and for some type of bodyguard duty. That's up to Reed. At the same time, Don will have more time on his hands, and there's no reason why he can't take over this part of the job."

Landis said, "Okay, if that's how you want to play it. Are your other boys happy?"

"Let's say a little nervous, having to come up with two and a half million in cold cash. That's a half million each they'll double within a few months."

"They can't complain about that, can they?"

"No, but they still get nervous. All they're risking are the profits they've made on previous deals, yet they put up some resistance. I had to lay it on the line for them, either put up or I'd get some others to go in for the full amount. Hell, if this goes on a regular two- or three-month basis, they'll be wallowing in tax-free money."

"Yes, well—you've got your reservation for tonight?"

"Yes. You'll drop me at the Firebird Motel in Santa Monica this evening. I'll be registered under the name of George Bannister. In the morning I'll take a cab to the airport and meet Al when he gets in. I should be back in about three or four days."

"Just in case she calls while you're away, what story did you tell Margaret?"

"That I'm going to Denver to see a client."

"All right, Charlie."

At five forty-five Landis, accompanied by one of his young law clerks, who carried a rather heavy suitcase, took the elevator to the underground garage, locked the suitcase inside the trunk of his Cadillac. The young man got in behind the wheel and drove the very short distance to the Ambassador Hotel. Landis went inside while the young man remained in the car, parked near the entrance.

At six-ten, Charles T. Valentine left his office and took the elevator to the street level. He exited the building on the Normandie Avenue side, walked down to Seventh Street, then to Mariposa Avenue, and entered the grounds of the Ambassador Hotel, went to the bar, and found Landis with a drink before him. Landis signaled the bartender, and Valentine ordered a bloody mary. Valentine drank it hurriedly, put the glass down, and said, "Let's get away from here, Paul. I don't like to be too far away from that suitcase."

Landis paid the check, and they left. On the parking lot, Landis led the way to the Cadillac. The young man stepped out, and Landis got in behind the wheel, Valentine in the passenger seat. "Thanks, Arthur," Landis said to his law clerk. "Sorry to keep you this late. I'll see you in the morning." And wondered what Arthur would think if he knew that he had been guarding a suitcase filled with two and a half million dollars in cash.

Traffic at that hour was heavy. Valentine was impatient and acted it, turning frequently to look out behind to see if any one special car seemed to be following. It was dark when they reached Santa Monica, and Landis took a final circuitous route to the motel to ensure against a tail car, more for Valentine's benefit. At eight P.M., Valentine checked in under his assumed name and carried the suitcase to his room. Landis, after a few parting words, left him.

Valentine then double-locked the door behind him and placed the suitcase on one of the twin beds. He unlocked and opened it for a final check. Under a suit, some shirts, underwear, pajamas, socks, ties, and shaving gear lay the twenty-five packages, each wrapped in heavy brown paper and tape-sealed. Each with a hundred thousand dollars in one-hundred-dollar bills. Two and a half million dollars. He pondered over the risk of a holdup, knowing full well he could easily be killed for what he was carrying. In earlier times, when the amount was a tenth of this, he hadn't been nearly this concerned, using commercial airlines, carrying a .38 for protection, until the airlines installed electronic search devices as a guard against skyjackings. No longer a problem since they began using the private plane to carry the money to the ranch.

He locked the suitcase and placed it under the bed, then ordered a light meal through room service, ate it leisurely, then undressed, turned on the television set, and watched two programs and the Eleven O'clock News, swallowed a Seconal, and read his copy of the *Examiner* until sleep overcame him.

As the first rays of dawn appeared in the east, Alan De-Witt stepped into the Cessna Skymaster 337, taxied to the south end of the runway, and took off. Three and a half hours later, 655 miles away, he landed at Tucson International and ate a second breakfast while his tanks were being topped off. Two hours and thirteen minutes later, he contacted the Santa Monica tower for landing instructions.

While the plane was being serviced for the return trip, De-Witt drank a cup of coffee and had his two thermos jugs filled. ATIS, Automatic Terminal Information Service, reported favorable conditions to Tucson. DeWitt bought four packs of cigarettes and returned to the plane, then saw the taxi pull up. Valentine got out, paid the driver, and lifted the heavy suitcase out of the cab. DeWitt went to him, and the two old friends exchanged handshakes, then brought the suitcase to the plane and strapped it to the rear deck. DeWitt did the walk around inspection, kicking the tires, removing the tank caps to be sure they had been properly filled, then checked the engine oil with the dip stick.

"Okay, Val," DeWitt said, satisfied, "let's grab us some sky."

Buckled in, DeWitt moved automatically through the pre-flight checklist, adjusted the altimeter and tested the controls. He set the brakes and pressed the starter. For all his backlog of flying experience, Valentine noted gratefully, DeWitt was a cautious pilot, particularly in a privately owned twin-engine turbo that, fully equipped with every modern navigational, communications, and safety feature, had cost better than $130,000. A beauty, Valentine mused, that could cruise at 220-plus miles per hour and had a safe flying range of 800 to 900-plus miles.

DeWitt was the total pilot now as he turned on the radio

and switched to ground-control frequency, listened to ATIS for a few moments for any last-minute changes in the weather, then reached for his mike.

"Santa Monica ground. This is Skymaster five-niner-six-three-Bravo at VIP with Information Hotel, taxi for takeoff."

The metallic voice responded through the overhead speaker. "Five-niner-six-three-Bravo, taxi to runway two-one and hold behind green Bonanza five-zero-Yankee."

DeWitt released the brakes and raced his engine slightly, moving downfield, braking beside and behind the Bonanza, next in line for takeoff. He set his brakes and throttled up to 1,800 rpms, then cut a magneto. He made a final check on temperature and oil pressure as the Bonanza got the word and took off.

"Santa Monica tower. Skymaster five-niner-six-three-Bravo, ready for takeoff."

Briskly, "Skymaster five-niner-six-three-Bravo, cleared for takeoff."

"Thank you." DeWitt moved into threshold position, watching for landing aircraft on the runway. Santa Monica did not cater to large commercial carriers, but was a mecca for business executives, pleasure craft, and student learners, which meant exercising even greater caution. One final traffic check, then a turn into the runway.

DeWitt pushed the throttle to red line on the manifold pressure gauge, and the Skymaster was racing along the smooth concrete path, straining, lifting, reaching skyward. They were airborne. Climbing at five hundred, he made a ninety-degree turn and continued to six thousand, altered course to southeast before climbing to eighty-five hundred, flying visual. They lit cigarettes and relaxed for the flight ahead. Valentine unstrapped one of the thermos jugs and said, "Coffee, Al?"

"Not yet. Help yourself. How do you like this bird?"

"Beautiful. Just beautiful."

"Want to take over for a while?"

"Maybe later. Hell, I haven't been off my ass in so long, I'm rusty."

"Come on, Val, this baby does everything for you except eat, drink, or smoke." He set the controls on autopilot. "Have any trouble putting the loot together, Val?"

"Not too much. A lot more than they expected, but figuring the profit margin, they went along. Everything okay on your end?"

"Yeah, sure. I'll take off tomorrow, meet Heck in Hermosillo, and fly him home to Guadalajara to pick up this Alessandro dude, then fly him to the general's *estado,* make the payoff and pickup, and head for home." DeWitt broke off, then said, "Hey, old buddy, why the hell don't you make one of those trips with me? You'd be good company. It's a long haul back solo."

Valentine grinned. "Hell, no, Al. I do a lot better sitting around biting my nails, waiting for the delivery in L.A. and the turnover so I can pay off our nervous investors."

DeWitt laughed. "I could give those guys something to be nervous about on that last leg from Hermosillo to the ranch. Man, that takes some tricky doing."

DeWitt stubbed out his cigarette and smiled. "That's why you're doing it, Al. Christ, you were always the best of the group at hopscotching and hedgehopping over, in, around, and between every obstacle in Korea."

"That was it, wasn't it, where it all was."

"The good old days, Al."

DeWitt's smile evaporated. "Good old days, my ass. Scrambling before daybreak, freezing our balls off, screeching through skies with our eyes half closed, fighting for the privilege of making it back so we could do it all over again the next day. If we were goddamned lucky. Good old days? Al, the good old days are now, today, this minute."

Valentine regarded DeWitt quizzically. "Getting to you, old buddy?"

"Maybe. And maybe it's old age creeping up on me. Hey, I'll take that coffee now."

Valentine unscrewed the thermos top and poured a fresh cup for DeWitt and refilled his own. DeWitt drank in quick gulps until the cup was empty, then handed it back to Valentine. "Val," he said, "how are you and Margaret fixed?"

"Fixed? If you mean financially, in good shape. Why?"

"Suppose—just suppose—we decided to wash up this whole deal after these next two trips."

Valentine studied DeWitt with almost clinical interest. "You're serious?"

"Well, Roy and I were talking it over just the other day. I think Roy would like to get married again, and I might just take this baby on a long flying trip, come back and maybe do the same thing. We're all pushing fifty, and this kind of cops and robbers is for kids, not old men."

Valentine shrugged and fell silent for a few moments, then said, "Well, if that's the way you and Roy want to go, I sure as hell won't complain too hard. My investors may get a little unhappy, but screw them. All they ever risked was money. They won't be any problem. My key people, well, they can go on operating, find other sources of supply, do it on a smaller scale. What about Heck?"

"I'll talk to him when I see him. I'm sure he's more than comfortable. Got a hunch he'll jump at it, with more to lose than the rest of us. Wife, two kids, home, the works."

"What about the others, Alessandro, the distributors?"

"Hell, Alessandro will always find contacts, that's his life's work. We'll talk to the Eastern people, let them set up their own deal with him. And yours out on the coast, if you want it set up that way."

"Sounds like it was more than just a little discussion you and Roy had. Then this one and the next one will be the last deals?"

"So far, they're the only two we've got set up firmly. We can wrap it up after that, go legitimate and stay friends. The old fearless foursome, scourges of the Korean skies. Okay?"

"Okay, Al. I've got enough, and laundering this kind of money gets to be a pain in the ass." He poured more coffee for both of them. "Shall we drink on it?"

DeWitt took the cup. "Cheers."

They stopped at El Paso, six hundred and twenty miles out of Santa Monica, to eat and refuel. Taking off again, Valentine broached the subject again. "You're really serious about cutting out, Al?"

"I wasn't kidding, buddy. After I take off for Mexico in the morning, you stick around and talk it over with Roy. Ever since he brought it up, I'm liking the idea more and more."

"I believe you. It's just that you came on so sudden."

"You thinking about changing your mind, Val?"

"Hell, no, not at all. Without you and Roy, I don't want any part of it."

"Okay, let's go then. We've got four hundred twenty-five miles to cover before we can really wet our throats."

5●

The Skymaster landed at the Wrayburn Ranch at 5:10 P.M. Agent Carlos Azuela, patrolling the road east of the ranch in a Dodge pickup, radioed the word in to Agent Max Arnold in Del Rio. In turn, Arnold phoned the message to SAC Jesse Tyler in San Antonio, who logged the information in the Wrayburn file and teletyped copies to Dallas and Los Angeles. The surveillance continued.

In the large house on the portion of the ranch that once belonged to the Bishop family, Don Reed felt totally out of place in the atmosphere of reunion between the three veterans of the Korean conflict. There was an open camaraderie, even affection, he had never shared with anyone, not in college nor with the men and women he had known and dealt with in the years that followed.

Listening to anecdotes, jokes, and laughter that passed between Chase, DeWitt, and Valentine, feeling the warmth and pleasure in their casual exchanges over drinks and the hearty dinner placed before them by the bustling Mexican servants, the realization that he was truly a loner struck at him very hard. Valentine, whom he had known only on the most formal, businesslike terms, was an entirely different personality, far more at ease, smiling, laughing uproariously at Chase's and DeWitt's quips.

When an occasional remark or question was addressed to him by Chase or DeWitt, it was hardly in the same genial vein, more pointed and direct, almost as though he were being interviewed or interrogated. Several times, it was Valentine who found it necessary to come to his aid with an answer, giving him a deeper feeling of inadequacy. At this point, he began to wonder why he was here at all since there had been no discussion of the upcoming operation and expansion.

After dinner, they returned to the huge central room, lavishly decorated with sofas and lounge chairs in smooth leather and animal hides, tall lamps, the glistening pegged floors covered with large and small imported rugs. On either end of the room, stairways led to an upper balcony lined with doors to six separate bedrooms, each complete with bath and dressing room. There were large vases of flowers on the tables and floors, the walls hung with tapestries, paintings, etchings, and engravings, spotlighted by beams of light recessed in the huge overhead rafters. Reed took note of the special placement of the largest painting in the room—a woman in her mid-thirties, dressed in riding clothes, leaning against the rails of a corral, a leather crop in one hand, smiling.

They sat in luxurious armchairs before a low table that held an elaborate silver coffee service and a tray of assorted liquors, cigars and cigarettes lighted, at comfortable ease; and although he was there with them, Reed felt no sense of being a part of them or their conversation—the stranger at the feast.

Now they began to discuss the upcoming shipment from Bogotá and the one to follow, referring to the cocaine and heroin as "goods," so that they might be talking about clothing, sugar, pots, pans, cattle, or any other commodity. Nothing beyond the second shipment. So Reed sat and listened to the details of the operation in which he was vitally interested and in which he was not included and felt that coming here had been a waste of time.

Then Chase turned to Reed and said, "We've added another thirty thousand acres to the place since your first visit here, Mr. Reed. Maybe you'd like to saddle up tomorrow and ride over some of it."

"Thanks, no, Mr. Chase," Reed replied. "I don't think I could last thirty seconds on a horse. I've never ridden one."

"Well, maybe Val and I'll show it to you from a car. Give you both a day in clean, fresh air."

Reed broke a small smile. "After L.A., I think I could use that."

"Fine, fine. You'll be going back with Val in a couple of days, so if there's anything special you'd like to see or do, let me know and I'll arrange it for you."

"Thank you."

At 9:30, he felt the weariness of the long day overcome him and, bored with the conversation he felt was too private to hold his interest, excused himself and went up to his room and to bed.

6•

At daybreak next morning, DeWitt and Chase removed the $2,500,000 from the suitcase and deposited $1,900,000 in the safe beneath the floorboards in Chase's bedroom on the ground level. The remaining $600,000 was divided into two flat metal containers. The two men breakfasted together, then carried the two metal containers outside to a station wagon and drove to the barnlike structure beside the landing strip. Ranch hands now wheeled the Skymaster out of the hangar. The containers were placed beneath the false flooring behind the forward seats, the floor screwed securely in place and covered with the carpeting.

In a hidden compartment beside the left seat, DeWitt placed a submachine gun. Beneath the control panel, he clipped a .45 automatic. Chase tossed in a two-suiter that DeWitt strapped into the luggage compartment in the rear. He warmed the plane up as Chase watched from the station wagon, then waved as he released the brakes and started toward the runway apron. A few minutes later, with visibility clear, he took off.

Don Reed was awakened by the sound of the Skymaster warming up. He got out of bed, drew the curtains, and stood at the window watching as the plane maneuvered toward the takeoff strip, wishing that he had been invited to go along and share that new, unique experience. He waited until the plane rose above the horizon, white with red trim, heading north. Then it circled and veered left out of his sight.

He dressed and went downstairs where a servant offered him a cup of rich, hot coffee. Valentine, who had probably been similarly awakened by the sound of the plane, appeared and they had breakfast together; eggs, slices of thick bacon, toasted homemade bread, flapjacks, and a platter of breakfast steaks. Reed ate sparingly, watching Valentine attack his food with zest. Chase had not yet appeared.

Reed poured another cup of coffee, lit a cigarette, and said, "Charlie, I don't see any point in me sticking around here for another two or three days."

Valentine looked up with a smile. "No? Relax, Don. It's good to get away from the rat race for a few days, isn't it?"

"I guess I don't know how to relax the way you can with your buddies. I feel out of the action, isolated."

"Three days won't kill you, and once Al gets back, you'll have all the action you'll want."

"I'm looking forward to that, but why don't I go back and get things set up with Hernandez and the new people I've got who are taking over from Butler. With two hundred kilos coming in, we'll have to arrange to bring in more of Simon's people to handle the milling operation."

"All right, Don, if you feel that's necessary. Give it one more day. Tomorrow, we'll have someone drive you into San Antonio for a flight back to L.A. Okay?"

"Okay," Reed said with relief.

With DeWitt and Chase talking retirement, Valentine saw no point in discussing his original reasons for bringing Reed along. After the second shipment there would be no need to transport large amounts of cash from Los Angeles in the future. There would, in fact, be no future for them in this business.

DeWitt headed first for Juarez International and received his landing instructions from the tower. He throttled back, glided in, and touched down smoothly, taxied to Customs

338

clearance, gave the universal switchoff signal to the cover-alled attendant by drawing a finger across his throat, set his parking brake, and cut engines.

He stepped out and greeted the uniformed, badged Mexican official, speaking to him in fluent Spanish. The official responded warmly and merely asked a few questions without examining the plane. Inside the building, they had a cold drink together: then DeWitt received weather information and filed a flight plan to Hermosillo. Moments later, he took off, landing in Hermosillo an hour and forty-five minutes later.

Hector Villanueva met him with a warm *ambrazo* as he entered the building. They stood together and talked while DeWitt kept an eye on the Skymaster and the attendants busy refueling it. Heck's first questions were of Chase, Valentine, and Margaret. "And you, Al?"

"As you see me, Heck, still going strong toward fifty."

Villanueva grinned. "Don't remind me."

"How's the leg?"

"As good as it'll ever be. A little stiff in the morning, loosens up a few hours later."

"Roy's hoping to come down with me one of these days very soon. A social visit, bring Val and Margaret along with us for a real wingding."

"Promises, promises."

"Mean it this time. How's Magda?"

"Magdalena is Magdalena. Beautiful as ever. You'll see her in Guadalajara."

"I'm looking forward to it. And the kids?"

Villanueva laughed. "They haven't been kids for a long time, Al. Benita is eighteen, looks like her mother. She's away at college. Paula is sixteen, an honor student, but a hellcat. What's with you, you old bastard?"

"Just getting older and meaner and still free-lancing."

"Man, you ought to quit and come down to Guadalajara to live. Nothing like it—"

DeWitt smiled and said, "Funny you should mention it."

"—and Magda'd have you married off inside three months."

"Well," Al drawled, "I'll give it some of my very best thinking and consideration, but anytime you and Magda decide to split—"

"You're right, Al. The older you get, the meaner, dirtier, and raunchier you get."

"Just a man with lots of experience and impeccable taste.

Hey, let's get the hell out of here and on our way. We've got three and a half hours in the saddle. What about Alessandro?"

"I left Estaban in Guadalajara at the Camino Real this morning to fly up and meet you. He'll be ready to go when you are."

"Tomorrow morning, early. Fill me in on this general in Bogotá, will you? I'd like to feel some reassurance I'm not going to get ripped off for the bread I'm delivering to him."

In Guadalajara, they removed the two containers and weapons and placed them in Villanueva's car. He drove De-Witt to the Camino Real on Avenida Vallarta and checked him in for the overnight stay. Heck dialed Estaban Alessandro's room, found he was out, and left a message for him to meet them for dinner and drinks in DeWitt's suite.

Villanueva then left to bring Magdalena to the hotel. De-Witt showered and changed, called room service and ordered a portable bar, drinks, hors d'oeuvres, and a boy to serve. He also ordered dinner for three in his suite for nine o'clock that night.

Heck returned with Magdalena, and the three enjoyed their reunion for two hours, when Alessandro returned. After introductions, Heck left to take Magda home. Alessandro and DeWitt discussed the trip to Bogotá, and Alessandro satisfied DeWitt's curiosity about General Mendenez. Later, Alessandro went to his room for a nap before their scheduled dinner at nine o'clock. DeWitt locked his door and slept in the bed beside the closet in which he had locked the containers of money, his .45 under his pillow.

Heck and Alessandro returned together just as the dinner arrived. It was a pleasant affair that lasted for two hours, when Heck left, promising to return to pick both men up at four in the morning. Alessandro then suggested a change in the flight plan. Instead of flying to Panama City, then on to Bogotá, they would stop at Tapachula International in Mexico, then Santamaria International in Costa Rica, then on to the Mendenez estate outside Parano in Colombia.

DeWitt did not question Alessandro's reasons for the revised plan, accepting the decision as necessary for purposes of security, relying on the Argentinian's expert knowledge of changing conditions—that certain officials had become greedier, in which case the risk of losing the money on the down leg, or the goods on the return trip, would have increased greatly. In that matter, Alessandro's superior judgment must be accepted.

They met, as arranged, at four A.M. DeWitt had studied his flight charts before going to bed. Tapachula, 759 miles, four hours and fifteen minutes. To Santamaria, 572 miles, three hours and fifteen minutes. To Parano, 736 miles, four hours. A total of 2,067 nautical miles, eleven and a half hours' flying time, weather permitting. Add another two hours for servicing would bring them to thirteen and a half hours. With a four-thirty A.M. takeoff, they should reach their destination at dusk.

At the airport, DeWitt replaced the containers of money beneath the flooring, secured his weapons in place. He checked the plane, filed the flight plan, and said good-by to Villanueva. With Alessandro beside him, he checked weather conditions, found them satisfactory, and asked for clearance, taking off without further delay.

Leveled off, Alessandro, a phlegmatic man who seemed to have little use for social conversation, for which DeWitt was grateful, fell asleep within a few minutes and did not waken until DeWitt received landing instructions from the Tapachula tower. He remained on board while the plane was refueled. DeWitt then filed his flight plan to Santamaria, had the thermos jugs filled, bought a bagful of sandwiches, and they were aloft with a minimum of time elapsed.

On the final leg of 736 miles, they flew through a cloud mass and unexpected turbulence. DeWitt got on the air, checking conditions ahead, and was given clearance to ten thousand feet. He flew at that altitude until they broke into the clear, remaining there for the next two hours.

Approaching Bogotá, DeWitt spread his area chart on his lap and studied it carefully, then began dropping lower, scrutinizing the surrounding sky for other aircraft. He dropped swiftly now, until houses and street and road traffic were clearly visible to the naked eye, then turned eastward, directed now by an alert Alessandro, who prompted him by picking out recognizable landmarks. Then, after a stretch of uninhabited forest, Alessandro pointed out the landing strip. "There, *señor*."

"I see it." DeWitt replied with secret elation. "I see it."

They were flying just above treetop level when he spied the mansion on their right, flew on beyond it, circled, and came in for the landing with light to spare. Beside the runway, as he cut power, he saw about a dozen armed men, a pickup truck, two jeeps, and a black limousine. At once, the men swarmed toward the plane, rolling several fifty-five-gallon drums of aviation fuel toward it.

DeWitt and Alessandro stepped down, then Al unscrewed the false floor, removed the two containers of cash, his weapons and suitcase, and placed them in the trunk of the limousine. He was exhausted. The idea of spending a full thirty-six hours sleeping and relaxing in these peaceful, wooded surroundings appealed to him very much, just as the thought that this and one more trip like it, bringing it all to an end, was pleasing him more and more.

He waited until the gasoline had been pumped into the tanks, then locked the plane. Two armed guards, Alessandro told him, would be on watch in shifts until it was loaded with the cargo and he was ready to leave—a moment DeWitt cherished. The flight back would be made alone, leaving Alessandro behind, something DeWitt looked forward to. The Argentinian could hardly be called lively company; conversely, his silent presence and ominous bearing were disconcerting.

They were driven to one of several guesthouses, barely within sight of the mansion, where General Gerardo Aramis Mendenez awaited them. Alessandro made the necessary introductions, and the general remarked his pleasure at their meeting and hoped Señor DeWitt (pronounced "Do-it") would be comfortable. In the morning they would discuss the business matter at hand. The general left, taking Alessandro with him.

Hot food and a bottle each of wine, Scotch, and a local liquor arrived moments later. DeWitt, more anxious for a hot bath and sleep, ate lightly and sent the two servants away with almost as much food as they had brought except for the coffee, liquor, and a bowl of fruit. He locked the bedroom door, placed the containers under the bed, and slept with the submachine gun and .45 beside him.

In the morning, breakfast arrived at nine o'clock. He was hungry now and devoured the food, drank three large cups of coffee. At ten thirty, the general arrived with Alessandro. DeWitt brought out the containers and permitted the general a view of the bundles of U.S. currency. Two aides were called in to carry the money away and, no doubt, count it.

This done, DeWitt was driven along a dirt road to a building well hidden by forest growth. The laboratory. Inside, stacked on two pallets, were the cocaine and heroin packed in small wax-coated, waterproofed cartons that would fit beneath the floorboards of the Skymaster. Two hundred kilos. Four hundred and forty pounds.

"The purest," the general said, not without some pride. "Nowhere else will you find purer."

There was little doubt in DeWitt's mind. At the ranch, the heroin would be stepped down, or adulterated, five times; the cocaine three times. One hundred kilos of heroin would become five hundred; one hundred of cocaine, three hundred. A hundred of each to Valentine would leave four hundred heroin and two hundred cocaine for their Eastern and Midwestern distributors, with room left for additional adulteration before selling it off to the dealers and street pushers.

"I would like to leave early tomorrow morning," DeWitt said, "and supervise the loading."

"At your pleasure, *señor*," the general said.

"Three o'clock loading, four-thirty takeoff."

The general nodded and gave orders to his aide.

DeWitt spent the rest of the day alone, sleeping, then a long swim in the pool, more sleep, a superb dinner served in his guesthouse, to bed at ten, and awakened by a guard at two-thirty. At planeside, the cargo waited. He instructed two workmen in its loading, packing the flat cartons tightly into the space, then screwed the floorboards over them, replaced the carpeting and was ready. At exactly four-thirty, he took off. Neither the general nor Alessandro was present to see him leave.

The flight back to Guadalajara, following the same route, was uneventful. There were only cursory oral examinations at each full stop, and at dusk, as planned, DeWitt landed in Guadalajara. Villanueva was at the airport to meet him, this time with two men, off-duty policemen, who would remain with the plane until DeWitt would take off early the following morning.

Now, unencumbered with the large sum of cash, the cargo well guarded, they had an early meal at the Villanueva home. Later, in DeWitt's suite at Camino Real, Heck took a sheet of paper from his pocket and unfolded it on the writing desk. "This is the new arrangement for the trip back, Al. People at a couple of the old stops are getting too damned nosey, jacking up the protection fees, so I've cut them out. Let's go over this together."

On the sheet was a carefully drawn map. "As best as I can figure it from a land road map, Guadalajara to Ahome, then west across the gulf to Puerto Escondido in Baja California, about seven hundred miles. Three miles north of the village is this dirt road within sight of a small church I've marked here with a cross. You'll come in low, throttled down, and you'll see a brown, shitty-colored pickup truck. Land on that road as close to the truck as you can. Four guys will help you refuel. No payoffs. I've already taken care of that."

"What about cops?"

Villanueva laughed. "The bag man, the one I paid off, is the chief cop. He'll be driving the truck with your fuel. He'll flash his badge on you for recognition. If you want to tip him ten or twenty, okay, just to keep him happy."

"All right. What next?"

"You fly north up the Baja, a *turista* on his way home. Then here—" indicating on the map—"you'll bear right until you're over San Felipe, where you'll see a fairly wide highway that runs north to Mexicali and an old narrower road that branches off to the east about forty miles north. Follow that one to this point here, a wide-open field with a large white house and two smaller ones on a hill. To the left of those three houses, you'll see a private road, but watch it. It's dirt and a little rough with some ruts, but not too bad for a hotdog like you. There'll be a truck with three men waiting to top you off. They've been taken care of, too, so load up and take off. From there, you fly north and east until you cross the border into Arizona, and you're on your own."

"Okay, Heck. It doesn't look too bad if I can count on those two roads and the guys you paid to be there. Let me check this out on my charts."

"I went over those places just before I met you in Hermosillo. They're not super landing strips, but they'll do."

From his suitcase, DeWitt got out his area charts, located the proper one, and began making notes on the map Heck had drawn for him. He checked these against a relief map of the border area, indicating his first, and alternate, choices to cross into the United States, using a red, then green, felt-tipped pen to mark both. He looked over his markings and said, "Okay, Heck. I think I'm all set now. Once this next deal is behind us, I'll be back with Roy and Val for that social visit."

"Hey, man, I'll be looking forward to that. I haven't seen either one of them in almost a year. Longer for Val."

DeWitt grinned. "You can count on it this time."

"I've heard that line before. Why should I believe it this time?"

"Well, let me tell you why." He paused, staring at Heck

for a moment, still smiling. "Heck, Roy, Val and I have been talking this whole lash-up over—"

"You've decided you want to bail out."

DeWitt was taken by surprise. "Now how in the hell did you guess that? You been practicing voodoo with the friendly natives down here?"

"Well, a guy starts moaning about pushing fifty, talks about maybe settling down, I've got to figure he wants to get this kind of pressure off his back."

"I'll be damned. I didn't know I was that obvious about it. Okay, let me ask a personal question, Heck. How are you fixed?"

"No sweat. Living in Mexico, I'm probably as well fixed as you, Roy, or Val. To be honest, I'm glad it's over. I don't like dealing with people like Alessandro, mixed up with revolutionary movements, looking over my shoulder most of the time. I've never really liked dealing in these goddamned drugs but—well, the money's been useful. If I believed in God, or a hereafter, I guess I wouldn't be able to sleep nights, but hell, I wouldn't have been able to do the kind of killing we did in Korea, either. So, if it's over, it's over, and I'm glad."

"What about Magda?"

"Magda?" Heck laughed without humor. "We never talk about it. Never have. What she suspects, I don't know, but she keeps it to herself. Mexican wives wouldn't think of interfering in a husband's business affairs. The kids don't know anything about it. I'm the only one who has to live with my conscience."

Weary as he was, DeWitt found it difficult to fall asleep. In the morning, he felt logy as he filed a flight plan to Hermosillo that he didn't intend to stay with, then climbed into the Skymaster and took off. He flew over Tepic, Mazatlán, Culican, and, approaching Los Mochis, radioed ahead, cancelled his VFR flight plan with Hermosillo, and went off the air without filing another.

He crossed the gulf at Ahome, followed Heck's map, found Puerto Escondido, and made a rough landing on the dirt road where the pickup truck waited. The refueling operation was tediously slow, but steady. DeWitt gave the man with the badge fifty dollars and took off, leaving a dust storm behind in his wake. Once aloft, he swallowed an amphetamine capsule to keep him alert.

The landing beyond San Felipe was a replay of the one at Puerto Escondido, and DeWitt was grateful to find the truck and manpower waiting to top off his tanks. Airborne again, fighting drowsiness, he began talking to himself to fight it off. "Now, Al, keep your fingers crossed. We're going to cross the gulf at El Golfo and squeeze in somewhere between Pincate and Quitovac. We'll be flying so goddamned close to the ground you'll feel like reaching out and scooping up a handful of sand. Just take it easy. You've done this before. Lots of times."

From El Golfo, he flew eastward, dropping lower until he seemed to be skimming the surface. Then, having crossed Gran Desierto, he flew between ridges and peaks, avoiding possible radar contact until he was across the border somewhere between Tubac and Bisbee. He swallowed another amphetamine, then switched his radio on to pick up Tucson ATIS and his exact location, headed north for a while, then east, beamed in on Tucson International. He landed there for a quick meal, lots of hot coffee, and a refuel, then took off for El Paso. Two hours and thirty minutes after leaving El Paso, he landed at the ranch just as the light was beginning to fail.

7●

Lying flat on the ground on the edge of a grove of trees some four hundred yards east of the private landing strip on the Wrayburn Ranch, Special Agent Carlos Azuela turned to his partner, Agent Juan Peralta. Both were dressed in ranch work clothes, both wearied from the long, long wait, but now it was there, the Skymaster, as it made its low-level approach, flashing its landing lights on, gliding in smoothly for the landing.

"Man," Azuela said admiringly, "that sonofabitch sure knows how to handle that baby."

"Yeah," Peralta agreed, "but right now I'm more interested in what he's carrying inside that baby's belly."

Through night field glasses, they watched as the plane taxied toward the hangar where a white pickup truck and a crew of four men waited. Once the plane was pushed inside beside the ancient Stearman biplane, it became impossible to follow the action. Then the tallest of the four men backed the pickup truck inside. Half an hour later, it emerged and drove in a westerly direction and disappeared from sight.

Azuela tapped Peralta on the shoulder. "Goddam. If we

had a search warrant and a crew of guys, I'll bet we could've caught us a hell of a load."

"Sure, sure. But what if all we caught was a big fat zip. Christ, we'd get ourselves spread out on every front page in the country. This'd make that Collinsville thing in Illinois look like a kid's playground."

"Okay, okay. Let's get back to the wagon and pass the word along."

It was a long way back to the extreme eastern border of the ranch where they had found a place to conceal the Toyota station wagon. In the darkness they stumbled and walked across Wrayburn land for almost an hour, crossed the dirt road, and found the car. Reaching Del Rio, Peralta relayed the word to Max Arnold. Arnold phoned the word in to San Antonio and learned that Jesse Tyler had left for the day. He repeated the message for the benefit of the tape recorder, which the night-duty man, Bob Cameron, played over the phone to Jesse Tyler, at that moment having a drink at his home before sitting down to his dinner.

"Okay, Bob, let's have it." Cameron cut the recorder in, and Tyler heard Arnold's voice. "Arnold here, phoning from Del Rio, relaying a message from Carlos Azuela. At approximately eighteen thirty-five the Wrayburn Skymaster put down on the landing strip; one passenger, unidentified, was met by four unidentified men in a white pickup truck. Thirty minutes later, the pickup and crew of four drove west and north toward the old Del Long Ranch. The pilot was picked up by another unidentified man in a white Cadillac and driven toward the main ranch house. Over."

Cameron said, "That's it, Jess."

Tyler grunted, then instructed Cameron to notify the night-duty man in the Dallas office and to send a teletype to the Los Angeles office, attention Lyle Carter.

In Los Angeles, the night-duty man read the teletype message to SAC Lyle Carter who, in turn, phoned Gene Morris. It was now eleven-thirty, and Morris decided against phoning McNeely at that hour. Next morning, when McNeely and Ycaza arrived, Morris was on the phone talking with Willis Ames in Dallas. After a few moments, he hung up, slid the teletype across the desk, and dialed Jesse Tyler's number in San Antonio.

McNeely and Ycaza read the teletype and waited for Morris to conclude his conversation. When he hung up, he said, "Okay, here's the drill. Dallas and San Antonio are certain there's been a delivery to the ranch. They know when the Skymaster took off, three days ago. They've checked airports in the area through FAA and found flight plans filed out of Juarez to Hermosillo, then to Guadalajara and south; then on return, a flight plan into Hermosillo was canceled en route, but no new plan filed until it landed at Tucson and refueled yesterday afternoon. It landed at the ranch at eighteen thirty-five last night.

"The pickup truck and four men who were the reception committee obviously weren't on hand merely to greet a returning vacationer, so we must assume the pilot, probably De-Witt, brought in his load of *harina* and *cereal*, a hundred kilos of each, if we can believe the intercepted phone messages. Somewhere down there, there's a milling operation going on which, considering the quantity involved, will take some time to cut and repackage before it can be shipped out or called for.

"Okay. So far, most of this is educated guesswork on our part, which isn't enough to get us a federal search warrant on a reasonable-cause basis, call out the troops, and go rooting over more than a hundred thousand acres to look for the junk. It could be anywhere by now, somewhere in one of half a hundred or more houses, buildings, and barns on that property. It would take an army to find it. I don't have to tell you we're also interested in where, besides L.A., it's being shipped to, and who's doing the buying.

"Ames has ordered more men into the area, and Tyler has them spotted around the ranch between U.S. 277 and the back roads, from Del Rio to Sonora and north as far as San Angelo, watching for any action into or out of the ranch. If the Skymaster takes off again, we'll have planes in the air as well."

"What do we do in the meantime," McNeely asked, "sit around on our duffs waiting for something to happen?"

"I was getting to that, Russ. Ames and Tyler both suggested I go to San Antonio, then into the area with Tyler. I asked him if it wouldn't be advisable to bring you and Ray along with me, and he thought that would be a good idea. If all our assumptions are correct, they'll have to start moving some of it out soon, and from what we have so far, L.A. would be a good starting point for a shipment. Let's put it up to Captain Esau and see if we can clear you both for the trip."

Esau read the teletype and listened to Morris as he repeated his conversations with Ames and Tyler. To Russ, "What's the situation here?"

"Everything is status quo at the moment, Captain. Butler is still in his house on Warren Canyon Drive; Don Reed has been checked back in at the apartment on Alicante. Valentine is still missing, but his car is parked in the underground garage of his office building. Still no sign of Moose Peterson or Cora Thomas. Everything that needs covering is being covered, including Tri-City's operation, and we've got our people out smoking out informant tips."

"All right," Esau said, "give me a little time to check this out with Chief Traynor. We'll need approval from the top for this. While I'm doing that, you might check out on the reservation situation to San Antonio."

"Myself alone, Cap?" Russ asked.

"You and Ycaza. You're a crew, remember? On your way out, see if Bob is around and send him in to me."

Barker had just returned from West Hollywood and went in at once to talk with Esau, who was at that moment concluding a telephone conversation. "Bob, I'll have to give this to you fast. I've got an appointment with Chief Traynor in thirty minutes."

He outlined the situation briefly, quickly. "I'm going to suggest to the chief that we send McNeely and Ycaza to San Antonio along with Gene Morris. I'm bypassing you on this for two reasons. One, I want you here to keep on top of the situation as we know it. Two, while I share your confidence in McNeely, I want to see how he would handle himself on his own."

Barker grinned and said, "I'm not exactly looking for a trip right now, Cap, and I would have made the same choice. You can count on him."

"That's what I'll be doing, and it won't hurt him if and when I propose to the brass that we jump him on the promotion list. Okay, I'm going up to convince the chief. Go out and talk to them and let them give you the rest of the details. I'll want Russ to report to you directly from the field."

Within an hour, they were summoned to Esau's office. Barker, Inspectors Walton and Garland were present to be briefed on the situation. Esau said, "We've got the approval from topside. Bob will take charge here while you're gone. If nothing happens down there within a week, I want you back here. Understood?"

"Yes, sir," McNeely said. "If everything else is in order, we should be taking off around noon."

"Good luck."

They returned to their office with Barker, and after making calls to Yolanda and Rachel, McNeely said to Barker, "If anything starts moving west, I'll phone you and keep you posted en route. When that happens, our crooks here have got to start moving around."

"Okay. For what it's worth, I've picked up an item for you from Johnny Segura, maybe nothing to it yet, but Johnny got it from a buddy of his in L.A.P.D. who spotted an old friend of yours back in town. Anson Talbot."

"Anse? I thought he was operating out of Newport Beach since he beat his rap here four years ago."

"So did I. I talked with the sheriff's people down there. They're sure he's been operating around there, but haven't anything to hang on him. I'm putting out a bulletin to all our crews to be on the lookout for him."

"Yes. Be interesting to find out what he's up to." And to Morris and Ycaza, "Well, let's get somebody to drive us to the airport."

8•

In San Antonio they were met by SAC Jesse Tyler and Agent Max Arnold, who drove them to Del Rio where they checked into the Lone Star Motel on the eastern edge of the town. Thus far, there had been no unusual movement in or out of the Wrayburn Ranch, as reported by Carlos Azuela who was coordinating the activities of the twenty-two men Tyler had moved into the area. Operating between Del Rio and San Angelo in various vehicles, all equipped with either radio or walkie-talkies, dressed as working ranch hands, laborers, migrants, sometimes posing as equipment salesmen, they were in constant movement on every road surrounding the huge ranch by day and night. Stationed just a stone's throw from the motel was an agent-manned radio car used to receive and relay calls from those on patrol and the San Antonio office in order to avoid using the phones in their rooms, which were tied into the central switchboard.

"So far," Tyler informed them, "we've got every road and trail covered from the outside, just waiting for some move, which we figure has got to come soon. If we're correct in our thinking, the stuff is there, and people outside are waiting for it. Unlike money in a bank, it gathers no interest until it's turned over. Washington and Dallas are just as anxious, even more so, to crack this thing once and for all, green light all the way."

"We're due for a break," Morris added. "We've been on it for damned near two years, and this is as close as we've ever gotten to pay dirt."

Tyler said, "Yeah," then, "Gene, in those clothes you boys are as conspicuous as three whores at a church social. I'm going to send Max out to pick up some ranch duds for you, then get you spread out in some of our ranch wagons and trucks to take you out for a look around. If anything comes up, I'll get to you on the radio."

Dressed in tan jeans, boots, and straw hats that were the universal uniform in the area, McNeely and Ycaza were driven through town, north on U.S. 277 to Sonora, then to San Angelo, south on the narrow dirt road on the eastern border of the Wrayburn Ranch, spotting an occasional building, some grazing cattle, familiarizing themselves with the terrain. The vehicles used by the surveilling agents carried sacks of grain and feed, ranch tools and equipment, and at intervals met with other agents to exchange loads in order not to attract curious eyes. On the first night, Ycaza slept in San Angelo, McNeely in Sonora. On the second night, they slept on bedrolls in their trucks, parked beside the road. Every hour around the clock, their driver-agent radioed in to report or pick up instructions, if any.

At dawn on the third morning, the first word came through from Tyler, a request that McNeely, Morris, and Ycaza meet him on Route 90, at a point four miles east of Del Rio, soonest. They arrived separately, Ycaza first, McNeely behind him, to find Jesse Tyler in a state of excitement. They waited for another fifteen minutes until Morris showed up. Drinking coffee from Tyler's thermos, he said, "Looks like we've got something starting. Here's the scam. At zero three-twenty a Ford Kar-a-Van, that's one of those mini-mobile homes on wheels, came into Del Rio, turned off on 277 north. Johnny Peralta was sitting about fifty yards south of the Wrayburn entrance, saw it go inside.

"He radioed the tags to me, and I ran them. Texas, four-William-nine-five-nine-two. Comes back registered to Billy John Gorman, with a San Antonio address. San Antonio PD has had him a couple of times as a juvenile, kid stuff, nothing serious. He's a male, Caucasian, thirty, five-ten, about a hundred seventy pounds, sandy-haired. With him, according to Peralta, is a female, Caucasian, no further identification; just caught a glimpse of her as they drove past.

"Okay. The way we read it, that Kar-a-Van with those two average people is going to haul a load out of there. A couple, tourists, off on a vacation somewhere. Everything normal, nothing unusual, just a couple of nice-looking, clean kids.

351

They'll make regular stops, travel at normal speed, take their meals at rest stops, and sleep in the van until they get to where they're going.

"My guess is, using a van of that type, they'll head west. If they were going north, chances are they'd use a panel truck or a big car. Whichever way they go, we'll be with them all the way, behind, in front, and in case there's a chance of losing them in city traffic, an occasional fly-over in a light plane.

"That's it, so you three stay close by in case the van moves out and heads west, in which case, they're yours. We'll give you a car and some walkie-talkies to keep in touch with our people. Now let's get some goddam breakfast with some decent coffee."

They waited expectantly all that day, loitering along 277, monitoring the radio and the talk-between-cars on the walkie-talkies. Tyler had a plane standing by at San Antonio International on the off-chance that the Skymaster as well as the Kar-a-Van would be used for transport, although they thought this would be unlikely.

The day passed. They ate sandwiches in their car, drank coffee from the large thermos jug, smoked innumerable cigarettes. Later, they took turns sleeping on the back seat while the third man drove slowly and listened to the radio. Morris was at the wheel at 0610 when the general alert was broadcast by Tyler.

"All vehicles, alert. Repeat, all vehicles, alert. The Ford Kar-a-Van, green body, white top, Texas license four-William-nine-five-nine-two has left the location, proceeding north on U.S. 277 at normal rate of speed. All cars previously designated to do so will report in and take action. Over."

Morris responded, reported his location seven miles north of the Wrayburn Ranch entrance and approximately two miles south of the 377 junction; that he would wait at the junction until the Kar-a-Van passed and pick it up at that point. The other tail cars, in turn, radioed their locations, with plans to make visual contact.

McNeely and Ycaza were wide awake now, with the promise of action. Morris speeded up and reached the 377 junction where he got out, went into the small store, and bought a supply of food: bread, processed meats and cheese, potato chips, candy bars, canned soft drinks and cigarettes, paper cups. There could be no planning for food stops since the van would no doubt be well supplied with everything necessary for its journey.

They ate hastily prepared sandwiches, washing them down

with the soft drinks while the storekeeper filled their gas tank. Morris again took the wheel, McNeely beside him, Ycaza on the rear seat. Morris saw the van first, moving north toward them at a modest pace.

"Here they come."

The van passed the 377 junction and continued on 277 toward Sonora, and Morris waited for a full minute before pulling out to follow, radioing in to Tyler. He drew up on the van to a point where its rear was within sight, then slowed to match its speed, pacing it. An occasional ranch vehicle and passenger car passed in both directions, then a large public bus, a truck carrying ranch laborers, several road freighters. But the green-and-white van kept steadily on to Sonora where it turned westward on U.S. 290, apparently headed for El Paso.

McNeely radioed the road change to the other surveilling vehicles and was contacted by the International pickup truck with two DEA agents. "We're three quarters of a mile behind you and holding."

A sedan, farther west at Fort Stockton, checked in. Another, coming up from Sanderson on 285, reported their position, with an estimated thirty-five-minute arrival time to make the meet. The Kar-a-Van moved on at a modest forty-five-mile-per-hour pace.

At Van Horn, it stopped for gas and a trip to the rest rooms. From sixty yards behind, using field glasses, Morris and McNeely were able to identify Billy John Gorman from Jesse Tyler's earlier description. The girl was about five-three, perhaps 115 pounds, below-shoulder-length dark-brown or black hair, dressed in tight blue-denim slacks, blue topper, and sandals.

Its tank filled, the van took U.S. 80 toward El Paso. Within sight of at least two DEA cars at all times, it drove through the city to the extreme western edge and checked into a large trailer park for the night. Gorman and the woman left the van singly to use the park's sanitary facilities, a practice followed by the tailing agents after the two had returned to prepare a meal from their stock of food. At ten o'clock, the lights were turned off, and the couple apparently turned in for the night.

Gene Morris telephoned Jesse Tyler and reported the situation, then returned and summoned the other agents for a conference. With the van's direction westward definitely established, it was decided to send the International pickup and the other sedan back to San Antonio, leaving the third sedan with Morris to continue the surveillance as far as it would take them. When the designated vehicles left to find a motel for the night before returning, Morris staked out his and the other sedan, arranged a schedule to observe the van through the night.

At five o'clock the next morning, lights came on in the van. Forty minutes later, it pulled out of the park and headed toward Yuma. The two tail cars alternated positions behind and ahead of the Kar-a-Van, never out of radio range. After one stop for a midday meal and gas, the Gormans proceeded steadily until they reached Yuma late that afternoon. Next to the trailer park was a motel where the agents, in shifts, were able to sleep in four-hour stretches. Again, Morris phoned Tyler in San Antonio to inform him of their progress. McNeely contacted Bob Barker in Los Angeles with the same information, now satisfied they were on the final leg of their journey.

"That's great, Russ," Barker said.

"What's new with you?"

"Not a hell of a lot, but we'll have some interesting pictures for you to look at when you get here."

"Of what?"

"It'll keep until I see you. Anything I can do for you?"

"It looks like we'll be getting in to San Diego fairly early tomorrow evening. How about sending a car down to take over the surveillance with the DEA team so that Ray, Gene, and I can take off and get a head start in the morning."

"Okay, can do. When you get in, check with the San Diego sheriff's office and we'll have the car waiting there to make the meet."

"Check, Bob, and thanks."

"Anything else?"

"No, I think that'll do it."

The following day was Sunday, and the van got a later start. Traffic was heavier on U.S. 80, and Gorman loafed along into El Centro, then was able to pick up speed most of the way into San Diego for another night stop, evidently moving on a carefully prescribed schedule. Other than the fact that the Gormans never left the Kar-a-Van at the same time, they appeared to be a young couple on vacation, not unlike others on the road, carefully observing posted speed limits and exercising road courtesy.

At four o'clock they were in San Diego. The van checked into a trailer park on the outskirts of the city. The two DEA men, Patton and Evans, checked into a motel directly across the road, and McNeely put in his call to the sheriff's office from their room. The two-man team sent down by Barker, Joe Gross and Dave Chesler, were waiting and were directed to the motel where they were introduced to their DEA counterparts, the van spotted for them. The briefing concluded, McNeely, Ycaza, and Morris then took off for Los Angeles, arriving at seven P.M. Ycaza picked up his car and headed for home. McNeely dropped Morris at his hotel, then phoned Rachel.

"Where in heaven's name are you?" she asked.

"Downtown. Can we have dinner?"

"Yes, of course. I've been so worried about you."

"I'm fine, nothing to worry about. Just tired. I'll be there as soon as wheels can bring me. Have a drink ready for me."

"Anything else?"

"Yes. A shower and some deodorant to get the smell of Texas off me."

"Texas!" He had told her only that he would be away on business, no more.

"Believe it. Give me about ninety minutes, then we'll make some sort of plan for the evening."

"I've already made our plan. I've got some steaks that are crying to be defrosted. Hurry home."

He lost no time getting to Manhattan Beach. In his house, he showered, shaved, and was dressed with minutes to spare. He dialed Harry Deliso's number, got no answer, dialed Steve Barrett, and came up blank. He tried Perry Roberts and found them all at Perry's house where he was playing host for dinner. After a few minutes, Deliso came on. "What's doing, Harry?"

"You talk to Bob or the captain yet?"

"Bob, yes, but he didn't tell me much, said he was saving it until he saw me, but I don't like surprises. What's the drill?"

"Oh, Jesus, Russ, we've been busy as hell. Got some photographs you'll want to see, all tied into Tri-City. Look, can we come over and lay it out for you later?"

"Not tonight, Harry. I'm too bushed for a long session. Capsulize it for me."

"Well, we've had a tail on Pete Rojas and shots of him making deliveries to a few places that don't deal in auto parts. Also, we've had a camera on Tri-City and picked up some shots of a few interesting callers. Nothing hard, but they all tie into the deal. That's as fine as I can draw it, but Bob and the captain have the blowups. I guess that's what he's got for you."

"Okay, Harry, and thanks. That's enough to hold me until tomorrow. I'll be in touch."

"Roger."

He hung up and went across to Rachel's house. After a warm embrace and welcoming kiss, they shared a drink while Rachel put the rest of the meal on the table.

As in the past, he gave her only a minimal account of his trip to Texas, but from his manner, she knew it dealt with something big and vital. He was on edge, like a boy with a huge secret that was hard to keep hidden, yet, from long association, she knew her curiosity would not be satisfied by questioning him. Only when it was over and became public property would he fill in some small details behind the press release.

They ate the meal, drank the wine, had coffee and brandy on the deck. It was a mild night with soft breezes, a welcome relaxation for both, sitting side by side in comfortable silence, until Russ said, "What's new at the shop?"

"Oh, the usual. Business has been holding up very well, and we'll be starting to get ready for our annual pre-inventory sale to make room for the new things I've got coming in. We'll be busy for a while going through our stock to get the sale items ready."

"No buying trips?"

"Not for a while. Why?"

"I'd like to reopen an old subject, let you try it on for size."

She guessed at once what the "old subject" would be, but said softly, "Which subject?"

"You. And me." When she remained silent, "I once asked you if you could ever marry a cop."

"And I said—"

"What you said was an evasion, neither yes nor no."

"All right, Russ. It wasn't so much an evasion as it was a—the insecurity, the uncertainty that would hang over our heads and lives."

"Which particular uncertainty?"

"The way it is now, this minute. You going off suddenly for several days, not able to tell me where you're going or when you'll be back. Of never knowing at what time on any given day or night I'd be made a widow by some hyped-up junkie or pusher who has an aversion to going to jail."

"Would it be so different married than the way it is now, Rachel?"

"I think so. A lot different."

"In what way?"

"Because as we are now, I love you. If we were married, I'd not only love you but become a part of a life I wouldn't want to lose. I might be able to cope with a breakup, but I don't know if I could go through widowhood a second time."

"Rachel—" he began, but she cut across his words.

"Russ, I'm with you for an occasional evening or weekend, and everything seems wonderful. Then you go off for two or three days and nights, and I don't hear a word. You're somewhere where you can't get to a phone, supervising a buy, on stakeout, God and your lieutenant or captain only know where. I live most of that time suspended in midair, wondering, waiting for Harry, Steve, Joe, or Perry to come to tell me you've been shot or killed. I know how it must have been for Carol, I can understand that now, what she went through—"

"Let's drop it, Rachel," he said suddenly.

Tears welled up in her eyes. "It's not that easy. I love you, Russ. I do."

"But not enough to take the risk of—"

"I'm not the one who is taking the risks, Russ. It's you, taking them every day, every night. You're out there like a big target, arresting the same people you've arrested before, people who know you, even hate or fear you. Any one of them can decide you're too dangerous to be alive—"

"Rachel, if you're asking me to quit—"

"I'm not even asking that. You've passed your lieutenant's exams and are on the list for promotion. When it comes, you can be transferred to some other job, administrative—"

"Rachel, Rachel, what would happen if Harry, Steve, and all the others did the same thing, ducked out into desk jobs? Who would be around to choke off the flow of dope that cripples and kills thousands of men and women every year, infects kids, turns them into thieves to get the money they need to support their habits. Christ, if you could only see in one night what goes on out in the streets, the battered people in broken homes, addicts undergoing withdrawal, willing to sell themselves to perversions, steal a car, hold up a store or filling station, mug a man on the street, snatch a purse, just to get enough for a lousy fix."

She shook her tears off. "Russ, I can't fight your arguments. I know it happens. I read about it day after day. It's just that I don't know what would happen to me if you became a victim. The thought alone destroys me."

"Then we go on as we are?"

"For now, yes. I could say 'no strings,' but there are. We both know that. Invisible strings."

He stood up and walked to the rail, staring out over the black ocean, trying to recall exactly when and where his marriage to Carol had begun breaking up; the days and nights she had had to spend alone waiting and wondering; the differences in women like Perry's Jo-Ann, Steve's Joyce; the rate of divorce among law-enforcement officers. Remembering his total sense of loss when he came home that day and found that Carol had left him, the emptiness in her wake; the new and entirely different Carol he had seen in Chicago recently, wife and mother, undoubtedly secure and happy as Mrs. Warren Deland.

The earlier spell, the mood, the joy of reunion with Rachel, had fled. They were here together, yet so far apart.

He returned to his lounge chair and said, "More brandy, Rachel?"

"I think not, Russ. I've got to be in early in the morning. Vicki is off tomorrow, and there'll be only Lilith and myself."

"I've got a long day ahead of me, too."

He left then, kissing her good-night, walking slowly back to his house. He fixed a drink for himself, carried it out to the deck, and sat there until he saw the lights in her house go off, then went back inside, undressed, and went to bed.

At 0730 next morning, McNeely met Gene Morris on the parking lot behind the Hall of Justice and rode up to the eighth floor with little more than a casual greeting in the presence of other sheriff's personnel. Ycaza was already in their office, a cup of coffee on the desk before him. Together, they went to Captain Esau's office where Inspector Garland and Lieutenant Barker were in conference. Esau looked up, smiled, and said, "Welcome home, gentlemen. Good to see you. Inspector Garland and I are tied up on another matter, so I'm going to ask Bob to fill you in until I'm free."

Barker stood up, holding a stack of 8 × 10 black-and-white photographs in his hands. McNeely, Morris, and Ycaza followed him back to their own office where he dropped the package of photographs on the conference table. "Look 'em over," Barker said, spreading them out. "While you've been gone, we've been adding to our rogues' gallery. Also, you'll find some overhead shots of the Tri-City layout we had Aero do for us, and the surrounding area."

There were shots of the Tri-City panel truck used for local

deliveries, some with Pete Rojas loading auto parts, traveling on streets and freeways, making stops at various garages, shots of the locations of each stop.

"And here," Barker said, handing over half a dozen photographs he had held apart, "are what we could call unscheduled or nonscheduled stops Rojas made."

These were stops made other than at garages; Pete in front of, and entering the Dos Hermanos Bar from the alley; a stop at Little Willie's Bar and Pool, operated by two known dealers in Carson, Willie Acheson and Jimmie Tice; Pete emerging with Acheson with Willie's hand on Pete's arm, both laughing; Pete carrying a small carton into Esposito's Bar on Whittier Boulevard in East Los Angeles; and at three other locations.

"Now for something with a charge in it," Barker said. He held up a single shot of a Cadillac entering the Tri-City yard, its license plate clearly discernible: 772-GUQ. The next shot was of the same car, parked at the entrance to the warehouse building, a male Caucasian at its side in the act of emerging.

"Recognize this dude?" Barker said to McNeely.

"Yes, sure. Anse Talbot," McNeely identified him. For the benefit of Morris and Ycaza, "We had him about four years ago for dealing. He got eighteen months and was out in twelve, then picked him up about two years ago, but he beat that one. Works with a dude named Del Foreman. After his last bust, they decided things were a little too hot for them around here and moved down to Orange County, working out of a pad in Newport Beach, but we've had word recently that Anse has been seen in L.A., and that could be very interesting, seeing him at Tri-City."

"And here," Barker continued, "a beautiful shot of Howie Reese, and this one of Fat Carl Huerta and his top runner, Freddie Silvero."

"What," Russ asked, "have we got besides pictures?"

"Addresses with telephones and utilities all checked out. Talbot and Foreman, Reese, Huerta, and Silvero. Five major distributors plus Tice, Acheson, and the Ruiz brothers, all in contact with Pete Rojas or Tri-City. Let's look closer. We know that there's been a shortage of coke and smack around here recently from the low quality and the upped prices, not exactly panic level, but it's a damned good indication of what's going on. With what those couriers on the way up from San Diego are carrying, this whole thing could open up wide. From what our undercover people report, a lot of pushers and dealers are scraping the bottom of the barrel, and we can buy that when we see distributors coming to Tri-City in person to see what they can scrounge from Hernandez.

"There's stuff coming in, we know, but not in any great quantity, maybe in single key lots, except for marijuana. The deal the inspector and captain are discussing right now is a couple of tons of grass the Antelope Valley crew got onto last night, trucked up from down south. They're setting up that bust for tonight.

"But our deal is big, one of the biggest we've had in this county, and we're not going to take any chances on blowing it." To Morris, "Where's the van now?"

"On its way up here now, if they're going by their previous schedule, taking it easy. I'd guess they should be in L.A. sometime around noon."

"Okay, we'll be in constant touch. We've alerted our Lennox, Firestone, and West Hollywood crews. We've got the stakeout on Tri-City and a tail on Pete Rojas. We've got tails on Reed, Butler, and Valentine. There's nothing yet on Peterson, Cora Thomas, or John Hall Ellison. Right now, they're nowhere, but when that van moves in and delivers, something, somewhere, has got to give. That's where it is."

"Where is my crew?" McNeely asked.

"Standing by at Lennox. Bill Hamlin's crew, except for those down in San Pedro, are with them. Something else. The other half of the block north of Tri-City's yard, on Seventh Street between Mesa and Reckord, is occupied by Trans-Pac Freighters—here, it's on this aerial shot—" showing the photograph. "We've been in touch with their security officer, a guy named Kevin Anderson, and if we need to get inside, we go to the Seventh Street gate, identify ourselves to the gate guard. He has his orders from Anderson.

"Also, we've got back-up on call as we need it, plus Aero, Special Enforcement, and Metro."

"What can we supply from DEA?" Morris asked.

"Besides your two men tailing the van, I don't know," Barker said. "I think we've got more than enough to handle it."

"Then," Morris said, "as soon as the van arrives, and your people take over, I'd like to pull our guys off and let them get some rest, then get back to San Antonio for the other end of this deal."

"Do it," Barker said.

Morris got on the phone to his local office and gave Lyle Carter a fresh briefing of the situation as of that moment.

When he hung up, he said, "Carter is calling Ames in Dallas and Tyler in San Antonio. I've got orders to stay with it here until the major bust goes down, then fly back to San Antonio for the raid on the Wrayburn place."

"Okay," Barker said, "let's get our plans set up to welcome the van."

9●

At six o'clock that morning, Walt Dyer awoke in the motel room he had been sharing for over a week with Cora Thomas at El Descanso Beach, about halfway between Tijuana and Ensenada. He shaved, showered, and dressed while Cora slept on, then sat on the edge of the bed and shook her shoulder gently.

"Uh—"

"Wake up a minute, baby, then you c'n go back to sleep," he said.

"What is it? What time is it?"

"Almost seven o'clock. Listen, I've got to go up to L.A., take care of a piece of business needs tendin' to. I'm takin' my car, an' I'll be back tonight or tomorrow. Anything holds me up, I'll call you. I'm leavin' you some money just in case I'm delayed. Okay?"

"Jus' you go on back to sleep. Get some breakfast later, go down to the beach. I'll be back almost before you know I'm gone."

"Okay. I'll miss you."

She smiled sleepily. "Okay. Be sure you come back."

"Don't worry, I will." He handed her two fifty-dollar bills. "That'll hold you till I do. If I get held up, I'll phone you, but I'll be back." He kissed her and left.

He drove north through Tijuana and, before reaching the border, stopped and put on his modified Afro wig and sunglasses. During his idyllic week at the beach with Cora, he had allowed his mustache to grow longer and thicker. He crossed the border without any trouble, stopped at a roadside diner for breakfast in Chula Vista, then continued on toward Los Angeles.

Chapter Twelve

1•

As usual on a working weekday, Simon Hernandez awoke in his Long Beach home at five o'clock. He got out of bed quietly in order not to disturb Benita and made his way to the kitchen where he put on a pot of coffee. He then went to the guest bathroom to perform his usual morning ritual shave, put on a robe, and returned to the kitchen. He removed two oranges from the refrigerator, peeled and ate them slowly, slice by slice, listening to the small transistor radio that was tuned to a Mexican language station while the coffee came to a boil.

He poured a second cup of coffee, then heard soft footsteps behind him and turned to see his seventeen-year-old daughter Teresa, his favorite, as she crossed the kitchen to the stove. "Good morning, Papa," she said, smiling over her shoulder.

Simon said, "You came in long after your mother and I went to bed. Why are you up so early?"

"You get up early every morning, Sundays, too, even though you don't have to." As he made a move to stand up, "Sit, sit. I'll bring the pot to the table. That's what woke me, the smell of it."

"So. Drink your coffee and go back to bed, eh?"

"Maybe. I haven't decided yet."

"Will your sister be home next weekend?"

"I don't think so, Papa. I talked to Alicia last night on the phone. She and one of her roommates are going to Santa Barbara to spend the weekend with her parents."

"Ah-h. I think when you go to college, you will become a stranger to us, like Alicia."

"Oh, Papa, she's not a stranger to us because she spends one or two weekends with friends. Mama approves. You're so old-fashioned."

She brought the coffeepot to the table and added some to his cup, then lighted a cigarette, saw her father frown, and stubbed it out after the second puff. He smiled his approval then and watched her with enjoyment as she began to drink her coffee, cherishing the quiet, rare moment alone with her. Young, alive, beautiful, and with so much of her life ahead to savor. Then Teresa reached over and turned the small radio off and Simon said, "Leave it on, *por favor*."

She smiled and frowned simultaneously. "What do you get on a station as small as that one?" she asked.

Simon's smile matched hers. "You wouldn't understand, *muchachita*. I enjoy the music and language of my youth. When I hear it, I am back in Mexico, among my own people—"

"Papa! You've lived in the United States for over thirty years. Mama, Alicia, and I were born here. None of us has ever *been* to Mexico. *We* are your own people."

"You are my family, *querida,* but my own people are in my homeland, Mexico, eh?"

"If we are a family, then this, where we live, is our homeland."

"To one who is American-born, American-schooled, yes. But to me, Mexico will always be my first home, eh?"

Teresa did not press the point. In the Hernandez home, Benita had insisted from the start that her home would be American, and Spanish would be the second language. In time, Simon had come to accept that even though his English was still accented. At moments such as this, alone with Teresa, he would have liked to tell her about his earlier years in Mexico, the good parts only; but even those good parts, to his American-born wife and children, would be somehow dreary and incomprehensible, even sordid.

No, they would not understand life in an overcrowded *vecinidad,* a family of eight living in two small rooms on the ground floor of a tenement facing a courtyard filled with drying laundry, scattered garbage and trash, chattering children, men and women arguing, drinking, fighting at all hours of day and night; child gangs, youth gangs; prostitution, gambling, and stealing. No, how could they understand hunger, squalor, community toilets, public baths, sons and daughters spending most of their time looking for work, turning into pimps and whores for a few *centavos*? Robbing drunks, peddling homemade *tortillas*, handmade scarves, buying household items to hawk on the streets; and always that emptiness in the belly that cried for food.

Another time, another world; yet there was that indescribable nostalgia on Simon's part to somehow be among those people of his youth, to experience the comfort in universality of language and customs, the fiestas, even the rituals of religious services that only his mother had any feeling for. Or perhaps it was the need to compare his life of today with the one of yesterday.

Until three years before he met Don Reed, Simon Hernandez had considered himself the most fortunate of men, this despite his early years of poverty. He was ten when his mother died. Almost a year to the day of her death, his father Tomas was killed when he slipped and fell beneath the wheels of a heavily laden farm truck, leaving Simon and his brother Pedro, who was then seventeen, to make their way alone. Four other children had died before they reached the age of five.

A month after Tomas's death, Pedro abandoned Simon and lost himself in the inner city. Simon, a naturally bright, inquisitive child, was taken into the home of Angel and Ema Vega, neighbors who lived in their own home next to the garage Angel operated with his son Augustin, who was twenty-two. There were three other Vega children of school age, and for the first time in his young life, Simon began to enjoy school and companionship.

Even more remarkable was his intense interest in mechanics, and at fourteen, he began spending his after-school hours at the Vega garage, assisting Angel and Augustin in repairing bicycles, motorbikes, and cycles, and prolonging the life of countless old cars and trucks with rebuilt parts cannibalized from wrecked vehicles. At eighteen, Simon was an expert mechanic in his own right, the owner of a Harley-Davidson motorcycle that had been wrecked and that he had personally rebuilt.

His life, stabilized by the Vega family, was a good one, but there was in him a restlessness that reached out for something bigger and better than the daily poverty of the people around him in the Lagunilla Market slum area of Mexico City; perhaps the same need that drove Pedro to escape. However, the thought of leaving the Vegas deterred him, even disturbed him, and it was not until he was in his nineteenth year that he finally decided to make the break.

Late one night, he returned to the garage, strapped his toolbox on the luggage rack of the Harley, a small canvas bag with some clothing on his back, and with his life savings, two hundred and forty pesos, took off, heading north. He left a note for the Vegas begging their forgiveness.

He wandered lazily for three weeks until he found himself in the seaport city of Guaymas, broke. He began looking for a job as a mechanic in every garage and boatyard, but there were no openings. Whereupon, he sold his beloved Harley and prized tools to a dealer for eighteen hundred pesos and began hitchhiking.

In Tijuana, a town he disliked intensely, he found a cheap room and rested from his travels. He ate sparingly and spent little, guarding his money carefully. For a week he roamed the streets, which were filled with American tourists and their sleek cars and with the slag heap of his own countrymen vying for American dollars: con artists, touts, pimps, whores, thieves, dope dealers and users, drunks trying to drown out the sordidness of their pitiful lives.

Soon, he learned of the traffic in human smuggling: delivering men and women across the border into the United States where there were jobs at better pay for a day's work than one could earn in Mexico in a week; or month. He met and dickered with Rosario Gomez, an agent for one such smuggling operation and eventually paid a thousand pesos to be delivered into the Mexican-American community in East Los Angeles. Of his seven hundred remaining pesos, converted into dollars by Gomez, he paid fifteen to Rafael Lopez for a week's room and board. Before the week was out, Rafael found Simon a job with a small garage whose owner allowed Simon to sleep on a cot in a back room used to store parts and other supplies and equipment.

Simon's expertise in rebuilding generators, distributors, water and fuel pumps, for use in repair jobs was an invaluable asset to his new employer, and within a year, his increased earnings permitted him to rent a room. He bought and rebuilt a wrecked Chevvy sports car and sold it for a three-hundred-dollar profit, then repeated the process with a Mercury sedan.

Within another year, he moved into a small apartment and found an eighteen-year-old waitress, a runaway from a Fresno *barrio*, who agreed to share it with him. From American-born Consuela Paredes, he learned to dress in better style and to know American customs. And to make love expertly.

He was twenty-two, grown into a tall, handsome man when George Aragon, from whom his employer bought new and rebuilt transmissions and other parts, discovered Simon and offered him a job at his Tri-City Auto Works in San Pedro. At one hundred dollars a week, thirty-five dollars more than he was earning in East Los Angeles. When his employer refused to meet the Aragon offer, Simon quit and moved to San Pedro. Consuela refused to move with him, and they parted amicably.

It was a much bigger job than Simon had imagined it would be, but he took charge with zest and met the challenge. He set up an assembly-line operation with Aragon's six Mexican-American mechanics, stripping down wrecked and abandoned cars for usable parts. Within eighteen months, Simon had added a paint and body shop to the Tri-City complex.

George Aragon and Simon got along exceptionally well, the former conservative, the latter moderate, temperate, and willing. Soon, Simon was invited to the Aragon home for dinner and to discuss business matters in a more relaxed, congenial atmosphere, made additionally pleasant by the presence of George's wife, Letitia. There were other such visits that followed and a few months later, in June of that year, he met their daughter, Benita, an only child, who had just graduated from UCLA.

Simon's meeting with Benita was an electrifying experience, but he remained wisely cautious. George and Letitia Aragon were American-born of Mexican extraction, both graduates of UCLA. Simon was not only an alien, but an illegal one. George had never asked him about his citizenship status, nor had Simon offered any information about this part of himself. He was unaware at that first meeting that his attraction to Benita was a mutual feeling.

His visits to the Aragon home became more frequent as time passed and, later, his invitations began originating with

Benita. There were weekends spent around the Aragon pool, picnics, movie dates in Long Beach and Los Angeles, a weekend in San Diego, another in Santa Barbara.

Three years later, Simon and Benita were married and George gave them their own apartment in the Aragon home. A year later, when their first child, Alicia, was born, Simon received a quarter interest in Tri-City. A year later, they were blessed with a second daughter, Teresa, and Simon became an equal partner.

When their children were ten and eight, Letitia Aragon, never a very strong woman, died quietly in her sleep. Benita was inconsolable, but the loss virtually destroyed George. He lost all interest in his work and remained at home with Benita and his grandchildren, walking them to school each morning, calling for them at the end of their school day, watching them at their studies and play. He began to fail, lost his appetite and much weight; then, fourteen months later, he died as Letitia had, quietly in his sleep.

The business, during this time, had suffered from George's absence. Simon, although an excellent mechanic and thoroughly knowledgeable in the operation for which he was responsible, was hardly a capable administrator. In the office, his bookkeeper, he discovered, was stealing cash and falsifying records. Merchandise was disappearing. Bills came due without the cash to pay them. He called in an accountant, who analyzed what was happening, then suggested that his entire office staff, shipping clerk, and delivery man be discharged at once and replaced. Desperate, almost on the verge of bankruptcy, Simon made the changes and began again to rebuild.

Times were hard during the next few years. The stock market fell; there was inflation and a recession. Simon turned his end of the work over to an assistant and began to move around more, calling on current customers and those Tri-City had lost through neglect, trying to make new contacts. Business picked up, but not enough. People were driving their old cars longer, and used parts for rebuilding became scarce, the competition in the new-parts field growing.

Now he began to buy old cars without questioning their ownership. Men and youths would appear with cars, ask and receive a few dollars for a quick turnover, then return a week later with another car to sell. These were taken in, immediately stripped down, the parts stacked in bins in the warehouse building. Numbered parts were altered or trucked at once to garages in Tijuana where there was a growing market. Bodies were compacted by the crushing machine and hauled off to large recycling mills. The police auto details came by as usual, but found little evidence of irregularity, since much of the work was done at night behind closed doors.

Then, as conditions became better, Simon met a man who had a proposition to offer. The man, Don Reed, had come to him through a garage owner both knew. At first, Simon was revulsed by the proposal Reed made, but Reed, dogged and persuasive, talked of the huge profits in which Simon would share.

"Why me?" Simon asked. "I know nothing of this business."

"You," Reed said, "because you know nothing of the business and are in the clear. No one will have any reason to suspect you."

"Except the people who will have to handle the goods."

"The same people who now handle the stolen merchandise you resell as legitimate goods."

Simon was thunderstruck that this Anglo knew of his operation; and if he knew, how many others knew?

"Don't look so surprised, Hernandez," Reed said. "The people you sell to know, but have protected you because they buy cheap and make a good profit. Your friend Jaime Castro is also my friend, and we have had many dealings together. Since he is your friend, he recommended you to me."

"How do you know I will not betray you to the police?"

Reed laughed at the suggestion. "And put your own neck in the same noose? I have looked into your operation carefully, Hernandez. You run an illegal business with illegal alien employees. You are married, have a wife, two daughters, a fine home. If I had looked deeper, I might even learn that you yourself are in the United States illegally and could be deported. So why should one friend betray another, eh?"

At that moment, Simon felt an urge to kill this man who could laugh and threaten so easily; yet he knew that danger too well. A man like Reed did not work alone. He must be a part of an organization, a *sindicato*, that would wreak swift revenge. "Let me think about this," he said.

"Of course. There is no hurry. Let us say in ten days, two weeks?"

"Two weeks."

"I will return then," Reed agreed, and left.

There was, Simon discovered, no way he could refuse without destroying everything he had built—business, home, family. Reed knew he had the ideal location, the manpower, and could bring in the necessary help, all illegal aliens, to adulterate the imported product and package it. A delivery system must be organized. Much the way stolen cars were dismantled, the parts sold and delivered. But dealing in dope was something else again.

Benita, happy with her home and daughters, knew nothing of the illegitimate operation into which her father's business had been turned, and now Simon must move a long step deeper into illegitimacy and secrecy. At the end of two weeks, he accepted Reed's proposition and became mill and warehouse for the narcotics operation.

"Go back to bed, Teresa," Simon said when she had finished her coffee. "You need your sleep."

"Papa," she chided, smiling, "I'm wide awake. I'm going to get dressed and ride my bike for an hour."

"And later?"

"And later, I'm going to have breakfast with mama, and she will deliver me to school, all safe and sound. After school I have a date to go swimming at the Bentleys with Donna and a couple of other girls."

"And boys?"

"And boys. Nice boys. Bobby Wilson, Brian Norcross, and Peter Hilton. You met them here at my last birthday party."

Wilson, Norcross, Hilton. When he was Teresa's age, seventeen, he had yet to hear the name of an Anglo. "I will go and dress now, too," he said. "There is something in my office I must take care of before the others come to take my mind from it."

Teresa kissed him. "Don't work too hard. I'll see you at dinner."

He reached his office before seven and looked over the weekly report that had been finished on Saturday afternoon. Everything seemed to be in order. He began signing checks that were attached to their individual invoices, then opened his safe and removed the large tin cashbox that he would need to pay his men the overtime for the week before and that would not be recorded in his records.

His private, unlisted phone rang at seven-thirty, and he knew it would be one of *them*. "Hernandez," he said into the mouthpiece.

"Simon?"

He immediately recognized the voice of Anse Talbot even though he had met him less than two weeks before. Brought

here by Reed, Talbot and the man Foreman would be re-
placing Butler and Peterson for the time being.

"Yes."

"Just had a call from Reed. Start getting your people lined
up. The shipment will be in late this afternoon, a heavy one.
If they work all night, tomorrow, and tomorrow night, they
can do most of it by Wednesday."

"Two whole days and nights? It is too much. They will
need to sleep, eat—"

"Let 'em sleep on mats or cots, for Christ's sake. They're
used to it. Bring food in for 'em. This is too big to hold over.
Reed wants the stuff ready to start moving out no later than
Thursday. I've got some hungry people lined up and waiting."

"I will have to pay extra—"

"Pay what you have to, but get 'em in there and get the
job done. Keep 'em locked in until it's finished."

"I will see what I can do."

"Don't just see, man. Do it."

The line went dead.

2•

For a few moments, Simon Hernandez sat and stared at the
papers on his desk, glowering at the silent telephone, angry
with himself, with those Anglo *hijos de putas* he was forced to
deal with, even though he had been made a rich man through
those dealings. Still, they were *basura*, cheap trash, no better
than those he had encountered during his youth in Mexico.
He thought of Benita, Alicia, and Teresa, who thought of
him as a man of character and dignity and wisdom, to whom
they had always shown the same respect they had given
George Aragon.

Ah, but what must be done must be done. He picked up
the receiver and dialed the number of Pete Rojas. The phone
rang seven times before he heard Pete's raspy voice grunt,
"Quien es?"

"Pedro. It is Simon Hernandez."

"Yeah, Mr. Hernandez."

"Listen carefully. It is tonight. You have deliveries to make
today, no?"

"Yeah. The stuff I put in the truck Saturday. About eight
stops to make."

"Notify your people first, then make your deliveries.
Gather the people and have them here no later than five
o'clock. This one is big. Very big. We will need them here
until Wednesday night."

"Jesus, Mr. Hernandez. Two whole days and nights?"

"Yes. We will make arrangements for sleeping and food. You must be very careful."

"Sure. I'm always careful. Okay, I'll begin now so they can get ready."

Pete hung up, lit a cigarette, and began the process of planning just how he would go about the job, whom he would call first, whom next. It was early, but he must reach his people before those who had regular jobs went off to work, give them time to call in sick.

Beside him, his latest girl, Estella—a whore he had taken in after her man had beaten her for holding out a portion of her earnings—lay asleep, undisturbed by the telephone or his conversation. A buxom warm body to use, her facial features marred by the recent brutalizing she had received.

First, then, he called Marcos Andrade and told him to be on the parking lot behind Lazarro's food market by no later than four o'clock and to bring his wife with him, prepared to remain away for two days and nights. Then, for Marcos to get in touch with his two neighbors, who did not have telephones, and have them at the meeting place at the same time. He would require the services of six couples for the job, who must make arrangements with friends, family, or neighbors to take care of their children until Thursday morning. *Bueno.* He lit a second cigarette and made his other calls. There would be no problems. The mill workers knew they would be well paid for their time. One hundred dollars a day for each person, less the fifteen dollars Pete would take from each (unknown to Simon Hernandez) for his services as labor recruiter, furnishing transportation and food (at no cost to himself).

He would plan to arrive shortly before or after five o'clock, unnoticed in the heavy flow of homegoing traffic, and help get the people set up in the back room. The eight Hernandez mechanics would also be present, armed with revolvers and shotguns, to stand guard while the milling operation was going on in order to prevent any possible attempt at a holdup, although such a thing had never happened. Yet the Anglo boss of Simon Hernandez insisted on this, so it must be done.

The people Pete Rojas had recruited, he could vouch for. All were illegals, the threat of deportation hanging over their heads. One or two had regular work, one or two held part-time jobs. The others were on welfare. And all had performed this service before. An opportunity such as this, at such high pay, was eagerly sought by all. None would dare talk.

What a business, Pete thought, that could pay so much money to so few people for so short a working period. A business he should be in for himself, if only he knew how, like Simon Hernandez. Two full days, twelve people, meant a twenty-four-hundred-dollar payroll, exclusive of the guards and the underboss, Solomon Quiroga. And with commissions of three hundred and forty dollars for himself besides his own extra pay for these two days—

What a business! Yet if it could not be his to own, it was best to work for those who could afford to pay so well.

Estella stirred in bed as he finished his last phone call. "Hey, you!" he called to her. "Get out of the sack and put some coffee on. Quick. I've got to get going."

3●

Shortly after noon, the Ford Kar-a-Van crossed the Orange–Los Angeles County line and continued northward on the San Diego Freeway until Billy John Gorman saw the tall revolving sign of the Sea-Vu Drive-In restaurant. "Hey, Lacy," he said to his wife, "we're way the hell ahead of schedule. How'd you like to sink your teeth into a good steak, some fries, the whole works."

"You gettin' tired of my home cookin', Billy John?" she asked with a smile.

"Well—" they had reached the exit ramp and he took it— "it ain't so much your cookin' as it is havin' to eat meal after meal cooped up in this here wagon. Almost like bein' back in jail."

"Excep' you didn' have me in jail to fix your meals."

"Yeah. That woulda sure made it a lot easier." He pulled the van into a parking space close to the building and parked. "Let's go."

"You think it's safe to leave the van out here on the parkin' lot all by itself?"

"Hell, in broad daylight, all locked up, we c'n keep an eye on it from the inside. C'mon, let's go."

"Okay, if you say so, but you know what they tol' us back there, don' ever leave it by—"

"They're a long way from here, sugar. Let's go."

The DEA team in the lead car tailing them had been caught by surprise by Billy John's sudden decision and was forced to continue past the exit ramp. Beyond it, Jim Patton pulled over onto the shoulder and came to a stop. In the second car, Joe Gross, some sixty yards behind, saw the van go off and Patton's car continue on. Gross took the exit ramp and pulled into a row behind and to the left of the van. "Get us a couple of hamburgers and something to drink," Gross called to Chesler, then contacted the DEA car by walkie-talkie and informed Patton and Evans of the situation. Evans rogered the message, and unable to turn back, Patton continued on for another mile to a point where it could park more safely and await word that the Kar-a-Van was moving out; bemoaning the fact that they had missed a meal opportunity.

At one P.M. in Lakewood, Moose Peterson's phone rang. He let it ring four more times before he picked up the receiver. It wasn't Eddie, he knew, since it didn't follow the prearranged system of communication between them: allow the phone to ring once, hang up immediately, then dial the number a second time. He answered now, assuming it would be a wrong number. "Hello."

"Moose?"

"Who is it?"

"Walt."

With mounting anger, "Walt? Where the hell are you, you spade bastard?"

Walt Dyer's laughter increased Peterson's fury. "Well, where the hell are you? What do you want?"

"Takin' your questions in order, I'm right here in L.A., and I want to get a message to your top man."

"What the hell are you talkin' about, my top man? If you mean Eddie, say so, but he won't talk to you."

"An' I don' want to talk to no Eddie. I mean your top man, the dude who sits on top of both of you."

"You sonofabitch! You freaked out or somethin', takin' a chance like this? You know who's out lookin' for you—?"

"Shut up an' listen to me, you honky mother. I ain't freaked out, an' I know exactly what I'm doin'. You listen now. I got Cora stashed away in a safe place you won't ever find. She's been with me a whole week—"

"You bastard—!"

"You better shut up an' listen to me, man, 'cause I got my hand around your throat, Eddie's, and that top dude of yours. Okay?"

"What the hell do you want?"

"I want you to get in touch with Eddie, have him pass the word on to Mr. Big. Mr. Don Reed. Yeah, I know his name, baby, an' you know where I got it from, right? So you tell

Mr. Reed it's goin'a cost him twenty-five big ones to close my mouth, an' Cora's, too. Tell him he's got to get it together tonight an' no stallin'. If he don't, I'm blowin' the whistle on all three of you. What's more, the sheriff's goin'a get a present in the mail. The gun that ripped Lloyd off, wiped nice an' clean, along with your name. And Mr. Eddie Butler's an' Mr. Don Reed's. You tell him that."

He waited for a reply, but there was none. Dyer, chuckling, said, "Okay, paddy, I'm hangin' up now. I'm goin'a call you again aroun' five o'clock, so you better have an answer for me. An' it better be the right one." He hung up.

Moose Peterson stared at the dead receiver clenched in his hand for several moments before his seething fury permitted him to replace it in its cradle. Sweat beaded his forehead, dampened his T-shirt, and moistened his hands. He stood up shakily and paced the length of the room, kicked a chair aside that was blocking his path.

That spade sonofabitch! He's got Cora, all right. That's how he got Don Reed's name. He's got all three of us by the balls. Jesus. I got to call Eddie. I can't handle this myself. That bastard's got a lock on us, and he's the only one with the key. Oh, man, man.

And running it through his mind over and over again, there was an underlying current of admiration for Dyer's craftiness. How had he managed to get Cora past the tails he knew were sitting on her around the clock, spirit her away to a hiding place? The bastard had to be some kind of a real stud to get her to talk, give him names. No wonder he had refused the contract on her for three grand when what he had sitting in the back of his mind was twenty-five thousand dollars. And there was no possible chance of learning where he had Cora stashed away. The sonofabitch had it figured right down to the wire. If it all came down to push and shove, Dyer would tip the cops to where she was hiding out, and that would give them a hell of a witness to hang them all on a conspiracy to commit murder.

It was one-twenty, and although he never went out of doors until dark, he would have to risk it, get to the phone booth in the shopping center and call Eddie. No other way. He was more wary than ever now about using his phone to make an outside call with the possibility of a tap on it; or, since it would be a toll call, that it would be recorded on paper for the police to find.

Moose slipped on a lightweight windbreaker over his T-shirt and went out. He saw no one until he hit the pavement; a few kids, two women carrying grocery sacks from the shopping market to their homes or apartments, a normal number of empty cars parked at the curbs, a man running a power mower across his lawn.

Two blocks down, he turned right toward the shopping center, its parking lot filled with cars, others moving in and out. There were a few things he needed, but that would have to wait now until this matter could be settled. He stopped at the Chevron station where the public booth he used was located, saw it was in use by a man engaged in heated conversation, gesticulating with his right hand. There was no one else waiting, and Moose paced back and forth to show the man his need and impatience, but the man was totally immersed and paid no attention to him.

On the far side of the Chevron station, in front of the open-windowed hamburger stand, Detective Sergeant Tom Soble sat behind the wheel of his unmarked car while his partner, Deputy Herb Rankin, waited for his order of two hamburgers, a Coke, and a root beer. Both were out of the sheriff's Lakewood station and were taking a Code 7 to eat before interviewing a John Sampson on nearby Chester Place, who had been strong-armed and robbed the night before, to try to get a better description than he had given immediately after the attack, then in a state of shock and incoherent.

As Rankin returned to the car, he noticed Soble staring intently in the direction of the Chevron station. "Something, Tom?" he asked.

"I don't know," Soble said. "Take a look at that big dude standing next to the phone booth, Herb, jeans and a dark blue windbreaker."

Rankin got into the car and placed the food on the seat between them, then glanced casually in the direction of the phone booth. After a moment or two he shrugged and said, "No bells. Never saw him before."

"I think we've had something on a dude like that recently. About thirty or thirty-two, six-two, two hundred forty pounds. No beard or mustache I can remember, though. A homicide APB. Hey, wait! Peterson. Moose Peterson. Wanted in connection with a dope ripoff. Lloyd. Whitey Lloyd."

"Hey, yeah. Without the beard, I remember the mugs on him. Do we talk to him?"

"No," Soble said. "I think it was an information wanted on

his whereabouts they asked for. Let's just keep an eye on him, see where he goes. Get on the radio to the station and give them the make. See what they want us to do about it."

The man in the phone booth had finished his call, and now Moose moved inside, dropped his coins, and dialed Butler's number. When it had rung once, he hung up, retrieved the coins, dropped them in the slot again, and dialed once more. On the third ring, he felt a sense of relief when he heard Eddie's voice. "Hey, Moose, what's up?"

"Plenty. I got to talk to you, Eddie, and fast."

"What's happened?"

"Look, I'm calling from outside. It's bad. My phone could be tapped."

"Come on, Moose, nobody's tapped your phone. You're getting hinky, for Christ's sake. Who the hell knows where you are?"

"Dyer. Walt Dyer, that's who knows. And I tell you it's bad. Goddamn bad, Eddie."

For a moment there was silence, then Butler said, "Listen. Go back to your pad. I'll be there as fast as I can make it, but I'll have to duck a tail."

"Yeah, okay. Make it as fast as you can."

He hung up and began walking toward Loma Vista Avenue. In the unmarked car, Soble placed the paper plate with his half-eaten hamburger on the seat and held on to his cup of root beer. Rankin slipped out of the car and walked along the pavement toward the service station. When Peterson turned up Loma Vista, Rankin waved to Soble, who started the car and pulled up beside him. Rankin slipped in and said, "He's on foot. Give him a few seconds, then turn left on Loma Vista. Any word from the station?"

"They want him, but no pickup. Tail and observe, call in his location. They're going to check with the Homicide guy who's on the case. He'll get in touch with us on the radio."

"Okay. We'll see Sampson later."

Soble backed out of the station and made the turn into Loma Vista. They saw Peterson lumbering along up ahead, and as he crossed the next street, they started moving along slowly. In the middle of the next block, Peterson stopped at 19141, turned to look back, then entered the paved strip beside the apartment driveway. Soble pulled up quickly. Rankin got out and crossed the street, looked up the driveway in time to see Peterson disappear into an open doorway. He moved toward it, entered, and found himself at the foot of a stairway. He took the steps two at a time to the second floor and peered around the corner. Peterson's back was toward him as he stopped in front of a door and used his key to unlock it, then went inside.

Rankin waited a few seconds, then tiptoed down the hallway, noted the number on the door, 26, and continued on to the near end of the hall where another stairway led downstairs.

Soble had the motor running when Rankin returned. "What've you got?"

"He's in twenty-six. The name board on the first floor lists twenty-six to a Norman Abbott. What's the drill?"

Soble grimaced. "Had a callback from the station. We're on stakeout here. Sergeant's sending somebody else over to talk to Sampson. We're to hold tight on this Peterson dude until we hear from Sergeant Ycaza at Homicide. I'll stay with the radio. Take a walkie-talkie with you and cover the back. If he moves, we tail and report location. That's all I've got so far."

"Oh, Jesus. I promised Marilyn and the kids I'd take them out to dinner and a movie," Rankin complained.

"Hell, hold off calling her. The downtown dicks may take over when they get here."

"Yeah, and I'll cover any bet you want to make that we're stuck with the deal."

"No bets. Get your ass out of here and keep an eye on the back entrance and the parking lot."

Ycaza, Morris, and McNeely were in their Hall of Justice office when the call came down from the watch commander in Homicide. Ycaza took it and a moment later signaled to Russ and Gene to pick up their phones and listen in. Together, they heard the details that Sergeant Soble had radioed in to Lakewood station.

"Yeah," Ycaza said finally, "that sounds like our boy. Get back to them and pass the word to stay with him, but don't pick him up. Have Lakewood keep the stakeout on until we send in a relief. Give me their unit number."

"It's David-five-Boy-thirteen-Sam. Sergeant Soble. I'll talk to Lakewood. Soon as you get lined up, call Soble and clue them in. Okay?"

"Roger." Ycaza hung up. McNeely said, "You'd better take it, Ray, while Gene and I hang in for some word on the Kar-a-Van."

"Okay. I'll see if I can pick up Danny Geiger and another team and get down there." Ycaza was out of his state of lethargy that waiting always produced in him. He slipped on his jacket and started for the door. "Anything comes up, I'll get word to you."

"You do that, and let's keep in touch. We may turn something up on our end."

Ycaza waved and was gone. The time was 3:05.

Eddie Butler, maneuvering his car through heavy traffic along busy Hollywood and West Los Angeles surface streets, was finally satisfied he had eluded his tail, then picked up the freeway at the National Boulevard on-ramp. At 3:21 he arrived at the Loma Vista address. He parked in the space beside Moose's '69 Dodge and went up the rear stairway to the second floor.

From his observation post behind the building, Herb Rankin watched, then followed. By the time he reached the upper floor, the hallway was empty. He tread easily to number 26, listened at the door and heard voices, then returned below and reported to Soble by walkie-talkie that the suspect, Peterson/Abbott, had company. Soble radioed the news directly to Homicide and was told to hold it, that Ray Ycaza would be in the area shortly and contact him.

Within seconds, the call came in from the dispatcher. "David-five-Boy-thirteen-Sam, cleared to contact David-three-Sam-two on Frequency C."

Soble rogered the call, switched his radio to Frequency C. "David-five-Boy-thirteen-Sam to David-three-Sam-two. Do you copy?"

"This is David-three-Sam-two, Ycaza. I copy you. What is your ten-twenty?"

"We're ten-twenty at one ninety-one forty-one Loma Vista Avenue in Lakewood. I'm covering the front, my partner has the rear. A couple of minutes ago a male Cauc about twenty-eight, five-eleven, one hundred fifty to sixty pounds arrived in a blue Ford sedan, tag Zebra-Zebra-Queen-four-four-seven and is inside first suspect's apartment. What is your ETA?"

"About ten minutes. Two cars, four men."

"Roger and holding."

"All right, Moose, calm down, will you?" Butler said.

"Calm down, my ass. That spade sonofabitch has us cold.

He's got Cora stashed away somewhere, and he wants us to come up with twenty-five grand tonight. Tonight, for Christ's sake."

"Cool it. Blowing up won't get us anywhere. What time did he say he'd call back?"

"Around five o'clock."

"Okay, let me try Don's number again." Eddie dialed the Alicante Drive number, and again there was no answer after ten rings.

Moose said, "This really blows it with Don. We'll be lucky if he gives us the time of day from here on in."

"Will you for Christ's sake settle down? You're getting me nervous. Stop pacing and take a drink. I can't think with you tearing things up around me."

Moose flung himself down in the one upholstered chair and glowered angrily. Eddie went to the window and stared out over the rooftops of several one-story dwellings and through a forest of television aerials in the direction of the shopping center. After a full two minutes he turned back to Peterson, still slumped down in the chair.

"Okay, Moose. I can't get hold of Don, and even if I could, I don't think he'd go for a twenty-five-grand heist like this. There's no doubt that Dyer's got Cora holed up somewhere, and she's a key witness if the cops get their hands on her. She talked once, she'll talk some more and bring Don into it this time."

"So?"

"So we're going to play it Walt Dyer's way. Did he put a time limit on when we're supposed to come up with the money?"

"No, just tonight was all he said."

"Okay. We'll wait for him to call around five. You tell him it's okay, that Don is putting the money together, but it won't be until sometime around midnight before he can turn it over to you. Tell him as soon as he's got it, he'll send me down here with it and to let him know where you can call him to tell him it's here.

"If he shows up here, we'll both be here to take him, work him over until he tells us where Cora is, then do him. If he wants you to deliver it to him, find out where. Either way, we'll get him and take care of him. Okay?"

It took a little while for Butler's plan to sink in, and when it had, Moose finally smiled, exhilarated with the thought of revenge on Walt Dyer. "Yeah," he said. "It sounds good. I just want to get my hands on that righteous sonofabitch. Just one last time."

"Okay. Relax until we hear from him around five."

4●

It was close to three-thirty when Pete Rojas finished all but his last delivery, saving the last one, to Rodriguez Garage, so that it would bring him close to Lazarro's Food Market by four o'clock, when his people were due to gather there. As he pulled his panel truck into the garage, he looked across Avalon Boulevard and saw that Marcos Andrade was already on the parking lot, waiting. Andrade's wife Celia was seated on the sidewalk bench at the bus stop with another couple.

Inside the garage, he opened the rear doors, removed a carton and several loose packages, and carried them to the parts counter where Benny Conteras checked the items in and signed for them. Moments later, Pete got into the truck and drove to Lazarro's parking lot to await the arrival of the last of his charges.

A few minutes later, Rudy Arboleya finished the tuneup job on Father Casimiro's eight-year-old Buick, which had been donated to him by Nestor Rodriguez four years ago. It was an accommodation job, and Rodriguez had authorized Rudy to draw the necessary parts without charge. Nor did Rudy object to doing the job for which he would not be paid. Father Casimiro had gone before the parole board to plead for Rudy's release and had also promised to officiate at his and Isobel's marriage.

Rudy drove the Buick from his stall to the rear parking lot and placed the keys under the rear floor mat as agreed, since the priest would be unable to pick the car up until sometime after six. He came back inside, checked his work log, and found no other jobs waiting, then washed the grime from his arms and hands and combed his hair. He was thirsty, but the vending machine was out of Coke. He told Johnny Lucero, the service writer, he would be back in fifteen minutes and went out the 223rd Street entrance and crossed over Avalon Boulevard to Lazarro's.

At this hour, Lazarro's was not crowded. Rudy walked to the rear of the store where the canned and bottled soft drinks were kept in a refrigerated cooler. He took a can of Coke, paid Jimmy Lazarro for it, ripped off the ringed aluminum tab, and drank directly from the can. And doing so, he looked out the rear window that overlooked the parking lot and saw Pete Rojas sitting behind the wheel of the familiar rust-brown Tri-City delivery truck.

This alone did not stimulate his curiosity until he saw a middle-aged Chicano couple approach the driver's side of the truck. The man called out to Rojas, who replied and waved his left hand toward the rear, then turned and apparently called out to someone inside the truck. The couple went to the rear doors, which were flung open from the inside, then an arm reached out to help the man and woman climb in. As they did, another pair of arms was extended to assist the heavyset woman. The truck remained parked in the same location, the door now closed.

Rudy dropped the empty Coke can in a carton beside the cooler and went out to the corner where he could better observe the rear of the truck. A few minutes later, another couple appeared and spoke to Marcos Andrade, who motioned them toward the truck. And now the same process was repeated. This time, Rudy was able to make out inside the truck at least six others sitting on wooden benches that lined the right and left sides.

Rudy pondered over the oddity of the scene for a few moments, then decided to act. Since it involved Pete Rojas, he concluded that this might be of interest to Ray Ycaza and, perhaps, Ray's Anglo partner. Now he crossed the street and went to the phone booth in the Gulf station, dialed Ycaza's office number, and was told that Ycaza was out in the field. "Can you tell me where I can get hold of him?" he asked.

"Well—not unless it's important," the man replied.

"Listen, man, I think it's important. It's got to do with something he and his partner are working on."

"Okay, give me a number where I can get back to you."

"Balls, man. I want to talk to Ray."

"You can't talk to him direct, mister. Give me your number, and if he thinks it's important enough, he'll call you direct. It'll only take a few minutes. That's the best I can do."

"Okay, but make it quick. Tell him it's Rudy." He gave the watch lieutenant the number at the Gulf station and stood waiting beside the booth.

The message was relayed to Ycaza by radio while he was en route to the Loma Vista location. "Did he say it was urgent, Ken?"

"He said it was important, and his voice sounded urgent. Something to do with you and your partner. Geiger?"

"No, probably McNeely. Listen, Ken, I can't stop now to make the call. I'm on to something hot. Get the word to

McNeely. You'll find him on the eighth floor, Narcotics. Tell him I said to make the callback. The kid will know who he is."

"Okay, Ray."

McNeely took the call, then dialed the number Ken Kelleher gave him. Rudy answered on the first ring. "Hey, Ray?"

"No, Rudy, it's Russ McNeely, Ray's partner. He's out on a job and asked me to call you. What's doing?"

"Hey, man, listen. I got something for Ray, looks funny as hell to me. Something with Pete Rojas mixed up in it, like what we was talkin' about last time, you know?"

"What is it, Rudy, and make it fast. I'm on a job, too."

Rudy related what he had seen. McNeely said, "Hold it for a minute, Rudy." He put the call on HOLD and dialed Bob Barker's number. "You have any report on Pete Rojas's location, Bob?" he asked.

"Yeah, about an hour ago. Our guys lost him, got trapped in traffic, and Rojas was out of sight when they got unsnarled. They're scouting the area now, hoping to pick him up again. Why?"

"I've got a call on my other line locating him on the parking lot of Lazarro's Food Market near the corner of Avalon and Two twenty-third. Tell your guys to contact the informant in the Gulf station across the street. He'll be standing next to the phone booth."

"Thanks, Russ. I'll get 'em on it right away."

McNeely depressed the button on the outside line. "Rudy, there's an unmarked car on its way to meet you at the Gulf station, should be there in a few minutes. Stay at the booth until it gets there just in case Pete pulls out. If he does, tell them the direction he took. Okay?"

"Yeah, sure."

"Did you recognize any of the people besides Pete?"

"One guy named Marcos Andrade and his old lady. The rest of 'em are from around here, I'm sure. I've seen a couple of 'em on the street. It looks like he's waiting for a full load before he takes off. I can see Pete from here. He's standin' alongside the truck now, lookin' at his watch."

"Okay, Rudy. Write this number down. If our guys don't make it in time, call me. If they get there before Pete leaves, tell them to call me on their radio. I've got to hang up now."

So did Rudy. And waited.

Less than eight minutes later, a dark-gray Plymouth pulled up alongside the booth, and Rudy pointed toward the Tri-City truck, then gave the driver McNeely's message. The man in the passenger seat reached for his mike while the driver pulled out and parked half a block away on 223rd where he could observe the truck and the action.

Rudy then returned to the garage. No new jobs had come in during his absence. He got out of his coveralls and waited for five o'clock when he would drive to the shopping center to see Isobel, do their marketing, then go home to dismiss the babysitter and give Robert his supper.

5 ●

At five o'clock, as usual, work at the Tri-City Auto Works came to a halt. Anita Frias, the one woman employee who worked in the small office at the rear of the retail store on the corner of Sixth and Mesa as telephone receptionist-typist-bookkeeper-billing clerk, covered her typewriter and plugged in an outside line to Simon Hernandez's phone. She retrieved her purse from a desk drawer and went out to her car. Moments later, the clerk in the Retail Parts Store locked the doors and left for the day, followed by the aged janitor.

What was not usual on this day was that the eight mechanics, once they had washed up, did not leave. Instead, they went to the warehouse building and reported to Solomon Quiroga, who was in charge of the warehouse inventory of new and rebuilt parts.

Quiroga gave two of the men a sum of money and a list of food, beer, and soft drinks to bring back. The other six men and two warehousemen gathered in the long, narrow room behind Simon Hernandez's office where two tables, four feet wide by ten feet long, were covered with clear sheets of hard plastic of equal width and length. When this was completed, Quiroga slid aside a panel in the south wall from which two of the men removed several cartons. From these, they began sorting out quart-sized plastic bottles of milk sugar and packages of procaine, lactose, and dextrose, for use in cutting the heroin and cocaine for which they waited.

Two of the other men were sent to the warehouse section to bring back cartons of Pliofilm bags, sealers, sifters, strainers, and measuring spoons. Simon Hernandez unlocked another bin and brought out two scales of the type used by pharmacists and that could measure anything from grams to ounces to pounds and kilos.

These were brought into the sorting room and spread out on the two long tables in equal numbers and quantities, within easy reach of the millers who would do the cutting.

When all was in order, twelve folding chairs, three on each side of each table, were properly spaced, a gauze face mask at each worker's place.

In one corner, a coffee maker and stacks of paper cups, plates, and plastic utensils were set up. Here, until Thursday morning, the millers, guards, Quiroga, and Hernandez would eat and drink. In the warehouse section, half a dozen folding cots and mattresses were placed in a row, and here the workers and guards would take two-hour sleeping breaks when their strength waned. Hernandez and Quiroga would share the leather sofa in Simon's office, relieving each other from their supervisory duties.

The operation was ready to receive the millers and the narcotics.

The first two men now returned with the cartons of food, which were placed on the coffee table and stored in the refrigerator. Quiroga then went to the storage bin and handed out several sawed-off shotguns and revolvers; these were distributed to the eight mechanics and four warehousemen. Each piece was loaded and checked by Quiroga and Andrade. While they waited for the arrival of the millers and Pete Rojas, the men went to the food table and had their supper, talking, laughing, joking. It would be a long two days and nights here, away from their families, but the extra pay would be sweet.

At four-thirty, the word they were eagerly awaiting came through to McNeely and Morris by land line. Dave Chesler reported that the Ford Kar-a-Van was now parked on the lot of the Van Ness Shopping Center in San Pedro. It had had its gas tank filled while the Gorman woman went into the supermarket, returned with a sack of groceries, and re-entered the van. Gorman then made a telephone call from the public booth outside the service station.

When he emerged, he asked the attendant for a road map, which he examined, then asked for more explicit directions. The attendant marked the map with a pencil or pen, and the Texan got into the van and drove it to the westernmost section of the lot and parked there, away from the more congested area. He then joined the woman in the interior of the vehicle where both could be seen preparing the meal they obviously intended to eat there. The DEA team was parked close by, and Chesler and Gross would soon be parked on the other side, bracketing the couple.

McNeely said, "Hold it where you are and keep in touch if anything moves. We'll get back to you."

McNeely hung up and turned to Gene Morris. "Looks like we're practically home."

Morris nodded eagerly. "Yes. We're running close. Let's get Barker and set this thing up."

McNeely dialed Barker's extension, and Barker said, "Okay, let's meet in the captain's office. He and Garland are waiting there for us."

Esau and Inspector Garland were informed of the van's location as well as the information McNeely had gotten from Rudy Arboleya concerning the movements of Pete Rojas. Garland said, "Nice. Very nice. Everything seems to be falling into place for a change."

"Remarkable," Esau agreed. Then, "It's my guess they'll follow a standard pattern and wait until dark to make delivery. From where they're sitting at the moment, they're within five miles of Tri-City. The call Gorman made was probably to alert them he's in the vicinity and to arrange the time of delivery."

"What have we got in San Pedro right now, Bob?" Garland asked.

"Two cars and four men staking the place out on a Code five, and we've asked the local cops to keep clear of the location. Deliso and Roberts, Barrett and Paul. We've got a tail on Rojas and those jokers he's got inside his truck, probably the milling crew."

"What about your crews and back-up?"

"All set and standing by at Lennox for the briefing."

"Okay," Esau said. "Inspector Garland and I have gone over the situation with Lyle Carter and the chief. We can go one of two ways. Let the van make the delivery, move in and make the bust, grab the junk, and collar everybody there. There may be some shooting, people hurt, even killed, some of theirs, some of ours."

He paused for a moment, then said, "We want to avoid that as much as possible. Those millers are just a lot of poor dupes, and we've got no real quarrel with them. The others are something else, an unknown quantity. If it comes to a shootout, it will hit the headlines like World War III, and we'll get all kinds of fallout, demands for investigations, minority-group protest marches, boards looking into trigger-happy cops for scapegoats.

"Or we can keep a continuing surveillance on the place, pick up the delivery people when they leave the location, hold them incommunicado until the thing is over. We have all the warrants we need, and it's only a question of manpower to conduct that kind of a widespread bust. Any suggestions?"

There was little doubt in the minds of McNeely or Barker that Esau had already formulated a plan to which he was already committed, but recognized it as his way of including his subordinates in a discussion, permitting them their viewpoints before making a definite decision known to them. Barker held back, and it was McNeely who spoke up first.

"If I may, Captain," he said, "it's quite possible that with the present short supply in the area, your second choice could give us a much better chance to pick up any major distributors who may be coming by to take delivery after the product has been cut. We have photographs of several, as you know, who have been seen in the vicinity—"

"That's true, Russ, but if our guesswork and assumptions are correct, that van is carrying one hell of a load of dope, and above everything else, we can't afford to take a chance that any of it will get past us."

"I don't think there's any way it can, Cap," Barker said. "For that matter, we could move in right now and take the van where it's sitting on that parking lot, grab the man and woman, too, but that would mean the Tri-City people and any distributors we might pick up would be getting another free ride."

Esau smiled and turned to Morris. "Gene?"

Morris shifted in his chair and grinned. "From our point of view, we want the evidence in that van for the purpose of convicting the couriers and the Texas group, but I can see the need to break up this local ring, and I go along with McNeely's suggestion for the continuing surveillance and what it can produce."

"That," Garland said, "was Carter's thought, and we're in complete agreement, so I don't see any point in discussing it further. John?"

Esau said, "All right, let's move on it." To Barker, "Get your people briefed and into position. Keep the two tail cars tight on the van until it arrives, unloads and leaves, then have it picked up. I'm going to set up a command post here—" indicating the area map—"beside this playground. The inspector will remain in his office and coordinate the information I'll be feeding back to him. Keep in close touch with me and I'll see you in the field. Let's go."

Barker, McNeely, and Morris were on their feet at once. Within moments they were on their way to Lennox station.

At Lennox, they had borrowed the larger assembly room normally used for briefing patrol units. Twenty-four narcotics detectives, chosen from the four zones, were waiting, reacquainting themselves with men they hadn't seen or worked with over a period of months, exchanging experiences, wondering about the job, evidently of major proportions, for which they had been brought together.

They quieted down as Barker, Morris, and McNeely arrived. McNeely unrolled a large map of the San Pedro area and thumbtacked it to a cloth-covered panel beside the blackboard, then put up a dozen 22 × 28 photographic blowups of the Tri-City installation, overhead shots taken by Aero Bureau's helicopter fly-overs, ground shots by cruising cars.

Barker began the briefing by introducing Gene Morris, then outlined the project quickly, spotted the Kar-a-Van at its present location, the two tail cars sitting on it, and the two cars presently surveilling Tri-City. On the map, switching back and forth to the photographs, he pinpointed the strike objective, the command post, and dispersal plans for each team, assigned the frequency and identification numbers to be used on their walkie-talkies.

He acquainted them, again using the photographs, with the industrial area surrounding Tri-City, the adjacent residential areas, the principal thoroughfares and side streets, their proximity to the nearest freeway; with the large warehouse buildings, marine supply houses, a foundry, junkyard, truck parking lots, miscellaneous small businesses sprinkled among them, the locations of public telephone booths to be used in case of emergencies. Many of the cars used would be personally owned and not equipped with official radios, hence the need to make certain their walkie-talkies had fresh batteries and were in perfect working order.

Barker then turned the briefing over to McNeely, who had been busy drawing up a roster of those present, assigning them in two-man teams and the unit designation of their vehicles. The assignments made, he asked, "Any questions? You've got ten minutes."

There were questions, and McNeely answered each as

briefly as possible; at the end of that period, he said, "That's it, then. I want every car fully equipped and checked, then double-checked. We'll be in communication by radio and walkie-talkie where applicable, so again, make sure your w-t's are in working order. When you're set, pick up some extra food and canned drinks. We don't know how long we'll be on this deal except that you'll be on duty until relieved, and that's about as much as I can tell you. You married guys call home and break the sad news to your wives, that you'll be away until relieved. Let's get going."

6●

At 5:15, the phone in Moose Peterson's apartment rang, and when he hesitated, Eddie Butler said, "Get it, Moose, and play it cool. You know what we want."

On the third ring, Moose picked up the receiver and growled, "Yeah?"

"Moose, boy, it's me," Dyer said.

"I know."

"What's the scam?"

"I talked to Eddie, an' he talked to Don. It's goin'a take some doin' to put twenty-five big ones together this late in the day, Walt."

Dyer's voice had a chuckle in it. "Don't go tellin' me your dude's got to go to a bank to get to his loot, man. He does a cash business—"

"I know, but he ain't stupid enough to carry it on him. He say's he'll have it to me by aroun' eleven-thirty or midnight, but you got to tell me where the broad is."

"Hell, man, I'll give her to you the minute you lay the bread on me. I'm takin' off outa these parts for good, so you c'n buy yourself another dude to do your future jobs."

"Okay. You want to be here around midnight?"

Dyer laughed. "You think I'm outa my skull, man? No, I do not want to be there aroun' midnight or any other time."

"Okay, where?"

"I'll call you aroun' midnight. If you got it, I'll tell you where the meet is. Got it?"

"I got it."

"An' lemme lay this on you. You come alone, man, just you an' the bread. I see anybody else, or you try to pull somethin' on me, you gonna get blown up on the spot. You read me, Moose?"

"I read you. This is on the level."

"It better be. An' you better be, too."

Moose hung up the receiver. "Well, you heard him, Eddie. We got about six hours to wait."

"Yeah." He thought for a moment, then said, "You got your piece?"

"Sure." He drew out the .38 from between the mattress and box spring. "I got the .45 in the trunk of my car, inside the spare tire."

"I've got mine on me. Go get the .45."

On the ground level, Herb Rankin saw the big man walk across the parking lot to the '69 Dodge and used his walkie-talkie to inform Tom Soble. Soble then contacted Ray Ycaza who, with Danny Geiger, was parked on the east corner, and informed him. Ycaza then transmitted the information to Pete Bramley and Dick Krasna, sitting in the alley and just west of the apartment house. Ycaza then called Soble and told him that he and Rankin could take off, to be replaced by his own teams. The exchange was made, and the two Lakewood detectives left the scene.

Bramley had moved into Rankin's position, and Ycaza took the parking space pre-empted by Soble's car. All four men settled down to wait.

Geiger said, "Why the hell don't we just go up and move in on 'em, Ray?"

"Because neither of 'em is the guy we really want, Danny, but if we need to, we've got the warrant for Peterson, and we think he's the only tie we've got to the triggerman who totaled Whitey Lloyd. If we get him, we're sure we've got the dude who iced Cruz Despues, and he's worth a hell of a lot more to us than these two crooks. Also, there's the chance that we can tie them all into conspiracy to commit murder. So it behooves us to watch and wait, which is the name of this screwed-up game."

At 5:35, the Tri-City panel truck came down Harbor Boulevard in San Pedro, proceeding north to Sixth Street, where it made a right turn, drove past Mesa to Reckord, made a left, and came to a stop at the closed and locked chain-link gate. A man on the inside opened the gate, allowed the truck to pass through, then closed and locked it.

In David-six-Adam-two, Harry Deliso broadcast the word to McNeely, who radioed the tail car that had followed Rojas to the location and dismissed it. He ordered the other cars to remain positioned where they were. Orders for any movement or action would probably come after dark. The photographic unit reported in. They had what they believed to be excellent film of the truck's arrival. McNeely then circled the area and returned to his original station.

Inside the Tri-City yard, the panel truck drove to the rear loading platform of the warehouse building and backed up to the dock. Pete Rojas leaped out, opened the rear door, and began to discharge his human cargo. An overhead door was raised from inside, and the twelve men and women went inside while Rojas parked his truck and entered the warehouse from the front.

Quiroga led the millers to a locker room where each was issued a suit of white coveralls. When they had changed, he took them to the cutting room where each chose a chair at the table where the work would be done. In the center of each table stood the scale. There was no need to issue instructions. All had been here before to perform this service. Six would work with the cocaine, the other six with the heroin.

They would do the sifting and mixing by hand, then weigh and package the adulterated material in quantities as directed by Simon Hernandez and Solomon Quiroga, who would monitor the scales to see that each bag contained the proper weight, down to the finest gram.

The sealed bags would then be cartoned by even weight in quarter- and half-pounds, some in pounds, for delivery to distributors on orders from the new number-two man, Talbot.

But for now, they all waited for the arrival of the Texas van, when the serious work would begin.

At 6:30, with dusk approaching, Captain Esau arrived in a solid-sided van and established his command post beside the playground on Mesa between Eight and Ninth Streets. Inside, working at a long table, he, McNeely, Barker, and Morris spread out their photographs and map of the area and pinpointed the various locations of the unmarked cars that had already been positioned.

"What about this north side of the block?" Esau asked.

"That's the Trans-Pac Freight outfit," Barker responded. "I've made arrangements with their security chief, Kevin Anderson, to give us access. I was on my way there just as you showed up."

Esau said, "I want you here with me, Bob. Russ, you and Gene take care of that, will you? We'll want to work somebody in there as soon as it's dark."

"Yes, sir." McNeely and Morris drove to the Trans-Pac entrance on Seventh Street and parked at the curb. Visible behind the six-foot-high chain-link fence that was topped with three strands of barbed wire was a guardhouse manned by a uniformed, armed watchman who sat behind a desk and monitored a panel board of lights linked to an alarm system that protected the entrance gates on Reckord Avenue, Seventh Street, and Mesa Street, as well as the doors and windows of the four rows of warehouse buildings.

The guard stood up and watched as the two men in civilian clothes approached the single gate next to the larger double gates used for truck traffic. Through a microphone, he called out, "This place is closed for the night."

McNeely held up his wallet to show his six-pointed star. The guard, one hand on the butt of his revolver, came outside to the gate. "We're officers on the job," McNeely said. "I'm Sergeant McNeely. This is my partner, Gene Morris."

"Oh, yeah," the guard replied. "Got orders from Mr. Anderson you'd be by." He opened the gate to admit them. "What can I do for you?"

"We want to get a look at your neighbor from the north side."

"Tri-City?"

"That's right."

"Okay. You'll have to sign the log book in the shack. After hours, everybody logs in and out in case there's any trouble. Insurance regulations."

"That's okay. We'll take a look now. Later, we'll send a couple of plainclothes deputies over to keep an eye on things. If there's any trouble, it will be on the other side of the fence, not here."

"Suits me fine."

They signed the log, went into the yard, and keeping to the shadows of the parked trucks and warehouses, crossed to the link fence on the south side, their view of Tri-City partially blocked by stacks of compacted car bodies awaiting the arrival of trucks to haul them away to the mills. At the extreme right stood the warehouse building, a large weather-beaten structure with no lights visible from the outside. On the far side was a series of work sheds, closed now. They saw no one, heard nothing. For all intents and purposes, Tri-City appeared to be shut down for the night; but McNeely and Morris knew better.

They returned to the guardhouse, signed out, and drove

back to the command post to report and await word on the Texas van.

At 8:40, the radio in the command post came alive with Dave Chesler's voice. McNeely took the mike and responded. "McNeely here, Dave. What's doing?"

"Looks like they're ready to move out, Russ. Interior lights just went out, the male crook is getting behind the wheel, lights coming on up front."

"Okay, Dave, stay with it, but not too close. Traffic in the area is reported to be fairly light, and he may make you."

"Don't worry. Patton and Evans will be right behind me, and we'll switch positions every half mile or so."

"Fine. Keep us informed, a running account."

"Will do. There he goes. I'll move out in a few seconds."

After a brief period, Chesler came on again. "Okay, Russ, we're into Pacific Avenue heading south at thirty miles per hour, Patton and Evans behind me."

And later, "We're approaching Front Street, now turning into Front, and I'm passing Patton. O-o-kay, we're turning north into Harbor Boulevard, looks like he's heading for the barn. No other traffic in sight in our direction. He'll be hitting Sixth Street pretty soon now. I'm cutting out. Over."

Then from Deliso, sitting on Sixth just north of Harbor, "David-six-Adam-two to Command Post. I've got him, Russ, going north on Sixth toward Reckord. Turning left on Reckord now, probably to the main gate. Over."

And from Joe Paul in David-6-Boy-3, "The van is at the gate, lights just flashed off and on twice. Man at gate, opening it, van is now inside, gate closed and locked, van heading for the warehouse building. Over."

Using his walkie-talkie now, McNeely broadcast the word to all units, then, "Walkie-one, what is your ten-twenty?"

Back came Perry Roberts. "We're ten-twenty in Trans-Pac yard. The van is inside, backing into the loading dock at the warehouse building. Four males talking to the driver, now entering the van, probably to help unload."

A full minute passed; then Roberts came back on. "That's the deal, Russ. Unloading has begun. Lights are on inside the van. We've just spotted a couple of other dudes with shotguns standing just inside the entrance. Over."

"Okay, Perry, stay with it."

While Esau, Barker, and McNeely evaluated the information thus far, Gene Morris was on the mobile phone to Lyle Carter, briefing him. They waited now for further word from

Roberts, and it came thirty minutes later. "Looks like it's over, Russ. The driver is inside the van again, lights on, probably ready to take off again. The woman is in the front compartment. Over."

"Okay, Perry, I'll take it from here." Then, "Attention all units. The van has completed its unloading and will probably exit the area shortly. This is for unit David-six-Adam-two. Do you copy?"

Harry Deliso came on. "David-six-Adam-two and I copy you."

"Harry, when he leaves, he's all yours. Go after him. Let him get far enough away from here, then take him. Hold both suspects at Lennox, no phone calls permitted, then get back here with Joe Paul as soon as you can."

"Ten-four."

The Kar-a-Van exited, taking the same route it had used to reach Tri-City. Harry Deliso, Joe Paul beside him, lay back a full block, lights on dim, then moved up quickly as the van entered the more heavily trafficked Pacific Avenue, lights fully on now. At the Harbor Freeway on-ramp, the van turned right, a much better situation now than before, with a heavier flow of traffic to give the tail car cover.

Deliso allowed two cars to separate his green Plymouth from the Kar-a-Van, its white top easily visible as it moved along the freeway at a modest fifty miles per hour. When they reached the turnoff into the San Diego Freeway north, the van moved into the right of center lane and rolled on through Torrance toward Lawndale, Hawthorne, and Lennox.

"Let's take the bastard, Harry," Roberts suggested.

"Hell, if we're going to book 'em at Lennox, they're being very cooperative. Get on the radio and ask Lennox for a black-and-white to take the mother."

Roberts got the radio room and put the message through, asking for a two-man patrol unit to make the meet on the freeway at the Imperial Highway on-ramp and make the stop just before the Century Boulevard off-ramp.

Minutes later, as they passed Imperial, Perry Roberts turned to peer through the rear window and said, "Looks like we've got our escort, Harry."

Via radio, they learned it was 31/Sam, and on car-to-car frequency, "Welcome aboard, Sam. You got any I.D. on you?"

"That you, Perry? This is Tom Logan. I was in the station

when your call came in, you lucky dog. Brought Norm Hart along for the ride. What's the drill?"

"The white-over-green Kar-a-Van with Texas tags up ahead. Take him off at Century. We'll be on your ass."

"Right where you always are, Narc. Ten-four."

Thirty-one/Sam spurted past the Plymouth and dropped into position behind the van. As they approached the Century Boulevard off ramp, Logan turned on his red flasher lights. When the van maintained its normal speed, on came the siren. The van slowed, its brake lights flashing; 31/Sam pulled up beside it, and Norm Hart waved it toward the off-ramp. It obeyed and curved off, then came to a stop on Century Boulevard.

Deliso braked the Plymouth behind 31/Sam. Logan and Hart were approaching the van on opposite sides, each with one hand close to his holster, the other holding a flashlight. As Deliso and Roberts came up behind Logan, Hart had the right door opened and was ordering the woman out of the van.

Gorman, smiling nervously, got out on the driver's side and said, "Hey, what's up, man? I wasn't doin' no more'n fifty."

"Would you mind stepping to this side, please?" Logan said politely.

"Sure." Gorman moved two paces away from the open door, eyes narrowed to slits as he saw Deliso and Roberts, in civilian clothes, backing the uniformed sergeant up. "Hey, what's the big deal, man?" he asked. "That's a lot of muscle for a speeding rap, ain't it?"

"May we see your driver's license and registration, please," Logan said.

Gorman pulled a wallet out of his jacket pocket and removed the inner plastic section. "Take it out of the sleeve, please," Logan instructed.

Gorman did so and handed it over. Logan examined the license and resgistration certificate by flashlight, then handed both to Deliso. Hart, meanwhile, had brought Lacy Gorman around to the driver's side. "Lord," she complained, "seems like a couple can't even enjoy a vacation trip 'thout cops bustin' things up for 'em." Ignored, she fell silent.

Deliso, satisfied, returned the license and registration cards to Gorman, who said, "We okay to go now?"

"I'm afraid not, Mr. Gorman," Deliso said. "You and the lady are under arrest under the California Health and Safety Code, Section one-one-five-oh-one, illegal transportation of narcotics—"

"Oh, come on, man. Go ahead an' search the goddamn van if you want. It's clean, and so are we."

"Turn around and put your hands on the van, legs spread out and back."

While Roberts patted Gorman down, Deliso read Billy John and Lacy Gorman their rights, then cuffed their wrists behind their backs and escorted them to Logan's vehicle, the rear section of which was wire-screened for prisoner transportation. Deliso followed Logan and Hart's black-and-white in the Plymouth, Roberts following in the Kar-a-Van.

The Gormans were booked at Lennox, and Deliso radioed the word to the command post, then started back to San Pedro with Roberts.

In the cutting room, the assembly-line operation had begun. The heavily taped cartons removed from behind the wall and ceiling panels of the Kar-a-Van had been brought inside and swiftly sorted out by the symbols marked in the upper left corner of each side: three red dots for heroin, three in green for cocaine. There were ten cartons of each, and each carton contained a single Pliofilm bag that weighed ten pounds. The heroin cartons were stacked along the north wall behind one table, the cocaine behind the second table.

Simon Hernandez went into his office and dialed Don Reed's number at the Alicante Drive apartment. Reed answered at once. "It's Simon," Hernandez announced.

"Is everything okay, Simon?"

"It has arrived. We have begun. I think we will be finished late on Wednesday night if all goes well."

"Good. Let me know when you are clear and the people gone. We will start contacting people to move a lot of it out at once."

"Yes." Simon hung up and returned to the cutting room.

Quiroga had opened the first carton of heroin, removed the single bag and weighed it. Ten pounds to the gram. He made a notation in a small notebook, then opened a carton of cocaine and repeated the process. The millers began the cutting process. Masks in place in order to prevent inhalation and addiction, they began spooning out the drug in proper amounts to adulterants, sifting everything through aluminum sieves, then strained through fine nylon netting secured on an eighteen-inch aluminum ring. In amounts of a quarter of a pound, drug and adulterants were then chopped and blended together on a square of thick lucite, using smooth, even strokes with thin-bladed knives until the powders were as one.

Solomon Quiroga took charge of the heroin table, while Marcos Andrade supervised the cocaine operation. It was important that no mistakes occur. The mixtures at the two tables were entirely different. To each pound of heroin, five pounds of a combination of procaine, dextrose, and lactose were added. To each pound of cocaine, only two pounds of dextrose and lactose. When completed, the one hundred pounds of heroin would become six hundred pounds, the one hundred pounds of cocaine, three hundred. And as each pound of heroin became six pounds, it was broken down into half-pound, pound, and kilo lots, bagged, weighed, sealed, marked, and replaced inside its individual carton. The cocaine was treated in a similar manner.

Simon Hernandez moved quietly from table to table, watching the overall operation. Quiroga and Andrade were skilled supervisors, the millers knowledgeable in their tasks. He went to the corner table and drew a cup of coffee, drank it, and went outside. In his office, two of the armed mechanics stood guard. He spoke to both, told them there was coffee inside, that they could go, one at a time, to refresh themselves.

Outside, the night air had grown cool but sweet as it came off the ocean, bringing a light fog with it. To the left and right of the double-doored entrance to the warehouse stood an armed guard. Two more were on walking guard, covering the front and sides of the building. Simon walked to the left, turned the corner, and went to the rear where the last two men were stationed. And came upon the one nearest him, who had a cigarette cupped in the palm of his hand.

"Put it out, *pendejo!*" he whispered sharply in Spanish. "There are as many eyes out there as there are stars, even though they are hidden by clouds."

"*Sí, Señor. Lo siento,*" the man replied abashedly.

"It is not enough to be sorry, only careful." Simon walked the rest of the way around the building and re-entered through the front, then wandered through the aisles of the darkened warehouse. He felt uneasy, as always during these operations. At this time in his life, when he had so much more to lose, there were never enough safeguards to give him comfort. Then what kept him at it, allowing himself to be used in such a way, risking prison for himself and disgrace for Benita, Alicia, and Teresa? And he smiled grimly, bitterly, knowing the answer to his own question. Greed. The money he had already accumulated, that which he could accumulate in the future; wealth he could not gain by legitimate means. For had it not been for Reed, Tri-City, without the administrative knowledge of his late father-in-law, George Aragon, would not be in existence today to provide the comforts he was able to give his family. And himself.

He went back to his office, past the two armed guards, and into the milling room.

From his observation post inside the Trans-Pac yard, standing close to the fence in the shadow of a freight trailer, Steve Barrett contacted McNeely by walkie-talkie. "Russ?"

"Here, Steve."

"A tall dude just circled the building from the front, talked to one of the two guards at the rear, made him ditch his cigarette, and kept going around. Far as I can make out, the two back here are armed with sawed-offs, probably handguns, too, but it's too dark to make that out."

"Yeah, Steve. Hamlin just checked in from the front side. He makes two at the front entrance and two on walking guard in the shadows, armed the same way. Can't tell what's inside, probably a damned armed camp and arsenal. Stay with it for now and keep in touch."

"Ten-four."

At 11:15 McNeely ordered Steve Barrett back to his car, then spoke to the other units to relieve their boredom. And his own.

At eleven-fifty the phone in Apartment 26 rang. Eddie Butler switched off the television set and motioned for Moose to answer. He hesitated, glancing from the phone to Eddie, then removed the receiver on the third ring. "Yeah?"

"It's me, Moose. You got it?"

"I got it."

"Who's with you?"

"Nobody."

"Okay. I'm downtown at the Greyhound bus station on Sixth and Los Angeles. You get in your car an' go there. You get there, an' you better be by yourself. You put the bread in one of those lockers, take the key. Then you walk out on the Los Angeles Street side an' start walkin' down Sixth toward Alameda. Somewhere along the line, I'll pop out on you, an' you just hand me that key an' keep on walkin'. You got that?"

"I got it. What about the broad?"

"I'll hand you a slip of paper with the address on it where

she's at. One more thing. You play it smart, Moose, an' don't be carryin' no piece on you 'cause I got mine on me. You make just one dumb move an' I'll blow you away. Understand?"

"I understand."

"Okay, start movin'. You blow this one an' there ain't no way you goin'a see the sun come up tomorrow." The line clicked and went dead.

"All right," Eddie said, "here's how we do it." He picked up the envelope into which he had earlier placed a sheaf of newsprint that had been trimmed out to dollar-bill size. "Put this in your pocket. We go out together, and I'll get to the place first, park on the other side of Sixth Street, somewhere around Wall. I'll keep an eye on you until he steps out to get the key from you. You hand it over and keep walking, just the way he said. He takes the key and gives you the slip of paper with Cora's address and starts walking back to the bus depot, and that's when I pop him and take off.

"They'll find him with a gun on him and the key. They'll check the locker and find the envelope with the news clippings in it and figure it for a ripoff. We'll meet back here later. Tomorrow, we'll pick up the broad and take care of her. Right?"

Peterson's head bobbed up and down in agreement. "Right," he said, "let's go do it."

In David-3-Sam-2, one among the dozen or more privately owned cars parked on Loma Vista across from the Peterson apartment, Danny Geiger squirmed in the passenger seat and said, "What the hell is that?"

Ycaza came alert. "What's what?"

"Dude coming up the street there, on the hustle, spade, Afro cut, denims. What the hell's he doing in this neighborhood walking all by himself this time of night?"

"Where?"

"Across the street, just passed the light, coming in this direction."

Ycaza moved across the center line of the front seat and watched as the slight figure advanced toward them, close to the building line on the other side of the street. As he passed beneath the light standard in the middle of the block, instinct, rather than positive recognition, caused an increase in his adrenalin flow.

"That's him," Ycaza said in a low, controlled whisper. "Ellison. Matches his stats except for the Afro and the get-up. Could be a wig. Get down out of sight, Danny. If he goes into that unit, it's him for damn sure."

Geiger slid forward and down in the front seat as far as space would permit. From his own position, crouching in the same manner, Ycaza watched from over the rim of the door as the slender man reached the open driveway at 19141, peered inside, looked to either side, then across the street, and turned in. On his walkie-talkie, Ycaza called Bramley and Krasna. "Pete, Dick, do you read me?"

"Loud and clear," Bramley replied at once.

"I read you," Krasna's voice came in.

"We make a dude, spade, Afro cut, just went up the driveway on foot. If he goes up the stairs to twenty-six, it's Dyer for sure. Get back to me and confirm. We'll be inside on the grounds, and watch it, he'll have a gun on him."

"Ten-four," Bramley and Krasna acknowledged.

Geiger had already unclasped the shotgun from its rack beneath the front seat and was out of the car, Ycaza beside him. They crossed the street quickly and looked up the driveway, then to the right. The slender man was not in sight, but at that moment they caught a glimpse of Krasna rounding the rear of the building, entering the doorway that led to the inside stairway. Ycaza motioned Geiger to the front of the building to guard the stairway there, then entered the doorway behind Krasna. Bramley was already inside, having preceded Krasna, and had now reached the top of the stairs, one step below the corridor.

Ycaza whispered to Krasna, "Get the shotgun from your car and get around to the stairway at the rear, cover the upstairs hallway from there."

When Krasna tiptoed out, Ycaza mounted the stairs to where Bramley stood against the wall. Bramley turned and whispered, "He's standing outside twenty-six with his back flat against the wall, like he's waiting for somebody to come out. Gun in his right hand."

Ycaza nodded. "Let's switch places. When I move, cover me."

Bramley moved down one step, and Ycaza moved up, now just below the corridor level, waiting for Dyer's next move.

It came suddenly when he heard a door open. Crouching low, he peered around the corner and saw Butler and Peterson in the act of emerging from 26. And as they did, the man Ycaza was certain was Dyer leaped away from the wall, revolver aimed at both men, heard him say sharply, "Back inside fast, or you both get it right here."

Ycaza leaped into the corridor, gun leveled in the direction of the trio. "Freeze! Police!"

Peterson, not completely in the open, leaped back into the apartment as Dyer's head turned toward Ycaza. Butler turned toward the open door to follow Peterson, but Dyer, standing behind him, grabbed Butler's arm and used him for a shield, fired two shots at Ycaza that struck the wall just above his head. Ycaza got off one shot and missed just as Krasna appeared at the other end of the corridor, his shotgun aimed at Dyer's back.

"Freeze! Drop the gun! Get your hands up over your heads!"

Dyer, partially protected from Ycaza's gun by Butler's body, wheeled and fired two shots at Krasna, whose shotgun roared at the same time Ycaza's handgun exploded, hitting Butler, while Dyer's body jerked toward the wall. His revolver fell to the floor as he reached for the wall, trying to hold on, then began sliding slowly toward the floor. Butler had fallen on his right side and was groping toward the open door when Peterson reached out and grabbed his right arm and dragged him into 26. The door slammed shut.

Dyer lay in a crumpled heap, bleeding from several wounds but still breathing, eyes rolled back up into his head, the Afro wig half off his head, hands clutching his abdomen. From the other apartments along the hallway, they could hear frightened cries of various tenants, voices calling out in anguish from the floor below, demanding to know what was going on up there. Geiger, coming along the hallway now, ordered those who were standing in their doorways in night clothes to stay in their apartments.

Ycaza called to Geiger. "Get to a phone and get an ambulance here and a back-up car from Lakewood. Then get out in back and cover the windows. Butler's hit, but Peterson may try to jump it. Pete, stay here with me. Dick, get the people back in their apartments." He picked up the .38 that had dropped from Ellison's hand and shoved it inside his waistband. "Let's move this dude out of the way."

They slid, rather than carried, Dyer's inert body about ten feet down the hallway, his eyes glazed, lips moving without sound. "Looks like he's going, Ray," Pete Bramley said.

"Well, there's nothing we can do for him right now, and we've got more work to do."

Now standing on either side of the door to 26, Ycaza called out, "Peterson, this is Sergeant Ycaza. Open the door, toss your guns out, then come out with your hands over your head."

There was no answer.

Again, "Peterson! If you don't come out in ten seconds, we're coming in. You know we've got shotguns out here. We've got an ambulance coming for Butler. Be smart and don't make us break in."

Two more doors opened along the hallway, and frightened faces, male and female, peered out. One man stepped out into the hallway, and Krasna called out, "We're police officers. Stay inside." Up the stairs came a large, robed, puffing man, anger written on his face. "What the hell's going on here, shooting the place up, scaring everybody to——" He saw Ellison's bleeding body on the floor then. "Jesus Christ! Blood all over the carpets. I'll sue——"

Ycaza said, "Police business, mister. Get downstairs and out of the way. There are guns inside that room." The manager paled and backed off.

To the doorway, "Last chance, Peterson. Five seconds and we're moving in."

There was no reply.

Dick Krasna said, "Christ, Ray, you're going to walk into one."

"Well, something's got to give. Back me up." He raised his right foot and placed it just below the knob. Krasna, directly behind him, was ready with his shotgun. Ycaza drew his foot back, then rammed it against the cheap door. It flew open as Ycaza threw his body to the left side.

But the expected gunfire never came. Inside, Peterson sat in the center of the floor, Butler's head and shoulders in his lap, tears welled up in the big man's eyes, staring down into his friend's unconscious face. Blood stained Peterson's jacket, shirt, and trousers. Butler's blood.

"All right, Peterson," Ycaza said, "it's all over for now. Let's go."

"You motherin' bastards," the big man mumbled. "You never gave him a chance."

Krasna bent down, felt Butler's heart, then his pulse. "He's alive, Ray."

They got Peterson to his feet, patted him down, removed his .38 and .45, and cuffed his hands behind him. Butler lay motionless on the floor. Ycaza said, "Who's your buddy outside?"

"He dead?" Peterson said.

"No. He might even make it. What's his name?"

"Walt Dyer."

"Where's he from?"

"Las Vegas."

Geiger and Bramley were back. "Ambulance and doctor on the way, Ray. Be here any minute now. Backup, too."

"Okay." To Peterson, staring down at Butler's white-shocked face, "This Dyer is John Hall Ellison, isn't he?"

"Go ask him," Peterson replied shortly.

"If he lives, we will. And we'll have a lot more questions to ask you and your buddy here if he makes it."

Peterson said, "Fuck you, pig. I got a right not to talk, and I ain't talking."

The Lakewood patrol unit arrived first with two deputies, then a second unit with their patrol sergeant. On their heels came the ambulance. Within a few minutes, Dyer and Butler were on their way to the Pioneer Hospital, the backup units along with Bramley and Krasna following.

"Let's go, Peterson." Ycaza and Geiger led him down to the car and started for Lakewood to book him. On the radio, Ycaza called in to Homicide and reached Lieutenant Kelleher.

"What's doing, Ray?"

"We got Dyer, Ken, and Butler, both shot, on their way to Pioneer. I've got Dyer's thirty-eight for ballistics tests, but he won't be talking for a while if he makes it at all. Same for Butler. We're on our way to Lakewood to book Peterson."

"Nice going, Ray. How would you like to have the rest of the night off as your reward?"

"You're all heart, Ken, but I'm going to stay with this dude for a while and see if he'll loosen up a little. Then I'm going to check on the other two at Pioneer and on the way in, drop Dyer's gun, along with Peterson's and Butler's, at the lab. One of 'em may be the piece that got Despues. After that, if there's still some of the night left, I'll take it off as my reward."

"Okay. I'll recommend you for sheriff's honors as the year's best hog for punishment. Keep in touch."

"And I'll be sleeping in all day tomorrow, so don't call me unless there's a national disaster."

Kelleher chuckled and hung up. There would be no sleeping in for Ycaza tomorrow.

Chapter Thirteen

1•

As the black of night began slowly to turn to slate gray, a heavy, chilly mist swept in across the ocean and virtually cut down the visibility of the cars that were parked around the Tri-City Auto Works to a bare minimum. The buildings, shed and stacked auto carcasses inside the yard were shrouded ghosts, and from his position in the Trans-Pac yard, Perry Roberts reported by walkie-talkie that the guards at the rear of the warehouse had moved inside. From the Sixth Street side, Harry Deliso reported that the guards in front of the warehouse had moved to new positions in the repair sheds.

McNeely and Barker conferred with Captain Esau and decided to remove all but four cars from the immediate area for the time being and keep the photographic unit in place. The conspicuous black-and-white units parked in the vicinity of the command post were ordered to pull back at least one mile and stand by. In groups of two, all units were given permission to leave their posts to get breakfast and fill their thermos jugs with fresh hot coffee.

And later, as the sky lightened, the busy harbor area came alive to begin its work day. First came the private cars of the warehousemen, truck drivers, mechanics, and clerks, then the heavy trucks, moving in and out of various yards to load or unload cargoes. In the Tri-City yard, four men came out of the warehouse building and opened several mechanics' sheds to give the appearance of normal activity, although they seemed more interested in watching the main gate and warehouse than engaging in any work at their benches.

At nine o'clock, the retail-store clerk and janitor arrived separately and parked their cars on the Sixth Street side. Moments later, the female clerk parked and entered the retail-store door. All were photographed by the unit cameramen. The delivery truck and private cars of those behind the fence remained parked in the yard.

By ten o'clock, all the deputies had had their quickly eaten breakfasts and returned to their stations, checked in with the command post by walkie-talkie, and settled down to await orders. At the end of each thirty-minute period, the four cars in direct observation of the Tri-City yard reported in, received a "Ten-four" acknowledgment, and resumed watch.

Shortly before noon, dark clouds moved in from the west, and by one o'clock a slow, steady rain began to fall. The four key cars were relieved singly then, and the afternoon wore on. Inside the cars, the atmosphere was no less dreary than the weather outside. Conversation, after being confined together for so long, had dwindled into silence, and the deputies took turns sleeping while their partners remained on the alert for any word that might come over their walkie-talkies from the command post.

The rain continued as night fell, and four more unmarked cars were moved into the immediate vicinity, along with a relief for the two deputies on observation in the Trans-Pac yard, who had been watching from inside the rear end of a trailer that had been backed up close to the link fence.

At six o'clock, Gene Morris was contacted on radio by his chief, Lyle Carter, and asked to get to a telephone and call in. He used the one in the command-post mobile van and made his call, then turned to Captain Esau.

"Sorry, Captain, but I've got to check out on this deal," he said to Esau, Barker, and McNeely, "and I'm going to have to get Patton and Evans and meet Carter in town. With the Gormans in custody, Dallas is concerned that Billy John may have had orders to call in as soon as the delivery was made. He may have done that from the Tri-City office, but Ames suggested that they may not have wanted a long-distance call to show up on Tri-City's phone bill.

"If he was supposed to, and didn't, the Wrayburn people will be getting suspicious and may become desperate enough to hide, burn, or bury the rest of the stuff. The ranch is under heavy surveillance, and Ames has ordered Jess Tyler to hit the place before dawn tomorrow. Ames wants us back there for the raid."

A deputy was assigned to drive him, Patton, and Evans to the DEA office.

Inside the cutting room, the work moved steadily throughout Monday night and Tuesday. At regular intervals, the workers were given two-hour breaks to eat and sleep. The laborious task of weighing, sifting, mixing, packaging, reweighing, and tagging continued on. Hernandez himself recorded the number and quantity in each completed carton in his inventory ledger.

At six o'clock on Tuesday night, Simon Hernandez telephoned Don Reed and informed him that the work was proceeding according to schedule and would be completed no later than five o'clock on the following morning. Reed expressed his satisfaction and told Hernandez he could start making small deliveries as soon as the cutting was completed and the people moved out, the yard returned to normal activities. Also, that he could expect "visitors" starting at two o'clock, a few who were most eager for their merchandise, and that he would hear from Talbot with explicit orders later in the afternoon.

Moose Peterson looked up sullenly when Ray Ycaza entered the corridor of the holding cells at Lakewood at eleven o'clock on Tuesday morning.

Before and immediately after his initial booking, Peterson had remained mute, and Ycaza decided to abandon the interrogation. Later, he had driven to the Criminalistics Lab where he left Dyer's, Butler's, and Peterson's guns for examination by the ballistics expert, with special instructions to check the test firings against the bullets removed from the bodies of Cruz Despues and Whitey Lloyd.

Now, having given Peterson some time alone to think matters over, he was back. The jailer unlocked the cell door, and Peterson levered himself upright off the bunk. "Let's go, Moose," Ycaza said.

"Where?"

"Somewhere private for a little talk."

"How's Eddie?"

"Let's go where we can be more comfortable."

"I'm comfortable right here."

The jailer moved inside the cell. "Come on, man, move it."

Peterson stared at the slightly built jailer with contempt. Ycaza said, "Make it easy on yourself, Moose. You can't fight the whole world, you know."

"Lousy pigs," Peterson snorted, and moved through the doorway. The jailer removed a pair of handcuffs from his belt, but Ycaza waved them aside. "We won't need those," he said. "Moose isn't going to give us any trouble. He's got more than he needs right now."

Between them, Peterson moved down the corridor into another, then to an interrogation room. A single overhead light, built into the eight-foot-high ceiling, was protected by a heavy wire screen. The room was windowless and contained a six-foot-long oak table, a strong wooden chair on either side. "Anything else, Sergeant?" the jailer asked.

"No, thanks." Then, "You might ask a trustee to bring us some coffee." And to Peterson, "How do you take yours, Moose?"

"Black."

"One black, one with a little cream," Ycaza said.

"Sure." The deputy went out, closing the door.

"Sit down, Moose, make yourself comfortable."

Peterson dropped into the chair, sagging, dispirited, chin almost resting on his chest. One arm rested on the table, fingers clenched into a white-knuckled fist, the other dangling at his side. Ycaza took out a pack of cigarettes and lighter, pushed them to the center of the table. "Have one," he invited.

Peterson hesitated, then said, "How's Eddie?"

"I talked with the hospital just before I came here. He's on the critical list, but the doctor I talked to thinks he'll make it unless some complication sets in."

Peterson expelled a small sigh and reached for a cigarette. As he lit it, Ycaza said, "Aren't you interested in your friend Walt Dyer?"

"He can go straight to hell for all I care."

"He really must have crossed you up—"

A knock on the door. It opened, and a trustee entered with two paper cups of coffee, the jailer behind him. The trustee left, and the deputy said, "Okay?"

"Fine. This'll do it," Ycaza smiled.

"I'll be outside the door."

When it closed, Peterson sipped at the coffee between draws on the cigarette. After a few moments, Ycaza said,

"Okay, Moose. You've had your rights read to you, heard the charges. You were given the opportunity to make a phone call and refused. That's your right, too. Let me tell you where we stand, sort of clear the air between us. We have your rap sheet—do you want me to read it to you?"

"Save your breath. I know what's in it."

"Okay. Your gun, Butler's and Dyer's are down at the lab being checked out by Ballistics. We're pretty sure one of them is going to tell us a story, and if we get what we think we're going to get, you're in for a very heavy fall. Right now, you can make it a lot easier on yourself if you tell us what we want to know before we find it out from Ballistics. That's where it's at right now."

Peterson glared and remained silent.

"Okay," Ycaza said, "I'll give you a little more. We know all about your and Butler's dope operations, and that you were dealing to Whitey Lloyd, now deceased, and believe that Walt Dyer, alias John Hall Ellison, was the hit man who blew him up. For you and Butler and the people you're working for. That puts all of you into a solid conspiracy to commit murder. If you don't talk to me now, one of those guns will. When it does, we won't need a damned thing more from you, and you'll all be in the same boat, up the creek and without a paddle."

"Don't bullshit me, cop."

"I'm leveling with you, Moose. We even know the top guy you've been working for. Don Reed."

Peterson's eyes opened wider at the mention of Reed's name. "And we know that Connie Moya and Cora Thomas are two of your telephone contacts. We also know about Simon Hernandez and his Tri-City operation, and within a matter of hours, we'll have all of them, including the cutting teams. Does that sound like I'm bullshitting you?"

The big man squirmed in his chair, leaned back and crossed one leg over the other. Ycaza said, "It's just about all over, Moose. You won't be helping Eddie any by holding out. When it comes down to push and shove, who do you think will go to bat for you? You've been there before. You know what happens, don't you? Every man for himself." And when Peterson remained silent, "Tell me, what do you think you owe Walt Dyer?"

The name and implication stirred Peterson. "That spade sonofabitch—" he began, then cut it off abruptly.

"That spade sonofabitch can put you in the joint for the

rest of your life, Moose, and Eddie along with you. You think Dyer will give you a second thought if he thinks he can buy even a month less of time?"

Peterson's mouth opened, then closed. In his life experience, he had been up against tough cops and prison jailers, had tasted brutality in its worst forms, seen it applied with force by prisoners against other prisoners in his tough world. He had known it from childhood in the streets, in schoolyards, at home from a drunken father and an indifferent mother. From Ycaza and the others last night, he had expected no less than death. And now he sat listening to the man who calmly outlined some—probably not all—of what he knew; and the facts he had stated so clearly, Peterson knew, could not be refuted. And wondered if—or how far—he could trust him.

"Well, Moose?" Ycaza prompted.

"If I give you Dyer, what do I get for Eddie and me?"

"You don't want any bullshit, do you?"

"You know it, man."

"Okay. Then you know I can't make you any kind of a deal right here and now. You know that all I can do is talk to my people, to the D.A.'s people, tell them the extent of your cooperation—"

"What about—suppose Eddie goes along with it, what can we come off with if we cop a plea?"

"I told you, it all rests with the D.A. and the judge. You know you can't buy a free ride, but neither will you get the limit, which you'll sure as hell get if you freeze up on us. Somewhere in between is all I can say for sure."

"Can I talk to Eddie first?"

"Nobody can talk to Eddie right now. He's on the critical list in intensive care, heavily sedated. Later this week, if he comes along, maybe."

"Okay, I'll wait."

"That's up to you. Just remember that if Ballistics comes up with what we're looking for, we may not need anything from you or Eddie and any talk of deals is off limits."

"Yeah." As Ycaza stood up, "When do you think you'll be hearing anything from Ballistics?"

"Almost anytime now, maybe tonight, tomorrow."

"You keepin' me here til then?"

"No. You'll be transferred to county jail on this evening's bus."

"What if I want to talk to you?"

410

"Just tell the jailer and give him my name. I'll arrange for him to call me."

"Okay. I'll think about it."

Late in the afternoon, sitting in his office on the eighth floor, Ycaza was summoned to the ninth by Lieutenant Kelleher and found him in Captain Sawyer's office. "How did you make out with Peterson?" Sawyer asked.

"Nowhere, but he's thinking it over, and he's got a hell of a lot to think about."

"He still at Lakewood?"

"Yes, but they'll be moving him to the county jail on this evening's bus. I've got a hunch he'll call me from there."

"Well," Kelleher said, "I don't think we'll need him any longer except to confirm what we already know." He handed Ycaza the ballistics report. "We just got that twenty minutes ago. It was Dyer's gun that killed Despues, also Whitey Lloyd."

Ycaza said, "That's confirmation enough. What's Dyer's condition?"

"Burr is on his way to Pioneer Hospital now to see if the doctors will let him talk to him. Last call we made there, they seemed pretty optimistic that he'll make it."

"Anything on Butler?"

"He's still a doubtful. Started bleeding internally and had to be rushed back to the operating room about an hour ago."

"Well, at least we know a lot more than we knew yesterday."

"That we do. Burr's going to hang in there just in case. Why don't you call it a day and take off."

"Sure. I want to call McNeely and let him know. Not that it'll do much good, but he'll feel better knowing we've got the crook who killed Casey Despues."

"Okay. Your report up to date?"

"Except for today. I'll look over my notes tonight and dictate it in the morning."

Back in his own office, he contacted McNeely by radio and received a simple, "Thanks, Ray. I'll pass the word along to the guys."

"You sound tired as hell. How's it going down there?"

"Status quo, and we're all tired. Still sitting on it. Our friend Gene Morris is on his way back to Texas. They're going to hit the ranch around dawn tomorrow morning."

"And I'll bet you're drooling to be there."

"No. Hell, no. What we're sitting on here is big enough, if

and when it goes down. Hey, I've got to sign off now. See you."

"Roger, and good luck."

At 0540 on Wednesday morning, Steve Barrett reached Russ McNeely at the command post by walkie-talkie. "What's doing, Steve?" he responded sleepily.

"Movement in the yard, Russ. The panel truck is warming up, no lights. Can't make out the dude in the dark, but I'm guessing it's the regular driver, Rojas. It's moving now toward the warehouse entrance, turning to back up. Could be they've finished the cutting and are getting ready to transport the millers back to their drop point."

"Stand by, Steve. I'll alert the other cars and get back to you." He turned to wake Barker and Captain Esau, who were asleep on their canvas cots, when Bill Hamlin raised him on the walkie-talkie with the same information, coming from the Sixth Street side. Barker and Esau, listening, poured coffee from the thermos. "Okay," Esau said, "let's move four cars out ahead of them to the drop point, have one car tail the truck to keep the others informed. After the drop is made, pick up the people and have them taken to Firestone for booking. We'll interrogate them later."

"Suppose," McNeely suggested, "we let the driver go and keep a tail on him. It's possible he may be carrying a package or two for delivery before he goes back to San Pedro."

"That's a good thought, but at this hour, it won't be an easy tail," Barker said.

"I'll put Perry Roberts and another man on it. Perry can tail a sparrow in flight."

"Do it," Esau said. "Move 'em out before Rojas loads up. Keep Roberts laying back of him."

Barker got on the radio to Firestone station and asked for a 240-Q, a transportation van to handle a dozen prisoners, to be parked in the vicinity of Lazarro's until needed. Russ, on the walkie-talkie, ordered Bill Hamlin's and three other two-man units to leave at once for the Lazarro location and stake it out for the arrival of the Tri-City panel truck, and to avoid taking the driver, since his absence might alert Hernandez to the possibility of his arrest. McNeely then assigned Perry Roberts and Harry Deliso to move from their positions on Sixth and Reckord and the Trans-Pac yard, to O'Farrell Street, facing Harbor Boulevard, where they would be able to spot the Tri-City truck as it passed that corner on the way to Front Street, Pacific Avenue en route to the Harbor Freeway.

Thirty minutes later, the panel truck drove out of the Reckord Avenue gate, turned right on Sixth to Harbor, left toward Front, its passage noted and reported by the three cars remaining on station.

As it passed the O'Farrell corner, Deliso radioed that he and Roberts were on target and moved out in its wake. Later, he reported his position on the Harbor Freeway, the panel truck in sight, proceeding northward. The time was 0625.

At Lazarro's Food Market, the building and parking lot were in semi-darkness except for the corner light standards and the dim night lights of the as yet unopened Gulf station. The four surveillance cars had been parked among others on two nearby residential streets, Hamlin and his seven deputies positioned in the alley at the rear of the parking lot, in doorways adjacent to the food market and across the street behind the Gulf pumps.

At 0700, Jimmie Lazarro arrived, drove into the parking lot, unlocked the rear door of the store, and entered. He began turning on the interior lights as he made his way to the front and unlocked those doors, ready for morning business. Moments later, his first customers, neighborhood women, two old men, began to arrive. The Gulf station manager and an attendant arrived to open up, and the two deputies stationed there were forced to move down the street into a doorway.

More people were appearing on the streets now, some driving to their jobs, others waiting at the corner of 223rd and Avalon for their bus rides. On either side of Avalon, the doors of other small business establishments began to open, and across Avalon, the metal door fronting the Rodriguez Garage was raised, its interior fluorescent lights turned on. With the government's extension of daylight savings time in force, the sky was still dull gray.

At 0725 the Tri-City panel truck came down Avalon and turned into 223rd, slowed as it passed the food store, then pulled into the parking lot. Pete Rojas braked to a stop, turned his head toward the interior, and called out in Spanish, "Quickly! Get down. Go home and keep your mouths shut."

Half a block down 223rd, Perry Roberts and Harry Deliso parked and watched. They saw the rear doors open from the inside and the passengers, six men and six women, emerge, climb down to the asphalt ground. Rojas at once made a U-turn and drove out again. Roberts took up the tail again.

They were alone now, the dozen millers, and began to move off the parking lot toward the pavement and to their homes; and then, suddenly, they became aware of the men approaching them in pairs, two from the rear, two from right and left, two from across the street. Dave Gomez, holding up his gold star, called out in Spanish, "Everybody! Stay where you are. Don't move. We are the police, and we want to talk to you. Keep still and no one will be hurt."

Startled, stunned by the sudden reversal of their fortunes, flush with the earnings of their labors, they obeyed. The muffled curses of the men were mingled with the quiet prayers and pleas of the women. While Gomez informed them that they were under arrest, Bill Hamlin called the prisoner van to the scene; weeping and protesting, they were placed inside the van and driven to Firestone station for booking and questioning.

A little over a mile away on Moneta Avenue, Pete Rojas parked his truck and went inside his house. At the corner of 235th and Moneta, Perry Roberts and Harry Deliso parked, radioed their location to the command post. On orders from McNeely, they settled down to await Rojas's next move.

At 0930, a dark green Impala came off Harbor Boulevard, up Sixth to Reckord, and stopped at the gates, sounding its horn. A man came out of one of the sheds, unlocked the gates. The Impala drove in and parked at the warehouse entrance. As the driver got out, Steve Barrett called in to McNeely. "We've got our first biggie, Russ. Dixie Norton, operates in the Sunset Strip area."

"Ten-four," McNeely acknowledged, then, "Myers, do you copy that?"

Bill Myers, parked on Ninth Street with Vic Lopez, came on. "We copy."

"Come up to the corner of Reckord and pick it up when it leaves. When you're sure he's headed for the barn, make the bust."

"Ten-four."

Fifteen minutes later, the Impala left, Myers and Lopez on its tail.

At 1000, a dark-blue Cadillac arrived, and Barrett reported in again. "Business is picking up, Russ. Male, black, about five-eleven, one hundred seventy-five pounds—hold it. I make him. It's Willie Acheson, Little Willie's Bar on El Segundo, Jimmie Tice's partner."

"Bingo! Solid gold," McNeely replied, and came to a quick decision. He sent one car ahead at once to stake out Little

Willie's Bar, and ordered Tom Loden and Gary Price, two black deputies out of Firestone Narcotics, to tail the Cadillac.

At 1030, after two hours of sleep, Pete Rojas awoke, drank the coffee Estella had heated for him, dressed in fresh slacks and shirt, and went out to his truck. Within a few minutes, he was parked on the lot behind the Dos Hermanos Bar on 222nd and Avalon. From their point of observation, Perry Roberts and Harry Deliso saw him walk around to the rear doors, then Harry reached for the mike and radioed in. Barker came on. "What's doing?" he asked. "Russ is sacked out."

"Rojas is at the Dos Hermanos. Looks like he's about to make a delivery."

"Okay. If he does, bust him and whoever is inside. We've got a couple of cars in the area. I'll get one of them to your location at once."

Rojas had carried one package inside, then returned to the truck, unlocked the rear doors again, removed a second carton, and returned to the rear of the bar. Moments later, a car drove up and parked behind the tail car. Roberts and Deliso got out and motioned Frank Delgamo and Manuel Ricardo toward the rear entrance.

Roberts and Deliso crossed the street to the front entrance and went in. Inside at the bar were seven males and one woman, all drinking beer, the thickset bartender mopping the bar with a towel. A jukebox was playing Mexican music without interference to a Latin newscaster out of Station KMEX on the television screen over the bar.

Deliso stood in the center of the room between the bar and a dozen tables; he had the patrons and barman in view. Perry Roberts went directly to the back room in which there were four pool tables, none in use at the moment. He moved into a short corridor with two doors on one side marked CABALLEROS and DAMAS, a third, PRIVADO. At the end of the corridor was the rear door, which exited to the parking lot. Roberts went to it, drew the bolt, and admitted Delgamo and Ricardo.

At the office door, Roberts listened and heard voices. With guns drawn, Roberts bracketed on either side by Delgamo and Ricardo, he knocked on the door and stepped to one side, heard George Ruiz's voice call out, *"Quien es?"*

"Open up, Ruiz. Police."

There was no answer. "Open it up, or we'll break it down," Roberts called out. Reaching to his right, he tried the doorknob. The door was locked. "Five seconds and I'll blow the lock off."

On the count of three, the door opened. George Ruiz, dark and smiling, stood to one side. Beside him and two paces behind stood Pete Rojas.

"What is it? Why are you here?" Ruiz asked.

"We want the two cartons Pete just delivered to you," Roberts said.

"Cartons? What cartons? There are no cartons here."

"Then we'll come in and look for them, George. While we're doing that, you can read this search warrant. If you want to spare us the trouble, you can also save yourself a lot of mess putting this place back together again. Is it a deal?"

Ruiz's smile evaporated. "You paddy bastards."

"Don't make it any tougher on yourself, George. Where are they?"

Ruiz turned and looked at Rojas with hatred. In Spanish, he called on God to witness the stupidity of Rojas, then cursed him to his dying day, which he hoped would occur very soon. While Ricardo patted Rojas down, relieving him of a .32 Colt automatic, Roberts and Delgamo followed Ruiz to his desk. From the lower left drawer, they retrieved the two cartons. On examination, one contained a full kilo of cocaine, the other a kilo of heroin, which they tagged and identified for evidence.

Further search of a small safe, concealed in the closet, turned up a number of balloons of cocaine, several of heroin, nine kilos of marijuana, and several thousand pills of various types. And over forty thousand in cash.

Ruiz and Rojas were handcuffed and led away. In the Tri-City truck, they found four similar cartons that would not reach their delivery points.

3●

On that morning, in her motel room at Descanso Beach in Baja California, Cora Thomas came awake early, now decidedly apprehensive over Walt Dyer's absence, having received no word from him. When he hadn't returned by Monday, she had checked through the Sunday edition of the Los Angeles *Times* and the Monday edition on Tuesday, the papers arriving one day late.

She got up, dressed, and had breakfast in the coffee shop, then returned to her room to dress for the beach on that brilliantly sunny morning. Taking her purse and the small transistorized radio with her, she decided in favor of poolside rather than the sandy beach. Stretched out on a towel-covered lounge chair, she turned on the radio and began applying a sun-resistant lotion to her splendid legs, arms, and upper body. Wearing sunglasses, her hair protected by a floppy straw hat, she lay back now to enjoy the music from a San Diego station.

In midweek there were hardly more than a dozen couples staying at the motel, half of that number lounging or breakfasting at poolside under umbrellas. On the hour, at ten o'clock, the newscaster came on, and listening to the international and national news, none of which was heartening or stimulating, she felt totally relaxed, although still with the underlying anxiety over Walt.

Then, as the news turned to the Southern California scene, she came to understand why.

"In Los Angeles, continuing the story of the shootout of two men wanted in connection with an alleged dope murder, the sheriff's department has been able to identify one of the wounded men as Walt Dyer, male, black, a resident of Las Vegas. Dyer remains in critical condition in a Lakewood hospital. The second wounded man has not as yet been identified, but further word is expected—"

Cora sat up, turned the radio off, gathered up her beach robe, purse, and radio, and went back to her room. She sat on the edge of her bed and began to consider her own situation. Walt, shot and in a critical condition. And Cora left stranded at Descanso Beach with— She turned her purse upside down on the bed. From her wallet, seventy-four dollars. Two dollars in loose bills. Sixty-three cents in change. She was without a car, with an unpaid hotel bill— She began to calculate; Saturday, Sunday, Monday, Tuesday. Four days if she checked out by noontime. Four days at eighteen dollars a day, came to seventy-two dollars, leaving her with four dollars and sixty-three cents.

The things Walt had bought for her, three dresses, two pairs of slacks, shoes, bathing suits, and lingerie, could be packed in the straw suitcase along with her cosmetics. But how could she leave here with only four dollars and sixty-three cents? The only alternative was to leave everything behind that wouldn't fit in her large straw bag. Walk up to the bus stop, get into Tijuana, and beat the motel bill. Without further thought, she moved quickly.

The straw handbag, bought locally, was roomy enough to carry her cosmetics, underwear, and two dresses. She wore the white slacks and blouse with matching topper, leaving all else, including Walt's clothes, picked up the small radio, and walked out past the office and toward the center of town. She was early for the noon bus to Tijuana and decided to have a light lunch. Sitting at the sidewalk table over a taco and glass of beer, she began to ponder her situation with greater clarity of mind.

Bus to Tijuana. Taxi across the border. Bus to San Diego, a city about which she knew little. On to Los Angeles, where she could make contacts, but where the police were looking for her. The house on Newton Street was out. It would be under surveillance. Her Pinto had surely been impounded by now; if not, someone would be watching it, waiting for her to return to pick it up.

Then it was noon, and the bus sighed to a stop at the nearby corner. Cora paid her check, boarded the bus, trying to reason her way out of the problem. At all costs, she must avoid Eddie Butler and Moose Peterson since, according to Walt, they had offered him a contract on her.

In Tijuana, her only desire was to get out as soon as possible. She took a taxi to the border, walked across without any problem, and there caught a waiting Greyhound bus marked for Los Angeles. As it neared San Diego, her concern over being spotted by Los Angeles police or sheriff's deputies increased, and at the San Diego bus terminal she changed her plans and caught a cab to the Cortez. She checked in, stripped, showered, and went to bed. She awoke at eight o'clock, ordered a small dinner in the coffee shop, and returned to her room.

She could hustle, she knew, but if she were picked up by local vice cops, her prints would come down from Sacramento and identify her as wanted. Los Angeles would send someone down to get her, charge her with complicity, conspiracy, bail jumping, and throw her back into jail. How light, she wondered, would they treat her if she gave herself up and cooperated fully?

She had more to give them than Walt Dyer, Moose Peterson, Eddie Butler, and Connie Moya. A prize plum: the name of the man with whom she had spent a weekend at Lake Arrowhead and who had introduced her to Eddie Butler. He was the man they would really want, the key dude sitting on top of Butler and Peterson. He had given her a phony name, and knowing it was phony, she had gone through his wallet while he slept on one of those three nights. His money wallet, complete with license and credit cards, had shown him to be David Rhodes. And in a credit-card wallet in his jacket pocket, another driver's license and more credit cards in the name of Don Reed. Obviously, the man Butler and Peterson worked for, the chief honcho the narcotics agents would be decidedly interested in. How much, she wondered now, would it be worth to the two detectives, Ycaza and McNeely? And how far would they go for her in exchange for this information?

She fell asleep then, thinking about these ramifications; when she awoke next morning, she came to a decision. She placed a person-to-person call to Sergeant Ycaza at the L.A. Sheriff's Homicide Department. The man who answered told the operator that Sergeant Ycaza would be in at ten o'clock and asked whether the caller would speak to anyone else.

"Is Sergeant McNeely there?"

"No," the man told the operator, "Sergeant McNeely is with another division. Can I have the party leave her name and phone number, and I'll have Sergeant Ycaza call her back when he comes in?"

The operator held while Cora decided. "The number, yes, but not the name," she said.

"Okay, I'll take that," the man said.

"The Cortez Hotel in San Diego, room 414. Tell him it has to do with a man named—Ellison. If he doesn't call by noon, I'll be checked out."

"He'll phone you before then."

She hung up, ordered orange juice, toast, coffee, and the morning paper sent to her room. There was no follow-up story on Walt Dyer. And now, waiting for Ycaza's call, she felt relieved that it would soon be over, wondering if she could successfully claim her car and personal possessions in the Newton Street house, the cash she had hidden away there. Six hundred dollars in hundred-dollar bills between the pages of a paperback copy of the *World Almanac*. She toyed with her breakfast, read the newspaper, scanned the Help-Wanted columns out of curiosity, chain-smoked, then dressed—and waited.

At 1005 her phone rang, startling her out of deep thought. She picked up the receiver with a trembling hand. "Hello."

"Hello. This is Sergeant Ycaza, Los Angeles sheriff's Homicide."

"Sergeant, this—this is Cora Thomas. I know you're looking for me."

419

"Yes, Miss Thomas, we are. You're in room 414 at the Cortez?"

"Yes, and don't send the cops to pick me up. I want to turn myself in to you."

"How do you want to do it?"

"I can catch a bus to L.A. There's one at eleven o'clock. You can meet me at the bus station there."

"That'll take hours, Miss Thomas. Do you have enough money for a ticket on PSA. There's one on the hour."

"I think I can just about make it."

"Okay, to International. I'll meet you there. Will you do that?"

"Yes."

4 •

Since the nine-thirty arrival of Dixie Norton, followed by Willie Acheson half an hour later, there had been only one other caller shortly before noon; a young heavyset white man whom none of the observers could recognize. Driving a 1970 Pontiac LeMans, he parked directly in front of the retail store, went inside, and remained for twenty minutes. When he came out, he was carrying several small packages. A 10-28 on his tags revealed no warrants or wants. His name and address were noted for possible future investigation, and it was decided not to waste a surveillance team at that time.

At 1300 Captain Esau conferred with Barker and McNeely and made his decision. "We've got Rojas and George Ruiz, and that presents a problem. If Pete was due to call in or show up back here after making his deliveries, our friend Hernandez knows, or will know soon, that something's gone haywire.

"Let's coordinate the hit for fourteen hundred. At the same time, have the teams standing by in town move in on Charles T. Valentine and David Rhodes/Don Reed, and have the people sitting on Norton and Acheson take them."

"What about any of the others who might show up here?"

"A bird in the hand, Bob," Esau countered. "No use stretching our luck. On the scale these people are operating, they've got to keep records—here, at Valentine's, or Reed's place. We've got the necessary search warrants, and we're bound to come up with what we need. How many men have we got to go with, Russ?"

McNeely scanned the assignment chart. "We've got eight men in four cars. The others are on stakeouts and surveillances. We've got Lennox, Firestone, and West Hollywood standing by and can draw on East L.A. and Malibu if necessary."

"All right," Esau said, "let's bring in four more of our people and roll eight black-and-whites. We'll move in, let 'em know we're here in force and mean business. Pass the word, Russ. Have them stand off a few blocks and report in. And put our eight men here on alert. They must be dragging low by now."

By 1350, Perry Roberts and Harry Deliso were back in San Pedro along with the deputies who had arrested the millers, which added eight more to those already on station. Four blocks away, eight black-and-white units were parked on Second and Pacific, each with two uniformed deputies, all awaiting the word to roll.

At 1355 all units were ordered to close in. They came in on Reckord, Sixth, and Mesa, facing the Tri-City yard on three sides, headlights and red lights turned on. Four uniformed deputies covered the north side on foot along the fence that separated Tri-City from the Trans-Pac yard.

Inside the Tri-City fence, the first mechanic who saw the array of black-and-whites shouted a warning to the others. They came out of their work sheds and stared with numbed surprise. At the main gate on Reckord Avenue, Captain Esau turned on his bullhorn. "Attention in there! We are police officers. I order you to open these gates. If you do not resist, no one will be hurt."

None of the startled mechanics moved.

"If you do not open these gates, we will break them down. You have ten seconds to—"

The mechanics turned as one, broke and ran toward the warehouse building. At that moment, the uniformed and plainclothes deputies moved. Some scaled the fence on Sixth, others entered the retail store. On Reckord, McNeely fired twice at the padlock that held the double gates together and threw them wide open. Esau's and Barker's cars moved inside, Roberts, Barrett, and two patrol units behind them.

McNeely, on foot, ran beside Esau's car to the warehouse door, tried it, and found it locked. Esau was out of his car and on the bullhorn. "Hernandez, this is Captain Esau, sheriff's department. You and your people are completely surrounded. I am ordering all of you to come out unarmed and with your hands up over your heads. No one will be hurt. If you don't comply, we will move in, in force."

Inside, the mechanics and warehousemen were gathered in a disordered knot before Simon Hernandez's office, chattering and cursing with fright and dismay. Solomon Quiroga, unable to quell them, himself sweating apprehensively, ran to the door and opened it. In Hernandez's office, he saw Simon sitting behind his desk, deep in resignation. Solomon closed the door, gesticulating wildly, his voice pitched to a near shriek. "Simon—Simon! *Madre de Dios*—they are here, the police!"

"I know, Solomon. I have heard them."

"The guns! Give me the keys to the guns, Simon!"

"No. The guns are to fight off thieves, not the police. They are too many, and we are too few."

"Simon—" Quiroga dropped his hands helplessly at his sides—"tell me what we will do. The men—our families—"

Hernandez's sigh fully expressed his defeat. "It is all over, Solomon. There is nothing we can do. I think we have both known that someday it must come to this. It was only a matter of time. If we resist, we will be killed. Go out and open the doors. Do as they say."

With one last plea, "Simon, our families, our children—"

"It is too late to talk about those things. Go and open the doors before they break them down."

Quiroga turned, slumped shoulders reflecting his total dejection. At the door, he turned and faced Hernandez. "Are you coming, Simon?"

Hernandez shook his head from side to side. "I have some things to do first. When they come, they will find me here. Go now, and close the door."

Quiroga sighed and went out. He walked with his head down, unable to return the anxious looks or answer the questions being thrown at him by the tense, excited mechanics and warehousemen. At the double doors, he removed the flat steel bar that stretched from one side to the other and stood it on one end. He turned then and said, "Quiet. I will open the doors and go outside with my hands above my head. If you are wise, you will follow me. If you do not, they will come in and take you, either alive or dead."

They heard the voice again. "No one will be hurt. If you don't comply, we will move in, in force."

The doors were thrown open, and Solomon Quiroga, hands held high above his head, walked out into the yard, the others behind him in single file. They were ordered to face the wall and were searched for weapons. None were found. They were then handcuffed, and all but Quiroga led to the waiting cars.

"Where is Simon Hernandez?" McNeely asked.

"Inside. His office."

"Who else is in the building?"

"No one. In the store—"

"We have them and the girl. Show me where the office is."

They went inside the building, Roberts preceding, Barrett following. At the door to Hernandez's office, Quiroga pointed. "In there, *señores*," he said.

Perry Roberts touched the knob; at that instant they heard the single shot. Perry's hand turned the knob and threw the door open, then drew back and to his left. There was no other sound from within the room. Gun in hand, McNeely moved in cautiously and saw Simon Hernandez lying slumped in his chair, upper body thrown to the right side, blood spurting from the left side of his chest. On the desk before him lay an open ledger.

At 1:10 P.M., David Rhodes, alias Don Reed, received his anxiously awaited call from Anse Talbot. "How do we stand, Anse?"

"We're okay, Don. Everybody on the list was called last night. Three were on fire and wanted to make their own pickups. Dix Norton, Willie Acheson, and Marty Paris. I sent one of my people in to pick up the six keys for Marty and have them here with me now. Dix and Willie made their pickups at nine-thirty and ten o'clock."

"I know about those. Simon called and told me they'd made their pickups."

"Okay. Pete went out early to take the cutters back, make a delivery to Ruiz, and a couple of other stops. I'm on my way to the marina to deliver the six to Marty Paris. He's got a mule coming in from Chicago tomorrow. We'll have most of it wrapped up by late this afternoon or tonight."

"Where are you now?"

"In a booth on Washington near the marina, but I'd like to unload all that bread as soon as I can."

"All right. Make the drop and meet me at the entrance to the Municipal Pier in Santa Monica at two-thirty sharp."

"Right on."

"Be careful, Anse. With Eddie down and Moose out of action, I want to revise our deal."

"Oh?"

"I'm going to have to lean a lot heavier on you and Del from here on. I'm sure you'll like the new deal. I'll tell you about it when I see you."

Talbot was pleased, apparent in his quickened response. "That's great, Don. I'll be there, two-thirty on the button."

Reed replaced the receiver, checked off the figure against the initials "M.P." on the adding machine tape, and pocketed it with satisfaction. He went to the kitchen and heated the coffee, smoked a cigarette, then drank the coffee. Checking the time, he slipped on his jacket and went out. On the parking lot, he got into his Mercedes and, as he turned the ignition key, first heard, then saw, a dark-gray car as it moved out of a space on his left and come down the aisle at an unusually fast rate of speed.

In that quick glimpse, he saw that the faces of the two men were concentrated on him, and instinct told him he was in trouble. Almost blocked now, too late to move forward as the gray car began braking to a stop, he glanced quickly to the rear, saw no car parked behind him. He threw the shift lever into reverse and backed into the rear aisle, braked hard, shifted into drive gear, and shot forward toward the other exit into Alicante Drive, tires screeching.

The dark-gray Plymouth raced ahead in the parallel aisle, and both cars reached the street at almost the same moment. Reed turned hard right, and the Mercedes slammed into the curb just as the Plymouth's front bumper rammed his rear left fender, forcing the Mercedes onto the narrow strip of pavement.

As the Plymouth's motor stalled on impact, the Mercedes leaped ahead along the pavement for some twenty feet, jumped the curb, and was in the street again, racing north on Alicante, the Plymouth more than a block behind. At the top of the hill, Reed turned left on Saratoga Drive just as the Plymouth's engine caught and started uphill in pursuit. At Saratoga, Fred Pace, at the wheel, made a two-wheeled left and shouted to Jerry Cronin, "Radio! And hold on, baby!"

Cronin grabbed the microphone and notified the radio room that David-4-Boy-1 was in pursuit of 1-0-4/King-Lincoln-Xray, a black over gray Mercedes four-door sedan. At once, the information was broadcast to all units in the vicinity.

Saratoga Drive was a narrow residential street that twisted and turned for six blocks until it spilled into Sunset Boulevard, which, at this hour, would be heavy with traffic. With siren activated, Pace floored the accelerator in an effort to close the distance between the Plymouth and the Mercedes, now a full two blocks ahead.

And as Reed approached the red traffic light at Sunset, his unconscious prayer was answered: The light turned green.

The Mercedes made a hard right, continued on for one short block, made a hard right, continued for one block, made another right, then left again. Seeing no movement behind him, Reed ran his Mercedes into a private driveway, braked to a stop, got out, and ran through the yard to an alley, through the facing yard, and emerged into a narrow, curvy side street that was empty of pedestrian or vehicular traffic. Seeing no sign of his pursuers, he walked casually downhill toward Sunset and, reaching it, went into a crowded coffee shop, sat down at a table, and ordered coffee.

When the Plymouth reached Sunset, the Mercedes was nowhere in sight. Fuming, cursing, Pace turned right without the faintest notion of which direction to take. Cronin was on the radio reporting their loss, which was similarly broadcast to the other units converging on the scene.

Twenty minutes later, a black-and-white unit found the abandoned Mercedes in the driveway where Reed had left it.

At 1:10 P.M., Charles Valentine, in his Wilshire Boulevard office, was preparing to leave for a luncheon appointment at the Windsor with his financial backers who were eager for news of his recent trip to Texas. At that moment, the phone rang. It was Paul Landis's secretary.

"I was just leaving to keep a one o'clock appointment, Miss Corliss," Charles said. "Will you please tell him I'll call him when I get back."

"I'm afraid this can't wait, Mr. Valentine," she replied. "Mr. Landis said it was extremely urgent."

"Put him on, please."

Landis came on, and Valentine learned then that in the predawn hours of that morning, Federal agents, armed with search warrants, had closed in on the Wrayburn Ranch and taken Roy Chase, Alan DeWitt, and two vanloads of ranch workers into custody. In the Del Long addition, they had found the balance of the cocaine and heroin, much of it cut to half strength, the rest still in pure form. All were being held in San Antonio. On being booked, Chase was permitted to make a call to his local attorney who, in turn, notified Landis only moments before.

Valentine, on the verge of panic, hung up, then went to the bar in the corner of his office and steadied himself with a stiff drink of Scotch. Any thought of a meeting, at this moment, completely left his mind. He returned to his desk, withdrew his keys, and unlocked the lower left drawer, which was separate and apart from the others—in fact, a steel safe. He turned the dial, lifted the cover, and removed an 8½ x 11 account book, then a file of handwritten coded notes.

From a wall cabinet, he took a large manila envelope and was in the act of inserting the book and material into it when he heard a knock on the door. "Paul?" he called out.

The door opened. It wasn't Paul Landis. Two men entered the office. Valentine recovered quickly. "I'm afraid," he said evenly, "you gentlemen have made a mistake. This is a private office."

So it appeared to the two men. A large single room, tastefully furnished in a style one would expect to find in a luxurious private home: its elegantly paneled walls hung with several large oils and numerous water colors; a curved, leather-topped desk, glove-leather sofa and matching side chairs, a bar, two period cabinets, one wall of book-filled shelves, a spectacular view of the mountains to the north.

The older of the two men said, "'Mr. Valentine? Charles T. Valentine?"

"Yes, but I don't—"

The man held out a thin black wallet and said, "I'm Sergeant Dicter, sheriff's department, Mr. Valentine. This is my partner, Deputy Robert Lance. We have a warrant for your arrest—"

5●

He was alone. And for the first time in years, afraid. After ditching his car and eluding his pursuers by taking refuge in the well-patronized coffee shop on Sunset, he huddled over his cup of coffee until he saw a uniformed deputy enter and look over the entire room, then leave. He paid his check, then and went to the men's room to smoke a cigarette and calm his nerves. Ten minutes later, on his way out, he saw the wall phone in the hallway, dropped a dime into the slot, and dialed Paul Landis's number.

"May I ask who is calling?" the receptionist asked.

"Tell him it's a client. I don't want to give my name on the phone. It's very important."

"One moment, please."

The male voice he next heard said, "Mr. Landis is out of his office at the moment. This is his associate, Tom McArthur. Perhaps I can help you."

Reed hesitated, then said, "Do you know the name Reed?"

"Yes. Mr. Landis thought you might be calling. In which case—"

"Where can I get in touch with Paul?" Reed demanded sharply. "Look, this is very important."

"I'm afraid you can't unless you leave a number where he can reach you when he returns from Texas. But I do have a message for you—"

"What is it?"

"Paul advises you to come into the office and allow me to make arrangements for you to turn yourself in. That will make matters a lot easier for him to—"

Reed replaced the receiver, trembling with anger. With prior felonies behind him, now involved in a major narcotics case that would make national headlines and the top networks, he knew he would be facing a minimum twenty-year rap. Big Casino.

Outside, he could see two patrol cars cruising east and west. He returned to the dining area, went to another table, and ordered a club sandwich for which he had no desire and another cup of coffee, toying with both, trying to formulate a plan of unilateral action. When, after thirty minutes had passed, he noticed two waitresses in conversation, throwing glances in his direction, he paid his check and left. Outside, there seemed to be no cop cars in sight.

He removed his sports jacket, folded it over one arm so that the dark gray lining only showed. He walked down Hancock Avenue to Santa Monica Boulevard, pacing his gait evenly so as not to attract attention to himself. On Santa Monica, he sauntered along, stopping occasionally to stare into a shop window, ready to enter the store in the event a cop car came into view. But he correctly assumed that the searchers would have concluded by now that he had left the area.

Again correctly, he reasoned that an all points bulletin had been broadcast, that every bus station and airport would be under close surveillance, his name, mug shot, and physical statistics distributed to auto-rental agencies.

In a small men's shop near Fairfax Avenue, Reed rummaged through the racks and finally decided on a pair of light-blue slacks and slightly darker blue jacket that fit his thirty-eight-long body without alterations, although the sleeves needed to be lengthened about half an inch. He told the salesman he would have it done when he reached his home in San Jose and wore the suit out, carrying his far more expensive sports jacket and slacks in a shopping bag.

His appearance was altered considerably by the change, but not enough, and his next stop was in a barber shop where he ordered his ample flow of hair cut down to "square" proportions, a request that left the barber somewhat aghast. On leaving the shop, he walked down a nearby alley and dropped the shopping bag into a large commercial-type trash bin.

So far, so good.

Feeling safer now, he continued to walk east on Santa Monica to Curzon Avenue where he was finally able to flag down an empty cab and tell the driver to take him to the downtown Convention Center. Reaching there, he paid the man and strolled to the nearby Holiday Inn and checked in under the name of Robert Drew, giving his home address as San Diego. Without luggage or car, he paid for the room in advance, bought a copy of the afternoon *Examiner* in the lobby, and took it to his room.

Christ, he thought to himself, if it had only happened after he had met Anse Talbot at the Municipal Pier and received the money he had gotten from Marty Paris. But as it stood now, that money was probably gone forever. There was no way by which, when the word was spread around, Talbot would make himself available with every cop on the lookout.

There was nothing in the paper to give him any indication of what had happened. Landis in Texas had an ominous note. He toyed with the thought of placing a call to Hernandez, even to Valentine, but without knowing the full extent of what was happening, he decided it would be foolhardy and dropped the idea for the moment.

It was now five-thirty. More than anything else, he wanted a stiff drink, but was afraid to risk a trip to the bar or order a drink sent to his room. The fewer people he came in contact with, the safer he would be; he wondered how long it would be before cops began showing up at hotels with mug shots, asking desk clerks if they could remember seeing that face.

He paced the room for a while and at six o'clock began tinkering with the unfamiliar television set, finally got it turned on. He listened to the Dunphy program on Channel 2 for a minute or two, then began switching to 4 and 7, then back to 2, but neither CBS, NBC, nor ABC furnished anything useful.

He lay on the bed and dozed fitfully. At eleven, he turned the set on again. Joe Benti on CBS had an item:

"—And out of San Pedro comes the word of a massive drug raid that took place earlier this afternoon, but there has been no confirmation from the police at this hour. This word was received by our reporter from an eye-witness nearby, but no verification from any law-enforcement agency has been forthcoming. It is believed here that they are keeping the lid on the story in order to carry out raids in other parts of the city and county. More later, as it develops. And now, turning to sports—"

So, Reed mused, they had taken Hernandez. And probably Valentine, unless he, like Reed himself, had been able to evade the net. The reason, no doubt, why Paul Landis had not been available earlier. Texas? Could it have extended that far?

Reed began seriously to assess his own situation without even the slightest glimmer of hope. Most certainly, he could never return to his apartment on Alicante Drive. The police had no doubt obtained a search warrant by now, and whatever he had there, clothing, furniture, about seven or eight thousand in cash, records kept in his own private code, would be in their hands and an around-the-clock surveillance maintained.

He emptied his wallet and counted out $1,250 in hundreds and fifties. In his trouser pocket, another $138, plus $1.16 in change. A total of $1,389.16. A checkbook with a balance of $2,143.88. Credit cards. But it was only the cash that counted.

And there was the house on Caribou Road, which he was reasonably certain the police had no knowledge of. Neither Landis, Valentine, Butler, or Peterson had ever been aware of the existence of his "safe house." But for now, his mind was in a state of confusion, and he knew he would have to put it all aside until tomorrow when he would be rested, his mind clear. His eyes closed, and he fell asleep on the bed fully clothed.

He awoke the following morning when the sky was bright, and it took him a while before he could orient himself to the strange room. And remembering, he groaned, sat up, and reached for his cigarettes. He stripped off his clothes and showered, but had no means to shave, then decided to allow his beard and mustache to grow. He used the hotel soap and his index finger to clean his teeth, then rinsed his mouth. He dressed again in the wrinkled suit, again checking his cash hoard. There was no follow-up on any news program to the rumor on the Eleven O'clock News of the night before. Reed sat on the edge of the bed, again trying to focus his mind on his desperate situation.

Since his last term in prison, he had decided that the theory of safety in numbers was a fallacy. He had, in fact, prided himself on being a social loner. Once he had put the gambling and prostitution business behind him and turned to narcotics, he understood the necessity of remaining as far apart as possible from the people he must deal with, limiting his association to the minimum few required; and the fewer the better. On rare occasions he had picked up a girl in a strange bar and taken her to an out-of-the-way motel, but there was never a repeat with the same girl. Only Hernandez, Butler, Peterson, Talbot, Landis, and Valentine knew of his Alicante Drive apartment, none of the Caribou Road house.

If he could get to that house undetected, there was money, over sixty thousand in cash, safely hidden in a strongbox beneath the insulation in the crawl space between the roof and ceiling over his bedroom. Also, there were the keys to three safety-deposit boxes, each in a different name, each in a different city, that held the rest of his personal fortune in cash. For that reason alone, he would never capitulate to Landis's suggestion that he turn himself in.

He must move, get out of this room, try to figure out a means of getting to the house on Caribou Road. He checked out, picked up a copy of the *Times* in the lobby, and walked to a nearby restaurant where he ordered breakfast and ate it hungrily. The paper gave no indication of the raid hinted at on television the night before. The meal finished, he left the paper on the counter, paid his check, and began walking, choosing the busiest streets he could find that led to the downtown area. He went into a drugstore and bought a toothbrush, paste, and a pair of sunglasses to add to his disguise, joined the throngs of pedestrians on the pavements, wandered through department stores, had lunch in a crowded sandwich shop. At five o'clock, he entered a movie house and sat through a double feature. At ten-thirty, he chose a seedy hotel for the night and slept until late the following morning.

6●

Ycaza met the PSA flight from San Diego and recognized Cora Thomas the moment she appeared in the doorway of the plane and started down the mobile stairs behind an elderly couple. He walked across the tarmac and reached for her elbow as her feet touched the asphalt.

"Hi," Cora said without further expression.

"Hi," he replied, smiling. "Welcome home."

"You're not going to put handcuffs on me, are you?"

Still smiling, "Not unless you try to overpower me."

She looked up, saw the smile, and somehow felt a measure of reassurance. Walking beside him toward the airport building, she said, "My car. Is it okay?"

"We had it moved from the parking lot after three days. It's safe. All we removed were the spoilable food items. After a few days, it can get pretty raunchy locked in a car."

"And the house?"

"Safer than any other in the city with somebody keeping an eye on it around the clock. Tell me, how did you pull that Houdini act of yours."

"Do we have to go into it now, Sergeant? I'd like to get a cup of coffee and a sandwich. Can we do that first?"

"Sure. You're a guest of the county again, you know."

"Don't I ever know it. How bad is it?"

"Let's get away from here. We can discuss it over the coffee."

They went out to his car, which was parked at curbside, and found a parking ticket anchored beneath the left windshield wiper. Pocketing it, he said ruefully, "You see, Cora. Nobody is above the law."

He unlocked the door, helped her in, and went around to the driver's side. Out of the airport and on Sepulveda Boulevard, he found a coffee shop and pulled in. Cora smoked a cigarette while they waited for her sandwich. "Do you want to start telling me about it, Cora?" Ycaza asked.

"I might as well get on with it," she said.

"You'll have to repeat it all when we get downtown. For the official statement you're going to make."

She nodded. "I know," and began relating the incident in the supermarket, meeting Dyer there, and how they had eluded the surveillance team.

"Where did you go from there?"

"Mexico. Tijuana to El Descanso, the El Paraíso Motel." She told him how Dyer had left her there to drive up to Los Angeles to "take care of some business," about which she knew nothing. When he failed to return on the next day, or the next, and didn't call to say why, as he had promised, "I got a little panicky about it. Then I heard about him on the San Diego radio, that he'd been shot and was in the hospital. I was running short of money and no place else to go, so I got as far as San Diego and decided to make the call. How is Walt?"

"He'll make it, and you're doing fine so far. Let's go back to Eddie Butler and Moose Peterson for a minute and—"

"I told you all I know about them. I even identified their pictures for you."

"Yes, I know, but what I want now is the name of the man they were working for, or with. You told us about him, remember? The man you met at the marina, the one you spent some time with at Lake Arrowhead. Then he introduced you to Eddie Rogers, who turned out to be Eddie Butler. I want that man's name."

"All right. The one he gave me first was a phony. I knew that right off. In my work, you get to know things like that. One night up at the lake, I went through his wallet while he was asleep. Just out of curiosity. His license and credit cards in the wallet were in the name of Don Reed, but he had another license and more credit cards in a separate wallet in the name of David Rhodes at an address on Alicante Drive in West Hollywood."

"You never saw him again?"

"No. After that, it was always Eddie or Moose."

"What about Connie Moya?"

"Not much. She's only a message drop, like I was until they rang in John Hall Ellison, Walt Dyer, on me. Connie's husband walked out on her, left her stranded with a couple of kids, and she needed the money."

"That's where it all begins and ends," Ycaza said, "with money."

"All right, it does, but that's what it's all about, isn't it?"

He let the question slide by. "Was it Butler, Peterson, or both who set Ellison, or Dyer, up with you, arranged for him to stay at your house until he wasted Whitey Lloyd?"

"Moose. Eddie wasn't there then, or later." She looked up and said, "Do you have them, Eddie and Moose?"

He hesitated for a moment, then said, "We've got Moose. Dyer is in critical condition, under guard in the hospital."

She noted his omission of Butler and said, "I guess that means Eddie is dead, huh?"

"He was shot at the same time Dyer was. He didn't make it."

She sighed deeply and put the rest of her sandwich down on the plate. "I've had enough," she said. "Let's go and get it over with."

7•

By six o'clock, McNeely, Barker, Esau, and Garland had eaten dinner at the Dutchman's and were back on the eighth floor of the Hall. Before gathering in Esau's office, McNeely went to his office and phoned Rachel.

"Where are you, for God's sake?" she exclaimed. "I haven't heard from you in ages. I've been worried."

"It will all be over by morning, I hope, Rachel. The most important case I've ever worked."

"Thank God for that. Do you think you'll be able to get a little time off when it's over?"

"It's never over, but I'll try for a whole weekend."

"What a big deal, but I'll plan on it. Maybe we can go away somewhere—"

"I'll do my best, darling. I've got to go now. Meeting coming up."

"Call me when it's over, no matter what time it is."

"I'll do better than that. If you hear someone creeping around your bedroom, don't scream. It'll be me."

"I'll count on it. Please be careful, darling."

By four o'clock, they had thoroughly examined the black ledger they had found lying open on Simon Hernandez's desk, a final act of defiance before he turned the Walther .380 on himself. The code names listed were obviously those of the ring's principal distributors, along with figures that had been rearranged to confuse the fact that they were telephone numbers. It took only a short time to add the figure one to each digit in order to determine the true number, then reverse their order. Thus, the original number 2714436 became 3825547; and reversed, 7455283.

With that solved, the telephone company, under urgent police emergency, supplied the true names and addresses of the subscribers. Five were in city jurisdiction, eight in county territory, and three were listed as public phone booths and of no practical value.

Meanwhile, there were precise data in Hernandez's ledger: figures indicating operations dating back for several years; quantities of *harina* and *cereal* received; inventories on hand, deliveries on certain dates to distributors listed only by initials, some dropped later, others added, but in no case more than sixteen.

Checking over the list of subscribers now on hand, some of which were not unknown to them, Esau said, "Before we set this up, Russ, I'm giving you first choice. Take your pick."

Russ quickly chose the largest of the two restaurants listed. "I'll take this one. Casa Mario at the marina, Captain. Mario Patricola, alias Marty Paris. We've been after that dude for at least two years and haven't been able to get enough on him to ask for a search warrant. Not even a parking ticket, jaywalking, or littering. I've got a hunch we'll find him dirty if we have an excuse to get inside his apartment on top of the restaurant."

"Well," Barker said, "no problem now with a legal warrant. Who do you want with you?"

"My own crew. Deliso, Barrett, Roberts, and Paul. And a two-man black-and-white for backup. We'll set it up for zero four hundred."

"Okay, it's yours. Let's get the rest of the operation organized."

Esau was already on the phone in contact with DEA's Lyle Carter and his counterpart at LAPD discussing ways and means of a joint operation. By 2100, all arrangements had been made, arrest and search warrants in the hands of each team leader. In each public place, at least one agent, sometimes two, entered as customers, ordered a drink or a meal, made an eyeball check of restrooms, exits, parking lots, and employees, then quietly left. Where applicable, black, Chicano, or white agents, dressed in the mode of the neighborhood, were used for that purpose.

Stakeouts were set on the four residences, and a single agent, Kimo Haolani, a Hawaiian, was chosen to make the initial approach on the Bell Gardens used-car lot where, in the process of examining the stock of vehicles, not only was permitted to try a 1970 Ford sedan, but rapped with the salesman convincingly enough to make a one-spoon buy of heroin.

Throughout the night, DEA, LAPD, and sheriff's men worked in teams from Malibu north, to Long Beach south, from west to east. They entered suspect bars and restaurants at closing time, moved in on the used-car lot with such sudden swiftness that there was little resistance. They made their searches, found a variety of narcotics, in some cases guns, made their arrests, and brought the suspects in for booking.

In one of the four residences, they found a high-level gambling setup, in another, the home of a well-known pimp, evidence of a countywide prostitution ring along with a heavy cache of cocaine and a small arsenal of guns. From a bar, they took three M-16 automatic rifles, later found to have been stolen from the National Guard Armory in Salt Lake City. And at the well-fenced estate of an upper-echelon distributor in Beverly Hills, they took him, his wife, and another

434

couple as his Bentley approached the electronically controlled wrought-iron gates.

At 0235, after the last customers left Casa Mario, McNeely, Barrett, Deliso, and Paul entered the restaurant, served Marty Paris with their search warrant, and discovered a cache of three kilos of heroin and three of cocaine inside a large attaché case, apparently waiting to be picked up by a courier for transport to Chicago. In a locked compartment of a safe, hidden behind a panel in Marty's private office, they found a substantial quantity of drugs in lesser amounts, no doubt for local distribution to a select list of dealers. Inside a locked metal box was the list—names, identifying code names, phone numbers—along with a total of $85,000 in cash.

A satisfying night's work.

8●

The work of the raiding officers continued well into the following day. Fully detailed reports had to be completed and approved, the overall results coordinated for examination by staffs of the U.S. attorney and district attorney's offices, where the charges would be carefully looked into to determine whether complaints would be issued, what further action would be taken. Attorneys for those arrested began appearing to request bail for their clients and inquire into the possibilities of plea bargaining for reduced charges.

At the press conference held at the Hall of Justice, a formal statement, prepared earlier, had been handed out to the reporters of the major and sectional newspapers, network and local television, and radio-station representatives.

In Captain Esau's office, coffee was more in evidence than congratulations as weary agents dictated reports from hastily scribbled notes, while Intelligence and staff discussed the probable effects of the roundup. Sorensen handed out copies of teletypes received from San Antonio and Dallas, where the raid on the Wrayburn Ranch had been significantly successful, with the principal offenders, Chase, DeWitt, and Varick in custody.

But in his long years of experience, John Esau looked upon the operation with less enthusiasm than most; at best, it was an interlude. There would be a temporary shortage of goods for a while and a "panic" of sorts created; but with the breaking of the story, others would step up their activities and the flow of drugs across the southern border and through airports would be increased to fill the demands at higher prices. Meanwhile, what goods were on hand would be further adulterated, and street prices would zoom upward. Addicts in desperate need would double their efforts to meet the rising cost, and the rate of burglaries, car thefts, robberies and purse snatchings would similarly rise.

A vicious, never-ending circle.

Esau ground out his cigarette, crushed the empty paper coffee container. Outside his office, he stopped at his administrative officer's desk. John Rivera looked up from the flow chart on his desk, a form he had devised to maintain close contact with the overall progress of the operation.

"How's it going, John?" Esau said.

"Very well, sir. The reports are coming in fast now. We've got it in hand. Should have it locked in by sixteen hundred."

"Good. Keep after it. I want the full story ready to turn over to the chief by no later than seventeen hundred."

"You'll have it."

The four field lieutenants were in their office, each busy at his desk rechecking his completed report before turning it in to Rivera. Esau walked past the communications room and down the hallway to the office that had been assigned to McNeely and Ycaza.

"What's doing, Russ?" Esau said.

"Just finishing up, Captain."

The captain sat down in Ycaza's chair. "Where's your partner?"

"On his way to County General to see if the medics will let him talk to Dyer."

"Must be coming along if he was in shape enough to be moved over from Pioneer."

"They seem to think so."

Esau nodded. "How do you feel?"

"Like a guy who hasn't had a full night's sleep in a month."

"It's been rough on all of us. You've got some time coming to you, and things may slow down for a little while. How about taking some of it to catch up on your sleep?"

"I'd like to, but—"

"But what?"

"Losing Don Reed. He's our hottest line into a conviction on Valentine, the chief honcho in the West Coast end of this operation. Less than an hour ago, Judge Kerr in federal court set his bail at a hundred and fifty thousand dollars. Paul Landis argued for a reduction and lost. He'll have Valentine out by noon. If we had Reed, I've got a strong hunch we could nail Valentine for keeps."

"Maybe," Esau said. "Well, we've got an APB out for him. Maybe we'll luck in."

"More important," McNeely suggested, "if we can grab Reed, I'm damned sure we can tie him into a murder-conspiracy charge on the Whitey Lloyd thing, along with Peterson."

"What is Dyer's situation exactly?"

"Last I heard, he's coming along. We can't see any problem there. We've got him cold, and Peterson to work on."

Esau sighed and nodded. Russ said, "I guess I'll be moving back to Lennox with my crew as soon as this one is buttoned up."

"That's something I want to discuss with you off the record." He paused, then said, "I'm thinking about making a few assignment changes."

McNeely waited. Esau would make his point when it suited him. "New promotion and transfer list will be out by the end of the month. You're on the top of the list for lieutenant, Russ. Congratulations."

Although he had passed his lieutenant's examination many months before, the captain's quiet announcement came as a warm and welcome surprise. McNeely looked up wearily and said simply, "Thanks, Captain."

"No thanks necessary, Russ. You're a damned good cop, and you deserve it. Of course," he added smoothly, "it means a change in your present assignment—"

"Does that mean a transfer out of Narcotics?"

"Not necessarily. I've put in a strong bid to keep you in the bureau. Question is, how do you feel about it?"

"That largely depends on what assignments are available. I'd hate to wind up behind a desk shuffling papers. Of course, I'd prefer to stay in some active division."

Esau smiled. "I was hoping you'd make that your choice. As it happens, we'll soon be having a vacancy of our own. I don't know how close you are to the grapevine, but Bob Barker will be moving into Special Enforcement until his resignation takes effect, and that leaves us with a vacancy in Zone II for a field lieutenant's rank and job.

"Also, Chief Traynor has gotten the sheriff's approval to expand our Narcotics Intelligence section in charge. It's yours if you want it. Along with that one, you'd take over supervision and training of all new men coming into the bureau."

After a few moments of silence, Russ said, "That's quite a

decision to make, Captain. Can I have some time to think it over?"

"Of course." Esau paused again, then said, "I'd hate to see you leave us, Russ. We need men with your ability and experience. Right now, we've got a lot of heavies on our hands who can feed us important information under proper interrogation. I'd like to put you in charge of that operation for the time being."

"No sweat. I don't need any more rank to handle that."

"Then let's leave it at that for the time being and, also, keep your promotion between us until the official announcement comes out."

"Yes, sir. Of course."

"Then that's it, Lieutenant," Esau said with a smile and an extended hand. "Congratulations. We'll have a longer talk later in the week."

In the outer office, a group was huddled around the radio, listening to the first break of the raid story, heard the comments of satisfaction by the sheriff and the chief of police and another by the head of the local DEA office, who augmented the local story with the tie-in to the Texas raid. A minute later, a deputy came in with a copy of the afternoon *Examiner,* its banner headline announcing:

MASSIVE COUNTYWIDE DRUG BUST

Russ phoned Rachel at three-thirty to apologize for not having been able to keep their rendezvous the night before and to arrange a consolation dinner date. He learned from Lilith that Rachel and Vicki were in town for a manufacturer's sportswear showing, "But they should be back by five-thirty, Russ," she added. "I'll tell Rachel you called."

"Thanks, Lilith." He hung up and sat at his desk trying to assess the full effect of the roundup. Roberts, Barrett, Deliso, and Paul, along with others, were at county jail interrogating the men in custody, each trying to fit the individual pieces into one overall picture. Tomorrow, he, Barker, and Billy Sorensen would review the reports and prepare a condensed version that Esau would deliver to Inspector Garland and Chief of Detectives Traynor, with copies for the undersheriff and sheriff.

Now that the physical part of the operation was done with, Russ felt the weight of his weariness. He re-read the preliminary report he had written earlier, inserted a few minor corrections and turned it over to one of the secretaries to retype. He had a cup of coffee with John Rivera, then returned to his office where he picked up the Rhodes/Reed file and began poring through it. A few moments later, Barker and Harry Deliso came in.

"What's doing?" Russ asked.

"You wouldn't believe it," Barker said. "We've got practically every interrogator tied up taking statements, and if it keeps up the way it's going, we're going to create the damndest paper shortage in the department's history. I've never seen a case where we've busted so many innocent people."

"Getting anything, Harry?"

"Plenty from the bargainers. They're pointing fingers in every direction, but we've got two key dudes who want a deal. Pete Rojas and Hernandez's foreman, Solomon Quiroga. Pete knows he's looking at a hard twenty-year minimum. This is Quiroga's first rap, but he's got a wife and seven kids. That gives us a nice edge on most of them." Deliso sipped at the coffee he had brought in with him, then asked, "Anything on Reed, Russ?"

"Nothing. He got away clean. Vanished in the rarefied atmosphere of the Sunset Strip. There's a team sitting on his Alicante Drive apartment."

"A waste of time," Harry commented. "He'll never show there again."

"Well, we've got an APB out on him, but I don't know how much that will help. By now he's probably changed clothes, bought a wig, and could be holed up anywhere. Except for this," he added, holding up the file.

"What is it?" Barker asked.

"His file. The address of his hideaway pad, Caribou Road in Malibu. Checking his file out, I don't think there's a snowball's chance in hell he knows we know about it. And it's just possible, now that he's on the run, that he'll try to make it there to pick up something he needs. Money, clothes, a gun."

"What are you doing about it?" Barker asked.

"I was just about to check with you and Glenn Toland about wiring Malibu into it. They know the area better than anyone else. I thought we'd send one or two of our crew along with them."

"I'm available," Deliso said. "It's our deal."

"I'll talk to Glenn about it," Barker said. "How about the three of us taking a ride out there and get it set up?"

"I'd like nothing more, Bob, but the captain asked me to get these reports in order. Why don't you and Harry handle it."

"Okay." Barker dialed Toland's extension in the field lieutenant's office and made arrangements to have two men from his Malibu crew move into the area and maintain surveillance on Reed's Caribou Road home. When he hung up he said, "Let's go, Harry. We'll check back with you, Russ."

9●

In late afternoon, lying on the lumpy bed in his cheap room, lacking a television set or radio, Don Reed decided to venture out and buy an afternoon paper. He found a news rack two blocks away and saw the blaring headline on the front page of the *Examiner*:

MASSIVE COUNTYWIDE DRUG BUST

Now he knew. Simon Hernandez was a suicide. Charles T. Valentine released on $150,000 bail. The San Pedro operation was gone, its employees and the milling crew in custody. Simultaneous raids elsewhere had netted scores more. In Texas, Chase, DeWitt, and Varick, along with thirty-four ranch employees, had been picked up in the DEA raid. Little wonder that Paul Landis had not been available.

But there was no mention of Anse Talbot anywhere in the story. Quickly, Reed went to the public phone booth outside the Chevron station on the opposite corner and dialed Talbot's local number. No answer. He hung up and dialed the Newport Beach number. Del Foreman answered.

"This is Reed, Del. Where's Anse?"

"Christ, don't you know anything?" Foreman said impatiently. "I haven't heard from Anse since yesterday. Soon's I heard the news, I came down here. All of Anse's clothes are gone, everything. And I'll be out of here in ten minutes, man."

"Hold it, Del. Do you know where I can get in touch with him?"

"Oh, man, he's gone, blown, taken every goddamned thing we had here with him. I'm a walking basket case, and I'm taking off right now." The line went dead. Talbot gone. The Marty Paris money with him. Par for the course. He should have known. You never trust anybody in the narcotics trade. Once it blows, it's every man for himself.

Now it was more imperative to get to Malibu and his stash in the Caribou Road house, his one last hope.

He walked back to his depressing room and lay on the bed waiting for nightfall. Never before had he felt so desperate and alone. He picked up the newspaper and began re-reading the story in detail, ticking off the names of the major distributors, scanning those of the lesser dealers that were totally unfamiliar to him, becoming engrossed in the most minute details of the arrests. With the feds involved, it was no longer a local matter; those apprehended would be tried by federal authorities, notably tougher to deal with.

Yet, underlying everything else, there was that faint glimmer of hope; he was still free, certain that no one knew of his "safe" house. All he needed now was the means to reach it. A car. A clean car that no one would be looking for. Clean out the cash and the keys to the safety-deposit boxes, pack some clothes and other personal possessions, and take off. Ditch the car in San Francisco, take a bus to Oakland or Sacramento. Hole up for a while until it would be safe to buy another car with newly acquired identification, move south to pick up the bulk of his money, then take off for Mexico or South America.

By the time the sun had set, Reed had worked out his plan of escape, polished it, and was satisfied. He was ready to move.

The street lights were on when he left his room for the last time. Outside, he walked toward Figueroa and the brilliantly lighted, banner-hung used-car lots. He passed by several that he considered too well patronized for his security needs, then found a smaller one just off the main thoroughfare on a side street. A lanky, bearded black man sat in a wooden chair that leaned on two feet against the front wall of a white board shack. HONEST JOHN'S. Used and Rebuilt Cars. Every Car a Bargain.

As he came off the pavement onto the lot where about thirty cars were parked in two neat rows, the chair dropped down on all four legs, the well-thumbed girlie magazine deposited on the chair seat, and Honest John was ready for business.

Along the front row, Reed come to a stop at the silver Camaro with the black vinyl top. Honest John unlocked it for him, and Reed got in, started the motor, and ran it for half a minute.

"Can we try it out?" he asked.

"Sure, man. That's what it's here for. Lemme just lock up the office."

Reed drove it for approximately six miles and appeared to be satisfied with its performance. They returned and dickered for another thirty minutes over the $980 asking price, but at the sight of $850 in cash, Honest John gave in.

There was no way Reed could avoid giving his name as David Rhodes since his license and other identification cards were in that name; but he felt little cause for alarm. The sales documents would not begin being processed until the following day, and by that time he hoped he would have no further need for the car.

The deal consummated, Reed drove away and into the nearest service station to have the tank filled, paying cash. Moments later, he was on the Harbor Freeway heading for the Santa Monica Freeway and Malibu.

Chapter Fourteen

1•

He lay flat on his back in the hospital bed, an intravenous tube in his left arm to feed him from the bottle stand beside the bed, his former cinnamon color paled to an ashen tan. Beneath the sheet, his body was encased in bandages and tape, with a small opening where a drainage tube had been inserted. Walt Dyer, his eyes half closed, mouth drawn in a grim line, was physically, mentally, and emotionally down.

The surgeons at Pioneer Hospital in Lakewood had removed two shotgun slugs from his body, one of which had come very close to ending his life. They had replaced lost blood, patched, sewed, fed him liquids, while sheriff's deputies kept a tight watch on him around the clock.

And when Walt Dyer returned to the conscious world, surprised that he had made it, he wondered to himself, *Why?* They had his gun, and he knew it would undoubtedly be checked out fully. They would discover that it had not only been used to kill Whitey Lloyd but the narc he had taken out earlier for Ernie and George Ruiz. Then why hadn't they allowed him to die? Why so much effort expended to bring him back into the world he had almost escaped, only to throw him into prison for the rest of his life?

If it were for Lloyd alone, there might be the possibility of eventual parole, but he was certain they would never forgive him the murder of a cop. Which was his own fault because Ernie Ruiz had lied to him, told him that Cruz Despues was a young punk who was trying to muscle his way into the narcotics traffic in Ruiz's turf. Mistake number one.

Mistake number two had been his own stupidity in not getting rid of the damned gun. On his way back to Las Vegas after taking Despues out, he had been tempted to stop and bury the .38 out in the lonely desert, but a fresh, clean gun was hard to come by at that time and the source of purchase always a clear danger. To burglarize a pawnshop or gun store, what with intricate burglar alarms, was even more dangerous since this was not Dyer's field. So he had kept the gun, hoping to replace it with another at some later date. Maybe an army .45 bought from a hardup soldier on leave in gambler's heaven. But he hadn't made the connection, and when he got the call from Peterson, through Ruiz, and needing the money, he had had to go with the same .38.

Ah-h-h, no use crying now. He had had it his own way for a long time. As a Las Vegas habitué, he knew that the odds had to turn against him someday—hard for a man to believe while he has a winning streak going for him.

Then they came in one night and moved him to County General Hospital, and he knew that soon, very soon, they would be coming to question him; and he knew they would have all the right questions.

When Ycaza came into the room, Walt Dyer's eyes were closed, feigning sleep, hoping to postpone the inevitable. Ycaza walked to the edge of the bed and stood looking down on the inert figure for a few moments, then said softly, "Dyer."

There was no response.

"Wake up, Walt. I want to talk to you."

Dyer remained silent. Ycaza put a hand on one shoulder and shook it lightly. Dyer's eyelids clamped down tighter with the pain he felt in his side and back at the touch.

"Come on, Walt. The doctor said you're in good enough shape to talk."

Dyer groaned. "Go 'way, man. I got nothin' to talk to you about."

"I think you have. Open up those baby browns and see what a pretty day it is. Full of sunshine and everything else good to look at."

"Oh, man, knock it off. I'm too down for that bullshit."

"Let's get it over with, Dyer. We've got your gun made, the gun you used to put two slugs into the back of Whitey Lloyd's head. You want to talk about that?"

"I don't wanna talk to nobody about nothin', man."

"Okay, Walt, we're going to stop playing cat and mouse, and right now. We've got you by the balls, and you know it. We know you did the Lloyd job, using an alias, John Hall Ellison, and we've got Harold Lawton, Lloyd's apartment manager, who made a positive identification on you while you were in intensive care at Pioneer.

"We also have Cora Thomas—" Dyer's eyes came wide open at the mention of her name. "That's right, Cora Thomas, who came up from Descanso Beach and turned herself in. We have her statement. We know exactly how you got her off that supermarket lot and took off with her. We know all about the yellow Torino, the works. Now you can try to stall all you goddamned well please, but you'll never get around everything we've got on you. All you're going to do is make it a hell of a lot tougher on yourself, sweating it out, and you sure as hell don't need that."

So far, there had been no mention of the Cruz Despues hit, and for a moment, Walt Dyer wondered if it were possible that they hadn't matched up the bullets. But no, these pig bastards were too smart to lay everything they had out in the open. Get him on this one, then lay the other one on top of the first. Yet what could he gain by holding back? They had him locked in on Lloyd tighter than a drumhead. If there was the slightest chance that they didn't have anything on him for the Despues thing—

"What do you want to know?" he said.

"Who set up the hit on Whitey Lloyd?"

"The big dude. Peterson."

"You do any work for Peterson before?"

"No."

"Then how did he get to you for this one?"

"Another dude gave him my number. He called me in Vegas. I drove down to L.A. to meet him, an' we set it up."

"He and Eddie Butler?"

"No. Just Moose. I never saw Butler till the night you dudes shot him. They tell me he bought it. That right?"

Ycaza nodded. "He bought it."

"You must be a better shot than the dude who got me."

"Let's get back to Peterson. He wasn't in this alone. Who else was behind this deal?"

"No way. I only talked to Moose, got paid by Moose. He set it up, fixed it with Cora for me to stay at her place."

"Okay. Who was the dude who gave him your number, put him in touch with you?"

There was no response now. "Come on, Walt. You've gone this far, go a couple of inches farther."

"Just for the hell of it, man, what do I get out of this, settin' these cats up for you?"

"I'll give it to you straight, Walt. I don't know. This isn't a two-bit rap we're dealing with. You took a man's life for pay. Not in heat of anger or self-defense. That spells premeditation, and it adds up to first-degree murder, but there's no death penalty in the state of California. I can talk to the D.A. and tell him you've been cooperative and willing to make a full statement. The rest will be up to him and the judge. That's all I can tell you except that whatever leniency is possible, you'll get."

"Ah, that's only more bullshit."

"It's all I can tell you. How about it?"

"Forget it. I said all I'm gonna say. I'm tired. Just get out an' let me alone."

"Not yet, Walt. Let me give you the rest of it." And Walt knew then that this man *had* the rest of it. "The gun that ripped off Whitey Lloyd was the same weapon that gunned down Cruz Despues, a sheriff's undercover narcotic operator." He watched closely for a reaction and saw it in Dyer's tensed facial muscles. "You killed a cop with that same gun, Walt, and if you think we're going to overlook that, you've got to have cotton for brains. You may not want to talk now, but you'll talk before long, bet on it. I want the name of the guy who set that hit up, and you're going to tell me who he is."

"An' if I don't?"

"You're going to take the full fall for the Lloyd hit, that's for damn sure," Ycaza said coldly. "For very damn sure. And we'll make sure that when you're sentenced, you'll be sent to the worst goddamned hole in the California prison system. We've checked you out pretty carefully. In the past, we can't find any record of your having done time anywhere in this country. You're a virgin. A young, good-looking cherry. Maybe you've heard of what happens to guys like you when they're tossed into a tough joint with a lot of hard-core, horny dudes—"

"Cut it out, you spic bastard!" Dyer screamed.

446

Ycaza smiled grimly. "You've heard, haven't you? You know what a gang rape is, don't you? Well, Walt, start thinking about it because you're damn well going to find out what it's like—"

"*Shut up, you motherfucker!*"

"Give me his name, Walt. That's all I want. A name. The least we can do is give you that much of a break, see that you get sent somewhere where you won't spend the rest of your life as a prison whore for a bunch of tough old bastards who only live for the day when somebody like you comes along."

It was all a lie, and Ycaza knew it, but to a man who had never seen the inside of a prison, knew only what he had heard or read about prison life, it was the most frightening of all lies. And Ycaza could see the lie working on Walt Dyer, the sweat beads rimming his forehead, the clenched fists, the body tensed despite the pain of his wounds as he strained his muscles.

And Ycaza waited.

And heard the name escape Dyer's lips in a near whisper. "Ruiz."

"Which one, Ernie or George?"

"Both. I didn't know the cat was a cop. They told me he was a hustler with a little bread tryin' to make it by takin' over a piece of their territory."

"How did they set it up?"

"A broad. She knew another broad this kid was into, or somethin'. She gave him a line about a big dope deal ready to go down. Somethin' in big figures that she'd lay out for him if he'd meet her at this bar, Moreno's. George got me a car he had somebody boost. I got to the parkin' lot an' waited. When he showed up, that was it. I took off, ditched the car, got into my own, an' drove back to Vegas the same night."

"How much did they pay you?"

"Twenty-five bills."

"How much did Peterson pay you for Lloyd?"

"The same. Twenty-five bills."

"Okay, Walt. I'll be back tomorrow morning with an assistant D.A. and a stenographer. Will you make a full statement then?"

Dyer nodded in agreement.

"You need anything I can get for you?"

"I'm low on cigarettes."

447

"I'll send a carton up to you on my way out. And I'll see you tomorrow."

"I won't be goin' nowhere," Dyer replied.

2 •

At home, Russ found the quiet solitude relaxing and pleasant. The sun was still warm, and the ocean looked inviting. On a late-afternoon workday, the beach was virtually deserted by city transients, and only a scattering of neighbors with their children were sprawled out on blankets and beach pads. He slipped on a pair of trunks and went down for a brief, restorative dip, then returned for a drink and a cigarette on his sundeck. For a while he dozed in the westering sunlight, then went in to shower and dress. At five-twenty he drove to Rachel's shop and found Vicki and Lilith just leaving. Rachel was at her desk checking duplicate orders for the goods she had purchased at the show.

They exchanged casual "hi's" while she continued her work. When she was through, he went to her, took her into his arms, and kissed her. She returned the kiss perfunctorily. "I've missed you," he said, and before he could apologize for the night before, she said, "I see you've been very busy," affecting a calm she didn't feel.

"Where did you pick up that scurrilous rumor?" he replied, with an attempt at lightness.

"On the radio, driving back from town. The big dope bust. That's the thing you've been working on, isn't it, the Texas trip tied in with it?"

Her voice was at the brink of annoyance, easily detectable. And he knew he should have anticipated it, aware of the strain his frequent, unexplained absences and necessary secretiveness created from time to time. As it had been with Carol from his first days in plainclothes: disappearing for a day or two, sometimes longer; sometimes phoning to break an engagement that had been planned with others days before; often unable to get to a phone until it was too late for more than an apology after the fact.

"I'm sorry, darling."

"I know. You're always sorry."

"Rachel, you know how damned hard it is for me at times. I'm not in a nice nine-to-five job where every minute of every day is the same well-ordered routine."

"Oh?"

"Just 'oh?' "

"It's just—just that I can never count on you to be where you should be. All I knew was that you had to go out of town. I didn't know if you'd be gone a day, a week, a month—"

"I didn't know that myself."

"—or if I'd ever see you again. You came back, and that was when I knew you'd been to Texas, then disappeared for another four days. Can you tell me this: Is it over now?"

"Just about. Only the cleanup details. It was big, Rachel, and very important, the biggest case I've ever been in on." He paused, waiting for some response, then, "How about dinner? You must be starved."

She seemed indecisive, then said, "All right. Give me another ten minutes."

"Sure. Go ahead."

Some of his earlier eagerness had left him, and he began to brood silently, yet knowing that the thing that had bothered Carol most was nagging at Rachel now, that unlike other men in normal, everyday jobs, so much of his work was kept deeply hidden within himself, so much he couldn't talk about outside his official family while an operation was in progress.

And the insecurity in the knowledge that at any given moment or any given day or night, off-duty time not excepted, some vengeful dealer or pusher might recognize him and cut him down—on a city street, in his car, on the beach, in a public restaurant. Although the possibility was remote, he believed, the possibility nevertheless existed for himself, for every man he worked with. For Carol then, for Rachel now. He had arrested several thousand men over the years, sent them to prison. How many were free now, out on the streets carrying the cancer of hate for him, he could not know; but they were out there somewhere.

Some had threatened him to his face, some by phone, their voices still recognizable, others anonymous and unidentifiable: "I'm goin'a get you, you honkey motherfucker." "You're a dead man, McNeely." "I'm putting out a contract on you, you sonofabitch." Threats that had not been carried out upon him as some had upon others. Or without a threat, as in the case of Cruz Despues.

"Five more," Rachel called out from the rear dressing room area while his thoughts continued to flow.

After their first drink at Bonnie's, Rachel resumed the subject. "You couldn't push a button on the radio this afternoon without hearing about it," she said. "I was even able to see the *Examiner* headline from the news racks, like the Korean and Vietnam headlines."

"Why don't we forget about it and enjoy our meal," Russ said.

She reacted swiftly. "Why can't we talk about it? It's been so important to you, hasn't it, all over the papers, radio, and television."

"Look, Rachel, I—"

She cut him off sharply. "You look, Russ. You can talk about it day and night with Harry, Steve, Perry, and Joe, but when it comes to me, I'm just like any other outsider, aren't I?"

"You're being childish about the whole thing, Rachel."

"Of course. I'm only a part of your life when it's convenient for you. Everything else is top secret as far as I'm concerned, where you go, what you do. As long as I'm here when you get back."

"Rachel—"

"Am I right or so wrong? And isn't that what happened between you and Carol, your way of holding back, keeping everything locked up inside you, unable to talk about it? For God's sake, Russ, do you think she, or I, would broadcast anything you told us about a case you were working on?"

"It isn't a question of trusting you, Rachel. Try to understand that much of what we do is putting little bits and pieces together to make a case or an operation work. It's like asking a writer to discuss his next book or movie with you while he's still trying to formulate his basic idea. We work with tiny threads—"

"Oh, damn it, Russ, I don't want to really *know*. I only wish you had confidence enough in me to talk, about even the unimportant things that don't matter, let me see the—the inside of you. For all the time we've known each other, what we've been to each other, I don't think I even know you. Not nearly as well as Steve, Perry, Joe, and Harry know you, what you feel or think."

He had never seen her so furious before, displaying genuine anger and outrage. And as with Carol, he knew no way to bring her back to her former calm.

"If you don't mind," she said, "I don't feel like eating now. Would you mind driving me home."

Anger begat anger, and he was all too willing to bring the unpleasantness to an end. In the car, neither spoke. Moments later, at the curb of her house, she said, "Good night. Thanks

450

for the drink," and ran up the stairs. He waited until she was inside, saw the lights come on, then drove the few feet to his own house. He went up and poured a stiff Scotch and drank it quickly, then poured a second and settled in his favorite chair, pondering over the sudden change in both himself and Rachel. He had planned, after dinner, to return to this very setting and tell Rachel of his upcoming promotion, of the possibilities it offered: assignment to replace Bob Barker as field lieutenant or, if backed with enough pressure from Esau, to take over the direction of the newly authorized Narcotics Intelligence section, either of which would be supervisory in nature, with more regular hours. And later, he had envisioned, while lying in each other's arms, he would again bring up the subject of their marriage. He hadn't had a real vacation in several years and would plan on at least a full month for their honeymoon, giving Rachel her choice of itinerary. But now, with that plan shattered, temporarily, he hoped, there was nothing he could do at the—

The phone shrilled him back to reality, and he lifted the receiver, hoping it would be Rachel. "McNeely," he said.

"Harry, Russ."

"What've you got, Harry?"

"I'm up here at the Latigo Canyon–Caribou Road junction."

"What's doing?"

"Nothing, except it's lonely as hell and colder than a welldigger's ass. The little store and filling station is getting ready to close down for the night, so I thought I'd make this last phone call. The phone's inside the store."

"What've you got up there?"

"I've got the car tucked away out of sight in a grove of trees. We've got Sam Jessup and Tony Berendo at the location, hidden somewhere in the boonies to watch for a car or a light in the house—"

"Isn't Bob with you?"

"He was until two hours ago. Got a call from Firestone on a half ton of weed supposed to be coming in from the south. Word was it's in, so he took off."

"Hold where you are, Harry. I'll get there as fast as I can."

"Hell, there's no need for that, Russ. I'm sure three of us can handle it. We're in touch with our walkie-talkies."

"I've got one in my car and nothing else to do. I'll buzz you when I'm close enough."

"Okay, Russ. Welcome aboard."

He hung up, put on a warm car coat against the chill night air up in the Malibu hills, and was on his way within ten minutes. As he pulled away, he heard his phone ringing, but resisted the impulse to return upstairs to answer. And passing Rachel's house again, he saw her lights were still on and wondered.

It was 2310 when McNeely was close enough to Latigo Canyon and Caribou Road to raise Deliso on his walkie-talkie. Ninety seconds later, he came into the junction and pulled into the service station next to the small store that had served the tiny hillside community for many years. Deliso stepped out of the shadows as McNeely backed the car and cut his lights, then drove around behind the larger structure.

"Hey, man," Harry greeted, "glad for the company. If we could have lights, I'd beat you a few games of gin rummy."

"You sod," McNeely said, "you've never seen the day or night you could beat me. What's doing below?"

"Jessup just checked in a few minutes ago. Nothing. Tony's out closer to the road, behind some hedges, just in case Reed tries to come in from the west."

"Well, we'll just sit and hope the bastard shows. You have anything in the glove compartment?"

"A few candy bars, some beef jerky, a couple of sandwiches, some potato chips, and two cans of Coke."

"What'd you do, buy out the whole store?"

"Damn near, between the three of us. Help yourself. The old man reminded me not to litter. Told me there's some kind of law against it."

"You'd better believe him." McNeely chose a Hershey bar from Deliso's hoard and began eating it.

"Thought you'd be too knocked out to come out tonight," Harry said.

"I was, Harry, but you know how great our Manhattan Beach air can revive a guy."

"Yeah, sure. Rachel have another date?"

"Uh, not quite. She'd had a long day in town and decided to get to bed early. What kind of sandwiches do you have in the bag?"

"Ham and cheese, and they're supposed to last until morning. Jesus, didn't you have dinner?"

"Sure, but you know how it is with us growing boys." He got out one of the sandwiches and tore into it hungrily while Deliso ripped the ring top from the Coke can. "That's a lunch you owe me, Lieutenant."

452

McNeely almost choked. "Where the hell did you get that?"

"Off the record. The record in Personnel. One of the chicks I know downtown is my own private spy. Congratulations, man. Or should I say 'sir'?"

"Thanks. I'll make life easier for you if you learn how to butter me up properly."

"You bastard. After what we've been through together, blood brothers, thick and thin, all that crap?"

"Rules are changed, Harry, old sod. We were in the peon class then. I'll be wearing that gold bar now."

"Boy, won't Perry and Steve be glad to hear all about this."

"You utter one word and I'll—"

Both walkie-talkies came on. McNeely picked his up and said, "McNeely."

"Berendo, *amigo,* and welcome to the party. Car coming up the hill from the west. Can't make it."

"Keep us posted."

"He's slowing down. Looks like he's casing thirty-six twenty-two. Could be the dude or a prowling burglar. He's just gone past the house, picking up a little speed. Dark-gray Camaro, looks like, can't make the tags from here. You ought to be picking him up in about forty seconds. Out of my range now. Over."

McNeely got out of the car and stood behind one of the two aged gasoline pumps. Deliso remained in the car, the volume on his walkie-talkie turned down low, waiting for some word from McNeely. Thirty seconds passed, then forty, now fifty.

"Russ?" Harry said into his instrument.

"Nothing, Harry. Jess, Tony, you on?"

"Copy you, Russ. No show?"

"No. He must have stopped somewhere between us, or pulled into a driveway. Let's take it on foot. Harry and I will walk down toward you. He may be heading down your way again. And watch it, the bastard could be armed."

"Roger. On our way," Jessup replied.

Deliso, listening in, locked the car and joined McNeely, bringing their flashlights with him. They started down the hill, Harry on the north side, Russ on the south, passing long stretches of hedges, concrete block or chain-link fences, peering into the few driveways without using their flashlights. As they came around the third bend in the road, they saw Tony Berendo standing just outside a pillared driveway whose gate stood wide open. Tony's left hand was waving them on, his gun in his right hand.

"Jess is inside. Haven't seen a damn thing on the way up," he whispered. "This gate was open. The only one open."

"Nothing on the way down," Russ began when Sam Jessup came down the driveway toward them, arms gesticulating, one pointing up the steep road that led to the house. "It's there, the Camaro. Parked up about two hundred feet. Hood's still warm. He's got to be in there somewhere."

"Or cutting across the back to get to thirty-six twenty-two," Deliso suggested.

"That's got to be it," McNeely agreed. "Let's get back down to thirty-six twenty-two. Where's your car parked, Jess?"

"About thirty yards below Reed's pad, off the road in a clump of trees."

"You carrying a shotgun?"

"Two."

"Okay. You and Tony go ahead, get your shotguns, then get around to the back of thirty-six twenty-two. Harry and I will take it from the front. He'll probably be inside the house by the time we get there. If you see a light anywhere at the rear, give us a call. We'll do the same from the front. Remember, this dude can tell us a hell of a lot we want to know, so let's make sure he can talk when we take him. If he comes up with fireworks, that'll be something else, but we want him alive if it's at all possible."

Jessup and Berendo moved out quickly, McNeely and Deliso following at an easier pace to allow the Malibu men to get on station. They approached 3622 cautiously. The heavy wrought-iron gate across the driveway was locked, the house, about sixty yards behind it, hidden from the roadside view except for about three or four feet of the second story and the crushed-rock roof that slanted toward them. To the right and left of the gate, the wall that surrounded the grounds was of white concrete block and about five feet high.

Deliso leaped up, got a handhold, and drew himself up and over the wall. McNeely followed, dropping in a crouch beside his partner. They moved along the outer edges of the paved driveway toward the darkened house without speaking. A few minutes later, the two-story structure was in full view, twenty yards ahead of them, beyond a circular driveway.

On his walkie-talkie, McNeely said, "Jess, Tony?"

"Copy you, Russ," Tony's voice replied. "Going over the rear wall now."

And moments later, "We're over, about thirty yards from the house. Pool and poolhouse on our right, a three-car garage on our left. Jess is checking it out. No lights visible, but there could be behind what looks like curtains upstairs."

"Okay. Find some cover and hold it until we know if he's inside. Let me know what's in the garage and pool house."

Deliso went on a scouting expedition at the front, keeping out of sight, and returned a few minutes later to report nothing on either side of the house. Then Jessup raised them again. "No cars in the garage. Nothing in the pool house except some tools, gardening equipment, some lawn furniture."

"Okay. Hold where you are."

They waited. The wind began gusting, chilling them through their heavy outer coats. Unable to smoke, they rubbed their hands and moved their bodies without moving their feet, trying to ward off the cold. It was 0210.

At 0225 Jessup raised them. "Tony just caught something that looked like a flash of light, upper story, rear window, a moving drape or curtain."

"Okay, Jess. We'll try it from the front. You and Tony get up to the rear door. If you hear shots fired, break in. Otherwise, hold where you are until we contact you."

"Roger."

"Let's go, Harry."

They followed the driveway to where it circled in front of the house, mounted the steps to the six-foot-wide veranda, and stood in front of the double doors. McNeely tried the knobs and found, as he had expected, the door locked, solid wood and immovable. As he moved along the right side to the walls of solid glass, nothing was visible behind heavy curtains. The veranda came to an end at the extreme right side of the house. Around the corner, at a height of about ten feet from the ground, were four small windows of leaded glass that provided daylight into what was either the living room, library, or den.

"Take a look, Harry." Deliso came to his side and peered around the corner. "What do you think? Suppose you stand on my shoulders—"

"No way, Russ. Those windows are solid. Let's try the back."

They walked around the side of the house to the rear and found Jessup and Berendo, their backs to the rear wall, one on either side of the three steps that led to the door. Jessup shook his head from side to side, indicating the door. "Locked tighter than a drum. The two kitchen windows and the four on the other side, too. Side windows are too high to reach. Only way in is through the kitchen windows."

"Scout the pool house and see if you can find a flat bar of some kind among those tools."

Jessup went toward the pool house and returned in a few minutes with a piece of metal that resembled a tire iron. Handing it to Deliso, "If this doesn't do it, why don't we just break this goddamned door in and rush him."

"No point in giving him enough warning to break out any heavy artillery he may have up there. Let's try the window."

Deliso began wedging the iron bar between the sill and the window ledge. After a few moments he turned and said, "It's in. I don't know how much noise this'll make when I force the lock, so be ready for all hell to break loose."

He began to exert pressure on the bar, levering downward. There was considerable resistance as the iron bit into the wood, then a sudden sharp *c-r-a-c-k!* as the lock at the top snapped. The four men flattened against the wall at the sound but, waiting, heard nothing from the inside.

A full sixty seconds passed; then McNeely formed his hands into a stirrup and signaled to Deliso with an upward nod of his head. Harry placed his right foot into the stirrup and raised himself up. Slowly, he moved the window upward until he was able to wedge his upper body inside the opening. He slithered through, turned and took the flashlight Jessup handed up to him, then disappeared from view. Ten seconds later he had found and unlocked the rear door.

Inside, McNeely said, "Harry and I will go up. Let me have your shotgun, Tony. You and Sam cover us from below."

Carrying the shotgun, McNeely tiptoed down the hallway, Deliso behind him flashing his light intermittently along the floor and into each room as they passed open doors. They paused for a moment at the bottom of the stairway to get their bearings. Jessup's shotgun at the ready position, Tony's service revolver in his right hand. Harry's flashlight was in his left hand, his .38 in his right. McNeely started up the stairs, Harry one step behind him and to his right.

At the second-floor landing, McNeely halted and pointed. Harry turned the flashlight off and looked down the hallway. At the bottom of the third door on their left they saw a razor-thin edge of light. They moved slowly, carefully down the center of the hall to avoid the several chairs and half tables placed against the wall, now guided only by the thin streak of light that escaped from the room.

Within twelve feet, the sliver of light they had had their eyes on so intently suddenly disappeared, and they were in total darkness. McNeely and Deliso came to an abrupt halt. At that moment, Harry brought his flashlight up and snapped it on. Simultaneously, the door was thrown open from inside, and Don Reed leaped out, gun in hand; and before McNeely could aim his shotgun, Reed fired twice in rapid succession. From behind them, Tony had found the light switch and threw it on. McNeely was lying on the floor, and Deliso, shocked at the sight of his partner, shot and bleeding, turned aside into a crouch and got off a single shot that missed Reed.

He could hear Berendo's voice calling, "Police! Drop it—" then Reed fired twice, the bullets thudding into the floor within inches of Deliso. Reed had turned and was racing toward the rear of the hallway, either to the window or the door on the far left. Harry aimed and fired three times, saw Reed stumble, reel, attempt to regain his balance, then fall into a crumpled heap on the carpet.

It had all happened in less than four seconds. Jessup and Berendo were kneeling at McNeely's side, and Harry ran to Reed, picked up the dropped .357 magnum that lay close to his body. Without more than a mere glance at Reed, he ran back to where McNeely lay. He had fallen on his side, knees drawn up, then rolled over face down, unconscious but drawing short, labored breaths. Berendo turned him over on his back. He had been hit twice, once in the upper chest, the other drilled into his lower left side.

"Oh, Jesus!" To Jessup, "Find a phone. Get an ambulance and a doctor rolling. Quick!"

Jessup was running down the stairs. Tony, standing between Harry and Reed, said, "Is he alive, Harry?"

"He's breathing, but I don't know for how long." He had opened McNeely's car coat and shirt, already blood-soaked. "Find a bathroom. Get me some towels, as many as you can find. Wet a couple of them."

Tony ran to the nearest bedroom and returned with several small and larger bath towels. Harry had ripped Russ's shirt away and applied the wet towels to both wounds, trying to stem the flow of blood. He mopped away as much of it as he could with the wet towels, then packed the dry towels over the wounds, bound a large bath towel over his chest and abdomen, holding the edges together with both hands.

Tony had gone down the hall to where Reed lay, knees drawn up in fetal position, groaning softly, eyes closed. He heard Harry shout, "Sam! Hurry up, for Christ's sake!" and walked back to Deliso's side and knelt down. Blood had begun seeping through the outer towels.

He heard Harry's low voice saying, "Russ! Russ! Hold on, boy. Hold on." Then Jessup, bellowing up from downstairs, "They're rolling!" Moments later, he was there beside them. "How is he, Harry?"

"Bad. It looks real bad, Sam. Christ, I don't know. He's in shock. I hope they get here in time."

Jessup looked up at Tony and, jerking a finger toward Reed, asked, "What's with him?"

"He's alive and moaning. Harry laid at least two into him."

"Not enough, the bastard," Deliso said. "If we didn't want him so much, I'd like to put another few rounds into his goddamned skull."

Jessup lit a cigarette for himself, then one for Tony. Harry, watching McNeely closely for some reaction, shook the offer off. "Go down and turn on every light you can find. Then find the gate control and open it."

Tony went downstairs. Seconds later, the house, inside and out, was blazing with lights, flooding the grounds and driveway. The gates were wide open, and when he came up again, he reported hearing sirens wailing their way up the canyon.

Lieutenant Toland and Patrol Sergeant Dick Ramirez were the first to arrive, leading the ambulance and a second unit with two Malibu station detectives. A middle-aged man wearing a topcoat over pajamas and carrying a black bag was ushered in by Sam Jessup while the ambulance men brought in two stretchers and several blankets. Another patrol car arrived, then a fire department rescue squad vehicle. In the roadway, several nearby residents appeared in night dress under overcoats and heavy jackets. Questioned, none had heard the shots fired and had been unaware of the incident until they heard the sirens. Nevertheless, deputies took down their names, addresses, and phone numbers for possible follow-up questioning.

An attendant returned to the ambulance for some plasma and the apparatus to administer it. Inside, the doctor had given what emergency first aid he could under the conditions, and moments later, McNeely was carried below, still unconscious, Deliso beside him, carrying the life-sustaining plasma. The doctor was kneeling beside Reed applying pressure packs to his wounds.

It was a tight squeeze inside the ambulance, with two

bodies on stretchers, one attendant, the doctor, and Deliso, but they somehow managed.

"How is he, Doctor?" Harry asked anxiously as they began to roll. "What are his chances?"

"Which one?" the doctor asked. Harry pointed to McNeely with an angry jab of an index finger. "I can't really tell at this point," the doctor said. "His pulse is fair, just fair, but he seems to be strong and healthy otherwise. I'd say he has a good chance." Then he added, "If there aren't any complications." He shook his head negatively and volunteered, "The other man, I won't even try to guess about him. He took one in the lower spine. Hard to say what's down there until the neurosurgeons look him over."

Toland had radioed the station, and by the time the ambulance wailed its way into the emergency entrance at Santa Monica Hospital, two operating rooms, nurses, and attendants were waiting, surgeons scrubbing.

Barred at the doors to the operating room where McNeely was being prepared for surgery, Deliso found a phone and called Captain Esau at his home. He then phoned Bob Barker and Steve Barrett, asked Steve to notify Perry Roberts and Joe Paul. He had begun dialing Rachel's number, then decided to delay that call until he had some word from the surgeons. The large white-faced clock on the wall at the nurses' station showed 0358.

There were no more calls he could think of to be made. Toland and Ramirez had remained behind at the house on Caribou Road and would handle matters there. He paced the hall for what seemed to him to be endless hours. A young night-duty aide brought him a paper container of hot coffee, and he drank it gratefully; and before he had drunk half of it, Perry Roberts came in, then Captain Esau with John Rivera. And as he began relating the incidents of the night, Steve Barrett arrived with his wife Joyce, Joe Paul, and Rachel Nugent.

Harry went to Rachel at once, holding her trembling hands in his own, apologizing. "I'm sorry, Rachel, I was waiting for some word before I called you."

Beneath her pallor of shock, she managed an automatic smile. "It's all right, Harry. Steve and Joyce stopped by for me. Is there any word yet?"

"He's still in the operating room."

He led her and Joyce to the nearby waiting room and asked a strange deputy to bring some coffee for them, then went back to the hallway and saw that Inspector Garland had joined Esau, Bob Barker just arriving. Once again, he gave them the details of what had happened on Caribou Road. Then a Santa Monica reporter and one from Los Angeles were there, asking for the story. Inspector Garland took them in hand while the others retreated to the waiting room.

At 0630, Garland, Esau, and Rivera left for the Hall of Justice to begin their daily routine, Esau admonishing Barker and Deliso, "Keep me informed. If there's anything Russ needs from our end—"

"We'll be in touch, Cap," Barker assured him.

At 0735, Deliso and Roberts, standing in the doorway, saw the gowned doctor walking toward the waiting room from the elevator. All eyes were on his tired, solemn face as he entered and looked around, searching for one who might be the nearest kin, then addressed the anxious faces as a group.

"I'm Doctor Aaronson, and I assume you are primarily interested in the officer. I'm sorry, I don't know his name—"

"Russell McNeely," Barker supplied. "How is he?"

"I'm fairly optimistic he will be all right, but it will be a while before he can return to duty."

"How serious is it, Doctor?" Rachel asked.

"Are you his wife, or a relative?" the doctor asked.

"His fiancée," Joyce Barrett said.

"In that case, you'll be able to see him for a few minutes as soon as he's brought into Intensive Care. Just a look-in. He'll be unable to hear or speak to you because he'll still be under the effects of anesthesia—"

"How serious is it, Doctor?" Rachel persisted.

"Foregoing purely medical terms, he was shot twice. One bullet nicked the upper part of his left lung. The other penetrated the lower left side of his abdomen. It was necessary to remove portions of his large intestine which had been perforated. The repairs have been made successfully, and if there are no further complications, the prognosis for his full recovery is very favorable. He will be here for several weeks, then there will be an indeterminate period of convalescence, after which, he should be able to return to an—uh, light-duty status. Full recovery should follow shortly. Now, if you will excuse me—"

At 0940, Reed came out of surgery. Two of the wounds had proved to be of minor concern. The third had torn into the base of his spine, and the prognosis was doubtful. The neurosurgeon suggested the possibility that Reed might be paralyzed from the waist down.

The team ordered to stand guard over Reed were in the hall outside the operating room waiting for him to be removed to Intensive Care. A private room had been set aside and the guard ordered for around-the-clock duty, one man inside the room to prevent a possible suicide attempt, the other immediately outside. The information was phoned in to Esau; then Barker and Deliso returned to the Caribou Road house. In the upper-floor bedroom where Dick Ramirez and another deputy stood guard, they found the reason why Reed had returned to his "safe" house. On the bed lay an open suitcase that contained a package, wrapped in heavy brown paper, containing $65,000 in hundred- and fifty-dollar bills that had been covered by a suit of clothes, some shirts and underwear, socks, and another pair of shoes. Also, a box of one hundred rounds of .357 magnum ammunition.

In the walk-in closet stood an aluminum stepladder. Above it was a square opening in the ceiling, a crawl space under the roof where the insulation had been placed, and used by Reed as his stash. From that hiding place, Toland and Ramirez had removed two high-powered hunting rifles with scopes, three brand-new Colt .38s, and a dozen boxes of ammunition. And two packages containing a kilo each of uncut heroin and cocaine.

Barker and Deliso verified the inventory, then packed it up to take downtown to turn in as evidence.

3●

It was 0840 when Moose Peterson was brought into the interrogation room at county jail. He hitched up his trousers and stood at the table opposite Ray Ycaza glaring suspiciously, a certain wildness in his eyes. His first words were, "How's Eddie? You can't get a goddamned thing outa these lousy screws around here."

"Take it easy, Moose. Sit down."

The big man stared down at the seated Ycaza, then settled his huge frame into the hard wooden chair. "How's Eddie?" he repeated.

Ycaza had reached into his jacket pocket and withdrawn a fresh pack of cigarettes and a book of matches. He lighted one, pushed the others to the center of the table between them. "Have one, Moose."

Peterson hesitated, eyes still on Ycaza's placid face, then took a cigarette from the pack, lighted it, and drew deeply. "How is he?" he asked again.

"I'm afraid I've got some bad news for you, Moose. Eddie

hemorrhaged twice and had to have surgery. He didn't make it the second time."

Moose crumpled, chin down, massive shoulders sagging. "Oh, Jesus. Jesus Christ." The words were choked sobs.

Ycaza sat watching silently, somehow understanding the big man's loss and agony, having felt it himself in Vietnam at the death of someone close to him, with whom he had shared meals, patrols, and fought beside. How much Eddie Butler and Moose Peterson had meant to each other, in whatever way, only Moose knew, but his anguish was genuine. He said finally, "They did their best for him, Moose."

Peterson turned back to him, his eyes opened wide, tear-filled. "Yeah," he said, not believing, "I'll bet."

"They did, Moose. The doctors weren't interested in who he was, what he did, or why he was in the prison ward. To them he was—"

"You," Moose said then. "You're the one who did him."

"It wasn't deliberate, Moose. The three of you had guns. We were in a shooting situation. You know that. You were there."

"Oh, Christ. Eddie—Eddie—"

"Let's face it, Moose. We didn't create the situation. You, Eddie, and Dyer did that." He waited, watching Peterson's suffering, then said, "Let's face it. He didn't have a lot to look forward to."

"Is that your out, cop? You rip Eddie off and tell yourself, 'Hell, it's okay, he didn't have a lot to look forward to.' That wraps it up so you can sleep nights, right?"

"It's not that way at all even though I'll never be able to make you believe it."

"Okay, okay. So you told me. Eddie's dead. Is that all?"

"No."

"What the hell else do you want? You inviting me to go to his funeral?"

"I'm afraid I can't do that."

"Then call the jailer—"

"I'm not finished. Something else I want to know."

"What?"

"About Ann Stennis."

"Who?"

"Ann Stennis. A stewardess for Mex-Am—"

"Go fuck yourself, cop. Go down to the goddamn morgue and ask Eddie."

"He set her up as a mule. She brought the junk up from Mexico City and turned it over to him. The beach at Playa

462

del Rey. There was some kind of a hassle, and he did her. We know that much. The thing I want to know is, why did he kill her?"

Peterson's lips were drawn into a grim, tight line. "Come on, Moose, let it out. Nothing you tell me now can hurt Eddie."

After a few seconds, Moose said, "Oh, Christ. You bastards never give up, do you?"

"You know the answer to that as well as I do. Look, Moose, you're in a tough situation, but you're still in one piece. You tell me what I want to know, I'll do what I can to help you. It won't be a hell of a lot, but however little it is, it'll be better than having me lean hard on you on the witness stand. Don't forget, we've got Dyer cold, and he gave it to us from the top of the page down to the bottom line.

"We know you brought him in from Vegas to make the hit on Lloyd. Not Eddie, Moose, you. You set him up with Cora on Newton Street. You paid him twenty-five bills for the hit. Later, you tried to get him to take a contract on Cora for thirty bills, but he was too hung up on her and double-crossed you—"

"Bullshit, he was that hung up on her!" Peterson spat out. "That spade fink took her off so he could blackmail us for twenty-five grand, that's what the sonofabitch was hung up on."

Ycaza filed it in his memory bank for future use in dealing with Dyer. "Let's go back to Ann Stennis," he prompted.

"Okay. Ann Stennis. Listen, nobody held a gun on her to take the job. She jumped at it, a thousand a trip, more goddamned money than she'd ever had or seen at one time. Made seven trips for Eddie; then she got smart, greedy. Told Eddie she wanted two grand a trip or she'd blow the whistle on him."

"So he took her off."

"Well, what the hell else could he do."

"She was pregnant at the time. Did Eddie know that?"

"Oh, man, look. If she was pregnant, it sure as hell wasn't by Eddie—"

"I'm sure of that."

"What makes you so goddamn sure?"

Ycaza almost smiled. "Well, let's just say it's a hunch, a guess."

"Go ahead, square, laugh. You're all alike. It's got to be your way, all the way, and everybody else is wrong. You can't see it no other way, can you? Well, let me tell you something, cop. In my whole life, I never knew anybody smarter or as good as Eddie. He was good to me, the best. We had something you never had in your whole square life—"

"Okay, Moose, but where did Eddie's smartness get him? Or you?"

Peterson had fallen into a brooding silence. Ycaza said, "Will you sign a statement on the Stennis thing?"

"What the hell for? You want to pin that on me?"

"No, Moose. I just want to close the book on it."

"Okay."

"I'll be back tomorrow with a stenographer. You'll give us the statement?"

"Okay."

"Is there anything you want that I can bring you?"

"Cigarettes."

"Okay."

At the reception desk, Ycaza found a message to contact Harry Deliso at the Malibu station. He dialed the number on the message slip from the desk and learned from the Malibu watch sergeant that Deliso and Lieutenant Toland had gone downtown and left word they would be at the Santa Monica Hospital later.

With mounting apprehension, Ycaza asked, "What's doing at the hospital?"

He learned then about Russ McNeely, feeling lightheaded and with a weakness in his knees. "Anything on his condition?"

"Nothing so far."

"Okay. Thanks," he said abruptly, "I'm on my way."

4•

When he regained consciousness sufficiently to tell the nurse in Intensive Care that his name was Russell Dennis McNeely, that he had been born in Chicago and his birthday fell on March seventeenth, he was moved into a private room and assigned nurses around the clock. The move itself was extremely tiring, and he was sound asleep even before he was aware the move had been completed.

When he next awoke, the first face he saw was Rachel's, sitting beside his bed amid the profusion of flowers behind and beside her. "Hey," he said in a low, uncertain voice.

She looked up from the book she had been reading.

"Hello, darling," she said, smiling, then rose and went to his side, held his hand tightly. "How do you feel?"

"I don't really know. Where am I?"

"Santa Monica Hospital."

"Oh. Yes. I think I remember someone telling me that years ago, while they were moving me. How are you?"

"Worried until now. You look much better than when I saw you yesterday morning. More color—"

"Was that when it happened, yesterday?"

"Yes."

"Who's minding the store?"

"Mine or yours?"

"Yours, while you're here."

"Vicki and Lilith, of course. And doing a very good job of it. As well as I ever did with it."

"Oh, Lord. I've given you a rough time of it, haven't I?"

"Not nearly as rough as what you gave yourself. That's enough talk for now. I promised to let your nurse know when you wake up. She's taking a coffee break." Rachel started toward the door.

"Wait a minute. She'll only shove a needle in my arm or give me a pill to knock me out again."

"For now, that's exactly what she's supposed to do."

"Good God, I'll turn into a hype before I get out of here."

"If you do, I'll see that no one busts you. I've got some great narc friends."

He smiled weakly, then looked around and saw the intravenous stand, its tube running down to where his arm lay strapped at his side to a covered board. Rachel warned, "Don't fool with that. It's busy feeding you."

"I'm already fed up. It's a long haul from the beach here, isn't it?"

"It's not all that bad, Russ. This is the first time since I've known you that I've been sure where you are and that you're in safe hands. No more now. I've got to call the nurse, else they won't let me sit with you alone again."

She leaned down and kissed his unshaved cheek. "And I've got to call your crew and tell them. Captain Esau wants me to report to him personally."

"So you've finally met Cap."

"I have, and we've been having some very interesting and pleasant talks. Also, with a man who tells me he's your partner, Ray Ycaza. He's been pacing the halls like a nervous husband with a wife in labor."

"Is he still here?"

"No, but I'm to call him, too. Good-bye now, darling. Don't be a fussy patient, and I'll be back tonight."

The nurse came in then and gave him a yellow capsule to swallow. "Are you in any pain, Mr. McNeely?" she asked.

"If I am, I'm too tired or sleepy to feel it."

"Good," she said, laughing. "I hope Miss Nugent comes to see you often. The effect is good for both of us."

He yawned. "We'll discuss the meaning of that more fully later," he said, and drifted off into sleep.

At four o'clock that afternoon, he awoke in pain, and the nurse quickly administered a shot of Demerol that brought him immediate relief, so swiftly that he wondered how many hospital patients became addicted in postsurgical care, marveling at the comfortable euphoria it produced. He slept again and awoke again at seven-thirty. Rachel was in his room arranging a floral piece that had arrived a few minutes before.

"Hi, beautiful," he called to her.

"Hello, darling." She carried the flowers to him to see, then kissed him. "How are you feeling?"

"Great. Like I don't belong here at all. Who are those from?"

She read the names from the card. "Ray and Yolanda Ycaza. And Ray is out in the hall waiting, pacing up and down. There'll be some others, too."

"Ask Ray to come in now, please? Before the others get here."

"Business as usual?"

"It's personal. An old friend. We were on patrol together—a hundred years ago."

"And went to Texas with you a lot more recently?"

"Ah, I thought Ray could keep a secret better than that, the blabbermouth."

"He likes me. I like him, too."

"I'm glad. He and Yolanda are very good people. Call him now, will you?"

"This one time, but talk fast. The nurse is having her dinner in the cafeteria. I'll wait in the hall and try to head her off."

"*Amigo*," Ycaza said, smiling broadly, "you just can't stay out of trouble, can you?"

"Just what I need, jokes. What's doing, Ray?"

"Just about ready to wrap it up. Statements from Walt Dyer and Moose Peterson, and we've closed the book on Ann Stennis. Butler did her. I hear Reed's in bad shape—"

466

"We're not going to lose him, are we?"

"No, he'll make it, but he'll never walk again. One of Harry's got him in the spine. Barker said he's sure Reed will spill his guts, which will take care of Valentine and tie Paul Landis into the deal. IRS Intelligence is sitting on the income tax evasion angle."

"Well, that should just about do it."

"Yeah. And we're a busted crew. I'm back in Homicide. What about you?"

"I'll have to wait a while before I can make any plans."

"Hey, let me help you."

"How?"

"That Rachel gal. She's something."

"I've got that in mind, too."

"Well, don't blow it."

"I don't intend to."

"Something else. Sawyer likes the way you work. I think if you ever decide to switch over, he'd be glad to make room for you."

McNeely laughed. "No way, *amigo*. There's one thing that'll keep me out of Homicide."

"What's that?"

"Your victims. They're beyond all help."

"Yes," Ycaza said. "Yes, you're so right."

That evening, on orders, he was limited to two visitors, and for only fifteen minutes, which hardly satisfied his MV crew. On the following day he was permitted to see Captain Esau, Barker, Inspector Garland, and Chief Traynor for a brief period.

The next afternoon, after a thorough examination by Dr. Aaronson and consultation with other staff members, the intravenous was discontinued, and Russ was placed on a light diet. He was more alert and able to receive additional visitors, and they came in groups and frequently. Ray came with Yolanda, bringing a basket of Mexican food he was not permitted to eat. Perry and Jo-Ann Roberts, Steve and Joyce Barrett, Joe Paul and Harry Deliso, Harry bringing with him a concerned Sharon Freeman. Barker, Garland, and Esau came, as did old acquaintances from as far back as his days in Patrol and Vice, men in uniform and plainclothes.

Books he could not read, candy he could not eat arrived daily, and so numerous were the flowers that he ordered them sent to the rooms of the less fortunate. And every day there was that special moment when Rachel appeared, telling

467

him by the expression on her face that he was indeed showing increased improvement.

On the day when he was permitted to get out of bed for longer than a few minutes, he moved around his room, assisted by his nurse and a peppermint-striped aide until he tired. He settled down in a wheelchair and sat beside the window, looking out on a bright, clear day and read the morning newspaper. An hour later, his first two visitors arrived together, Rachel and Captain Esau, to perform a small, intimate ceremony. Esau withdrew an official document and read his name from the sheriff's promotion and transfer list, then handed Rachel a small jewel box. She removed a pair of gold lieutenant's bars from it, pinned them to his pajama collar, and kissed him. Esau offered his congratulations with a firm handshake and left them together.

"Well, Lieutenant McNeely, how does it feel?" Rachel asked.

"I'll know when I feel well enough to give someone an order. At the moment, no different than I did earlier this morning."

"We saw Dr. Aaronson on our way in. He told us you should be ready to leave here in about a week or ten days. Chuck and Bonnie have been asking for you, dozens of neighbors, too. You'll have plenty of company once I get you home."

"That sounds marvelous, 'once I get you home.'"

"And I mean, you'll be in bed or out on the deck most of the time. No strenuous walks, no swimming, no jogging, no food that will upset your tender tummy. Strict orders."

"Sounds like you should be wearing these gold bars, but I'm great about taking orders from properly constituted authority."

"I'm glad you've been properly trained. Okay, darling, you've had enough excitement for this morning. Just lie back and rest while I read my morning mail."

There was little rest for him that afternoon when visiting hours began. Toland and Jessup first, Roberts and Barrett next, then Deliso and Sharon Freeman, Bill Hamlin and Joe Paul, all with congratulations on his promotion and with additional gold bars to celebrate the event. Others followed, and at six o'clock the nurse finally cleared the room of all but Rachel. A few minutes later she left to have dinner with Harry and Steve. While they were gone, Bob Barker came in and asked the nurse to allow him to talk to Russ privately.

Barker pulled the armchair up beside the bed and, noting McNeely's expression of heightened anticipation, said, "Relax, man, your blood pressure's showing."

"Come on, Bob, what's with Reed?"

"Well, taking it from the top, we've got confirmation on his condition. Paralyzed from the waist down. He'll be confined to a wheelchair for the rest of his life. Garland and I had a long session with him this afternoon. He's ready to talk, make any kind of a deal to get him into a federal prison hospital. We'll have a complete statement from him sometime tomorrow."

"How much did he give you?"

"Just about everything. He'll implicate Valentine and the Texas group. He's admitted to conspiracy in the Lloyd ripoff, along with Peterson and the late Mr. Eddie Butler. We picked up Anse Talbot at the airport here, and Orange County sheriffs nailed Del Foreman. What's even better is that Paul Landis is involved up to his neck and will probably be indicted for criminal conspiracy and evasion of income taxes for several years back. IRS is deep into that one."

McNeely was totally relaxed now. "Well, that about wraps that end of it up. Have you talked to Ray?"

"Haven't had time. What's doing there?"

"A home run with the bases loaded. He's got Dyer cold on the Lloyd hit as well as the one on Cruz Despues, with the Ruiz brothers tied into that one on conspiracy. Peterson fingered Butler for the Ann Stennis murder. Looks like we're going to be spending a lot of time testifying in court."

"Yes, well—it'll be time well spent if we can wrap this one up. Hey, take care of yourself. I'll be checking out at the end of this month, but I'll be flying down to testify when the trials come up."

"I hate to see you go, old buddy."

Barker smiled and emitted a sigh. "In lots of ways, I hate to leave, but that's how it goes. You think you're going to like my job?"

"I don't know yet. I'll have to try it on for size first."

"It'll fit, and you'll like it. Zone II's the best."

"If I get it, I hope it stays best."

"It will. I'm counting on it. So is Cap. Anyway, take it easy. I'll be looking in on you before I take off."

Barker left, and Russ dozed off for a while. Then Rachel and Harry returned. "Where's Steve?" he asked.

"Waiting out in the car for me," Harry said.

"What's your rush?"

"Got to get back to the grind, man. Nothing's stopped since you've been goofing off in bed, you know."

"What've you got going?"

"Uh-uh. Just back off and get used to your gold bar and new assignment."

"I don't know of any yet."

"You'd better start thinking about one. You can't go running around with us peons anymore, Lieutenant."

"Knock it off, will you? I won't be out of action forever, and I'll still be around to burn you. What have you got on tap for tonight."

"Threats, threats. Okay. Steve and I are meeting a cabin cruiser coming up from Baja with a load of assorted junk. We're working it with Customs."

"The marina?"

"Yup. Forty-two-footer, been out for a week. Four dudes making like a fishing party."

"Where'd the tip come from?"

"Forget it, Lieutenant," Harry said with an elfish grin. "I meant to tell you this before, but I didn't want to set your recovery back. The captain and Barker officially turned the MV crew over to me the other day, and I don't know if I ought to be dealing out confidential information to an outsider. Relax, baby. Let Rachel hold your hand and soothe your fevered brow. See you tomorrow if I'm free." He turned with a smile and a wave of his hand and was gone.

"Think of that," Russ said. "I practically broke that viper in as a narc."

"He's right, you know," Rachel said quietly. "There comes that time when one has to decide he must cut old ties."

"That has a very ominous ring to it."

"Not necessarily. Sometimes it's for the best. Bob Barker—"

"You almost sound as though you're thinking of cutting a tie of your own."

"As a matter of fact, I've been deliberating about one for several weeks."

Russ suddenly experienced a sinking feeling, remembering the last night they had shared at Bonnie's, its disastrous ending. "Don't you want to hear about it?" she asked.

"If you want to talk about it."

"Don't look so down, Russ. It's not all bad."

"What?"

"The offer from the Delta chain."

470

He looked puzzled. "What offer?"

"I told you about it."

"I'm sorry. I can't recall it now."

"One of your problems has been not paying attention to anything unless it has to do with your job."

"Since I'm practically unemployed at the moment, or between jobs, I promise you my undivided attention."

"I'll hold you to that. The Delta chain operates sportswear shops in dozens of suburban shopping centers and wants to come into Manhattan Beach. It makes sense for them to take over a going business and eventually change the name than to start from scratch as a competitor and divide the business, if they can. So, the offer, and a very good one."

She paused for some reaction from him, but he remained silent, his eyes intent on her face. "On my last trip East, they contacted me and made a tentative proposal. Which I turned down. Since then, they've made several inquiries. The last one was at the sportswear show here ten days ago."

"And?"

"I said I would consider it."

"I'll be damned. I'm sure you never told me that."

"Only because you haven't been around for me to tell you much of anything until this happened to you. That and other things."

"Like what?"

"Like how sorry I am I blew up that night at Bonnie's. I made a fool of myself, losing my temper. I wanted to tell you about Delta and that I'd marry you if you still wanted me, but something happened. That big case broke, I was tired from a long day in town, and I'd been so damned worried about you being away and not hearing from you. Adding it all together, I simply blew my top."

"Rachel, please. It was all my fault. You were right about me keeping things locked up inside, unable to confide in you." He paused, then said, "That night, if Harry hadn't called me just as I got home, I'd intended walking back to your house to tell you that, apologize, tell you about the promotion and my intention to take the Intelligence job Esau is setting up—"

"I know about that."

"How could you know? I didn't know about it myself until that afternoon."

"Oh, not that you were going to take it. Just that it had been offered to you. As a matter of fact, I had the idea I was being asked to encourage you to take it instead of the field lieutenant's job. Don't look so surprised, darling," she added, smiling. "Things have been happening on the outside while you've been cooped up here. I've been making a few new friends. Like with Captain Esau. In fact, I had dinner with him and Roberta the night after you were brought here. Later, the Garlands dropped by, and we got along famously. When Henry and Ella left, John told me all about it, and—"

Russ exploded. "Henry? John? Good Lord, nobody ever calls them by their first names!"

"I do," Rachel said evenly. "They asked me to. So did Ella and Roberta."

"Rachel, Rachel. You're not to be believed."

"Yes, I am, and you'd better believe me. I've decided to sell the shop. Just now. If Delta will give the girls a nice contract to stay on."

"And what about you. And me."

"I thought we'd decided that some time ago, just a matter of when we'd get around to it. I can't see much sense in operating two households if I'm going to get rid of the store. It's really silly for me to pay rent when you own a much larger home. Of course, it needs a lot of redecorating, but without a shop, I'll have lots of time. And money. I really do have a feel for decorating, Russ, and it'll give me something to do while I'm waiting for you to come home—"

He knew she was running along on his decision to take the Intelligence assignment; that she was right. There does come a time when one must cut away the ties to yesterday and move into tomorrow.

To the living, there must always be a tomorrow waiting; without it, of what use is today?

He listened, holding her hand while she talked on about the quiet wedding she was planning as soon as his period of wanted for them, hearing only expectancy and hope in her voice.

For tomorrow.